Borderline Dreamtime

Borderline Dreamtime

BOOK TWO OF THE LANDMINE CHRONICLES

Luke Mitchell

Borderline Dreamtime

Spiderwize
Office 404, 4th Floor
Albany House
324/326 Regent Street
London
W1B 3HH
UK

www.spiderwize.com

ISBN: 978-1-907294-93-8

When the power of love overcomes the love of power,
the world will know peace.

Jimi Hendrix

CONTENTS

1

ON THE ROAD AGAIN

Midnight on the beach, Saint Valentine's Day, Cambodia, 2005.

F ree of thought, I joined my palms prayer-like in front of my face, closed my eyes and found myself tottering on the brink of a great abyss. I jumped and disappeared into a deep emptiness, a thoughtless state where there was awareness but no sense of separation. I remained silent and sat doing nothing. Time passed. I eventually noticed a slight tension in my face and realized that I was smiling. It was just then that a palm frond crashed to the ground behind me, prompting my heart to slam against my ribs.

The return to my physical location was fragmentary at first − snippets of sound and shards of silver light. My eyelids blinked and then snapped open. I sighed and drew in a deep breath as if it were my first. The world of name and form rushed in to capture my soul. I was back on the moonlit beach in Cambodia. A faint hiss escaped from my lips as I cursed my misfortune. '*Ssshit!*' It was the last place on earth that I wanted to be.

I was distracted from my terrible predicament by a curious hermit crab, popping its head out of a hole in the sand. It ducked out of sight when a big hairy spider scuttled by.

Is that thing poisonous? I wondered, as my eyes followed the bandy-legged spider's movements for a few moments, until it disappeared out of sight. I closed my eyes again and listened to the cicadas shrill droning in the undergrowth. I heard a dog howl. My eyes opened in time to catch sight of a lightning bolt streaking across the sky beyond the horizon. A distant boom followed seconds later. I looked away from the flickering skyline and saw a dog walking at an angle along the seashore. I whistled and received a short bark in return.

'Come here, boy,' I called.

I clicked my tongue against my palate and gently slapped the sides of my upraised knees. The dog drew closer, sniffed footprints in the sand, circled me, and began to growl.

'Och, there's no need for that,' I said softly. 'I won't harm you. Come over here.'

Unconvinced by my soothing voice, the pye-dog snarled. Fur bristled between bony shoulders and pointed teeth glistened in the bright moonlight. I experienced a moment of trepidation. I knew it was unwise to let the animal smell fear. If it attacked, it would probably be the end of both of us. I inhaled through my nose, slowly exhaled and my uneasiness subsided.

'Come on now, boy, there's nothing to be afraid of,' I said, at the same time thinking, who the hell am I trying to kid?

The dog was an obvious consequence of countless spontaneous liaisons, the end product being something that resembled a cross between terrier and whippet. I noticed a row of teats hanging below the mongrel's ribbed belly. The full moon's silver-blue light made the bitch's fur glow softly and accentuated dark paws, shiny eyes and a white blaze upon her forehead.

I extended my right hand. She sniffed it in search of some kind of olfactory clue as to my identity and intentions. A whiff of my scent was all it took for her to determine that I posed no immediate threat. A rough tongue gave my fingers a welcome lick.

'That's it, girl. Yes, yes, I know. You're friendly, aren't you?'

I'd won her confidence. Enthusiasm incarnate, she nuzzled into my ribs.

'Take it easy, girl.'

I placed my hands on the sides of her head and rubbed a pair of twitching ears, one of which was slightly torn. An animated tail wagged with a life of its own. Had I had a tail it would also have been wagging. I was overjoyed to have a bit of company.

I patted the sand and tried to coax the bitch into sitting down in front of me. She tilted her long head. Her inquisitive eyes gazed at my face and then looked towards where I was inviting her. Message received, she turned around three times and sat down at my feet. Settling in to the situation, she yawned, curled up, put her muzzle on her forepaws and lay facing away from me towards the shimmering sea's expanse.

I leaned forward, stroked the fur on her back and looked up. Encircled by a ring of moisture, the moon gazed down at me. I raised my hands to my face. They smelled of damp dog. The mongrel's presence had a calming effect upon me. I began to think about the tens of thousands of years it had taken for human and canine to form their relationship. I envisioned man the hunter, surrounded by darkness, sitting by a blazing campfire and throwing scraps of food and bones to a pack of barking scavengers. I wished that I had a fire. I took a plastic lighter out of my denim shirt's breast pocket. I lit it and stared at the pointed orange flame until it burned my thumb. 'Ouch!'

I looked up again. I could tell by the moon's position that time was passing, albeit slowly, in this, the longest night of my life.

'Ooofh!' I let out a deep groan, raised my arms above my head and straightened my aching back. A dull pain had settled in my knees. Taking great care, I unfolded my crossed legs and straightened them.

Bloody hell, I thought, kneading my thighs, I'd give anything to walk away from here and get back on the road again.

Association summoned up an old blues tune from my brain's jukebox. I could hear the twangy string and harmonica intro to Canned Heat's perennial classic, 'On the Road Again'. The song came to me like an echo from a previous lifetime and I couldn't remember the last time I'd actually heard it. The idea of being on my feet again, let alone on the road, had taken on the dimensions of an impossible dream. My eyes hosted mirages of strolls on the heather-clad banks of fast flowing rivers in the Scottish Highlands.

In the rain and snow... Al 'Blind Owl' Wilson's falsetto voice called from beyond the grave and opened a sluice gate of nostalgia. Comforting domestic scenarios projected themselves on to the screen of my mind. I envisioned myself in Oban, coming home from work on a cold winter's night to a warm kitchen. My belly rumbled at the thought of a delicious chicken curry, cooked by my wife, Jean. 'You'll never guess what I heard today.' I could hear her excited voice delivering a juicy morsel of local gossip, as I sat reading the evening newspaper in front of an open fire, while my grandchildren played at my slippered feet.

And my dear momma left me when I was quite young... My mother had died on the night I was born. *Lord have mercy on my wicked son...* As the lonesome boogie played out in my head, a poignant vision was withdrawn from my memory. My mind drifted back in time to Sri Lanka, to the morning I'd asked Angus, my twin brother, why it was that he and his friends decided to drive Rolling Thunder, a single-decker Mercedes bus, six thousand miles overland from Scotland to Nepal in 1973.

'It's over thirty years ago now,' said Angus, after he'd considered my question, 'but I can still remember that there were a number of reasons that made us head east. I suppose the idea of smoking dynamite dope, which cost next to nothing, was one of the obvious ones. The more subtle motives ran a wee bit deeper than that. As far as I'm concerned, it was LSD that delivered the idea of India to my mind more than anything else. Western logic will never satisfy the cosmic curiosity that is sparked by the LSD experience.

Only the East can do that. Generally speaking, turned-on baby boomers had become disenchanted with the West's increasingly materialistic and fatuous value system, which was engrossed in the basic utilities of life and knew no other guiding principle than that of more of everything. The acid-dropping hippies weren't interested in accumulating things. They wanted to live for the moment and refused to adopt the roles, pre-established behaviour patterns and social conventions that their post-war parents' society wanted to impose upon them. Disillusioned with the two-dimensional world, psychedelic misfits began to look east for the answers to life's bigger—'

I remembered interrupting my brother's flow of thought by saying, 'Hold on a minute. What exactly do you mean by two-dimensional world?'

Angus replied quickly, 'The world people inhabit when caught up in the demands of modern life – you know, making money, struggling to get ahead, rushing from here to there, having little or no time left to take a good, long look at life and its deeper meanings. That's why we used to call straight people squares.'

'People like me, you mean?' I asked.

Angus's smile had been almost sardonic when he'd answered, 'Yes, Hamish, if you want to put it that way, people like you.'

I said, 'Bit of a judgemental attitude if you ask me.'

'Not really,' Angus had objected. 'It's just a fact that, for large numbers of people, there is simply no time for a spiritual dimension in their busy lives. For most people life is happening on a rather flat plane of physical existence.'

'I still think you're being judgemental.' As I recalled my own words they dredged up the gutsy feeling of anger that had accompanied them and the strong impression of how arrogant and smug my brother had appeared to me that morning. Angus's eyes narrowed as he listened to me say, 'It's…it's like you think that you're better than other people just because you were lucky enough to have the time and money to live the life you were able to live.'

'It had nothing to do with luck,' Angus objected again. His voice rose slightly and he tapped a forefinger on the wooden table in front of him to emphasize his words. 'We had the choice, and we had the guts to make it. That choice eventually brought me on to the spiritual path, a path of lifelong learning. Just because…'

I waved my hands palm up in surrender and said. 'Alright, alright, I get the point. Keep your hair on.' Angus had a shaved head. 'I was a square living in the second dimension while you and your hippy gang were getting stoned, listening to Jimi Hendrix and going where no man's been out of his mind enough to go before.' I thought that was funny and so did he because we shared a brief laugh.

Angus continued. '*Yeah, man,* ' he raised his right hand and made a peace sign with two fingers, 'something like that. But there were a lot of other things factored in to the equation. The hippy dream that we can live as one was wearing a bit thin due to the Vietnam War, the Nuclear Arms Race and the brutal murder committed by the Hell's Angels in front of the stage at Altamont, round about the time when The Stones were requesting sympathy for the devil. Even the great imaginer, John Lennon, said in a *Rolling Stone* interview that the dream was over. But we weren't quite ready to stop dreaming because, during the late Sixties and early Seventies, hippies began returning to Europe from the East with fascinating travellers' tales that were so inspirational we could not help but get caught up in them. Apart from that,' he added, 'there was no armed conflict in Afghanistan during those years. The only Western incursions taking place in that wildly beautiful country were peaceful ones. An army of European dharma bums that wanted to make love, not war, was travelling overland to India and Nepal, so we decided to do it in style in our very own magic bus. Tripping on the long and winding road that led to Kathmandu was the hippie era's rite of passage. We wanted to cut society's umbilical cord and break away from its future-orientated mindset so that we could be free to live in the present – where life is really happen—'

'*Arrrgh!* ' I groaned in pain and the memory vanished. Only a few minutes had passed. Unaccustomed to sitting cross-legged, I'd developed a severe muscle cramp in my right thigh that required urgent attention. I stretched my leg again and massaged the ache away. Unwanted images of what would happen if I made a wrong move gushed into my mind. A loud bang and then…and then nothing – I wouldn't exist anymore and neither would the dog.

The raw taste of acid bile rose in my throat. My tongue felt thick as it rolled across the roof of my dry mouth. Heart-palpitating anxiety gripped me for a few minutes until I brought it under control by breathing deeply.

I thought about Jean and reckoned about six hours must have passed since she'd fallen asleep in our beach hut, leaving me free to slip away for a smoke – the simple act which had caused my life to now hang in the balance. Responding to an unconscious signal, my right hand groped in my shirt pocket for my cigarettes. The thought of having only five left prevented me from lighting one. Something in the back of my mind anticipated that I would become a lot more nervous as the night wore on and therefore more desperate for a nicotine fix.

On the horizon, storm clouds were bubbling up, their grey edges picked out by flickering lightning. The air had become eerily silent. The ocean of time stretched out before me like a sheet of fantastic elastic extending to infinity. I closed my eyes and found myself passing through the mental transit lounge that led to the psychological escape hatch. Fuelled and ready for blast off, my twin brother's life was waiting to transport me into dimensions beyond the known. I was once again about to be diverted from my precarious perch upon the landmine, triggered when I sat down on its detonator button and now primed to explode if...*if*...*if*...*if.* The word echoed and faded in my mind. Relief moaned in my throat

Seconds later, I heard a faraway rumble.

March 21, 1973.

The journey down from Scotland had begun slowly, due to snow and ice on the M74, especially on an elevated section of dual carriageway that passed through the Pennines. The further south Rolling Thunder travelled, the better the road conditions became. The bus was a few miles south of Birmingham – doing eighty miles per hour in the outside lane – when her stellar-galactic paint job caught the attentions of a couple of motorway cops. They were driving a white Land Rover, with checked orange and lime green decals covering its side panels.

The cops tailed the single-decker Mercedes bus for five minutes and observed how its driver, who must have seen them in his rearview mirrors, managed to slow down very quickly to fifty without applying the brakes. They pulled out and overtook. A flashing blue light came on as the Land Rover decelerated in front of the bus and indicated that it should stop in the breakdown lane.

With a wheeze of compressed air, Rolling Thunder's concertina doors folded open. One of the policemen looked away from the crowned skull and crossbones that was spray-painted over the bus's radiator grill and requested that the driver step outside and bring any relevant documentation with him. He did as requested and handed over his driving licence, insurance and vehicle registration form. The cops examined them closely and discovered that the bus belonged to the brown-skinned young man standing before them – none other than Mr Raj Gupta. The police officers could find nothing that was out of order except the Indian Scotsman's waist-length hair and the rather vacant look in his green eyes.

Raj pulled his grey wool cap down to his eyebrows and watched the cops examine his driving licence as if it were a letter informing them that their families had been abducted by aliens. He had his back to the inside lane of the M40 and was being buffeted by displaced air and noise, thrown off by a nose-to-tail line of articulated lorries emitting gouts of black diesel smoke as they roared south, bound for London. He turned up his black donkey jacket's collar and nodded his head repeatedly, pretending to be interested in the stony-faced cops' lecture about speed restrictions and road safety.

The grimmer of the two noticed Raj's inattentiveness. He made it clear that he wasn't exactly pleased to see this by saying, 'Mister…,' he glanced at Raj's driving licence, '…Gupta, are you listening to us?'

'What…eh…eh sure, man,' answered Raj, raising a leather-gloved hand to stifle the greater part of a yawn.

'Listen, son, my names not man,' said the policeman, who was in his mid-twenties and therefore about the same age as Raj. 'In case you don't realize it, we clocked you doing eighty miles an hour back there. We could charge you for speeding, but I've decided to let you off with a caution. Do you understand what I'm saying?'

'Yes, officer, I am very pleased to be informing you that I am understanding the English language most perfectly, sahib.'

'Are you trying to be funny?'

'No, sir,' Raj lied, shivering and looking up into the man's eyes, who at six foot three was about a head taller, 'I'm sorry for breaking the speed limit.'

The cop looked at his colleague and they both smiled, as if laughing inwardly at some privately shared and immensely satisfying joke. Still smiling, he turned back to face Raj and said, 'That's more like it.' He then glanced up at the bus passengers' faces framed in the tinted windows. They were peering round the edges of red tartan curtains and weren't exactly doing a good job of concealing the fact that they were extremely interested in what was going on with their driver. The traffic cop handed Raj back his papers and said, 'I notice you have some nice-looking young ladies on board. It would be a shame if I had to scrape their pretty faces off a concrete pillar under a flyover and all because you got a bit carried away with your driving skills, while imagining you were Stirling Moss. You with me on that, Mister Gupta?'

Raj was thinking that the man must have donated his sense of humour to an Oxfam shop. He answered. 'Yes, sir, I understand. I'll pay more attention to the speedometer in future.'

'I wonder why it is that I'm experiencing difficulty believing that,' said the cop with the hat on, whose unremitting stare had been fixed on Raj for a couple of minutes. The skin round his eyes was so pouchy he looked like he was wearing a diver's mask. As an apparent afterthought he added quickly, 'You don't have any illegal substances on board, do you?' His eyebrows shot up, indicating that his suspicion meter had just kicked in to high alert mode.

'Eh... eh no, man, eh... I mean no...sir.' Raj felt his bowels loosen and envisioned sitting down on a warm lavatory seat.

'Right then, *Mister Gupta.*' The policeman chuckled, appearing to find some amusement in the sound of the name. 'I hope you're telling the truth for your sake.' He exhaled a big cloud of vapour with a pronounced sigh to demonstrate how much his patience had been tried. 'You can go now. Have a safe journey.' He paused for a second and then asked, 'Where are you headed?'

'India,' answered Raj, relief coursing through him like water in a flushed toilet.

'*India?*' echoed the other cop with an unpleasant snort. He scratched his five-o'clock shadow and ran a finger round his regulation blue nylon shirt's tight collar. 'No offence meant,' he said sincerely, 'but if it's Pakistanis and Indians you're looking for you can save yourself a lot of fuel by visiting Birmingham's town centre.' He smiled again. 'Have a good trip and stay away from the wacky tobaccy when you're driving. You hear me?'

'Yes officer,' replied Raj, 'I hear you. Thanks.'

Twenty miles further along the motorway, Rolling Thunder lurched when a back tyre blew out. The rest of the afternoon was spent in a service station's parking lot, searching the bus for the bright red hydraulic jack with black steel wheels.

'Where the fuck is it?' asked Murphy, addressing nobody in particular. 'I saw the fucking thing two days ago.'

'I dumped it,' announced Nina, gripping one side of her lower lip between her perfect white teeth.

Murphy looked up from inside of the luggage hold. 'You did what?'

Nina tightened the belt on her knee-length sheepskin coat and then tugged nervously on a strand of her dyed black hair. 'I threw the jack away to make space for the things I want to trade with the pygmies in Afghanistan. I thought that big heavy red thing was something for a disabled person.'

Murphy crawled out of the hold. He sprang to his feet, pulled off his green woollen cap, shook out his long dark hair, looked into Nina's waif-like eyes and shouted, 'You stupid fucking bitch, there aren't any pygmy tribes in Afghanistan!'

'B...But you said it was a...a good idea to buy lighters to—'

'You daft—'

Nina drew back her right hand and, like an old-fashioned Hollywood starlet, slapped him hard on the face before he had a chance to say anything else. 'Don't you dare raise your voice and swear at me again or...or...or you can start washing your own dirty underwear.'

Murphy's left cheek began to turn pink and his eyes started watering. 'What the—'

'Hey, you guys, what's going on?' asked Angus, fastening the buttons on his waterproof jacket as he approached the couple.

Murphy turned to face him, put his right hand to his smarting cheek and answered, 'This fu... I mean, Nina threw the jack away in Glasgow.'

Angus looked sideways at Nina and said, 'You didn't... Did you?'

Nina was clutching at her sheepskin coat's white lapels and staring at Murphy like she'd just found him on the sole of her high-heeled boot. She lowered her long artificial eyelashes to half-mast and remained silent.

Angus could see that she was close to tears. He stepped up to her and drew her close. 'Never mind, Nina,' he said, 'we can buy another one. It's not a big deal.'

She began to sob on his shoulder. Angus glanced at Murphy and jerked his head, signaling for him to get lost.

'Welly, well, well,' said Murphy to Angus, employing a bit of droog-speak from Stanley Kubrick's satirical science fiction film, *A Clockwork Orange*. His thick mane of hair blew over his face as he walked towards a line of parked trucks in the hope of borrowing a jack.

Nina lifted her head from Angus's shoulder and gazed at Murphy's retreating back with the eyes of a lovesick cow.

A few days were spent in London, visiting banks to change thousands of pounds into American dollars, applying for visas, paying for international motor insurance, which wouldn't be worth a sou in Afghanistan, and obtaining *carnets de passage,* documents that function like an insurance policy which agrees to pay duty should the vehicle fail to leave a country after a designated period of time.

One afternoon, Angus and the crew drove over to Hackney to visit Raj's Pakistani uncle, who'd supplied them with hundreds of kilos of cheap Border hash during the past couple of years. Rolling Thunder was parked a couple of blocks away – just in case.

Over a pot of strong tea, Suleiman Khan's three veiled and sobbing wives explained as best they could, none of them spoke much English, how it had happened that their husband had been arrested for his part in a heroin importation scam. One of his cousins had been sending him crates of leather footballs from Karachi – lined with plastic packets full of smack.

Worried that Uncle Sulei's house might be under surveillance, Angus wandered over to the living room window. He stood for a while beside the thick curtains, looking out into the street, where he studied a clean-shaven man in a high-visibility vest, who was sweeping the gutter. Angus could hear the brush's stiff bristles making small scratching noises against the concrete kerbstones. The tall man's alert eyes glanced up at Angus and then he quickly returned his attention to the gutter, which was clean. There was a rectangular bulge in his dark blue dungaree's bib pocket. Angus turned to Murphy, who was sitting on a stuffed armchair rolling a joint, and said, 'Hey, man, there's a street cleaner outside.'

'So what?' Murphy asked.

'The street's as clean as an operating theatre and he has a walkie-talkie stuffed in his pocket.'

The church clock facing the square struck five and it was six very nervous-looking hippies who slipped out of the back door a minute later.

Saturday morning, it was business as usual up at Acid Mike's apartment in Notting Hill Gate. Sandalwood incense smoke drifted up from the brass base of a three-foot-high Buddha statue in a corner of Mike's living room. *We all sit around and meditate...* The Asian-influenced sound of Quintessence twanged out of the stereo.

'Hey, man, you're looking good,' said Angus to Mike.

The LSD dealer's bearded face was suntanned and he was wearing his trademark tie-dye shirt and trousers. He was puffing on a joint, loaded with so much resin it was starting to drip. His refined voice soon grew excited when he began speaking about his dream of buying a farmhouse on Ibiza.

'I just returned yesterday,' he informed Angus and his friends, who were seated on cushions around a low wooden table. 'I spent two weeks there after watching *More*.'

More was a film directed by the iconoclastic film-maker Barbet Schroeder, with an original musical soundtrack by Pink Floyd. At the time, *More* was enjoying a modicum of success and would later be dubbed a Sixties cult classic, an accolade that perhaps had more to do with the movie's innovative soundtrack and excellent photography than the story, which follows the exploits of an uptight German junkie who overdoses on heroin in the closing scene.

'It was the Mediterranean scenery in the film that caught my attention,' continued Mike. 'When I arrived on the island, I was surprised to find that it was even more beautiful than I'd hoped for, with the added plus of lots of acid-dropping freaks to hang out with and supply.'

'Ah...*supply*,' interrupted Murphy, eager to get down to business. 'Now that you mention it, we were just wondering if you—'

'The answer is *yes*.' Mike chuckled and passed Murphy the joint.

Jenny, Alice and Nina left the guys to their own devices and set off on an expedition that took them first to Kensington High Street, to check out the latest fashion trends, and then down through the bustling Portobello Road street market. Walking in the direction of Ladbroke Grove they shopped around for glad rags and then sat around in the *Third Eye Bookshop*, where they browsed for esoteric books and drug-related literature to supplement Rolling Thunder's library.

'Shall we get this one?' asked Nina, holding up a paperback copy of Paramahansa Yogananda's *Autobiography of a Yogi*. The book had a black and white photograph of the longhaired, androgynous-looking Indian author printed on its orange cover.

'Yeah,' answered Raj's girlfriend, Alice, looking up from Hermann Hesse's *Siddhartha*, 'he looks really groovy, man.'

'This is a must,' enthused Jenny, thumbing through Aleistair Crowley's *Diary of a Drugfiend*, her light-hazel eyes twinkling like polished amber.

'Love the title,' commented Nina, who had a red paisley patterned shawl wrapped like a turban around her head.

'Hey!' Alice exclaimed, squinting through her pink, heart-shaped sunglasses at her plastic Mickey Mouse watch. 'We better get moving or we'll miss this afternoon's Pink Fairies concert under the Westway flyover.'

At the same moment, Angus, Murphy and Raj were blowing Maui Wowee marijuana and cutting a deal with Acid Mike for ten thousand trips of 'Window Pane' LSD, a transaction that would leave behind a trail of blown minds that stretched all the way to Kathmandu and beyond the beyond.

That evening, Acid Mike did something very uncharacteristic. The tight-fisted dealer splashed out on seven tickets and took Angus and his friends to a theatre on Shaftesbury Avenue to see the American musical *Hair*.

Halfway through the performance Murphy and Mike decided they'd heard enough about mystic crystal revelation and the dawning of the Age of Aquarius to last them for a lifetime.

'We're going for a drink,' said Murphy in a too loud voice.

Mike and Murphy rose noisily from their front stall seats and stamped out of the theatre. Angus and the others were enjoying the show and, towards the end of the performance, joined the cast on stage when invited to sing along to 'Let the Sunshine In'.

On Wednesday afternoon, Angus and the gang met up with Mike in the Princess Alexandra on Portobello Road for a farewell pub lunch. During their meal, a loose arrangement was made to meet up with the acid dealer on Anjuna Beach in Goa towards the end of the year.

The following evening, everybody was in high spirits when, just after dusk, Rolling Thunder rumbled down the ramp of the Dover-Calais ferry. Nobody among the bus's crewmembers had ever been out of the British Isles before. Now here they were, after three months of preparation, on the Continent of Europe. Everything looked different: the buildings, streetlights, road signs, even the highway appeared newer and tidier than in Great Britain.

Their excitement quickly turned to horror when Raj turned left on the first roundabout he encountered and then found himself driving on the wrong side of the road. The bus was almost involved in a head-on collision with a German beer lorry speeding to catch the ferry they'd rolled off five minutes before. Raj stamped down hard on the brake pedal. There was a loud screech. The smell of burning rubber filled the bus's interior as smoke from the tyres was sucked in through the ventilation system. As the bus swerved and lurched into the breakdown lane, the truck roared by with its horn blaring.

'Raj, ya fucking idiot, you nearly got us all killed,' shouted Murphy, hair flying as he ran up to the front of the bus.

'I'm sorry, Murph, I forgot what—'

'Forgot, my ass. Get the fuck out of that seat.' Murphy jerked an aggressive thumb towards the back of the bus. 'You're banned from driving for a week.'

Raj adjusted his lopsided woollen cap, stood, and made way for 'Cannonball' Murphy, whose driving skills did not inspire anyone's confidence – he'd been done for reckless driving when he was twelve. Gears crunched as he slammed the vehicle into reverse. The back wheels mounted the kerbstones edging the roundabout, prompting the release of a communal groan. The road was quiet and Murphy managed to steer the single-decker on to the correct side of the highway without another perilous encounter. They were heading north instead of due east because everyone wanted to visit Amsterdam.

It was midnight when, within sight of a well-preserved windmill two kilometres west of central Amsterdam, Murphy parked under some leafless trees in a carpet centre's empty parking lot. Everyone else on board had crashed out. He switched off the lights.

'Oofh!' Murphy barked his shin on the corner of a heavy suitcase that had been left on the floor. 'Who the fuck...?' He spat curses as he made his way through the darkness to his sleeping compartment. He lay down beside Nina and began snoring just as he remembered he hadn't smoked a beddy-bye-bye joint.

Murphy and Nina were smoking a grass joint and checking out the Dutch going to work in the early morning rush hour. It had snowed during the night. Lines of cars were queuing up in the slush at a nearby traffic light, their exhaust systems puffing out clouds of vapour like boiling kettles on wheels.

I want to live. I want to give. I've been a miner for a… Turned down low, Rolling Thunder's radio was tuned to a local radio station and was whispering Neil Young's 'Heart of Gold'. Lust was in the air, blending with the marijuana smoke drifting above the stoned lovers' heads in the driver's cockpit. Dressed only in a baggy pair of Y-fronts, Murphy was toying with the idea of returning to bed with his girlfriend, to better express how he felt about her naked form sitting opposite him. His feelings were beginning to show and Nina was pulling his leg about it. Their laughter was interrupted when somebody rapped on the bus's side panels. Murphy stubbed out the joint in the driver's seat ashtray, and then pressed the big red button that controlled the concertina door. The door hissed open. Standing in six inches of snow were two uniformed police officers, both of whom were wearing fur hats. One of them was a woman. She was the best-looking female cop that Murphy had ever laid eyes on. Her long straw-coloured hair spilled out from under her black hat. Her big, blue, baby-doll eyes were staring at Murphy's groin. His protuberant cock was pushing the front of his formless white underpants out to create a mini pup-tent. The woman's creamy cheeks blushed before she turned away. Her colleague, a tall clean-shaven Dutchman with a square jaw and cold blue eyes, looked Murphy up and down, shook his head, cleared his throat and said in English, 'Good morning, sir. It's forbidden to park here. You will have to move your vehicle immediately.'

Never the one to miss an opportunity to blurt out something inappropriate, Murphy smiled as his erection wilted. 'Aw, right, officer,' he said. 'Ehm…aren't you supposed to be wearing clogs?'

The policeman didn't blink an eye as his breath clouded the cold air in front of him. 'Sir, we could issue you with a parking ticket in excess of two hundred guilders.'

Murphy didn't have a clue how much this amounted to in real money, but it sounded like a lot.

The cop bent his head at an awkward angle and peeked behind Murphy. Nina sat facing him. Her long naked legs were crossed. Due to the cold air flowing in through the open door, her volleyball-sized, milky-white breasts had dark brown, puckering nipples on them that resembled brass tipped bullets. She winked at the street cop. A loaded silence reigned supreme for a few moments, broken only by the radio announcer's voice in the background who said something in double Dutch and then played The Eagles's first hit single, 'Take It Easy'.

Well, I'm running down the road trying to loosen my load...

Angus had been lying in bed listening to the exchange. He dressed, hurried out the door of his sleeping quarters and came to his stoned, big-mouthed friend's assistance.

'Morning, officer,' he said brightly to the cop. 'Sorry for any inconvenience. Give us five minutes and we'll be out of here.'

'All right, sir.' The policeman was finding it difficult to break out of the spell cast by Nina's enchanting gaze for she was looking at him with love-at-first-sight eyes. 'Five minutes will be fine. I wish you a pleasant stay in The Netherlands.'

Apart from Britain, there is no other country in Europe where English is spoken as fluently, willingly and universally as in Holland. The Dutchman grated his consonants but still spoke better Queen's English than the two Scotsmen combined. He began to walk away towards his co-worker, who was stamping her feet and rolling a cigarette.

'See you later, officer,' called Nina.

The street cop turned to see her standing stark naked, legs apart, waving him goodbye from the bus's open door. He waved back, his beaming pink face as polished as his black leather boots.

Grinning, Murphy turned to Angus and said, 'Man, these Dutch bobbies are really cool.'

Angus looked down at his friend's bagged-out underpants. He shook his head and said, 'Well, you aren't. One of your big hairy snooker balls is hanging out of yer drawers.' He pointed. 'Look at the state of you. What are you? Some sort of flasher? If this was England, you'd have been nicked.'

'Oops!' Murphy adjusted his Y-fronts.

'Aw, man, I thought that bobby was gorgeous,' cooed Nina.

'What's with the pair of you this morning?' Angus asked. 'Nina, put some clothes on, you'll catch a cold. Come on, we better move it before the fuzz come back and fine us.'

Angus drove the bus along Prins Hendrikkade and crossed Damrak in front of Amsterdam's elaborately turreted central railway station. Everyone else on board was running on stoned sightseeing mode. Dressed up in her sparkling white finery on a bright sunny morning, the city, steep sloping roofs quilted in snow, shone at her best.

'What the...?' Angus stamped on the brake pedal and uttered an oath under his breath as cyclists criss-crossed through the dense traffic in front of him, obeying a Highway Code tailor-made to fit their individual requirements. He pressed down on the centre of the steering wheel and sounded the powerful air horn. A heavily pregnant young woman, wearing a cream-coloured artificial fur coat with a small child squeezed into a customized chair on the back of her bike, had manoeuvred between the bus and the car ahead just as Angus was about to lift his foot off the brake. The blonde-haired mother dismounted and leaned her bike against the bus's stainless steel bull bars, while the little kid stared up at Angus with the eyes of a curious puppy. The cyclist knocked on the glass-panelled door. Angus pushed the red button and cold air tainted by the smell of exhaust fumes rushed into the bus's warm interior. He looked down and noticed that the cyclist had on a pair of yellow-painted wooden clogs. Oblivious to the blaring car horns all around her, anger flared in her eyes. When she spoke it sounded like there was a table tennis ball-sized lump of chewing gum lodged in her throat.

'I'm sorry,' said Angus. 'I don't understand Dutch.'

'I said you nearly deafened me and my daughter with your *Godverdomme* horn. Please show some respect.'

Taking her time, the irate woman returned to her bike, remounted and began making her way through the slow moving lines of traffic.

Hemmed in by fascinating buildings, most of which were built during the 16th and 17th centuries by merchant princes, the inner city's narrow, curving gridiron streets, flanking canals, were a bus driver's nightmare. Angus drove back over to the west side of town and parked Rolling Thunder on a piece of wasteland on the edge of a seedy neighbourhood.

After switching on the vehicle's mega-decibel alarm system, it was time to go for a walk on the wild side in Amsterdam's Old Side, home to some of the city's extreme contrasts, including the fleshpots of the famous Red Light District. On the way, the crew popped into *Green Zone*, a cannabis café situated in a narrow lane near to Dam Square. It took the rest of the afternoon to sample several of the intoxicating items listed on the small establishment's 'alternative menu'. Sitar music twanged in the background as hash brownies were washed down by marijuana-flavoured coffee.

Angus and his friends were stoned out of their gourds by the time they stumbled out of the café and headed for the labyrinthine sex-for-sale quarter.

The Red Light District turned out to be a somewhat sleazy area where coloured neon lights lent the scene a spurious air of glamour. Some of them only a few feet wide, crowded alleyways were lined with sex shops selling anatomically explicit videos, go-go bars with suggestive names, massage parlours and tantalizingly lit windows, framing seated transvestites and semi-naked female prostitutes. Not all, but many of these women's faces were as hard and brittle as the glass they gazed through, waiting for their next client to knock on the door.

'Fuck a duck, look at her.' Drawn by a male-attracting magnet, Raj stood transfixed in front of an ultra-violet lit window that was draped with red velvet curtains. He was looking up into a longhaired Asian woman's electric eyes. She was performing a provocative, burlesque disco dance to a beat that nobody else could hear. Dressed in a G-string and a see-through wonder bra, which was struggling to contain a pair of ripe breasts, she pumped her lithe hips in mesmerized Raj's direction.

Alice jerked him away from the window and said in an anguished voice, 'You bloody moron, you're embarrassing the hell out of me, standing there with your daft tongue hanging out.' A tear of frustration escaped from her left eye, slid down her cheek and dropped into the dirty slush at her booted feet. 'You're supposed to be with me. *Remember?*'

A glassed-in exhibit in a human zoo, the caged vixen danced on. Her cold eyes, tinged with purple reflections, were directed towards Angus, who was sitting on a cast iron street bollard set into the pavement beside the spot where Raj and Alice had been standing a moment before. The prostitute smiled down at him in a way that suggested it was easy, when involved in the business of satisfying men's lust, to develop a scornful attitude towards the very appetite she was exploiting.

'Hey, Romeo,' called Jenny from along the narrow street, 'do you want us to come back and collect you in half an hour?'

Angus caught up with Jenny and Murphy just as a black junkie pulled on Murphy's jacket sleeve and asked in an American accent, 'Hey, man, you wanna score some China white?' He held up a paper wrap in the grimy fingers of his left hand.

Murphy glanced into the man's glassy eyes and said, 'Listen, you dirty little bawbag. If you don't fuck off immediately I'm going to chuck you in there.' He nodded towards a canal's murky waters.

'Fucking asshole,' hissed the junkie, disappearing into the shadows of a recessed doorway.

By 11:00 p.m. the crew were on the Paradiso Club's wooden dance floor. It was the first time Angus had been at a large public gathering where people smoked joints openly. There was so much cannabis smoke clouding the air, one only had to inhale deeply to get high. Up on the stage a group of talented African musicians, wearing sequined outfits of brightly reflective colours topped off with matching pill box hats, were laying down a bass-heavy blend of Fela Kuti-style Afro funk. Everyone in the packed venue was on their feet doing the Amsterdam double-shuffle, shake your booty hop.

The club was located in a converted high-roofed church which, going by the stifling temperature, completely lacked a decent ventilation system. Heat produced by the dancer's bodies was rising up in competition with large drops of condensation dripping down on their heads. Sweating like lumps of cheese on a hot plate, Angus and Jenny headed for the bar. After pushing their way through a boisterous crowd of revellers, he ordered plastic beakers full of ice-cold Heineken beer.

Upstairs, on the balcony, they sat down on a wooden step and looked over the guardrail to check out the writhing mass of humanity below them. The drummers in the band were hammering out a percussive bombardment and the whole place was reverberating to the rhythm of the brass section's horns. All around, people were skinning up joints.

Angus turned to Jenny and yelled. 'Man, this has got to be the most civilised place I've ever been!'

'What?' she hollered back.

Angus shouted louder. 'This place is brilliant!'

Jenny nodded her head in agreement. Her long blonde hair fell forward and shadowed her impish face. Bright reflections from the multi-coloured, stroboscopic light system flashed and glittered in her brown eyes.

As if obeying a subliminal command, they both stood up simultaneously and began moving to the music.

'That was far out. I'd really like to meet that guy. He's on acid for sure,' enthused Nina, the following afternoon, as she exited the National Vincent van Gogh Museum, arm in arm with Murphy.

'Don't be so daft,' he chided, looking down into her sparkling eyes. 'Albert Hofmann, the Swiss chemist who first synthesised LSD in nineteen-thirty-eight and accidentally ingested it through his fingertips five years later, before taking a historic trip on his bicycle, was still a twinkle in his dad's eye when old Vince popped his clogs in eighteen-ninety at the tender age of thirty-seven.'

'Oh wow, man, I didn't know that,' said Nina in a voice as sweet as honey. 'He must have been loaded. Those paintings of his are worth millions.'

'They are,' agreed Murphy, 'but Vincent van Gogh only ever sold one painting in his lifetime, even though he painted more than two hundred during the last ten years of his life. The guy died a pauper's death and not long after his paintings began to fetch high prices on the international art market.'

'Man, what a bummer,' said Nina, tugging nervously at a strand of her black hair. She tilted her head to one side. This was a coquettish ploy, which she often employed to make herself look innocent and more attractive. Nina's body language served her well, because Murphy fell for it. He pulled her closer and kissed the seductive smile off her lips.

They hurried through the rain and, a few minutes later, entered the Rijksmuseum. It was time to view what Rembrandt van Rijn's obsessive eye had been observing during the 17th century, when the artist's deft hand had applied paint to canvas with brush and palette knife to create his unsurpassable masterpieces.

That night, the crew were back on the dance floor – in the Melkweg (Milky Way) Club. More compact and with a lower ceiling than the Paradiso, the atmosphere was intimate. Everyone was up for popping an acid. Murphy handed out tiny semi-transparent squares of LSD.

Expect the unexpected. Angus remembered Acid Mike's words just as he was about to swallow the trip. The savvy dealer had emphasized that these were powerful hits of LSD and the importance of being in a meditative and peaceful setting to enjoy the most benefit from what he'd described as 'going molecular' doses. Angus decided to heed turned-on Mike's advice, because no matter how he looked at it there was no way he could envisage the noisy, smoke-filled club as being a peaceful and meditative setting. He nibbled off half the square and deposited the remainder in his corduroy shirt's breast pocket.

The first band to hit the stage were a group of skinny musicians dressed in uniform black leather. Their name was painted in fluorescent colours on the bass drum. The Skilletriks played an up-tempo mix of skanking rock steady, held together by tight bass licks punctuated by ear-splitting controlled feedback and the occasional burst of shimmering light-up-your-brain-circuits guitar. The band's catchy beats were impossible for a dancer to resist. Angus looked up at the elevated stage and could have sworn he saw static shooting from the lead guitarist's fingers as he coaxed wild emotion out of his red

Gibson. He was glad he'd elected to only take half a dose of acid, because towards the end of The Skilletriks set he was beginning to feel like an electrode that had been struck by lightning.

To Angus's right, a circle was beginning to form around four individual dancers. He stopped moving to the music and took hold of Jenny's hand. His vision was blurred. When things came into focus he was surprised to see Murphy, Raj, Alice and Nina had removed all their clothes and were bopping around like a mini tribe of frenzied Picts possessed by the spirit of the Celtic God of good times, Lord MacDoolally. A couple of heavyweight bouncers, with slicked-back hair and no necks, waded through the crowd and moved in to break up the spectacle. Minutes later, the six trippers were bundled out of the front door, pushed across a bridge spanning a frozen canal, and warned not to return. As a result, the naïve young Scots woke up to the fact that the liberal Dutch were not as free of social limitations as they would have liked to believe.

In bitterly cold contrast to the Milky Way Club's stifling heat, the slush-covered streets no longer seemed quite so inviting. The ousted revellers felt like they'd been banished to the North Pole. Murphy was clasping his freezing private parts because someone had stolen his tartan trousers and Alice was hopping mad because she'd lost one of her expensive platform-soled boots.

'Help ma fuckin' Boab!' Raj exclaimed, patting his jacket pockets, 'some manky bastard's nicked ma wallet.'

Their breath rising in plumes into the freezing cold air, the shivering Scots walked by a glass-fronted police station, which had it been located in Glasgow would have been a lot busier seeing as how it was a Saturday night. Across the road from a multi-storey car park, they caught a Number 10 tram and headed west down Marnix Straat. To the sounds of a bell clanging and steel wheels rumbling along the tracks, intermittent showers of blue sparks poured down from overhead electric cables as the tramcar wound its way into the future. The surrealistic journey back to the bus had begun as the Earth's crust was cooling. When they reached Rolling Thunder the Mesozoic era had come and gone taking the dinosaurian reptiles of the time with it. Completely zapped out of their chronological minds, the crew arrived back at their spaceship just in time to surprise a couple of junkies from Planet Skag, who were preparing to break into the bus. Murphy, who was still bare-legged, gave chase but strong visual hallucinations, coupled with uncontrollable knees and ankles, prevented him from catching up with the scurrying alien scavengers.

Seated around Rolling Thunder's collapsible dining table, it was back to the Stoned Age. The beetle-browed Neanderthals smoked a few joints and gawked at each other.

By the light of a flickering candle, Murphy unfolded a map of Europe and looked up from it. 'Does anyone here fancy hitting the road and heading for India?' he asked, running a finger along his moustache. Nobody said a word. The spirit of Long John Silver took possession of Murphy's vocal chords and he tried a different approach. He raised his voice and growled, 'Well, shiver me timbers! Gather round me hearties. It be time to set sail for warmer waters.' Captain Murphy looked each member of his motley crew in the eye. 'All those who want to stay here in the port of Amsterdam and risk walking the plank, say nay.' The crew remained silent. 'All those in favour of upping-anchor and steering a steady course to Chappatiland, say aye.'

'Aye!' Everybody cheered and stamped their cold feet in approval.

'Hey, man, who is going to steer the ship?' Raj asked, his slurred words rolling from his tongue in a cloud of marijuana smoke.

Angus was nominated to take command of the good ship Rolling Thunder, because he was the only one to score any points on the 'Can you remember your name?' test card. He tightened his seat belt, turned the ignition key, gunned the engine, brought the bus round in a wide arc and steered on to a deserted street lined with parked cars.

Ten minutes later, the single-decker was about to enter the space age. Commander Angus Macleod spoke into a microphone that was hooked into the sound system. 'Mission Control, this is Rolling Thunder. We're ready for blast off.'

Hoots, howls and whistles greeted his announcement as they zoomed down a slip lane, which brought them on to a highway that girdled Amsterdam's outer limits.

'Ten, nine, eight...' Angus began the countdown. '...three, two, one...' The rest of the crew joined in. '...*zero!*'

Angus spun the amp's volume control east. Loud and proud, Canned Heat boogied out of the speakers. Each time Al 'Blind Owl' Wilson delivered the highway anthem's lyrical hook, everyone on board joined in the chorus, singing at the top of their voices, 'I'm on the road again.'

2

RANCID RUM BABA

Insects strummed and whirred, the sounds coming to my ears in oscillating waves. The penetrating din brought my awareness back to the beach. I lit a cigarette and drew deeply on it. Exhaling a cloud of smoke, I watched as it was carried off on warm air currents wafting in from the sea. I glanced at my wrist and remembered that, in a moment of uncontrolled exuberance, I'd thrown my watch away. I asked myself if time really was an illusion, built upon the strength of three words: past, present and future. Words that, as Angus once described them to me, are nothing more than thoughts, trailing behind the ever-changing flux of life which is all happening now.

As far as I was concerned, the present was the last place that I wanted to be – not difficult to understand taking into consideration that there was a landmine's detonator button merging with my numb left buttock, a dull ache spreading from my lower back through every cell in my body and nothing to quench a thirst that made my tongue feel like a dry sponge. I looked out to sea. Water, water, everywhere, nor any drop to drink. A line from Coleridge's *The Rime of the Ancient Mariner* floated up to the surface of my conscious mind and I remembered how I'd studied that depressing story as a teenager in secondary school.

So much for the past, I thought. The future isn't exactly looking too bright either. Illusion or not, I'd be happy to entertain it. But how the hell can I with this bloody thing under my arse? One wrong move and boom – I'll be blown to bits.

'Ugh!' My stomach convulsed at the thought of what that meant. I dry heaved and broke out in a cold sweat. The dog sleeping in front of me whined in her sleep. My paranoia was so corporeal it had penetrated into her slumber. 'No', I whispered, knowing full well that to dwell on my awful situation would drive me mad. I longed for physical movement.

Temptation beckoned me to smoke another cigarette but I reasoned that with only four left I'd be wise to ration them. 'Ah-ha!' I chuckled, realizing that I hadn't quite given up hope, or why else save my cigarettes? 'Yes', I muttered, 'I'm going to make it through this.'

A memory loop unwound itself and I began humming the tune to an old Kris Kristofferson song, 'Me and Bobby McGee'. I fell silent when I remembered the line about freedom being just another word for having nothing left to lose. I pondered upon its meaning for some time. What the songwriter had intended to convey in his prose was not so clear to me, but I was certain that the only freedom available to me in that moment was the freedom to roam where I wanted in my mind. I closed my eyes and visualized how Rolling Thunder must have looked as she headed east along the highway. The peripheral sounds of insects and the sea faded to be replaced by the astral wind whistling in my ears.

Up ahead, I could see the bus's back lights, glowing red in the dark as it sped along a three-lane highway. I drew closer and saw my reflection, mirrored in the back window's tinted glass. I was flying through the cold night air like a DC Comic superhero. *Whoosh!* I passed through the window and found myself standing behind Angus and his girlfriend, Jenny. I looked out through the broad windscreen and saw a line of reflective lime-green studs, marking out a traffic lane. The catseyes looked like they were being sucked in by the speeding bus. I was on the road again.

It was five in the morning. The slipstream whined in the background as Rolling Thunder shot along an Autobahn in West Germany. Huge industrial complexes lined the sides of the broad road like neon-lit film sets from a sci-fi epic. Oil refineries' towering stacks belched orange flame and clouds of toxic smoke into the night sky.

Sensory input levels were moving into the red on Angus's reality meter. Grinning like a lunatic riding on a moonbeam, he kept his eyes on the road and his hands upon the wheel. Jenny sat by his side in the passenger seat as they flew through what appeared to be a tunnel composed of flowing lines of orange-hued fluorescence.

'Ugh!' Angus gasped. His body shivered and his scalp prickled. He glanced behind him.

'What is it?' asked Jenny.

He answered, 'I just had the weirdest sensation.'

'Like what exactly?'

'Like...like creepy, man. Like somebody just walked over my grave.' He pressed the back of his neck between his shoulder blades. 'For a moment there I could have sworn someone was standing behind me and looking over my shoulder.'

Jenny peered round and shrugged. 'Nobody here but you and me, darling.' She laughed nervously. 'It must have been a ghost.'

'Hey, you just read my mind,' said Angus.

'You're tripping.'

He turned to his right and faced her. 'Look who's talking.'

The light, rising from the dashboard like yellow vapour, gave Jenny's face a spectral hue. Her glittering eyes shone with excitement. She was still sky high on LSD, even though several hours had passed since she ingested it in Amsterdam's Milky Way club.

They shared a brief laugh together and then she posted a cassette into the player's slot. It was *Happy Trails* by The Quicksilver Messenger Service, one of the finest albums of the psychedelic era by a San Francisco band.

Got a brand new house by the roadside... A twenty-five minute marathon version of Bo Diddley's 'Who Do You Love?' began. Jenny rose from the co-pilot's seat and stood behind Angus to give him a shoulder massage. *Who do you love...?* There was no doubt in her mind who it was that she loved with all her heart, which was beating in time to the fantastic music cranking out of the speakers. Her journey east was only just beginning, but she already felt like she was flying into uncharted regions of the galaxy.

'*Yeeeheee!*' She screeched in delight as John Cipollina's guitar playing ripped through the air.

'*Yeah! Yeah! Turn it up!*' From the back of the bus, the rest of the Rolling Thunder tribe could be heard voicing their enthusiasm.

Jenny turned around and said, 'They're dancing.'

Angus glanced up at the rear-view mirror and said, 'Far out, man.'

He returned his attention to the highway, thinking that this was the very best of times.

Sunrise an hour away, the Autobahn was like a living organism being nourished by fast cars streaming onto it via feeder lanes.

Time sped by and a grey morning gave way to clear skies.

After filling up with diesel at a motorway service station, Angus pulled into a large parking area adjacent to a transport café. The crew disembarked like jellyfish being poured from a bucket. Dirt-speckled snow covered the ground. Everyone took a few deep lungfuls of what passed for fresh air in the region – thin oxygen mixed with carbon monoxide.

Children waved to them from passing cars' back windows, whilst pasty faced motorists peered out from behind the windscreens of their Mercs and BMWs, in a world that could have been designated Auto Planet.

Angus looked up at the pale blue sky and imagined how the scene might appear to a space traveller using a telescope to observe life on the smog-covered globe. He heard an unearthly voice in his head. *Apart from a few sentient aquatic species, no other intelligent life forms exist down there.*

Register this planet as being home to a grade two mechanical civilization. Carbon units control primitive, fossil fuel-burning, motorized land, sea and air vehicles. Temperature levels are rising due to atmospheric contamination and loss of sun-reflecting ice on melting polar caps. The biosphere has been destroyed to the extent that it will soon be unable to support organic life. Set co-ordinates for Alpha-Centauri. Droid, get the kettle on. I'm dying for a cup of tea.

'Hey, Angus,' called Raj, who was stamping his moccasined feet in the dirty snow. 'Do you believe in intelligent alien life forms?'

Angus employed the strange voice he'd just heard in his head to deliver an answer. 'Affirmative. Looking at you earthling, I can see that the DNA we seeded on this planet three billion years ago has produced a new life form. Whether or not it is intelligent is at present being debated by the galactic council.'

Raj drew closer to Angus and looked into his eyes. 'And here's me thinking I'm the one who's left the planet. What the fuck are you rattling on about?'

Angus grinned and gazed into the black holes at the centre of Raj's luminous blue-green eyes. His Indian friend's hair was matted on one side and sticking out spiky on the other. Tucked into his patched Levi jeans was a black T-shirt with a large, fluorescent-orange marijuana leaf emblazoned on the front. Printed over the seven-pointed leaf in bold violet letters were the words 'LEGALIZE IT'.

Angus looked over Raj's shoulder and saw a green and white Porsche, with a couple of Autobahn *Polizei* in olive-coloured uniforms sitting in its black leather contoured seats. As the sports car purred by, an electric window slid down, affording the curious cops a clearer view of the dishevelled longhairs, standing around in the snow in front of their fantastically painted bus. Angus saw their lips moving and imagined what they might be saying.

'*Achtung,* Johan,' said one cop to the other, 'look at those guys. How come those scruffy freaks have such nice looking girlfriends?'

'Beats me, Klaus. British plates. Probably a bunch of drug dealers going by the looks of them. Any smokes left? I'm dying for a cigarette.'

Officer Klaus searched in the glove compartment. His colleague took one hand off the steering wheel, smiled at Angus, gave a friendly salute and hit the gas pedal. The Porsche sped off in true high-performance style, bound for life in the fast lane, its back lights glowing bull's-eye red.

The motorway café smelled of burnt sausages, sauerkraut, fried eggs and stale tobacco smoke. Angus and his fellow travellers drank mugs of stewed coffee, passed a fat spliff under the Formica-surfaced table and pretended not to notice the disapproving stares that the other breakfasters were directing their way. Murphy stubbed the grass joint out in a spotless white ceramic ashtray and then put the cardboard roach in his mouth. He nodded towards a heavyset waitress in a grey plastic work coat, jabbering excitedly into a telephone while glancing towards them, and said, 'Something tells me we should get the fuck outta here before those friendly cops return – minus their smiles and jangling six pairs of shiny handcuffs.'

Back in the driver's seat, Angus stepped down hard on the accelerator when he saw a police car speeding down the opposite side of the Autobahn with its blue lights flashing. An overdose of caffeine flipped the switch of a reserve energy source. Eyebrows touching his hairline, Angus kept on trucking down the highway. Cars shot by on the outside lane like coloured tin cans riding on a high-speed conveyer belt, some moving so fast the bus was buffeted by displaced air. Angus felt like he was sitting on the prow of a high-powered speedboat, cutting through asphalt waves with black spray fanning out on both sides. He decided to enhance this exhilarating sensation by ingesting the half trip of LSD left in his shirt pocket from the night before.

By mid-afternoon, everyone else had crashed out. Towards evening, Raj appeared when the bus drove by the exit lane for Mannheim, Rolling Thunder's birthplace.

'How's it going, Captain?' Raj asked.

'Absolutely amazing,' replied Angus. 'I feel like an astronaut.'

To aid the driver's concentration, Raj produced a small circular mirror with a razor-bladed line of sparkling amphetamine powder upon it.

'What the fuck is that?' Angus enquired, glancing away from the road.

'Whizz,' answered Raj.

'Speed! Hey, man, you know I'm not into that shit.'

'Come on, it will keep you going. It's a tradition amongst long-distance drivers.'

'Tradition my ass, the only thing that shit is good for is rotting your gums.' Angus gave a broad smile to reveal two even rows of gleaming teeth, winked at his friend and said, 'Okay, just this once.'

Raj held the round mirror under Angus's nose as he blocked a nostril and vacuumed up the white line through a short length of plastic straw. *'Oocha-kamboomba!'* he cried, gripping the wheel with both hands. The amphetamine crystals caused bright blue sparks to dance behind his eyelids when he blinked. His gums began to tingle.

Raj sat down in the passenger seat and rolled a joint. He lit it, took a few puffs, passed it to Angus and then went back to bed.

The blood red ball of the sun shone in the side mirrors as it descended towards the industrial horizon near Stuttgart. It began to rain. Fifty kilometres past Munich, Angus made another stop for fuel. After paying for the diesel, he bought fresh coffee from a hungry dispenser machine that ate Deutschmark coins like it hadn't been fed for a week. Angus stretched his legs and gave the windscreen a clean using a bucket of soapy water with a dead cockroach floating in it.

'Hey! Du langhaariger Affe! Schau mal was für eine hübsche Braut!'

Angus was busy topping up the engine's cooling system with antifreeze when a couple of skinheads shouted abuse at him, as they drove by in a black VW van. Unaware that he was being called a hairy ape and a pretty girl, Angus responded by giving a friendly wave. The black van's horn blared as it sped off towards the Autobahn, from where the whine of vehicles being driven at high speed growled and whooshed.

The traffic that choked the motorway by day had diminished by early evening. Amplified by the bus's hollowness, the engine droned like a hive of angry bees as Angus drove east into the night. Now and then somebody would surface, make him a cup of instant coffee and then leave him to it.

On the Austrian border, near to Salzburg, the guards manning the checkpoint brought to mind a meeting of Gestapo officers. They were dressed in black, ankle-length leather coats and knee-high boots. All that was missing to complete the chilling picture were black-and-red swastika armbands and silver death's heads on their gold braided military caps.

Angus stood in front of a cluttered metal desk in an overheated office, while an unhurried customs official sat with a magnifying glass in his steady hand, examining half-a-dozen passports with an air of impersonal professionalism.

What's he searching for? Angus silently asked. Germs?

He glanced up at the time, dripping Dali-style from the warped hands of a large functional clock, which appeared to be melting as it floated like a chronometric sun above a paper sea of Xeroxed photographs that were tacked to the wall to form a rogues' gallery. From a neighbouring room came the slow clip of someone single-fingering a typewriter accompanied by loud intermittent bursts of white noise, emitted from a shortwave radio delivering police bulletins.

'Alles in Ordnung,' said the customs officer, a hint of a smile upon his tight lips, the creases of his blue cotton shirt immaculate. He returned the passports to Angus and said in perfect English, 'You and your sleeping passengers may now enter the Federal Republic of Österreich.'

Relieved to be back in the driver's seat, Angus drummed his fingers on the leather-bound steering wheel and let out an impatient sigh. 'Fucking borders, bad idea, man,' he muttered, waiting for the weighted, horizontal, red and white striped metal pole in front of the bus to be lifted. A stony-faced guard waved him through.

Angus checked the dashboard clock. It was nearly three in the morning.

The road widened and he overtook a slow-moving articulated lorry with chrome hubcaps. Its black cab was studded with small blue lights. The truck driver glanced down as the bus passed and raised a hand in greeting. He then flashed his headlights. Angus steered onto the inside lane.

Two hundred kilometres later, snowflakes, as big as hexagonal slices of bread, began to swirl out of the sky and spiral onto the windscreen. The falling snow reduced the vehicles ahead – few and far between – to a mere fuzz of red light. The glistening whiteness created by the bus's headlights began to dazzle Angus. He eased up on the accelerator. The slower he drove, the more sluggish he became. His field of vision narrowed and shortened to a few metres. He decided to throw in his driver's gloves just outside of Graz, the second-largest city in Austria after Vienna. He pulled off the highway and continued for a few minutes until he reached a residential area. With a squeal produced by damp brake pads he parked next to a skip full of builders' rubble, within sight of a row of tall, faceless apartment blocks. He cut the engine, stood, stretched his arms and gave Rolling Thunder's illuminated dashboard an affectionate pat. He then switched off the lights and stumbled through the darkness on his way to bed. Jenny woke up and gave him a neck rub. He lay with his eyes closed, still seeing the highway's white lines flashing before him, like a repetitive Morse code message minus the dots. His hands gripped a dreamy steering wheel. The lines faded. He let go. All that remained was the clicking of hot metal as it cooled down and contracted.

It was still dark when Angus awoke. Jenny lay sleeping by his side, her scent soft, warm and inviting. The bus was in motion. He kissed Jenny on the forehead, rose out of bed, pulled on a tee shirt and made his way to the front to see who was driving. Raj was behind the wheel.

'Where are we?'

'Ninety klicks west of some place called Thessalonica.' Raj picked up and then offered a joint that had been smouldering in the ashtray.

'*Thessa* what? Where's that?'

'Greece.'

'Man, how long have I been out?' Angus asked, puzzled.

Raj shrugged. 'I've no idea. Murphy drove for a while. Alice had a go when we were in Yugo—'

'What? But Alice doesn't know how to drive.'

Raj chuckled. 'Yeah, man, you're telling me. She'd only been behind the wheel for five minutes, on a quiet stretch of road, when she nearly crashed into the back of a cement-mixer truck.' He glanced down at the dashboard clock. 'I've been driving for six hours now.'

Angus sat in silence for five minutes, watching the bus gobble up the road. He still felt bone tired. 'You alright to keep driving?' he finally asked.

'Yeah, man, I'm cool with that,' assured Raj. 'Everything's under—'

'Don't say it,' snapped Angus, knowing from experience that Raj saying he had everything under control was a precursor for disaster.

Raj's bespectacled face looked up, a broad smile separating his lips. He was wearing a peaked, dark green, Glasgow Corporation bus driver's hat, a farewell present from his father. 'You worry too much,' he said. 'Go back to bed.'

Angus removed his clothes and snuggled up to his girlfriend. He held her close. Her damp scent flooded his nostrils. She moaned. Ten minutes later, the intensity of her moaning ratcheted up several passionate notches.

Warm sunlight filtered through tinted glass and shone on Angus's face. He opened his eyes, turned on his side and saw that Jenny was gone. The bus was stationary. From outside came the sound of raised voices. He dressed quickly, pulled on his canvas baseball boots and went to investigate.

The rest of the crew were standing around at the side of a two-lane road, having a heated discussion with a platoon of helmeted men. The soldiers were dressed in military issue fashion statements and carried sub-machine guns slung over their shoulders. Angus could read the tension in their body language, tight jaws, nervous eyes and hastily smoked cigarettes being ground into the asphalt by booted feet.

'What the fuck's going on?' Angus asked Jenny.

She pulled him over to one side of the fracas and whispered, 'We drove over the border from Greece into Turkey ten minutes ago. Now these jokers flag us down saying we entered the country illegally.'

'Did we?'

Jenny screwed up her face in annoyance. 'Of course not, we had our passports stamped at the frontier.'

'So what do they want?'

'Guess.' Jenny looked down at her right hand. Angus followed her gaze. She rubbed a thumb back and forth across a forefinger.

Murphy approached them, an irritated expression cut into his face. He flapped his arms in a gesture of frustration. His mouth twitched with anger as he spoke. 'These guys are claiming the bus's papers are invalid.'

Angus's jaw dropped. He stared into a fenced-off field where a bored-looking black heifer had its tail raised in an arc. Its bowels eliminated a steaming olive brown jet of bovine diarrhoea. 'That's absolute bullshit.'

'Try telling that to the camouflage monkeys.' Murphy wiped sweat from his face with the bottom of his black and white op art shirt.

The Turks had enough English between them to string together a couple of sentences, the contents of which spelled out trouble – with a capital T.

Rolling Thunder received an armed escort to the outskirts of a small, terracotta roof-tiled town called Ipsala, which was built around a whitewashed hill fortress.

Angus and Murphy were led by two uniformed men into an austere grey edifice that housed the Turkish border authority for the region. The building was, in appearance, the kind of place where papers are given an official stamp and legal documents are issued.

The lads were unceremoniously pushed into a room where they came face to face with the man who was calling the shots. He was seated on a revolving leather chair behind a broad ostentatious desk that was so big Angus wondered how they'd managed to get it in through the door. On the wall behind the official hung a sepia photograph of a sallow-skinned personage with a pencil line moustache. He looked like an effeminate insomniac. The man sitting before them had the same coloured skin, although his moustache was more exuberant. Dressed in a pompous, braid-embellished uniform, like that of a Latin American dictator, it was easy for Angus to imagine him pacing a corridor in Buckingham Palace, as he waited impatiently for an audience with the Queen, before being decorated with a RHA (*Right Horribilis Anus*) medal. In other words, he appeared ridiculous to Angus, which did not mean he wasn't dangerous.

The Turk looked up from the sheet of paper he was studying, drew thoughtfully on a cigarette and blew a thick plume of what smelled like toasted hippo droppings in the Scots' direction. The acrid reek blended with the ripe pong of flatulence and whiff of typewriter oil that hung in his corrupt domain where, day in day out, he exerted his influence. The uniformed bureaucrat hacked up some mucus, spat into a convenient brass spittoon and got down to business.

'Please be seated,' he said, speaking heavily accented English, delivered in a quiet voice. He smiled smugly, confident in the knowledge that no matter how inaudible his words, they still carried a lot of clout.

'Well now,' he began, after a few loaded moments of silence, not a flicker of expression in his dark hooded eyes, 'it seems that you are in serious trouble. You have broken Turkish law by importing a vehicle into the country without the correct documentation.' He paused for effect, cleared his throat again and spat towards the spittoon. He missed. A thick gobbet of green phlegm splattered on to the bare concrete floor. His head gave an irritated nod and his leather chair creaked a complaint as he leaned forward and said, 'I have to inform you that your illegal activities could lead to... How should I put it? ...an expensive and time-consuming legal process. Unless, that is, a separate financial arrangement can be agreed upon.' With a thin ugly smile he added, 'I can assure you that the wheels of Turkish bureaucracy can grind very slowly...' His words trailed off as he blew a doughnut-sized smoke ring across the desk and stared at Angus and Murphy with something that looked like ironic humour in his dark eyes.

The light in the drab office took on a sinister aspect, as if the man's words had somehow altered the physical structure of the room to make it suffocatingly small. In the thick silence the swishing ceiling fan sounded suddenly loud.

The customs officer squinted at his fake gold watch, signalling that he was too vain to wear spectacles and that more important matters awaited his urgent attention. He shrugged, as if to say that he cared little for the outcome of their meeting, and then lit another hippo shit filter-free cigarette from the stub of his last one. A cracked actor, he sat smiling to himself on the stage set of *Daylight Extortion*. It was a B-movie that left the lads with only one question to be answered – how much does it cost to get out of here?

'I'm not fu—'

Before Murphy had a chance to blurt out something that could get them locked up in Sodomy Central Prison, Angus slid a baseball-booted foot across his friend's and pressed hard. The journey up to this point had been a case of surfing along on the crest of a very high wave. Now, to avoid wipeout, it was necessary to hang ten and play along with the sly Turk's game.

Angus and Murphy were very aware that, to a man like the power-broking border official sitting before them, it could not have been made more obvious that they were a pair of drug-crazed hippies cruising freedom's shore, even if they'd been wearing bright orange sandwich boards with big black letters stencilled on to them, proclaiming in Turkish, 'STONED OUT OF OUR MINDS'. The last thing they needed was for a quantity of illegal narcotics to be discovered on the bus. Even had they been clean, they both knew with gut-wrenching certainty that the Turks were quite capable of planting something on them.

Eating a very large helping of rancid rum baba, the Turkish equivalent of humble pie, and paying a bribe was the only intelligent course of action. The corrupt official settled on five-hundred American dollars. It was a blatant rip-off, but the two Scots grovelled in front of the customs man, apologizing profusely for having broken his trumped up laws, while he puffed on his rancid cigarette and patted his moustache as if it were a pet dormouse. He took his right hand away from his face and began tapping out a dead man's dirge with his fingertips on the wooden desk until he gave a forced dry cough and rose wearily to his feet, signalling that the interview was over. He ushered the two hippies out of the cobweb-netted throne room of his fiefdom with a contented yawn and then his face split into a grotesque smile. He was obviously delighted to have the cash in his pocket and glad to be rid of the scruffy foreigners who, after having paid his unofficial tariff, had no place in his world.

Outside, under the bright light of day, Angus and Murphy looked up at freedom's sky and breathed a deep sigh of relief.

Murphy shook his head not quite believing what they'd just been subjected to. 'What a fucking bastard that guy was.'

'Yeah,' agreed Angus. 'You're not joking. I hate fuckers like that.' He turned to Murphy and slapped him on the back. 'Come on, man, let's get out of here. It's time to check out Istanbul.'

3

TURKISH DELIGHT

A week after driving off the ferry at Calais, Rolling Thunder joined the heavy flow of traffic snaking its way through Istanbul's suburbs. Scenes of urban sprawl assaulted the travellers' eyes. Surrounded by garish billboards, proclaiming the merits of new, improved soap powder and the latest models of cars, factories were pouring out monochromatic clouds of grey smoke from red brick chimneystacks. Flat-roofed warehouses gave way to shabby office blocks and then grime-stained residential areas, intersected by streets with no names and peopled by throngs of tawny-faced pedestrians. Scattered throughout were white-painted mosques, their minarets adorned with shiny brass crescents that reflected dull sunlight.

All of Raj's driving skills were brought into play as he steered through traffic that was tied in drunken sailors' knots. Any notions he'd entertained about there being something remotely resembling a highway code in that part of the world were sucked out of the window to float off on the hot clouds of hydrocarbon emissions, streaming out of a multitude of blackened exhaust pipes.

A human element was also at play within the low gear soundtrack created by the downtown gridlock. Above the motorized thrum of overheating engines, apoplectic drivers vented their frustrations via an orgy of horn blowing. The resulting cacophony rising into the polluted air was deafening, a herd of stampeding mechanical beasts yowling and bellowing in protest at having been brought to a standstill.

Raj was gripping the leather steering wheel so tightly his knuckles were turning grey from the pressure. His pink tongue was sticking out the side of his mouth in concentration as he inched Rolling Thunder's gargantuan bulk along narrow streets, congested with American fifties-style Dolmus taxis and tramcars that crawled along as if they were on their way to a funeral.

Up in the bus's observation bubble, the girls were taking in the sights and sounds of Near Eastern urban chaos. They were smoking a joint of Malawi laughing grass, their girlish voices warbling with euphoric laughter.

Meanwhile, Raj was breaking out in a sweat. He took a right turn into a steeply inclined lane, flanked by small cafés. Under dusty awnings, the cafés' patrons sat outside on low wooden chairs, lazily sipping coffee as they browsed newspapers and smoked tobacco through snaking tubes that stemmed from water-cooled pipes. Raj turned right again and drew to a halt behind a London Transport bus. The double-decker was painted Day-Glo orange and parked on the opposite side of the main road from the Blue Mosque, in front of an establishment called The Pudding Shop.

As far as the hot, chocolate-flavoured pudding went, the sugar-loaded, black jellified rice goo that the café produced and sold in glass desert bowls was at the very least a cure-all for the munchies. Clientele-wise, the place was a backpacker's Mecca. During evening hours, the neon-lit bar was crammed with a mixed bag of hippy itinerants and local men in white shirts, who sat around eating, smoking and drinking glasses of Turkish coffee that was so thick you could have spread it with a knife. More than anything else, The Pudding Shop was a platform for the telling of road stories and exchanging snippets of information relevant to the dauntless traveller. The air hummed with multilingual chatter. If that wasn't interesting enough one could spend time checking out the notice board. It was as thick as a mattress with notes that had piled up over the years. Written on scraps of paper, the messages ranged from, 'Bobby Moustache, I've got your medicine. Meet me outside Yener's café at midnight', to, 'Space for three riders back to UK, £25 a seat, non-negotiable. Magic Bus leaves from across the street Friday, 10 a.m. sharp. Sorry, no junkies.'

Sorry, no junkies. I opened my eyes for a moment, looked out over the sparkling sea and smiled what I suppose might be described as a melancholic smile. I inhaled deeply and let out a pensive sigh. My brother's voice continued talking to me, narrating his story, as clearly as though he were sitting beside me on that deserted beach. I closed my eyes and returned to Istanbul and concentrated on Angus's description of how it had been in 1973.

Back then, without the aid of guidebooks, overland travellers were obliged to view the world as it really is − a complex cultural and topographical jigsaw puzzle, the interlocking pieces of which form mountain ranges, canyons, valleys, rivers and borderlines. Everyone in The Pudding Shop was open to a good conversation about new developments on the overland trail.

A decade later, with the arrival of cheap air travel, the prerequisites of having a courageous heart and adventurous spirit to reach hitherto difficult to access destinations would become obsolete. The time needed to traverse a continent would be reduced from days, weeks or even months to a few hours spent looking down through the clouds at anonymous landmasses, where contact with the fascinating human beings who inhabit those places was made impossible – even if one was fortunate enough to have a window seat.

Murphy talked to a tall Frenchman who had run foul of a gifted psychic woman. She was employed by the Indian customs at the Wagah border checkpoint, and had an impressive track record for busting hippy smugglers. The Frenchman had paid for this information with a one-year jail sentence. The clairvoyant had singled him out and, after a thorough search, it was discovered that a kilo of Kashmiri hashish was secreted in the soles of his Sherpa boots.

Seated below a large peace sign, painted on one of the Pudding Shop's walls, Jenny bought twenty grams of fresh opium from the Frenchman's shifty-eyed girlfriend, who had a gold stud set in her left nostril and said *très bien* to almost everything.

Angus was none too happy to hear about Jenny's purchase. He did not enjoy smoking opium because it left him with a headache. He was also concerned that if the crew got wasted on the narcotic it would mean spending more time in Istanbul than he felt necessary.

The following morning, awakened by loudspeakers echoing across the city as muezzins called out the day's first prayer, he rose out of bed to find his apprehension from the evening before made manifest. During the night, his companions had puffed their way on to the 'Oblivion Express' and, asleep on the down-bound train, were now living in suspended animation, going station to station, far away in the Land of Nod.

One cup of instant coffee later, Angus was rummaging around in a hidden compartment behind the sink. He found what he was searching for; a small glass jar containing the LSD stash. Angus swallowed a tiny gelatine square and placed another in a corner of his wallet, just in case he needed to refuel on his solo psychedelic adventure trip in Istanbul.

The doors of perception hissed open and he stepped out on to the pavement. It was just after dawn and it was cold. There had been a light dusting of snow during the night.

Early morning traffic was beginning to build up in the streets by the time he wandered into the Kapali Carsi, a vast roofed-in bazaar, selling everything from wooden false teeth to stainless steel chastity belts with reinforced padlocks attached. The souk was a riot of clashing colours and noises. The whole building was permeated by the pungent aromas of a great variety of spices, piled up in neat little multicoloured volcanoes outside of merchants' shops.

For an hour or so he wandered aimlessly, enjoying invitations from shopkeepers, tailors and carpet salesmen to examine the merchandise on display more closely and find out what *'the last price'* was. When he began to see everything with increased clarity and hear people's compulsive thought patterns, buzzing like hornets on the attack, he decided to seek out a less contaminated atmosphere to hang out and let go in.

The Turkish sun had risen above Istanbul's rooftops to cast bright light on the streets. The smell of coffee and freshly baked bread hung in the cool air. It was just another busy morning of hustle and bustle for the city's inhabitants. Angus gave a ragged shoeshine boy a ten lire note so that he would stop pestering him to polish his suede boots.

He allowed himself to be carried by the river of life's current as it flowed along the crowded cobblestone streets. Viewed through his psychedelically expanded retinal circus rings, the pedestrians surrounding him went through a metamorphic meltdown, which made them appear like microorganisms dancing in a Petri dish.

He turned a corner and, from a distance of about a kilometre, saw the grand cosmic bubble of curving masonry and brick that is the Sultan Ahmet, or Blue Mosque as it is commonly known. Built during the early years of the seventh century and named after the Muslim sovereign who'd ordered its construction, the magnificent mosque with its six towering minarets is western Istanbul's most defining architectural feature. To Angus's turned on mind, the masterpiece of Islamic architecture looked like a nuclear reactor surrounded by streamlined white missiles. He felt inexorably drawn towards the huge building.

As Angus drifted across Sultan Ahmet Square he decided to have a 'Talk to God' experience. He let the second dose of acid melt on the tip of his tongue. The tiny gelatine square tasted like out-of-sight Turkish delight. *LSD!* He had to control himself from shouting it out loud.

To one side of the mosque's main entrance, wooden shelves provided a place for worshippers to deposit their shoes. Barefoot, Angus bowed his head in reverence and walked under the arched doorway. Inside the enormous house of prayer he was immediately overwhelmed by feelings of harmony and grace. The ambience within the masjid was suffused by an air of calmness that he found welcoming, especially as he was by now hallucinating like a madman. He felt like he'd wandered into a new world.

Sunbeams from the east streamed through stained-glass windows set high above in the curving edges of the main cupola. The filtered sunlight reflecting on the walls created a mysterious light show of moody colours. Beautiful blue and white Iznik tiles, set in complex interlocking floral patterns, adorned the high walls. The ceramic tiles appeared fascinating to his astonished eyes. There were thousands of them, each one an expression of the same creative impulse. This added to the overall impression of the many millions of skilled artisans' hours that must have been poured into this monumental house of Islamic worship. In apparent defiance of the laws of gravity, massive pillars supported domed ceilings, one built upon another until reaching the central, uppermost cupola.

Overall, electric blue permeated the dim light within the Sultan Ahmet. As the creative state of Angus's eyes increased he wandered around examining intricate testimonies to the talented craftsmen who had helped create the huge building. He stood on a thick red carpet and gazed up into the centre of the main cupola. It converted into a portal leading to the unknown. He broke away from its magnetic pull when his neck muscles began to ache.

Like the individual instruments in a cosmic orchestra, the sound of echoing voices harmonized into one unified hum. Angus's sense of self was in such a state of dissolution, he felt like an oxygen atom being carried on Almighty Allah's breath. His body began performing a peculiar repertoire of actions. After shrinking to an atomic particle it would then blow up and expand like a hot air balloon. Unable to remain standing, he sat down in a quiet corner. He tied his long dark hair up in a topknot and then religiously wrapped his head in a turban, formed from the black cotton scarf that he'd been wearing around his neck. Overcome by awe, he knelt on the carpeted floor and then prostrated himself. The carpet was warm on his forehead and smelled of disinfectant. He remained in that position and watched a circle of bright colourless light open up in the centre of his mind. His inner eye looked into the middle of the dazzling brilliance and saw what appeared to be the hollow end of a thick cable. He was sucked into it. Picking up speed, he shot down a tunnel, its curved opaque interior as smooth as glass.

When the rushing sensation of accelerated motion was reaching the point of becoming unbearable, Angus flew out the end of the tube and found himself floating in space. There wasn't a sound. He looked around and saw that he was surrounded by what looked like rainbow-coloured footballs. They were radiating high frequency transmissions that related to the source, purpose and laws pertaining to all of life. More and more translucent globes were popping out of astro sockets identical to the one he'd exited from a moment before. Then the realization struck him that he also was a sphere of light. Eyeless, he could see. Looking in the direction he sensed as being down, he saw that he was hovering high above the surface of a glowing white sun, its curving horizon endless. He once more started to pick up speed and plummeted towards the solar giant. A feeling like you get descending in an express elevator came over him. There were no distances on earth like he was now covering in his expanded mind. As Angus drew closer, he perceived that the massive sun was an illusion created by the gathering together of trillions of rainbow globes like himself. A space opened up for him. He took what he instinctively knew to be his own place in the infinite community of spheroid spirits and became an intelligent cell in the brain of a great cosmic being. Suspended in a state of extreme ecstasy, every particle of his soul was bathed in bliss. He remained there for what seemed like an eternity – in reality, the time it takes for the All-seeing One to wink.

Angus sat up straight and it then occurred to him that, during the whole time he'd been in the mosque, not a soul had paid the slightest bit of attention to him. It was as if he did not exist. Worshippers passed by focused on themselves, practising the lost art of remaining silent. The strong aura of sacred geometry, along with the edifice's immensity, inspired him to look within and connect with that which is greater than one's normal ego-bound condition.

Time appeared to pass. Angus opened his eyes and began to examine the palms of his hands. Their lines swirled around in phantasmagorical combinations that contained worlds within worlds. Specks of dust, lodged in his fingerprints' deep crevices, became entire cities, some ultra-modern, while others appeared medieval. Zooming in to one of the latter, women dressed in sackcloth came into view. *'Gardiloo! Gardiloo!'* He could hear their warning cries as they emptied night soil out of open windows into the feculent streets below, where pedestrians waded and staggered through a swamp composed of human waste, trying to dodge the airborne shit raining down on their heads.

Like a visionary Einstein, he marvelled at the illusions created by the time-space continuum, pure relevant phenomena in themselves. He experienced himself as a miniature cosmos, his expanded consciousness an infinite sky within which nebulous thoughts drifted by like stellar nurseries. He saw directly that everything, including his illusionary self, was a play of light and sound constantly transforming in a singular continuous flux. His exhalations and inhalations corresponded exactly to the universe's most fundamental law of expansion and contraction. All there ever was and all there ever would be was contained within the atomic moment.

Grateful for this revelation, Angus joined the faithful as they faced Mecca for *Salat al-Zuhr*, the early afternoon prayer. He mirrored the worshippers' movements as they prostrated themselves in obeisance to the all-powerful will of Allah. There was something simple and potent about such a communal act of humbleness performed in such magnificent surroundings.

Some of the pious wept openly, a common occurrence among devout Muslims. These devotional practices were performed with the minimum of fuss, humility being a virtue that was actively exercised by the faithful on a daily basis.

When the people around him began to take on the appearance of fuzzy holographic images coloured by their individual personalities, Angus sat back against a marble pillar. He closed his eyes and the acid took him higher than he'd ever been before. He felt like a glass onion being peeled to its selfless core. Like the exhausted fuel tanks on a rocket, layer after layer fell away as he blasted into deep inner space, bound for the kernel of truth. For an instant he became a tiny soap bubble, vanishing down an eddy in the stream of consciousness until it dissolved into a silent vastness, a witnessing awareness that contained the world. This was his first real glimpse of a reality greater than that of the individual − a reality which was both transcendental and more fundamental than that of religions and philosophic systems.

When Angus returned to the world of name and form, he did so knowing that his individuality was a sensory mirage, something to play with and experience, that's all. He'd seen that he was only a wave on the surface of an eternal ocean. It was through the grace of God that life had been breathed into his body so that he might, for a few fleeting moments, be allowed to dance upon the earth and experience the illusion of separateness.

It was early evening when Angus exited the mosque. He collected his desert boots, bent down, put them on and fumbled as he tried to remember how to tie his laces. He stood, took a few unsteady steps, turned and raised his eyes to observe a robed muezzin on a small balcony, set high up on one of the mosque's towering white minarets. Turbaned, the man began to call the faithful to prayer, prompting flocks of startled pigeons to fill the sky. *'Allaaaagh hoooo Akbarrrr!'* The muezzin's amplified voice echoed over Sultan Ahmet Square. The plaintive sound, its eerie spirituality and the poignant message it carried needed no translation as it resonated within the psychedelic tripper's heart, making him think that Islam was right in saying that there is only one God. As far as holy names went, Allah sounded as good to him as any other, but it was the idea of oneness that appealed to him in that particular moment.

Angus stood for some time and watched the sun go down behind the rooftops of Istanbul, a city that, in many ways, formed the gateway to the East.

The sky was darkening by the time he entered a cheap restaurant situated under the Galata Bridge, a pontoon bridge that spanned the Golden Horn. A vacant plastic table by a window was wiped clean for his use. He sat down and ordered a plate of butter bean stew from a corpulent waiter wearing a stained white apron. Angus looked out over the Bosphorus and watched the lights of Eastern Istanbul twinkle on the water as traffic rumbled overhead and the floor beneath him swayed as the sea moved beneath it. The food, when it arrived, tasted so good he asked for a second helping and then a third and then finally a fourth. Stuffed to the point that his full belly made him look like he was six months pregnant, Angus settled the bill and wandered out into the street. Gas from the high-protein stew was already beginning to expand in his alimentary canal.

A lingering sense of being mysteriously linked to everything and everybody stayed with Angus as he farted his way back to the bus. His flatulent sonic booms echoed in the narrow streets. Pedestrians staggered and reeled in the gaseous aftermath of his passing.

Propelled by his spluttering, gas-powered rectum, his pace quickened and he began to wonder what his friends were getting up to. He reached the bus and, when its concertina door opened, the fragrance of fresh coffee drifted out into the cold night air.

'Hi, man', said Raj from the driver's seat, a Fabulous Furry Freak Brothers comic lying open in his lap. He stretched his arms and yawned, a vacant expression on his face.

Angus stepped inside Rolling Thunder's cosy, cocoon-like interior and found the rest of the crew sitting around the dining table, recovering from the nullifying effects of the previous night's opium session. He sat down beside Jenny, who was wearing a swirling psychedelic dress. Her normally wavy blonde hair was damp and lay flat against her head and slender neck. She smelled of orange blossom-scented shampoo and her own natural odour, which came to Angus's frozen nose like olafactory treasure. He inhaled deeply and sighed.

Jenny curled an arm around his neck and asked, 'Where have you been all day?' She pulled him close and gave him a wet kiss on the cheek that slalomed onto his lips.

'Oh...you know,' he answered, 'just out and about having a mind blowing experience.'

Jenny peeked into her lover's eyes. 'Looks to me like you're still in the process.'

He smiled. 'Yeah, I'm still pretty buzzed out. I took two of Mike's Window Panes.'

'Two!' She drew back from him. 'What on earth was that like?'

'Man, it was like a cosmic family reunion. I spent the whole day in the Blue Mosque. Even went so far as to join the Muslims in their prayers.'

Unsure what to make of this, Jenny changed the subject. 'We're off to the Turkish baths. Would you like to come along for a scrub-a-dub-dub?'

'Can I take Donald with me?'

'Who's Donald?' she asked, gathering the ends of her hair together to slip them through a black velvet band.

'My rubber duck.'

'I'm sure that can be arranged, my darling. As long as wee Donald doesn't mind getting his vulcanized feathers wet.'

'What are we waiting on?' Angus rose to his feet and farted loudly. 'Let's go.'

Now that the sun was long gone, freezing cold air blew in from the Sea of Marmara to chill the city streets. Still high, Angus giggled to himself as frost burned in his nostrils. Pedestrians, exhaling white puffs of breath as he passed them on the pavement, were transformed by LSD into smoke-belching steam locomotives that, due to the minimalist cartoon-like expressions he projected on to their blank faces, could have been related to Thomas the Tank Engine.

The baths had been built in Roman times. Judging by the amount of green mould on the ceilings, the place hadn't seen a fresh lick of paint since Pontius Pilate washed his guilty hands in the hall of judgement and sealed his fate.

Shrouded in steam, stout masseurs, with arms as thick as elephants' trunks, stood waiting in attendance. Water vapour was pumped into partitioned cubicles via an archaic plumbing system that gurgled and groaned. Beads of condensation ran down the white tiled walls like an army of tears.

Muscles made pliable by intense heat were worked on by individual strongmen and subjected to the kind of punishment that Mohammed Ali had been capable of delivering at the peak of his walloping career – and that was just for starters. Once softened up, the next stage of the painful process involved being bent and stretched into an involuntary variety of contortions.

When the punishment squad felt the time was right for a horrible surprise, the client, naked except for a skimpy towel to cover his or her private parts, was requested to lie belly down. Heels were picked up while a heavy bare foot applied pressure to the coccyx. It was time for the mother of all spine crackers, the Marquis De Sade reverse back bend. Angus's eyes almost popped out of their sockets when he heard and felt every vertebrate in his spinal column crunch into disharmony.

Just in case any part of one's skeleton was accidentally left in its correct anatomical position, the bare torso boyos soon put paid to that. Standing on their victim's red raw back, the mad masseurs performed their personal rendition of the Turkish Highland fling. If getting in touch with one's early incarnations as invertebrate species was the goal, it was indeed the perfect regression therapy. Angus experienced sensations that he had not felt in over fifty million years and was reminded of the time when he was a jellyfish washed up on the shores of the Black Sea. Had the burly bunch of sadists, now posing as masseurs, been living in the late fifteenth century they could have practiced their trade down in the Alcázar of Toledo's torture chambers – under the watchful eye of the Spanish Inquisition.

When a large wooden box, containing wire toilet brushes and what looked like industrial-sized, double-ended, black rubber dildos, was hauled out from under a five-ton marble slab that served as a massage table, Murphy shouted, 'Okay, boys, hold it right there!' This brought an abrupt halt to the proceedings, and in all probability quite literally saved his companions' skins as well as his own.

With no desire to risk undergoing a possible life-threatening assault, the Scots hurried off in the direction of the changing rooms.

Thanking the masseurs profusely for an experience they would be unable to forget for as long as they lived, the wobbly kneed hippies paid their fees, including a healthy tip, just to keep the gorillas sweet. They ran out of the hammam as fast as their bruised and twisted legs could carry them. Clouds of steam rose from their heads as they made their way back to the bus.

'I can hardly walk,' complained Angus, as he hobbled along the street hand in hand with Jenny. 'I can't believe I actually paid someone to beat me up.'

4

RUSSIAN ROULETTE AND MONOPOLY

After his run-in with the Istanbuli masseurs, Angus required forty-eight hours to regain any real sensation in his legs. He spent the next couple of days in the back of the bus as Rolling Thunder headed east along the E23 highway.

Alice and Nina almost jumped ship in Ankara when it turned bitterly cold. Murphy and Raj convinced them not to catch a flight back to London by saying the weather would clear up in a couple of days and telling them that they couldn't live without them. The girls were naïve enough to believe such nonsense and settled into practicing Transcendental Meditation. A handsome Englishman had turned them on to the Maharishi Mahesh Yogi's technique during their last evening in The Pudding Shop, when everyone else was too stoned to notice. The charming spiritual hustler had charged Alice and Nina fifty dollars each for their secret mantras. The girls began droning like a pair of contented bumblebees, while their boyfriends looked on like happy honey farmers. A somewhat less harmonious scenario was taking place between Angus and Jenny. They were embroiled in an ongoing argument about her continuing to smoke opium. Everyone else had decided to give the narcotic a miss because it was a downer.

Istanbul was three days behind and daylight was fading fast as snow flurries began to intensify and thicken. Raj was sitting in the hydraulic driver's seat, steering the snow-chained bus through what was to become a white-out blizzard in northeastern Turkey. Darkness fell and neither telegraph poles, road signs nor the highway east could be seen for the snow. During particularly strong gusts of wind, Raj could not see more than a few metres beyond the windscreen. The engine roared in second gear, kept there to retain traction on the slippery road.

Mother Nature was flexing her mighty muscles in a show of raw power by dropping billions of tons of snow over the land and turning the dial on the environmental deep freeze to minus fifteen degrees centigrade. Not to be

42

outdone, Lola, the fickle Goddess of Fate, contrived to make the bus run out of fuel in the middle of colourless nowhere. Located on a high plateau, 6000 feet above sea level, the next dot on the map was a town called Erzurum. A red warning light had been glowing on the fuel gauge for ten minutes. Raj doubted that the single-decker would make it to the next petrol station. There had already been a heated debate as to whose fault it was that there was not enough diesel in the tank and how it came to happen that the reserve storage cans were all empty. When the engine shuddered and then cut out, Raj steered to the hard shoulder. Rolling Thunder skidded to a halt beside a snowdrift. The hazard lights were switched on. Their orange flashing reflected off the snow outside, providing stroboscopic illumination until Nina broke out a box of candles from her trading supplies. In such extreme weather conditions a flat battery was something to be avoided at all costs and it was therefore the bus's internal lights were not switched on. The ambience inside the bus would have been cosy had it not been for the chilling fact that the temperature was dropping rapidly.

According to the map there was a petrol station a few miles further along the road. Angus and Raj volunteered to go on a fuel hunting expedition. Armed with a thermos flask full of scalding hot tea, reinforced by a quarter bottle of rum, they put on olive green, army surplus parkas, pulled the fur-lined hoods tight around their heads and set off down the snow-covered road, carrying two empty jerry cans.

Twenty minutes later, they hitched a ride on the first vehicle to come their way, a Skoda truck loaded with oxyacetylene gas bottles. Inside the stiflingly warm cab, it became immediately apparent that the bearded driver was drunk on arrack, a potent alcoholic beverage made from fermented dates.

'*Assalaamu aleikkum.* My name Zaloo,' said the trucker, introducing himself as he glanced towards a bottle, rolling back and forth on the floor. He smiled broadly at Angus and Raj to show off his many gold teeth and then prodded his chest with a grubby finger. 'Me Kurd.'

His two passengers thought he said turd and grinned at each other. Raj entered the spirit of the occasion by pointing at himself and saying, 'Me Scottish.'

Zaloo's bloodshot eyes opened wide. 'Ah-ha! Scottish whisky very, very good!' He was breathing alcohol fumes that were practically flammable.

Angus shouted, 'Look Out!'

The driver spun the wheel and the lorry veered away from the edge of a dangerous curve, full beam headlights momentarily cutting a bright swathe through wind-driven snowflakes to illuminate thick low cloud.

'Ah-ha-ha!' Arrack-sodden Zaloo cackled and reached into the insides of his padded nylon jacket. He whipped out a big rusty revolver... *Boof! Boof! Boof! Boof! Boof! Boof!* ...and quickly discharged six bullets into the roof of the cramped cab. The Kurd laughed uproariously, delighted with his personal demonstration of what a badass macho cowboy he was. Angus and Raj's nostrils contracted from the stifling stench of cordite. They turned to face each other and swore they would never again let the bus run out of fuel. Caught between the extreme possibilities of freezing to death or being vaporized if the madman decided to reload and pop a few slugs into his highly volatile cargo, clanking a couple of feet behind them, the two friends hung on to their seats as Zaloo steered his lorry on its sickeningly erratic course.

Half a bottle of arrack and a long incomprehensible conversation later, artificial light shone through the wall of whiteness in front of the truck's cracked windscreen. It was a petrol station. Zaloo waved and began reloading his gun as Angus and Raj jumped to the ground. Gears crunched and a horn blared as the truck disappeared down the road.

Gas cans in hand, the two Scots made their way over to a shuttered office. The door was locked.

Raj asked, 'What the fuck are we going to do now?'

'Have a drink,' suggested Angus, squatting down in the snow. He removed his thick woollen gloves with his teeth and then unscrewed the Thermos's cap and poured some of its steaming contents into a plastic cup. After taking a sip he handed the rum tea to Raj and said, 'What about Mister Zaloo?'

'The guy was pure mental,' declared Raj. 'I thought we'd had it when he started firing his gun into the roof.' He laughed, drank some tea, sniffed and cleared ice crystals from under his nose with the back of a gloved hand. 'What a story though, eh?'

'You're not joking,' said Angus. 'Kerouac's *Dharma Bums* and *On the Road* ain't got anything to compare with Zaloo, the trucker from hell who drinks Molotov cocktails and plays Russian roulette when he's loaded all six.' He rubbed the palms of his bare hands together, blew on his fingers, glanced over at his friend and shouted, not loudly, about four out of ten, 'Hey, you greedy Indian shit, don't drink all of that.'

Raj grinned wolfishly and passed the empty cup to Angus for a refill. Small feather-like snowflakes drifted down from the sky and settled on their clothes. Behind them, with much clattering of bolts, the petrol station's office door creaked open. Wearing a fur hat with earflaps, a thick woollen jersey and stained long johns tucked into black rubber boots, a bleary eyed pump attendant emerged from the shadows. He couldn't speak a word of English. It took a fifty-lira note to cross the language barrier. The Turk switched on the diesel pump and then a second fifty-lira note inspired him to telephone for a taxi. Half an hour later, a battered black Peugeot estate car, driven by a wild-eyed man who had obviously learned to drive by studying car-chase scenes in Hollywood movies, careened to a halt beside the illuminated petrol pumps.

It was starting to register in Angus and Raj's minds that it was eastern Turkey's night of the mad motorists. Before they were delivered back to the bus, Anton, the chain-smoking cabby, deliberately let his vehicle spin out of control on three separate occasions, each time embedding the steaming radiator grill of his Peugeot in a snowdrift. Angus and Raj had to get out into the bone-chilling cold to help free it. They spent more time pushing the car than they did sitting in it, which was the whole idea because the taxi's meter was running – fast. When they reached their destination, Anton badgered them into paying an extortionate fee, ten times above what it should have been due to his charging by the minute instead of the kilometre.

Savage winds whistled under an oyster-grey sky as Rolling Thunder growled into Erzurum's main square, deserted except for a gang of noisy children drawing wooden sleds behind them. Apart from the childrens' excited cries the whole place seemed to be holding its breath. It was as light as it was going to get for the next few days. The town's narrow crooked streets were lined by slant-roofed buildings. Long icicles hung from eaves and snowdrifts banked up against walls that had been built from volcanic rock, which was as black as coal and added to the general air of gloom that hung over the place.

The exhausted travellers slept for several hours as the wind blew steadily from the northeast and plastered the bus with snow. By mid-afternoon four feet of snow had settled on the small city, a snow so thick it could hardly be said to have settled at all, rather piled up and set like icy concrete, which lowered the outside temperature until it dropped into a new sub-zero dimension called minus twenty-five degrees centigrade.

Later that day, when the crew awoke, it was difficult to emerge from the bus due to the amount of frozen snow that had built up outside of the door.

In a local café that smelled like a skunk emporium, the crew huddled around a potbellied, cast iron stove. It was fuelled by dried cow-dung, wood being in short supply in the region. A thick cloud of acrid, mustard-coloured smoke hung below the large rectangular room's rafters. Illumination was provided by a single, piss-yellow bulb, which was dotted by dead flies and suspended from the ceiling by a dusty, twisted cord. The light bulb cast jaundiced light on the unrendered concrete walls, coated with a film of grease and grime. The floor was strewn with soggy sawdust. From behind a long bar counter, made from cement-splattered wooden planks stretched between two rusty oil drums, Turkish saz music buzzed out of a blaring radio's cracked loudspeaker. Served by a slavering humpbacked waiter, the establishment's coffee had all the physical attributes of hot, dark brown gloss paint. Pale, dull-faced patrons, who looked like they'd spent their lives in a dungeon counting grains of sand, sat around chattering to each other. Their conversations were interrupted by sporadic loud squawks produced by a brood of scrawny chickens who had invaded the café to escape from the bitter cold. The filthy birds flapped around and clucked frantically as they shat on woodworm-riddled chairs and tables that looked like rejects from a council tip.

By using international sign language, it was ascertained from the locals that the Bazargan border crossing into Iran was closed. Angus stomped slush and chicken shit from his boots as he talked to the gorilla-like proprietor who was biting chunks from a huge overripe banana. The hulking brute threw the fruit's bruised yellow skin over his left shoulder for good luck and then, using a bestial concatenation of grunts, barks and howls, communicated that it usually took a few days for bulldozers fitted with snowploughs to clear the pass when it snowed so heavily.

Back on the bus, the crew settled into a Monopoly-playing marathon. The players passed 'Go' on numerous occasions, ended up in jail for no other reason than bad luck and built up property portfolios. Street war broke out in Mayfair when it was discovered that Lord Murphy, CEO of the Monopoly Corporation, was embezzling money from the bank.

Plans were made for an excursion, which didn't go further than talking about it, to nearby Mount Ararat. According to tradition, the conical mountain was the setting for two of mankind's most important events. A discussion ensued about the origins of man, Adam and Eve, and why it happened that the divine gardener evicted them from the Garden of Eden, generally believed to have been located in Mount Ararat's foothills.

'It was Eve's fault,' commented Murphy. 'She shouldn't have been hanging out with a snake and stealing apples. Everybody knows how uptight gardeners get about their Granny Smiths.' He looked at Nina, who he'd been having sporadic arguments with since they left Scotland. 'That's women for you, always upsetting the fuckin' apple cart.'

'Male chauvinist pig,' snapped Nina, dismissing his comment with a wave of her ringed fingers. 'I think the only sin Adam and Eve ever committed was beleiving that sin exists in the first place. Anyway, at least Eve wasn't selfish like you. She shared the apple with her boyfriend.'

'What the fuck are you talking about? I don't like apples and I'm not a pig.'

'Oh yeah?' Nina placed an index finger on the point of her pert nose, pushed it up and went, *'Oink, oink, oink!'*

'You cheeky little—'

'Hey, cool it you guys,' Angus intervened. 'You're starting to sound like you've been married for twenty years.'

'Yeah,' agreed Alice, 'he's right. You two are blowing up in each other's faces so often you should change your names to Nitro and Glycerine.'

'Ha-ha, very fucking funny.' Nina's cheeks reddened with anger.

The conversation moved on to an incident that occurred some time later in Biblical history. Raj explained. 'After spending forty days and forty nights out on the ocean, a seafaring farmer called Noah, who bred and collected animals as a hobby, dropped anchor over Ararat's submerged sloping flanks. It was there that his ark was believed to have come to rest when the waters of the great flood started to recede.'

'What a load of fucking bollocks,' said Murphy, having decided to direct his hostile attentions towards his friend. 'You've got to be stupid if you believe that Bible shite.'

'Och, you just think you know everything, Murphy,' said Alice, snuggling up to Raj. 'Jesus was really cool, man. He was a hippy and he died on the cross for our sins.'

And all the coloured girls say...

'Yeah, right,' scoffed Murphy to the sound of Lou Reed's *Transformer* album playing in the background, 'Jesus might've died for somebody's sins, but they weren't mine.' He raised his chin in a show of defiance. 'We're descended from an ancestor which we share in common with the apes and that's all there is to it.'

Cool saxophone notes drifted out of the speakers.

Nina flicked the fringe of her long black hair out of her eyes, leaned over the dining table, patted Murphy on the crown of his shaggy head and said, 'Looking at you I'm forced to agree with your Darwinian logic, because you look like a hairy monkey.'

Murphy pushed her hand away with more force than necessary. 'That's not what you said last night,' he countered, licking the edge of a cigarette paper suggestively.

'That was different,' protested Nina, whose fashion note was a red tee shirt with 'MAKE LOVE NOT WAR' printed over her bulging breasts. 'Anyway, why can't you keep it here and now?'

Hey Joe, take a walk on the wild side...

'Okay then, I will,' said Murphy. 'Right here and right now I'm telling the lot of you that it must have been raining African lions and Great Danes for those forty days and nights when old Noah was sailing on the extremely high seas. Mount Ararat rises from a plain that is almost two kilometres above sea level and its cone shaped summit peaks out at a little under seventeen thousand feet. And in case you're wondering how come I know that, I read about it in a *National Geographic*.' He lit the joint he'd been rolling, blew smoke at his five companions and continued. 'I wonder how that trickster, The Lord, who works in mysterious fucking ways, managed to come up with so much water to deliver such an inordinate amount of precipitation. If you ask me, going by the appearance of the local populace, Captain Noah must have let a few monkeys loose in the region, who eventually joined the human community, got married, settled down and had a few monkids. These Erzurumites, or whatever the fuck they call themselves, are so simian in appearance they could have applied for jobs as extras during the making of *Planet of the Apes*.'

Nina patted him on the back. 'You must feel right at home then.'

Everybody laughed except Jenny, who'd had a thoughtful expression on her face during Murphy's brief lecture. 'I was just thinking about Adam and Eve,' she said. 'If they hadn't eaten the forbidden fruit they'd have continued to live like animals. They might have been happy but they wouldn't have known it. I reckon God planned it that way right from the start and that's why he told those guys to stay away from the tree of knowledge. That was a smart move. The best way to get anyone interested in a thing is to prohibit it. Adam and Eve were tricked into believing they could eat the forbidden fruit and get away with it. But they didn't, and they paid the price for disobeying their creator.' Jenny smiled and then concluded. 'I believe that the moral of the story is that God has sown the seed of desire for knowledge in us, his human creations. To achieve that knowledge you have to work for it. There is no shortcut. It's worth striving for because if you don't know you're happy, that happiness is worthless.' She lit an incense stick, waved it about like a magic wand and asked, 'Can I tempt anyone into playing another game of Monopoly?'

Angus glanced across the table at Jenny and found himself host to an unexpected wave of admiration for her.

'Yeah me,' said Raj in reply to Jenny's question, 'as long as I get to be the battleship.'

'I've already claimed it,' said Alice, holding up the small lead counter.

'Hey, that's mutiny.' Raj tried to grab the tiny grey ship out of her hand.

Alice laughed. She had a tendency to laugh for the slightest reason and now she had a good one.

Murphy began stacking up piles of brightly coloured bank notes on his side of the table. 'I'm the fuckin' banker,' he proclaimed, daring anyone to challenge him.

'You're so vicious…' Nina sang along to Lou Reed and looked poison-tipped stilettos at her boyfriend.

'You hit me with a *flowerrr!*' chorused the rest of the crew.

During four days of board games, a cabin fever outbreak was kept at bay by inhaling hashish smoke. As sticky as toffee, local hash, scored in the Chicken Run Café, came in thin, bendy strips wrapped in red cellophane paper. Cursing like a fishwife, Nina eventually threw all the boxes containing the games out into the snow when her boyfriend was, once again, caught red-handed stealing money from the Monopoly bank. *Old habits die hard*, was a throwaway line that definitely rang true in Murphy's case.

It was early morning on their fifth day in Erzurum. A cheer went up when news came through that the Bazargan Pass leading into Iran was open.

Under a brooding sky the colour of ashes, the deserted town square's thick silence was ruptured when Rolling Thunder's engine roared like a wounded beast and strained for a moment until she broke free from the snowdrifts that had built up against her side panels. Soon, she was slowly winding her way along a freshly gritted road, heading towards the frontier.

So let me be who I am and let me kick out the… To the sound of fiercely anti-establishment Detroit rockers, MC5, kicking out the jams, the bus rocked and rolled as she ascended into the pass by way of a treacherous series of bends. A weak sun broke through grey clouds. Mountains reared to the north of a landscape scoured clean by an abrasive wind and swathed in thick blankets of snow. The scene reminded Angus for a moment of Scotland and how, over a decade earlier, it was a winter such as this that had taken the life of his beloved stepfather, Daniel. When he felt the snow chains on the tyres key into the frozen powder covering the road, he let go of the memory and focused on his driving. The bus crested a steep hill. Gripping the steering wheel tightly, he eased up on the accelerator in order to avoid going into a downhill skid. When he heard the snow chains rattling against asphalt he pulled into a lay-by and parked.

Raj and Murphy took the stainless steel chains off the wheels and stored them in the luggage hold. Angus and Jenny walked over to the edge of a steep embankment to admire the view. Arm in arm, they stood and surveyed a vast snow-covered panorama.

'Man oh man,' said Jenny. 'Isn't that a wonderful sight?'

'Yeah,' Angus agreed, 'it certainly is. And it's great to have you by my side looking at it.'

She snuggled against him.

The sky was by now almost cloudless, the air crystal clear. In the foreground stood a massive outcrop of rock, which was home to a towered citadel. In the far distance, Mount Ararat and its twin peak rose up like extinct white volcanoes. Forming a backdrop to a scene that was both timeless and perfect, the pale blue sky deepened to ultramarine on the horizon.

'Mother Nature has fantastic tits,' shouted Murphy from behind, pointing towards the twin mountains.

Jenny cringed and whispered to Angus, 'Has it ever occurred to you that your mate's got a bit of a one-track mind?'

'No, never,' he answered. 'What makes you say that?'

Iran's roads were better surfaced than those of her Turkish neighbour. Driving along them, it soon became apparent that Iranian bus and truck drivers had signed a suicide pact with one another. Maniacal kamikazes, piloting six-wheeled, ten-ton coffins, were as common as distance markers on the highway to Tehran. Positioned on the roadside and placed every five kilometres, the white-painted markers counted down to the capital, which on a journey of over nine-hundred kilometres did little to relieve the monotony. Crisscrossed by thick, sagging electric cables supported by towering pylons, on some stretches the road narrowed down to such an extent that it was only wide enough to accommodate one and a half vehicles. If an uninitiated driver was foolish enough to imagine he was the one instead of the half, it was highly probable he'd find himself saying hello to the spirit in the sky quicker than it took to say 'Holy Insh'Allah'.

Although the Francophile Shah was still hanging on to power in Iran, Tehran's wide parallel boulevards, crammed with British-manufactured Hillman taxis, did not create the impression that the city's numerous mosques were going to be converted into discotheques any time in the foreseeable future. There were plenty of cinemas, showing Hollywood films and doing good business, judging by the long lines of patrons queuing up outside on the pavements. The movie houses stood in stark contrast to the mosques that, although huge in comparison, appeared somewhat forlorn and neglected. Their minarets were lined by green light bulbs that were switched on at night, creating a visual effect that was unearthly.

On first take it appeared that half the city's population was marching around in antiquated military uniforms, gold epaulettes being the ultimate fashion accessory of the time. The rest of Tehran's citizens seemed content to dress in biblical Old Testament costumes. If one was a non-military female, life outside of the home was viewed from a burka's eye slit.

Murphy, who had been studying a group of burka-clad women as they stood by a traffic light, rose up from his window seat and switched on the microphone that was plugged into the bus's sound system. 'Good afternoon—' Feedback howled out of the speakers. Murphy bent forward and adjusted the amp's volume control. 'Good afternoon,' he began again, pretending to beckon Nina with his left hand. 'Madame Hezbollah,' he said as if surprised to see his girlfriend, 'please come into my shop and try on one of these baggy, white satin prayer robes that have just arrived from our Ku-Klux-Klan wholesaler down in Alabama?' Nina looked away when he picked up a discarded tee shirt and dangled it in front of her face. 'Yes siree, you'll have enough room under one of these burkas to conceal a couple of bazookas and a brood of screaming children. Buy three and I'll chuck in a funny pointed hood and face mask for free. Buy a dozen and one for a cousin and I'll throw in a pair of stiletto-heeled sand—'

Angus jammed on the brakes at a busy traffic intersection. Murphy stumbled backwards and fell against the windscreen, bringing an abrupt end to his spontaneous performance.

Near to a tall grey concrete building, bristling with a sinister array of aerials and a fleet of parabolic antennae, just off downtown Tehran's tree-lined Sharah-e-Pahlavi Boulevard, the roadrunners checked into the renowned backpackers' haven, The Amir Kabir Hotel. Early the following morning, they moved back to the bus because of the racket rising up from the all-night garage downstairs, the bedbugs, cockroaches and mosquitoes, the communal seatless toilet that didn't flush behind a door without a lock on a u-shaped terrace that was infested by rats, and the paranoia. They'd had to stick their heads out the window when blowing a joint in case the uptight management got wind of it.

No visit to Iran's capital is complete without a tour of southern Tehran's Grand Bazaar. Having expanded and evolved over centuries, the souk encompasses an area of approximately ten square kilometres, making it one of the biggest public marketplaces in the world. The services of Hadi, a gangling teenager with gleaming white teeth and ears that stuck out from under his oily black hair like tan-coloured butterfly wings, were employed to navigate through the maze of winding streets and narrow alleyways that form the bazaar. Hadi claimed to have learned English from listening to Voice of America broadcasts on his transistor radio and watching spaghetti westerns which, upon hearing his Texan accent, wasn't hard to believe.

'Y'all stay close together now, folks,' he drawled as he led the travellers through an inconspicuous sandstone archway.

Angus was to later recall the bazaar's main entrance as being deceptive in the extreme. The arched gateway gave no hint of the thriving commercial colossus behind it.

'Wow, man, this is amazing,' cooed a saucer-eyed Nina upon encountering the first section of the bazaar they walked into, the gold market. Shops, fronted by display windows illuminated with dazzling light, were a temporary perch for all manner of filigreed gold jewellery. Inside the well-stocked stores, women in jet black burkas haggled from behind face veils with crafty-eyed salesmen. These sometimes-vehement disputes were centred on the price of golden bangles, brooches, rings, necklaces and any other kind of adornment made from the precious yellow metal that behind-the-scene artisans produced for their masters. Captivated by the beauty of these creations, the small group had to be herded together by Hadi for fear of anyone straying and becoming lost.

'Come, come this way,' called the young guide, beckoning with an eager hand. 'I want to take y'all to my uncle's teahouse.'

He ushered the Scots into the confines of a small café, its cushioned furnishings made from recycled iron reinforcing rods.

'*Salaam.*' The robed proprietor greeted them bowing from the waist, hands interlocked across his stout rotund belly, his big teeth flashing under the light of flickering fluorescent tubes.

It would soon become apparent that Hadi belonged to the biggest family in the country because in the dozen or so establishments he took the Scots to, there stood a beaming 'uncle' waiting to receive them.

'This is really brilliant,' said Alice, sitting down by a round table with a shiny, red and white checked, vinyl tablecloth. She pouted her lips, looked into a highly polished brass ashtray and applied lipstick that was the colour of arterial blood. 'You know...I haven't had a bad vibe from anyone since we entered the bazaar.'

It was true. The amicable bazaaris were going out of their way to welcome the young foreigners into their midst. Curious Iranian students, viewing the outlandishly dressed Westerners as emissaries from the capitalist world, greeted them with smiles and bombarded them with ridiculous questions pertaining to the Scots' homeland that revealed more about their own country than the one they were enquiring about. The most common question being, *Have you met the Beatles?*

'Yeah, I was just thinking the same thing myself,' said Raj in response to his girlfriend's enthusiastic comment. 'Everyone in this place is really cool, man.' He paused to bite a chunk out of a pastry that had just been delivered to their table. It was dripping with rose-scented honey. 'Mmmh, this stuff is delicious – perfect for the munchies.' He wiped his sticky mouth on a serviette. 'Let's smoke a joint.'

'Cool it, man,' cautioned Angus, looking up from a plate of abghoust beef stew. 'That French guy we met back in Istanbul told me a story about some guy who got five years for smoking a spliff in Iran.' He glanced around. 'And he didn't get time off for good behaviour.'

'He's right,' agreed Murphy. 'The bizzies here are into torture. Fuck knows what they'd do if they managed to get their dirty hands on European chicks behind a prison cell's locked door.'

'That's really heavy, man,' said Jenny, suddenly nervous. 'I'm dying for a smoke but maybe we better wait till we're back on the bus.' She stood up and called to Hadi, who was over at a counter having a discussion with the proprietor about his commission for delivering the foreigners to him. 'Hey, Hadi, come on, man. We want to go to the clothes market.'

'Hold on a minute,' said Angus, his mouth half full with beef stew. 'I want to finish my lunch.'

If bustling crowds of shoppers was an indication of success, business was booming. The scene on the streets was becoming more congested as the day wore on. The Scots brushed up against a jostling stream of chador-clad females and rubbed shoulders with youths dressed in wide-lapelled jackets and skin-tight jeans. Their risqué female counterparts wore patent leather boots with platform soles, mini-skirts, too tight blouses and headscarves. Military personnel bumped into grey-bearded clerics, their robes billowing as they hurried by on urgent holy missions. Sweating porters, backs bowed under monumental loads, vied for space with muscular deliverymen, blowing whistles to clear a path for the rubber-wheeled trolleys they hauled behind them, their eyes bulging as they heaved at loads better suited to carthorses. Marauding gangs of street urchins weaved in and out of the throng under the watchful alert eyes of policemen, who hung around in groups on street corners, fingering the trigger guards of the automatic machine pistols they had slung over the shoulders of their fatigue-style, dark blue uniforms.

'What a bloody din!' Raj's shouted complaint was drowned out by the percussive cacophony created by dozens of metalworkers' hammers, battering out pots, pans and water carriers in the heart of the copperware market.

Minus brothels and bars, every kind of social institution had its place in the bazaar's precincts. Its warren of passageways and arcades were home to thousands of shops and stalls. On the wider streets stood mosques, banks, madrasas, restaurants, steam baths and even a fire station with ancient, red-painted, Leyland fire trucks that were so well maintained they would have been considered prized exhibits in a British Transport Museum. Interspersed throughout were neat, well-swept squares centred on tiered fountains spouting jets of water, creating cool oases of calm in the heart of the hot clamorous marketplace.

Host to every strong smell, bright colour and loud noise created by God and man, the Scots were relieved when they exited the souk and returned to the relative quiet of the street outside.

Angus looked north into the distance and, through a bank of yellow smog, could make out the Alborz mountain range's snow-capped peaks, reflecting the late afternoon sunlight.

'Here you go, Hadi,' said Murphy, handing over a few hundred-rial notes.

Hadi's long eyelashes blinked in disbelief. 'Hop diggedy dawg, pard, you're a goddamn son of a gun!' he exclaimed, barely able to hold back the tears of gratitude glistening in his dark eyes. 'A thousand thank yous. May the all-merciful Allah shower his infinite blessings upon y'all. You've given me enough money to feed my entire family for a month.' He turned and bowed to each of the Scots in turn. 'Thank you, thank you, thank you my Scottish brothers and sisters.' All elbows and knees, the tall youth turned away from his generous benefactors and, with a skip to his step, joined the crowds milling around outside the bazaar.

'Aw, how cute,' sighed Nina, watching him merge with the thronging pedestrians crowding the pavement. 'I really liked him.'

'Me too,' chimed Alice, her red lips curving into a smile as she raised a hand to shield her face from the descending sun. 'Did you see his eyes? They were like a gazelles. I wish we could take him with us.'

'You've got to be fuckin' well joking,' said Murphy, overhearing their comments. 'We better get back to the bus for a smoke quick, before the pair of you completely lose the plot.' Murphy stepped aside to let a breathless old man pass by. Red-faced, he was pushing a rusty wheelbarrow, its cargo a bleating billy goat. 'Jesus,' continued Murphy, 'the way you two are going on, I'm tempted to agree with that guy who said that sobriety is the greatest intoxicant.' He slipped his arms round his female companions' slim waists.

Nina pushed him away, saying, 'I'm not sure, but I think it might have been Oscar Wilde who said that. But I know for certain that he did say that no man has real success in this world unless he's got a woman to back him. So don't speak down to me, you big lump that you are!'

'Huh!' Murphy was gobsmacked.

Alice twisted and unhooked herself from his other arm. 'Right on Nina,' she called, raising a clenched fist in front of Murphy's surprised face. 'Women's lib rules!'

The times they were a-changin'.

The last stop in Iran was Meshed, a small city 900 kilometres east of Tehran. On Meshed's outskirts, roadside vendors sold the most delicious halva in the world. Raj stopped the bus so that he could nip out and buy three kilos of the sticky sweet made from crushed sesame and honey.

Meshed turned out to be an easier going and more culturally interesting place than Tehran. The holy city played host to many Shia pilgrims, who flocked into the superb gold and turquoise domed mosques that lay to the sides of the city's dusty streets. The holy buildings were surrounded by fluttering green banners emblazoned with black, curlicue Arabic calligraphy. It was adjacent to such a place of pilgrimage that a very significant meeting, with one of kismet's puppets, was about to take place.

I opened my eyes, then clapped and rubbed my hands together. Disturbed by the noise, the dog lying at my feet woke up, cocked an eye at me and then went back to sleep.

The vertebrae in my neck creaked and clicked when I looked up to observe the swollen moon. I stretched my arms and noticed that my surroundings were drenched in an unsettling, cold stark light. A chill ran down my spine. I massaged my thighs. The urge to stand up was close to overwhelming. My shoulders slumped. I began to feel miserable.

'Bloody hell,' I cursed out loud. 'This is depressing.'

I sat up straight, crossed my legs, placed my hands on my knees palm up, closed my eyes and flew back in time to Iran. I could hear the clamour of a busy marketplace.

5

DIRTY ALI

Raj, Murphy, Alice and Nina went shopping for groceries in the constricted lanes of Meshed's old souk area.

Angus and Jenny were supposed to be keeping a vigilant eye on the bus but – blinded by love – their attentions lay elsewhere. Jenny's opium supply had run out and, much to sex-starved Angus's relief, they were making love again. As far as he was concerned, it had been well worth the wait. They'd been together as a couple for over two years and carnal desire still burnt hot in their hearts. Fiery temperaments caused them to become embroiled in the occasional inflammatory argument with each other, counterbalanced by their shared feelings of mutual trust. Minus the opium, they got along like a flamethrower in a fireworks factory.

Basking in the warm afterglow of their lovemaking, Jenny took hold of his still tumescent penis and gave it a squeeze that produced a bead of glistening sperm. She moaned low in the back of her throat and purred like a big cat. She raised her head and they looked into each other's eyes, feeling so at one it seemed strange they should be in separate bodies.

She said, 'You know, for a minute there I could have sworn I felt the earth move.'

Heart still pounding in his ears from his exertions, Angus lay on his side and ran a gentle finger round one of her swollen nipples to trace out an idle circle. 'Yeah, Jen, I felt that too. Amazing, wasn't it?'

The bus shuddered.

'What the hell was that?' Angus asked, sitting up in alarm.

He pulled on a pair of shorts and hurried outside to investigate. A few moments later, he returned.

'It wasn't the fucking earth we felt moving, it was the bus. Some rotten bastard's slashed the front tyres.'

The morning was gone and the heat had risen to an almost unbearable level. In the bazaar, the rest of Rolling Thunder's crew were having their senses bombarded from all directions. With little in the way of a breeze to dissipate the pungent smell of everything from cooking spices to sun-dried salted fish, the baking hot air was as thick as treacle and consequently hard to breathe. Loaded down with supplies, the four Scots exited the noisy souk and walked along a dirty alley. It led on to a wide street, where asphalt bubbled in the midday heat. Seeking shade and something to quench their thirst, they entered a quiet teashop and sat down at a wobbly table that only had three legs due to the fourth having been decimated to a ragged stump by a gang of ravenous woodworms.

Seated in a corner and dressed in white cotton robes, three elderly men were smoking sweet-smelling tobacco through a ghalyun. The gurgling sounds produced by the water-filtered hookah pipe helped create a soothing ambience. A young waiter smiled bashfully as the four foreigners spoke to him in a language he did not understand and pointed enthusiastically at pictures on a laminated menu card to order ice-cold soft drinks, yoghurt soup, flat brown breads spread with strawberry jam and macaroons sprinkled with grated coconut.

'*Salaam*, my friends, how are you this fine afternoon?' The cheery male voice belonged to an Iranian seated at the table next to them who, going by the deep wrinkles etched round his eyes, appeared to be in his late fifties. In spite of his crumpled, patched-at-the-elbow, dark blue business suit with a fatigued red rose hanging from a bent lapel's buttonhole, there was – in an old fashioned kind of way – something of the gentleman in the man's appearance. His thick mop of silver-grey hair was combed straight back from his broad forehead. His face twisted into a mask of geniality when he flashed an engaging smile, which prised his fat lips apart to frame nicotine-yellow false teeth that were too big for his mouth and conjured up images from a nature documentary about hyenas. 'My name is Ali Khatib,' said the stranger. 'Would you be so kind as to allow me to join your esteemed company? That way I'll eliminate the need of craning my neck in order to converse with you.'

Welcoming Mr Khatib into their midst, the Scots made space for him. They then proceeded to fill the quiet with animated chatter. It soon became apparent that the Iranian was a witty and amusing conversationalist. Raj thought he looked like a haggard version of Jack Nicholson with a big nose. Like the American film star, Mr Khatib was also an actor, albeit a social one. Ali had been playing his role for so long he delivered a polished form of method acting with such panache he could have charmed the knickers off a Carmelite nun on her way to vespers. It was therefore that he encountered little difficulty when it came to persuading the spaced-out hippies to take him back to their bus for a smoke of something, which he described as being the key to paradise.

When Angus was introduced to Mr Khatib, he smelt mothballs first and then a rat. The Iranian gave off an air of depravity, like the stench of rotten beef served up on mouldy garlic bread. Angus could not put his intuitive finger directly on whatever it was about the newcomer's personality that he didn't like, but he instinctively drew back from him.

When Ali passed around a pipe of pure opium for his newfound friends to share, Angus let it go by him. He cringed as he watched Jenny inhale a lungful of the narcotic's sweet-smelling smoke. It was, however, impossible not to join in the laughter that followed Ali's sordid anecdotes about his predilection for having passionate sexual encounters with a variety of four-legged lovers. In order to better illustrate how to go about the tricky business of shagging a camel Ali took of his jacket and rose to his feet. Hands behind his thick neck and pumping his groin like a go-go dancer in need of a hip replacement; he gave a ludicrous impersonation of himself unabashedly humping his favourite dromedary. Ali's stories were further embellished by his mimicking the sounds made by female camels, sheep and donkeys in the throes of sexual ecstasy, due to his highly developed skills in the realm of animal husbandry. He roared, baaed and hee-hawed until his listeners' laughing muscles began to ache. From that afternoon on, he was dubbed 'Dirty Ali'.

The animal lover adopted a more serious tone when he explained how he needed to leave Iran − in a hurry. Ali lacked a passport but he possessed money − lots of it. He placed 10,000 Danish kroner on the table saying that he wished to be transported to Kabul.

'Take it.' He handed the money to Murphy. 'I am willing to pay this exorbitant sum to be smuggled over the border into Afghanistan.'

Murphy held the money up to the light in order to better scrutinize it. The ten thousand-kroner notes were so crisp they could have rolled off the printing press that very morning in Copenhagen. As Murphy examined the bank notes, Angus could hear his friend's mind, clicking like the beads of an abacus, as he quickly calculated exchange rates.

Angus faced forward and rotated his eyes sideways to observe Dirty Ali, who was so busy watching Murphy it presented Angus with an opportunity to really study him. The cartilage of the Iranian's hooked nose was twisted, as if broken and then inexpertly set. Tiny pupils sat at the centres of deep-brown eyes, their whites tinged by iodine yellow, lending them a feral quality. His face's jaundiced skin was deeply lined; not so much from exposure to intense sunlight, but more because it had been well lived in. The thick-knuckled fingers of his right hand tapped the table with an impatient, angry rhythm.

Murphy nodded in approval. 'It's real, definitely not counterfeit.'

Angus stole a glance at Murphy, caught his friend's eye and signalled to him with a barely perceptible shake of his head.

Murphy continued without missing a beat. 'But I'm sorry to have to tell you, Ali, it's not enough.'

There was a momentary silence. Tension crackled in the air like static electricity before a storm.

Ali's nostrils flared and his thick eyebrows pinched together. He became a player who'd forgotten his lines, but not for long. '*Not enough!*' A fine spray of spittle flew from his mouth. 'By the holes in the Prophet's socks, peace be unto him, d-d-d-darn you, boy,' he spluttered, the words shooting from his mouth like needle-pointed darts propelled by foaming saliva. 'How...how can you say that? I...I'm offering you a small fortune to perform a relatively simple task.'

'If it's that easy, you shouldn't have any difficulty finding someone else to take you.' Murphy let a provocative smile cross his lips.

Ali rose to the bait. '*Twenty!*' His voice quivered with indignation. The wattles of skin under his chin waggled to expose lines of grey stubble; testimony to using a blunt razor to shave, failing eyesight, lack of a mirror, or perhaps a combination of all three. 'I'll give you twenty thousand to take me to Kabul.' His voice went up a couple of octaves. 'Take it or leave it,' he concluded with a thump of his fist that made Angus's coffee mug jump up from the table.

This was indeed a lot of money for the Iranian to offer for what he was requesting, enough to pay for fuel, food and good times for everyone on board the bus for two months.

Murphy was not quite ready to let Ali have his way. He picked up the money and waved it in front of the Iranian's unfocused eyes. 'How come you're in possession of such high denomination Scandinavian bank notes here in Iran?'

Ali lowered his head in mock humility. 'Ah, my dear Mister Murphy,' he said, adding gentle emphasis to the name, 'that is a good but not entirely unexpected question.' He paused to allow a measured silence, as if his answer required careful consideration. 'It's a long story. Perhaps if I became a paying passenger on your splendid omnibus,' he said, smiling a flatterer's smile, 'we could find the time needed in order to relate it to you. What do you say, my friend?'

My friend, thought Angus, chuckling quietly. Who does this twisted toerag think he's trying to kid?

Angus hadn't taken his eyes off Ali Khatib since he'd entered the bus. There was something in the Iranian's cunning manner that ignited a strong feeling of disquiet in him. Like a scab, a layer of suspicion was beginning to form in his mind. Yet, in spite of his unarticulated misgivings about the man, he found himself warming towards what he viewed to be the perfect incarnation of a first-class incorrigible rogue. There was definitely something not quite right about Mr Khatib but, for the moment, he elected to lay his misgivings aside.

When it came to a vote Angus gave his head an affirmative nod. Dirty Ali was welcome to travel with them as far as Kabul. Ali pulled a wad of cash out of his underpants, peeled off another ten notes and handed them over to Murphy. Ali then went off to collect his worldly possessions.

One thing was for sure, Dirty Ali liked to travel light because, when he returned twenty minutes later, all he carried with him was a scuffed brown leather briefcase.

'I thought you were supposed to be guarding the fucking bus while we did the shopping,' complained Murphy, pumping a brand new hydraulic jack's lever.

'Yeah, man, I'm sorry,' apologized Angus, slackening the wheel nuts with a monkey wrench. 'I got waylaid.'

'I might've fucking well guessed.' Murphy grinned and then said, 'Hey, man, that's the wrong tool for the job.'

'I know,' said Angus. 'I couldn't find the cross bar.'

'I wouldn't be surprised if that stupid bitch, Nina, tossed it away, thinking it was a grave marker. *Ooopfh!*' Murphy groaned loudly as he lifted the wheel off.

'What's up with you, Murph?' Angus asked, rolling the replacement wheel into position. 'Had enough of Nina?'

'That's a fucking understatement, if ever I heard one. *Women*, love 'em and leave 'em. Relationships really aren't my thing, man.' Murphy stood up and wiped sweat from his eyes with an oily rag. 'Come on, Angus, tighten up those nuts and let's get the fuck outta here. My brain's starting to boil.'

Ruined tyres exchanged and stowed in the luggage hold beside the four remaining spares, Angus sat down behind the steering wheel, turned the ignition key, engaged the clutch and stepped on the accelerator. Meshed was left behind to swelter in the heat as Rolling Thunder hurtled out of town in a cloud of swirling dust.

The highway cut a long black line through a stretch of hardpan desert, broken in places by dunes, broad bands of grey shale and snow white gypsum flats. Ten kilometres from the Afghan border, the sun's crimson fireball was beginning to impale itself upon a distant mountain range's spiky outline. Nightfall fast approaching, Angus spotted a date palm grove by the edge of a wadi carved out of the harsh landscape by a river that had dried up and disappeared. He swung the bus off the road in the palm grove's direction. The place had the makings of an ideal overnight campsite.

Everyone disembarked and began to busy themselves with various tasks as the last light of day manifested itself as an ozone-orange glow on the horizon. Venus began to shine bright beside a waxing moon – cut in the sky like a crescent-shaped silver slash on a cobalt-blue canvas.

The temperature dropped from hot to chilly within half an hour. Angus and Murphy collected fallen palm fronds. Raj used a small axe to chop them into manageable pieces. The girls set up a portable gas ring outside of the bus and began to prepare a meal. Ali slumped against a boulder and promptly fell asleep.

After a dinner of brown rice mixed with spiced vegetables, a metal tripod was erected over the fire to suspend the copper kettle used to boil water for tea. The campers brought out cushions and lay around watching the circle of flames lick the blackened kettle's round bottom. Tiny bats skimmed over their heads, screeching in delight at the unexpected feast provided by the airborne insects attracted by the fire's glare.

Ali sat in the firelight preparing pea-sized pellets, pared off from a cricket ball-sized sphere of opium. For the occasion, he'd produced a special pipe from inside his battered briefcase, never more than an arm's length away from him at all times. He called the pipe a *vafoor*. Its thirty-centimetre-long tapering black stem had been carved on a lathe from a piece of wood so dense it would have sunk if placed in water. The pipe's white porcelain bowl, stained to the colour of old ivory from years of use, was decorated by cursive Arabic script in dark blue glaze. From the grooved join, where the stem had been screwed into the oval-shaped bowl, hung a golden chain, at the end of which swung a thick solid gold needle used for cleaning the smoking implement when necessary. To light the pipe, Ali used a long pair of pincers to lift a glowing charcoal from the fire and applied it to a *bast* (small bead of opium) placed beside a tiny hole in the porcelain bowl. He explained how the sound made by the sputtering opium was music to the *taryaki's* (opium addict) ears and that some adept smokers knew how to convert this gizz sound into music, whereupon he played a short rendition of 'Rule Britannia' upon his smoking *vafoor*. Pleased with his performance, he smiled to himself and offered the pipe to whomever in the circle gathered around him wished to partake of it.

'So, Ali,' said Murphy, exhaling a jet of warm smoke into the cool night air. 'I think now is as good a time as any to tell us the story of how all those crisp Danish bank notes arrived in your drawers. What do you say, *my friend?*' he asked, affecting Ali's style of speech.

The Iranian looked at him and produced a thin smile, which completely lacked humour.

Nina voiced a little encouragement. 'Yeah, come on, Ali, tell us a story.' She pulled a tartan blanket around herself, a loose strand of black hair bobbing on her forehead in the desert breeze.

There was a brief moment of silence in which all six Scots gazed intently at the Iranian.

Obviously pleased to be the centre of attention, Ali nodded in assent and then, like an over keen amateur actor performing too vigorously, laughed loudly. When his laughter subsided he said with oily charm, 'Oh well, if you insist.'

He loaded his pipe for the third time and applied a red-hot charcoal to another black pellet, which sizzled and bubbled on the porcelain bowl. Satisfied that it was drawing well, he passed it to Jenny who sucked on it as if it were a nipple supplying desperately needed sustenance. A zephyr stirred the overhead palm fronds, rustling them to produce a percussive sound, like a multitude of Lilliputian drummers beating upon thimble-sized drums.

The fire's flames died down, leaving red embers to glow in the darkness. Draped in a brown woollen shawl, Ali looked like a wizened old shaman. The lines on his face became more pronounced in the shadows, making it appear as if it were criss-crossed by a black web. He cleared his throat and modulated the sound of his voice to resemble a creaky hinge on a dungeon door; a rasping, subdued tone that made his listeners draw closer in order to hear the full contents of his quietly spoken words.

'In a previous lifetime,' he began, 'I was a king. That's why tears come to my eyes whenever I see royalty on television, for it reminds me of what I no longer am.'

The girls tittered when they heard the storyteller's absurd opening statement about himself. Momentarily taking on the facial expression of a wrathful deity on a Tibetan *thangka* (scroll painting), Ali glowered in their direction, bringing their indiscreet sniggering to an abrupt halt. In the distance a nocturnal predator greeted the night with a gastronomic howl that prompted Ali to continue with his campfire tale.

'I was born over half a century ago in the fair city of Isfahan, within sight of the *Si-o-she Pol*, a famous bridge with thirty-three arches that spans the Zayandeh Rud River's shallow and slowly flowing waters. As far as cities go, Isfahan was quite picturesque and a pleasant enough place to grow up in, or so it seemed.

'My father, Achmed Khatib, was a renowned carpet weaver who specialized in the creation of what are known as Bakhtiari carpets. Born under the shade of a black kilim tent in the desert, his ancestors were from the pastoral nomadic Bakhtiari tribe. My paternal grandfather had passed on his skills to him; thus continuing the age-old tradition of handing down the secrets of the weaver's loom from generation to generation. It was therefore natural that my father wished to transfer his craftsman's heritage to me, his only son.

'Achmed's magic carpets, as he liked to refer to them, were woven either with hypnotic repeat patterns or complex concentric medallions contained within an oblong lattice. His silk thread creations were much sought after by collectors, who travelled from many distant parts of the world to purchase his works. When visiting my father's shop, these well-dressed businessmen would pay him thousands of dollars for the fruits of his labours. Haggling over the price of his carpets and striking a bargain was, for my father, the most enjoyable aspect of the business. It was not uncommon for these sometimes-heated disputes to take up the whole of an afternoon. I was gifted with an innate aptitude for learning foreign tongues. These drawn-out discussions helped me hone my linguistic skills by listening to the foreigners speak amongst themselves. A sponge for the spoken word, I'd learned by the age of ten not only the trick of understanding foreign languages but also how to grasp foreign concepts. My astute father encouraged the development of my talent because his clients paid little heed to my presence, taking me for a feeble-minded simpleton, a role which I took much enjoyment in performing. Knowing how to hold one's tongue and listen has many advantages. It was thus that I was able to relay back to my father to what extent the carpet buyers were willing to go with their bids.

'As the years slipped by like thieves in the night, my father became ever more obsessed with his magic carpets. When my dear mother died suddenly from a brain haemorrhage, may she forever rest in peace, my father was infected by a mysterious affliction; the kind that makes a man feel guilty if he's not endlessly employed. He threw himself into his work with increased fervour and became a...a...' Ali grappled for the right word. '...*workaholic.*' He continued. 'Every day my father spent long hours weaving the spellbinding magic of his craft. He strained his eyesight by working under candlelight in the evenings and as a result his eyes were left permanently crossed.' Ali paused for a moment to cross his eyes, casting a cockeyed impression of how Mr Achmed Khatib must have looked. Evidently satisfied with the smiles that appeared on his listeners' faces, reflecting crimson in the warm roseate glow cast off by the campfire, he returned to his narration.

'My industrious father was immensely pleased to have me as his apprentice working faithfully by his side. Dressed in a thick green robe and wearing a camel hair cap upon his shaved head he'd spread his arms expansively, look around his shop and say, 'Just think, Ali, my son, one day all of this will be yours.' I, in turn, would take in the interior of the oblong, window-fronted room containing piles of neatly folded carpets, the two looms where we toiled all day, the round brass table surrounded by tasselled donkey bag cushions where my father would sit arguing with his customers for hours on end and ask myself, by the infinite vision of the Prophet, on whose name be praise, is this it? Is this as far as my life will go?

'In the early days of my apprenticeship I surrendered myself to my father's wishes. Having little in the way of personal ambition, I was quite content to do my father's bidding. Work all day, eat and sleep, was about the extent of it.

'One weekend, an old school friend, who was home on vacation from Shiraz in the south of the country, where he worked as a ladies hairdresser, asked me if I'd like to accompany him to a soirée. For the lack of anything more entertaining to do, I walked with him to an affluent neighbourhood in Isfahan's northern suburbs. The owner of the house was a wealthy police commissioner who had gone to the capital with his wife and left his eldest son in charge of the two-storey gated mansion that was his home. We passed through a long vestibule, flanked by fluted Doric columns, and entered the building's spacious interior. American big band music played over a pair of large loudspeakers positioned on each side of a staircase, which was made from the finest white marble and appeared to float up from the marvellously designed, circular entrance hall. I liked the music. It sounded so fresh and luxurious in comparison to the dreary religious songs and military tunes I was used to hearing on the state-sponsored radio stations broadcast from Tehran. Under the glittering light cast by a crystal teardrop chandelier, which wouldn't have looked out of place in a Venetian palazzo, young people of both sexes mingled freely with each other, a social phenomenon I had never before witnessed. Beautiful unveiled damsels laughed without restraint. They were wearing makeup, something I'd only seen before in foreign magazines. To my innocent mind, it was all very exciting.

''Come,' said my friend, grabbing a drink from a passing tray, 'come with me.' He took my hand and led me up the staircase. We entered a large candlelit sitting room where a group of young people were reclining on ponderously ornate furniture and overstuffed bolsters. Some of the women were not fully clothed. Nobody present seemed to care about what would normally have been regarded as outrageous behaviour. Remember, the events I am describing happened a long time ago, in a society where shaking hands with a woman in the street was frowned upon.

'There was a strange cloying smell in the air, similar to that of roasted groundnuts. I soon discovered it was 'The Remedy' – the affectionate term used by Persians when referring to opium. Within a few minutes I had inhaled the vapours of the drug via the stem of a brass pipe, its base enamelled with scenes from a Chinese garden. I lay back on a chaise longue. The drug took possession of my soul and lifted me high above the mundane goings-on of the world that lay beneath the puffy white clouds I soon found myself floating upon. A delectable dark-eyed maiden caressed my face with such gentle fingers I could have sworn my cheek had been brushed by a butterfly's wings. I had entered paradise. A tangible feeling of sensuality permeated the room's smoky atmosphere although, I might add, the most tactile manifestation of this was the occasional fleeting touch. For the most part, physical contact was kept at an inhibiting minimum.

'Suddenly, I felt chilled to the core, as if I were a naked castaway stranded on an iceberg. Sensing my discomfort, my old school friend went in search of something hot and sweet to drink. Minutes later, he returned with a cup of steaming tea, loaded with sugar to counter the opium's side effects.

'The Chinese pipe came round again. Being ignorant of the art and mystery of opium taking, I sucked greedily on it, inhaling more than I should have. For a while I lay with my heavy head propped up by a supportive arm. I stared fascinated as everyone and everything in the room displayed an aura of purple and lime green. The music, filtering up from the loudspeakers at the bottom of the staircase, sounded as if it were coming from a great distance away. I closed my eyes. The outside contours of my body melted into nothingness. I dreamt that I was a chrysalis, attached by gossamer threads to a wooden beam in a warm dark loft. Metamorphosis complete, I cracked open and, transformed into a moth, flew to my annihilation inside a brilliant white ball of flaming light.'

Overcome by his own story, Ali stopped speaking for a moment. He glanced at his rapt listeners. No one said a word. No eye left Ali's face. He sighed and continued. 'Next thing I knew, my friend was shaking me. 'Come on, sleepy head, it's time to go home,' he said, his voice jovial. My eyelids felt thick, my thoughts muddled. Patterned daylight filtered into the room through lace curtains. Looking around, I saw that the other guests had already left. Spell broken, the room had lost its magic and appeared untidy. The place stank of stale tobacco smoke and was littered with empty bottles, overflowing ashtrays and wine glasses. Many of the glasses were half full...or half empty, depending on one's perspective, mine being the latter as I was in a particularly saturnine mood that morning.

'Many of my contemporaries used The Remedy as a weekend recreational drug, smoked moderately in the company of friends. In my case it was different. I began to smoke opium every day – alone. In those bygone times, the substance was relatively cheap and easy to procure in the unpaved alleys hung with washing behind the old bazaar. Soon I was addicted to the dark, pernicious sap bled from the opium poppy's unripe seedpod. If a person has never been dependent on opium they cannot understand what it means to crave the drug like an addict does. It possesses your soul. One day you wake up with a gnawing sensation in your guts, which makes you feel nauseous, and the realization hits you that you're hooked. I began to see my life measured out in little black beads and puffs of smoke.'

Angus noticed Jenny nodding in agreement. He recoiled at the thought of what was going on in her stoned-out mind. Ali rambled on and Angus returned his attention to his words.

'Work in my father's shop continued unabated for some time. Slowly, the closed environs of the workplace became claustrophobic for me. I felt like I was trapped in a glassed-in cage, empty and colourless in comparison to the blissful world that I inhabited at the end of my pipe. The depth of my obsession with the drug paralleled that of my father's fascination with his carpets, which had by then dropped all semblance of being magic for me. We began to have arguments about my lackadaisical attitude. Soon the day arrived when I could stand it no longer. I walked out of my father's workshop, never to return. My newfound freedom allowed me to pursue my pipe dreams all day long. With what little money I'd managed to squirrel away, I rented a small apartment in a poor neighbourhood. Thus began my descent into the netherworld of opium addiction.

'Most of my days were spent on my back, smoking and poring through a mountain of books. I learned Latin. I read the ancients, the moderns and the in-betweens. I consumed literature the way a glutton devours food. Why, I've even read you notoriously frugal Scots' intrepid Robert Burns and know from my own bitter experience how true his words were when he wrote, *'The best laid schemes of mice and men, go oft astray, and leave us nought but grief and pain, to rend our day.'* However, it was closer to home that I found the poets and writers that I grew to admire. Jalaluddin Rumi, Omar Khayyam and Farid ud Din Attar were the flowers of Islamic culture whose fragrance came to my mind as attar, the scent of roses. Din Attar was my favourite Persian poet by far. A spiritual subversive, he broke with the Sufi tradition of secrecy and openly expounded mystical doctrines about oneness that clashed with Islam's extreme dualism. This was encapsulated in Din Attar's most famous pronouncement: *'I am the Truth'*. That declaration was judged by the intolerant religious justice system of the time to be iniquitous and, just like your prophet Jesus Christ, he paid for it. In his case by being imprisoned for eight years, after which time he was condemned to death, whereupon he was flogged, mutilated and then what remained of his still living body strung up on a gibbet to be decapitated. If nothing else, this serves to illustrate that not only is a prophet rarely recognised in the land of his birth, but also he is, more often than not, vilified and then crucified for his revelation by the very people he sought to enlighten.

'Well now, I see I've digressed from my story, so I'll round off this preamble by informing you that as a child, during the twelfth century, Din Attar studied theology at a madrasa in Meshed, which was attached to the shrine of Imam Reza, a Shia martyr. This particular gold-domed holy spot is pivotal to my tale and one which I will return to later on in my narrative.'

'What the fuck does this auld fart think this is,' muttered Murphy from the side of his mouth, 'a fucking lecture or something?'

The storyteller, pretending not to hear this slur, spat in the fire. Upon taking up his story from where he'd left off, his voice assumed a more solemn note, that of an anchorman announcing the death of a popular monarch or head of state. 'Hear me when I say that Persia once produced the finest strain of opium in the world. That I am a connoisseur of the drug is something that I do not take a great deal of pride in. I've travelled as far afield as Laos and Burma, searching for the sticky black gold extracted from *Papavor somniferum* but, alas, nothing I sampled could compare to the nectar I smoked during the days of my youth in Persia.

'Calamity entered my life by way of a Royal decree. The great Shah, Muhammad Reza Pahlavi – may God roast him in hell – broke with the age-old tradition of opium poppy cultivation in my country. A custom, I might add, that had been kept alive since Alexander the Great introduced opium to the people of Persia over two thousand years ago. Why, it was not so very long ago when it would have been viewed as uncivilized not to offer a visitor a dish of charcoal and opium upon them entering one's home. In Europe also times and attitudes have changed. During the nineteenth century, the widespread use of opium played a crucial part in the Romantic Movement, and sparked a creative revolution in the minds of a generation of European artists and writers. Nevertheless, the Shah embarked upon a vile campaign to eradicate all the poppy fields in Persia. His masters in Washington spurred him into action because of their fears concerning the refinement of opium into heroin, a much more dangerous drug which, when first synthesized, had been mass-produced by Bayer in Switzerland and then mass-marketed in the form of cough medicine, until it was discovered to be extremely addictive and then criminalized. From there criminal elements belonging to the underworld took over and began to distribute it. In the major population centres of America large quantities of cheap heroin started blowing on to the streets in a lethal snowstorm. The heart of the matter had little to do with addicts injecting the white poison into their disappearing veins in shooting galleries. Those, those...' Suddenly, Ali's voice grew louder as old enmities seized his imagination. 'Those damnable Yankee hypocrites and the blatant propaganda they broadcast all over the world.' Spittle flew from his mouth. 'If the truth about their double-dealing politics ever gets out and becomes public knowledge, the United States of America will be recognized for what it really is, the land of the global barbarian pirates and home of the schizophrenic bloodsuckers. I wouldn't put it past the plundering devils to invade this country when the world's oil supplies begin to dry up.'

I yawned, stretched my back straight and recalled the morning when Angus had narrated Ali Khatib's story. We'd been sitting together by the sea in Sri Lanka when my brother had paused for a moment to add a comment. 'You know,' he'd said, 'back in seventy-three, while we sat around the campfire listening to Ali, I didn't take very much of what the old bugger was saying seriously, especially his rant about the Americans. Years later, I began to realize there had been more than a little truth in what he'd said. I was thinking about it earlier this morning when I was listening to the radio. There's a lot of sabre-rattling going on in Washington just now about Iran's nuclear programme but it could be, like Saddam Hussein's nonexistent weapons of mass destruction, some kind of political subterfuge. Perhaps Ali was right about the Americans and they will eventually invade Iran.' Angus was sitting cross-legged on the sand. He picked up a small pebble, tossed it towards the sea and concluded, 'One thing's for sure; he definitely hated them.'

I heard my own words echo in my head from when I'd responded by saying, 'Yes, you've made that pretty obvious. Your Dirty Ali sounds like a raving anti-American lunatic to me.'

Angus had become uncharacteristically serious for a moment. 'Ali was a lot more than that. He was the most depraved man I ever had the misfortune to run into in my entire life. Like many a wicked person he came to an evil end.'

'Why?' I asked. 'What happened to him?'

Angus shook his head, remembering something that obviously troubled him, but all he'd said was, 'I'll get around to telling you the gory details, but for the mean time I'd like to continue with his story from where I left off.'

'Go ahead,' I said, 'you've got me hooked.'

Angus had then cleared his throat and, after adopting a gravelly voice to fit the role, he returned to Ali Khatib's story.

I glanced around the moonlit beach in Cambodia, closed my eyes and found myself back in the Iranian desert close to the Afghan border in 1973.

'Why,' said Ali, 'many a so-called respectable American's fortune was made from trading in opium. I know for a fact that Warren Delano, the millionaire paternal grandfather of Franklin D. Roosevelt, the great American president who led his country into victory in World War Two, made huge sums of money by being a senior partner in a company which owned a fleet of ships that ferried opium across the South China Sea. Their British counterparts won Hong Kong by launching an opium war, which gave a conniving gang of Zionists the exclusive right to drug an entire nation. The corrupt British monarchy disgraced the crown by inviting those Zionist bandits to Buckingham Palace and honoured some of them with Knighthoods for being such great developers. Great developers indeed, they ran one of the biggest drug-dealing operations in—'

'For fuck's sake, Ali,' complained Murphy more loudly than previously, 'you could have warned us this was going to turn into a history less—'

'*Ssssh!*' Raj shook his head and put an index finger to his lips.

Ali nodded to Raj, acknowledging his gratitude for silencing Murphy on his behalf and continued. 'As I was saying, before I was so rudely interrupted,' he glanced at his antagonist and flashed him an alligator smile, 'Shah Pahlavi, under pressure from the west, banned opium production in my country. The American government and their cronies were worried about the hundreds of millions of narcodollars cascading into the coffers of political groups whose ambitions were contrary to their own.

'The sometimes central role that the narcotics trade plays on the political chess board is by no means a novel one. Over seven hundred years ago in Northern Persia there lived a Shia Muslim ruler called Ala Al-Din, who came to be known as the 'Old Man of the Mountain'. He was a drunken maniac who trained an elite group of young killers to go out and murder his enemies. Ala Al-Din thus spread terror throughout the Mohammedan world and obtained notoriety among the ranks of the infidel Crusaders, because no man, however powerful, could escape death once exposed to the sheikh's enmity. As a reward for carrying out their homicidal duties, Ala Al-Din provided his psychopathic henchmen with hashish-fuelled sex orgies in pleasure gardens flush with voluptuous maidens, whose sole purpose in life was to bend over backwards, or forwards if requested, in order to cater to every whim of the intoxicated exterminators. These hatchet men of the Medieval Middle East became so accustomed to using the drug that they performed their deadly missions while still high on hashish. The killers came to be known as the 'Hashisheens' or, as we say in our times, 'Assassins'. This appellation has stuck to political hit-men and hired guns over the centuries, although, it must be said, it's hard to imagine modern-day assassins smoking a joint before clocking into work in the morning.'

Everyone, including Murphy, laughed at the thought of such a preposterous image. Ali used the brief interlude to take an immense draw on his pipe. Raj threw what remained of the chopped up palm leaves on the campfire. As the flames rose up into the desert night's cold air, so did Ali's voice, invigorated by the effects of the opium.

'In more recent times, introducing narcotics into the ranks of an opposing army has been accepted as a legitimate way to undermine the strength of the enemy. After all, who cares about participating in warfare when they're flying high in an endless sky without the aid of a noisy fighter jet?

'And so it came to pass that the Shah, with the help of Persia's armed forces and Savak, the dreaded secret police, managed to destroy almost the entire opium crop in Persia. Supplies began to dwindle and soon ran out completely, resulting in inflated prices. Persian dope peddlers had to turn to Baluchi smugglers in the east of the country to supply them with the goods of their trade. In exchange for petrol, Afghan bandits traded opium that was much adulterated with glucose. Addicts began to be thrown into prison for committing what had become a serious criminal offence.

'Searching for and obtaining the drug became an increasingly expensive and dangerous full-time occupation for me. Opium can be a particularly cruel mistress if she is not available to extinguish the searing flames that torment the addict's soul. In times of short supply, I took to scraping out the *sougte*, resin that had built up on the inside of my *vafoor*, to prepare a smoking mixture called *sheerah*. This pure essence is the dope fiend's true beloved.'

Ali smacked his thick lips, as if it were gourmet food he was describing rather than a narcotic. He sighed, ran a hand over the stubble on his chin and then pressed on. 'In order to support my habit, I stooped to levels of moral deprivation I could previously never have imagined might exist. I became a jissom jockey, prostituting my young body and peddling my anus to the highest bidders and, if necessary, to the lowest also. No matter who they were or what they looked like, if they had the money I let them have their way with me in hotel rooms, in the back of automobiles or in the shadows of dirty back alleys. They subjected me to all manner of sexual perversions. Countless pederasts grunted, groaned, drooled and slaked their desire as they sodomized me and pumped their lust into my young body. During those years my anus was, at times, so distended from frequent penetration I dreaded going to the toilet to relieve myself.' Ali screwed up his face as if he'd swallowed a gallon of citric acid and then continued. 'Night after shameless night I performed fellatio, sucking the putrid sap out of a petrified tree stump forest of rancid phalli. Sucking on a dirty old man's swollen cock is a disgusting experience that requires, requires... How should I put it? A certain detachment from reality. A mental state which is easily achieved when good opium is available. However, it was during and after that traumatic period in my life that I began to seek out the company of animals for the fulfilment of my own sexual needs. From bitter experience I've learned that animals are indeed beasts, but it is only man who can be transmuted into a monster. Four-legged lovers are so much more innocent than their two-legged masters.

'Some say that time is an illusion but, illusion or not, the Lord of Time waits for no man and he certainly didn't wait for me. One day I awoke to the fact that fifteen opium-addled years had drifted by, taking with them my youthful looks and vigour. My sexual favours were no longer as sought after as they once were.

'For the first time in my life I made up my mind to break free from the shackles that my heartless mistress bound me with. I pleaded with an uncle to help me get the monkey, who clung to my shoulders with iron claws, off my back. Asking my father, still alive at the time, was out of the question. He'd disowned me years before out of broken-hearted frustration when he'd caught me sneaking out of his house, his life savings stuffed into a basket, clutched in my thieving hands. My Uncle Asaf, a widower with one eye and a black leather patch over an empty socket, the result of a motoring accident, was sympathetic. He agreed to assist me in kicking my addiction on one condition; I give my most solemn word never to touch the vile substance again. I gave him my promise, only half believing it myself.

'My uncle, a committed Muslim who sincerely believed that no act of charity would go unrewarded in Paradise, locked me behind a thick steel door in the cellar of his house. Once a day he supplied me with a meagre ration of unleavened bread, a boiled egg and a jug of water. In the gloom of that damp cellar, with only a stinking chamber pot for company, I went through the living hell of opiate withdrawal for two weeks. As Jelaluddin Rumi once wrote, *On Resurrection Day your body testifies against you.* I found out the painful truth contained within that statement during the first few days of my self-imposed imprisonment, when my flesh was crawling and my brain had become a nest of seething black vipers. I banged on the inside of the rust-covered door so hard, begging to be let out, that my knuckles bled. My body felt like a bruise. I was tormented by nightmares whose horrifying sensations would not leave me. I sat on the edge of my sweat-soaked mattress, praying to God for mercy. The All Merciful was listening. My prayers were answered. Slowly, I began to feel better. When the day arrived for Uncle Asaf to unlock the cellar door, I climbed out of that dank hole into the dazzling sunlight and realized, as they say on birthday cards, that it was the first day of the rest of my life. I was a new man.'

A moment passed before Ali spoke again. When he did, his voice was a little lighter. 'A few months later, I met and eventually married a local Parsee woman named Zahra, may Allah keep her memory fragrant. In time, she gave birth to Gholam and Halim, our two handsome sons, and our lovely fair-haired daughter, Haniyeh. My wife taught me the art of personal discipline, not in words but by setting an example. With a firm hand on the rudder of the little ship that was our family, she steered a steady course towards heaven on earth. Zahra's presence also brought with it an air of humour, buoyancy and gentleness that lit up our apartment as if sunlight were shining through a big hole in the ceiling. Her heart of purest gold more than made up for what she lacked in the way of physical beauty, which does not mean to say she was ugly. A little plump perhaps, but to me she was a veritable goddess. Her kind eyes shone with a scintillating light that came from within. Her soft skin was as cool and smooth as the polished marble of a Michelangelo statue.' Ali sighed. 'My beloved Zahra.' His voice softened with nostalgia. 'For the first and only time in my life I enjoyed normal sexual relations with a woman. Our trysts in the bedroom were uncomplicated and full of reciprocal sensitive emotion.

'I took up employment in a cousin's carpet shop. Kemal was a kind and generous employer who had a smile for everyone, may Allah extend his infinite benefits to him. He prefered the life of a bachelor and had no family of his own. Due to the nature of his business he travelled a lot, leaving me to run things in his shop, situated across the great square that fronts Isfahan's Masjid-a-Shah Mosque. I felt so grateful for my new life that I would visit the four-hundred-year-old mosque every morning before work, to give thanks for the bushels of blessings showering down on my humble head. Each day, at lunchtime, I would sit in an alcove outside the masjid to enjoy a lunch that my beloved Zahra had prepared for me the evening before. Leaning back against the cool tiled walls, I'd listen to the birdsong that filled the rose-scented air and contemplate the mosaic surfaces in front of me. Like the ancient artisans' craftsmanship, my life seemed perfect.

'For the amount of hours I put in at Kemal's carpet shop, I received little in the way of financial reward. At the end of each month the few rials I had left over from my meagre salary were saved for the children's birthdays, when my little angels would be presented with a new set of clothes or, if need be, a pair of leather sandals. The years passed, leaving me to enjoy the existence of a happy and contented family man.

'Life went on, much the way as it does for most of us. I settled into a comfortable routine, wherein one day was much the same as the last. One evening, about ten years after I married Zahra, I decided to take a different way home after work, following a route that led me through a tangle of narrow streets behind the old souk. It was there that I ran into Kabir, an acquaintance from my previous life as a drug addict. A man of convivial temperament, he was happy to see me looking so well. Need I mention that Kabir was still dependent on opium? Once near, his somehow haunted, deep-set eyes betrayed the fact that he was still a user. His eyelids drooped with the weight of his addiction. We stepped into a convenient teashop for some refreshment and a friendly chat. One thing led to another and he ended up asking me if I'd like to accompany him back to his nearby apartment to share a bowl or two of opium. For the life of me, I still don't know why I succumbed to the temptation. All I do know is that I did.'

Ali fell silent. He lit another pipe in the now familiar manner, took a long draw on it, blew out a cloud of smoke and watched as it was carried away on the updraught caused by the campfire's red-hot coals

Murphy let out a bored snort, yawned and said, 'I've had enough of this shite. I'm away to my scratcher.' He stood, let rip a resounding fart that sounded like a bassoon and then stumbled off in the bus's direction. Ali glanced up at his receding form and if looks could have killed Murphy would have been stone dead before he reached Rolling Thunder's concertina door.

The girls had passed out from smoking opium. Angus and Raj sat sharing a joint of sweet-smelling Lebanese hash. When it was finished they rose to their feet and covered the sleeping women with woollen blankets.

Ali sat with his pipe in hand, facing the faint crimson radiance cast by the campfire's embers. The fire spluttered and sent a small cloud of sparks sailing into the night. He bent forward and used his pincers to select a small burning charcoal to reignite his pipe, then puffed away contentedly for a few moments until the narcotic's calmative vapours registered their effects upon his haggard face. His half-closed eyelids lent him a somnolent look. Observing Ali, Angus realized he smoked the black poison with the regular frequency that some people smoke cigarettes and reckoned he must be going through a quarter-ounce a day.

When Ali's pipe was host to nothing more than cooling ashes, he pulled it out of his mouth, exhaled a long whooshing sigh and then remained silent for so long Angus wondered if he was going to continue. When Ali did pick up the thread of his story, his voice was low and without inflection.

'Back at Kabir's modest, second-floor bachelor apartment, we settled down on mattresses, shared a pot of mint tea and lit a well-used opium pipe. Due to over a decade of abstinence, I had become unaccustomed to the narcosis produced by the drug. Feeling drowsy, I laid my head on a soft cushion and drifted off to a place somewhere between the land of my dreams and sleep.

'Suddenly, I was awoken from my blissful slumber when the whole apartment started to shake. In the small kitchen, pots and pans clattered to the floor. Slowly I came to my senses, at first unsure of what was happening. Dragged from the depths of narcotic-laden sleep, Kabir was sitting on the floor, a look of shocked bewilderment on his drawn face. Outside on the street, people were screaming. Their anguished cries made me realize that something terrible was taking place.

'Another more powerful earth tremor shook the foundations of the building. Dust fell down upon our heads from a large crack that had appeared in the ceiling. I rose unsteadily to my feet from the mattress on the floor, knocked over a small wooden table and then rushed out of the apartment without pausing to say so much as a word to Kabir.

'The electricity supply had been cut off. A tremor struck when I was half way down the dark stairway. I had to hold on to a metal banister with both of my trembling hands in order to prevent myself from tumbling over. My breathing was coming in rasps and echoed in the stairwell. There was a taste of bile in my mouth. I felt sick with fear. By the time I ran out into the street, I was wide-awake. Pure terror had purged the opium from my bloodstream.'

Ali's voice became even more subdued, his eyes focusing on the cataclysmic events he'd witnessed. Angus and Raj leaned forward and cocked their heads to facilitate catching his quietly spoken words. 'The scene outside was one of pandemonium,' he said in a voice that was barely a whisper. 'Ruptured mains spewed huge jets of water out of fissures in the pavement, inundating vehicles that had skewed around and, tilted at crazy angles, been abandoned in the street. An exceptionally violent shockwave threw me to the ground. People's tormented cries filled the dusty air as they desperately tried to cling to something that was not moving. I stood up and started running in the direction of my neighbourhood. A large warehouse caved in, enveloping me in a cloud of cement dust. I must have looked like a ghost. All concern for my personal safety had evaporated in the heat of the moment.

'My dust-covered body seemed to move on its own. It kept to the centre of the street, winding its way through the chaos.' Ali's tone turned deadly serious, to fit the mood of the story to come. 'Concern for my family completely absorbed the attentions of my mind. The closer I drew to the vicinity of my home, the worse the devastation became. The streets were blocked with fallen debris from collapsed buildings. I clambered over wreckage and could hear cries for help rising from below along with the smell of butane gas.

'When I finally reached the area where I lived, it looked like photographs I'd seen of the Blitz in World War Two. A huge pile of smoking rubble with twisted steel girders sticking out of it was all that remained of the three-storey apartment block that had housed my family.

'All around, groups of survivors huddled together in numb silence, their faces stiff with terror and incomprehension. The only illumination came from a half moon, partially obscured by a thin layer of cloud. I recognized neighbours. Approaching them, I enquired frantically if anyone had seen or heard anything of my family. Nobody would look me in the eye, for they were too afraid to see their fear reflected in my own. They just stood there staring at the ground, from whence the cause of so much destruction had arisen. I remember thinking that they resembled a herd of frightened cattle, their heads weaving from side to side, somehow sensing that it could be their turn next to enter the slaughterhouse.

'When I realized my family was more than likely buried under the misshapen scrap heap that had once been the scene of the only true happiness I'd ever known in my life, a bolt of ice cold lightning struck me in the guts and turned my entrails into freezing jelly. I began to tear at the rubble with my bare hands. Even in my agitated state I soon realized that my desperate efforts were futile. Employing heavy machinery was the only way to untangle the twisted mass of reinforced concrete beams that had been the wrecked building's main weight bearing composites.

'The following evening, the crushed bodies of my beloved Zahra and our three children were recovered from underneath the debris. Death's cruel hand had been at play and I could only identify them by the tattered remnants of blood-smeared clothing that hung from their broken husks. Once so full of life's vibrant energy, death had transformed them into life-sized, disjointed rag dolls whose stuffing had been squashed out of them. My wife's hair was matted by blood and pressed into a big hole in the side of her smashed skull. My beautiful fair-haired daughter, Haniyeh, had lost a leg. I cursed the world and everything in it, and I cursed the day on which, forty-six years earlier, I had been born.

'My spirit crushed into the very earth I trod upon, I walked away from the scene. I turned at the end of the demolished street to take one last look at the place where the veritable mainstay of my life had been cut by the shears of fate. It was an area of Isfahan that I would never return to.

'Memories and the bitterness in my heart were my sole companions as I wandered aimlessly, leaving the authorities to the grim task of burying my family along with the hundreds of other victims who had perished in what was later to be referred to as the region's most powerful earthquake in over a century. As far as I was concerned, my family had returned to where they'd come from, the bosom of Almighty Allah. God opens doors and people disappear through them, sometimes, as in the case of my loved ones, never to return. A vague notion began to enter my distraught mind that all was as it should be. That my family was seemingly too good for this malign world was a thought that had often troubled me. Now they were safe forever, far away from the vicissitudes of life, merged in the all-encompassing love of the Holy One.' A teardrop glistened in the firelight as it seeped from Ali's right eye and worked its way down his cheek until it shrank to nothing before it reached his chin. Ali acted as if he didn't notice this physical manifestation of his sorrow and continued talking without a pause. 'If I asked anything of my God, it was why I had been left behind to suffer the grief of such a soul-destroying loss. To this day I've never received a clear answer to that question, perhaps because it is beyond the wit of man and it is only omniscient Allah who understands such things. And thus it became another of life's dark mysteries to live through without knowing the reason why.

'Why? Why? Why? I repeated that word for weeks, until it sounded like an incantation. If you think about it long enough, you'll conclude that existence simply *is* and there is no why to it. Although I know that, I still haven't reached a place in myself where my heart can totally accept what happened.'

Ali Khatib fell silent for a few moments to allow the weight of his softly spoken words to register. He looked up, slowly focusing as if from a great distance. His face was contorted by despair and regret. Ali's slumped shoulders, the hurt in his glistening eyes and the sadness etched in every line of his face spoke volumes and told Angus much about the storyteller's damaged psyche. Minutes passed and, as he sat observing Ali, it occurred to Angus that, contrary to popular belief, time doesn't heal everything. In Ali's case his injuries had turned septic, gangrenous even.

The Iranian poked at the fire's glowing cinders with his metal pincers and then, after setting the tongs aside, picked up his narrative's dangling thread. 'When I returned to Kabir's apartment, I found him in the kitchen, stooped over a small charcoal brazier grilling mutton kebabs. Less than a day had passed since I rushed out of there, yet to me it felt like a lifetime. He offered to share his meal with me. I refused, having no real appetite – at least not as far as food was concerned.

'After explaining what had befallen me, I asked him for some opium. The voice of reason, he said, 'My dear friend, are you sure you know what you're doing? Perhaps you should take some time to think things over.' I told him that was, in fact, the source of my problem. I wanted to escape from my depressing thoughts, not move further into them. Somewhat reluctantly, Kabir gave me what I requested. I prepared a pipe immediately. My long absent black mistress's powerful arms reached out and embraced me. A month later I was as addicted as I had been in the years of my youth.

'Work for me became a thing of the past. Any semblance of a normal life disappeared out the same exit door my beloved family had vanished through. A number of well-intentioned friends were sympathetic towards me, understanding to a certain degree my need to escape the painful reality that had become my life. In the long run, my constant troublemaking would have exhausted the patience of a Sufi saint.' Ali let out a conceited chuckle and said in a voice full of pride, 'Why, my serpentine manoeuvres could have beguiled a snake charmer's wits to the point of tying them in convoluted knots.' His voice was suddenly tinged by resignation when he announced, 'My benefactors tired of me when they realized with practical certainty that I was an irredeemable drug addict. I had once again moved far beyond the boundaries that form the essence of most people's sanity, my sole purpose in life being to seek oblivion by drawing deeply on my opium pipe.

'By hook or by crooked hand, I procured the funds to pay for my deep-seated habit. Opium was the perfect mistress who supervised my labour intensive apprenticeship in deceit and larceny. My drug-fuelled imagination devised ever more ingenious methods to obtain the cash I so desperately needed. Sometimes, when my sticky fingers attached themselves to some real money, I used it to travel out of Persia in my quest to find the best that the world's poppy fields had to offer. Last year I returned from South-Vietnam, where they call opium *dau sac*, crazy smoke. A month ago I came to Meshed after overstaying my welcome in Kerman in the south of my country.

'Within a week, the police in Meshed had arrested me twice, both times for petty theft. On the second occasion they confiscated my passport and set me free after a night in their stinking cells, seeing me more as a social nuisance than anything else. In a bygone era my thieving hands would have been chopped off as a punishment for my larcenous transgressions. It occurred to me that, if I was apprehended again, perhaps the authorities would not be so lenient with me. Receiving a harsh beating at the hands of the police was the least of my concerns. What worried me was the idea of having my opium supply cut off.

'In relation to the world, my only remaining dream was to travel once more to Afghanistan where, apart from opium being dirt cheap, I would no longer be part of a repressed minority, who are treated like the scum of the earth. I've often thought that Kabul would be the perfect place to live out the remainder of my smoke-filled days and drink deeply from the well of contentment that opium delivers me to. In Afghanistan the cost of living is negligible and, if you pay your bills, the Afghans mind their own business and leave you alone. All that I needed was a lucky break to make it happen. For the first time since losing my family I returned to the mosque, praying to God to present me with an opportunity to make my dream come true.

'Omnipotent Allah deemed fit to grant me a boon because, ten days ago, I came across two well-dressed Danish couples exploring the inextricable maze of Meshed's main bazaar. I approached them and established an immediate, easy exchange composed of banal commonplaces and pleasantries. I offered my services as a guide. They accepted. It did not take me long to worm my way into their confidence and discover that the Danes were wealthy people of a kindly disposition, gullible enough to place their trust in one so perfidious as my wicked self. Within a day of meeting them, the unwary foreigners inadvertently let it be known to me that they had in their possession rather a large sum of money.

'The Scandinavians' reason for visiting the Holy City of Meshed was that they wished to purchase quite rare and expensive nineteenth century rugs called Farsibaffs. In Copenhagen the four Danes were mutual partners in a furniture shop that catered to the expensive tastes of the city's more affluent citizens. Wishing to invest in some valuable carpets, they'd eventually travelled east to Meshed, where they'd heard, quite rightly, that prices were more reasonable than in other parts of the country. The uninitiated foreigners were suitably impressed by my extensive knowledge concerning the densely floral-patterned exotic rugs they so diligently sought after.

By the following afternoon, we were seated round half-a-dozen or so fine examples of Farsibaff and Turkibaff carpets, whose names derive primarily from the weaves and knots employed in their creation. I demonstrated my expertise by picking out the better made rugs and elucidating why one was superior in quality in comparison to another.

'When negotiations with the carpet dealer began in earnest, I took Jan, the tall fair-haired spokesman of the group, to one side. 'Jan, my friend,' I said, my voice low as if I were letting him in on a big secret, 'I advise you to stall a little. Don't show the colour of your money yet. Say you'll think it over and return later. That way you'll save yourself a fair amount of expense.'

'Jan winked at me. 'Thank you, Ali,' he said, his boyish face breaking into a toothy smile, 'I won't forget how much you've helped us. It's a good idea. We'll follow your wise counsel.'

'It was a good notion. Unfortunately, not for the reasons the foreigners believed it to be. What I told the Dane was, in fact, true. To the calculating carpet salesman, the amount of money involved in such a transaction would have appeared to him as the equivalent of a Saudi sheik's ransom. He would not want to jeopardize the deal for a few extra rials in his pocket. Just before we left the carpet shop, the anxious owner was already dropping his price. He'd have dropped his drawers and presented his arse for the sum involved, but that was unnecessary as I had other plans for the money. We left the premises and walked down the street. The Danes were talking excitedly. Turning to me at one point, Marika, Jan's big-busted wife, put her arm around my shoulders and drew me close.

''Ali,' she whispered in my ear, 'there will be a good commission in this for you.'

''You're so kind,' I said, feigning embarrassment. 'Do as you wish. For my part, I am only too happy to help you. It's my way of making you welcome in my country.'

'When I'd escorted the Danes back to Meshed's most expensive hotel, a tall modernistic building with a fleet of imported American automobiles parked in front of it, they paid me twice as much as I'd originally asked for my fee. This did not make my plan to rob these fine people of everything of value that they had upon their persons any the easier to carry out. What little conscience I had left flickering in my deceitful heart was snuffed out by reminding myself that, to these foreigners, it was only money. To me it was a ticket to a new life. There was to be no turning back on the execrable path I'd chosen to tread.

'The following morning, my design began to fall into place when, for the last time, I played out my role as the Danes' tour guide. They had the cash payment for the carpets with them as prearranged. I took them to a pleasant tea garden for refreshments – the first part of my plan. You see, the proprietor of this particular establishment was an old acquaintance of mine with whom I'd had some dealings in the past that had turned out to be mutually beneficial for us both on a financial level. The evening before, I'd visited his café and offered him all the money I had in my possession to drug the foreigners' drinks. Unable to refuse the cash incentive, more than he earned in a month, he agreed to do as I requested. What he put in the Danish people's tea was a dangerous hallucinogenic drug called LSD.

'Let me explain. A few months before, in Tehran, I'd exchanged a *lool* (18 grams) of poor quality opium for ten orange pills. The trade had been done with a group of young European travellers...' Ali glanced at Angus and Raj. '...like yourselves.' He produced a cough to clear his throat and then said, 'When one of the youths handed me the tablets, he told me to enjoy my trip. I'd taken this to mean that upon ingesting the stuff I would feel so intoxicated that I might fall over things. Not wishing to injure myself, I swallowed two of the small pills while sitting on the edge of my bed in a cheap backstreet hotel. At first I thought I had been cheated. One hour later, I felt like my body had been taken over by the spirit of Satan. I had to lie down and when I did I saw that the ceiling appeared to be melting. I could have sworn that the faces of the damned were coming out of the walls. An eerie chorus of anguished human wailing assaulted my ears. Just when I thought the sound would drive me insane, the unsettling chorus slowly faded away like a dying breeze and then I almost jumped out of my skin when I realized that there were little winged devils and jinn flying about the room. I could hear foul-mouthed demons' lusty cries as they fornicated under my cot. I got down on my knees and prayed to Allah to stop the hellish visions. My plea to the almighty fell on deaf ears because, when I looked up, the horned Son of the Beast stuck his horrible head out from behind the drawn curtains and howled in a diabolical voice that I was indeed possessed by his father, Beelzebub. I was terrified out of my wits. In order to calm myself down, I smoked a bowl of opium. Lying back on my mattress I was enveloped in a foul-smelling fog. Suddenly, I found myself inhabiting the body of a giant copper-skinned cockroach that was scuttling around in the city's sewer system. The horrible thing's quivering antennae mirrored the state of my trembling nerves. It was a living nightmare and an experience that I would most definitely not wish to repeat again, even if I were offered enough gold to make me as rich as King Solomon.

'When the Danes had finished their drinks,' said Ali after a pause, 'I suggested we move on to the next part of the tour. We were going to visit the shrine of Imam Riza. I'd kept the best until last because this holy memorial is, for the faithful, one of the great places of pilgrimage in the Shia Muslim world. It suited my impious purposes perfectly.

'Outside of the mosque, we removed our shoes. I could see the drug was starting to have an effect on my victims. In between bursts of untimely laughter, they were talking enthusiastically about the spiritual vibrations of the place. It was time to make my move before the situation became uncontrollable. Seeking out a quiet corner, I sat the Scandinavians down on a stone bench. My tone was solemn when I explained how it was customary to remove all valuables from one's person before entering the holy shrine. I also told them that, in accordance with tradition, all layers of upper body garments had to be removed. Now then, these foreigners, although naïve, were not altogether stupid. Upon hearing my last request, they glanced nervously at each other, not quite knowing what to think. They turned to me, seeking some sort of reassurance. This predictable eventuality was something I was well prepared for. Cutting the perfect pose of innocence, I spoke with contrived honesty and watched as their looks of apprehension quickly changed into the kind of faces advertisers use to promote a new brand of toothpaste. A picture of irreproachability, I informed them that although I loved to worship at the holy shrine, it would be no problem for me to wait outside and guard their valuables until they were ready to leave. Exuding a compelling quality of sincerity, I played my nefarious part well. Their apparently unfounded worries evaporated like spit on a hot frying pan. By this time, the LSD was really taking hold of them. They were becoming unnaturally buoyant and laughing to themselves like four nursery school children enjoying an outing to the zoo. Handing me their bags and clothes, they wandered off – hand in hand – in the direction of the shrine of Imam Riza, babbling away in Danish, a strange tongue, I might add, that I'd never felt inclined to try and master.

'It does not require a lot of imagination to picture what sort of reception two blonde foreign women, with their large bouncing breasts exposed, would receive upon entering a Muslim Holy of Holies, where photography and non-believers are barred. I didn't wait around to find out. Using a black plastic bag I had with me for the purpose, I threw all their possessions into it. When I reached the street, I could hear a great hullabaloo of shouts and screams arising from within the shrine's precincts. As I hurried along a back alley, I had to suppress the devilish laughter that was straining to erupt from my throat at the thought of what must have happened to those poor gullible tourists. I wondered for a fleeting moment if perhaps the great blasphemer had taken control of my soul, that I'd somehow managed to embrace evil in its totality and, having done that, I was left with no other choice than to resort to the devil's means to survive. One thing was certain; the Danish travellers' trust in strangers would no doubt lie in tatters at their well-shod feet for the remainder of their lives.'

There was a pause, not long, a few moments, and then Ali said, 'My robbery turned out to be an even greater success than I'd imagined possible. Back at my lodgings, I spilled the contents of my victims' bags out onto my bed. A large sum of money lay next to four expensive watches, an assortment of diamond encrusted jewellery and leather wallets containing a dozen major credit cards.

'After putting on a straw hat and dark sunglasses to disguise myself, I went to visit a dealer in stolen property to whom I'd sold valuable items in the past. On my way I dumped the foreigners' clothes, bags and empty wallets in an open sewer. Two hours later, I returned to my room, feeling like I was the lucky winner of a state lottery jackpot. My new life had begun. I locked the door, thinking it prudent to lie low for some days. After a week of overindulgence, my opium supply eventually needed replenishing. It was when returning from my supplier that I ran into Raj, Mister Murphy and their two charming lady companions in the teashop.

'Now that I've narrated the story of how I came to acquire the foreign currency, I realize that perhaps I've let my tongue run away with me more than I might have wished. Maybe it's been unwise of me to reveal certain characteristics about my self that you, my dear listeners, could, quite justifiably, deem fit to view as untrustworthy. Let me put your minds at ease concerning this matter. Due to my good fortune, I am in absolutely no need of money. Therefore, you have nothing to fear. Allah, the Munificent – may He shorten my tongue – has once more provided for my simple needs. Peace, and may God's compassionate blessings be showered upon you.'

With that, Ali's tale drew to a close. He was greeted with silence. Angus and Raj sat looking at him for some time, watching as he busied himself with his pipe.

'Thanks for telling us your story, Ali.' Raj stretched his arms and yawned. 'It sounds to me like your life has not been an easy one.'

Ali remained silent, shrugged fatalistically, flashed a twisted smile that could have been a grimace and then drew on his pipe. He exhaled a jet of smoke and sat staring into the smouldering fire like a bleary-eyed sphinx.

Angus caught Raj's attention and moved his head in such a way as to indicate that it was time to take a little walk. The two friends stood up and ambled off.

Once out of earshot, Angus turned to Raj in the darkness and asked, 'So, what did you make of that then?'

'Well, to be honest,' replied Raj, 'I kind of felt sorry for the poor guy, losing his family and all. I had a lump in my throat listening to that part of his story.'

'You've got to be joking.'

'Why do you say that?'

'Because the man's a fuckin' verbal bagpipe blowing a hot air lament.'

'Come on, don't you think you're being a bit hard on the guy?'

'Hard on the guy!' Angus aped, pulling down his zipper to take a piss. His urine splashed on to the sand. *'Mmmgh,'* he groaned in relief and said, 'I wouldn't be surprised if he made the whole thing up. All that nonsense about the Shah and Allah the Almighty, he's probably never been in a mosque in his life. The man's a mass of contradictions with a drug-fried brain. I mean to say, what self-respecting Muslim would tell a tale like that about himself? He doesn't even have a beard to hide his bald-faced lies behind.'

'Don't you trust him?' Raj asked.

'I wouldn't trust that guy as far as I could spit. You know what they say; you can never trust a junkie.'

'Is he a junkie?'

'Have you dented your helmet or something? Of course he is. Open your eyes, Raj. The heavyweight force of his addiction must have steamrolled any trace of a conscience he ever had out of existence long before you or I were born.'

'You really think so?'

'Of course I do. Ali is bad news. Man, by the time we get rid of him he'll have the girls hooked on that shit he's smoking.'

'Yeah,' agreed Raj, 'I know what you mean. I'm giving it a miss from now on.'

'You know, I'm worried about Jenny. She's developing a real taste for that stuff.'

'I noticed. What are you going to do about it?'

'I don't know, man. I really don't know.'

'Maybe it's time to put your foot down.'

'You're probably right. But if I say anything along those lines she'll just start rattling on about being a free spirit and how I have a judgemental attitude.'

'Sounds just like Alice,' said Raj, nodding his head thoughtfully. 'She lays the same trip on me sometimes. Anyway, one thing's for sure, you're not very keen on Dirty Ali, are you?'

'No, it's not that,' answered Angus. 'He's the sort of interesting character I find difficult not to like. He reminds me a bit of your Uncle Sulei. So bad he's good, if you catch my drift. Thing is, I've got this gut feeling about Mister Ali Khatib that doesn't bode well.'

'Och, come off it, Angus. You worry too much. We'll be dropping him off in Kabul before you know it.'

At the thought of where they were headed, the two friends turned and stood shoulder to shoulder, facing the infinite shadowy expanse to the east.

'Afghanistan,' said Angus. 'We'll be in Afghanistan tomorrow.'

'Yes, I know. I can hardly believe it myself. I can hear destiny calling to me.'

'Oh yeah?' Angus let out a short laugh. 'Let me guess what she's whispering in your ear. 'Come on big boy, fuck me harder.' Raj, you're becoming a romantic in your old age.'

Raj draped an arm over his friend's shoulders and chuckled. 'And you're turning into a cynic. But you know what I mean, don't you? We've come a long way together. Haven't we?'

'We sure have, man. Look at where we are now. It's so limitless and free, like we're the only people in the world.' Angus thought for a moment and then said, 'I've been meaning to ask you. What's up with Murphy?'

'What do you mean?' said Raj, continuing to stare out into the darkness.

'Haven't you noticed he's been acting pretty uptight recently?'

'Not really. Murph's a funny bugger even at the best of times. Just don't take him too seriously.'

'That's just it, Raj. Murphy is serious and that's not like him. Freeze-your-nuts-off glances and caustic comments have been flying thick and fast between him and Nina since we left Scotland. And he's becoming more aggressive than usual. I mean to say, look at the way he behaved in front of Ali tonight.'

'Yeah, I hear what you're saying. When he stood up and farted in front of the old boy in the middle of his story and said he'd had enough of listening to his shite, that was really uncool.'

'Right! And it was Murph, more than anyone else, who wanted to take Ali on board as a fare-paying passenger in the first place. It's as if— '

'There's something I've been meaning to talk to you about for some time.' Raj sounded anxious and seemed to be on the brink of saying a great deal, but chose to say, 'No…no, it doesn't matter, forget it.'

'What doesn't matter?' Angus asked, turning to face Raj whose shiny hair reflected faint silver starlight.

'Nothing...I...I...I mean s-s-something,' stammered Raj, 'but I don't feel like speaking about it right now.'

Angus could feel his friend's nervousness and was puzzled about its source. 'Are you feeling alright, man? You know I'm always here for you.'

'I know that and I appreciate your saying it.' Raj shook his head, as if he didn't trust himself to say anymore. 'Maybe some other time, forget it. Okay?'

Angus wondered if whatever it was might have something to do with Murphy, but decided not to pursue it. A few seconds of uncharacteristically awkward silence passed between them and then he said, 'Yeah, sure. No problem. What were we talking about? Oh yeah, Afghan—'

A pair of shooting stars flashed across the sky in front of them. Angus thought he heard them whoosh through the earth's atmosphere as they burned up.

'Hey, man!' Raj exclaimed. 'We can make a wish on that.'

'Aye, Raj, that we can.'

Angus thought about it for a moment, and then he wished that Jenny would stop smoking opium.

Not far from where they stood a wild animal yowled.

Raj bumped against Angus and asked nervously, 'What the fuck was that?'

'I don't know,' answered Angus. 'But it sounded like an Iranian werewolf.' He clapped Raj on the shoulder. 'Come on, man, we've got a long day ahead of us. We better catch some sleep.'

When they returned to the campsite, there wasn't a ripple in the air, the breeze having died out along with the fire that Ali remained gazing into. He was locked in a silent communion with the ashes, as if they were telling him that in time everyone would turn grey, cool down and die, just like they had.

Angus and Raj walked silently over the sand to the bus and left Ali to his thoughts and the three sleeping women to their dreams.

Out in the loneliness of the desert, the mountains to the south were outlined by a lightning flash. A wild beast let out a long howl. There was something dreadful about the sound, as if contained within it was a tale of untold suffering down through the ages. Angus's shivered. He was tired. When he lay down, sleep came swiftly.

6

THE CRIPPLED MUSICIANS
OF THE BAYON

Cambodia.

I was thinking how I would have given anything to lie down and sleep when the dog that was snoozing on the sand in front of me woke up, sprang to her feet, threw her head back and bayed like a wolf howling at the moon.

At first I hadn't a clue what all the fuss was about – until I heard the sound of an engine. I bent forward, turned my head to the right and saw full beam headlights strafing across the beach. My initial thought was that Jean had sensed that I was in danger and somehow organized a search party. As the vehicle drew closer I realized how unlikely this was and started waving my arms in the air. The dog barked furiously and lolloped towards the speeding vehicle. Through the glare, I could make out the box-like form of a short wheelbase Land Rover. The moon's silver glow was reflecting off its oblong windscreen.

I shouted. 'Hey! Hey! Stop! Stop! I'm over here!'

It was just then that the driver swerved towards the sea to avoid hitting the dog. The Land Rover's wheels ploughed into the water and threw up iridescent silver-grey fans of spray.

'Oh no!' I groaned, realizing that the driver had been distracted and wouldn't see me. I hollered, 'You stupid bloody dog get out of the way!'

'*Aieejah! Waaghee! Yahee!*'

I heard alarmed shouts. The Land Rover's windows were open and I caught a glimpse of a woman's face. Over the combined noises of the yelling, splashing water, the guttural growl of a straining diesel engine and the excited dog's barking, I caught a trace of the peculiar tinkle-tong-clonk of traditional Cambodian music. The Land Rover passed by and continued on its way with the barking dog in hot pursuit. The vehicle receded into the distance and the twinkling red dots created by its rear lights faded and disappeared.

My soul screamed in pure frustration. 'No! No! *Nooooo!'*

Despair snaked into my mind and then slithered south into my guts, where it congealed into vitriolic jelly. Bilious fluid rose in my dry throat.

Out over the moonlit sea's expanse, thunder boomed. Cumulonimbus cloud formations were rising up to form thunderheads on the horizon. Illuminated from within by bolts of lightning, the clouds flickered and glowed acid pink. I saw them as ominous harbingers of calamitous events, a line of mushroom clouds billowing up in the aftermath of thermo-nuclear detonations.

The breeze was maturing into a wind and swelling up the sea in its path. On the shoreline, an arm's length away from the water, I could see a small dark spot. It was my watch, cast away earlier when I'd allowed myself to indulge in a moment of impulsive excitement. I regretted having done that. Inhaling deeply, I puffed out a loud aggravated breath. Wound up tighter than a clock's mainspring, my anxiety manifested as a nervous tick under my right eye. Knowing what time it was had suddenly become the most imperative piece of information in the world.

No thinking, no time. I heard my brother's words inside my head. Yes, I reasoned, Angus was right. The denser my thoughts, the more real the impression that time is crawling by like a sick lizard.

In spite of that I was unwilling to accept Angus's assertion that time was a repetitive play, being performed for all eternity by dream actors on an imaginary stage in the theatre of illusion. How can I believe that time is an illusion, I asked silently, when overloaded seconds, separated by leaden intervals, are bearing down on me with their combined weight?

I was drawn away from my ruminations by the reappearance of my doggy companion. She was panting and her tongue was dripping saliva as it hung from one side of her smiling mouth.

I shouted, 'You stupid bloody bitch, this is your fucking fault!'

The dog stopped dead in its tracks, ears twitching like biological antennae. She then tilted her head and produced a friendly bark.

Compassion flared in my heart and my frustration evaporated. My voice softened. 'Och, come here girl. I'm sorry. I know it's not your fault.'

I reached out and rubbed behind her ears. Unaccustomed to so much affection at the hands of a human being, the mongrel made excited whining noises through her damp nose. Satisfied with the attention, she turned around three times before plumping herself back down in the sandy indentation she'd vacated ten minutes before. She lay on her side and gave herself an energetic scratch with the outstretched paw of one of her hind legs.

Fleas, I thought in alarm. My ankles began to itch.

My mind went into reverse and returned to the Land Rover, more specifically, to the music I'd heard coming out of it as it drove by, for it reminded me of when I had heard similar music two weeks earlier, played in an environment more conductive to its appreciation. I did not exactly think about it − I had a sudden vivid recollection of a busy street by a river in a small Cambodian city, shimmering in the midday heat.

The countryside was littered with rubbish. On the outskirts of many towns and villages there were fields covered in discarded plastic bags. This had left me with the distinct impression that the Khmer population seemed to be completely unaware of the fact that plastic doesn't dissolve when it rains. It was therefore, upon arriving in Siem Reap, that Jean and I were pleasantly surprised by the city's well-tended gardens, litter free streets and general air of social orderliness. Located 250 kilometres northwest of Cambodia's capital city, Phnom Penh, Siem Reap is situated near to the country's western border with Thailand. Amongst other things, this easy-going settlement serves as a dormitory for tourists visiting the nearby ancient city of Angkor. The colour of dung, a shallow river, almost stagnant in the hot season, winds its way through Siem Reap like an aquatic serpent. Its neatly mowed, grassy banks are adorned with local government signs declaring in English, 'DO NOT WASTE OUR VALUABLE NATURAL RESOURCES'.

When my wife read that she exclaimed, 'My God! Don't tell me they're referring to that stinking open sewer that passes for a river round here.'

'Come on now, Jean,' I said, as we walked along the cracked pavement that flanked the riverbank, 'it's not Scotland, you know. They have droughts in this part of the world. The locals value their water, no matter how dirty it is.'

'Well, maybe you're right, for once,' she said, 'but I have to say you're starting to sound like one of those bloody environmentalists. I hope to God you're not thinking of voting for the Greens in the next election. Charles Skinner, our local Conservative MP, needs all the votes he can get. I don't want you wasting yours on weirdoes who hug trees.'

We continued along the side of the road and passed teenage couples sitting on wooden benches. The shy oriental lovers exchanged meaningful glances with each other and giggled shyly. Behind them, a herd of grey concrete elephants stood on the grass, their empty eye sockets blind to the endless stream of three-wheeled motorized rickshaws passing on the street.

'Taxi, taxi, you want taxi?' The baseball-capped drivers called out their moneymaking mantra.

Outside of a Buddhist temple with a steeply slanted roof, a small group of saffron-clad monks sat on stone steps chanting in unison. Their droning voices drew my attention. I stopped for a moment to take in the scene and admired the ornately carved and brightly painted spirit houses in the courtyard. Well into the upper thirties, the air was thick with humidity.

'Come on, now,' said Jean, urging me to keep moving. 'I'm dying for a cold drink. Let's go round to the Blue Pumpkin Café for a glass of that iced tea.'

We made our way over to the area surrounding the town's old market, walking along narrow streets lined with Chinese style houses, currency exchange offices, bookshops, art galleries, massage parlours and westernized cafés catering to the tastes of foreign tourists, French ex-pats who like croissants with their *café au lait* and American aid workers with dollars to spend. By the time we reached the Blue Pumpkin Café, we'd been accosted by at least a dozen beggars, most of whom were either blind, diseased or had one or more limbs missing. I took pity on them and began handing out low denomination Cambodian riel bank notes like they were flyers advertising a free beggar's banquet. I was soon surrounded by a small crowd of sad-eyed unfortunates, who were serenading me with a heart-rending chorus of desperate pleas.

Jean's voice was full of chagrin when, over the heads of the scroungers, she cried out to me. 'For God's sake, you bloody idiot that you are, get away from them! Can't you see their hair is filthy? For crying out loud, you'll get lice!'

The Khmer begging population was in a deplorable condition. Many were landmine victims.

My eyes sprang open and I felt goose pimples rising on the skin of my arms as I remembered, for what seemed like the umpteenth time, that I was sitting on top of such a device. I snapped my eyes shut and summoned up powerful images to block out the present.

From what I'd read and heard I knew that Cambodia as a whole was still, in many ways, struggling to come to terms with its recent history. I'd seen the dark cloak of past catastrophe, hanging over Cambodia like a shroud. A chilling reminder of what happened in the mid-seventies when the country began to be torn apart by Pol Pot's madcap vision of creating a new civilization to rival that of the ancient Khmers of a thousand years before. Like a high-speed newsreel, I watched my mind produce a condensed visual report on how Pol Pot's dream quickly degenerated into a nightmarish agrarian concentration camp, where people were executed for wearing spectacles and rotting corpses were used as manure.

'That's the last thing on earth I need to think about,' I muttered, shaking my head as if the movement could make the ghastly images disappear. I took a few deep breaths, concentrated my thoughts and looked back in time to the cloudy morning when Jean and I paid eighty American dollars for a couple of three-day passes to gain admittance to the hundred square kilometre park that is the site of Angkor's various temple complexes. Within an hour of arriving in the grounds, we were standing inside the magnificent Ta Prom temple, where tall trees' roots grow out of the cut stone walls like huge wooden tentacles. I recalled how we stood listening to a young, immaculately dressed tour guide explain to us, in perfect English, how in Khmer Rouge times the buildings had been turned into field hospitals to shelter the wounded.

'Over there,' said the young man, pointing to a large rectangular courtyard, 'if you look carefully, you will see faded brown marks on the flagstones. Those are bloodstains.' There were sighs of appreciation from the tour group as they captured the scene with their digital cameras. The guide smiled and then said, 'Pol Pot's army executed people here. The soldiers saved bullets by using farm implements and bamboo spears to dispose of their enemies. Sometimes,' he added, 'counter-revolutionaries were fed to crocodiles – while still alive. We will now move on to...'

'Jesus bloody Christ,' complained Jean, having heard enough about Cambodia's horrifying past to give her nightmares. 'The way this guy's rattling on, you'd think he was proud of what happened. He'll be telling us next about how many bombs the American air force's B-52s dropped on them back in the twentieth century. It's high time we got back to Scotland and civilization. That's the trouble with countries that lack culture; they don't show *Neighbours* or *Friends* on the telly. I dread to think about how many episodes I've missed since we left home. Maggie's been keeping me up to date with her e-mails, but that's not the same as watching the programmes. If Angus hadn't bought us those bloody tickets we'd be back home in Oban by now.'

I paid little attention to my wife's diatribe – I'd heard it all before – or the guide's running commentary. I'm a civil engineer and I was therefore fascinated by the huge blocks of cut stone that had gone into the sacred building's construction and the seamless accuracy employed to set them in place.

The following morning, I rented a motor scooter and returned to Angkor's temples, alone. Jean had decided that it was a far more appealing idea to visit an air-conditioned hairdresser for a rinse and have the chipped varnish on her long manicured nails repainted into the bargain. It was fine with me. I was used to her complaining to the extent that I sometimes enjoyed it in a strange kind of way, but it was also nice to get away from her voice from time to time.

I spent hours in the Bayon Temple, marvelling at the majestic beauty of the many Buddha-like faces set into the imposing stone towers that crown the ancient edifice's central elevated platform. Encrusted in grey and jade green lichen, their weathered countenances, entwined with creeping vines, smiled down upon me as their wide-open eyes watched the tourists and the centuries pass.

A sweating, scarlet-faced man, wearing a thick tweed suit and a black baseball cap, approached me and asked for a cigarette. He was German and informed me that he was an archaeologist working on a nearby restoration project, funded by his country's government. We sat down with each other for a smoke and I had it explained to me how the man who was behind the construction of the fantastic temple was called Jayarman the Seventh.

'On being crowned King in 1181 AD,' said the archaeologist-turned-historian, 'Jayarman adopted the idea that he was a living Buddha. How he managed to tie this notion in with the millions of hours of enforced slave labour that were employed to create this grandiose monument to his greatness is anybody's guess.' He suddenly stopped talking and looked absently at the cigarette lodged between his dirty fingers. It had gone out, having burned down to its filter.

'Would you like another?' I asked, offering the packet.

'What? Oh...no, *nein danke,* I limit myself to one a day.' The archaeologist took off his salt-stained black cap and scratched his head. 'Now then, where was I?' He tugged at his right ear and then put his cap back on. 'Ah yes, as I was saying, Jayarman the slave master thought he was a Buddha and most definitely succeeded in creating a piece of heavenly architecture, as I'm sure you will agree.' I nodded in accord. The archaeologist stood up, shook hands with me and said, 'You'll have to excuse me. I must go and see how my workers are getting along.' He glanced at his wristwatch. 'Leave them alone for more than five minutes and the lazy devils are liable to lay down their tools and start playing cards. *Auf Wiedersehen* and thanks for the cigarette.' He raised his right hand in farewell, turned and walked away.

I watched him quickly descend the temple's steep main staircase with a skill born of practice and wondered how he could bear to wear a thick woollen suit in such a humid tropical climate.

The sun had reached its zenith, making it too hot to walk around without risk of heatstroke. I decided to seek out a bite to eat from one of the many corrugated tin-roofed restaurants that were located across from the temple and situated under the shade of tall peepul trees.

Mournfully exquisite music drifted up to meet me as I made my way down precipitous and, in some places, disintegrating, cut stone steps. Curiosity won out over hunger. I was drawn to the source of the music, as if under a spell.

The Crippled Musicians of the Bayon were seated on a woven mat, playing their sublime celestial melodies beneath a willow tree's drooping branches at the side of a dusty pathway. I discovered the group's name by examining the cover of a CD, taken from a small carton that was strategically placed beside a gruesome pile of pink plastic prosthetic limbs that the boys in the band had disconnected from their bodies before settling into their musical groove. The music alone warranted a monetary donation, but obviously the artistes saw fit to create a macabre display in order to wring out even more financial sympathy from their transient audience.

I fished in my khaki short's pockets for a moment, then bent forward to drop a thousand riel note into a wooden donation box, which bore a little sign that informed me that each one of the Khmer men was a landmine victim. I'd then stood up straight and let my eyes rove over the musicians' impassive faces. The men wore uniform red *kromahs* (traditional Khmer scarves), wrapped turban-like around their heads and bore the same gentle facial characteristics I'd come to associate with their mild-mannered countrymen. Eyes closed, if they were fortunate enough to have any, the smooth unlined masks of their expressions betrayed not a hint of the terrible suffering and painful fate they must have endured during their lifetimes. One of the players performed a violin solo, while his fellow musicians created a pitter-patter background of rhythms on small hand-held drums and a bamboo xylophone for him to launch into inspired musical flight. His bow stroked his finely tuned instrument's two strings and flew up and down the Khmer five-tone musical scale. He continued on the same melody adding soaring embellishments. The violinist's adroit playing was so full of intense feeling it produced a knot of empathetic emotion in my throat. I was flabbergasted that such heavenly music could be created by people who'd lived through hellish agonies, produced by a world gone violently insane. The emotional impact of the scene was too much for my sensibilities to handle. Tears came to my eyes. Wishing not to embarrass the players with a public display of emotion, something which I'd been told was viewed all over Southeast Asia as being extremely bad manners, I walked away.

The band played on without missing a beat. Like an amicable spirit, a superbly delicate tune accompanied me as I strolled along a dusty track. My heart registered that I might never again be so moved by listening to music. The haunting melody was eventually obliterated by the strident high-pitched sawing made by male crickets rubbing their legs together to produce a penetrating din, which rose from within the shadows of the sweet-smelling secondary forest that flanked both sides of the path.

Now, two weeks later, the crippled musicians' music had come back to haunt me or, viewed from another perspective, awaken me to the situation I found myself sitting in. It seemed to me in that moment that dying wasn't the worst thing that could happen to me. The idea of dismemberment cast the impression in my mind that it would be a far more terrible fate to endure than a run-in with the Grim Reaper.

I opened my eyes and gave my four-legged friend a reassuring pat as she slept. One of her back legs tried to relieve an itch on her side. Off target, it pawed at the air.

About seven metres from where I sat, I could see the strap of my watch sticking out of the sand. Maybe it's a blessing that I don't know what time it is, I thought.

Lightning flashed. I looked out to sea. *Ba-doom! Ba-doom! Ba-doom!* Thunder rolled like kettledrums in a symphony orchestra's percussion section, drumming me out of my awful predicament and propelling me into a trans-dimensional jump, back into the borderline dreamtime.

7

HOTEL RUMI AND THE BIG PICTURE

The day began slowly. Over brunch in the palm grove it was decided that it would be prudent to conceal Ali for the border crossing into Afghanistan. The bus's shower basin was lifted out of its place and he was squeezed into the secret stash compartment. It turned out to be a good idea.

When they reached the frontier, a pair of battle-dressed Iranian customs and immigration agents, carrying short-barrelled Heckler and Koch submachine guns, boarded Rolling Thunder for a quick check before the bus was permitted to cross the borderline and leave the twentieth century behind.

The Afghan border guards were a different breed altogether. Dressed in patched, Keystone-Cops style serge-blue uniforms, the ruddy faced men had colt revolvers jammed into their worn, brown leather, Sam Browne holsters. An unshaven man with a discoloured glass eye hurriedly stamped everyone's passports with entry visas. It was soon made clear that the Afghans were eager to get down to the business of persuading the hippy tourists to buy some hashish from them. Cannabis was still legal in Afghanistan, but that would change in 1974 due to anti-drug pressure from the United States. 'Number One' was the guards' sales pitch although, even had a potential customer been in possession of an imagination with the stretching power of knicker elastic, it would have been difficult to designate the mouldy chunks of hash on offer to any category other than that of 'Pure Rubbish'. Murphy purchased a cigarette packet-sized piece for five dollars.

Next, it was the moneychangers' turn. 'Change money, change money, you change money', they chanted enthusiastically, waving wads of dirty bank notes that were so worn they looked like they were ready to disintegrate. The local currency was called Afghanis and the exchange rate that day was 55 for one American dollar. Raj bought enough of the well-fingered paper money to fill a shoebox.

Approximately ten kilometres into the country, Angus drove into a small town called Tir-Pol for a tea break. A composite of turbaned locals, made up of camel-herders, farmers, labourers and tramps, stood around in the *chai-chana* (teashop), gawking at the bellbottom and kaftan-clad hippies as they sat sipping on egg timer glasses filled with heavily sugared mint tea. Little more than a brick-walled bunker with a sagging corrugated iron roof, the teashop reeked of home-grown tobacco and the sickly stench of unwashed male bodies. The rank air was swarming with squadrons of large blue bottles. Crazed by the stink they were staging a re-enactment of a Second World War air battle. Kamikazes flew out of dogfights and completed their suicide missions by crashing into their human enemy's ears, nostrils, blinking eyes and open mouths. Everybody was relieved to return to the bus's more sterile environment before anyone was unfortunate enough to choke on a mouthful of buzzing blowflies.

Ali was left in the stash for another twenty minutes. Angus made good use of this time by driving over some potholes that were so big they were verging on craterdom.

Murphy called out a complaint from the back of the juddering bus. 'Hey, man, what the fuck are you playing at? Take it easy or you'll ruin the suspension!'

Angus pulled over to the side of the road, by the banks of a swollen river spanned by a concrete bridge. Springtime snowmelt, from the Sefid Kuh Mountains to the north, had created a glacier green torrent, which had uprooted small trees in its path and risen so high it was level with the bridge's underside.

Pulling Ali out through the hidden compartment's narrow hatch was like freeing a fat genie from the neck of a bottle. His normally tidy mop of swept-back grey hair was dishevelled to the point of making his head look like a paranoid porcupine. His dark blue polycotton suit looked even more crumpled and formless than before. It was obvious how he'd passed the time in the cramped space.

'Tut-tut,' complained a slant-eyed Ali, dabbing his brow with a sweat-stained handkerchief that he produced from his scuffed leather briefcase. 'By the seat of the Prophet's pantaloons – on whom be peace and prayers – I've just been subjected to a punishment from Hell down there. I could hardly breathe.' He coughed into his right hand and cleared phlegm from his throat. 'My God, the bumping was driving me mad. Praise be to All-Seeing Allah that I had the foresight to take my pipe along for company, for it helped ease my discomfort. I don't know if I would have been able to cope without it.' Ali dusted himself off and tottered off to the back of the bus, muttering what sounded like a repetitive prayer as he went, which was in fact a string of Parsi profanities.

A broad smile stole across Angus's face. He gave Raj a sly wink when he heard Dirty Ali voice his displeasure, thinking that it served the thieving reprobate right.

Back on the road, the girls stood behind Angus holding on to the driver's seat as they joined in with David Bowie singing, *'Ch-Ch-Ch-Changes'*. It sounded hunky-dory, but Murphy wasn't having it.

Alice protested when he edged past her, pushed the eject button on the cassette player and tossed the tape onto the shelf above the windscreen. 'Hey, man,' she whined, 'we were really getting into that.'

'I can't stand Bowie and his fuckin' melodramatic, bisexual bullshit,' was Murphy's irreverent response. 'The last time he brought out a record they were giving away free lipstick with it. The way you lot are going you'll be singing along to that twat Gary Glitter next.'

'I like Gary Glitter,' retorted Nina, staggering as the bus swerved to avoid a braying donkey that was wandering along the middle of the road.

'Aye, that'll fuckin' be right,' spat Murphy. 'Move over.' He pushed a cassette into the empty slot, cranked up the volume for maximum eardrum pounding and then said, 'Listen to this, man! This is real music!'

'Oh, oh, pass the earplugs,' commented Angus, depressing the clutch pedal with his left foot and shifting up into top gear.

There was a loud static hiss coming out of the sound system and then the bus's smoked-glass windows shuddered in their frames when The Doors blasted out of heavy-duty speakers playing 'Break on Through'.

'Yeeeeah!' Murphy roared with glee.

You know the day destroys the night...

Angus had to admit that the savage raw power unleashed in Jim Morrison's vocals better suited the wild scenery passing by outside.

Arms that chain us, eyes that lie... The song's lyrical content conjured up images so potent that it was understandable why the, by then deceased, 'Lizard King' had been described by one journalist as being a hippy reincarnation of Edgar Allan Poe.

Break on through, break on through, break on through, yeah!

The roadside panoramas were vast. To the north stood ranges of jutting stark grey mountains, stretching into the distance like frozen waves on a dehydrated ocean of ridged sand. To the south was a bleak brownish-yellow lunar landscape, dissected by bleached pebble-strewn gullies, marking the passage of streams that had dried up long before man first observed the heavens and invented time. Dust devils twirled like whirling dervishes and died within sight of black-tented nomad camps, surrounded by camels munching on sparse patches of sallow grass under a fierce blue sky, where buzzards wheeled on the lookout for carrion.

The people who inhabited the wilderness wore colours that matched the landscape, the most predominant being khaki. Overloaded, floridly painted trucks trundled by, rocking and pitching precariously as cheering passengers hung on to anything that stopped them from falling off to meet certain injury or death on the road below.

Herat was a small town, alive with the sounds of commerce. Vendors sang the praises of their merchandise, spread out before them on barrows or collapsible tables by the sides of dusty streets lined by stunted trees. The most valuable goods on display were silver fox furs, leopard skins, glassware, sturdy leather sandals and small discs of sour-smelling hashish, similar in quality to what Murphy had bought at the border. Most of the other items were household utensils made from stainless steel, aluminium or brightly coloured, moulded plastic. 'Made in China' was the predominant brand name. These mass-manufactured wares seemed incongruous in an ancient town where people had been living for over three thousand years. Appearing equally anachronistic, decrepit rusty buses chugged out black clouds of dirty, soot-laden diesel smoke, alongside dented old American cars with patched treadless tyres. Traffic trundled over carpets, laid out in the street by their owners in order to age the rugs quickly. Mud-brown adobe brick buildings lined the streets. Many of them were in such dilapidated condition it was easy to imagine that they'd been standing there when Alexander's armies marched through Herat on their way east.

Much more in rapport with Herat's general antiquated ambience were the buggies that served as all-purpose taxis. The carriages had shiny brass mudguards and velvet sunshades and were drawn by emaciated horses. The scrawny animals' reins were adorned with little silver bells, producing a lively merry sound that underscored the suffering the poor blinkered beasts of burden endured at the hands of their whip-wielding masters. Judging by the speed these men drove, they apparently envisioned themselves to be charioteers involved in a never-ending race. An animal rights activist's nightmare, the moral concept of being kind to four-legged creatures would have found little purchase in the hearts of these rugged men – had anyone been naïve enough to try and introduce the idea to them. All that the insensate tonga drivers appeared interested in was forcing every cubic centimetre of drawing potential out of the half-a-horse-power biological engine that their nickering nags represented.

Herat was pervaded by a tangible Wild West feeling, an anarchic quality that was characteristic of many frontier towns in the region. Robed tribesmen, sporting a variety of innovative turban styles, walked around in sandals whose thick black rubber soles had been cut from car tyres. Slung raffishly across their narrow shoulders were long-barrelled, flintlock *jezail* rifles, their heavy wooden stocks decorated with elaborate inlaid patterns made from mother-of-pearl. A wild glint in these noble men's often sky blue eyes cast the impression that they were capable of shooting off a cat's whiskers at a hundred paces – in the dark. Their souls were more intact than the clothes they wore. Often, their tattered robes were held together by washed out patches of different-coloured cloth. This in no way hindered the aloof warriors from striding along the street with a magisterial bearing, their turbans' tails drawn over the bottom half of their faces.

To Angus, the Afghans were as exotic as lions in a drive-through zoo. He'd never seen anything like them and quickly fell in love with these proud men's defiant spirit who, steeped in a tradition where every physical gesture was interpreted as a symbolic measure of their level of dignity, bowed to no one other than the Almighty Allah. At first the Afghans seemed unapproachable, but Angus soon discovered that hidden behind their stern faces and medieval chivalry were friendly souls who enjoyed nothing better than to share a laugh. Angus had never before felt so at home in the company of strangers – strangers who guarded their reputations to the point of sometimes committing suicide due to status anxiety. They also practiced hospitality towards foreigners religiously.

It struck Angus that he was perhaps witnessing one of the last social bastions in the world where wisdom was valued more highly than gold. On first take it was easy to perceive the Afghan men as being churlish and heartless, especially in respect to the way they maltreated their animals – that is, if one did not take into account that most of Afghanistan is composed of hostile terrain, wherein survival is the main theme of daily life and thus they were totally in tune with their environment. If a man was not unyielding and psychologically bulletproof, in a world where material life had been reduced to its bare essentials, he would ultimately perish for his weakness.

The few young women in Herat who dared to break with tradition and wear headscarves instead of veils had sparkling eyes and fine-boned faces and, in some instances, a thin black line tattooed around the perimeter of their lips.

Angus brought the bus to a standstill outside of a two-storied building with a cockeyed sign suspended from a pole that was set into the wall above a low arched doorway. The sign read, 'Hotel Rumi'. Taking into consideration that English-speaking citizens were in short supply, it was highly unlikely that any pun had been intended. From the outside, the Rumi Hotel looked like half a dozen giant loaves of brown bread set at right angles to each other. Square holes had been punched into the metre thick walls to form windows.

Upon entering the building, Ali proceeded to become embroiled in an argument with the robed proprietor, a neat little man who sported a long bushy beard, had thick tufts of grey hair sprouting from his ears and nostrils, and wore a cracked steel-rimmed monocle, which pried open and magnified his right eye. Most Heratis speak Persian as a first language and the two of them were clucking away at each other like a pair of truculent cocks. When it reached the point of coming to blows, Murphy intervened by pushing his way between them.

He enquired forcefully, 'What the fuck is all the fuss about?'

Ali answered, 'This thief wants to charge us too much money.'

'How much is too much?'

'Fifteen dollars a day for four rooms.'

Murphy handed the hotel owner a hundred-dollar bill.

The Persian's eyes blazed with a vicious yellow intensity and then flickered like a neon tube ready to explode. 'This is madness. You can't—'

Murphy cut him off. 'Shut the fuck up, man. It's not even your money.'

Ali fumed at loosing face in front of the proprietor, who, in one appreciative shot, fired off his entire vocabulary of English words to express his gratitude.

'Congratulations to meet you. My name Rabah.' He placed a hand over his heart in the local gesture of greeting. 'Thank you.'

'No problem, man...I mean, Rabah,' said Murphy, offering his right hand.

Ali, his face a furious mottled red, stormed off in a huff.

For the most part, amenities in the Hotel Rumi occupied the realm of non-existence. The dried cow dung floor surfaces filled the whole building with a distinct barnyard smell. The hotel's cell-like rooms were almost bare. The sole furnishings were the kind of beds that are called charpoys in India, rough wooden frames strung with hemp fibre rope to support thin coconut fibre mattresses. Flanked by two porcelain footprints, the toilet was a hole in the floor that gave a rectum's eye view of a pile of stinking faeces, mounting up under the building in preparation for a herd of hungry pigs to pass by for lunch, when they'd gobble the whole disgusting heap up in the space of a grunt-filled minute and squeal in pleasure as only pigs can do in shit. When Angus noticed this organic waste recycling process he took a mental note to stay well away from Afghan sausages in the unlikely event that he came across such a sacrilegious culinary phenomenon in a predominantly non-pork-eating Muslim country, where contact with swine is the ultimate abhorrence as they are considered the most unclean of God's creatures.

Angus soon discovered that bacon and pork sausages were not on the dining room's menu. All that could be ordered up from the misspelled bill of fare was scrambulled, booled or freed eggs with cheeps or breed and gootz meelk yoogurt. Rosed lam and rabid stoo had been crossed off. Alas, the hotel's cook had gone on holiday to Kandahar six months previously, never to return. The management would have apologized for any inconvenience caused by the chef's disappearance, but they too had headed southeast with the cook.

Deserted, pretty much summed up the Rumi Hotel's social environment. As soon as he'd received money in advance, Rabah, the proprietor, vanished without a word of farewell. On the Scot's second day in the unstaffed hotel, it was discovered that Rabah was a contestant in an ongoing chess tournament, taking place in a nearby teashop. The competition had been running for twenty years and was showing signs of coming to a decisive conclusion, within the next few weeks or so. Barring an outbreak of fire in his hotel, there existed nothing else under the shifting sky that could force Rabah's attention away from the marathon and the chessboard's faded black and white squares.

Despite the Hotel Rumi's fetid smells, lack of décor and thickly barred windows that gave the impression you were in a medieval prison, the girls loved the space and privacy that their rooms provided in comparison to the bus's cramped quarters. Alice and Nina laid out all their things on the functional built-in shelves and soon began making excursions into the market for incense, flowers and coloured scarves to decorate their temporary nests. Jenny accompanied them if she wasn't lounging sedately on her bed with her pipe or off into Ali's room for some smoking companionship, with the Persian chattering away enough for both of them. There were no other guests in the hotel and consequently the girls flitted from one room to the other, drinking tea and smoking joints while planning their next trip to the old bazaar, a big dusty building with vaulted ceilings.

The one luxury that the Hotel Rumi did provide was a commodious, oval-shaped, copper bathtub with clawed feet, which was located beneath an open skylight in an upstairs room. It didn't take long before the tub became Angus and Jenny's personal hot spot. The first time they used it, Angus employed the services of a posse of dirty-faced little boys to act as water bearers. He'd found them outside on the street, where they were playing football, using a tightly bound bundle of rags as a ball. The bathwater was heated in a rusty oil drum supported by bricks over a wood fire in the hotel's backyard. The barefoot boys ran up and down the stairs using aluminium pails to convey their liquid cargo. Once the copper tub was half-full of boiling water, Angus and Jenny stripped off and immersed themselves in the rust-coloured water. When the young Afghans caught a glimpse of Jenny's hot pink nipples, they began running up the stairs carrying buckets of steaming water like their lives depended on it. Angus ended up having to pay the excited boys a fifty Afghani bonus to make them perform a reluctant disappearing act. Otherwise, he and Jenny would have been boiled alive due to the water bearers' overenthusiastic efforts.

One evening, just after sunset, Rabah took a break from the chess tournament to visit his hotel. He was plodding along a corridor like a school janitor, inspecting God only knew what, when he bumped in to Alice and Nina, who employed their none too proficient skills in the use of international sign language to communicate with him.

Dressed in scanty undergarments, that served only to display more tantalizingly the generous proportions of their voluptuous bodies, the two young women gathered Rolling Thunder's crew together to announce the three-fold message that the proprietor had conveyed to them. To begin with, Rabah had made it perfectly clear that he did not approve of the girls running around in the Rumi Hotel in their underwear. Second, judging by the way his monocled eye followed their every movement, and the speed with which his prayer beads ran between his thumb and forefinger whenever he drew close to the girls, Rabah wasn't being entirely honest with himself about this. Last, but not least, tonight was the night of Herat's monthly social highlight. An American movie was going to be shown in a nearby cinema that was situated across the street from the Behzad, the town's biggest backpacker hotel.

Dirty Ali, made conspicuous by his absence, was the only one who wasn't interested in going. He had more important things to do. He'd skulked off to his private upside-down universe – a place where a cracked plaster ceiling could become a suitable screen to project an image of himself in the role of emir, flying in a private jet over the dream rivers flowing through his fabulous desert kingdom, where fields of ripe opium poppies swayed in the breeze.

Angus stared around at the eager throng. The long line of men queuing up outside the social hall made it clear that this was essentially an all-male event. That is, apart from the two unveiled moustachioed matrons sitting by the entrance in front of garishly coloured Hindi film posters, depicting big-breasted heroines in halter-tops and cruel-eyed villains, brandishing huge swords that looked like they could cut a car in half. The fat ladies were doing a fair impression of a toothless hippo transvestite duo as they collected the twenty Afghani entrance fee from each of the moviegoers.

Due to Muslim sensitivities, Jenny, Alice and Nina had put on long dresses and covered their hair with cotton shawls, an act of foresight which helped ward off the curious stares that were coming from the Afghan brotherhood's direction. Wherever the young women went in Herat they were like magnets to the inquisitive. None of the attention directed their way was hostile. More often than not it was quite the opposite. Sometimes there were so many kisses being blown their way, the draught caused dust clouds to swirl up in the street.

Inside, the hall-cum-cinema was fairly humming with excited anticipation. Everyone made themselves comfortable by sitting down on the thick carpets and stuffed cushions that the management had provided for its patrons. Large water pipes, glowing with charcoals, were being loaded up with lumps of hashish to enhance the experience of viewing the motion picture.

The hippies sat down next to a large projector that was supported by a sturdy metal table.

A roar of applause rose into the smoke-filled air when the lights flickered out. Cheering turned to booing when it was realized a false start had been brought on by a blown fuse.

The projector looked like it had been manufactured when Charlie Chaplin was too young to grow a moustache. With the grinding of metal gears, thirsty for a spot of lubricating oil, the ancient contraption rattled into sputtering life. When the lights went out for a second time, only a murmur passed through the crowd. There was a faint smell of burning dust when, like a beacon on a foggy night, the noisy projector's lens threw a conical beam of bright light across the long room, illuminating the thick clouds of smoke that were belching off a dozen or so hubbly-bubblies that were gurgling like a tribe of contented babies.

The screen went white. Starting from ten, a series of Roman numerals counted down to zero on its smudged surface. Any expectations that Angus and his companions had been entertaining about the nature of the big picture they'd come to see were completely blown out of their liquid imaginations' swirling waters when, in big black capital letters, the film's title appeared on the screen – 'ROBIN HOOD'.

Murphy's disgruntled voice rose above the loud bubbling sounds produced by a large hookah pipe. 'Aw no, man, we've been ripped off!'

Made in 1922, Douglas Fairbanks was cast in the leading role of this black and white epic of the silent film era. An orchestra composed of various local musicians, sitting cross-legged below the screen, provided the spontaneous live soundtrack. Banging on drums, twanging on strings and blowing on anything that made a noise, the music these bravura players created was unlike anything Angus had ever heard before. What was even more incredible was that the non-stop hullabaloo matched the moving pictures perfectly, if − and this was a big IF − the viewer was completely stoned out of their mind. Fortunately, this was the case. Otherwise the music would have sounded like an amplified cat and dog fight, taking place on top of the strings of an out-of-tune grand piano.

The film's opening scene flared on to the screen. Medieval soldiers in white uniforms carried spears as they marched over a drawbridge. The Earl of Huntingdon, soon to take up the mantle of Robin Hood, appeared in the grounds fronting a magnificent castle. The audience knew straight away the man had the makings of a hero. A vociferous roar of approval rose up from the stoned-out spectators and reverberated from the hall's rafters. Dressed in a groin-hugging leotard and a ruffled white shirt, Robin's attire gave off the impression he'd just left a fancy dress party being held at the local gay bar. Doffing a woodsman's felt cap adorned with a pheasant's tail feather, he greets Lady Marian Fitzwalter, the movie's love interest, when she wafts in through an open portcullis. A quintessential embodiment of medieval femininity, her Ladyship's holding her skirts up to avoid the dust.

Judging by her magnificent mane of wavy dark hair, topped by a glittering tiara, Lady Marian had just returned from an appointment at the castle's hairdressing salon. Her appearance provoked a full-throated roar of approval. Alerted by the whistling of their countrymen, the Afghan orchestra fell silent as its members gazed up in awe at the noblewoman's image. She looked ravishing in a tight-waisted, bosom-hugging, snow-white, ankle-length dress. Without a veil, her whole face and neck were exposed. She was most definitely risqué for Afghanistan. The way some of the men in the audience groaned in ecstasy, one could easily have been led to believe that her Ladyship had actually descended into their midst via a greasy fireman's pole, dressed only in her birthday suit. A damsel in distress, Lady Marian was a trifle upset.

Richard the Lion Heart had roared off to spend three years with the Crusaders in the Holy Land, leaving Merry Olde England to Bad Prince John and the wolves. When Good King Richard wasn't riding over the sand dunes on his charger in pursuit of Saladin's army, he was hanging out with his Knight Templar buddies in the vast system of catacombs that honeycombed the sacred ground beneath old Jerusalem. It was there that the king and his sadistic friends committed unholy acts to entertain themselves. They enjoyed nothing better than pouring molten brass down the throats of heathen Saracen prisoners. Luckily for Angus and his companions none of the Afghans present twigged that the English King was an infidel maltreating their Muslim ancestors, or it might have turned into a lynching party.

Hoots of derision, catcalls and jeering greeted Sir Guy of Gisbourne's villainous countenance when his debauched features filled the canvas screen. A fusillade, composed of fruit, bottles and pieces of garbage, was hurled in the direction of the wicked-looking evildoer's face, whereupon it bounced off the screen and rained down on the musicians' heads. This caused another abrupt temporary halt to their orchestral manoeuvres in the dark.

Sir Guy soon made it clear that he wanted to start up an extortion racket, which would tax the country's peasantry into the muddy ground.

'Fucking fascist bastard!' shouted Murphy, who was by now totally caught up in the movie's simplistic plot.

The scene was set for Robin to swing into swashbuckling action. His dalliance with fair maidens became a thing of his decadent playboy past. Beneath the screen, the members of the spontaneous ensemble played their instruments with an accelerated gusto. Robin set off to Sherwood Forest in Nottinghamshire to organise a small army of like-minded freedom fighters. A rallying call went out, urging all peasants to join the revolution in order to fight the good fight against the forces of evil.

Word spread that wild times were to be had in that neck of the woods and soon the insurgent militia's ranks began to swell. There was an air of bonhomie and gaiety permeating the camp. Freed from the constraints of family life, the rebels were really starting to party hearty − so much so that they decided to call themselves The Merry Men.

Murphy crumbled a half-ounce of good quality Afghan hashish into the projectionist's silver-bowled narghile pipe in an effort to make him a merry man as well. There was soon so much smoke pouring off the hookah's charcoals it created a localised version of a pea soup fog in the cinema. Angus and his friends were getting well and truly blasted while Friar Tuck, the cheery Franciscan monk, sorted out the merry men's personal problems with his wise, albeit unorthodox, counselling methods. The corpulent Holy Man was in the midst of having a guffaw about life's absurdities when his thick-jowled face began to undergo a metamorphosis, which was well beyond the technical limitations of Hollywood's special effects department in the nineteen twenties.

'Aw for fuck's sake!' Raj shouted in alarm. 'Friar Tuck's having a fit!'

The jovial friar's chubby countenance blistered and then melted away to nothing, leaving a blank screen in its place. An acrid smell of burning celluloid filled the hall. Angus looked up to see that there was as much smoke pouring out of the ancient projector as there was coming off its operator's water pipe. Staggering clumsily to his feet, the perplexed projectionist pulled himself together and switched off the lamp. *'Bokon! Pedarsag!'* Cursing loudly, he freed a burned-out length of film from the overheating machine. He then began stumbling around in the darkness with an electric torch in his hand, searching for a flat, circular film canister. It took him five long minutes to feed another roll of film into the contraption's chattering gate. The clamour rising from the disgruntled audience sounded like a noisy cattle auction.

The beam cast by the projector's high wattage lamp bored through the smoke and the movie started rolling again. The ragtag orchestra produced an uncoordinated fanfare. A whole section of the film was missing. Nobody in the hall gave a hoot, because by now the action had begun in earnest. The Afghan ensemble's percussion section began banging up a storm.

Robin Hood and his Merry Men had been robbing the rich and giving to the poor. When Sir Guy of Gisborne got wind of this communistic madness, he massed an army and marched on Sherwood Forest in search of the insurgents' camp. Fortunately for the greatly outnumbered partisans, the invading army's ranks were made up of imbeciles carrying crossbows, a deadly but clumsy weapon which is slow to reload. The soldiers were hopeless when it came to hand-to-hand combat.

When Robin Hood entered the fray he did so with the fighting skills of a one-man army. He began taking out the enemy like the Terminator, the Gladiator and the new James Bond, all rolled into one.

Thump! Thump! Thump! An irregular bass drumbeat provided the sound made by Robin's white-feathered arrows as they thudded into the enemy ranks. Intoxicated spectators began diving for cover, afraid of being struck by the stray arrows that were apparently zooming out of the screen.

'This is so far out, man,' squealed Nina in delight, watching the scene with a slack jaw.

'Absolutely brilliant,' agreed Angus, who was stoned enough to believe he was watching a state-of-the-art Hollywood production, filmed in glowing Technicolor.

When King Richard returns to England and finds out what's been going on while he was off murdering Arabs, he thanks Robin for destroying the axis of evil and restoring democracy to the country during his absence. Lady Marian, who'd done nothing in the film but sit pretty, clasps the pearls strung round her slender neck and titters in the background when Robin Hood makes light of the fact that he's become a champion of the people. Down in the dungeon, Sir Guy's got the sulks.

Order restored, the Merry Men return home to their families and, with an air of reluctance, hang up their camouflage tights along with their bows and arrows. Friar Tuck, Allan-a-Dale, Will Scarlet and Little John were the only men left looking merry because they'd gone round to the Bowman's Arms to get plastered and chat up the busty serving wenches.

'THE END' appeared on the screen and a tremendous crescendo of discordant sound rose from the Afghan orchestra.

The lights came on, signalling that it was time to face reality. Murphy didn't quite manage. 'Man,' he gasped, 'that was the best fucking movie I ever saw in my life.'

Raj was also finding it difficult to change wavelengths and tune in to channel normal. 'Yeah, man, see that gorgeous chick, Maid Marian? I'd marry her in a minute if she asked me to. I'll bet she won an Oscar for her performance.'

The three wobbly girls giggled and hung on to their boyfriends' arms as they joined the throng of men waiting to exit the cinema. Outside, the cool spring air cleared their heads somewhat. Anticipating rightly that a munchie outbreak was imminent, street vendors had set up stalls to sell candyfloss and sweets dripping with honey. The sugary treats were displayed under the dazzling brilliance of acetylene lamps, beacons for swarms of airborne insects. Everybody bought a bag of sweets to ward off a low glucose attack.

Raj was still excitedly babbling on about the film. 'You know, Robin and the boys were just like the Afghans. So many foreign armies have invaded this country and got their arses kicked for their efforts.'

Alice, transformed by the hash filter clouding Raj's vision into a medieval princess, slipped an arm around his thick waist. 'So, Raj,' she said, 'getting all philosophical after a night out at the cinema?'

'He's got a point, though,' added Angus. 'The people in these parts have been involved in guerrilla warfare for so long they practically invented it.'

'I suppose you could say that,' commented Jenny. 'But if you ask me, I don't believe the Afghans like fighting. Ali was telling me last night that they love poetry and, like the Romans, are very fond of roses. He knows them better than we do and considers them a peaceful people at heart. What do you think, Alice?'

'I thought Robin Hood was really sexy,' answered Alice, dipping in to a bag of sugar-coated peanuts.

'Oh wow, man, so did I,' agreed Nina, speaking through a sticky beard formed from pink candyfloss. 'The guy was hot. Did you see that bump in the man's pants?'

'I used to have a pair of underpants with 'Home of the Whopper' printed on them,' said Murphy, lighting a quickly-rolled joint.

'Home of the very average would've been more accurate,' quipped Nina.

'Fuck you, Nina!'

'Fuck you too, Murph—'

Angus intervened. 'Hey, cut it out, you two.'

Raj mumbled to nobody in particular. 'I still think Maid Marian was gorgeous.'

Alice let go of his arm. 'Well...if that's the case, maybe you should bugger off and go and look for your damsel in distress,' she suggested.

Jenny stopped in her tracks, looked around and said, 'I think we're walking in the wrong direction.'

Angus nodded in agreement. 'You're right.'

Everyone turned and headed back along the street. Horses' hooves clip-clopped and harness bells jangled in the background.

8

HERAT TO MAZAR-E SHARIF

Angus would have been happy to stay in Herat for at least a month. It was without doubt the best place he'd visited so far on the journey. Every morning he'd rise early and set off to explore the town's precincts and its surrounding countryside. To the east stood an ancient mosque which, although in a state of disrepair, was still an impressive sight due to its enormity. Its four towering minarets leaned at slight angles and were faced off with jade-coloured tiles, many of which had fallen to the ground leaving red bricks exposed. Further east, dusty roads narrowed into country lanes, where squat flat-roofed dwellings dotted the landscape. Tall cedars, pistachio, almond trees and trellised grapevines surrounded the fortified houses. Spring's arrival had brought fruit orchards into full blossom. The brown earth was carpeted with pink, yellow and white flowers, creating the impression of pastel-coloured snowfall. The warm air was filled with the scent of wildflowers and tall weeds that gave off a fragrance similar to that of parsley. At the edge of each orchard were wooden beehives. Swarms of small brown bees were out and about performing their natural task of cross-pollinating the blossoms. A humming buzz was the living soundtrack for viewing a pastoral scene that had changed little over the passing centuries.

Angus sat on a dry-stone wall and contemplated the scenery. It occurred to him that the idea of creating a modern industrialized society had not yet gained a foothold in that part of the world. He hoped it would remain so. It seemed perfect as it was. His attention was drawn from his musings by a shrill whistle.

Dressed in rags and blowing on a tin flute, a young barefoot goatherd was walking in his direction. He wore a filligreed skullcap on the top of his head, which had been shaved to prevent lice infestation. His dark eyes shone with curiosity when he looked up and noticed that there was a longhaired foreigner observing him from the shade of an enormous, gnarled fig tree. Angus raised a hand and said, 'Hi.' The lad smiled self-consciously, muttered a greeting and returned his attention to a small herd of goats which, when viewed from Angus's perch, appeared like an undulating black, brown and white patchwork quilt. One of the bleating animals, a devilish-looking creature with curly horns, jumped up on to a wall and began to feast on a flower-covered branch. *'Haagh!'* The goatherd shouted and cast a well-aimed pebble.

As he passed below, Angus looked down and saw that there was a red five-pointed star embroidered on the crown of his cap. Six years later, in 1979, Angus would remember that red star and the terrible symbolic meaning it would come to represent in the minds of the Afghan people when Russia, fearing an American attack on Iran, invaded Afghanistan. The land invasion was vanguarded by the heavy Soviet T-62 tanks that rolled over the frontier with Uzbekistan into northern Afghanistan's Balkh Province. From there, armoured divisions pushed southwest and eventually rattled into Herat. The ancient town would be pulverized by shellfire, turning what had stood for over three thousand years into dust. The beautiful orchards and vineyards that Angus once admired would be chopped down for firewood to cook the invading Red Army's rations. Herat's well-tended fields, producing harvests of golden corn, would be sown with mines, some of them disguised as toys. Many of the villagers living in those fort-like houses that Angus had walked by would be dragged outside and shot dead in front of their innocent children's eyes, for no greater fault than being in the wrong place at the wrong time. The survivors would live underground in buried sewage pipes and tunnels. Young lads, like the flute-playing goatherd that Angus had exchanged a greeting with, would be enlisted into the ranks of the mujahedin, where they'd learn how to move like shadows in the night and drop Molotov cocktails into communist tanks' open turrets. Unable to withstand the Afghan's indomitable fighting spirit, the Soviet army, like countless conquering armies before them, would eventually be defeated and forced into a clumsy withdrawal. It was to be a pyrrhic victory. In ten carnage-filled years, over one and a half million Afghans, twenty-five percent of the country's population, would be slaughtered by Mother Russia's armed forces.

Back in the spring of 1973, all that was a nightmare waiting to happen. If a seer had approached Angus and told him what was going to transpire in that wonderful land in the near future, he would have found it hard to believe.

As Angus strolled back into Herat on that particular morning, some part of him did register that he was witnessing a scene that would one day be remembered like a fantastic dream. Nobody gave it much thought at the time but, by the end of the twentieth century, it would begin to sound incredible that there had existed a time when tens of thousands of peace-loving hippies had journeyed through Afghanistan and cashed in their travellers' cheques. With the arrival of the eighties the country would begin to be plagued by invading imperialist armies, civil war and crackpot jihadists, all of whom, it would seem, were hell-bent on returning Afghanistan to the Stone Age.

It was business that brought Rolling Thunder's wheels into motion again – dope business. Raj met an anarchistic hippy traveller called Claude in the bazaar one morning and invited him round to the Rumi Hotel for a smoke. Born on the West Indian island of Guadeloupe, Claude had a flat-nose, nut-brown skin and shoulder-length dreadlocks bound up by a headband. He'd been riding around Afghanistan on a brown stallion for over a year and looked like a renegade Comanche, an image that was enhanced by the ivory-handled Colt .45 sticking out of his rainbow-coloured waistband.

The Guadeloupian informed the Scots that the best quality hashish in the country could be purchased very cheaply in a town to the north called Mazar-e Sharif. He threw a finger of sticky black hash on to the table and said, with more than a trace of a French accent, 'Check it out, mon. That's the crème de la crème.' He flashed a broad smile. 'Let's keep it high, mon.'

The potent hashish was the exotic substance that a dope smoker's dreams are made of. It smelled intoxicatingly sweet and, when smoked, released the mean green tang produced by ripe marijuana buds at summer's end. As for the high, it was out of this world.

Originally it had been planned to travel south towards Kandahar but, after meeting Claude, the route that would eventually take the Scots on to Kabul ran in the opposite direction. When Ali heard this, he complained at first, but for the most part he was content to kick back and puff on his opium pipe.

It was a hot afternoon when Raj drove the bus out of Herat. Angus sat with Jenny, up in the Perspex observation bubble, looking back as the last buildings of the city disappeared in the distance amidst a wavering heat haze boiling up from the landscape. The next time Angus saw Herat was on television – by then reduced to a formless wasteland strewn with rubble.

Bound for the Sabzak Pass, Rolling Thunder wound her way up into the Paropamisus Mountain Range. From the opposite direction swaying lorries rumbled past. Loaded with huge bales of cotton, they looked like puffy loaves of bread on wheels. Afghan men hung on to the bulging cargo like human barnacles and cheered at the sight of the fantastically painted Mercedes bus as it drove by.

In places the road became so narrow there was barely enough space for two vehicles to pass. There were no crash barriers. Mangled and rusting wrecks lay strewn at the bottom of deep gorges. It became a strict rule that whoever was behind the steering wheel was forbidden to smoke joints until he was relieved.

Two-hundred kilometres from Herat, the asphalt road deteriorated into a rock-strewn dirt track which ascended to over 2,000 metres above sea level. The views to be had from such lofty heights were spectacular. Weathered grey mountain ranges rose out of the desert below, resembling a fleet of gigantic alien battle cruisers, lined up and anchored in a sand-coloured waterless ocean, waiting to go to war. The endless sky stretched off into the distance where, on the eastern horizon, tiny ridges formed by white clouds guarded what appeared to be the end of the world.

Ali and Jenny sat for hours chatting away about all and everything.

Jenny's physical condition was in a state of rapid decline. Her olive skin was losing its vibrant, healthy glow and taking on the bleached colour of a withered sunflower left in permanent shade without water. Because of her gaunt skeletal appearance, Raj and Murphy had taken to calling her 'Voodoo on a stick' behind her bony back. Framed by the mass of her still beautiful wavy blonde hair, her face looked like a skull covered with a thin layer of semi-transparent membrane. Set deep in their sockets, her glittering eyes were losing their shine. Angus was beginning to give up on her. He watched as she drifted further and further away from him. She had given up caring about anything except her pipe. Their sex life, once so full of fire, had burned out. As her dependency on opium grew their friendship was slowly diminishing into an amicable truce.

Angus found it easy to blame Ali for putting temptation in front of his girlfriend, although in his heart he understood that it was not quite so simple. All Angus really wanted to do was hold her hand as they tripped through the light fantastic. Alas, that was not meant to be. Jenny was destined to inhabit a shadow-filled netherworld, where she dreamt her dreams alone.

The Number One slot of the on-the-road-top-ten was held by Santana's *Caravanserai* album – a perfect soundtrack for a drive through mountainous desert terrain punctuated by overnight stays in serais, where the travellers shared the company of cameleers, caravanners and the occasional friendly bandit. Outside in the darkness, camels fed and slept, hitched to iron rings set into the adobe walls. The female dromedaries could be heard roaring as Dirty Ali visited each of them in turn and, with the aid of a wooden stool and a big jar of Vaseline, treated himself to an orgy of midnight humping.

On the third afternoon of their journey to Mazar-e Sharif nobody could be bothered to cook. In the vicinity of a town called Dowlatabad, Murphy pulled the bus up in front of what passed for a truck stop in the region. The place was a conglomeration of tin-roofed shacks decorated with bent and rusty, bullet-riddled Coca-Cola signs.

As soon as the gypsy travellers stepped outside of the bus, they could smell something cooking. Mouths watering, they sat around a table made from a warped wooden door supported on breeze blocks, its dirt-splattered surface home to a swarm of buzzing flies, apparently upset about having to vacate their mating ground. A squadron of them haloed Ali's head like jet fighters stacking up before landing on an aircraft carrier's flight deck. Unperturbed, Ali ordered six plates of fried rice. Angus should have known that it was a mistake to eat at such a roadside dump. He'd noticed that the grumpy-looking proprietor had enough dirt under his fingernails to fill a flowerpot.

When the food arrived it looked clean enough, although the black cracks in the crockery looked like bacterial highways. The emptiness in everyone's stomachs overcame any warning signals put out by their logical minds. From a neighbouring table a pair of curious ethnics stared on in disbelief as the foreigners ate like starving pigs at a trough. The greasy food tasted delicious – that is, until it was discovered that pickled goat's eyes were buried underneath the piled up rice.

'Mmmmh, delicious,' hummed Ali, crunching down on a glazed eyeball. Yellow gunk trickled from a corner of his mouth.

Nina looked up from her half-eaten plate of food and then performed an excellent impersonation of the rubber-necked girl with the lime green face, who was possessed by Satan in *The Exorcist*. A jet of vomit erupted from her mouth and splashed over the wooden table.

Thanks to lunch at the truck stop from Hell, Rolling Thunder's progress was severely hampered on the next leg of the journey. The bus's toilet was soon overflowing with intestinal waste and therefore emergency stops were required every half hour, so that crewmembers could relieve themselves by the side of the cracked concrete road. Ali, who had the constitution of a sewer rat, found it all very amusing, but nobody else on board was laughing. Jenny slept through the whole episode.

Fringed by vast cotton fields and the occasional patch of hemp, Mazar-e Sharif was a large bustling town more or less equidistant from the frontiers of Turkmenistan, Uzbekistan and Tadzhikistan. Of ancient Persian origin, the local population were mainly light-skinned Tajiks.

Unlike the rest of the crew, Jenny and Ali were unaffected by dysentery. Once a secure spot had been found to park the bus they set off to explore Mazar's enormous blue mosque.

Meanwhile, the rest of the crew desperately tried to find something to eat that would not appear at the end of their digestive tracts a few minutes after they'd finished swallowing it. Ali's opium came in handy, it being a natural curative for diarrhoea. Pushing a little pellet of opium up into their rectums, burning like they'd been dipped in chilli sauce, dammed the flow better than any prescription drug available.

On their second day in Mazar-e Sharif, Angus, Murphy and Raj started checking out where to buy a load of hashish to plug a different kind of hole, the bus's stash compartment. Claude, the Guadeloupian they'd met in Herat, had given them the address of a man called Sayyid Abbas Rouhani, who ran a moneychanger's shop that was just round the corner from the central post office on the opposite side of the street from the main bazaar. He turned out to be an affable, denim-clad Pashtun with a pockmarked face – smallpox epidemics had, until recently, been common in the region. His age was indeterminate. He could have been anything between thirty and fifty. His hairline was receding and, like his wispy burnt-red goatee, dyed with henna.

'Assalaamu aleikum' – peace be unto you. Sayyid stepped forward and shook hands with a moist grip. 'Please, be seated,' he said, indicating several leather cushions scattered round a low table in a corner of his commercial premises, a ground floor office that did not appear to be doing any business. 'I'll order tea.'

In the same instant, Raj supplied the standard response to the moneychanger's welcome, the traditional Muslim greeting that reassures a stranger that he is safe. *'Wa aleikum assalem wa rahmatullah wa barakaatuh'* – and upon you the peace and the mercy of God and his blessings. He said this with such natural ease, his two companions' jaws dropped.

The Pashtun nodded at Raj in acknowledgement, walked over to the front door and opened it. He spoke Dari, the Afghan dialect of Persian, to a skinny, snot-nosed child with prominent ears and skittish eyes who was sitting outside on the pavement.

Murphy tugged on the sleeve of Raj's Bedouin djellaba and in a whisper asked, 'Where the fuck did you learn to say that?'

Raj winked. 'Dirty Ali's Arabic class. Now nobody will be able to mistake me for a Sassenach.'

'What do you mean?' Angus enquired.

Raj replied, 'Haven't you noticed that the English always expect everyone else in the world to speak their language?'

'Probably a hangover from the days of the British fucking Empire,' remarked Murphy.

'Hey, man,' said Angus, 'I want to learn to speak Arabic too.'

Five minutes later, the little boy entered the moneychanger's office and set down a copper tray on the circular wooden table. The glasses of heavily sweetened black tea were topped off with a dollop of thick cream. Sayyid handed the pitifully thin urchin a few coins. Head bowed low, the boy crept away as if he'd committed some punishable offence.

'An orphan,' said Sayyid Abbas without prompting, turning his full attention to his foreign visitors. 'How may I be of service to you gentlemen?' he asked, fingering a string of shiny black beads, his broad smile conspirational.

Angus enquired, 'Where did you learn to speak such good English?'

Sayyid chuckled and then answered, 'My father, Muhammad Abbas Rouhani, taught me your language as a child. He graduated from Cambridge with honours over forty years ago and is still teaching English in Kabul University today.' Then, after a pause, he said, 'He's an old man now, but he still speaks fondly of the magnificent gardens and trees surrounding Cambridge University...oh yes, and the beautiful river.'

It was left to Raj to explain what they were after. The Pashtun tore cellophane from a green and gold flip-top packet of cigarettes and offered them around. Everyone politely refused what was an obvious local status symbol.

Sayyid lit up and puffed on a king-sized Dunhill menthol, inhaling smoke through his nostrils as he thought things over. 'Please,' he said, a silver grey exhalation of tobacco smoke curling out of his big nose as he threaded his worry beads through the fingers of his right hand, 'if you would be so kind, come back this evening. I will have something to show you gentlemen by then.'

Sayyid tapped some ash on to the grey cement floor and, while the foreigners made their exit, studied his cigarette's glowing tip.

The Pashtun was as good as his word. When the three Scots returned to his shop, Sayyid the moneychanger had half-a-dozen sample slices of black hashish waiting for them. They sat around the office's low wooden table for a heady hour, drinking tea and smoking the produce on offer. The piece that finally came out on top was similar to what Claude had shown them in Herat.

'How much is this one?' Raj asked, exhaling a lungful of delicious smoke.

'Ah, *that*...is number one quality.' Sayyid, a salesman at heart, was handling the situation like he might be able to sell five or ten kilos − if he was lucky. He picked up the finger of hashish in question, broke it in half, held it under his nose and said, 'This is very expensive, my friend. You have very good taste.'

'How much is very expensive?' Murphy's tone was aggressive

Before the Afghan answered, he studied Murphy for a brief moment, a look of amused tolerance on his face. 'It costs around two hundred dollars a kilo,' he said, making an open-handed gesture that suggested his offer was a fair one. 'It all depends on how much you purchase.'

Raj gasped. 'Two hundred dollars a kilo? That's not ex—'

Angus discretely stamped on Raj's foot.

'Say a hundred kilos.' Murphy was now on the managing director's cushion.

'A hundred kilos,' repeated Sayyid, a slight twitch appearing under his right eye. 'That's a lot of valuable merchandise. If you pay a deposit, I can sell it to you for…say…one hundred and fifty a kilo.'

Murphy reckoned the Pashtun would be getting it for fifty or sixty dollars. He asked, 'Say we buy five hundred kilos?'

Sayyid raised a sceptical eyebrow and asked, 'Are you serious?' His nervous twitch was registering on the Richter scale.

Murphy opened a leather satchel. He then threw two brick-sized wads of Afghanis on the table in front of Sayyid and said, 'Listen, man, I'm as serious as a fucking nuclear bomb. How much for five hundred kilos?'

Angus smiled at Sayyid to let him know that they were still friendly. The Pashtun smiled back nervously. He lit a cigarette, glanced across the table at Murphy and stammered, 'One…one…one hundred and forty per kilo.'

A sly expression darted across Murphy's face. 'A hundred and ten and I'll give you fifteen thousand dollars as a deposit.'

The Pashtun had sweat breaking out on his brow from the strain of doing quick arithmetic in his head. *By Allah,* Angus imagined him thinking, *these Scottish kafirs are no fools.* Sayyid exhaled smoke through his nostrils, looked up and studied the grey cloud as it drifted towards the ceiling. His lips quivered and Angus realized that Sayyid was suppressing a smile. The man was accustomed to bargaining and was enjoying the intensity that came with it.

'Yes, my friend, a little difficult perhaps, but yes…yes, I think it can be orchestrated,' said Sayyid, with the conscious pride of one who has mastered a difficult idiom in an intense transaction. He added, 'But for one hundred and twenty five…last price.' The Pashtun said this reluctantly, melancholy almost, as if he were weary from living in a world that forced him to agree to financial terms so grossly unfair they caused him pain.

This guy's brilliant, thought Angus.

Murphy shrugged. 'A hundred and twenty is the most I'm willing to pay.'

'No, my Scottish friend, that is not enough.'

'Oh well,' said Murphy, placing his half empty tea glass on the table as he rose to his feet, 'I suppose...'

'Wh...Where are you going?' asked Sayyid, gesturing with his hands for Murphy to sit down again. 'You haven't finished your tea.'

'A hundred and twenty!' blurted an incredulous Raj.

'Yes, yes, my friends, it will be difficult, but I can do it for one hundred and twenty...two dollars.' Sayyid smiled at the Scots as if awarding them a prize. *'Last price!'*

Murphy stretched out his hand to shake on it. 'You've got yourself a deal. How long will it take you to get it together?'

Sayyid's eyes darted around for a moment before he answered. 'I cannot say for certain, but I believe it will take three or four days...maximum.'

'That's cool with us, Sayyid' said Murphy, brimming with self-confidence. 'We'll return in five days, how does that sound?'

'Excellent, my Scottish brother, excellent.'

A week passed and the Pashtun was two hundred kilos short of filling the order.

'I am sorry, my friends, it will take another forty-eight hours,' said Sayyid, twisting a strand of his thin beard between nicotine-stained fingers, an apologetic smile fixed on his lips.

'No problem, man,' said Murphy in an unconvincing voice.

It had been raining all day. Mazar's rutted streets had been transformed into muddy quagmires. The air was solid with moisture and felt like cool liquid against the three Scotsmen's dejected faces. Water trickled down inside the raised collars of their plastic raincoats as they trudged across Mazar's central square on their way back to the bus.

On board Rolling Thunder, the air hung heavy with lassitude. A decision was made to move out of town. After a short drive, Angus parked the bus in a clearing by a forest of coniferous evergreens shrouded in mist.

Time was passed smoking, drinking coffee and playing card games.

The following afternoon, Ali lurched out of the door and disappeared. He returned in the early evening with a large ball of opium wrapped in plastic. There was a weary smile upon his unshaven face and dark pouches beneath his hooded eyes, baggage from voyages over a sea of sleepless nights.

By now boredom had gotten the better of everyone on the bus. When Ali's pipe went round, they all drew heavily on it with the exception of

Angus, who had made a vow never to smoke opium again for as long as he lived.

While everybody else was lying around semi-comatose, Ali and Angus sat at the dining table, playing chess. The Iranian was winning as usual. Angus cupped his chin in his hands, leaned over the chessboard and concentrated on his next difficult move. He'd already lost his queen when a rook swooped in to carry her off.

When Ali spoke, his voice was a pleasant baritone. 'Would you like me to make you a cup of coffee, my friend?' He flashed a benign reptilian smile.

'Sure, man.' Angus was only half with his reply. He was staring at the chequered board where, frozen in mid-battle, his shambolic and decimated army awaited his command.

The gentle whoosh of gas, the watery clunk of the copper kettle being placed on the cooker and then, five minutes later, Ali returned with a mug of coffee. The steaming liquid was thick enough to be mistaken for hot crude oil and had globules of what looked like powdered milk floating on its surface.

Angus took an apparently defenceless castle and then Ali sped the game to a decisive close with a series of rapid checks, delivering the *coup de grace* with his queen. 'Check and mate,' he said with a victorious chuckle for the eighth time that evening. 'Would you like a return match?'

'Why not?' Angus shrugged, resigned to the fact that he'd never be able to beat the Iranian at chess.

'Drink your coffee,' encouraged Ali.

Angus looked up from the chessboard and Ali smiled at him for the second time in ten minutes. Angus thought that he detected a certain cunning to the upward curl of Ali's lips and a small bubble of suspicion burst in his head. He wrote it off as misdirected paranoia, a side effect of smoking too much strong hashish, and forced the uneasiness from his mind. He sipped on the sickly sweet beverage and started to roll a joint. Ali set up the board for another match. By the end of the game Angus felt suddenly tired, exhausted. His eyelids felt as heavy as lead weights.

Next thing Angus knew, he was slumped over the table. He had to force his eyes open. His vision was blurred, but not so fuzzy that he could not see that Ali was gone. There was a sharp stab of pain in the pit of his stomach. Two words ripped through the thick fog that was clouding his brain − *the money*.

The cash for the dope deal was in a black plastic bag, concealed in a hidden recess behind the kitchen sink. Finding it difficult to keep his balance, Angus staggered over to look for it. Queasiness rose on top of the ache in his guts. The plastic bag was still there, but the cash was gone − all forty thousand dollars of it. He threw up into the stainless steel sink, which was full of unwashed crockery.

Angus shook Murphy, who was lying on the floor, and shouted, 'Murphy, Murphy, wake up, man!'

'Ugh!' Murphy's cracked open a bloodshot eye and was immediately awake.

'Ali's ripped off the dope money,' said Angus.

Murphy sat bolt upright. Raj, lying on the couch beside him, started to come around. He stammered, 'Who…who's…rip…ripped who off?'

Angus stumbled towards the driver's seat trying to organise his jumbled thoughts. He sat down, turned the ignition key and gunned the accelerator. Murphy and Raj held on to the back of his padded hydraulic chair as he steered the bus towards the asphalt road. One of the back wheels bounced over a large rock, jarring the whole vehicle.

'What the hell's going on?' Jenny's voice called from behind.

'Your fucking pal's run off with our money is what's going on,' was Murphy's angry reply.

Angus ignored the exchange and kept his attention on the road. He switched on the wipers and dashboard ventilation fan to clear the build up of moisture on the windscreen. When the bus reached Mazar-e Sharif's outskirts the headlights picked up a figure in the distance hurrying down the road. Angus pulled up alongside the man and realized it wasn't Ali.

'The bastard must be hiding in the woods,' said Murphy. 'Turn the bus around.'

It was on their fourth run into Mazar that Raj shouted, 'Stop!'

Angus slammed on the brakes. Murphy stumbled forward and banged his head on the windscreen.

'What the fuck is it?' Murphy shouted, rubbing his forehead.

'I think I saw something,' said Raj from behind the driver's seat.

Angus turned and looked up at him. 'Come on, man. What did you see?'

'I…' Raj hesitated.

Murphy grabbed Raj's right arm and shook him, saying, 'For fuck's sake, *wake up!* What the fuck did you see?'

'I…I'm not sure. I'm double stoned.' Raj shook his head. 'I thought I saw a flash of something.'

Angus slammed the gear stick into reverse. 'What kind of fucking something?'

'Like…like a lighter.' Raj looked out of a side window. 'Stop…stop! It was round about here.'

Angus steered the bus over to the wayside and then opened the door. The three Scotsmen hit the ground running and headed into the undergrowth. It was pitch dark.

'Ooofh!' Murphy nearly broke a leg when he tripped over a felled tree. 'Raj,' he groaned from the ground, 'go back to the bus and get some fucking torches.'

Angus sniffed the air and said to Murphy, 'Hey, man, do you smell something?'

'Yeah, fucking pine trees.'

'No, not that—'

'Opium!'

'You got it.'

Murphy rose quickly to his feet. 'That fuckin' junkie. He must be close by.'

'Right,' agreed Angus, 'and he's so hooked on that shit he just had to have a smoke to calm his nerves.'

Raj returned with three flashlights. One of them had flat batteries.

'He's here,' said Angus.

'Who?' Raj asked.

'Your fucking dad,' said Murphy.

Puzzled, Raj looked around. 'My father?'

'Hey, Raj,' said Angus gently, 'pull yourself together, man. This is serious. We caught a whiff of opium smoke.'

Murphy added, 'Dirty Ali's nearby. I can feel it in my goolies.' He grabbed his groin and gave it a shake.

'Okay,' said Angus, 'Me and Murphy will take the torches and sweep the ground in front of us. Fan out. Try not to trip over anything.'

'That's alright for you to say,' said Raj. 'You guys have got the torches.'

Murphy gave Raj a shove in the direction of the woods. 'Shut up and do what you're told.'

'Hey, don't you—'

'Cut it out you two,' said Angus, switching on his torch.

It took twenty minutes to locate Dirty Ali. He was cowering behind a bush, a terrified, damp, bedraggled fugitive, cringing like a nocturnal animal caught under the bright light of day.

'I…I'm…s-s-sorry,' he spluttered from the shadows, his voice quivering with mortal dread. 'As the P-P-Prophet Mohammed, p-p-peace be upon him, is my judge, I…I just wanted to take care of your financial interests by depositing the money in a s-s-safer place.'

Murphy shone the torch's beam in the Iranian's face. Ali's mouth twisted into a reassuring smile, which might have taken months to perfect, while studying his lips in a mirror. It was a good try but, unfortunately for Ali, not good enough for Murphy.

'You fuckin' toerag!' Murphy stepped forward. He was wearing his dark brown Doc Marten lace-up boots. His right foot shot out from under him and delivered a karate-style kick to Ali's face. The thief keeled over and lay still, splayed out on top of a clump of wet grass. A grey thread of saliva dribbled from a corner of his half-open mouth. His false teeth had flown from his gums. Caught in the beam cast by Angus's torch, they lay stark and forlorn on a bed of rust-coloured pine needles. Murphy bent down and picked up the dentures. He squinted his eyes, studied them for a moment, grimaced and then tossed them away.

With much huffing and puffing, the three young men carried the unconscious thief back to the bus with the briefcase, containing the stolen money, wedged in his sodden suit jacket. By this time all of the women were up and about.

'What have you done to him?' Jenny asked, her face taut with alarm.

'Be quiet, Jen,' Angus advised. 'He's okay. Murphy knocked him out.'

Ali was bound and gagged. For want of a better place, he was dumped in the shower room. Angus, Murphy and Raj went outside.

'What the fuck are we going to do with him?' asked Raj.

'Let's chuck the thieving bastard down a gorge and let the fucking wolves feed on his carcass,' replied a venom-spitting Murphy.

Angus shook his head. 'We can't murder the guy.'

Murphy and Raj exchanged a brief but, to them, meaningful glance.

Angus caught it. *'Well...can we?'*

'Li..Listen, we need to think this over,' suggested Raj. 'Sayyid will probably have the gear by tomorrow night. We have to get rid of Ali by then. Let's sleep on it. We can discuss it in the morning.'

Nobody slept well that night, least of all Ali whose muffled groans went on until dawn. Over a breakfast that nobody was interested in, with the exception of Murphy, the fate of the Iranian was decided.

'Look,' said Angus, displaying the dregs in the bottom of his coffee mug from the evening before. A residue of tanned sludge lay in the curve of the tilted mug. 'The bastard slipped me a Mickey Finn.'

Murphy glanced at the mug and then at Angus. 'Sherlock, your powers of deduction amaze me,' he said, splashing milk over a bowl of cornflakes as if they were on fire.

Ten minutes later, Ali was hauled out of the shower stall. His eyes were those of a spooked animal. Blood from his damaged nose had caked in his nostrils. He was having difficulty breathing. A hole was cut in his gag so he could suck water in through a straw. He was taken outside, where a thick ground mist hung in the still air. After untying the nylon cord, which had cut livid furrows in his wrists, the three Scotsmen led the shaking Iranian into the dank, dark, dripping woods.

'Don't hurt him.' Jenny's plaintive voice called out from behind them, piercing the forest's dense silence to fall on deaf ears.

The four men walked for some time before the Scots found what they were searching for, a large boulder with a bowl-shaped hollow underneath it. Ali's wrists and legs were bound again and then he was lifted into the small cavity.

'N...N...Now what?' Raj stammered, looking questioningly at Angus.

'We need to leave him some water or he'll die of thirst,' replied Angus.

Murphy was all for leaving him to do just that. A heated debate ensued. In the end, Raj and Angus's more humanitarian standpoint prevailed. Raj went back to the bus and soon returned. Three plastic water bottles with straws sticking out of them were placed close to Ali's head. Raj left a small kitchen knife on the ground to give the thief a fighting chance to cut himself free from the blue washing line that bound him. Dirty Ali was horror-stricken. He was gasping like a fish out of water in the midst of an asthma attack. His body began to jerk spastically. A dark stain spread out on the front of his mud-splattered trousers from where he'd pissed himself. His eyes rolled back into his head to such an extent that it suggested he was observing his own erratic brain patterns.

Before anyone could stop him, Murphy kicked Ali in the face. The Iranian sensed it coming and tried to dodge the blow. Too slow, his physical reaction worked to his own disadvantage. The heavy workman's boot smashed with a sickening thud into his left eye. Angus and Raj had to wrestle Murphy to the ground to stop him from having another go. Ali was, once again, out for the count. Grey vitreous ooze flecked with blood seeped from his damaged eye.

'For fuck's sake, Murphy, wh...wh...what's got into you?' Angus asked, trying to catch his breath. 'If you keep that up you'll kill the fucking guy.'

'It...it wouldn't be the first time,' said Raj in a faltering voice.

'Shut the fuck up,' spat Murphy, jumping on Raj, fists flying.

'What the...!' Angus shouted as he gripped Murphy's muscular upper arms and tried to haul him off of Raj, who was pinned to the ground. 'What the fuck's going on? Tell me Raj, what the fuck are you talking about?'

Angus pushed Murphy to one side and pulled Raj up into a sitting position. Raj's damp ink-black hair hung over his shoulders in limp tendrils. The blood had drained out of his face, leaving it with a sickly green pallor. He was quivering with terror as he remembered the ghastly sight of a man, head split down the middle by five pounds of razor-sharp Sheffield Steel. With tears in his eyes, Raj sat staring at the ground, until he looked up and glared at Murphy. He stabbed a finger at him.

'That...that fucking headcase, he...he...' Tongue thick with fear, long dormant words erupted from Raj's mouth as he blurted out the story of how Murphy had murdered Jack Kilroy in Glasgow, after the notorious gangster had ripped them off for half a million pounds that was never recovered.

Angus stood and listened, trying with difficulty to digest what he was hearing. He opened his mouth to speak, but changed his mind and remained silent. He was shocked, not just by the suddenness with which Kilroy's murder had been revealed to him but also by what his two closest friends had been getting up to behind his back.

'I...I...I...oh...oh...' Raj's words disintegrated into an incontinent torrent of vowel sounds and then turned into a string of staccato sobs. He pushed his tightly balled fists into his eyes, trying to stem the flow of tears.

Angus looked quizzically at Murphy, who appeared like a stranger to him. 'Man,' he growled, the word reverberating in his throat, 'you mean...' His mind teetered as he struggled to find the words. A nauseating dread lurched through him and his intestines writhed like the coils of an angry snake. 'You mean to say you topped the fucking guy in the street with a meat cleaver?'

Murphy tossed his long hair out of his face, smirked arrogantly and said in the filthiest Glaswegian accent he could muster, 'Dead fuckin' right I did. That rotten bawbag deserved it.' He hacked up some phlegm and spat on Dirty Ali. 'Anyway, man, what are you getting so worked up about? That piece of shit, Kilroy, nearly fucking well killed you. You should be grateful to me for taking care of the bastard for you.' He jutted out his unshaven chin, defying Angus to contradict him.

A heavy silence fell between them, as tangible as a granite tombstone.

It took a few minutes for some past and present observations to coalesce into a clear picture in Angus's mind. Now he understood what had driven Murphy to become overly serious and aggressive during the past few months. Now he knew what Raj had wanted to tell him in the Iranian desert the night Ali had narrated his life story. Knowing Murphy, Angus reckoned that he'd probably coerced Raj into remaining silent. Angus realized that, up until then, he'd been living in the belief that he and his two friends hid nothing from each other that really mattered. Now the illusion had been shattered and the stark reality that replaced it made him feel like he'd aged several years within the space of five minutes.

Angus stood for a long time, looking down at Raj and Murphy, storing the memory, another incongruent piece in the jigsaw puzzle of his life. Murphy, as unassailable as a silverback gorilla, crouched by a rounded boulder. He was twiddling his thumbs and avoided Angus's gaze by looking up into the trees and saying nothing. When it suited him, he'd always been capable of producing a thick wall of silence around himself that Angus found impossible to penetrate. Raj sat cowering, like a dog about to be punished, his face alive with muscular twitches and tremors.

Shoulders stooped with the onus of what he'd heard, Angus walked away and left them there, a murderer, his accomplice and perhaps their second victim. His footsteps fell heavily, as though the profound responsibility and burden that came from sharing his friends' dark secret was pushing him down into the mire. The forest floor squished under his boot soles as he made his way back to the bus. He went inside and picked up a packet of cigarettes and a blue plastic lighter with a lime-green marijuana leaf printed on it. Jenny saw immediately he was very shaken up.

'What happened?' she asked, twisting her hands. 'You...you haven't done away with him have you?' Her words were riddled by anxiety.

Angus shook his head. He glanced over at Alice and Nina. They were huddled in a corner like frightened wide-eyed sheep waiting to be transformed into mutton. Nina bleated, 'Where's Murphy?'

Angus began to turn and Jenny tried to take hold of his arm. He pulled away from her as if she were a plague carrier. He headed off back into the woods to try and tame the disturbing thoughts that were kicking a steel spiked cannonball around in his head.

Encapsulated in a thick bubble of disbelief, Angus sat down on a soggy, moss-upholstered boulder in the centre of a clearing and struggled with the uncomfortable feeling that this appalling situation had been rolling towards him for years. He probed deep in the pit of his soul for an answer as to how Murphy could have murdered another human being, no matter that Jack Kilroy had been a particularly vile one. Murphy's a fucking maniac, was the only conclusive thought he could come up with.

A dispiriting chill crept over Angus. He put a hand to his chest and could feel his heart thumping. He looked up when a light breeze stirred the treetops, inducing in him a giddy, momentary vertigo. Cold sweat was starting to bead on his forehead. Bile burned his throat. His stomach heaved and he wondered if he was going to throw up.

A raven swooped down and landed on a nearby rock. The big black bird shook its shaggy throat, spread one of its wings and dug its sharp beak into glossy plumage to rid itself of a flea. The raven turned its head and blinked at Angus with translucent grey eyes, as if unable to make up its mind whether he was a predator or prey. An unsettling, sharp croak pierced the forest's silence. With a rustling of feathers, the bird flew off.

Blades of sunlight slashed through the pines, dappling the scene with multitudinous shades of green. On another morning the sight might have been enchanting. Blind to the beauty that surrounded him; Angus lit a cigarette, took two drags on it and threw it away in disgust.

9

ABU AAJIR, GOO GOO GAJOOB, BAMIYAN AND BUZKASHI

On the beach, Cambodia.

'*Kraa! Kraa!*' I looked up towards the source of the sound and saw that a crow had alighted on a palm frond. 'I don't bloody well believe it,' I said out loud. I spoke to the bird. 'Were you sent by Angus?'

'*Ca-ra, ca-ro − that's right,*' cawed the big black bird from the shadows.

I shook my head and let out a weak laugh. I tried to concentrate on the present, but instead found myself returning to a place in the past where there existed a cluster of fond memories. I recalled the afternoon when my brother told me that crows were his favourite species of birds.

'Why?' I'd asked.

Angus answered from the other side of a bamboo table, 'A number of reasons.'

'Like what?' I said, thinking that he was pulling my leg.

'Well…for a start, crows speak a language that's quite easy for humans to understand.'

I looked at him and tried to figure out if he was being serious or not. 'You're joking?'

'No,' said Angus, 'I'm not. Here in Sri Lanka it's illegal to keep a crow as a pet.'

'Really? How come?'

'Because it's an easy matter to train crows to steal things,' said Angus.

'Is it?' I asked, unconvinced.

'To be honest,' he replied, 'I'm not hundred percent sure. It was one of the Tamil gardeners who told me that. What I do know for certain is that the seed of the holy bodhi tree will only germinate if it passes through a crow's digestive tract.'

'That's interesting. How on earth did people figure that out?'

Angus shrugged. 'I suppose by keeping their eyes open and observing crows.'

'What's so special about bodhi trees anyway?' I asked. 'I'm not even sure what a bodhi tree is.'

'It's a member of the banyan family. Look, there's one over there.' Angus pointed to a tall bo tree, about twenty metres from where we were sitting in the garden of *The Retreat,* the meditation centre that he and his wife owned. At the tree's base there was a small stone shrine that was home to a white marble Buddha statue.

'Oh,' I said, 'you mean a peepul tree.'

'Yes.'

'Why are they holy?' I enquired.

Angus answered, 'Because it's the tree under which the Buddha attained enlightenment more than two and a half thousand years ago at Bodh Gaya in the northeast Indian province of Bihar.' He added, 'I've been there a couple of times. It's an inspirational power spot. If you can see beyond the crowds, you can still feel Gautama the Buddha's presence. The last time I went there was to see His Holiness the Dalai Lama. Unfortunately, he didn't put in an appearance because he was unwell. Nonetheless, Lara and I still had a fantastic time. Bodh Gaya's a great place to meet wonderful people, especially Tibetans.'

'So,' I said, shifting position in my creaking rattan chair, 'you were telling me about how you...ehm, communicate with...' I couldn't help letting out a nervous laugh. '...crows.'

'Yes, I was, although it's usually a case of them talking to me.'

'Oh, I see,' I said sceptically. 'And what do they say to you?'

'The crows are messengers. They deliver warnings.'

'Warnings!' I repeated forcefully. 'What kind of warnings?'

'Well...usually things concerning natural occurrences. You know...storm coming, it's going to rain, that sort of thing. Occasionally they notify you if somebody in the neighbourhood is going to die.'

'Come off it,' I said. 'You're having me on.'

'You think so? Watch this. *Kaaraaw!'* Angus made a loud, dry, cawing sound.

'What—?'

'Ssssh!' Angus cut me short and put a finger to his lips.

A moment later, a large black bird swooped down from a tall Washington palm and landed on the wooden table in front of us. I have to admit that I was thunderstruck. I was also amazed at the bird's size, especially the length of its curved yellow beak. Its glossy black feathers shone with oily rainbow colours in the bright sunlight. The strange-looking bird did not appear to be in the least bit apprehensive as it pecked at the leftovers from lunch.

'Caraw,' Angus cawed softly.

What I took to be some exotic species of raven looked up, went *'krak-caw-coh-cra'* and then flew off.

I rose unsteadily out of my rattan chair. I was flabbergasted. 'Jesus bloody Christ!' I exclaimed. 'How in God's name did you do that?'

Angus chuckled. 'I told you. The crows are my friends. They bring me messages.'

'Bu…Bu…But what did it tell you?'

'She – *it* was a female – told me that there's a big wave coming.'

'She…she…she said what?'

'You heard.'

'A big wave coming!' I could feel my forehead creasing in puzzlement. 'What's that supposed to mean?'

'I haven't the faintest. The meaning of a crow's message is not always immediately apparent. It's bad news for sure because only one of them showed up.'

'But—'

'But nothing. Sit down. Relax.'

I did as I was told. 'Next thing, you'll be telling me about UFOs and little green men.'

'I'm getting around to it,' said Angus. 'How did you know?' His eyes narrowed and he stroked his chin. 'Let me guess. You're becoming psychic.'

'Sitting around with you, watching you talk to a big black crow with a huge yellow beak, it's hardly surprising, is it?'

'No, it's not. Don't forget we're Highlanders, and Highlanders have always been known for their gift of *Second Sight*.' Angus opened his eyes wide to lend emphasis to the expression. 'Anyway, didn't I tell you?'

'Tell me what?'

'That the raven is my totem.'

'Get away with you,' I said. 'You'll be telling me next that you're Big Chief Angus, last of the Hebridean Mohicans.'

'No, I won't,' he disagreed. 'I'll be telling you that wild ravens often live over thirty years. Many ornithologists recognize them as being the most intelligent avian species. In the Hindu tradition they are sacred to Shiva and Kali. The Arabs call the raven *Abu Aajir* – the Father of Omens. Celtic healers use the raven's spirit to summon the spirit of the banshee, a Gaelic word that means 'fairy woman'. The Vikings—'

'All right, all right,' I said, waving my hands in front of me, 'I get the bloody picture. Where the hell did you learn all that?'

Angus smiled. 'Last night on the internet.'

'What?' For a moment I felt confused. Then I said, '*The internet? What...what...*you mean to say that you—?'

Angus finished the thought for me. 'Made the whole thing up? Yeah, Hamish, I did.'

'You stupid idiot,' I said, raising my voice a little. 'What about that big bloody raven?'

'That...that...that was Polly, Jeep's pet parrot.' Angus was finding it difficult to control his amusement. 'The wee man used vegetable dye to colour its feathers and lent it to me so I could set you up. We captured the whole thing on video.' He bent forward and howled with laughter.

'You did what?' I asked, looking around the garden.

'Hey, Jeeps,' called Angus, sitting up in his seat, 'you can come out now.'

Loud laughter erupted from a nearby bush.

'You manipulating bastard!' I cursed, starting to see the funny side of the situation. 'You scared the shit out of me with that damned bird.'

Suddenly, Angus stood up and reached over the bamboo table. He then took hold of my shoulders and stared into my eyes.

'Wh...Wh...What the bloody hell is it now?' I asked, spooked by the intensity of his stare.

'Next time a bird talks to you, listen carefully to what it...it says.' Angus spluttered and then began laughing like a madman.

Now, weeks later, I could hear my brother's laughter ringing in my head. Remembering what Angus had said, I looked up to the crow, who was watching me from above. 'Well then, what's the bloody message?' I asked in a gentle voice.

'*Tok, tak, tuk – be here now,*' answered the crow.

For fuck's sake, I thought in alarm, I'm going nuts.

The dog, sleeping at my feet, woke up. She blinked at me and then, spying the crow in the palm tree, sprang to her feet and started barking.

'Aw no, not you now, be quiet!' I ordered.

'*Woof, warf, grrrr – I don't like birds,*' said the dog.

'*Kra – bye,*' called the crow, taking to the air.

The dog continued to bark.

'Hey, c'mon now girl, there's no need for that.' I reached out a hand. She licked it. I bent forward as far as I felt it was safe and patted the sand in front of me. The dog turned around three times, settled down and put a paw over her eyes, as if to say the moonlight was a hindrance to her sleep.

I sighed. 'Well now, that was an interesting little interlude, wasn't it? What the hell's going on? I've started talking to myself. There's nobody here to listen to me.' I looked around. 'Is there?' I reached for my packet of cigarettes. 'No, I'll save them for later.' *Tok, tak, tuk – be here now.* I remembered the crow's message. 'Here and now! I don't want to be in the bloody here and now. It's the there and then that I need.'

I moved my head slowly from one side and the other to relieve the stiffness in my neck. I then closed my eyes and returned to my twin brother's past.

It was midnight in Mazar-e Sharif. Sayyid guided the bus as Raj reversed it into the interior of a vast warehouse that was stacked to the rafters with bales of cotton. On the centre of the grey concrete floor and illuminated by a solitary light bulb suspended above it, lay a wooden pallet. Stacked upon it was half a metric ton of primo-dreamo Afghan hashish. Each of the five hundred oblong slabs was neatly wrapped in green cellophane.

It took two hours to stash the cargo, the last twenty kilos going in with a tight squeeze. The Pashtun had spruced himself up for the occasion.

'Check out the platform footwear,' said Murphy to Angus in a hushed tone, nodding towards Sayyid's feet. He had on a ridiculously thick-soled pair of brown leather sandals and pink socks. His blue tartan shirt was threadbare. The yellow kipper tie that hung from its worn collar was dotted by tea stains and the freshly pressed pair of Levi's that he was wearing were, judging by the way the jeans were bunched around his narrow waist, three sizes too big for him. Sayyid's outfit was topped off by a black astrakhan cap.

Murphy whispered in Angus's ear, 'Hey, man, dig the woolly hat. Do you think he'll give it to me if I ask him for it?'

Angus shrugged and, stepping forward, gave Sayyid the balance of his payment. The Pashtun mumbled to himself as he counted the money with long nimble fingers. When he'd finished, Angus said, 'Here' and handed him two thousand dollars.

'What is this, my friend?' asked Sayyid, tugging nervously at his wispy beard. 'You've given me too much.'

'That's a small symbol of our appreciation. It's been a pleasure doing business with you, man.' Angus offered his right hand.

The Pashtun shook it firmly and, clutching a thick wad of money in his left hand, made a slight and dignified bow. He straightened his back and said, 'Rest assured the feeling is mutual. Thank you for your patience, my friend.'

He stumbled forward and embraced Angus. For a brief moment the cultural chasm that separated them was bridged by heartfelt respect.

Murphy, whose idea it was to give an extra two thousand dollars to the dealer as an added incentive to keep his mouth closed, watched the tactile exchange and smiled wryly.

Sayyid noticed Murphy looking at him with an air of detached curiosity and a strange smile on his lips. He turned away from Angus, took off his astrakhan cap and handed it to Murphy, saying, 'Please, my friend, take this as a token of my friendship. *Safar-e-khosh,* have a safe journey.' He turned back to Angus and said, '*Zinde bashi,* long life to you.' Then he said to all three Scotsmen, '*Khuda hamrahi shumyan!* God be with you all!'

'Hey,' said Raj, turning to Murphy as he tried on his new hat, 'that really suits you, man. It makes you look like a right numpty.'

Murphy ignored Raj and his comment, and made a point of pushing past him to board the bus.

Raj muttered under his breath, 'Fuckin' asshole.'

By mid-morning of the following day, Rolling Thunder was headed south in the direction of Bamiyan. Wrapped in cloud, hillside forests thinned out and gave way to a broad desolate valley hemmed in by towering mountains. The scene looked like it had been carved by a colossus's hand, using a glacier's bevelled edge to gouge out a stark natural masterpiece of bleak emptiness.

Ali's treachery and the shocking repercussions that followed were still fresh in everyone's minds. Nobody was in much of a mood to take in the dramatic scenery passing by outside. Angus had hardly spoken to Murphy since they'd dumped the Persian under a rock and when they did their words did not come easily, their few brief conversations stilted and uncomfortable. The mood inside the bus was claustrophobic and suffocating, as if every atom of air had been sucked out of the atmosphere by a black hole. Raj put the Beatle's *Magical Mystery Tour* soundtrack on in an effort to cheer everyone up.

Your mother should know... Paul McCartney's merry voice made Angus cringe. The next track, 'I Am the Walrus', didn't cut the audio mustard either. When John 'The Egg Man' Lennon sang about custard dripping from a dead dog's eye, Angus's thoughts returned to Dirty Ali and he wondered if the Iranian was still breathing. A dull ache began to throb in his left temple as he recalled how the Glaswegian gangster, Jack Kilroy, had walloped that side of his head with a baseball bat. 'For fuck's sake,' he cursed out loud, shuddering at the thought of Murphy splitting Kilroy's head in half with a butcher's knife.

Crabacocker fishwife, pornographic priest—
Angus hit the player's eject button and threw the Beatle's cassette out of the window. He then took a few quick hits on a joint and entertained a stoned fantasy about the tape he'd just thrown away. He pictured the plastic cassette as it flew through the air and then tumbled helter-skelter into a ravine. It landed at the feet of a twenty-eight year old Afghan shepherd called Abol Hussein. High above, the sound of the passing bus's straining engine receded into the distance. Abol's narrow slanting eyes looked away from his small herd of bleating fat-tailed sheep and stared at the cassette in disbelief. He picked it up and put it in his tobacco pouch.

Later that day, when Abol Hussein returned to his one-roomed lean-to shack, he showed his find to his skinny wife and five young children. That evening, the Hussein family went round to see Sheikh Azim Handeez Haji, the corpulent village headman. Abol handed him the tape and explained how it had fallen out of the sky. The beturbaned chieftain finger-combed a few grains of soggy white rice from his black, shovel-shaped beard and then studied the undecipherable writing on the cassette.

'Praise be to the Weaver of the Web of Appearances for He is the All-powerful Inbreather and Outbreather of Infinite Universes,' said Sheikh Handeez, his fervent eyes bulging in their sockets. *'Al Allah Il Allah. Muhammad rasull Allah'* – There is no God but God and Mohammad is his prophet. Surely this is a message from above. Praise be to the Giver of Peace.' The headman stood to one side. 'Come in my children, come in.' He ushered the family into his spacious home.

The whole village was summoned to listen to the divine recording. A superstitious hush fell over the villagers as they stood waiting to hear God only knew what. Sheikh Handeez turned up the volume control on his brand new Hitachi radio cassette player and John Lennon's voice came on singing about a pornographic priestess who'd let her knickers down. The sound caused a symphony of neural firings from the cerebellums in the back of the villagers' skulls that zapped into their brains' frontal cortices. There was a collective gasp of astonishment and cries of incredulity from different parts of the large room, the walls of which were hung with prayer rugs and photographs of the Kaaba in Mecca. Nobody could understand a word of English, but everyone present understood the universal language of great music. The inspired Afghans threw their hands in the air and began chanting *'goo goo gajoob, goo goo gajoob,'* assuming them to be the Almighty's holy words. Who knows? Maybe they were, thought Angus, wishing that he hadn't thrown that particular Beatles cassette away.

Further on up the long and winding road, he jammed a John Mayall tape into the empty slot. The father of the British blue's scene lent a true blue voice to the chilly undercurrents flowing through Angus's heart. Peter Green's supernatural tremolo guitar echoed through the bus as the cracked and disintegrating asphalt track it was jouncing along was transformed into The Bluesbreaker's hard road, ribboning its way up into the mountains towards the snowline.

Angus's spirits began to lift. His ears were popping from the altitude as he steered round the 3,000 metre high Shebar Pass's hairpin bends. Leaning to one side at an extreme angle, the bus crunched over a small landslide of shattered rock and scree, a result of torrential rain earlier that day. The road narrowed to a dirt track ledge with crumbling edges and then, for a thirty kilometre-long stretch, deteriorated further when it became little more than a glorified mule track. Angus felt his stomach yawn when he looked down to his left into sheer drops, at the bottom of which ran raging cement-coloured torrents. Driving conditions became even more hazardous when the rocky track was made slippery by a barrage of hailstones that pinged off the bus like ice bullets fired from a Gatling gun.

The engine whined in low gear as Rolling Thunder descended a forty degree slope on the road. If nothing else, downshifting and working his way up through the gears served to keep Angus's attention focused in the present, well away from the abhorrent thought that one of his best friends was a killer.

Over sixty metres tall and carved into a cliff face, the grandeur of Bamiyan's two megalithic seated Buddhas was cause for an excited outbreak of chatter on the bus when they first came into view. Fifteen hundred years before, Kushan masons had laboured long and hard to carve the tallest Buddha statues in the world out of a reddish-pink limestone cliff's vertical face. On first take, their principle function seemed to be that of dominating the valley's landscape. At this they succeeded magnificently.

History had not been kind to Bamiyan's Buddhas. They'd been defaced by Genghis Khan's gunners when they'd used the statues as targets for cannon practice. The statues' future prospects were also bleak. Twenty-eight years after Angus and his friends rolled into Bamiyan, the Taliban would arrive on the scene, fire rockets at the Buddhas for days, and then, ignoring pleas from the international community, dynamite them into non-existence. This destructive act was ordered by an Islamic council composed of Muslim clerics, some of whom possessed the most intelligent minds of the Stone Age. The holy patriarchy viewed the monuments as an affront to Islam and proclaimed that they were heresies carved in stone. Attitudes had changed in a region where Buddhism once enjoyed its greatest flowering.

Jenny and Angus stood at the Bamiyan Buddhas' feet and stared up at their faceless heads that had in ancient times been gilded in gold.

Angus could taste the damp, bitter, limey taste of the stone at the back of his throat. He commented, 'Kind of ugly, aren't they?'

'Well...they're not exactly beautiful,' Jenny replied, taking a few backward steps, 'but they are incredibly big.' She took a few more steps away from the towering megaliths to gain a better perspective, tilted her head back as far as it would go and gasped out, 'Wow! They're absolutely mind-blowing.'

By way of narrow and worn steps, hewn out of rock, it was possible to ascend to the flat top of the tallest Buddha statue's head. Once there, Angus sat with his five companions and looked out over the fertile landscape, stretching out below them like a chequered carpet.

Wearing fur-lined hats, Chinese-looking Hazara farmers, said to be descendants of Genghis Khan's Mongol warriors, tended neat rows of vegetable crops and melons laid out in plots throughout the whole valley. The small fields were separated by low mud walls and intersected by narrow lanes and irrigation ditches that ran with muddy water, which was being diverted from a nearby river, creating a criss-cross tapestry of dark brown background with orderly green furrows, interspersed by the occasional line of bright floral colour.

Iron-grey clouds drifted in over distant mountain peaks, the sunny day having changed its mood by mid-afternoon. The atmosphere began to thicken, readying itself for a downpour. The rain came slowly at first, drops pattering on to the vegetation's leaves. There was a sudden bright flash, a simultaneous crash overhead and then the sky opened to produce a deluge. Water ran in rivulets over the cliffs, gushed in ditches and transformed tracks into muddy streams. Short-lived, the cloudburst rinsed away the dust, rejuvenated the entire valley and left behind a brilliant rainbow as a signature.

Angus and his friends watched as thin clouds of vapour began to rise from a rural scene that was home to sprawling, dune-coloured, fortified houses circled by tall cypress and poplar trees. Angus mused that the ancient monks, who'd lived in the ten Buddhist monasteries that had once existed at this junction on the Silk Road, had chosen Bamiyan because the place had a palpable uplifting ambience about it. This imbued him with the sense that there was something eternal taking place behind the string of fleeting events that compose an individual's life – a something which definitely wasn't history.

Back at the bus, a crowd of urchins dressed in mud-stained rags began to gather round. Their innocent eyes sparkled with enthusiasm. Nina could not resist breaking out one of her cartons of trading goods. Dressed in an orange boiler suit and wearing a green tartan bonnet jammed on her head, she began handing out necklaces made from coloured plastic beads. A riot broke out when the kids started fighting about who got what. The openly curious Hazara women congregated to watch their children kick up a rumpus. Dressed in long skirts, loose blouses and coloured headscarves their faces had narrow eyes, flat noses and broad cheeks. They laughed amongst themselves, staring in amusement at the strange foreigners and their outrageously painted vehicle as if the Scots were visitors from another world, which in many respects they were.

The limestone cliffs were honeycombed by caves, some of which had thin grey streaks of smoke drifting out of them, a clear signal that people inhabited many of the larger grottos. These damp hideaways had once been home to over five thousand hermit monks, until they were cast out by Arab invaders in the ninth century. The caves were interconnected by narrow-stepped passageways, creating a maze that was easy to lose one's way in.

On their second day in Bamiyan, a family of cave dwellers invited the travellers to come and share food with them. These people had little in the way of possessions or money, but what they did have was gladly shared with the young foreigners. Their home was situated underneath what had once been a seated Buddha statue. The limestone figure had been carved out of a rock face. Centuries of erosion had succeeded in reducing it to a conical lump.

There was a wonderful sunset that evening. Surrounded by mischievous giggling children, Angus sat in a cavern whose steep walls showed faint traces of ancient Buddhist frescoes. He looked out through the natural frame created by the cave's mouth. The sun hung above mountain peaks like a polished orange egg until it sunk out of sight, leaving behind fingers of light to fan across the sky and tint purplish-grey clouds with shades of red.

Drawn by a mouth-watering aroma, Angus turned away from the fading orange glow on the horizon and found that bowls of rice pilau and scrumptious mutton stew were being passed around. Word soon spread that there was a party going on. Half a dozen musicians showed up and immediately swung into melodious action. The thudding of drums and shrill whistling of pipes echoed off a cavernous ceiling blackened by centuries of cooking fires. By nightfall, over a hundred people had joined the gathering.

Most of the menfolk were partial to a puff on a water pipe loaded up with sweet smoke. As the night wore on, social barriers dropped and the festivities became less restrained, with not a drop of alcohol in sight. The Hazaras danced, laughed, sang and encouraged the foreigners to participate in their celebration of life. Angus felt like he'd come home to his long-lost tribal family. Everyone roared with laughter when an elderly couple strutted around a blazing fire, like two ancient birds of paradise performing a mating ritual. The male pumped his arms and stamped his feet, while the female lifted a veil to reveal a toothless smile. The old grandmother's timeless eyes shone with a vigour that contrasted sharply with the deep lines etched into her wrinkled face.

A fair-haired *Kochi* gypsy, with a drooping Fu Manchu moustache and amber-coloured eyes, passed a pipe of smoker's gold to Angus. He drew deeply on its stem and blew a jet of fragrant hashish smoke towards the dancers. The previous days' troubling occurrences drifted off into the slipstream of the past as he settled into enjoying this most wonderful of get-togethers with his friends.

Over the next few days, Nina, Alice and Jenny distributed all of Nina's trading goods amongst the local populace. Nina was in her element, dashing around sharing her gifts with young and old alike. Never before had a hundred pounds, spent in a Woolworths store in Glasgow, delivered so much joy, colour and happiness into so many lives. Meanwhile, much to everyone's amazement, Raj was making a name for himself with the local cricketers by displaying his dexterity with a cricket bat.

When the morning came for Rolling Thunder to finally drive off along the narrow poplar-lined avenue that led away from the flat agricultural area in front of Bamiyan's Buddhas, she did so with an escort of cheering children trotting alongside her until their legs gave up on them.

The road began to wind down between snow-capped mountains in sets of treacherous switchbacks. Three tyres were shredded on a twenty-kilometre stretch of the Hajigak Pass, which was little more than a narrow lane composed of rutted gravel and sharp rocks set in dried mud.

By late afternoon, Kabul came into view. To the northeast lay the soaring peaks of the Hindu Kush mountain range, which separates the vast Central Asian steppe from the arid deserts of the south.

The bus entered the capital from the north and merged with a disorganized line of traffic heading downtown. Russian-built Kamaz trucks, painted like fairground attractions, were adorned with flashing lights strung around the boat-prow boxes above their cabins. Red-eyed drivers steered these groaning metal hulks past wooden wagons with rubber tyres, drawn by blinkered horses whose masters held the reins between their toes, freeing up their hands to either wave to people or shake a fist at them.

In the old part of the city, adjacent to the bird market, a secure place was located to park the bus. The walled-off scrap yard charged a five dollar a day parking fee, which seemed reasonable enough to Angus, but was very expensive in local terms when taking into account that an Afghan civil servant earned ten dollars a month.

Overnight bags slung on their shoulders, the three couples made their way across a rust-stained girder bridge, spanning a murky dark brown effluence that was the Kabul River. A talkative tout in denim attached himself to the small group and led them to the city's Westernized section, where they checked into Hotel Nasir-ud-Din, an unpainted, five-storey, ferro-concrete building. After a good deal of haggling with a stubborn, narrow-eyed Uzbek receptionist who only had one arm, his right having been amputated at the shoulder, Angus and Jenny managed to acquire a room on the fourth floor. It came with a small balcony, which faced the steep hills backing the city's old town.

Angus glanced around the neat room and threw his canvas bag on the double bed, which was made up with fresh white cotton sheets. He then opened an unpainted aluminium door and stepped outside. 'Man, look at this place,' he commented, leaning forward against a rusty guardrail, 'it looks just like The Flintstones.'

The sun had set and darkness was creeping in. Lights were beginning to come on and shine out from within, what looked like, hollowed out boulder homes, similar to those in the American cartoon series about a group of cave dwellers who dine on brontosaurus burgers washed down with Carnosaur Cola. Angus smiled, imagining Fred Flintstone calling out for his wife Wilma, while his friend Barney Rubble's legs blurred like twirling Catherine wheels as he disappeared round the back of a prehistoric bowling alley. He remembered what Fred used to shout out when he was excited.

'*Yaba-daba-doo!*'

'What?' Jenny gave Angus a puzzled look as she joined him on the balcony. She glanced up at the diamond-shaped, tissue paper kites wheeling in the pink twilight sky.

'*Yaba-daba-doo.* Meet the Flintstones, they're a modern Stone-Age family. Remember?'

'Oh, yeah, right.' She sniffed the air. 'Man, what a delicious smell, it's making my stomach growl. I'm famished.'

The flavour-rich aroma of skewered mutton kebabs and herbs rose up from the street below where vendors, wearing flat, felt, *pakol* caps, were grilling their offerings on charcoal braziers fashioned from recycled oil drums. The portable grills were mounted on wobbly, wooden trolleys that were rolled around from corner to corner on buckled bicycle wheels. Apart from kebabs and fried rice, most Afghan street food was an unidentifiable insalubrious stew that looked like a bubbling broth made from putrefied offal. Angus took it as a good sign that Jenny was feeling hungry and hoped her carnal appetite would also return – last encountered in Meshed before it disappeared in a thick grey cloud of opium smoke, drifting in the sky over eastern Iran.

It was a Friday afternoon when Angus, Murphy and Raj walked over to Kabul's Ghazi Sports Stadium to watch a game of *buzkashi*.

Twenty-three years later, in 1996, when the Taliban moved up from their stronghold in Kandahar to take over the country's conflict-scarred capital, the stadium would gain international notoriety as a public execution ground, where whip-wielding, black-turbaned Taliban militiamen imposed one of the strictest interpretations of Sharia law ever witnessed in the Muslim world. Minor infringements of these Islamic religious regulations were dealt with by enforcing Draconian punishments. Men, found guilty of sodomy, were executed in the middle of the stadium by having a ton of bricks dropped on their bare heads from a mechanical digger's giant shovel. Afghan women, who had committed such crimes as learning to read or laughing out loud in public, were given severe beatings or, if it was their unlucky day, had their hands chopped off. A bullet in the back of an adulteress's head was viewed as a just reward for sacrilegious sexual misconduct.

In 1973, the Talibs were still just an idea fermenting in the minds belonging to a cabal of Islamic zealots based in Pakistan. During the seventies, Kabul's sports stadium hosted more civilized sporting events. *Buzkashi* is a traditional Central Asian sport. A team player's objective is to gain possession of a headless goat carcass, which has been pickled in brine to prevent its disintegration, and use it to score a goal. This is achieved by pitching the carcass into a target circle, located at the far end of the opposing side's end of the playing field, which more resembles a battlefield due to the combative tactics used in the game.

Angus, Murphy, Raj and a few thousand spectators looked on as the two teams, turbans tied under their chins, mounted sturdy horses that were bred and trained for this kind of sport. Five minutes into the match, it degenerated into a brutal free-for-all. Holding onto a heavy blood-spattered carcass before dropping it into a painted circle at one end of the grassy field was something the other side's players were hell-bent on preventing. A stiff leather horsewhip, used to smack adversaries in the face, was a standard accessory that was liberally employed by all team members. Shooting an opponent with a handgun could earn the offending player a blood red card, signalling instant expulsion from the game.

Ghazi Stadium was wired for sound. Broadcasting live from the match, a local radio announcer's voice screamed out of a loud public address system. *'Yes...yes, Dostum, an unpredictable player at the best of times...some of you will remember he changed sides during the last tournament...has passed the goat to Shah Ahmed Massoud. Brilliant play! Massoud's grabbed it by the hindquarters. He's galloping up the field. Foam is spraying from his horse's mouth. I can't believe it...he's...he's scored! Wallah o Billah! It's Kabulis one, Kandaharis zero, and we're only ten minutes into the game. The crowd is going wild. Fans are running on to the pitch and discharging their muskets in jubilation. Oh, no...what's this? Shah Massoud's fallen off his palomino stallion. Oh dear, oh dear, oh dear, there's a large curved dagger sticking out of his back. Wearing a blue knitted skull cap and matching robe, Ruhollah Yazdi, the referee, is pulling at the reins of Mullah Omar's mount. The big, black whinnying brute's the size of a park statue. The horse that is, not Mullah Omar. As everybody knows, the two men hate each other like tyres hate punctures. Yes...no...yes...Ruhollah Yazdi is handing the one-eyed Mullah a red card. Banned for the next three inter-city matches. It's a sad day for the sporting world when it comes to this. By the mount of Mohammed, may God surround him with His prayers, what's this? A mob of Kandahari supporters has invaded the pitch. They're...they're running towards the ref! Mullah Omar is a popular player in these parts. Stone the martyrs! Ruhollah Yazdi has been wrestled to the ground. Kandahar's captain, Gulbuddin Hekmatyar, is brandishing a sword. Good Lord, he's chopped the referee's head off. There's blood gushing everywhere. What a mess. Bismillah! I don't believe my eyes. The clouds of dust are settling. Well, I'll be the son of an infidel. The decapitated body is being trampled into the ground by the hooves of the Kandaharis' horses. The match has degenerated into a diabolical shambles. Looking at the hands of time, I see it's three-thirty p.m. Time for a word from our sponsor, Jannati Tyres, the company that keeps our country rolling and value friendly service above all else. That's all we've got time for today, folks. I'll be back again next week. This has been Hassan Zahedi reporting to you live from Kabul's Ghazi Stadium for Radio Afghanistan. Thanks for tuning in. Don't touch that dial.'*

'For Christ's sake, this is worse than a Rangers and Celtic match,' shouted Raj above the commotion going on in the stands. 'We better hurry up and get the fuck out of here.'

'This way,' said Angus, pointing to a flight of steps leading to an exit.

'Ah-ha!' A tall, broad-shouldered Afghan hooligan with a Palaeolithic face, a pelican's beak for a nose and a beard like a black haystack, jumped in front of the fleeing Scots. He grabbed hold of Murphy's shirtsleeve. With a fanatical twitch of the eye he laughed like a human jackal and then called to a nasty looking bunch of men, who were sporting more facial hair than a ZZ Top convention. 'Shit from the belly of a whore! Infidels! Kafirs!'

Crunch! Bone splintered and blood gushed. Before he had a chance to say anything else, Murphy head-butted his antagonist in the face and broke the man's huge hooked nose. The Afghan crashed to the ground like a felled tree. 'Come on!' Murphy yelled over his shoulder and then dashed down the stairs.

A minute later, Murphy, Raj and Angus were racing neck and neck along a narrow street. Their pursuers' angry shouts spurred them into the human equivalent of a full gallop. Fuelled by pure adrenaline the fleet-footed Scots zoomed off like rockets. Startled chickens squawked and tried to take to the air in sudden fright. The Afghans soon gave up the chase.

10

CLOSE ENCOUNTERS IN THE DMT ZONE

The moon was full in the sky over Kabul. Thanks to the girls chatting up a wealthy shopkeeper in the Shar-e-Nav district, the Scots were invited to a party being held in the city's most affluent neighbourhood. A block away from the presidential palace, a high brick wall, capped with razor wire, surrounded the sprawling whitewashed house. A remnant of colonial optimism, its numerous balconies, cusped gables, leaded-glass windows, thick stone chimneys, bell tower and sheltering conifers set in neat lawns, cast the impression that one was looking at a Swiss chateau. Passing between ornate wrought iron gates, Raj gave a curt salute to an armed guard, whose white-helmeted head popped out of a sentry box that was painted in black and green diagonal stripes.

If the house appeared large from the outside, it seemed enormous on the inside but, as far as parties go, it was a lacklustre affair. Soft jazz music played from unseen speakers. The air smelled strongly of cigar smoke. Well-heeled Afghans from Kabul's *haut monde* wandered from room to room, dressed up in outfits that had been fashionable when Bill Haley and The Comets were rocking around the clock.

Sitting in a cavernous public room, where the lighting was bright yet intimate, Angus could see that Murphy and Raj felt ill at ease, even though the black leather chairs their backsides were squeaking on were designed for comfort.

'Hey, guys,' said Murphy, rising to his feet, 'let's split. Sitting on my arse and nibbling on dainty cucumber sandwiches, while making polite conversation with a bunch of stuck-up twats, isn't my kind of scene.' He pulled up his black leather jacket's collar and looked ceiling-ward as if what was taking place around him was too much to bear. 'This is like listening to people describing their acid trips, like really fucking boring, man.'

Angus glanced over at Jenny. She glanced back at him and crossed one slim leg over the other. Pale-faced, the only colour in her otherwise monochromatic complexion was the purple slash of lipstick on her thin lips. With a jerk of her head she tossed her hair out of her eyes and then began loading her glass pipe with opium. She was definitely settling in to the situation. The sight of her made an unsettling chill rise from Angus's guts and spread through his body. He looked up at Murphy and said, 'You, Raj and the girls go ahead without us. We'll catch up with you back at the hotel.'

Raj and Murphy nodded in assent, raised a hand in farewell and walked over to collect Alice and Nina, who were standing in the centre of the room with a flock of male admirers circling them like tuxedoed buzzards.

It had not been the best of days for Angus. Before breakfast, he'd had a row with Jenny over her drug habit. He'd realized he was wasting his breath, stamped off in a rage, gone for a walk to cool off and lost both his shoes in a mud patch on the corner of Koch-e-Morga, better known as 'Chicken Street', although why was a mystery because there was never a hen in sight. Lined with tourist shops selling knick-knacks, rugs and ethnic clothes, it was necessary to traverse Chicken Street to get over to the modern Wazir Akbar Khan section of town. An early morning downpour had turned the muddy street into a river of quicksand that had the suction power of a megawatt vacuum cleaner. It was a local downtown pastime in Kabul to watch unsuspecting pedestrians lose their footwear in the gunk. Angus had looked up from his sludge-covered feet to see a crowd of local men, clapping their hands and jeering at him. Faces grinning, they were loitering outside of a butcher's shop, where skinned animals' purple flesh hung surrounded by swarms of big black flies. It was embarrassingly obvious to him that the men were delighted by his shoeless predicament. Afghans love a practical joke – especially when it's a foreigner who is the butt of it. Angus let go of the recollection, but not the foul mood that had accompanied him all day, which was now hanging over his head like a cloud of poison gas.

A young man in a white apron approached and then pushed a metal tray with glasses of bubbling champagne under Angus's nose. He shook his head and the waiter moved on to a small group of mini-skirted Afghan women, who were laughing loudly as they studied a painting of naked, preposterously well-endowed, black men, dancing around a blazing campfire.

Angus turned belligerently towards Jenny and noticed that she'd been distracted from her opium pipe by something going on in a corner of the crowded room. He followed her gaze and saw a tall, lean, flat-chested woman with a very pale complexion whose spindly legs were encased in a pair of skin-tight, black leather trousers. Angus studied the woman's nervous movements until she stooped over in a corner and vomited into her red handbag. The sight disgusted Angus and prompted him to rise to his feet. 'If

I'm not back in three days, send out a search party,' he said over his shoulder, walking off and leaving Jenny to her little glass pipe and her own devices. He knew from experience that her honey-coloured eyes, wavy blonde hair, fine-featured face and aura of mystique would guarantee her an attentive male audience that would soon be wasting its best lines on her.

Boredom drove Angus to explore the rest of the house. Drinks in hand, numerous guests were standing around in runner-carpeted corridors and arched doorways admiring stuffed wild animals in glass cases, the most impressive of which was a huge, glassy-eyed Bengal tiger, its dark lips drawn back in a frozen snarl to display a signal red tongue and ivory-coloured incisors at least six inches long. The big cat's fur was scraggy and moth-eaten and it reminded Angus of the rainy afternoon Jenny and he had dropped acid and visited Edinburgh zoo. As he'd stood transfixed observing a magnificent tiger slowly pacing a barred cage, its massive shoulders shifting with each ponderous step, an old drunk, who smelled of cheap whisky, had leaned into Angus and whispered in his ear, 'If you were walking unarmed in the jungle and saw one of those hairy beasties, you wouldnae have to look at your watch to know what time it was, because you'd know it was five minutes too late.' The old man had then staggered off, chuckling merrily to himself.

The memory and the guests' excited chatter faded as he wandered further into the building. The house was labyrinthine. Long hallways were intersected by short ones that led to dozens of chambers, big and small. The rooms he passed through were uniformly high-ceilinged, boasted carved, gold-painted mouldings and were decorated with the occasional patterned carpet, headless stone statues and earthenware urns, home to desiccated palms that were turning brown from lack of water. He walked up to an ancient grandfather clock. It stood in a corner, ticking somnolently until he looked into its face and it suddenly stopped. It was exactly midnight. Slightly spooked, Angus moved on. His footsteps echoed on the black and white-chequered floor tiles and he felt for a moment like a solitary chessman crossing a life-sized chessboard. The memory of the last time he'd played chess made him flash on Dirty Ali's battered face. He pushed the thought out of his mind and entered a windowless room that was the size of a tennis court. The place reeked of linseed oil. The walls were hung with dozens of paintings. They were illuminated by dim brass spotlights, fixed to overhead racks and suspended from the ceiling by rusty chains intertwined by yellowing flex.

Paying little heed to the laws of perspective and painted in a semi-impressionistic style, employing bold harsh brushstrokes to apply lurid colours, so intense the overall effect on the viewer is vulgar, the paintings illustrate perfectly the repressed nature of the artists' personalities, was how Angus imagined an art critic might have described the various gaudy canvases hanging on the walls. Some of them depicted desert scenes, where camels stood silhouetted in shiny black before impossibly garish sunsets, composed of thick layers of bright orange and deep crimson oil paint that seemed to bleed out of the canvas. Others were painted in bizarre abstract styles, the kind that looks like a psychopath's brain, after it has been savaged by a school of ravenous neurotropic piranhas. All of the canvases were set into heavy wooden frames, producing an impression of weightiness as they strained to contain a riot of colours

The only painting that he felt drawn to portrayed a plump, veiled belly dancer, arms akimbo, frozen in time in front of an audience made up of leering turbaned men who were seated on floor cushions. The picture was suffused with a raw masculine excitement that struck Angus as irresistibly suggestive.

Due to his disposition that evening, he felt like the whole building was devoid of any real spirit, as if it weren't somebody's home but rather a soulless museum, displaying an exhibition of art works whose theme was 'Systematic analysis of stretcher, canvas and paint wastage in Kabul'.

Drawn by the sweet green smell of hashish, he crossed the threshold of a candlelit room and came upon a half-dozen or so ethnically dressed, middle-aged hippies puffing on a hookah pipe. One of them looked up, a fat lady with a flushed face, and asked him in Dutch-accented English if he'd like to join them. They were smoking tobacco laced with hash oil. Made by squeezing the oily essence out of cannabis plants' flowering tops, this powerful substance, ten times stronger than conventional resin, soon had Angus legless. His thoughts drifted back to the paintings he'd looked at earlier and he began to change his mind about them to the extent that he would have bought the belly dancer picture, had it been up for sale. His awareness returned to the present when a hip-looking couple sat down beside him on a white leather sofa that was fitted into a corner of the room.

'How's it going, brother? Enjoying the party?' asked the strikingly handsome man with a North American drawl.

'Yeah, I'm beginning to,' Angus replied, trying to focus his eyes. 'If you'd asked me half-an-hour ago I'd have said something smart like, I'm having about as much fun as a marathon runner trying to cut his legs off with a blunt knife.' He shrugged self-consciously. 'Man, that hash oil is strong shit. I'm—'

'Whoa there, brother,' said the newcomer, grinning broadly to show two lines of perfect white teeth that looked to Angus like they'd been set in place by an expensive German dentist, 'with an accent like that there's only one place you could've come from. You're Scottish...right?'

Angus's eyebrows shot up. He adopted a Highland twang and replied, 'Och, aye. Hoots mon the noo. I'm as Scottish as a haggis, wearing a kilt and sporran on a braw moonlicht nicht, doing the Highland fling to the skirl of the pipes at a Burn's Supper, being held in my castle on the banks of Loch Ness. How does that grab ye, Jimmy?'

'Like...far out,' said the man, extending his hand. 'But my name's not Jimmy, it's Orion.'

Angus shook the proffered hand. 'Angus, Angus Macleod, nice to meet you, man.'

'I'm also Scottish,' declared Orion, swirling the red wine in his glass. 'Two centuries ago my forefathers from Clan MacDonald left the homeland to begin a new life in Nova Scotia.'

'Two hundred years ago!' Angus frowned. 'That must be where you got your excellent long-term memory from.'

Orion peered into Angus's bloodshot eyes. 'Are you being sarcastic?'

'Ehm... maybe...eh...I'm pretty stoned, man.' Angus ran his hands through his long dark hair. 'Yeah, I suppose I might have been.'

'Are all Scottish people as mordant as you?' asked Orion's female companion, who'd been listening to the exchange.

Angus's brow creased as he thought about it. 'Naw,' he replied, 'not really. It's just that we Scots have a tendency to rib people. You know, joke about things to stop each other taking life too seriously.'

She nodded in understanding. 'Yeah, I can dig it,' she said, twirling the long stem of her glass between her ringed fingers.

'This is Dawn,' said Orion, introducing his wife, who had the assurance that wealth can bring but lacked the arrogance that so often accompanies it.

Her long eyelashes fluttered and a perfectly lipsticked mouth smiled. 'We're Canadians from Vancouver,' she announced.

Even in the subdued light, Angus could not help noticing that the couple were well-dressed. They both had on Cuban-heeled snakeskin cowboy boots. Orion had a neat beard, tinged by a few grey hairs at the chin, and looked to be in his early to mid-forties. He wore a neat chamois leather outfit with his fair hair tied back in a ponytail. Doe-eyed Dawn was the fortunate type of woman whose appearance doesn't change over time, who will still look thirty when she is sixty. She wore her black, auburn-streaked hair pulled back in a tight bun at the back of her finely shaped head. Tucked into the slim waist of her suede leather bellbottom trousers was a cobalt-blue cotton shirt. She had enough pearl buttons undone to expose the edges of a pink bra and a few centimetres of tanned cleavage, which looked like a crevice in the Grand Canyon to Angus's sex-starved eyes. He looked away, afraid of being caught staring and having his curiosity correctly interpreted. The Canadians wore silver jewellery, inset with lapis lazuli. When Dawn raised her wine glass up to a passing servant and indicated she would like a refill, candlelight sparkled on her ring-encrusted fingers and splashed prismatic colour across the ceiling.

Accompanied by a few stares, Jenny sauntered into the dimly lit room and wandered over to join them. She was wearing a red satin miniskirt, matching top and black leather, high-heeled bootees. She looked like an anorexic play-pet of the month, who had just stepped out of the Nosferatu Club's pin-up calendar.

When Angus introduced her, Orion stood and gave Jenny a European double kiss on her concave cheeks. Dawn remained seated, reached over and shook her thin hand.

Orion and Angus started to talk about music. Jenny admired Dawn's jewellery while they sparked up a conversation about local customs and clothes.

A dignified Afghan, who had the hooked nose of an Arab, ambled over. He bowed towards Jenny and Dawn, stood straight, put his hands behind his back and said, 'Good evening, ladies.' He was wearing a long, dark green, silk-embroidered shalwar shirt over black trousers. He had a white satin scarf wrapped around a tasselled, red fez on his head. Fadi, a close friend of Orion's, was the party's host. Angus had noticed him hovering in the background like a discrete maitre d' in a posh restaurant, only stepping into the fore to provide a guiding hand, friendly smile or agreeable word for his guests.

It soon became obvious to Angus that Fadi was a great lover of all things Western, especially jazz. Angus had been aware of the strangely haunting melody playing in the background with cool trumpet in the lead. A stranger to this type of music he asked what it was. Fadi became enthusiastic and explained how *In a Silent Way*, by Miles Davis, was his favourite long-player.

Angus relaxed into the situation and started to chat with the host about the paintings he'd looked at earlier on in the evening.

'Did you like them?' Fadi asked, his veined eyes protruding to such an extent they looked like they were trying to escape from their sockets.

'Ehm...well...some of them were very...*interesting*,' answered Angus diplomatically.

Fadi's wide sensual mouth curved into a knowing smile. 'I'm aware that most of them are dreadful,' he admitted, 'but painting for me is a hobby that I enjoy immensely.' He paused and then added a reflection. 'In Afghanistan poets, musicians, singers and warlords have always been honoured, but never painters.' He smiled again – almost bashfully. 'Besides, my paintings bring a bit of colour into the house.'

'Yes,' agreed Angus, 'you can say that again. It must have taken ages for you to paint them all.' His voice became eager. 'I liked the belly dancer.'

'You did?' Fadi's voice was incredulous.

'I liked her so much I'd be willing to buy her from you,' said Angus, realizing immediately that he was getting a bit carried away with himself.

'I'm sorry,' apologized the Afghan, 'like God, my pictures are not for sale.'

'No problem,' responded Angus, feeling somewhat relieved, 'I understand.'

Fadi sat down beside him on the leather sofa. 'I do give my paintings away as gifts, though.' He smiled benevolently at Angus and put a reassuring hand on his knee. 'Come round tomorrow afternoon and you can pick up the belly dancer.'

Angus was astonished by the Afghan's generosity. 'Man, you don't have to do that,' he objected.

Fadi stood. 'It's my pleasure.' He nodded to the Canadians and Jenny, then scanned the room for a moment before saying, 'You must excuse me, I have to attend to my other guests.' He smiled down at the four foreigners, his eyes lingering on Jenny's crossed legs. 'I wish you all a pleasant evening,' he said and then quickly walked away.

'Man,' said Angus, turning to Orion, 'I can't believe it. The guy just gave me a painting.'

The Canadian put a hand to his mouth to cover laughter.

Angus asked, 'What's so funny about that?'

'Fadi gives his paintings away to anyone in Kabul who wants to have them,' replied Orion. He spluttered. 'He...he...he's got to be one of the worst p-p-p...painters on the p-p...planet.'

Dawn laughed quietly and added, 'Like most artists, Fadi hates to have criticism directed at his work by people he thinks are unworthy to judge. The thing is, as far as he's concerned, that encompasses just about everybody.'

A bottle of red wine was opened to celebrate the occasion. They touched glasses and drank.

After spending about an hour in each other's company, Orion glanced at the slim stainless-steel watch on his left wrist and then said to Angus and Jenny, 'Would you guys like to come back to our place for a smoke of something special?'

Angus had heard that line before and knew from experience that it usually led to the opening of some interesting doors. He rose unsteadily to his feet, looked at Orion and Dawn, gestured with his right hand and said, 'After you.'

A ten-minute walk along tree-lined streets later, they entered a two-storied house on a corner through an arched wooden door that was decorated with pointed brass studs. They climbed a spiral staircase and Dawn unlocked a steel door. She stepped aside, motioned for Angus and Jenny to enter, and then said in a mischievous voice, 'Welcome to our humble home.'

Angus realized she'd delivered a jocular understatement as soon as he stepped inside and saw that there was nothing at all that was modest about the place. He stood in the centre of a large, opulently furnished, circular room and gazed around, feeling like he'd been transported into another world. Orion was, among other things, an antique dealer. The place was a veritable Aladdin's cave full of dark red and deep blue Afghan carpets, embroidered cushions, brass lampshades and stone statues. Hanging on the walls were curved daggers in bejewelled scabbards, polished elephant hide shields and silk tapestries depicting scenes from Mogul emperors' courts. Everything looked valuable and appeared to be of museum quality.

Now that there was more light available, Angus could see that Dawn used heavy make-up to cover a rough complexion. In his opinion, she needn't have bothered because he found her fascinating, to the point that he had to stop himself from ogling her big busting bombshells from Vancouver that, judging by the way they kept bouncing around, were probably held in place by a living bra. His eyes followed Dawn's swaying hips and tight derriere as she went off to make tea in the kitchen, her monumental breasts preceding her exit like a catamaran's pointed prows. Meanwhile, her husband made his two guests comfortable around an octagonal brass table engraved with concentric rings of swirling calligraphic script, exotic enough for a Sotheby's auction of Middle Eastern antiquities.

Dawn returned with a pot of tea and, while she poured it into white china cups, Orion supplied a few details about their lives. They spent six months of the year in Afghanistan, the other half travelling the world or living at their cabin on a pine-covered islet not far from Vancouver Island. In subsequent conversations, the Canadian would reveal that he was a heavy-duty mover, shipping out two to three tons of hashish from Afghanistan every year.

Angus and Orion immediately formed a deep connection that was so natural they could have been long lost relatives. Angus glanced over at Jenny and Dawn, who were by now seated on the opposite side of the low table. They were sipping green tea and chatting quietly. It appeared to him like they were enjoying each other's company.

Orion reached over to the centre of the table, opened an intricately carved wooden box and retrieved a jewel-studded circular tin. He asked Angus, 'Ever tried DMT?'

'DMT,' repeated Angus. 'What's that?'

'This,' replied Orion, opening the small container to display its light brown contents, 'is one of the most amazing psychedelic substances in the world. Dimethyltryptamine can be created synthetically in a laboratory, but the waxy paste you see here originated in the Amazon Basin. I spent three months in the rainforest with an old Ecuadorian shaman called Don Cabeza,' he said wistfully. 'We drank the psychedelic brew ayahuasca together, used mind-blowing hallucinogenic snuffs and smoked DMT, which the old man extracted from various plants using biochemical processes that had been taught to him by his teacher. Shamanic rituals have been centred on these psychoactive drugs' use over a time span that stretches back into prehistory. Before I parted company with him, Don Cabeza gave me this DMT as a gift.'

'Wow!' Angus exclaimed. 'That sounds far out. Is it dangerous?'

Orion nodded his head thoughtfully. 'Well,' he said, 'I believe it would be irresponsible to suggest that there are no risks involved in smoking DMT, but I'd be lying if I said the risk wasn't worth taking.'

'Yeah, I can dig that, man.' Angus chuckled. 'But what does it do to you?'

'Come on,' said Orion, 'you know there's only one real way to find that out. Would you like to try some?'

Observing the eager smile on the Scotsman's face, the Canadian must have known immediately that he would not have to repeat his question. He looked away from Angus and said, 'Jenny?' She tossed her thick blonde hair to one side and then nodded.

Orion picked up a transparent glass pipe and placed a smidgen of the sticky substance on the fine wire mesh in its bowl. The DMT looked like damp brown sugar and had a very distinct, plastic-like, chemical smell to it, not unlike model glue. He instructed, 'After inhaling the smoke, try and hold it in for as long as possible before exhaling.'

Orion put a gas lighter's blue flame to the pipe's bowl. Angus drew heavily on its stem and held the smoke deep in his lungs until his eyes began to bulge. He coughed out the smoke and immediately felt a tremendous rush of energy course through his body. His head felt like it was going to explode and, in a manner of speaking, it did. Overlapping, spinning discs, formed from a spectrum of vibrant colours, throbbed inside his skull. He fell back onto some cushions. His mind sonic-boomed through a cerebral cyclone and was sucked into the centre of a rotating mandala. Rainbow light gave way to a pulsating brilliant whiteness. The glare in his inner vision faded and was replaced by what appeared to be purple velvet curtains. He hesitated before moving on to what lay beyond. His ears filled with the sound of cellophane paper being crushed and then he heard a strongly accented Irish voice say, 'Begorra and bejabers, how are you doing? Popped in for a visit, did you?'

Angus found himself staring into the bemused eyes of a dwarf who was dressed in a shiny red suit with a bright green bowler hat on his head. Angus gazed around and realized that he was sitting cross-legged on the wooden floor of a circular room with a domed ceiling that pulsed with a violet light, the source of which could not be discerned. 'What the fuck!'

'Now now, laddie,' cautioned the gnome, 'mind your language, you're a guest here. No need for that, tee-hee-hee.'

Angus sensed movement behind him and turned to see another similarly attired dwarf performing an impromptu jig. A green top hat fell from the midget's head to reveal a bald patch with a silver star painted on it.

Angus soon discovered, much to his amazement, that there were four abnormally small men in the room. Their eyes shone with a spectral glow.

'Leprechauns!' he exclaimed.

The four dwarves began laughing uproariously. They started to dance and kick their stubby legs in the air. They joined hands and formed a circle around Angus.

He stammered, 'Wh…Wh…Where am I?'

The dwarfs began to sing with lilting Irish voices. 'Round and round and round we go, where it stops, nobody knows. Round and round and round we go. *Rrrr…r…rr…rrr…*' Their voices sped up, as did their circling, until their bodies blurred in movement. Angus was sucked up into a vortex. He spun through the centre of the domed ceiling and next thing he knew he was floating in space. An infinity of stars spiralled up into the Milky Way. Galaxies spun and expanded while comets hissed by, leaving behind trails of sparkling crystals. His vision of time and space was so perfect that had he been able to write it down in mathematical formulae, it would have signalled Einstein's nemesis. Lacking paper and pencil, he opened his eyes.

Orion and Dawn were looking down at him.

'How did you get on?' asked Orion.

Angus sat up. 'Man! That was like a fucking bomb going off in my head!'

The Canadian couple laughed at his inarticulate outburst.

'I can't believe it, man,' said Angus, shaking his head. 'I just met four leprechauns and then flew through the universe. And now, apart from feeling a bit spaced, I feel completely normal.' He turned to Orion and asked, 'How long was I gone?'

The Canadian shrugged. 'Maybe ten min—'

'Oh, *wow!*' exclaimed Jenny. She sat bolt upright. 'That was incredible. I've just been in an old-fashioned amusement park. There were people dressed in Victorian-style clothes, riding wooden horses on a carousel.' She placed her long fingers on her temples. 'Everyone in the park was drunk. I could smell the alcohol. The women had Indian war paint on their faces.' She ran her fingers through her hair, shook her head and said, 'That was really, really weird, man.'

'Sounds interesting to me,' said Dawn, fixing her gaze on Jenny. 'I've visited that funfair too. There's a Hall of Mirrors you can walk through that shows who you've been in previous incarnations.'

Angus's ears pricked up. 'Do you guys believe in past lives?'

'We've been left with little choice in the matter,' answered Orion, a hint of resignation in his voice. 'That is, taking into account that the Buddha was reported to have said that there is no soul and therefore no transmigration of the soul. Nonetheless, both of us have experienced things that have led us to consider our present existence as a link in a long chain of lives. Each time we die we take our latent tendencies and potentialities with us. The wheel of life and death turns and we are born again with our karmic baggage, and then we resume the journey from where we left off.'

'The way I see it,' added Dawn, 'is that who and what we really are may be beyond anything we can imagine. It's occurred to me that it could be the case that only a small part of me lives as this being I call Dawn. Simultaneously, in a different dimensional reality, I might be living in another world that is just as real as the one we are in here.' She went on. 'I remember reading something about a Chinese sage, called Chuang-Tzu, asking himself whether he was a man dreaming he was a butterfly, or whether he was a butterfly dreaming he was a man.'

'Yeah, I've heard that one before,' said Angus. 'But who were those midgets I met?'

'Maybe a throwback to your Celtic roots,' suggested Dawn.

Orion thought about it for a moment before he said, 'Perhaps they exist in dimensions that can only be reached through the door of the subconscious by means of a DMT transference. Don Cabeza taught me...' Orion hesitated. 'No, no that is not how it was. Don Cabeza *showed* me that the world has a centre, which exists simultaneously inside of everyone in the form of a vertical axis. It's like an elevator that allows you to travel up and down. Depending on where the elevator goes, you can see into and experience different dimensions that vary in nature from celestial to infernal. I suspect that those dwarves you encountered exist in the borderline dreamtime, the place where the conscious merges with the unconscious. From our own DMT sessions, I can tell you that some of the entities Dawn and I have run into are of a rather more sinister nature.'

Even though it was warm in the cosy room, goose bumps appeared on Jenny's arms when she heard that.

'The thing is, I really don't want to colour your experiences too much by filling your heads with my stories and theories,' concluded Orion, tapping some more DMT into the glass pipe's bowl. He nodded towards Angus. 'Want to try a stronger dose?'

Angus was in no doubt that he wanted to indulge in another transdimensional, quasi-quantum leap. Jenny was looking a bit pale around the gills, but allowed herself to get carried enough away on Angus's enthusiasm to take another flight into the DMT zone.

By the time Angus exhaled his third lungful of acrid-tasting smoke, his brain was singing like a well-cast Tibetan bell. For a few moments there was an intense sensation of pressure on his temples, accompanied by an itchy tingling on the back of his neck. His scalp tightened, as though an elastic headband had contracted around his skull. His ears popped as he flew between the pillars of infinity, riding on a winged anaconda's back. The rushing in his ears faded and was replaced by a crackling rustle.

All of a sudden, in the centre of Angus's inner vision, there appeared an ant's head. Its mottled skin was a pinkish brown colour. The creature's eyes were as black as polished coal and multi-faceted. Angus could see that each octagonal segment held his own face as a reflection. As if possessing a life of their own, two long antennae twitched on top of the insect's head. Angus intuited that if their ends touched, something significant was going to happen. It did. There was loud sizzling crash, like an electric power line being struck by lightning, followed by a blinding flash of sharp blue light. Angus was disconnected from his body. He became an incorporeal presence catapulted into a black void. *It would be irresponsible to suggest that there are no risks involved in smoking DMT.* Orion's words came out of the darkness and it registered in the back of Angus's mind that he'd overdosed and was now dead. Floating in limbo, he experienced a bout of intense fear and paranoia. He had no body, but still he could feel. Nebulous clouds of colourless mist began to swirl and thicken. He could sense rather than see that there were amorphous spirits moving around him. A face appeared. It was Daniel Macleod, Angus's dead foster father. Daniel smiled enigmatically and then called out, *'Gregara!'* Angus remembered the word from the stories told to him as a child on Iona. It was the Scottish outlaw, Rob Roy Macgregor's, cry of victory. Hearing his foster father's voice reinforced the idea that he'd stepped over the threshold of death.

The mist parted in front of him and Angus felt movement. Disembodied, he knew not how it was possible to experience motion, but he did. He was shooting forward at great velocity. Up ahead, bright balls of luminescent colour began to appear. They blurred into wavering lines as he shot past them at hyper-luminal speed. Then…nothing, he was pure emptiness. The sensation of separateness was gone. There was no more 'I' to experience, only an experiencing. A cool breeze blew and he knew it as himself.

A vibrant blue sphere became visible in the distance. Eyeless, he gazed at it and was enthralled by its beauty. An invisible magnetism pulled him towards it. He drew closer and recognized Earth. He was struck by its cosmic isolation in space. *Home*, he thought, as he began a tumbling descent. There was no fear, only detachment. A curved shadow moved over the vapour-shrouded planet as it turned on its axis orbiting the sun. He sped by the moon, close enough to see steep grey mountain ranges rising from the sides of deep boulder-strewn craters. He passed through thick cloud and looked down at twinkling pinprick patterns of electric light. It was a city. A curving line of river, streets and buildings came into focus. Air rushed. *Wroom!* He thudded back into his body. For some time he lay with his eyes closed, watching patterns swirl and pulse behind his eyelids, while his spirit savoured the lingering peace of the void.

'*Eeeeegh!*' Jenny screamed.

The sound slashed into Angus's consciousness like a cut-throat razor, but his detached frame of mind helped him to remain calm. He sat up slowly and looked over to where Jenny was laying spread-eagled on top of embroidered cushions. Her eyes were wide open and her jaw was moving up and down. Orion and Dawn hurried over to her side. Jenny began to weep.

'Jen, what's wrong? What happened?' Angus asked, drawing closer as he placed a reassuring palm on the centre of her heaving chest. He couldn't help noticing that her breastbone only had a very thin layer of flesh covering it. He flashed on the emaciated horses that pulled the tongas around town.

In between tear-filled sobs, all Jenny managed to say was, 'They stuck something in me.' She held up her left arm and used her right hand to knead nervously on her bicep. When she removed her hand, her arm did indeed look swollen and inflamed.

Dawn rose to her feet and hurried off into the kitchen. Seconds later, Angus heard a hiss of gas and then the watery clunk of a kettle being placed on the cooker.

After a strong cup of hot tea, Jenny composed herself enough to light her little opium pipe. A few puffs later, she lay back on the cushions and began to narrate in a quiet, monotonous voice what had happened to her. The others sat beside her and listened in silence.

'There was a vibrating hum,' she began. 'It was a comforting sound, like the idling engines below a passenger ship's deck. Then the humming grew louder and louder, until it was all there was. The gentle hum had turned into an aggressive roar. Then, suddenly, as if someone had thrown a switch, the roaring quickly faded into a quiet electrical buzz, interspersed by the occasional metallic twang.

'I found myself standing in front of what I took to be thick velvet curtains but, when I touched them, they felt like soft plastic. The material was glowing with a reddish golden colour. Something moved behind them. I experienced a moment of panic. In spite of my apprehension, I pushed the fabric aside. There was an electric crackling sound and next thing I knew I was strapped into some kind of stainless steel dentist's chair. It felt warm with no edges, only smooth curves. I tried to move my head, so that I could see where I was, but I couldn't because there was a tight band over my forehead keeping my head locked in position. My eyes started to hurt. I wanted to blink but found it impossible because they were being held open by clamps.'

Jenny stared into space, her eyes apparently following the wisps of opium smoke drifting in the room. Angus noticed her eyelids were red and puffy. He took this to have come from her crying.

As if in a trance, Jenny began to speak in a droning tone, as though she was trying to control and rationalize what she described. 'All of a sudden, a face entered my vision. It looked like a giant lime green grasshopper's head, or how I would imagine a praying mantis to look close up. Its eyes were orange with black pupils. There was a high-pitched clicking sound coming from its curved mouth, which opened to display two lines of serrated teeth. A long, thin, red tongue shot out of its mouth. It made a slurping sound.' Her voice rose. 'It licked my face. The clicking sounds grew louder.'

Jenny's body shuddered. Angus looked over at Orion and saw that he had a concerned expression on his bearded face. The Canadian raised his eyebrows, as if to say he was as surprised as anyone else in the room to hear what she was describing.

Jenny's voice became more emotional. 'Up until that point I'd felt, for the most part, neutral to what I was seeing. It was matter of fact, like I was watching a weird movie. Like...like the visions I was seeing belonged to somebody else.' She pressed on, 'The mantis creature moved out of my vision and I just sat there staring around, wishing I could close my eyes and get the nightmare to stop. The ceiling was curved, lit from the sides with a violet light that was radiating from some hidden source. The mantis reappeared, accompanied by an ant-like creature. Man, he was scary, with rough pink skin and a long beaked mouth that had little brown tusks on each side of it. His eyes were big, black and shiny. I could see motion in them, reflecting other beings moving around in the room. The ant creature was also making clicking sounds, although deeper than those of the mantis, like sticks tapping on a tight drum skin. I sensed that the two creatures were becoming keyed up because their clicking intensified. For a moment, another being came into my line of sight. He was shorter than the other two, had grey waxy skin, a round smooth forehead, large, black oval eyes and a pointed chin. He didn't have a nose or ears and there was a bad odour coming from him, like smelly socks…no, no, more like wet cardboard boxes.' She paused and nodded once. 'Now I remember. The thing smelled of ammonia, like a dirty urinal.'

Angus sniffed the air, but all he could detect was the metallic whiff of Jenny's fear, which was only marginally weaker than the cloying scent of the patchouli oil that she wore as a perfume.

Jenny hung her head and spoke in a hoarse, breathless whisper. Her listeners leaned in closer so as not to miss anything she said. 'I heard the sound of rubber wheels rolling over the floor. A big machine with a central column, its top rounded, came into view. It was covered in tiny flashing neon-blue lights and, as far as I could tell, was made from the same smooth material as the chair I was strapped into. Suckered arms stretched out of the column, like an octopus's tentacles. They were flailing around and seemed to have a will of their own. I felt terrified. Really man, I don't like to say it, but I'll tell you anyway. I thought I was going to shit myself.' Jenny paused for a moment, put her hand under her backside, breathed an audible sigh of relief, gave a self-conscious smile and returned to her close encounters. 'I knew the creeps were aware of my fear and I could intuitively sense that they had the ability to enter my mind and affect my thought patterns. They stood staring at me without moving. I received a strong silent communication from them that I was the subject of an experiment. They knew all about me. Like, man, they communicated non-verbally that they'd been waiting on me to show up so that they could do whatever it was they wanted to do with me. I began to worry that they were going to have sex with me. My heart started beating like a bass drum. I thought I was going to have a bloody heart attack or something. The two insect creatures made some more intense clicking sounds and then the giant ant stretched out a thin arm with a red pincer-like claw on the end of it. He grabbed hold of one of the machine's tentacles and pressed its pointed end into my arm. It really hurt, like someone had injected sulphuric acid into my veins. I freaked out, screamed and next thing I knew I was back here with you guys.'

Jenny massaged her arm. After that evening, she would knead her left bicep whenever she felt tense or nervous.

She refilled her opium pipe while Angus spoke to the Canadians about what Jenny had told them. He asked Orion, 'Who are these creatures? Are they aliens?'

Orion gave his beard a few contemplative strokes before answering. 'I believe that thousands of years ago our ancestors used potent psychoactive plant preparations to gain access to supernatural realms. If you think about it, how else could ancient man have imagined four-armed elephant-headed gods, the Great Sphinx of Giza, dragons, chimera and many other mythological entities? One could surmise that it was such visions that laid the foundations for early religious ideas about the existence of heaven and hell.' He paused and then continued, his brow creasing in concentration. 'The thing is, when one experiences these hallucinations, if that is in fact what they are, what's disorienting about them is that they appear to be as real and solid as us sitting here now.'

He turned and spoke to Jenny. 'I've seen the Greys before. The ones I saw were about four feet tall, very thin with limbs that didn't seem to have any joints, like they were made out of rubber. I once saw the same kind of being but twice as tall with cream-coloured skin. I had the distinct impression that it was female. She was wearing a long black cape with a sparkling collar fastened round her elongated neck. I was with Don Carlos Cabeza in the jungle at the time. When the shaman became aware of her presence, he whistled and she disappeared. During one of my ayahuasca sessions with Don Cabeza, I met machine elves whose job it was to design new flowers. On another occasion I found myself pushing against a transparent rubber wall with bright orange humanoid creatures on the other side.' He looked into Jenny's eyes and slowly shook his head. 'I have to admit, though, I've never heard anyone describe anything similar to what you've just experienced.'

Dawn poured fresh tea into their empty glasses. She nodded thoughtfully. 'Yes, but remember what San Francisco Frank told us. He said that the Greys were abducting humans to obtain the hormonal secretions they needed to sustain themselves because their own race was doomed due to a collapse in their digestive system and genetic structure.'

'Jeez, whoa down, Dawn,' cautioned Orion. 'Everybody knows that Frank swallowed way too much acid with Kesey and the Pranksters, to take anything he said seriously. Last time I saw Frank he was on his way to Tikal in Guatemala, raving on about the Mayan calendar and how the world, as we know it, is going to end in December, two thousand and twelve.'

'Yeah, maybe you're right,' Dawn agreed. 'Besides, that's almost forty years from now. That's a long time to wait to find out if there was any truth in what Frank said.' She concluded, 'Besides, people who go on about the end of the world being nigh are usually the ones who lack enough imagination to see what might be coming next.'

Orion glanced at his wristwatch and then spoke to Angus. 'It's getting late,' he said. 'We have a guest room.'

Angus rose from a leather cushion. 'Thanks for the offer, man, but I think we both need a breath of fresh air.'

Dawn looked up at him. 'Are you sure?'

Angus nodded. 'Yes. But I'd like to see you guys again before we leave for Pakistan.'

Orion stood up. 'Of course we'll see each other again. Come round anytime. We're in most afternoons.'

Sunrise was half an hour away. The air was fresh. Jenny clung to Angus's arm as they made their way along Kabul's deserted streets. Every time a dog barked, Jenny jumped. She also made a point of walking around any dark shadows they encountered on their way back to the Hotel Nasir-ud-Din.

Put my arms around ya, like the circles going 'round the Sun... A scratched and warped copy of Big Brother and The Holding Company's *Cheap Thrills* was blaring out of a battered Philips record player when, over brunch at 'The Place With No Name', one of Kabul's numerous hippie hang-out cafés, Angus shared his and Jenny's DMT experiences from the previous evening with his friends.

'Leprechauns, fucking aliens,' scoffed Murphy, looking up from a dog-eared issue of *OZ* magazine. 'Sounds to me like you guys flipped right out.'

By the sceptical looks being directed their way by Alice, Nina and Raj, Murphy had given voice to their sentiments entirely.

'You guys just don't understand,' protested Jenny. 'What Angus described to you is true. That DMT paste is pure psycho-dynamite. You can't imagine what it's like until you've tried it. It...it...it's like ten seconds and...and boom, you're peaking out on the strongest acid you've ever had in your life.' She shook her head. 'As far as I'm concerned I never want to smoke the bloody stuff again. I don't mind admitting that it scared the shit out of me.'

'I wouldn't mind trying it,' said Raj, mumbling through a mouthful of muesli. 'Hey, Angus, man, why don't you ask your Canadian pal if you can buy some from him?'

'Hey, Raj, man,' said Angus, 'did your mother never tell you it's bad manners to speak when your mouth's full?'

Croaking in the background, Janis Joplin's whisky-soaked voice sounded like a bow being drawn across an untuned violin's strings as it delivered a rendition of George Gershwin's 'Summertime'. The record started clicking louder than previously and Janis sang the same thing, repeatedly: *Don't you cry – don't you cry – don't you—*

Murphy shouted out, 'For fuck's sake! What a fucking racket!' He called to the tall Afghan-America proprietor. *'Sharif!'*

Wearing a grease-stained apron and a Mexican sombrero, Sharif rushed out from the kitchen and said, 'I'm on it, man. I'm on it.' He lifted the record player's arm and then dropped the stylus down on the middle of a different track, where Janis Joplin was in the midst of pouring her frustrated heart out and asking the world, with an apparently limitless vocal range, why it is that love feels like a ball and chain?

After her DMT session, Jenny became more withdrawn and insular. She completely stopped smoking hashish and steered well clear of all hallucinogens. She'd recently discovered Tolkien's *Lord of the Rings* and enjoyed nothing more than to lie in bed all day long, puffing on her opium pipe as she read about Frodo, his friends and their adventures. The dark forces pursuing the hobbit, as he made his treacherous journey toward his destiny, held a special fascination for her. She could relate deeply with Gollum and his obsession with the ring of power. In her case the ring's seductive qualities had been replaced by a narcotic and her inability to resist it.

During the next few days, Angus spent as much time as possible with Orion and Dawn, who were in their mid-forties and therefore twice as old as he was. The well-travelled Canadians took obvious pleasure in sharing their many fascinating experiences with him. They were by far the most sophisticated people he'd ever formed a close relationship with. He was happy to note that they, in turn, enjoyed his company, although why he was not quite sure, reasoning that it might have something to do with his being Scottish.

On their last afternoon together, Angus told Orion about the half-ton of hash he and his friends had stowed away on the bus. The Canadian wrote down a New Delhi telephone number and handed the slip of paper to Angus.

'If the hashish is good quality,' said Orion, 'you'll be able to sell the lot to this man for at least twice what you paid for it. Just don't hand it over until the money's on the table. Get the picture?'

'Sure, man,' Angus chuckled. 'Thanks, but I wasn't born yesterday.'

Orion glanced at Angus, as if to say he'd heard that throwaway line before. After an attentive pause, he said, 'It's still easy to make an expensive mistake in this part of the world. The Eastern mind is cunning and has devised ways of ripping-off even the most seasoned of Western dope dealers. As far as the Pakistani businessman I'm sending you to is concerned, you will appear to him like a new kid on the block and therefore fair game. So don't you forget that one can never be too careful.' He handed Angus a cigarette packet-sized soapstone box and said, 'Here, I'd like to offer you this as a parting gift.'

Angus opened the box. Inside was a small tin containing about ten grams of DMT paste, a little glass pipe and a sheet of neatly folded, yellow silk thread paper.

'What's this?' asked Angus, unfolding the paper.

'That's a number in Canada that you can use to get in touch with us. We'd both like to see you again.'

The previous afternoon the Canadian couple had explained how they'd founded a small community of close-knit friends and family. They'd pooled their financial resources and bought the twenty square kilometre island they lived on when they were in their homeland.

Heartfelt hugs were exchanged when it was time for Angus to leave. The rest of Rolling Thunder's crew were keen to hit the road at dawn the next morning and head for the Khyber Pass.

Orion gave Angus one last hug, the kind any self-respecting grizzly bear would have been proud of. He then stood back from Angus and said, 'Happy trails, brother. Enjoy the DMT.' He winked. 'Oh!' he exclaimed, suddenly remembering something. 'Did you return to Fadi's place to pick up that painting?'

'Yeah, I did,' replied Angus, nodding. 'I'm beginning to wish I hadn't, because it takes up a lot of space and nobody else on the bus likes it.'

The Canadians laughed.

Dawn stepped forward, kissed Angus on both cheeks and lent some words of caution. 'Keep an eye on that girlfriend of yours. I don't think Jenny's aware of how hooked she is on that crap she's smoking.' Dawn hugged him one last time, as if he were her only son going off to war, and then whispered in his ear, 'Remember. India is not a country. It's an exalted state of mind that has to be dreamed into existence.'

11

THE KHYBER PASS WELCOMES YOU

S oft pearly light was seeping across the sky when Rolling Thunder's crew arrived at the scrap yard car park, located across the street from Kabul's bird market. Raj poked a sleeping night watchman on the shoulder and then, once awake, tried to persuade him to unlock the large padlock that secured the metal gate. It took ten minutes of arguing to convince the grizzled old man, whose false teeth rattled when he spoke, that he should open the lock. The dispute was centred on how much money was owed to him for guarding the bus.

Murphy settled it by handing the man five 100 Afghani notes. 'Now open the fuckin' gate, you stupid old bastard,' he spat, 'or I'll do it myself.'

The foreign words were wasted on the obstinate Afghan's ears, but the grimy bank notes broke through the language barrier and worked their magic. Laying his rusty blunderbuss to one side, the quarrelsome watchman retrieved a big brass key from inside the folds of his underpants. By the stench that rose out of them, they hadn't been washed since the British Raj closed the laundry and left town in a hurry in 1841 after a tribal revolt, which turned out to be a mistake. Of the 17,000 British soldiers, women and children involved in the mass exodus, only one man lived to tell the tale. Ghilzai tribesmen massacred everyone else. The sole survivor was an army surgeon. He was spared because the Afghans wanted him to take a message back to his masters in London. Doctor William Brydon did just that but, as history shows, nobody listened to the Afghans' warning about the price to be paid for invading their country. Fortunately for the Scots, times had changed and they drove out of town without further incident.

The outskirts of Kabul were disappearing in the distance when, as red as a stop sign, the sun's glowing disk floated up from behind a long line of smoking, conical-shaped brick kilns. Traffic thickened as the morning wore on. To the left of the highway and fringed by sugar cane fields, the Kabul River's banks were encrusted in chrome-yellow sulphur deposits. Low-lying outcrops were caked in cracked phosphate mud that had dried out under the harsh sun. The spiky, ice-blue encrustations looked like exposed coral reefs.

A short mountain pass was crossed, a barbed wire-encircled hydroelectric plant passed and then it was downhill all the way. The road descended through a series of twisting curves to the last town of any importance in the country, Jalalabad.

The crew were hungry and decided to stop for breakfast. The surrounding countryside was dotted with orange groves and within a minute of stepping out of the bus, Raj returned with a gunnysack full of sweet, grapefruit-sized oranges that he'd bought for a dollar.

Jalalabad was a large, spread-out town. Many of its houses had small hibiscus-filled gardens in front of them and others walled-in courtyards from where the sounds of domestic life echoed out onto the streets. Being springtime, flowers were blooming everywhere, giving the place a cheery, life-affirming ambience.

Pashtun tribesmen roamed the streets. They wore thick *pakol* caps, brown or black woollen waistcoats, light-coloured tunics and matching trousers with shawls wrapped around their waists to form thick cummerbunds. In their hands they carried Kalashnikov rifles as casually as bowler-hatted Englishmen do their umbrellas. Their weapons were the only sign that they were connected to modern times. These tall men's leathery, sun-scorched features reflected the harsh mountain deserts they inhabited. Often sporting henna-dyed beards, their narrow, hawk-nosed faces were home to deep-set taciturn eyes that rarely blinked. Capable of quick, calculated reactions, they were men of few words. If one was respectful towards the Pashtuns, they paid little heed to one's presence, at most a nod of recognition. On the other hand, any sign of disrespect could easily have been interpreted as a request to be given a permanent out-of-body experience. The Pashtuns were similar to other Highland peoples in that loyalty to the clan and personal honour were held in high regard. Following in their footsteps, at a respectful distance, the tribesmen's wives and daughters were faceless ghosts in cornflower-blue burkas, often to be seen balancing yellow-coloured calabashes upon their heads.

Under a pomegranate tree, where a few of last season's dried out fruits hung like ruptured Christmas decorations, Angus and his companions sat down around a wooden table and ordered food from a street café waiter. They ate in hungry silence from thick clay bowls full of thick curd, sweetened with wild bees' honey, and drank in the town's peaceful atmosphere. Away from the main road's hubbub and exhaust fumes, Jalalabad was like many other places in Afghanistan in that the technological progress that covered much of the planet had gained little purchase in a region where a well-shod horse was still seen as the most practical form of transport.

Back on the highway, scraggy, mange-infected camels grazed by the roadside.

It was early afternoon when Raj parked the bus in a small field a kilometre from where the Khyber Pass officially began. The crew disembarked and joined a slow-moving queue of truck drivers and foreigners, standing outside a cinder-block frontier post, waiting to have visas and vaccination certificates checked. The Afghan immigration officer, a short, bald man with broken yellow teeth, whose job it was to inspect foreign nationals' documents, didn't even bother to look at them. His hands ran on automatic as he stamped passports with scarlet ink, his bulging bloodshot eyes never still for a second as he mentally stripped Alice, Jenny and Nina of their clothes.

Alice's lips scarcely moved when she whispered in Jenny's ear, 'Man, this guy's a real fucking wanker.'

Jenny smiled at the leering Afghan and whispered back, 'Yeah, poor thing, when he dies he'll probably get reborn as a toilet seat.'

Alice and Jenny giggled wickedly. The immigration officer grinned at them, obviously delighted that the young women were apparently enjoying his company.

Rolling Thunder was in motion again. Raj was driving on the left hand side of the road for the first time since he'd left England. The highway narrowed and descended into a gorge. A large roadside notice declared that it was a punishable criminal offence to enter this stretch of road during the hours of darkness. Raj glanced at the dashboard clock. It was ten past two. When the bus passed under a huge cut stone gateway with turreted cannon emplacements, he looked up and caught a glimpse of a big black and white sign that said, THE KHYBER PASS WELCOMES YOU.

To the left of the two-lane asphalt road, where the only form of crash barriers that existed were white-painted boulders, a precipitous chasm was home to hollow rusting vehicle wrecks, semi-submerged in the swiftly flowing, mud-coloured Khyber River. Battleship-grey clouds drifted into dark brown crags, their outlines sticking up like pointed teeth on the exposed jawbone of a gigantic fossilized predator.

Angus and Murphy sat up in the bus's observation bubble, dizzy from the copious amounts of hashish they were smoking through a long-stemmed water pipe. Music was bubbling out of a small pair of stereophonic speakers. Their Satanic Majesties were playing '2000 Light Years From Home', one of The Stones' better attempts at going psychedelic and a perfect soundtrack for the alien landscape passing by outside.

The music phased and faded. Kettledrums rolled. Mick Jagger's voice whispered eerily, *It's so very lonely...*

Angus pointed in the direction of a distant, perforated cliff face. 'Hey, look at those caves up there. Do you think people live in them?'

'Where do you think the smoke's coming from?' enquired Murphy. 'Volcanoes?'

...you're two-thousand light years from home.

A loud high-pitched whine rose up from the engine compartment, located at the back of the bus.

Murphy asked, 'What the fuck's that?'

The bus was slowing down.

'I haven't the faintest,' replied Angus, cocking his head as he listened to a rough downshift of gears. 'It doesn't sound good. We better go and check out Captain Raj. You never know what's going to happen when he's behind the wheel with his Glasgow bus driver's hat on, telling everyone on board that he has everything under control.'

Murphy stood up and banged his head on the underside of the Perspex bubble. 'Ouch!' He rubbed the crown of his head and then said, 'Come on, man, let's go downstairs and see what's going on.'

Raj steered the bus on to a convenient strip of gravel and cut the engine. He applied the hand brake with his left foot and spoke over his shoulder when he heard his friends approach. 'I think a belt just broke.'

The girls watched from the windows as Angus, Murphy and Raj stepped outside, walked to the rear of the bus and unlocked the oblong, slatted aluminium hatch that gave access to the engine. Raj took a quick look inside, made a noise like he'd stood on a six-inch nail, turned and said, 'What a drag, man, the main fan belt is gone.'

Angus asked him, 'What do you mean *gone?*'

Raj shrugged. 'Disappeared.'

'Shit,' spat Murphy.

'We have a spare,' said Angus heading back inside to fetch the T-shaped key to unlock Rolling Thunder's storage holds.

An hour later they'd found everything – except a spare fan belt.

'Who the—?'

'Don't start,' cautioned Angus when he saw that Murphy was getting ready to blame everyone else but himself for the missing spare part.

'What now?' asked Raj, looking east in the general direction of Pakistan. 'Without a fan belt we're fucked. The engine will overheat in no time on this road. I've not been above third gear for the last ten kilometres.'

A truck roared by, its horn blasting. Displaced air shook the bus.

'Maybe we should head back along the road to see if we can find the broken belt,' suggested Murphy. 'It can't be more than a kilometre since it came off.'

'You hope,' remarked Angus.

Raj asked, 'Did you see that place we passed about ten minutes ago?'

'What place?' said Angus and Murphy in unison.

Raj replied, 'The big wooden shed that looked like it might be a garage.'

Murphy and Angus glanced questioningly at each other and then, without so much as a word, started walking back along the road. Fifteen minutes later, they found the broken belt by the wayside. Accompanied by the sound of the river rushing in the gorge, they continued walking for about an hour. Traffic was intermittent. When Angus stuck his thumb out, nobody stopped to give them a lift.

A bent-over Pashtun Methuselah, with a tumour the size of a cricket ball on his neck, was mounting a wobbly bicycle when the two Scotsmen showed up in front of what passed for a breakdown repair shop in the region. He seemed anxious to ride away, but when Murphy pointed to the broken rubber belt and waved a crisp ten-dollar note under his hawk-billed hooter, the old fellow liked the smell of it so much he let his bike clatter to the ground.

Murphy held his black leather wallet up and gave it a shake. 'Amazing how this stuff works, no matter where you are.'

Mumbling to himself, the Pashtun mechanic unlocked a riveted padlock and pushed a wire mesh gate to one side that wouldn't have kept a headless chicken out of his tin-roofed workshop. Quarter of an hour later, he emerged from the shadows. He held the fan belt aloft and exposed his pink gums in a toothless smile to show that he was pleased with a job well done. He'd pinned the broken belt's frayed ends together with a pair of industrial-sized, tempered steel staples.

'Well,' said Angus wearily, 'temporary at best, but if we're lucky it should take us out of the pass.'

Murphy patted the stoop-shouldered Pashtun on the back and then handed him the ten-dollar bill, which quickly disappeared into the baggy groin of the man's trousers, little more than dirty cotton rags.

'What is it with these old guys and their smelly drawers?' asked Murphy, flapping at the air in front of him.

The sun had vanished behind a bank of swiftly racing cloud, the atmosphere suddenly muggy and leaden as it filled with an electrical charge. A few drops of rain pattered on the workshop's corrugated tin roof. The Afghan started jabbering in Pashto while he pointed at the darkening sky, his hand shiny with black oil.

Murphy looked up and then turned to Angus. 'What the fuck's he on about?'

Angus scratched the back of his head and shrugged. 'The weather?'

Both the Scots turned and looked questioningly at the mechanic, signalling a communication breakdown. Stepping closer to them, the old man took hold of Angus's left wrist and tapped the face of his Timex watch. He let go of Angus's wrist and drew an oil-stained finger across the folds of his chicken skin throat. Then he walked over to his abandoned bicycle, bent over, pulled it upright, straddled the saddle and rolled away in the direction of Afghanistan. The bike began to gather momentum. The old mechanic's legs started to go up and down like pistons. He peddled well for a man of his years. Before he disappeared round a bend in the road, his bearded face looked back. He waved, shouted *'Allah-u-Akbar'* (God is great), and with that he was gone.

A thrush that had been warbling from a nearby bush fell silent.

'Ehm, Murphy.'

'What?'

'Something tells me we should not be hanging around in the Khyber Pass at this late hour of the afternoon.'

'I think you're right,' agreed Murphy, glancing up and down the deserted road. 'Let's get a fucking move on.'

During the time it took to jog back to the bus, the only vehicle that drove by was a rusty Land Rover. Minus doors and windows, it was spluttering like an internal combustion asthmatic and left behind an expanding trail of black diesel smoke.

Angus stopped to catch his breath and coughed when a wisp of oily smoke caught in his throat. He took in his surroundings. Deep blue shadows were emerging out of the gorge to ascend the mountains' steep slopes with unencumbered ease.

'Hey, Murphy.'

'What?'

'It's getting dark.'

'Your powers of observation amaze me.' Murphy, out of breath, was relieved to see the bus in the distance. 'Thank fuck,' he gasped.

A cold wind was blowing up from the gorge. The Kabul River's rumbling took on a more ominous note.

As they approached Raj, he shook his head, raised his arms in the air, shouted, 'Where the fuckin' hell have you two been?', and then lowered his arms. His tone softened. 'You've been gone for nearly three hours.'

Adopting the theatrical manner of a stage magician, Murphy whipped out the fan belt from behind his back and handed it over. *'Ta-raa!'* he exclaimed, bowing from the waist.

'Not bad at all,' said Raj, examining the thick rubber belt in the fading light. 'But it's going to be another story fitting it in the dark. I'll have to make a few adjustments. It's a bit shorter than it should be.'

'No problem,' said Angus, trying to keep the mood positive. 'I can rig up a couple of spotlights.'

An ancient Volvo bus rattled by with passengers hanging out of its glassless window frames. Its horn wailed in one long agonizing note, producing a sound like an air-raid siren. Jenny was nowhere in sight. Alice and Nina were standing around and staring up at the dark grey mountains like a pair of senile lost sheep.

'Come on girls, how about making yourselves useful?' suggested Murphy. 'I'm bloody well starving.'

The young women gave vacant smiles and disappeared inside the bus.

Soon, the smell of frying onions filled the damp evening air. Angus switched on a pair of twelve-volt spots that he'd wired to the batteries. Raj started to work on the engine with a large adjustable wrench, which gleamed brand new in the artificial light. Murphy leaned against the bus and began to roll a joint.

A few minutes later, the crack of a rifle shot echoed in the distance. A bullet whizzed through Rolling Thunder's windscreen, leaving a neat round hole surrounded by frosted Perspex. The bullet continued on its trajectory, ploughing through three inches of compressed synthetic fibre until it was brought to a halt by a tempered steel spring coiled inside the back of the hydraulic driver's seat. One adrenally elongated moment later, a second bullet took out the windscreen completely.

Inside the bus, Alice and Nina began screaming like they were being scalded to death. Frozen on the spot, the three Scotsmen stared at each other like hypnotized deer caught in the headlights of a fast approaching vehicle. Angus snapped out of it and pulled the spots' electrical cables off the batteries, plunging them into darkness.

'Eeeeegh!' Nina sounded as if she was trying to top Alice in an operatic screeching competition.

Murphy yelled out to them, 'Switch the fucking lights off!'

The bus's internal lights went out in the same moment that more shots were fired − *'Brrrrp!'* − from an automatic weapon. Angus caught a flash of flickering orange light, high up on a precipitous cliff on the other side of the gorge. Bullets buzzed in like angry lead hornets, perforating windows on both sides of the bus. The slugs ricocheted off rocks. Close enough to feel the breeze of its passage, a squashed bullet whanged over Angus's head and thudded into the centre of a super nova starburst painted on the side of the bus, where it left a small indentation.

The girls were still perfecting sound effects for a ghost-train when Murphy crept into the bus with Angus close behind.

'For fuck's sake, *shut up!*' shouted Murphy.

Angus could make out Alice's outline in the almost pitch darkness. She was kneeling beside Nina, who was jerking on the floor like a decked shark and whimpering. He noticed a strange metallic taste in his dry mouth – coppery, that of fear. He asked, 'Where's Jenny?' There was no response, just the Khyber River's thunderous roar rising up from the gorge. He squeezed past the girls to reach his sleeping compartment. He found Jenny under a blanket. She was fast asleep, oblivious to the chaos around her. He shook her awake.

'Wh…Wh…What the hell are you doing?' Jenny complained.

Pulling her down beside him on to the floor, he hissed in her ear, 'For Christ's sake, how the fuck can you sleep through this? We're being shot at.'

'Who…? What—?'

Before Jenny had a chance to say anything else, Angus bundled up some blankets and hauled her towards the door. When they stepped down on to the road automatic gunfire chattered out. They crouched as a hail of bullets splattered into stone about ten feet above their heads, showering them with falling gravel.

'C'mon!' It was Murphy's voice. 'We've got to move away from the bus.'

The six Scots crawled up the road and took shelter behind a pile of limestone boulders about a hundred metres from Rolling Thunder's shadowy form. Raj switched on an electric torch. 'For fuck's sake,' shouted Murphy, grabbing it out of his hand and clicking it off, 'what're you trying to do, get us all killed?'

Alice was the only one who'd had a near miss. A gash ran at an angle across her left cheek where a bullet had grazed her. The bottom of her left earlobe was dangling, nearly severed off. She was bleeding. The blood was reflecting like black paint in the gloom. *'Maaa! Ma!'* Terrified, she was crying for her mother. Nina had bashed her right eyebrow on a sharp edge, leaving a deep cut that would require stitches.

Raj did his bit by creeping back on to Rolling Thunder to collect a bottle of antiseptic and some bandages.

Angus turned to Jenny. She lay curled up like a lap dog at his side. Her right hand grasped her left bicep protectively. She was sound asleep.

Murphy peered at her and commented with impressive calm, 'Good old Jen, she won't let a few flying bullets disturb her dreams, now will she?'

Everyone giggled, helping relieve some of the tension. Their eyes had adjusted to the lack of light and they sat for a few moments gazing at each other. Alice and Nina had taken to using a lot of mascara in Kabul. They appeared to Angus like a pair of paranoid panda bears out on a midnight romp a long way from home.

Murphy asked, 'Raj, have you any idea where we are?'

Raj's reply cut through the gloom. 'The Khyber Pass.'

'I didn't think we were in Clydebank. I mean in relation to fucking civilization.'

'Oh…yeah…right…ehm…the pass is approximately fifty kilometres long and we've come about half way.'

'Oh, that's just fucking great,' said Murphy, chuckling. He was apparently thriving on the chaotic situation, as if it served no other purpose than to vaporize life's banalities and bring him to the place where he felt strongest – the present. 'That means we're in the middle of fuckin' black nowhere with the trigger-happy fuzzy-wuzzies using us for target practice.'

Angus grunted. 'Thus spoke MacMurphy, last of a long line of Glaswegian soothsayers.' Now that the gunfire had stopped, and the original shock of being shot at had worn off, he was beginning to feel more secure.

'Do you think they'll come down and murder us?' asked Raj, his neon-green eyes blinking like stroboscopes.

'No way, man,' answered Murphy, completely oblivious to the nervous breakdowns taking place around him. 'I reckon this is just early evening entertainment for the wild bunch before they get into a bit of serious goat shagging.'

'I…I…really hope you're right, Murph,' said Nina's timid voice from behind him, her arms hooked around his waist. 'I'm ab-ab-absolutely shitting myself, man.'

'M…Me…t-too, I want to go home,' stammered Alice, her soft Scottish lilt brittle with fear.

More bedding was retrieved from the bus along with one of the bottles of whisky saved for special occasions. A cork popped. Raj grinned in the darkness, the white of his teeth showing astral blue. He took a healthy swig from the bottle and then passed it to Angus. Liquid gurgled in the neck of the bottle as he gulped down a mouthful of whisky. He smacked his lips when the alcohol burnt a coarse welcome path down his throat then flushed all the way to his toes. 'Ahhh…just what Doctor MacFeelgood ordered,' he said, as the fiery liquid's heat coursed through his veins and helped him relax. The taste of whisky stirred a childhood memory about Iona and how his stepmother used to make him toddy when he caught a cold. He pushed the recollection from his mind by taking another shot of medicine and then another.

'Hey, pass the booze, man,' complained Nina.

Angus was hanging on to the bottle like a suckling infant. When he reluctantly passed it to Nina and Alice they knocked back shots of whisky in turn. They laughed nervously when Murphy shook the almost empty bottle and said in a posh Scottish accent, 'I say chums, who is responsible for this outrage?'

Angus lay on his back and stared up at the sky. Not a star could be seen. Jenny snuggled up against him. He inhaled deeply. The night smelled of damp stone, tar and diesel oil. Well, he thought, I was looking for adventure and now I've found it. He let out a sniggering laugh.

A match flared in cupped hands and then Murphy's voice came out of the murk. 'What the fuck are you sounding so happy about?'

'I was just thinking about what a great time I'm having,' answered Angus.

'Aye, right,' Raj chuckled. 'I'm going to send my maw a postcard tomorrow. *Pinned down by sniper fire in the Khyber Pass. Wish you were here. Lots of love. Your wandering son.*' Raj glanced over at Murphy, who was crouching in the darkness. 'Hey, man, is that a spliff you're hogging?'

'Yeah,' said Murphy, making an exaggerated sucking sound. 'Why? You want some?'

'Don't be daft,' replied Raj. 'Pass it over.'

A glowing red dot floated through the darkness. It hovered and brightened when Raj drew on the joint.

A voice cried out in the distance and was answered seconds later by the far-off yapping of a jackal. The sound echoed in the mountains before an eerie silence descended, complete except for the dense rumble rising from the gorge, where the churning Kabul River coursed over rocks and collided with boulders, following its inexorable easterly course towards Pakistan.

'Angus, Jenny, wakey, wakey.' Murphy shook the couple as they slept under dew-soaked blankets.

In the pre-dawn light Raj had installed the temporary fan belt. Minus half a dozen windows and her windscreen, Rolling Thunder was roadworthy again. Murphy had cleaned out shattered pieces of Perspex from the rubber-sealed window frames to avoid the danger posed by flying fragments. Alice and Nina, who hadn't slept a wink all night, had thrown together a sparse breakfast of hot coffee, fresh orange juice, bread and boiled eggs that were so hard they might have been white pebbles.

Everyone bundled up in coats and hats to ward off the cold air that rushed through the bus when it picked up speed. The wind made the bus's red tartan curtains flap and crack like whips.

The pass snaked up into the Safed Koh mountain range, where cotton-wool clouds lodged in craggy folds. On higher stretches, thick ground mist cut visibility down to less than ten metres.

A few kilometres later, vehicles with their headlights on, approaching from the opposite direction, began to emerge from the fog, sailing by too close for comfort. Raj was clenching the steering wheel so tight his hands looked like claws. His peaked bus driver's hat was pulled down tight on his head and he was wearing diver's goggles to protect his eyes from airborne insects.

Shrouded in mist, small flat-roofed villages began to appear. Wedged into gullies at the foot of crumbling eroded cliffs, the settlements seemed more like natural growths than things formed by man. Desolate yet ruggedly beautiful, the landscape would have been fascinating to the crew had it not been so cold. With almost no fat on her body to protect her from the rushing wind's penetrating chill, Jenny's teeth were chattering.

Eardrums crackled when the bus crawled up and over the Khyber Pass's highest point. On the river's opposite bank deserted railway tracks crossed cantilevered bridges and disappeared into deep tunnels. Raj drove past the turnoff for Landi Khotal. Everyone was crying out for a cup of something hot, but the small mud-walled town had something forbidding and uninviting about it. Known as a smuggler's haven, Landi Khotal was home to many of Pakistan's most successful drug dealers and well on its way to becoming one of the biggest heroin production centres in the world. Strangers were made most unwelcome there, the locals being suspicious of all outsiders, believing them to be foreign intelligence gathering agents, trying to locate the whereabouts of clandestine laboratories. With hundreds of millions of dollars at stake, paranoia ran high in the region, where the only law in evidence was that imposed by the end of a heavy calibre gun barrel.

Raj slowed the bus to a crawl as it approached an old fort, situated a hundred metres from the road. The stone fortress appeared to be in remarkably good condition, especially taking into consideration that it had stood for over a century in such a hostile environment. Sandstone in colour, parts of the fort's crenulated walls were highlighted in white. A wooden drawbridge's chains shone black as if they'd been coated with gloss paint the day before. The place appeared to be deserted.

In close proximity to the stone fort, a caravan of about two dozen heavily laden, two-humped Bactrian camels was emerging out of a valley. The beasts of burden were swaying from side to side and escorted by robed figures. The scene was timeless, ancient yet new, fresh like the sun's rays that strafed through the uniform grey cloud ceiling above the procession, bathing it in a stark unearthly light.

The sun's warmth began to disperse the clouds, lifting the curtains on a vast panorama to the north. Like searchlights breaking into a world of grey shadows, diagonal sunbeams brought colour to the high ridges of range upon range of mountains stretching off into a continuously expanding horizon. When a shaft of sunlight caressed a snow-white mountaintop, the peaks glowed with a fiery orange light, as if ignited by the sun's passion.

Angus sat beside his shivering girlfriend and gazed out of the window as an invisible, man-made borderline was crossed and Afghanistan turned into Pakistan.

With a squealing of damp brake pads, Rolling Thunder ground to a halt outside of a frontier checkpoint surrounded by split sandbags that were oozing yellow, diarrhoea-like gunk. Khaki-uniformed Pakistani border guards, wearing dark red berets adorned with silver badges, stood by a smoking brazier warming their hands. Their backs were turned to the road, where a line of six-wheeled Bedford petrol tankers was filtering by on its way into the pass.

A sergeant, with three golden stripes sewn on to the right arm of his olive green sweater, marched towards the bus. Gravel crunched under his spit 'n' polish boot soles and his tight black leather belt creaked from the weight of his bulging belly. His stiff mechanical movements made him look like some kind of cartoon character. Brandishing a swagger stick and speaking pukka English, delivered in a clipped military-style manner, he soon made it clear that he was none too happy to see a windowless bus full of hippies emerging out of the Khyber Pass at this early hour of the morning. Well-informed, he knew where the bus had spent the night. Raj watched his fisheye reflection in the sergeant's mirrored sunglasses as he tried to explain what had befallen them. The belligerent man would hear none of it. Instead, he blasted Raj with his garlic breath as he yammered about impounding the bus and locking the longhaired lawbreakers up in his frontier post to teach them a lesson.

Now that the travellers were on the edge of the Indian sub-continent, a powerful religious movement was beginning to make its presence felt. The cantankerous sergeant was the first disciple who bowed to the will of Lord Bakshish that the Scots had encountered since their run-in with the crooked border official in Turkey. Although, it must be said, bureaucratic devotees all over the world venerate the God of Corruption, whose power is rooted in the abuse of office for profit and has the sanction of an ancient custom which has become a way of life. At first, the sergeant pretended to be morally upright, a standard ploy used by the crooked deity's converts. Murphy produced a bottle of whisky. The sergeant's eyes lit up. In that parched region a bottle of Chivas Regal could grease the thirsty hinges of most doors. With that and a little lubricant in the form of a hundred dollar bill, the gate leading into the country swung open without a squeak.

'Welcome to Pakistan,' said the sergeant, acting as though his performance up until that point had been nothing more than a ridiculous practical joke. He gave a salute as the bus drove away, unable to suppress a quick tight smile that passed under his well-oiled handlebar moustache.

Angus sighed with relief. Apart from him, everyone else on board had been so caught up in the bribery scenario that they'd forgotten they were sitting on top of half a metric ton of very illegal hashish.

Mother Nature soon made it clear that borderlines were a man-made concept that was alien to her. The mountains in Pakistan looked much the same as the ones in Afghanistan. Supple long-stemmed trees grew out of cracks in giant-sized boulders perched at impossible angles on the steep inclines of high-sided gorges with rocky moraine piled high at their feet.

Murphy called to Angus, 'Hey, man, check this lot out. Those sullen-faced shite-bags look like they'd slit your throat for a penny.' He nodded towards a line of scowling, fair-skinned Afridis as the bus edged past them on a congested stretch of road. They were carrying Russian-made Mozin-Nagant carbines, a bolt-action rifle known for its ruggedness. The ectomorphic tribesmen were remarkably tall and had cruel faces lined by aggression and cunning. They wore exceptionally large cotton turbans on their heads and cartridge belts, filled with finger-length bullets, strapped across their narrow chests. Some walked barefoot, while others wore boots with more holes than leather. They were making their way along the roadside, leading a coffle of moth-eaten pack mules laden with wooden crates. The animals flared nostrils had been cut to increase their oxygen intake when crossing high-altitude passes where the air was thin. Following behind, at a respectful distance, were heavy-footed women in voluminous, russet-coloured dresses. Wobbling layers of fat hung pendulously from their pale faces. Their thick black hair was pleated and beaded with lapis lazuli.

All of the women were obese. In a skinny society where food was scarce they represented the ideal of feminine beauty. They were gathering mule droppings to be used as cooking fuel. The dung was flattened into patties and then deposited in woven baskets slung over their backs.

Murphy was right in his observation. Afridis are consummate smugglers who are taught from an early age to trust no one, including close family members, and are notoriously treacherous. As lean and mean as the world they inhabit, Afridi warriors have a vindictive nature and are crack shots who rank alongside the most ferocious fighters in the world.

The highway began to descend into more level terrain. Raj slowed the bus down to a snail's pace when fording sections of the road that were flooded. Flowing sheets of gurgling, reflective water ran over the asphalt on its way to join the main river in the valley below. Swollen by cataracts rushing down from the mountains, many of the tributaries that normally flowed through conduits had burst free to cover whole sections of low-lying countryside. Some short sections of the highway had been completely washed away, leaving the bus to trundle over a road surface as bumpy as a riverbed.

PESHAWAR 10 MILES, declared a road sign peppered with rusting bullet holes. Tall poplar trees began to line the highway. Their long finger-like branches pointed skywards and were covered in shiny, grey-green leaves that shook and whispered in the breeze, reflecting the sunlight as if they were made of beaten tin. Apple orchards in full bloom surrounded stumpy, oblong stone houses rendered in dark red mud. With only arrow-slits for windows, these thick-walled cuboid structures dotted a lawless frontier land where living behind solid defences had proven over time to be the best way to survive.

Bullock carts loaded with neatly bound stacks of cordwood held up the flow of traffic as rural scenes gave way to Third World urbanization. In an angular tangle that resembled giant spiders' geometric webs, overhead electric and telephone cables criss-crossed the sky. The grating sounds of mechanized society rushed into the bus, carried on air warmer than that of the high altitude mountain road that had been left behind.

Angus observed his fellow passengers. Nina sat staring into space. Her eyes were large from unfinished crying. She appeared to him like a small, frightened creature, alone and a long way from home. Her skin was ashen, her expression numb. There was a deep cut clogged with congealed blood over her swollen right eyebrow. She was chewing on a broken fingernail.

'Hey, Nina, are you all right?' Angus asked her.

She nodded absently and returned to biting on her nail.

He turned his head to look at Alice. The wind rushing through the bus was blowing her black hair away from her pallid face. Her right cheek had a bloodstained bandage covering it. Her damaged ear lobe was exposed and caked with dry blood. In a state of delayed shock she gazed over at Angus with eyes puffy from crying. There was a bewildered look on her face, as if she'd just listened to Swahili recorded backwards at high speed and been asked for a translation by a Chinaman. Her lips skinned back in an uneasy smile, which looked to Angus like a silent scream.

Murphy, the Hashisheen, was toking on a joint and staring out of a window frame with an air of detached curiosity. He immediately sensed eyes upon him, turned to face Angus, cocked his right eyebrow, shot him a flinty-eyed glance and returned his attention to the scene passing by outside.

Wrapped up in a tartan woollen blanket, Jenny was asleep and leaning into Angus's side. Her face was so pale the dark mole below her right eye stood out like a spot of black ink on a sheet of white paper. Angus eased himself away from her, rose to his feet and walked to the front of the bus.

When he reached Raj, he put a hand on his shoulder. Raj looked away from the road for three seconds, glanced up at him and smiled wearily. He returned his attention to the road, spun the steering wheel and cursed under his breath at the erratically driven car ahead that had stopped in front of him for no apparent reason. He pushed the brake and clutch pedals to the floor and Angus pitched forward. Upon regaining his balance, Angus studied his friend's face in the large, rear-view mirror. Raj had taken off the diver's goggles and replaced them with a pair of round-rimmed sunglasses that were perched precariously on the end of his nose. Exhaustion was registered in the deep creases around his bloodshot eyes. His lank jet-black hair hung down in greasy strands on both sides of his face, lending him the appearance of an intellectual Druid with a strong suntan.

'How's it going?' Angus asked.

'I'll be glad to get the girls to a doctor. Apart from that, I'm dreaming of a hot bath and clean cotton sheets.' Raj tooted the horn at a crowd of cheering schoolchildren in navy blue uniforms and said over his shoulder, 'How about you?'

'I feel a bit burnt out,' answered Angus. He pointed to a huge pile of rubbish that was smouldering by the roadside. 'Man, look at the state of this place. It's filthy.' The bus was entering Peshawar's congested downtown area. The streets were chock-a-block with every form of wheeled transport invented by man. 'If Herat looked like the Wild West, this has got to be the Wild, Wild West.'

'Yeah, I see what you mean.' Raj waved to a couple of kids who were standing on a street corner and shooting at the bus with their fingers. 'There's definitely a lawless vibe about the place. Looks like some kind of oriental Dodge City, where the cowboys wear ten-gallon turbans and anything's yours if you can come up with a fistful of dollars.'

'I hope so,' commented Angus. 'Let's see if we can get our hands on a new windscreen to start with.'

Raj nodded and said, 'You don't miss your windscreen till the wind's blowing in, right?'

'That's right, pal. *Hey!*' Angus pointed towards a three-storied, concrete building with a red neon sign outside displaying the words 'Hotel Kentarab'. 'Pull in over there. That looks like a decent enough place to spend a few nights in.'

Raj parked the bus beside a ruptured pavement, which looked like it had been pushed up by an earthquake to form a military style obstacle course. Angus negotiated the broken paving slabs and entered the hotel. He returned a few minutes later and said to Raj, 'It's cheap and cheerful with nice clean rooms.'

Raj asked, 'Do the rooms have baths?'

'All modern conveniences, sahib,' replied Angus, affecting an Indian accent. 'We will be having hot and cold running water, with very nice sit down toilet to be placing your most holy bum upon.'

As it was to turn out, it was a good thing they checked into a comfortable hotel. Rolling Thunder and her crew were destined to spend a lot more time than a few days in Peshawar.

12

TRANSCENDENTAL DRIFT

Cambodia

A raindrop splattered against my forehead. I opened my eyes, half-expecting to see camels being led along the shoreline by turbaned Pashtun tribesmen, rifles slung over their shoulders. The beach was deserted.

I looked up. Heavy rain clouds were being blown in from the sea. They loomed overhead like vaporous barges, preparing to dump their wet cargo on the parched land.

I gazed at the sea, no longer illuminated by the moon. Earlier in the evening, squid boats had lit up the horizon with halogen floodlights. They were no longer visible. Strange, I thought, as the humid atmosphere pressed against my face.

Without moving her head, my mongrel friend opened one eye, blinked and whined. Her nostrils flared and an ear flipped up as she sensed a change in barometric pressure. She stood, staggered, stretched her legs, gave herself a head-to-tail shake and, without so much as a glance to acknowledge my presence, walked off along the beach.

'Hey! Where are you going, girl?' I called after her. 'You can't leave me here on my own.'

The dog turned, let out a short, sharp bark of farewell and continued on her way. I tried whistling, but to no avail. Surrounded by an air of canine capriciousness, the bitch kept walking away from me like a deserting lover.

Raindrops the size of marbles began to fall, throwing up little craters in the sand. A strong wind, blowing in off the sea, set off an alarm bell in my mind. A squall was brewing. The sea was rising. It had already come up on to the beach far enough to repossess my watch, now no longer visible. I tried to recall how high the tide had risen on previous evenings and felt certain it had never come up as far. A roll of surf crashed on to the beach. Panic's cold grip tightened around my heart and made it pound fearfully. Shit! I cursed silently. What the bloody hell will happen if the sea reaches me?

Ten minutes later, streaks of lightning ripped across the sky, followed intermittently by booming thunderclaps, so loud their sonic impact rattled my eardrums. The rain strengthened and turned into a torrential downpour. I was soaked to the skin.

Cold and lonely, I fell into a well of self-pity and began to weep. I sat in the gloom, wondering what I'd done to deserve such a miserable fate. Salty tears ran down my cheeks into the corners of my mouth. Incidents from my past sprang into my mind. I felt an ache in the knuckles of my right hand, as if the pain still lingered with the memory, when I saw myself breaking my perverted foster father's jaw with a knockout punch. *Shut up, you stupid bitch!* I cringed when I recalled my angry voice, shouting at Jean when her nagging became too incessant for me to bear. My heart throbbed faster at the thought of smacking my eldest daughter on the backside with a hairbrush, because she'd covered our pet Corgi dog with red spray-paint and then drowned the poor animal in the washing machine – trying to clean it before mummy came home from the gym. I felt guilty about the time I'd hurled abuse at my business partner back in Oban, when our submission to build a town council housing scheme was rejected. I remembered reacting in an extremely aggressive manner towards Angus when he knocked me into a mindless state by slapping me on the face and a dozen other occasions when I'd lost my temper. When you think you might die at any given moment there still seems to be enough time to regret your mistakes, but even combined the effects of those incidents did not equate a reason for me to be riding through hell on top of a landmine in the pouring rain.

I thought about Lara, Angus's wife, and how I'd derived great pleasure from being in her company. My twin brother lived with such intensity that I sometimes found him contradictory and perplexing to be with, whereas Lara helped me to relax and accept myself.

I remembered, in great detail, events that had taken place on a wonderful day, two months earlier, in Sri Lanka, on December 12, 2004. It was the day Angus had invited me, Jean and Lara to the large coastal town of Galle for a special lunch to celebrate our fifty-third birthday.

Built by the Dutch in colonial times, Galle's fort area is an oasis of calm in relation to the hustle and bustle that accompanies life in the scruffy new town's commercial district. In recent years, many of the old buildings in the Galle Fort vicinity have been purchased by foreign investors and converted into either boutique hotels or private residences. The birthday lunch had taken place in the newly opened Galle Fort Hotel, a luxurious location by any standard.

It was Angus's custom to give rather than receive presents on his birthday. When we'd finished our five-course meal, he popped the cork from the third bottle of Dom Perignon that afternoon and presented Jean and I with a pair of first-class, round-trip tickets to Cambodia. Brimming with champagne, fluted glasses were raised in a toast.

By the time we wobbled out of the air-conditioned hotel, all four of us were quite drunk. Outside, in the narrow cobbled street, it was sweltering. Angus led Jean into a nearby jeweller's shop to buy her a gift. This left Lara and I with some time on our hands. We decided to go for a digestive stroll.

'Good afternoon, madam,' called a tall, gaunt man from the shadows of a small teashop that was shaded by a brown canvas awning.

'Oh, hullo, Faisal,' said Lara, glancing up from tugging at the creases in her forest-green cotton dress. She straightened her floppy straw hat and enquired, 'How are you today?'

'I'm not too bad. Can I invite you and your companion in for a glass of ice-cold ginger beer?'

'Oh, I'm sorry,' she said, turning towards me. 'Hamish, let me introduce you to a very dear friend of mine, Faisal.'

Dressed in a spotless white robe, prayer cap and scuffed tennis shoes, Faisal stepped out into the street. He raised his left hand to shade his eyes, offered his right to me and said, 'I'm very pleased to make your acquaintance. I'm in no doubt that you are Master Angus's twin brother. Am I correct?'

'Yes…yes I am, but how did you know?'

Faisal ignored my question and said, 'Please be so kind as to grace my humble premises.' He bowed his head and extended an arm towards his teashop. 'There will be no charge.'

I was struck by the man's genuine humility. There was something childlike and playful about him. This was counterbalanced by a mature glow in his tender brown eyes which spoke of hard-gained wisdom. I felt inexplicably drawn to him, as if Faisal were a glowing sun and I a shadow-filled planet in need of light.

'No you don't,' protested Lara, grabbing my elbow as I stepped towards the teashop's doorway. She then looked at Faisal and said, 'We drank way too much champagne this afternoon and we're going for a walk. I'm sorry. It will have to be some other time.'

Faisal chuckled. 'Ah, Lara, I almost had Mister Hamish here charmed and now you've broken my spell.' He smiled bashfully at her. 'You know me. I always enjoy a good chat.'

'Yes, I'm very much aware of that and that's why we're not going to sit down with you. This is the first time in a week that I've had Hamish to myself and you're not going to steal him from me.'

'Very well then, as you wish,' said Faisal, feigning disappointment. He tilted his narrow head and studied his long fingernails. 'Besides, it will soon be time to go to the mosque for *Salat-al-Asar*, late afternoon prayer. I must wash my face and hands.' He glanced at his black plastic wristwatch. 'Time has a way of running away with itself and when it does it waits for no man. Meanwhile, the Compassionate One waits all eternity for us, his children, to return to his infinite heart. And on that note, I bid you both good afternoon.' Faisal gave a curt bow, turned and quickly disappeared into his teashop.

Arm in arm, Lara and I continued walking slowly along the deserted street.

I remarked, 'What a charming fellow.'

'He is indeed,' she agreed. 'Faisal always succeeds in making me feel that most of the world's Muslims are being judged unfairly in the West, because of the scare-mongering that fuels the war on terror. Here in Galle the Muslim community is well-respected. Like most people, they just want to be—'

'Left in peace and get on with their lives?' I said, cutting her off.

'How did you know I was going to say that?' she asked.

'That's what nearly everyone says these days,' I replied.

Lara let go of my arm, looked at me and asked, 'Do they?'

'Of course *they* do,' I said, 'but most people also know that Islamic extremists would be overjoyed to see the West go up in flames.'

'Let's not get into that,' suggested Lara, squeezing my arm. 'And let's not forget that one man's terrorist is another man's—'

I butted in again by finishing her sentence. 'Freedom fighter? But that's also a—'

It was Lara's turn to cut me off. 'There is no *but*,' she said, her voice sounding a little strained. 'Cliché or not, it's true. Leave it at that.'

I did.

A V-shaped sweat stain had appeared on the front of my short-sleeved, blue nylon shirt by the time Lara and I reached Galle Fort's grass-covered western sea wall. We sat down on a wooden bench, the green gloss paint on its slats cracked and peeling. The bench was shaded by a tall eucalyptus tree, the fragrance of which reminded me of Vicks VapoRub. For a while we sat looking out past the palm-encircled Galle lighthouse, sentinel of a wide bay whose distant shore's most outstanding landmark is the twenty-metre-high Peace Pagoda, a pure-white, circular, Buddhist shrine.

A pleasant sea breeze brought freshness to the humid air. The situation would have been perfect had it not been for one thing – I was in the midst of experiencing an unexpected bout of jealousy. When Angus walked off with Jean, he'd had his arm wrapped tightly around her slim waist. More than a little tipsy from drinking a lot of champagne, she had giggled like a happy teenager by my brother's side. Not entirely immune to the effects produced by the alcohol myself, I began to settle into a gloomy mood. Lara sensed this and turned to face me.

'That's really not necessary, you know.'

'What isn't?' I asked, a little uncomfortable in my skin.

'You feeling resentful, because Jean was obviously enjoying the attention Angus was paying her,' answered Lara, attempting to soothe and cajole me with the softness of her voice.

The highly developed sense of intuition that both Angus and Lara often demonstrated still, at times, caught me by surprise. I found this ability easier to accept in Lara. Had it been my brother putting me on the spot, my defences would have shot up like a porcupine's quills.

'I'm sorry,' I said. 'It's just that Jean never laughs like that with me, no matter how hard I try to please her.'

Lara gave a gentle knowing chuckle. There was a hint of resignation in her voice when she said, 'Don't let it worry you. It happens to everyone…me included. Jealousy is an issue most couples have to deal with in one form or another. Once you understand that the root of jealousy is primarily grounded in comparison, you'll also realize that there's no need to compare, because every person is unique.' She tilted her head, smiled at me and concluded, 'Even if it happens, as in your case, that you have a twin.'

I tried to protest. 'But I don't—'

'No!' she objected. 'I'm sorry to cut you short, but I won't have you make a fool of yourself by denying the fact that you often match yourself up against your brother.'

The truth made itself evident by delivering an empty feeling to my full stomach. 'It's true,' I confessed.

'That's the spirit,' she said, patting my left shoulder in a comforting gesture. 'In all of our relationships with people, but most especially with our partners, it's important not to take them for granted. I've made it one of my personal disciplines to view Angus in a new light every day because I know that if I don't, it won't be long until the rot sets in.'

'Yes,' I agreed, 'I know what you mean.'

'Relationship karma is what I call it.'

'*Karma,*' I echoed, the word said in such a way that it indicated I was unaccustomed to using it. 'Angus has spoken to me about cause and effect. Do you really believe it's true that you reap what you sow?'

'I don't know if *believe* is the right word, but it will do,' she replied. 'Karma is like throwing a stone in a pond. The ripples spread out, reach the water's edge and bounce back to the spot from where they originated.'

I ran a hand over the bald patch on the crown of my head. 'I can't believe it's that simple.'

'Don't think too much about it,' she advised. 'In the middle of the night when you're curled up tight, it will come to you.' Lara laughed softly and I remembered the long-forgotten John Hiatt song that she'd stolen that line from. Her eyes looked past my face when she noticed a shabbily dressed woman heading towards us. 'Oh, oh,' she said in a voice that was almost a whisper, 'here comes God dressed up in one of his favourite disguises.'

When the skinny beggar saw that she'd been spotted, she raised a grimy hand with dirt-caked fingernails to her open mouth. Malnutrition had shrunk her dental arch and left her with two rows of buckled teeth. There was a tiny infant wrapped in the folds of her faded brown sari. The woman stood in front of us as though bewildered as to how she'd come to be there.

Lara said, 'Move over.'

I did as requested and she gestured with her hands for the impoverished mother to sit down between us. A painful smile came to the woman's cracked lips and, after a half-hearted protest, she complied.

Her warm body smelled of baby puke. I shifted uncomfortably towards the edge of the bench and sat with my legs crossed and arms folded. I focused my attention on a nearby seagull. Yellow-beaked and yellow-eyed with grey and white plumage, the big gull was puffing up its feathery chest and waddling about like a pompous five-star general inspecting his troops. Unnerved by a youngster chasing a red ball, the seabird squawked and took to the air.

I turned my head when a colicky cry arose from within the folds of the beggar's tattered sari. Lara spoke a few words of Sinhalese. The woman nodded and then handed over her squealing infant, its tiny light brown hands clenched in fists. Once in her arms, Lara gently rocked the crying baby to soothe it into sleep. Soon, Lara and the women were engaged in a lively conversation, the contents of which were lost to my ears because I didn't understand a word of the rapidly spoken language. I looked on as they began giggling like old friends in the midst of amusing reminiscences about their adolescent escapades.

Lara returned the sleeping baby to its mother's waiting arms, rummaged in her small leather shoulder bag and then produced a tight roll of hundred-rupee notes, bound with a thick rubber band. She handed the money over to the beggar.

'Ahooogh!' The woman gasped as if suffering a heart attack. Tears squirted out of her eyes.

Lara placed a reassuring arm around the poor soul's heaving shoulders, her fragile frame wracked by sobs. It took the distraught woman a few moments to compose herself enough to dry her eyes with a corner of her threadbare garment and then stand up. Clutching the baby to her breast, she bent down, mumbled and touched Lara's sandaled feet and then mine. There was a half-astonished, half-grateful smile on her dry lips. She paused to take a lingering look into Lara's eyes before hurrying off, a lot more energetically then when she'd first shuffled up to us, employing the tired gait of the destitute.

I turned to Lara and found myself captivated by her physical appearance. I'm not quite sure why, but I felt like a young lad on his first date. There was something eternally youthful in her face that I knew was born of her positive spirit. How different she is from Jean, I thought, engaging her eyes for a moment.

I looked away when a fishing boat, returning to port, hooted its horn as it chugged by the lighthouse on the corner of the harbour wall. Hopeful gulls wheeled and cried in the air, eager for a free meal cast away by the fishermen, busy on deck sorting through the day's catch.

For some time we sat sharing an amicable silence which, as far as I was concerned, barely extended past the thin veneer of the superficial – inquisitive thoughts were scurrying around in my mind. I was waiting impatiently to ask a question, which I soon blurted out. 'Do you think giving that poor creature a lot of money will bring you good karma?'

As soon as I said it I knew I'd committed a major faux pas.

Lara was visibly shocked by my query. 'For goodness sake, no, I don't,' she said, shaking her head as if trying to dispel my question from her mind. 'I see it as unfortunate that many Westerners, who've lived in the East for a long time, become inured to the beggars' plight to the extent that they ignore it. I feel blessed that I still recognize the personal needs of the poor and I wish it to remain so.'

A burst of loud rock music caught her attention and she shifted position on the bench to see where it was coming from.

One man washed on an empty beach... On the street behind, a Toyota pick-up rattled and hummed slowly by with U2's 'Pride' blaring out of its open windows.

Lara chuckled. 'Perfect timing,' she said. 'That's one of my favourite songs.' She turned away from the street. 'Whatever way one looks at it, the greatest moral challenge that faces today's rich and educated is the elimination of extreme poverty. In these times of plenty it's a collective disgrace that anyone should have to beg in order to survive.'

In the name of love... Bono called out and the Edge's staccato guitar echoed.

I kept my voice low and respectful. 'I'm sorry. It's just...it's just that I thought that karma was—'

'Listen,' she said, interrupting me, 'karma is created by the mind, which in turn is conditioned by the past and it is this mechanical process that compels you to repeatedly re-enact the past. If one enters into the realization that one is not really doing anything at all in life, that life is simply being lived through you, that your spirit is a pure witness separate from the mind-body complex that acquires and creates karma, then my dear friend, you are free of karma.'

I had no idea what she was talking about and found that my lack of understanding was making me nervous. I felt like smoking a cigarette. Out of respect for Lara, who like my wife detested the habit, I suppressed my craving. I suspected Lara could see my discomfort with the situation but for reasons of her own she chose to remain silent.

I tried to approach the law of give and take from a more familiar standpoint, that of my brother. 'Angus said he never gives money directly to poor people on the street, because he thinks that kind of charity simply perpetuates the poverty it aims to eradicate.'

Lara looked out to sea and thought about this for a moment before responding. 'I'm aware of that, but that's just one of many points he and I choose to differ on. Angus believes that the poor need inspiration – not handouts. He also believes that becoming rich is the best way to help them. Sometimes I suspect he's right. Anyway, I'm sure he's told you about the free clinics he founded.'

'Yes, he has,' I confirmed.

She smiled wryly. 'Personally, I still believe in giving to beggars on the street, even though Angus thinks it only helps them forget about their plight for an hour or two.'

I could not resist fingering my cigarette packet.

'Go ahead and smoke,' said Lara. 'As long as we're outside, it doesn't bother me.'

I quickly placed a Marlboro Light in my mouth without lighting it and remarked, 'I think what you gave that poor woman will do a lot more than help her forget about her problems for a couple of hours.'

She nodded in agreement. 'Yes, I'm sure it will. But, perhaps more importantly, it's also the love and respect I gave her as a fellow human being that will help her on her difficult journey through life, not only the money. The more I learn to give, the more thankful I am for learning life's true arithmetic. One plus one makes one, if you catch my transcendental drift.'

I did. She'd finally gotten through to me. 'You know...' I tried to keep my voice steady, but was not very successful because I felt deeply moved by her words. 'I think that you...that you have a wonderful attitude.'

'Good of you to say so,' she said, her voice playful, her face impassive. 'One of the biggest problems existing in the world today is that most people have forgotten the language of the giver. Those who do not recognize how important it is to be generous in life are, in a way, already dead inside and it's only a matter of time until their body will follow them. I feel grateful whenever life presents me with an opportunity to give, because it lets me know directly that I am alive and moving in the current of life.'

I was captivated by the singsong sound of her voice and the wonderful sentiments carried upon it. She spoke with a lilting Irish accent that rounded her words, making them roll into a melodious flow. I didn't want her to stop speaking because I felt that I was close to understanding something important. I edged closer to her on the bench, my mind busy trying to come up with an interesting theme that would keep her talking.

'I'm still not clear on this karma business,' I said, shaking my head and crinkling my brow dramatically. 'Could you shed a little more light on it for me?'

She gave me a curious glance and then her intelligent eyes, green like the patina of old bronze, shifted to the right as she thought about her answer before giving it. 'The theory of karma is vague at best, but it does teach responsibility and definitely helps when it comes to rising above man's animal-like behavioural tendencies. But then again, Buddha is reported to have said that trying to understand the workings of karma is impossible, even going so far as to declare it one of the 'Four Imponderables'. So maybe it's a good idea not to think too—'

'What are the other three?' I asked.

She put a hand to her mouth, hiccupped and then answered, 'I haven't the faintest idea.'

'Oops...sorry to interrupt your line of thought,' I apologised. 'What were you saying?'

'Eh...ehm...shit! I've forgotten.' Lara took off her straw hat and set it in her lap. 'Got it!' She nodded thoughtfully. 'The concept of karma is one of the most potent controllers of human behaviour this world has ever known. Religious power brokers and priests installed the fear of divine retribution into people's hearts to make them easier to manipulate. Spiritual remedies to cure the effects of bad karma have always been a part of organized religion.' She adopted a stern and heavily affected voice. 'Donate generously to the house of God and all of your sins shall be forgiven.' Lara snorted derisively and her tone became scornful. 'People have been brainwashed into believing that sort of bullshit for centuries.'

'Yes,' I agreed with a chuckle, 'I was never much of a churchgoer myself. But not so long ago you would have been burnt at the stake for saying such things.'

She sniggered. 'Well I'm sure I'd have given the Inquisition a run for their money.'

'Maybe you did,' I said, 'in a past life.'

'Perhaps,' she said.

I raised an inquisitive eyebrow. 'Do you really believe in reincarnation?'

Her face was creased by a broad smile, as if I had asked precisely the question she was most eager to answer. 'I was wondering how long it would take you to get around to asking me that. My answer is yes, but not in the way that you understand it.'

'Really?' I said. 'I'm not even sure what I understand about it myself.'

'I'll tell you then. You think that reincarnation means that when you die your personality survives and is reborn into another body.'

'Yes...yes, Lara, you're right. I...I thought that's what reincarnation was. Am I mistaken?'

'The way I see it,' she said, 'the personality doesn't even survive while we are alive, because we are not one but many. I am not the same person that I was yesterday and neither are you. So, taking that into account, which one of those shifting personalities will live on when we die? The child, the youth, the middle-aged or the old person on the verge of senility, which one will it be? I don't think it is any of them because it is not personality but rather unfulfilled desires that supply the energy for a new person that seeks a body to be reborn in. I'm not saying the same person dies and is reborn. I'm saying that residual memories, unfulfilled desires, fears and addictions do.'

'Addictions?' I repeated questioningly, fingering my packet of cigarettes. 'How can addictions be born into a body?'

'Easily,' answered Lara. 'Imagination is the greatest magician. Just as a dream can reproduce waking states, so too can the after-death state replicate such experiences. If you were addicted to substances like tobacco while alive, the craving for tobacco will live on after you are dead.' She paused and looked into my eyes. 'I just thought of something.'

'What?' I asked.

'It might be a good idea for you to quit smoking.' She winked at me and then continued. 'Being identified with the body creates new desires and hence what the Buddhists and Hindus call The Wheel of Life and Death keeps turning round and round until the mechanism of bondage is clearly seen.' She took hold of her straw hat and began feeding the woven brim through her fingers. 'A person who wakes up from the dream of life and death sees that up until that point they have never arrived anywhere, sees – like a mouse on a treadmill – that they've been constantly running on the spot.'

'Jesus!' I exclaimed. 'This is starting to sound like a bloody nightmare.'

'Well,' she remarked, 'I daresay it is, if you're living in a war zone, or holding a newborn baby in your hands that is dying from malnutrition. Nevertheless, I ask you, does it feel to you like you're living in a nightmare?'

I looked around. The late afternoon light added a surreal quality to the scene. Nearby, a small group of elderly men were sitting in a loose circle on the grass. They laughed together at a shared joke. A young couple strolled by, the breeze ruffling the woman's canary yellow saree. They were watching a toddler in front of them pedal a blue plastic tricycle. Their faces beamed with parental adoration. Over by the ramparts, two little boys and a girl in a pink dress were playing marbles on a patch of sand. The children's high-pitched voices were carried to my ears on a gust of wind. They were arguing, yet the sound affected me like soothing music. I glanced at Lara. She smiled enigmatically. Her eyes shone like polished emeralds and I was once again struck by her grace and charm.

I answered her question. 'No, it doesn't feel at all like I'm living in a nightmare. In fact…in fact, it feels to me like I'm in heaven.' As soon as the words left my mouth everything changed. Suddenly, I felt ashamed – of what I did not know. The presence of this inexplicable and entirely unexpected feeling in my chest prompted me to ask, 'Are you sure that we won't one day be judged for our actions in the future?'

'Yes, I am,' she replied, looking at me curiously, 'because it would be like a never-ending trial in the Supreme Court and not even God would have the patience for that. The only yardstick that will ever be used to measure our spiritual progress is the extent of our ability to love. That is why there is nothing more important than knowing how to give and receive love.' She looked up and pointed to a buzzard coasting on a thermal. 'When that bird took off and flew high in the sky its shadow disappeared. That doesn't mean the shadow no longer exists, because when the bird lands its shadow will reappear and be just as distinct as it was before. In much the same way, the repercussions from our actions may not always be visible but that does not mean that they are not there and accompanying us through life. This is why it is said that to know what you've done in the past, look at what you are now. If you want to know where you are going to be born next, look at what you are doing now. You see how it always comes back to this moment?'

I nodded absently, my mind preoccupied with joining the existential dots.

Lara took one look at the puzzled expression on my face and let out a spluttering laugh. There was something in her laughter that unsettled me and spurred my imagination to produce a bizarre fantasy – about Angus and my wife – that was without doubt based in my insecurity in regards to Jean's fidelity.

Like Lara and I, Angus and Jean were also in the midst of a discussion, although their topic was based on a far more down-to-earth matter. They'd spent almost two hours in the jeweller's shop. In the end it had been a case of Jean choosing between two equally desirable adornments: a string of natural pearls or a solid gold necklace with a jewel-studded pendant. She went for the latter, thinking that it better suited her long black hair and tanned skin. The fact that it was four times more expensive than the pearls had also influenced her decision.

They stood on the concrete pavement facing each other.

'No way. I won't do it.' Angus's voice was playful but firm.

'Och, come on. What harm will it do?' Jean pointed. 'Look, there's a nice wee hotel over there. It would only take half an hour.' She paused for a moment, smiled seductively and then said, 'An hour would be better.'

'It's out of the question. There's no way I'd cheat on my wife or do that to my brother. For crying out loud, it's our birthday.'

'I know that, and that's why I want to give you something special.' She reached forward and locked her hands behind his neck. 'You wouldn't need to worry about it.' She pulled his head towards her face. 'I know all about discretion.' She sighed. 'God knows, I've been practising it for long enough.'

He looked into the dark pools of her sultry eyes and had to admit to himself that he was tempted, but he could not cross the boundary that had been marked out by the love and respect he carried in his heart for his wife and me. He pulled away from her. Jean's fine hands, her fingernails crimson and perfect, fell despondently to her thighs.

'Listen, I'm flattered by your proposal,' he admitted, 'but at the same time I'm kind of shocked. How could you think of doing this? Hamish loves you more than anyone else in the world. What more do you want?'

'I want you.' Frustration blazed in her eyes. 'Hamish is a bloody fool who isn't capable of coming up with what I need.' Her face softened as her pointed tongue licked her lips. 'Come on. I know how to make your eyes water.'

Angus believed her and grinned at the thought of it. Jean smiled as if she knew his mind.

He took hold of Jean's left hand and gave it a tug to try and snap her out of her mindset. 'Let's go,' he said. 'It's time to find our partners. You behave yourself now, please.'

She leaned into him as if her spine had collapsed, her surprisingly firm breasts pinning his right arm against his side, her hot breath in his ear whispering, 'I'd suck you dry, Angus Macleod.'

He wondered if she had silicone implants, then let go of the thought and her hand, saying, 'Pack it in, Jean.'

She relented. 'Thanks for the necklace, darling.'

'The pleasure's all mine.'

Taking hold of Jean's hand once more, he guided her along the deserted darkening street. Her high-heeled slip-ons clicked sexily on the cobbles and echoed off the old town's walls.

'Angus?'

'What?'

'Just remember, the offer is permanently open for you.'

'That's enough for today,' he said, unable to suppress a laugh.

I heard Lara say, 'Hey, Hamish, where are you?'

'Huh...oh, sorry,' I said, snapping out of it, 'I was just thinking about something.'

'You looked like you were a million miles away,' she said. 'What on earth were you thinking about that brought such a worried expression to your face?'

'Nothing special,' I replied in a voice that did not sound very convincing. 'I was just wondering how Jean and Angus were getting along.'

Lara's unblinking eyes locked onto mine. She made an impatient noise with her tongue, shook her head and then turned away to look in the sea's direction, where the last sliver of sun was slipping beneath the line of the horizon.

Then, as if obeying a silent command, we both stood up and brushed wind-blown sand from our clothes. Lara put her floppy hat on and bent the brim up at the front. She then took hold of my right hand and we walked away from the bench

We were crossing a grassy embankment when, from a pair of funnel-shaped loudspeakers housed in the window frames of a mosque that looked like a protestant church, a muezzin's amplified voice called out. He was yodelling *azan*, inviting the faithful to *Salat-al-Maghrib*, the prayer said immediately after the sun sets.

Lara unexpectedly stopped in her tracks, turned towards me and placed her right hand on my chest above my heart. I was surprised to see that there was a grave expression etched upon her face. 'Listen,' she said in a solemn voice. 'When it happens that you find yourself going through intense suffering, discipline yourself to see that everything is an illusion, for the cause of most of our sorrow stems from viewing the dream of life with emotional involvement.' Her green eyes fixed on me with a curious distress, as if she feared what the future held for me. 'If you reach what you believe is the end and you feel afraid of that finality, practice the *now*.'

With the rain hissing in my ears and falling on me in sheets, I wondered if somehow she'd had a premonition of what lay in wait for me a few weeks later.

Practice the now. Lara's words of advice echoed in my memory and suddenly I became acutely aware of how my mind only spoke about the past and future, but never the present, where life actually takes place. The realization prompted the spirit of sadness that had been haunting me to leave my heart, to be replaced by a feeling of deep acceptance.

I began to laugh, softly at first, then louder, like a drunken Highlander attending a wild ceilidh. My laughter subsided and then I shouted at the sky, 'Now! Now! *Nowwww!*' Lightning flashed, thunder clapped and the wind whined as it blew in from the sea. *'Yeeeeah!'* I continued to shout at the top of my voice. 'Bring it on!'

I'd stopped shivering. The warm rain began to feel like a cleansing shower. I felt pressure in my bladder. The zipper on my shorts jammed. I didn't want to risk blowing myself up by tugging on it. *'Aaaagh!'* I groaned in relief as I pissed in my pants. The hot urine on my inner thighs succeeded in bringing me in contact with how it felt to be a little boy again. This emotion was counterbalanced by my recognizing that to try and figure out the karmic reason why I was now in a terrible life-threatening situation was indeed, as the Buddha said, imponderable. I stopped thinking about it, and then suddenly realized that whether or not I was willing to entertain the possibility that some kind of rebirth process came after death, it was being made shockingly clear to me that within the fabric of my own lifetime there was a simultaneous series of births and deaths taking place.

'That's right, Hamish,' Lara's gentle voice spoke inside my head, 'that is how it is. Remember what I told you. If you shy away from death, you will inevitably shy away from life as well. Never forget that the only thing to fear is fear itself and that reality is fuelled by the NOW!'

The word snapped me back into the moment. Dripping wet, I looked around, took in the whole crazy scenario and asked myself how it was that Lara and Angus had come to such liberating insights in the first place? The answer came back that their karma had led them East in search of more spiritually fertile soil, to a place where their souls would be formed and moulded by the impressions gathered there, especially deep in the heart of Mother India.

13

PLACE AT THE FRONTIER

Peshawar, Pakistan. May 1973

A s legend would have it, Canibol, the ancient, Indo-European, dog-headed deity, was sitting in his Himalayan cave, feasting on a mountainous pile of tiger kebabs. When Canibol came across a piece of fatty cartilage that was too tough to chew on, let alone swallow, he spat the gristle out and it landed in Pakistan's Northwest Frontier Province. That particular spot became known as Peshawar, a Pashto word which means *'place at the frontier'*.

Peshawar was the sort of town where anything could be purchased – for a price. Everything from armoured cars to bootleg copies of Led Zeppelin's latest album was up for sale – everything, that is, except windscreen and window replacements for a customized Mercedes bus.

'Six fucking weeks,' gasped Murphy in shock, when the bespectacled manager of an international spare parts depot informed him how much time would be needed for the Perspex windows he'd ordered to arrive from Germany.

The entire crew was upset about the prospect of spending a month and a half in a city they'd originally intended to bypass. It was the last straw for Nina and Alice who, showing distinct signs of fraying at the edges, decided they'd had enough on-the-road adventures. A local doctor had stitched Alice's left earlobe back together again, but the deep cut on her cheek was not healing well. She'd taken a course of strong antibiotics, yet the wound remained septic. Freaked out by their plight, the two young women decided to travel by train to Islamabad and from there catch a flight back to London.

Apart from Angus, nobody was sorry to see them go. On the contrary, the prospect was received with relief, because under stress the two young women had caved in, making their combined presence a burden rather than fun to have around. They were griping ceaselessly and suffering from nervous disorders, made evident by a permanently twitching muscle under Alice's right eye and Nina's cough, which made a horrible tearing sound in her congested lungs. She was chain-smoking her way through four packets of cheap, cardboard-filtered Russian cigarettes a day.

Raj and Murphy were not even attempting to conceal the fact that they were looking forward to being unattached again. They didn't consider themselves the marrying kind. 'So many flowers in the garden,' Murphy was fond of saying, 'why get hung up on one?'

What was ironic about the situation was that Alice and Nina were just the kind of women who fall for men who are aren't interested in developing a strong emotional bond. They were acutely aware of their lovers' uncommitted attitude and, during their last days together, made a point of letting Murphy and Raj know this in no uncertain terms. Angus, for his part, made an effort to steer clear of the blue emotional sparks that were flying around. He had enough problems of his own to deal with. Jenny was so stoned on opium she could not be bothered to get out of bed and therefore was absent when the time arrived to walk down to the railway station to see Alice and Nina off.

Angus, Murphy and Raj were suddenly surrounded by a battalion of shouting tea vendors, carrying big aluminium kettles as they tried to get in one last sale before the train left the station. Bang on Pakistani time it was three hours late for departure. Jets of scalding steam squirted out of the black iron locomotive's stainless steel pistons as they brought the train's wheels into motion. With an ear-piercing shriek of its klaxon the engine began to huff and puff like an angry dragon as the dust-covered train drew away.

Dressed in white cotton kurtas, Alice and Nina gave unenthusiastic waves from their first-class compartment. As thick and black as tar, their Bridgette Bardot-style eye makeup contrasted sharply with their waxen complexions. The girls' pasty faces were as grey and washed out as the dirt-streaked window they stood glaring through. They stared so pointedly at Raj and Murphy, Angus was surprised his mates' hair didn't start smouldering. The girls looked to Angus like a pair of woebegone spooks on their way to a funeral, yet at the same time they still appeared train-stoppingly beautiful and he hoped to see them again some day. He stood beside his two friends, waving until the back of the green brake wagon disappeared down the railway tracks.

'Thank fuck for that,' said Murphy, making it perfectly clear how he felt about Nina's departure.

'Well,' said Angus, as they walked out of the station into the bright light of day, 'I can't fail to notice that you two seem fairly pleased with yourselves to be bachelor boys again.'

'Oh, aye,' said Murphy, pricking up his ears, 'that wouldn't be a touch of envy in your voice that I detect now, would it, sahib?'

'Not really,' replied Angus, sidestepping a bearded old man, who was bowing silently on a prayer rug placed in the middle of the narrow pavement, 'it's just that Jenny has turned into an opium addict.'

Murphy's dark eyes opened wide in a parody of amazement. 'Oh dearie me, Angus-kins, you don't fuckin' say.'

Angus ignored Murphy's sarcasm.

'I saw that coming,' commented Raj, as they walked by the line of tall iron palings that fronted the station. 'You should've put your foot down in Herat. Now that she's hooked on that shit it's going to be a real bummer to get her off of it, even if she wants to, which I seriously doubt.'

Angus asked, 'What do you suggest I do?'

'All you've got to do is tell her to pack it in, or else pack her fucking bags and fuck off,' was Murphy's no-nonsense suggestion.

Angus had a sinking feeling in his guts that Murphy was right, but he was unwilling to admit it. 'Easier said than done,' he said, stepping over an open manhole in the middle of the pavement. 'I can't just dump her here in Peshawar, now can I?'

'Why the fuck not?' asked Murphy.

'Because...because...I don't fucking know. Because I still love her, I suppose,' confessed Angus, realizing that his voice sounded higher than usual – Murphy was making him nervous.

Murphy looked at Angus as if he were crazy. 'Love? What's that supposed to mean?' he asked. 'It's such a vague fucking word – *love!*' He spat the word out as if it were the name of a debilitating disease with no known cure for the afflicted.

Angus shook his head. 'I don't agree. I think love is a flexible word that can signify many things.' Upon hearing this, Murphy's lips curled in disgust, but Angus continued. 'In this case it means my complete and sincere respect for another human being and it also means that I will not abandon Jenny in a place like this.'

Murphy looked questioningly at Raj. 'Is this guy for real?' he asked, jerking a derisive thumb at Angus. 'Nature hoodwinks his otherwise perceptive mind with the oldest genetic trick in the book, to bolster the survival of the species, and now this fucking idiot thinks he's in love with a junkie.' He twirled an index finger by the side of his head.

Raj shrugged nervously and turned towards the idiot. 'Have you tried talking to her about it?'

'Of course I have,' answered Angus in exasperation, flustered by Murphy poking fun at him and embarrassed by his own obvious naivety. 'It's like talking to a fuckin' zombie. I just can't break through that thick fog she's living in. How about you guys giving me a bit of back up? She's your friend as—'

'*Back up?* Listen to you,' scoffed Murphy, pulling a comically shocked face. 'Never get involved in a boy and girl story is what I always say. You made your bed of roses so don't start complaining to me about the thorns.'

'Thanks a fucking lot, Murph, I don't know what I'd do without you.'

Murphy laughed and gave Angus a hearty slap on the back. 'Don't mention it, pal. Glad to be of assistance.'

'What about you?' Angus asked Raj, who'd stopped to observe a herd of about two hundred long-horned cattle, making its way along the cowpat-splattered street.

'I'm sorry, man,' Raj shrugged again, 'I more or less see your situation the same way as Murph. I enjoy having Jenny around.' He added, almost apologetically, 'She's been a bit lazy lately, but apart from that I'm cool with her.' Raj grinned toothily and nudged Angus's shoulder. 'Don't worry. You'll work it out, pal.'

Raj's cheerful manner made Angus feel like a loser. It couldn't have been made clearer to him that, as far as his love life was concerned, he was on his own. A nagging thought chattered in the back of his mind. An awkward self-consciousness had entered his relationship with Jenny that signalled to him that they didn't know each other, and perhaps themselves, as well as previously imagined. The confusing thing was that this only served to make him feel more attracted to her. It felt like he was tethered to her with a cord, invisible to everyone else but him. Yet that cord bound him with a physical reality which reminded him of the ball and chain he'd heard Janis Joplin singing about. Like many a young man, Angus was living under the illusion that sex was the culmination of intimacy. The thought that it might not be was beginning to creep into his mind. At times, he longed to speak about this with his friends but, due to Raj and Murphy's cavalier attitude, he found this impossible and was left to carry his heart's burden alone.

'I'm sorry guys,' said Angus, realizing he might not be the best of company. 'This relationship thing is making me feel a bit melancholy.'

'Aye right, dear,' chuckled Murphy, 'head like a melon and a face like a fuckin' cauli.'

It was an old line, but it managed to bring a smile to Angus's lips.

They continued along Sethi Street for a couple of blocks until they reached Chowk Yaadgar, Peshawar's main square. Crowds of people were lining the pavements, obviously waiting for some spectacle to take place. It was midday. For the lack of anything better to do, the three friends joined a group of bystanders on a street corner and stood around waiting for something to happen.

They did not have to wait more than five minutes before a brass band paraded into the square. The musicians were marching like a clockwork Salvation Army orchestra wound up on amphetamine. They strode past knocking out a lively racket, which made absolutely no concessions whatsoever to even the most basic concepts of melody. The discordant din, the musicians' accelerated mechanical movements, their comic opera uniforms, plumed hats, and a few quick tokes on a fat joint of Afghan hash managed to propel the Scots into an uncontrollable laughing fit.

Following close on the band's worn boot heels came dozens of burly men who were stripped to the waist and quite literally whipping up a storm. Sweat mixed with blood as the bare-chested men flailed themselves with a variety of flesh-rending implements that ranged from homemade whips, with fish hooks attached, to car aerials. There was nothing new about this excruciating practice, which can bring its adherents into a state of sacred ecstasy. In fourteenth century Europe, public displays of self-flagellation began to take place in Germany. It was believed that by flogging oneself with a metal-tipped whip for the sins of humanity, God would relent from sending virulent plagues to decimate the population.

Judging by the cries of appreciation rising into the warm air, the local Pakistani populace sensed the frenzied flagellants' ecstatic self-transcendence, their longing to free the spirit from the bonds of physical reality.

Murphy asked, 'What the fuck's all this about?'

'Beats me,' answered Raj, who was leaning against one of Peshawar's rare traffic light poles. 'Maybe we should ask one of the natives?'

Everyone in the immediate vicinity was transfixed by the gory demonstration of extreme worship, and therefore unable to come up with an answer that went beyond 'Very brave Shi'ites.'

Someone bumped into Angus from behind. He turned to see a filthy, wrinkle-faced leper who was minus a nose and hands. Set deep in his nightmarishly eroded face, his milky eyes were so opaque Angus couldn't tell if the man was blind or staring blankly at him. The leper's cracked lips and swollen tongue were working to produce coherent words that sounded like they were emerging from a grave. The poor wretch was holding an empty tin can between twin arm stumps. Angus donated a handful of change. The coins clattered into the tin and caught Murphy's attention.

'Hey, man,' said he, turning away from the procession and glancing at the beggar, 'did you hear the one about the leper who was losing at poker?'

'No,' answered Angus. 'What happened?'

'He threw his hand in.'

'For fuck's sake, Murphy, that's not funny,' complained Angus, chuckling.

He looked back towards the street and discovered that rabid eyes were staring at him with a barely concealed challenge behind them. They belonged to a tall, balding Pakistani who stood before him with what looked like a stainless steel knitting needle sticking through his cheeks. Dark rivulets of blood ran down from the man's face and over his hairy chest to soak into the waistband of his white cotton trousers. Extracting the long steel pin from his cheeks, he quickly pushed the pointed implement through his nose. It was clear the man was in great pain by the way his bloodshot eyes bulged and stared at infinity. There were raised veins pulsating in his neck. Not a sound escaped from his lips – they were stitched closed with thick black thread.

'Hey, Angus,' said Murphy in a loud voice that rose above the noise on the crowded pavement. 'I think it's time we split the scene.'

Murphy was right. Another Muslim penitent was heading their way, whacking a curved sword against his bleeding forehead. The metallic scent of fresh blood tainted the air and an aggressive force began to emanate from the crowds of spectators, whose cries had strengthened and coalesced into a continuous roar of endorsement.

The three Scotsmen hurried off. A ten-minute walk later, they entered the Qissa Khawani Bazaar, known locally as 'The Street of the Storytellers'. The souk was a semi-circular construction composed of arched arcades shaded by hessian awnings. Due to the flagellants' procession and it being a local holiday, the market was unusually quiet. Exotic aromas rose from food stalls, prompting hunger drums to beat out a rum-tum-tum rhythm in the Scots' empty stomachs. Since his acid trip in Istanbul, Angus had not felt comfortable eating meat, but that warm afternoon he could not resist the mouth-watering smells wafting off the sizzling hot coals, above which the stall owners barbecued lamb chops and cooked succulent chicken tikkas. Spoiled for choice, they all three ordered chappli kebabs, a local delicacy in the form of a spicy beefburger sandwiched between juicy red tomato slices, garnished with green chilli sauce and served up on flat buttered nan bread. The delicious feast was completed by gorging on dollops of pink, rose-flavoured ice cream topped off with a generous sprinkling of crushed pistachio nuts.

Stuffed to the point of feeling nauseous, the trio headed for Café Kaput, a back street teashop with a painted sign outside proclaiming in English 'NON-MUSLIM FOREIGNERS ONLY'. This had obviously made the place rather unpopular amongst the locals. The windows were permanently boarded up, after having been smashed during the night on several occasions. The proprietor, Heidelberg Heinz, was a crazy bespectacled German hippy. Heinz had a bronze Russian samovar on the go all day long to boil the water for his green tea, which he dished up in brightly glazed china. The clientele were a mix of European travellers, dope dealers and a pair of regulars suspected of being American undercover narcotics agents because they always wore mirrored sunglasses, spoke Urdu fluently, asked lots of questions and never supplied any answers.

Apart from the expat community's watering hole, Green's Hotel, which was more like a motel, the kind you drive into and drive out of half an hour later with a hundred kilos of hashish loaded in the boot, and the National Hotel, a notorious junkie hangout, Café Kaput was the only alternative meeting place in town. To the ambient soundtrack supplied by Tangerine Dream, Amon Düül, Popal Vuh, Can and local *qawwali* music cassettes, patrons hung around for hours, eating Heidelberg Heinz's baked beans and drinking his special tea, spiced with powdered cannabis flowers.

One evening, a week after they'd arrived in Peshawar, Angus confronted Jenny about her opium addiction. It came as a surprise to him when Jenny expressed the desire to try and kick her drug habit. She confessed to feeling like she'd been sleeping her way through the journey since Istanbul and now wanted to experience consciously everything that was going on around her. Raj and Murphy put in an appearance and, contrary to what they'd said some days before outside the railway station, offered to lend moral support to both of their friends.

'Why don't you try coming off it slow and easy, a little less each day?' was Murphy's suggestion, which, as it turned out, was how Jenny went about weaning herself from the drug. Throughout the following two difficult weeks, Angus, Murphy and Raj supported Jenny by helping her sort out her daily dose and including her in all of their activities, so that she never felt lonely. During this period, Angus began to notice that Jenny was constantly scratching her arm where she'd imagined aliens to have inserted something into her body during her DMT session in Kabul. He spoke to her about this and it was then that Jenny revealed that she'd been having nightmares, inhabited by unearthly creatures who wanted to have sex with her.

The weeks drifted by. A daily routine was adopted, which usually included a visit to the Café Kaput. Angus and his friends became accustomed to the sporadic crackle of gunfire and the occasional stuttering thud of a heavy machine gun, knowing that it was either guests at a wedding party, getting carried away with the celebrations, or arms dealers demonstrating the weaponry on offer over at Ammo Avenue. The Scots had given this name to an unpaved street on the edge of town where the tools of war were sold. Ammo Avenue was a partitioned ammunition dump, lined with open-fronted shops displaying wares ranging from bazookas to boxes of German potato masher grenades left over from World War II. Dressed in baggy trousers and long loose shirts with thick bullet-studded bandoleers strapped across their chests, Pakhtun customers often went outside to fire off a banana clip of 9mm ammunition into the air to test prospective purchases, submachine guns being the must-have of the time. Angus wondered why it was that falling bullets didn't injure somebody. He entered a shop, where custom-made Sam Browne holsters hung from the rafters like a colony of tan-coloured fruit bats, and asked a weapons salesman about the dangers posed by hot lead and brass raining down from the sky. Looking up from a box full of rusty bayonets the man shrugged and answered, 'Everything is in the hands of Allah the Almighty.' He winked at Angus and then said, 'The wind blows the bullets away.' It wasn't windy.

For a few days Murphy toyed with the idea of buying an AK-47. When Raj and Angus got wind of this they managed to convince him that it was not in the interests of love and peace to invest in what is perhaps one of the world's greatest weapons of mass destruction, whereby he eventually dropped the notion.

Jenny weaned herself from opium and after a month she was down to using a smidgen of the substance in the evening to help her sleep. For the first time in weeks she began to have an appetite for food again and, much to Angus's delight, she quickly began to put on weight. Raj and Murphy were happy to see the return of her cheeky sense of humour.

During daylight hours, Jenny and Angus would stroll around Peshawar's streets for hours on end. Strategically placed, the city had been a commercial and cultural crossroads for thousands of years. Transient civilizations – Arab, Indian, British, Greek, Mogul, Turkish, Mongol and Persian – had left monuments as a testimony to having passed through Peshawar at various times in its history. The compact city had a half million inhabitants. With the arrival of the Russian invasion of Afghanistan in 1979, refugees would flood in; setting the stage for a population explosion that would quadruple the city's inhabitants in less than a decade. Six years before those calamitous events were set in motion the two young lovers still had room to move. They strolled hand in hand, exploring Peshawar's busy streets, oblivious to the holes being drilled into their backs by the hawk-faced men who sat on their haunches by the wayside, or walked behind them holding pinkies and clicking tongues against the roofs of their mouths in disapproval, because they viewed the foreign couple's physical signs of affection as an insult to their manhood.

During the evenings, Angus and Jenny spent a lot of time bouncing on top of their hotel room's double bed, making love and trying to figure out how to prevent the iron bed frame from squeaking like an excited metal pig. Angus eventually paid a small fee to have the offending noisemaker removed from their room. After that, the only disturbing sounds the other guests had to put up with were the two lovers' joyous cries, echoing continuously through the corridor until dawn.

Early one morning, after seven weeks in Peshawar, there was a knock on Raj and Murphy's hotel room door. Half asleep, Raj opened the door and found himself looking down at a delicate-featured little boy.

'Yes, what is it?' Raj asked, rubbing sleep from his eyes.

The boy smiled up at him. 'Hello sir, please to be coming to my father's shop. Windows are waiting for you.'

It was the best piece of news the Scots had received since entering Pakistan. Two days later, Rolling Thunder was back on the road, bound for Lahore.

14

A TALE OF FIVE
SUBCONTINENTAL CITIES.

Angus and his friends spent a day in Lahore. As far as they were concerned, it was twenty-four hours too long. The noisy city was a festering boil on the face of the planet. During the afternoon, oppressive heat drove the thermometer's mercury well above the forty degrees centigrade mark.

After an early night, they were back on the road. India was only thirty kilometres away. The sun broke over the city like a sizzling fried egg. Rolling Thunder's air-conditioning system was set at its coolest level. This didn't prevent Angus's sweat-soaked shirt from sticking to his back. He'd thought that hitting the road before dawn would avoid rush hour traffic. The idea quickly evaporated as the heat rose from a million vehicles – stuck in a gridlock that was thronged by pedestrians who traversed the congested streets and broken pavements with the physical stamina of urban tri-athletes. The air was thick with exhaust fumes. Rumour had it that all three members of Lahore's 'Clean Air Club' had been found dead in their beds back in 1971. There were unconfirmed reports that the environmentalists had been gassed with carbon monoxide after they'd aired one too many complaints to the government's Minister for the Environment.

After several near misses with cars, apparently driven by blind lunatics, Angus swung on to the main highway heading east out of the city. Breathing a sigh of relief, he engaged the clutch and shifted up from second gear for the first time in an hour. Worried about blowing the cylinder head gasket, he glanced at the temperature gauge. Its thin white needle was hovering a millimeter below the red. The bus picked up speed and air rushed into the vents to cool the hot engine.

'Man, that was close,' muttered Angus under his breath, when he saw the temperature gauge's needle edge down to level out at eighty-five degrees.

Five kilometres from India, the already slow moving traffic ground to a complete standstill. From his elevated position in the driver's seat, Angus could see that a bottleneck had formed in the distance.

Sometimes the lights all shining on me... His attention shifted to the music coming out of the bus's sound system. The Grateful Dead were playing 'Truckin''. Normally he liked this ode to being on the road, but in that moment it sounded inappropriate. Leaning over to his right, he hit the eject button on the tape player.

Murphy shouted a complaint from the back of the bus. 'Hey, man, we were listening to that.'

Angus glanced round and shouted back, 'It was getting on my nerves. I'll put it back on when we're trucking again.'

The bus was lurching forward at a one kilometre an hour crawl. A million millimetres later it reached the cause of the traffic jam. A wooden wagon, dangerously overloaded with curved terracotta roof tiles, had been too much weight for the skinny horse pulling it to bear. The beast of burden had died of exhaustion in the middle of a busy intersection. Tipping to its rear, the two-wheeled cart had pulled the frail creature up by its harness to leave it reared up on its lifeless hind legs. The bus drew level with this pitiful sight. Angus turned to his left and looked through the window. Gazing back at him, the dead nag's eyes protruded out of their sockets. Grey mucus drooled from its dust-caked nostrils and a long pale tongue hung to one side of a mouth lined with greenish-yellow rotten teeth.

The traffic had ground to a halt again. Angus took a hit on a joint and sat staring out of the window at this grotesque caricature of death, as if it were a monument to horror erected by an insane town council. After what seemed like a very long minute, the dead horse's features no longer appeared gruesome to Angus. He reasoned that it was probably a relief for the animal's spirit to be set free from a bag of bones that had to suffer a daily routine of physical hardship and abuse.

Angus closed his eyes and imagined where a dead horse's spirit would like to roam. He visualized a vast rolling plain covered in lush green grass and wild flowers, a line of snow-capped mountain peaks in the distance adding a sense of high places with unobstructed views. A blaring car horn brought Angus back to his senses. Taking one last look at the horse's head, he let the clutch pedal up and the bus eased forward. From behind came the sound of Jenny squealing in fright as the lifeless creature's face passed by.

Angus shifted up through the gears and, as the bus picked up speed, he thought about how the dead carthorse was a symbolic encapsulation of how he'd perceived Pakistan as a whole. The country seemed to be on the point of dying from fatigue. Pakistan's fractured society lived in a parched and overpopulated land, which appeared to be collapsing in upon itself from carrying the enormous weight of tens of millions of poverty-stricken people. India was only a couple of kilometres away and he hoped it was not going to be more of the same.

Angus parked by a narrow canal. After a perfunctory check by khaki-uniformed, Indian immigration officers at the Wagah border crossing, the bus's carnet, passengers' passports and inoculation certificates were found to be in order. Rolling Thunder and her crew were permitted to cross over the frontier into India with the minimum of fuss.

Driving along the long straight road that ran between the two neighbouring countries, Angus felt a weight lift off his shoulders. He glanced up at the tall jacaranda trees spanning the road, their fern-like leaves creating a tunnel of shade. In full bloom, the trumpet-shaped flowers of these deciduous trees were of such an intense, vibrant purple they looked almost artificial.

He lowered the driver's side window. Damp air wafted in, suffused by the organic smells of cow-dung cooking fires, decomposing vegetation, burning slash piles, fermenting fruit, termite-chewed wood and the sweet scent of frangipani flowers, an appreciated change after the oxygen-starved air of Lahore. It felt like he was emerging from a period of incubation in a hot, cramped womb and entering into an altogether different, cooler, more expansive world.

The bus drew to a halt when it encountered a large herd of dark grey water buffalos crossing the highway. As they lumbered past, the bulky beast's eyes stared from their huge swaying heads. A little boy played the role of herdsman, whistling and shouting at the horned cattle as he guided them over the asphalt. Every now and then he'd apply a bamboo switch to a buffalo's thick hairy hide if it began to stray too far from the bovine procession. One large female, with swollen udders, stopped in the centre of the road. She turned and bellowed anxiously. A young bull calf trotted out from between a stand of tall, yellow-stemmed bamboos and kicked his hind legs in the air in a display of youthful vitality. He ambled up to his mother's side, gently nudged her and then they continued together in pursuit of the herd. The young lad looked up at Angus and raised a hand. Angus waved back, marvelling at the passing of this rural scene. He was left asking himself where else in the world would it be accepted that a herd of water buffalos was allowed to bring the traffic on an international trunk road to a complete standstill?

Murphy called out, 'Put some music on.'

Angus pushed The Dead's cassette back into the player's slot and 'Truckin'' came back on. *Lately it occurs to me...* He raised the volume and hummed along to the melody. He glanced at a large black and white road sign. AMRITSAR: 16 MILES. ...*What a long strange trip it's been.*

He recalled a conversation he'd had with Orion and Dawn in Kabul. The Canadian couple had spent many years travelling in the subcontinent. Dawn had coined an expression that he'd liked: India is not a country. It's an exalted state of mind that has to be dreamed into existence. Gazing ahead, he realized there was probably a strong element of truth in what she'd said. He had the distinct impression of somehow having been there before in a forgotten dream or a previous lifetime. An old memory came unstuck from his brain's flypaper and floated into his conscious mind. Angus burst out laughing when he remembered his mysterious childhood friend, Amah, who had told him so much about her life in India. His relationship with Amah had been the source of a lot of trouble with his parents. *'Shit!'* Angus cursed out loud as he spun the wheel to the left. The bus swerved, almost sideswiping a bullock cart.

'Here, you want a toke on this?' Jenny's voice asked.

A slender hand, holding a long conical joint, appeared in front of Angus's face. The aromatic smell of good quality Afghan hash drifted up from its smouldering end. He took the joint and inhaled a lungful of its fragrant smoke. He blew a cloud against the bug-spattered windscreen and turned to gaze up into Jenny's smiling honey-coloured eyes. His eyes looked down. She was wearing a tight yellow tee shirt. Nothing else. It was short, very short.

'Hey, man, keep your attention on the road.'

Angus did as he was ordered, while Jenny stood behind him, kneading the muscles in his shoulders with her adroit fingers.

'I noticed you were laughing to yourself,' she said. 'What's so funny?'

Angus took another drag on the joint and replied, 'I was just remembering something from my childhood days on Iona.'

'Like what exactly?'

'Well, I was thinking about how I must have driven my parents up the wall.'

Jenny's fingers probed deeper as she enquired further. 'Why was that?'

Angus chuckled before answering. 'I had this big fat Indian lady who was my friend.'

'What's the big deal about that?'

'She was invisible to everyone else except me.' He let out a spluttering laugh. 'You...you have to understand, I was a right wee nutter.'

'Excuse me, Angus Macleod,' said Jenny, bending forward to kiss the crown of his head. 'Did I hear you speaking in past tense just now, or am I mistaken?'

Busted flat in Baton Rouge...

The Grateful Dead played on and the two young lovers sang along to 'Me and Bobby McGee'.

There was a cloudburst. Angus switched on the wipers. They clicked in time to the music.

First stop in India was Amritsar. Compared to the dirt and chaos of Lahore, the small city was a relatively clean and peaceful place.

The main attraction in Amritsar for visitors and pilgrims alike is the Golden Temple, holy of holies for members of the Sikh religion. Like a sentinel of faith the temple is set in a tranquil pool that is home to giant carp. Throughout the day the waters reflect the temple's image in a constantly changing play of light and shade. These waters gave the city its name, Amrit-sarovar, the pool of nectar.

It was during their time in Amritsar that Angus and his friends realized it was becoming too hot to travel south to Goa. Therefore, the decision was made to head for Kathmandu in Nepal. Everyone was eager to seek out the cooler climes of the mountains, but the Golden Temple was such a beautifully serene place they felt a little time could be spared to enjoy it.

Gilded with a ton of gold, the temple's domes radiated yellow light during the day. In the evenings, inside the temple's massive refectory, rotund Sikhs served free dhal and chapattis. Dressed in orange robes and armed with spears, the temple guards sported long beards that hung down to their bulging bellies. The Scots were familiar with turbaned Sikhs; in Glasgow they represented the most industrious section of the city's large Indian immigrant community.

Guru Nanak had founded Sikhism in Lahore 500 years earlier. As a child he'd demonstrated his linguistic skills by writing out a poem in twenty-five different languages. During his teenage years he began to wander far and wide, seeking out the company of mystics, mullahs and ascetics.

Legend has it that one hot afternoon he'd dived into the river Baain to cool off. When he resurfaced – three days later – he was, as one could easily imagine, a changed man, having undergone a profound, underwater, spiritual experience. The aura of enlightenment that was radiating from Nanak acted as a magnet upon those who were spiritually inclined and soon the guru had a large congregation of seekers and disciples gathered around him. In Sanskrit,

India's ancient Indo-European language, the word for disciple is *shisha*. The word later became 'Sikh'.

Big on civil rights, Guru Nanak was centuries ahead of his time. He campaigned against the social inequalities and institutionalizing of prejudice represented by a caste system that had existed for 3,000 years, a system which he recognized for what it was; an identification with a form that obscures the light which is the spiritual essence of each and every human being. He was also opposed to idolatry, recommending to his followers that they should throw their holy statues away and tune into the living god residing in their spiritual heart. Later in life, the radical guru turned to farming and lived in the world as a hard-working family man who'd married and fathered two sons. An agricultural commune was formed and the master's shishas were encouraged to follow his example and sing along to the songs he was fond of composing. Half a millennium later, his tunes are broadcast through loudspeakers in the Golden Temple. Although they could hardly be described as being foot-tappers, Guru Nanak's hymns are still very popular.

Raj became enamoured with Sikhism and bought a stainless steel Punjabi bangle, which he began to wear on his wrist as a good luck charm. It was because of his reluctance to leave Amritsar that over a week was spent there.

Each day, before dawn, Raj would jump out of bed and set off for the temple. Under the boughs of a very old tree, said to dispel sorrows, he'd sit and watch devotees clean the temple with milk and water in preparation for another day of worship. It was there, under the ancient tree's shade, that Raj befriended a retired history teacher called Mohinder Singh. Mr Singh was a talkative old gentleman who always wore a black turban and he taught Raj much about the sanctified place from which he derived so much pleasure visiting.

According to Mr Singh, the huge tank of water that they sat beside had once been a pond in a forest. The Lord Buddha had passed by the spot 2500 years before and remarked to the monks who accompanied him that the place had a vibration that was conductive to meditation. During the sixteenth century the pool's waters were found to have miraculous curative qualities and the task of enlarging the pond began. Eventually paving stones were laid around what was fast becoming a place of pilgrimage. As for the Golden Temple, its history was one of triumph over extreme persecution, especially at the hands of the various Islamic dynasties that once ruled India. Over the centuries, Muslim soldiers desecrated the sacred site on numerous occasions. Ignoring and displaying none of Koranic Allah's compassion, they'd gone so far as to one time drain the pond and fill it with rubble and rotting carcasses. As if this weren't enough, provocatively attired dancing girls were hired to perform within the temple's hallowed precincts. Massa Rangar, the military governor responsible for these particular violations, paid for them with his life. Riding into town, two avenging Sikh youths beheaded the governor and bore off with his head impaled on a sword. Thus began a cycle of violence where reprisals and brutalities were visited upon the Sikhs for decades to come.

'Yeah, yeah, history is a nightmare, from which I'm trying to awake,' said well-read Murphy. He was quoting James Joyce after listening to Raj enthusiastically bombard him for days with various stories from the temple's past. 'Listen up, Raj. We've been discussing your new role as star fucking pupil.' Murphy used a small towel to wipe sweat off his face, for it was hot and sultry on the bus. 'If you want to hang out any longer with your Sikh history teacher, you can catch up with the rest of us further on up the road.'

Raj didn't have to think too much about the prospect of staying on alone in Amritsar. With her engine running, Rolling Thunder and her crew waited outside the Golden Temple's iron gates, while Raj hurried across a stone bridge and then the inner courtyard's chequered marble tiles to bid Mohinder Singh a fond farewell.

The next stop was New Delhi, a city where progress was measured in rising decibel levels and thickening clouds of blue smog. The sun was high in a hazy sky and New Delhi was a picture of civilization gone seriously wrong. What was new about Delhi was anyone's guess. It is one of the oldest cities in the world and full of things that one rarely sees in the modern world – bicycle rickshaws, Muslim men with long black beards and wooden-wheeled carts, hauled by a variety of horned beasts. Everything about the place seemed either aged or ancient, except for the bands of hollow-stomached child beggars who, in spite of their impoverished existence, appeared to be uninhibitedly happy, accepting unquestioningly with a genuine smile the indignities and privations a hard life had doled out to them. They were everywhere and roamed the capital's congested streets, subsisting on what they could forage from piles of fetid rubbish or what they could hustle on crowded pavements, where people's financial sympathies could best be played upon.

Millions of people were living below the poverty line in tin-roofed shacks, jammed together for mutual support to prevent them collapsing into a filthy rat-infested heap. Over time, separate shantytowns had merged to form enormous conglomerates that spread like a sea of wretchedness, where the downtrodden clung to life like barnacles on a rusty sewage pipe. Incubators for diseases like typhoid, which is transmitted through oral-faecal contact, the festering slums stood in stark contrast to Delhi's more opulent neighbourhoods, home to foreign embassies and inhabited by the rich one-percent who controlled ninety-nine-percent of India's wealth. Fronted by well-clipped hedges, lush tropical gardens and manicured lawns with sprinkler systems gushing like fountains, the buildings that housed the ruling classes appeared palatial from the crew's moving perspective.

The bus cruised along broad avenues, flanked by lines of smooth-trunked royal palms, heading for the city centre. It soon became apparent that New Delhi was the kind of place where the blatantly wealthy got richer by the minute. In public, the well-off appeared as shadowy figures, who peered out of their imported air-conditioned limousines' darkened back windows to watch poor unfortunates, rolling along the pavements on wheeled planks, their legs flattened by a steel hammer to further their careers as professional beggars.

A land of extremes and stark contradictions, India's capital contained them all. Anarchy ruled Delhi's highways and byways under the watchful eyes of squadrons of scrawny, leather-necked vultures. These hawk-eyed scavengers either drifted on thermals quartering the sky or perched on high vantage points, hissing and lashing out at each other like winged serpents as they waited for something or someone to die in the streets below. This was a common occurrence in Delhi, which according to statistics is the most dangerous city in the world for road accidents. A bus crash with fifty fatalities was usually described by the local press as a *minor mishap*. In this seething environment, honking vehicles' rear-view mirrors had been made obsolete by intuitive drivers who cared nothing for what lay behind, only forward and into the fray with the light of battle in their crazed eyes.

Enveloped by swirling clouds of dust and unfiltered exhaust fumes, everything stopped for the ubiquitous holy cows, who took full advantage of their sacred status. The cows caused traffic jams as they wandered aimlessly like sleepwalkers and chewed on discarded bamboo broom handles, plastic bags, cardboard boxes, all kinds of rubbish and anything else that jammed into their smiling mouths. Superstitious motorists reached out of their windows to pat the urban bovines on their dung-caked hindquarters for good luck. In the midst of these standstills naked beggars relieved themselves in the middle of the road and stood in malaria-breeding gutters, cleaning their teeth with yellow twigs harvested from the neem tree. They stared blankly into space and, like the holy cows, seemed untroubled by the celebration of human filth and noise taking place around them. The air was so polluted it occasionally caused flocks of small birds to be asphyxiated in mid-flight. The gassed birds would drop from the sky like feathered hailstones and bounce off people's heads as they stood in disorderly queues, waiting for hours to board groaning, ramshackle buses that were already so crammed with sweating passengers they resembled wheeled slave ships.

Viewed by the international community as a backward nation, India was decades ahead of the rest of the world's countries in terms of overpopulation, recycling rubbish, creating unbreathable air and poisoning rivers, thus presenting a vision of how things might be for everyone in the future if birth control is not implemented and rampant economic development reigned in.

At night, one had to watch the uneven pavements for coverless drains that released a foul stench into the dimly lit streets. It was easy to break a leg in these deep holes. In some sections of the city pedestrians were forced to walk in the road because the pavements were blocked by tattered, sackcloth tent colonies. It was in these human cesspools that destitute squatter families, blanketed in a noisy lethargy and fatalistic acceptance, lived in a squalor that was so deep they were drowning in it. People in rags cooked food scraps in soot-blackened iron pots over smoking fires, defecated in open sewers, traded in salvaged garbage, fornicated in the shadows, slept in front of shops whose corrugated metal shutters were lowered and locked at night, gave birth to malnourished babies and died hoping for a better deal next time around.

In the heat of the day sweating ice wallahs hauled rumbling, steel-wheeled trolleys, loaded with frozen blocks that were insulated from the hot sun by brown hessian sacks sprinkled with wet sawdust. Buzzing around them like a swarm of aggravated metal insects, lines of scooters weaved in and out of the thronging traffic. A popular and practical form of transport, the weight they often carried kept their squeaking shock absorbers permanently compressed to their limits. Angus gazed out of the bus's side windows in fascination and watched as a stressed-out father in an acid-pink turban and matching cotton robe desperately tried to keep his balance as he manoeuvred his overloaded scooter through the slow-moving traffic. Behind him, sitting side-saddle, was his obese wife. Dressed in a sequined blue sari, she was serving up breakfast from the passenger seat to her brood of bright-eyed children who, like a circus act, hung on to the pillion, giggling as they fed their pet vegetarian mongoose titbits from an aluminium tiffin-tin.

Jaw clenched in concentration, beads of sweat tumbled from Raj's forehead as he drove along a clogged, arterial road leading into the heart of the city. He had to wait at a busy intersection for five minutes until a traffic cop, wearing a spotless white uniform and pith helmet, blew his whistle and waved the bus on. Raj circled Connaught Circus three times, and then headed north towards old Delhi. Halfway there, he pulled into the entrance of a fenced-off compound called 'The Tourist Campsite'. The grassy rectangle of waste ground was surrounded by a rusty iron fence and decrepit five-storey mansion blocks. Ripe with rot and decay, the sick buildings looked tired and sagged from the weight of over a century of use. Their exhausted faces were peeling off from their underlying brickwork like rotten flesh, the only effective cure for their malaise – a visit from Doctor Demolition and his five ton wrecking ball. The good doctor was nowhere in sight and, as if to conceal the buildings' facial disfigurement, large hoardings covered them. The billboards were plastered with adverts proclaiming the merits of tooth-whitening powders, skin-whitening creams, shoe polish, hair-restorer, government sponsored family planning, Thumbs-Up, an Indian soft drink that tastes like Coca-Cola with ten times as much caffeine in it, and the latest Bollywood movies.

The Tourist Campsite became headquarters for the next few days. The Scots pitched a large, circular, army surplus tent, while the city droned around them like a huge bee with a blocked nose. When their temporary khaki-coloured home was erected and the guys secured, Angus kicked back on a canvas bed and began reading Robert Heinlein's *Stranger in a Strange Land*. The sound of traffic faded to a distant wash and the multiple realities existing around him crumbled and gradually disappeared as he was absorbed by the world of science fiction.

Delhi was extremely hot. During the afternoons, excited mercury atoms were pushed up to dizzying heights within the thermometer's glass confines. In the evenings, the air was cooler and slightly less polluted.

Priority number one was to sell the bus's illicit cargo of hashish. This turned out to be a relatively uncomplicated task. The contact, which Orion had given Angus in Kabul, was a good one. Over a three-day period, the hash was transported by taxi, forty kilos at a time in canvas bags, to a dingy office that was situated in a nameless alleyway behind Main Bazaar in the seedy Paharganj area. Upon delivery, each shipment was paid for in American dollars by a great, blubbery whale of a Pakistani man, who had the sanguine complexion of a heavy whisky drinker and wore a sweat-stained green robe the size of four-man tent. A week after arriving in Delhi, the deal was done. The MacDopes had more than doubled their original financial investment.

Just off Connaught Place was a grey concrete market building, about the same size as a cavernous aircraft hanger, called Mohan Singh. It was a meeting place for hippy travellers. Air-conditioned milk shake bars provide blaring rock music and a cool spot to sip on an ice cold drink, while blowing some dope with a few like-minded souls. It was here that Angus became acquainted with chillum smoking. The durable, clay, conical pipe was the preferred implement of the sub-continent's hash-head population, because it had the equivalent power of a shotgun blast when it came to delivering THC into the smoker's lungs.

No government agency had done a survey on the incidence of lung cancer amongst regular chillum smokers, but Angus reckoned it was probably high. It was therefore that, upon taking up the practice, he listened to a seasoned smoker's advice and began eating lots of buffalo milk curd to create a protective layer of phlegm on his pulmonary system.

While overdosing on banana lassies and practicing with the chillum, the temperature outside continued to soar. Fierce afternoon sunlight baked the asphalted streets to the extent that tar stuck to the soles of one's shoes like black chewing gum. This severely hampered dodging out of the way of speeding Harley motorbike taxis whose loud, stuttering exhaust pipes were pouring out more black smoke than a coal-powered electricity plant.

New Delhi was left behind to swelter in its cacophonous mix of straining internal combustion engine sounds, multiple odours and suffocating smog of yellow-coloured air. This was most definitely not the kind of India the young Scots were in search of.

An unscheduled stop was called for in the city of Lucknow. Murphy, in the midst of humming along to Steppenwolf's 'Born to be Wild', bounced a three-wheeler motorized rickshaw off the stainless steel bull-bars mounted on the front of the bus. It was clearly the rickshaw driver's fault. He'd performed a spontaneous U-turn in the middle of the road right in front of Murphy's shocked eyes as he slammed on the bus's brakes two seconds too late. Badly shaken but miraculously without injury, the dishevelled driver, his livelihood transformed into a crumpled wreck, stood up and started tearing out his thin, greasy, black hair.

A couple of khaki-uniformed members of the local constabulary witnessed the accident from a nearby police station, a Third World cinder block construction with holes punched in its walls to serve as windows and a tattered Indian tricolour flag fluttering above a palm leaf roof. The sandaled policemen waded into a straining mob of gawking spectators and sent them scurrying by wielding long cane lathis.

Seeing an opportunity to make a spot of bakshish, the two cops approached the foreigners and circled them like a pair of insolvent buzzards who'd just spotted a fat piggy bank by the side of the road. Raj greased the crooked wheels of justice by handing over a bundle of crumpled, hundred-rupee notes to one of the police officers, whose mouth appeared to be filled with blood due to the betel nut he was chewing. The money was quickly pocketed and the two policemen began grinning like happy chimps, displaying bright red teeth and gums, badly corroded over the years by their daily intake of lime powder, which was added to their betel concoction to bring out the flavour.

Lingering handshakes were the order of the day, except for the rickshaw driver, bald and bleeding due to his own efforts, who received a hard slap on the back of his head for causing the charming tourists so much trouble. The poor fellow looked so crestfallen that Angus, assuming correctly that none of the bribe would reach him, slipped a few hundred dollars into his grimy hands when nobody was looking to pay for his ruined vehicle. The appreciative driver held the paper money to his lined forehead with both hands. His eyes filled with tears as he gazed heavenward, hoping perhaps to catch a glimpse of Goddess Laxmi, the Hindu deity associated with wealth, for it was surely her that had smiled on him and showered her material blessings upon his humble, blood-encrusted head.

Over a century before, Lucknow had been the thriving capital of Asia's wealthiest kingdom, which was ruled by the Nawabs, an extremely liberal group of Shi'ite Muslims who'd developed a taste for aesthetic culture, pleasure gardens and fabulous palaces filled with harems of beautiful nautch girls. There was still plenty of crumbling architectural evidence to support the claim that Lucknow had once been India's most prosperous pre-colonial metropolis, compared by Victorian Era European travellers to Constantinople and Rome. To the Scots, Lucknow was just another over-crowded city lost in a somnambulistic daydream, where some of the descendents of the flamboyantly dressed Nawabs had been reduced to wearing dirty rags and begging on rubbish-strewn street corners. Angus looked out of the bus's back window and watched Lucknow fade away like the city's former glories.

Situated on the western banks of the River Ganges, Benares (Varanasi) was once called Kashi (City of Life), a typical Indian paradox because Benares is the place to be if one is a Hindu and you happen to be dead. A crossroads between the grossly physical and divinely spiritual worlds, taking one's last breath in the holy city is said to be very auspicious, guaranteeing liberation from the endless cycle of death and rebirth. The Ganges is perceived by Hindus to be a living stream imbued with their spiritual dreams and overflowing with their religious symbology. The flux of contradictions that is India manifests itself magnificently in this slow moving river, so polluted with industrial waste one could develop photographs in its noxious waters. Hindus believe that taking a holy dip in the Ganges is a remedy for relieving oneself of heavy karma, which sinks down to join the millions of tons of sludge and human waste on the river bottom that has built up over the centuries from millions of Indians dumping their raw sewage into the water.

The Scots fell in love with the city as soon as they arrived in it. After parking the bus in a builder's yard, they checked into the Vishnu Rest House. The rooms reeked of DDT powder but the warm welcome they received from the management more than made up for the unpleasant chemical smell.

Ten minutes later, they hurried along a busy street that led down to the river. Scenes passed in a blur. Children playing hopscotch on a corner. Tailors bent over foot-pedal-powered Singer sewing machines in dilapidated shops. Turbaned merchants weighing out grains on brass scales counterbalanced by rocks. An old man in a spotless white dhoti emptying a plastic bucket of soapy water over a pair of howling dogs, locked together by their swollen genitals. Black baby pigs squealing in delight as they frolicked in a muddy puddle. Mangy feral cats pursuing a rat as big as a hare. A lumbering bull elephant with an orange trunk whose stately stride was marked out by a clanging brass bell strung around its wrinkled neck. A long line of stoop-shouldered men queuing outside of a thatched hut, waiting patiently to purchase betel nut and tobacco. Housewives with kohl-eyed babies fastened to their swollen breasts, or wedged into their wobbling rings of waistline fat, passing on the only currency they had in abundance: gossip. A naked Mongoloid toddler chasing a red rooster. Laughing women in saris balancing water pots upon their heads like bulbous copper crowns. A blind beggar playing a one-stringed instrument as he stared up at the sun, his sightless eyes ridged with scabs that were cracked and weeping pale yellow pus. And an ancient yogi, who had exhaled his final breath a week earlier, sitting in the full lotus position on top of a vermin-infested rubbish heap.

Dead Hindus couldn't still life's vibrant pulse as it coursed along the narrow *gallies* (alleys) that led down to the ghats (steps) on the riverbank. A non-stop procession of vivid and spectacular impressions flooded in through the young travellers' eyes to inundate their imaginations as they stood facing the world's holiest river.

'Wow, man, look at that! It's the Ganges!' Angus exclaimed, as if he were the first to discover it.

'It's the colour of diarrhoea,' said Raj, looking over the flowing expanse of light brown water, as wide as three football pitches lined end to end.

'It fucking well smells of shit around here,' commented Murphy, wrinkling his nose.

'It does,' agreed Jenny, sniffing the humid air, wonder brimming in her eyes. 'But can you feel the vibes?'

'*Yeeeah!*' chorused her three companions.

For the following week Angus, Murphy and Raj walked down to the burning ghats every morning. Once there, they'd share chillums of hashish and watch as Hindu priests cracked open corpses' skulls with curved knives to allow spirits to escape the mortal coil like fine ribbons of smoke.

Jenny, who was clean when she arrived in Benares, became depressed after visiting the funerary ghats for the first time. She began to venture out on her own and soon started to explore shadier districts of the city. Before long, she gravitated to one of the city's numerous opium dens. It was in such a dive that she became acquainted with a lizard-eyed Bengali called Pagel. He was a smack addict in his late twenties who would, in all probability, graduate from being a mainliner to a flatliner before he turned thirty. Pagel introduced Jenny to a close relative of Opium. Her name was Sister Morphine. Jenny took to the drug like an opiate does to mu opioid receptors. By the time she left Benares, Jenny was chasing the dragon just as fast as it was pursuing her. Unknown to the rest of the crew at the time, she purchased a kilo of the analgesic opiate for 4000 rupees and then stashed the light-brown-coloured powder in a cushion on board the bus. From then on, her sticky fingers were constantly dipping into her plastic bag of brown sugar and she never ceased to wonder how come the stuff tasted so good.

A week into his stay in Benares, Angus dropped a hit of LSD after breakfast. He spent the afternoon alone at the Manikarnika burning ghat, where he sat on top of a huge pile of stacked firewood. From this elevated position he looked down and studied the mournful yet fascinating spectacle of life's thin layer being scorched off to reveal death's charred skeleton, as an endless procession of cadavers were cremated in funeral pyres.

Even after death the rich appeared better off than the poor, for it was only the wealthy who could afford to pay for enough wood to completely transform their corpse into a small pile of grey ash. The less fortunate were merely reduced to a smouldering heap of burnt bone, scorched gristle and melted fat that would be unceremoniously swept into the nearby river as soon as the fire went out.

Unlike the West's sanitized version of death, whereby it is hidden away in a box like an obscenity from which everyone must be protected, Mother India has made a show out of mortality. The ghat stank of *ghee* (clarified butter) and burnt human flesh, a smell that reminded Angus of fried bacon. A thick shroud of sorrow hung over the place, the kind of grief that makes life more real and its shadow, death, a living presence.

'Satya Hey, Satya Hah' (God is Truth), chanted a passing procession, a dead body wrapped in a sheet carried upon the sturdy shoulders of four bearers.

It appeared to Angus that he could see the life history of the people milling around below him, mostly men dressed in white, the Hindu colour of mourning, and the casual events that had led them to be on the ghat at that specific juncture. For a few fleeting moments he understood perfectly how their movements were preordained and manipulated by an invisible intelligence, which was both supreme and benign, an all-knowing presence that propelled everyone to foster and fulfil their individual destinies and then die at their appointed time. His vision brought with it the inconvenient realization that everything he did in life – down to the smallest detail – carried a responsibility whether in thought, word or action.

Uncomfortable in his skin, Angus's spirit detached itself from his body, floated up into the phantom skies and entered the astral realm, where he encountered a variety of wraithlike spirits that moved around him like fine silk scarves dancing in the wind. When the solar stone began to sink towards the hazy horizon, Angus re-entered his physical shell.

A breeze came in from the river and blew a thick cloud of smoke in his direction. The reek was pouring off a corpulent woman's corpse. Its scorched elephantine legs were sticking out of a funeral pyre and dripping fat. The cadaver's long grey hair had caught fire. The stench of singed hair filled Angus's nostrils. Coughing and spluttering, he rose unsteadily to his feet and began to climb down from the pile of firewood that had been his perch for the last few hours. *Boof!* There was a dull thud when intestinal gasses in the dead woman's stomach exploded. Angus ducked instinctively as bits of sizzling flesh flew over his head. It was high time to take a stroll along the riverbank.

Away from the crowds, Angus found a quiet spot to sit and view the sun setting on what, for him, had been a most remarkable day. The residue of LSD molecules, playing pinball wizard in the cross-town traffic coasting through his brain's synaptic channels and curvilinear galleries, were by now running on cruise control. He felt relaxed enough to give his neurotransmitters a booster of high-octane DMT in order to shift up into inter-dimensional overdrive. He took out his little glass pipe, placed a smidgen of brown paste in the bowl and gave it a light. He felt the surge of blood as it carried tiny DMT messages into his cerebrovascular system. Three lungfuls of smoke later, he heard the echo from the Big Bang as his mind blew apart into a sparkling cloud of sub-atomic particles.

Eyes wide shut, he could see through his eyelids. He stared in dumbstruck fascination as the turbid Ganges transformed into liquid ribbons of light that twisted together to form a rope of white-hot plasma, which shone brighter than a thousand splendid suns.

Over on the other side of the brilliantly dazzling river, a city began to appear where only a moment before an endless expanse of neatly ploughed fields had stretched away into the distance.

Angus could feel the planet turning on its axis beneath him. His eyes blinked open and he looked towards the horizon. The flaming fireball of the sun was low in the sky. He heard it hiss in delight as it caressed the earth.

He closed his eyes again and once more the astral city appeared. It was more clearly defined and soared up from the ground to incredible heights. In the midst of the city stood a massive domed structure that glowed with an unearthly blue light. A spire rose from its curved apex like a gold-tipped spear. Upon it fluttered a bright yellow banner, emblazoned with two entwined serpents that were brought into motion by the flag's undulation. Tiny white specks, that Angus took to be a flock of pure-white doves, circled the gigantic cupola. The high-pitched trill of Tibetan bells quavered through the ether and sung in his ears. He gasped in astonishment when he saw winged beings hovering in the sky above the city's fantastic edifices.

The vision faded. For some time, Angus continued to sit with his eyes closed, listening intently to insects communicating at frequencies that were normally beyond the human range. He opened his eyes and looked over the Ganges at empty fields shrouded in misty shadows. In the twilight he stared up into a cloudless dark blue sky. Bright stars began to spring forth. He imagined he could hear them roaring like nuclear furnaces even though they were light-years away.

Angus's inner eye flashed back on a scene he'd witnessed the evening before. Walking back to his hotel, he'd lost his way in the maze of gallies that led up from the ghats and found himself in a cobblestone alley lined on each side with emaciated beggars who were crying out for alms. They were victims of an abject poverty so crushingly subhuman that the only escape from their Dantean reality was through death's portal. The poor unfortunates raised their begging bowls and bleated in unison, *'paisa, paisa, paisa,'* in the desperate hope that a few coins would come their way to help ward off starvation. A wave of nausea overwhelmed Angus as he recollected the stench of human misery that had risen off those wretched people, a putrid smell of sour sweat, unwashed clothes and shit. His own life unfolded before him. Mirrored in his fragmented but intensely reflective mind he saw what a hollow, pleasure-seeking lifestyle and purely selfish attitude he'd adopted, leaving him with an outlook wherein having a good time was all that really mattered. He felt like God was rebuking him without saying a word.

The cerebral cortex is the outer part of our brain where most of our thinking goes on. Angus had neon-yellow lightning bolts flashing across his. Contemplations on self-indulgence caused a victorious, guilt-laden army of thoughts to swarm over the battlefield of his psyche. Sensuality's dwindling forces were beating a hasty retreat. 'Fucking shit!' Angus cried out. He saw what he was with sickening clarity – a self-serving hedonist. A peculiar yearning arose in his soul which he had never known before – a desire to put something back into life instead of always being on the take.

Pictures of working in a charitable organization that served to the needs of the poor materialized in his remorseful mind. Starving brown-skinned infants surrounded him. Swarms of flies pooled around their pleading eyes as they watched their Scottish saviour mix up some powdered nutritional supplement. He spoke out loud to the potbellied toddlers. 'Here kids, eat this.' Angus was so caught up in his humanitarian fantasy that he actually held out an imaginary aluminium soupspoon. It was dripping with white creamy liquid as he tilted it towards a hallucination of malnourished children's open mouths.

'Good evening.'

Angus nearly jumped out of his guilt-ridden skin when he heard a gentle voice deliver this greeting in the semi-darkness. Raising his head, he looked up into a pair of intelligent eyes. Silence hissed in his ears for what felt like an eternity.

'Goo…Goo…Goo…Good evening,' stammered Angus, only just remembering how to respond in kind to such a social exchange.

'My name is Swami Ram,' declared the stranger.

The light was fading fast, but to Angus's psychedelically-fuelled brain the softly spoken man appeared to be suffused with ethereal light. His face, although heavily shadowed, was curiously alert and radiant.

Angus's guidance system switched on to autopilot. 'Angus…Angus Macleod,' said he, offering his hand. The swami glanced down at the hand and then raised his own, prayer-like to his face in the traditional namaste greeting. He squatted beside Angus, who found the man's presence familiar, as if he were in the company of a lifelong friend.

As the gloaming converted into starlight, the troubling countenance of remorse once again rose up from the depths of Angus's consciousness. He turned to the man and, needing to exorcise the demon of shame from his mind, blurted out the first things that came to him. 'Swami Ram, I've just realized what a selfish person I am. I feel mixed up and guilty. What...what should I do?'

The swami said nothing at first. Angus let the silence sink into his soul. He studied Swami Ram's profile, the high-bridged nose, short chin, the smooth brow. Only one eye was visible from that angle and it was closed. When Ram turned to face Angus, his eyes opened and shone as if illuminated from within by reflections from a celestial world.

'Do not be worried, young man,' said the swami, with not a hint of condescension in his voice. 'What you are experiencing is natural enough. If you choose to, you can view it in a positive light and see it as the dawning of maturity in your heart. Your confusion is healthy, for it is often the case that we are more enlightened when we are confused, and lost in the dark when we are confident. As to what you should do, that is indeed a tricky question.' He produced a cough to clear his throat. 'My suggestion is that you begin to meditate.' Ram looked intently at Angus, who felt like he was being scrutinized by an alarming intelligence. 'If you really do care about your fellow man then the first thing you must learn to do is curb your appetites, especially greed for all things material. Personal greed is the root cause of so much of the suffering that exists in the world today. When the people of this world realize the power of love and overcome the love of power and desire for material things, then no one will want for anything they really need and peace will reign supreme in all its glory.'

It was the first time in Angus's life that anyone had ever spoken so directly to him about such matters. Although the swami's words were recognizable as language their content was obscure to Angus's mind, but his soul understood – knew without memorable knowledge – exactly what the man meant. Angus could feel the compassion radiating from him, not some kind of feeble sympathy, but a powerful force that had the capacity to heal emotional wounds, soothe a troubled mind and vanquish the past by laying it to rest. A lump rose in Angus's throat. A gentle sob floated out of his mouth and for a few heartfelt moments he wept silently, grateful for understanding Ram's message.

Soon, another question hatched in his mind and flew from his lips. 'There seems to be so much unnecessary suffering in the world. Isn't there something else that I can do to help besides meditate?'

'Angus, you're mistaken if you believe that the gentle art of meditation is something which exists apart from life. The point is that, although wishing to help people less fortunate than yourself sounds like a commendable thing to do, you will not succeed in your endeavour unless there is a radical shift in conscious awareness. It is not so much a question of what you can do to alleviate the suffering that exists in the world, but rather what you can refrain from that really matters. Suffering is caused by indifferent selfishness, insularity and personal greed. When understanding dawns and you see that it's time to uproot and destroy these causes then suffering will begin to cease. If your desire to assuage mankind's afflictions is sincere, then you must develop and perfect the one tool which you have at your disposal that can truly help – yourself. To meditate means to bring a quality of awareness into every act you perform and in so doing those acts are transformed into something wonderful.' He added, 'As your understanding of the mystery of life grows you will begin to realize that everything is predetermined. Yet, at the same time, you will see that you are always free not to identify with the body and not be affected by the pains and pleasures that come as a consequence of the body's activities. It is often the case in life that in order to allow the right thing to happen you have to get out of your own way. Find your true self by becoming a witness and then you will be free.'

Over towards the city a temple bell clanged with brass clarity and, at the stately rate of a megaton a minute, the Ganges flowed by as quiet as the voice of God.

After a long and apparently thoughtful pause, Swami Ram emitted a faint sigh and then said, 'What I am about to tell you may sound like a cliché to a mind moulded and made rigid by logical thought. However, it's your heart's intrinsic intelligence I'm addressing when I say: life is a constant flow, with no beginning and no end. Don't allow the doors of birth and death to lead you into believing otherwise.' He nodded towards the river's broad black shadow and continued. 'Life is as unstoppable as *Ganga Ma*, Mother Ganges. Born in a Himalayan glacier she sets forth into the world as a trickle, turns into a stream, expands into a cataract and then, fed by tributaries, matures into the great waterway we sit beside now as she continues on her inexorable journey to merge with the ocean. She exists in the past, present and future simultaneously. Yes, that is how it is and, if we are fearless, we can plunge into the river of life's depths and experience reality directly – *here and now*.'

The swami stood, walked down to the riverbank and dived into the Ganges. Angus had been so captivated by the sound of Ram's soothing voice it took him a moment to take in what had happened. Understanding came with the speed of a lightning bolt. He was thunderstruck.

A thin layer of low-lying mist had moved in to filter the starlight, making the sky appear like a massive hospital x-ray, pin-holed by flickering light. Angus rose up unsteadily. He could see nothing of the swami. The splashing sounds from his swimming were quickly fading away. Angus sat down again and noticed his ears were buzzing. In the distance Swami Ram called out – '*Om, nama Shaivaya*' – and then there was only silence.

The holy man's dramatic exit had torn a big hole in Angus's reality screen and left its tattered remnants blowing in the winds of change. His mind struggled to define Swami Ram but failed and so he quickly became an enigma to him. For want of anything better to do he rolled a joint. He struck a match. Flame erupted out of its sulphur-coated tip with a pop and a hiss. He stared in amazement at a red giant going supernova. 'Ouch!' He burnt his fingers. Six blinding starbursts later, he remembered to light his joint. He smoked it down to its cardboard roach, closed his eyes and entered the trance part of transcendental. Next thing he knew, the sky to the east was beginning to lighten into the pale grey of a false dawn. Flabbergasted at how time had shot by unnoticed, he stared at the river for half an eternity before he stood up and discovered his limbs were stiff from sitting still for so long.

He wandered along the riverbank and made his way back to the Vishnu Lodge Rest House. High-pitched temple bells rang out, rupturing the silence as they heralded the arrival of a new day.

In many ways Benares became a crossroads in the four Scottish travellers' lives. From the sacred city on the banks of the Ganges the individual paths they were to tread for some time to come set out in different directions.

When Angus returned to the rest house that morning and opened the door to the room he shared with Jenny, there was an unfamiliar smell hanging in the air. Jenny had caught the dragon. The small room had two rickety wooden chairs, a cracked window lending a rooftop view and a low double bed. Jenny was sprawled out on the bed's foam rubber mattress like a soporific wraith, a thin white sheet wrapped around her waist. By her side was a small, soot-blackened square of tinfoil that she'd used to heat up a sticky line of morphine powder, before inhaling the narcotic's stupefying fumes through a biro's hexagonal plastic tube.

'What the fuck is this?' Angus asked, picking up the discarded dragon-chasing kit.

Jenny's eyelids fluttered open as her body stirred. She turned onto her right side, leaned her chin on a thin arm and stared up at him with a catatonic gaze that was as vacuous as a stone statue's. In the dim light Angus could see that there were black shadows under her eyes and a trickle of saliva dribbling from the corner of her mouth. Semi-comatose, her answer came as a question and was surprisingly concise, although it contained little information in regards to his query. 'Why don't you fuck off and mind your own business?'

She moaned, rolled over to face away from him and muttered, 'I'll do what the hell I want.'

Jenny's words pierced Angus's sensitive eardrums like burning needles and blistered his brain like scalding oil. He stood by the bed and studied the curving delicacy of her naked back. Anger flared and seethed within him and he struggled to control his emotions. He kept his distance, afraid that if he drew closer he might be tempted to slap her.

He shook the square of aluminium foil in her direction and said in a level voice, 'I thought you were finished with this shit.'

'Fucking arsehole! You're just…ego tripper…' Her words became garbled.

A heated row ensued, which didn't end until Jenny fell into a sea of incoherent ravings and sank into unconsciousness. It was the most words they'd shared in a week and it was obvious to Angus that their roles in respect to each other had become that of adversaries rather than allies. He stormed out of the room, slammed the door behind him and stomped off in search of some breakfast.

For obvious reasons he'd failed to mention his mysterious meeting on the riverbank. Like an earth-filled pot planted with bulbs and stored in darkness, Swami Ram became a secret left to flower in a hidden recess of his heart.

Under the watchful eye of an elastic-limbed yogi, Raj had taken up practicing hatha yoga. He rose each morning at dawn to go off to a yoga school where he performed a series of body-contorting asanas and breathing exercises in front of Ananda Ganapati Lund, his teacher. Mr Lund was an adept who could bend his body into an om symbol and, like many a man in his profession, was totally preoccupied with seducing his female students.

Murphy had become embroiled in an ill-fated love affair, which would end when he left Benares. His latest flame was a tall, slim, copper-skinned Algerian siren called Mohini. Her almond-shaped eyes were the colour of conkers and smouldered with lust. Mohini had cheekbones sharp enough to slice leather and was as skinny as a kite and beautiful, if one could see beauty in a cut-throat razor's glinting edge. She'd been living in the holy city for over a year, learning to play the sitar. With a tongue as finely tuned as her ethnic instrument, Mohini was involved in an ongoing argument with Murphy about his macho attitude. Their heated disputes were punctuated by intermittent bouts of noisy lovemaking. The Vishnu Lodge's manager had already threatened to call the police due to the infernal racket coming out of Murphy's room at all hours.

When Murphy wasn't raising huge amounts of hell with Mohini, he would accompany Raj and Angus down to the ghats after drinking a marijuana concoction called bhang lassi. Flying high, they'd watch life and death rub up against each other on the banks of the Ganges while, overhead, vultures circled languidly, coasting on thermals without so much as the quiver of a wing. Angus kept his third eye open in case Swami Ram showed up but the enigmatic holy man failed to put in an appearance.

By the end of June the sun's implacable rays were beating down with such ferocious intensity pigeons evaporated in mid-flight and roasting stone temples sweated concrete bullets. A shimmering cloud of humidified heat lay over Lord Shiva's city like the lid on a continental pressure cooker, which produced a roasting clamminess so profound it rivalled that of an overheating, nuclear-powered Swedish sauna. The scalding syrupy air was almost unbreathable. Even the flies and vampiric mosquitoes were somnambulant.

The stifling temperatures prompted the Scots to head for the hills. They had reached a point where it was difficult to remember what a cool breeze felt like. A journey up into the mountains would refresh their memories as well as their fatigued bodies.

15

MONKEY BUSINESS

Cambodia.

The rain was falling with a steady mechanical hiss. I was soaked to the skin. I took off my denim shirt, wrapped my cigarettes and lighter in it and then placed the bundle to one side. The thought of warm tobacco smoke filling my lungs appealed greatly to me, but I knew that lighting up in the torrential downpour would be impossible. I looked out over the restless sea, a mirror of the ocean of nervous anxiety I was drowning in. I couldn't remember a time in my life when I'd felt as washed out as I did in that moment. My hands dug into the wet sand and I wished I could lie down on it. I groaned in frustration. My aching shoulders felt like they were in the grip of iron tongs. *'Aaaarrgh!'* I let out a long scream to disperse the tension. It was a primal howl compounded of shivering angst, fury and the desire to be free of the awful fix I was in. It felt good to let it out. *'Rrrrrggh!'* I roared like a lion escaped from a cage after years of captivity. And then my roaring turned to laughter. What made me laugh was the recollection of a line from a story that Angus had told me. 'That's enough of your monkey business.'

India, July, 1973.

The southwest monsoon's thick grey clouds were moving steadily northward and preparing to inundate India. It was the middle of the afternoon. Raj had the air-conditioning going full blast, as he drove towards Raxaul on the Indian border.

Angus checked a small thermometer that was glued to the outside of one of Rolling Thunder's passenger seat windows. It was forty-three degrees centigrade. He looked down as the bus edged past gangs of Rajasthani labourers, repairing stretches of pot-holed asphalt. The gaunt-faced men were dressed in ragged shirts and threadbare trousers, stained by mud to the colour of used teabags. Angus wondered how they could stand the heat. Only a few of them wore cotton turbans to protect their heads from the sun. They stood indolent and deadpan as they smoked beedies. The women, who laboured beside them, were built like kick-boxers. They wore mirrored skirts and skimpy tops that glinted in the sun and left the bottom half of their breasts exposed. Their muscular arms and ankles were adorned with heavy silver bracelets that jangled as they swung pick axes with the tireless enthusiasm of Klondike prospectors digging for gold.

Travel documents were checked at a small customs post by three impeccably-dressed Nepalese officials, who somehow managed to remain cool in their stiflingly hot workplace.

A red-painted, aluminium security barrier was lifted and the bus continued on her journey north. For a while there was little to distinguish the sun-scorched landscape from that of the country that had officially been left behind. Parched flatlands, with a few glimpses of cultivated green, gave way to impenetrable graceless jungle.

Rolling Thunder sounded glad to be gobbling up kilometres again. The engine's growl intensified as the bus began to wind her way up into a mountain range, which had been formed over fifty-million years before, when India broke away from a massive proto-continent and rammed into Asia's soft underbelly.

An endless course of hairpin bends snaked up through the mountains that formed a natural border between the two countries. By late afternoon the bus had risen above the torrid temperatures of the alluvial plains below. The all-too-familiar sight of shattered vehicle wrecks lay at the bottom of thousand metre deep gorges, lending a far better admonition to drive carefully than the bent out of shape road signs that stood by the wayside. The light began to soften and cast pastel tones on the stark landscape. It was getting dark by the time the road levelled out. Angus sat alone in the observation bubble gazing at splintered, craggy basalt mountain peaks that were silhouetted like black paper cut-outs against the background of a deep purple sky. A handful of stars dotted the heavens, flickering as if powered by a fluctuating electricity source. Kathmandu was only a few hours' drive away.

In 1973 Kathmandu was the world's major Mecca for dope-smoking hippies. Hashish and marijuana were legitimately sold commodities – made illegal later that year – dealt out by government-sanctioned retailers with names like *Shiva Shakti Cannabis Shop* and *Eden Ganja Centre*. Not only were hash and marijuana legal, a lot of it was high-quality produce, sold at very cheap prices. The MacDopes were in heaven. They spent their first week in

Kathmandu smoking hashish from the moment they woke up in the morning until they passed out late at night.

The Nepalese capital was a relatively compact city that had not given way to uncontrolled urban sprawl. This made it a pleasant and easy place to explore by foot. Thousands of foreign freaks wandered the streets and hung out in cafés. Unfortunately, the town-planning department had not woken up to the fact that the open sewers that flanked the unpaved streets were a disease-breeding eyesore. The gutters flowed with a dark green bacteriological gunk which, had it been collected and canned, could have been sold to a rogue state as a major component in the manufacture of biological weapons. Amoebic dysentery was rife amongst the droves of hippy travellers who inhabited the city's lodges. The Scots were not immune to it.

Due to excessive pot inhalations, the MacDopes were prone to frequent munchie attacks. The entrepreneurial spirit of the local Nepalese had cottoned on to the foreign visitors' gastro-psychosis and set up bakeries, selling sugar-loaded cakes to cater to the ravenous cannabis crazies' needs. The apple pie topped with whipped cream, served up with coffee at the Flying Pig Café, was delicious, albeit loaded with enough parasitical microbes to turn a stalwart rat's bowels inside out. The three Scotsmen contracted amoebic dysentery after eating the apple pie and, had a casual observer caught sight of them while visiting their hotel – built entirely from wood and situated opposite the Ganesh Sthan Temple – that person might have been left with the impression that they were training for a cross-country race as they sprinted for the squat-down toilet at the bottom of three flights of narrow stairs. Jenny was unaffected by this debilitating malaise as she rarely ventured out of her room to eat anything. She was content to read books or lie flat on her back staring at the ceiling, out of her mind on the morphine that had anaesthetized most of her physical sensations including hunger pangs.

'If we're going to stay in Nepal, we have to rent a place with a kitchen and cook our own food,' croaked Raj, clutching at his bloated belly one morning, like an overdue pregnant mother in labour – giving birth to a ten-gallon oil drum. He was barely able to sit up in bed after a weeklong bout of diabolical diarrhoea that had left him, and his two mates, weak at the knees and totally lacking intestinal flora.

Back on their shaky legs, the three Scotsmen went for a four kilometre walk that brought them to Swayambhu, a rural community that lay on the western edge of the Kathmandu Valley. Situated below an ancient temple that had been built on top of a conical hill, the village had taken its name from the elevated structure, which was called Swayambhunath.

Enquiries were made amongst the friendly villagers and it was soon discovered that near to the temple a two-storey house, built from dark grey stone that was covered in ivy and set in its own grounds, was available for rent. The five-roomed building had no electricity. Water could be hand-drawn from a well outside of the kitchen door. Upstairs there was a bedroom with a small veranda that looked down into a well-tended garden, where there was enough space to park the bus. At the Nepalese rupee equivalent of two hundred American dollars a month the place wasn't cheap, but it was a dream come true.

By the end of July, the Scots were settling into what would become their home for over a year.

On a clear day, a white line on the horizon marked the edges of the Himalaya mountain range. The surrounding countryside presented endless possibilities for hikes in a rural Xanadu, where the modern world had not yet managed to cover over the landscape with concrete, steel and asphalt. The size of an open book, fantastically patterned butterflies fluttered around on flowering bushes, accompanied by big black bees whose loud buzzing could be heard from some distance away.

Jenny was not immune to the effects of such an inspirational environment. Most mornings she climbed the 365 steps, flanked by copper prayer wheels and carved stones, that led up to the temple. Swayambhunath was a high-energy power spot with commanding views of the surrounding countryside, which brought tears of appreciation to her pin-prick-pupil eyes. Angus, Raj and Murphy's pupils were quite the opposite, dilated to the max due to their frequent LSD sessions.

At least twice a week Angus and his two friends would drop acid and trip around the temple. Its environs were the perfect setting for mind-blowing experiences. Beneath the shade of trees that surrounded the sanctuary, massive, whitewashed Buddha statues sat in stately repose. Above them and facing towards the four cardinal points were all-seeing eyes. They were painted on each side of the square base of the monkey temple's towering spire, which was strung with lines of flapping green, yellow, red, blue and white prayer flags and illuminated at night by pale green electric light. Between each pair of eyes was a curling question mark, the Nepali character for number one, symbolizing unity or signifying that the single way leading to spiritual enlightenment could be found if one followed the Buddhist path.

There were two unpleasant natural hazards that were occasionally encountered in the neighbourhood. First and foremost were the temple's simian inhabitants, who flourished in great numbers in Swayambhunath's grounds. The light brown Rhesus monkeys had white chests, narrow shoulders and orange eyes that darted around, furtively searching for a spot of mischief to perpetrate. The spunky monkeys were highly organized rip-off merchants. They would attack in troops and employ guerrilla tactics to steal anything shiny or edible. Extremely aggressive, quite a number of the monkeys were infected with the dangerous rabies virus. The Scots took to carrying thick sticks to ward off the slavering disease carriers. Murphy's stave was more like a cudgel. It didn't take long for him to get into the swing of things. He became very proficient in putting his club to good use and took to calling the process shillelagh bashing, harking back to his Celtic roots. Word soon spread through the gibbering simian grapevine that contact with Murphy was life threatening. Whenever he showed up carrying his shillelagh, one could hear the monkey lookouts' agitated chattering high up in the trees as soon as they caught sight of the human monster from hell with the waist length hair.

'Come on, then, you hairy fuckers. What are you waiting for?' Murphy would shout his challenge, but the furry tribe wasn't up for having their skulls cracked. They stayed on their branches looking down at him with petrified expressions etched into their pink faces.

Roaming packs of vicious pye-dogs were the second group of animal pests in the region. These stray mongrels would bite a stranger in the leg for no apparent reason. Like the monkeys, many of them were infected with rabies. Being bitten by one of them was something to be avoided at all costs. If one didn't, it meant a daily trip to a hospital in Kathmandu to receive a series of immunoglobulin shots in the stomach for the following two weeks. According to rumour, the injections were extremely painful.

When Murphy killed a couple of drooling, rabid bow-wows, by employing vicious blows to their heads with his cudgel, his reputation rapidly spread through the canine community as well. After that, any dog that spotted him gave a quick yelp, stuck its tail between its legs and scampered off in the opposite direction.

Viewed from a distance and using a little imagination, the Swayambhunath temple resembled an outer space communications centre. Its gilded spire was composed of thirteen horizontal golden discs that, depending on who one listened to, symbolized either the spiritual worlds or the stages on the path leading to Nirvana. Inside the temple, it was definitely inner space that the maroon-clad Buddhist monks were endeavouring to stay in close contact with. Most afternoons, a small group of the shaven-headed sangha congregated in a windowless room to play discordant music. Using a variety of instruments, including brass cymbals, thigh-bone trumpets and hand drums made from human skulls, the boys in the band of spiritual brothers reproduced the sounds made by the body's organs as it went about the daily business of staying alive. For the most part, the monks kept to themselves, their curiosity about the hippy invasion limited to the occasional shy glance.

Evenings drifted by down at the *Rising Moon*, a cosy café that had been adopted by the foreigners who lived in and around the village. Over a hot bowl of *chang*, an alcoholic beverage made from fermented barley, and the occasional chillum loaded with fresh Nepalese temple ball hashish – a combination that was as potent as a mule kick in the head – the conversations that filled the establishment's smoky air with chatter were often far-out and amusing.

On one particular evening, a thunderstorm rolled over the Kathmandu valley, unleashing salvos of veined lightning. Angus sat outside the teashop, watching Mother Nature's dramatic lightshow illuminate the darkness with her zillion-watt zigzag performance. He was joined by a longhaired New Yorker who had a drooping moustache and mutton-chop sideburns that were shaved into points to accentuate his jaw line. His name was Professor Vogel. What the talkative Jew was a professor of nobody seemed to know. However, his nickname, 'The Prof,' suited him. He looked like a youthful Albert Einstein on a foggy night and, just like an absent-minded professor, he had a habit of repeating himself. In his early thirties, he was a tough bagel who, if he was to be believed, narrowly missed being burnt in an oven.

Heavy rain began to fall and pelt off the overhanging tiled roof above their heads. Angus pulled up his woollen jacket's collar and stared at the curtain of water falling from the overflowing gutter. Meanwhile, The Prof proceeded to deliver an anecdote – in this instance an abbreviated version of his life story.

Angus listened patiently as The Prof told how he was of Polish extraction and how he'd inherited his resilient genes from parents who had, according to him, been held prisoner in the Nazi slave labour camp at Auschwitz-Monowitz. He claimed to have been born in Auschwitz's Barracks Number 2 in 1942, although he bore no physical evidence of this.

The Prof caught Angus glancing at his uncovered arms and said, 'I was too young to have a number tattooed on my wrist.'

Angus nodded, his expression revealing neither belief nor doubt. 'Go on, man,' he said, 'I'm listening.'

'My mother perished in the Auschwitz-Birkennau extermination camp,' continued the American. 'She was killed by the hydrogen cyanide gas that is produced by crystallized prussic acid when it comes into contact with air. To the sound of screams rising up to greet them like choral music from hell, the deadly pellets were dropped through a hole in a gas chamber's roof by fiercely anti-Semitic, Latvian *Shutzstaffel* troops who were possessed by a diabolical vision of a racially ordered empire.' He blinked. 'My mother was gassed to death…gassed to death…until she was left foaming at the mouth and bleeding from the ears.' He turned to Angus and took a firm hold of his arm. 'They gassed my mother to death with Zyklon B, man. Can you imagine what that must have been like?'

'Holy shit!' Angus was genuinely shocked by the horrible images produced by the man's words. His hand trembled slightly as he lit up a half-smoked joint.

'There was nothing holy about what those monstrous fiends did,' remarked The Prof, letting go of Angus's arm. 'IG Farben's atrocious patented product, Zyklon B, which was originally intended to be used as an insecticide, was sold by the truckload to the SS by a Polish poison gas salesman. When the war was over, that bastard went on to pursue a career in one of the world's biggest organized religions. He rose in the ranks and attained the exalted position of regional director and soon had corrupt politicians queuing up to kiss his ring of power.'

Angus found this piece of information incredible, although the sincere tone in the Jew's voice convinced him that he was perhaps telling the truth. He coughed out some smoke and offered the hash joint. The Prof took three hits on it, pinged the smouldering nub into a puddle and continued with his story. 'Via a brick chimneystack, connected to the furnace that had incinerated her corpse, my mother went up in smoke. Her hot ashes were carried off upon the ill winds blowing over European skies at the time. As a result, my mother's molecular remains were inhaled by countless other human beings, gaining her a certain kind of immortality.' He once again turned to Angus and, for a brief moment in the semi-darkness, smiled enigmatically, as if pleased with his personal brand of warped philosophy. 'A certain kind of immortality,' he repeated quietly, before delivering some more gruesome information. 'By the time Soviet troops swarmed across Poland and liberated the camp, during the last days of January nineteen-forty-five, my father and I had been reduced to hollow-eyed, pale-skinned wraiths. Battle-hardened though they were, many of the Russian soldiers wept openly when they saw wasted corpses piled in ghastly heaps between the camp's wooden huts and the emaciated condition of the hundreds of prisoners who'd somehow managed to survive. Many of those starving people died within days after eating beef stew, because their bodies were unable to absorb fat. Due to the bitter cold and the need to build up our strength, my father and I remained in and around the camp and small neighbouring village called Oswiecim until early spring.'

The Prof eyes misted over when he depicted how his father had looked when they'd staggered out of the six square kilometre concentration camp. 'I was only a little boy at the time, but I can still remember holding papa's bony hand and looking up into his skull-like face that was…was all…all eyes,' he stammered. 'The…there was a yellow Star of David sown on to the right arm of his filthy oversized jacket, which hung loosely on his skeletal frame like that of a scarecrow.'

The Prof blew his big nose into a handkerchief, wiped his eyes and went on to tell about how, as refugees, he and his father had hitched rides on military vehicles and horse-drawn carts across a war-torn Europe and eventually made their way to Belgium. 'In Antwerp,' he said, 'we made contact with a distant relative, who worked as a diamond cutter in the Jewish ghetto. My father borrowed money from him and promised to pay it back at fifty percent interest within a year. We then caught a train to Rotterdam in the Dutch province of South Holland. From there we made our way to an office in the seaport, where we booked passage on an Atlantic steamer and immigrated to the United States.

'The Atlantic crossing took two very long weeks, during which time papa and I suffered terribly from seasickness. The morning that I first set eyes on the Statue of Liberty, rising out of the mist in New York harbour, was perhaps one of the most memorable in my life. It was a wonderful and inspiring sight. Even now, I get choked up remembering how my father pointed to the broken shackles being trampled by the Lady of Liberty's left foot and how his voice was hoarse with emotion when he said, 'Look, my son, the nightmare is over. We are free at last. If only your mother were here to share this moment with us.'

'Five years later, my father married a New York banker's daughter and went on to become a successful arms dealer. He made a fortune supplying sophisticated weaponry to Israel. By the time I was eighteen, I was his right-hand-man,' he added proudly. 'That is, until the arrival of the Vietnam War when, due to my expertise in the handling of weapons, I was called up to go and fight in a conflict where I stood a good chance of getting my ass blown off by the gooks, people who I had nothing against except the fact that they'd probably want to kill me for invading their country. Now,' he concluded, 'I'm a goddamned draft dodger hiding out in Nepal.' Sensing rightly that the young Scotsman sitting beside him was not entirely convinced by his story he added with greater conviction, 'A few years back, I returned to southern Poland and visited Auschwitz.'

'What was that like?' Angus enquired.

The American shook his head slowly. 'It is the most evil place on earth. *The most evil place on earth,*' he repeated loudly. 'A black silence permeates what's left of the camp that sends shivers up my spine just thinking about it. The few birds that you see in the trees go about their business without so much as a cheep. It's as if they know what went on in the Nazis' death factory, which will forever remain as a filthy stain on mankind's conscience because over a million innocent people were murdered there, most of them Jews like myself.'

Well and truly stoned, Angus shuddered.

The American concluded, 'I know it might sound strange, but I think everyone should visit Auschwitz, because it is a living reminder of the fact that we're all only a few steps away from becoming monsters.'

The rain ceased.

One thing was certain: The Prof had the gift of the gab. He was a non-stop talker who could have competed in an Olympic talkathon and taken the gold. If one had a subject, he was guaranteed to have a tale to match it, even if he had to fabricate it on the spot.

The Prof's big-nosed face and lively eyes were momentarily illuminated by the flash from a perpendicular lightning bolt, which had just struck a distant tree, setting it on fire. 'Do you know,' he said to Angus, having decided to move on to a less depressing subject, 'that up on the temple's main square there are a couple of circular brass plates set into the floor? If you take your shoes off and put a foot on each of them, things can pass through your body.'

Angus smiled wryly at the American, whose head was capped with a red Nepalese felt hat embroidered with a Tibetan double dorje, a symbol of spiritual power. 'What? What do you mean, *things can pass through your body?*' he asked, returning to the pragmatic scepticism of his Scottish intellectual heritage.

'I know it doesn't sound plausible,' said The Prof, 'but I'm telling you, what I'm saying is the truth. Why, the other day I was standing on those brass plates – high on mescaline – when a hummingbird, a moth and a dozen bumble bees flew right through my body. What a buzz I got.'

Angus burst out laughing.

'You goddamned cynical Scotsman,' chuckled the American.

Just then, the Rising Moon's wooden door swung open. The lively hum of excited conversation, clatter of dishes and a swathe of pale yellow light washed out into the night. Framed by the doorway, Murphy and Raj's silhouettes were caught for a moment, lit from behind before they stepped outside.

'Evening,' said Raj, looking towards the American, who responded with a nod.

Cool to the point of indifference, Murphy glanced at The Prof and said to Angus, 'It's stopped raining. You coming?'

Angus stood, shook hands with The Prof and said to him, 'Thanks for the company. I'll catch you later, man.'

The Prof rose to his feet, headed for the open door and said over his shoulder, 'Pleasure was all mine, Angus, pleasure was all mine.' He raised a hand in farewell. 'Goodnight, you guys.' He stepped inside and closed the door behind him.

On the way home, Angus told Murphy and Raj about The Prof's experience up at the monkey temple.

'Sounds like a load of fucking nonsense to me,' said Murphy, writing it off as over-the-top ravings from a man whose hold on reality was, in his opinion, down to a broken fingernail. 'The guy's right off his rocker,' he continued. 'The other night he was trying to convince me that he and his dear old dad survived the holocaust by drinking soup made from grass, worms and chicken feathers. Cuckoo fuckin' feathers more like. He actually managed to produce crocodile tears when he was telling me this and all the time I was thinking to myself, this wanker is lying through his gold-capped teeth.'

'I don't think it's quite like that,' disagreed Angus. 'It's just that The Prof experiences difficulty when it comes to separating fact from fiction.'

Murphy screwed up his face like somebody had let off a smelly fart and spat to one side. 'In other words he's a fucking liar. I've said it before and I'll say it again; you can't trust anyone who's over thirty.'

Raj was less sceptical. 'Why don't we drop a window pane of acid tomorrow morning and go and check out those brass plates for ourselves?' He paused for a brief moment and then said, 'Oh…I just remembered, after I've done my asanas.'

'Oh aye, Raj,' commented Murphy, stopping dead in his tracks, 'can't start the day without your yoga, not with Buddhahood waiting just around the corner for you.'

'Don't be so fuckin' sarcastic,' snapped Raj, turning to face him. 'It makes me feel good,' he declared, his tone rising defensively. 'What's wrong with that?'

Murphy grinned, pleased to have provoked a reaction. 'Sorry man, I didn't mean to offend you,' he lied, giving Raj a friendly shove. 'I was only rattling your cage.'

'Well you've fucking well succeeded,' fumed Raj. 'Satisfied?'

Murphy started walking again. 'Anyway,' he said over his shoulder, 'this bliss trip you are on is just a repackaged version of the heaven myth, custom-made for naive hippies.' He let out a spluttering laugh.

'You stupid bastard!' Raj shouted at his back. 'What the fuck are you laughing at? Yoga's a lot better for your mind than all those intellectual books you read,' he said in his best holier-than-thou tone.

Murphy turned and began walking backwards. 'If you're referring to me reading Dostoevsky's *The Brothers Karamazov*,' he said to Raj, 'I have to agree with you. That fucking book is doing my head in because I can't keep track of all those Russian names.'

'Good!' Raj snapped again.

Angus asked, 'When are you guys getting married?'

'We haven't quite made up our minds yet,' said Murphy, adopting a camp tone. He stood still, grabbed Raj's left hand and asked, 'Have we, darling?'

Raj pulled his hand from Murphy's grip and replied through gritted teeth, 'No we fucking well haven't. We just can't seem to decide where to go for our honeymoon.'

Angus and Murphy laughed. Raj didn't.

Over to their right, the sound of a monkey screeching arose from within the thick clouds of mist shrouding the Swayambhunath temple. A common enough occurrence, Angus thought nothing of it at the time. Soon he was to remember the high-pitched shriek as an omen.

The following morning began in a way that passed for normal in those heady times. After breakfasting on homemade muesli, the three Scotsmen drank local coffee, passed a smoking chillum around the kitchen table and filled their lungs with hashish smoke. Still seated, each of them ingested a strong dose of LSD and then joined hands to chant *'Hum'*, a Tibetan syllable Raj had read about in a Buddhist book. The sound's vibration was supposedly powerful enough to awaken a serpent-like coil of psychic energy, called Kundalini, which lies dormant at the base of the spine. In Murphy's case, the humming awoke the uncomfortable sensation of feeling like a complete idiot.

The acid came on in waves. Raj suggested that they walk up to the monkey temple to investigate the mysterious brass plates that The Prof had informed Angus about.

'Hold on a minute,' said Murphy. 'Shouldn't we do something about these fuckin' flies before we leave?'

Murphy's proposal was reasonable enough. Squadrons of big black flies were buzzing around the kitchen and crawling over a pile of dirty dishes that were stacked high beside the sink. The lads rolled up old copies of *International Times* and *Frendz*, and then went to work on the flies. Half way through the blue bottles' last stand, Raj put down his improvised fly swatter and began to cry.

'What's up with you?' Angus enquired, puzzled by his friend's flowing tears.

Raj heaved a frustrated sigh, the kind which suggests something important is going on that nobody else has observed. The sound was so deep Angus was surprised that lava didn't start bubbling up out of the cracks between the kitchen floor's slab stones.

'This is really heavy, man,' sobbed Raj, sitting down on a rickety wooden chair that looked like it might collapse at any moment.

'What is?' Angus asked, noticing that his Indian pal's face had taken on purple hues.

'The flies, man,' replied Raj. 'They have as much right to live as we have. Wiping them out like this is creating heavy karma for us.'

'*Heavy fucking karma!* What a load of bollocks!' Murphy remarked, whacking a large blue bottle into a reddish-yellow splotch against one of the kitchen's windows. 'If you ask me, you've been reading too many spiritual books.'

There was truth in what Murphy said. Ever since Raj had discovered the Evans-Wentz translation of the *Bardo Thödol,* or the *Tibetan Book of The Dead* as it is commonly known, he was constantly quoting from its pages. This ancient treatise, used widely in Tibet and recited on the occasion of death, is addressed as much to the living as it is to the dead or dying. Implicitly, it is a text that lays out guidelines that can assist one to live life well and, in so doing, die a good death. It teaches that the mind is the source of all things and contains within it the possibility of enlightenment, leading to freedom from the repetitive cycle of birth and death. Raj was mightily impressed by the *Bardo Thödol.* He considered it a gift, given by the Tibetan people to the rest of humanity.

'Here, take this.' Murphy held out a hand. On his palm was a tiny square of LSD.

Angus thought rightly that Raj was on the edge of falling into that most chaotic of psychological states, a bad trip, and was not so sure about

Murphy's cure-all for a bummer. Before he could say anything about it, Raj had swallowed his second powerful dose of acid that morning.

Angus and Murphy went back to swatting flies with the panache of a pair of sword-wielding gladiators. Raj sat with his head in his hands, crying a river of rainbow-coloured tears. Ten minutes later, he screamed, jumped to his feet and then ran out of the front door. Murphy shouted after him, 'Don't come back without a takeaway from Wun Lung's Chinese restaurant.'

As intended, his ridiculous demand elicited a burst of laughter from Angus, who looked over at Murphy and saw a smiling, Asiatic-featured garden gnome with red hair and an orange moustache. 'Ehm… Murph, fancy a smoke?'

'Is this daft questions half-hour or what?' Murphy asked, binding his thick hair into a ponytail with a rubber band. 'Where's the chillum?'

'What about Raj?' Angus enquired, suddenly remembering that all was not well with his Indian brother.

'Looks like he's gone AWOL. Let's smoke some dope, then we can go look for him,' suggested Murphy, as he sat down at the table to prepare a pipe mix. He glanced up at the wall where the painting that Angus had acquired in Kabul was hanging. 'Hey, man, your girlfriend is winking at me.'

Angus looked around the room. 'What?'

'The belly dancer, man, she's giving me the come on.'

'Aw, her,' said Angus when he realized who Murphy was referring to. He gazed up at the broad, garishly painted canvas in admiration. 'She's a beaut, isn't she?'

Murphy let out a spluttering laugh. 'You've got to be joking, man. Everybody else around here thinks that thing is a fucking eyesore. You should take it outside and burn it.'

Angus looked away from the painting and said, 'No way, man, that's a masterpiece.'

'Masterpiece my arse,' said Murphy. 'It's pure rubbish!'

'You know what your problem is, don't you?'

'No I don't,' replied Murphy. 'Tell me.'

'You haven't developed a taste for art.'

'Yeah, right, like fuck I haven't. That painting of yours isn't art. It's a multicoloured fart from the fifth dimension.'

Murphy's absurd abstraction, and the fact that the whole room was beginning to appear to Angus's eyes like it had been freshly painted by Jackson Pollock, prompted him to put a tape into the ghetto blaster and push the play button. Captain Beefheart's *Trout Mask Replica* stormed out of the speakers.

One chillum and ten minutes later, Beefheart and The Magic Band's bizarre musical antics had the two trippers filling the room with loud volleys of uproarious laughter.

'Turn it up man,' pleaded Murphy. 'I love this bit when somebody says, *'I run on beans'* – fucking laser beans, man.'

Another bout of gut-splitting laughter ensued that soon had them doubled over and gasping for air.

'What's all the noise about?'

Summoned by the sounds of mirth and discordant music, Jenny had emerged from the blissful world she inhabited in her citadel of dreams. Dressed in a knee-length silk kimono, she stood at the top of the stairs and looked down upon the scene. Her thick blonde hair was piled up on top of her head like a golden crown. The paleness of her skin stood out in stark optic contrast against her jet-black garment. Despite the overuse of make-up, there were charcoal-grey shadows under her eyes.

'Oh, oh,' said Murphy in a hushed theatrical voice, 'pass the garlic. It's Dracula's daughter. She's risen from the dead.'

Jenny tilted her head, thrust out her lower lip and wedged her balled hands into the top of her narrow hips. 'I heard that, smartass,' she hissed, as she appeared to float down the stairs, her vulpine eyes pinning Murphy to the spot, 'and it wasn't funny.'

'Sorry, Jen,' he apologized, crossing his fingers in front of him. 'Just don't go out in the sun, or you might get burned to a crisp.'

Angus burst out laughing. Jenny pretended to be angry, glared at him and realized what condition he was in. She looked around and enquired, 'Where's Raj?'

Angus said, 'He's gone to Wun Lungs for a Chinese takeaway.'

'Don't be so daft,' she said, unable to suppress a smile. Her face was alight with a mid-morning bout of good humour. The evening before she'd caught a taxi into Kathmandu and scored an ounce of pure heroin from a bent Nepalese doctor for the sum of one hundred dollars. 'Want a cup of fresh coffee?' she asked.

The two Scotsmen nodded numbly, their blown minds perceiving Jenny as a cross between a blonde Geisha and the Prince of Darkness's favourite concubine. All that was missing to complete the picture were puncture marks on her slender neck.

The winged eel slithers on the heels of today's children... In the background, the King of Weird, Captain Beefheart, warbled out the madcap lyrics to 'Beatle Bones 'n' Smokin' Stones'. The jarring melody sounded pleasantly insane.

'*Strawberry fields forever,*' chorused Angus and Murphy.

The three sat sipping on hot coffee with Angus and Murphy blowing on juicy joints as the morning drifted by in a cloud of phantasmagoria and psychedelic music. When Jenny's favourite song, 'White Bird', by It's A Beautiful Day, drew to a thunderous close and the room fell silent, she sloped off to her lair for the day's first line of smack.

Angus and Murphy deliberated about going out for a stroll and then stumbled out into the garden. After the dim light of the kitchen, it was dazzlingly bright outside. The midday sun gave everything a hard-edged radiance, as if the world were made out of shattered glass.

By this time they had completely forgotten about their original plan to visit the temple. They set off in the direction of the hills. Angus had to concentrate to walk in a straight line because the LSD was affecting his cerebellum, the part of the brain that controls balance.

He asked, 'What about Raj?'

'Och, he'll be fine,' replied Murphy, cleaning his dark blue, wire-rimmed sunglasses with the hem of his black and white skull and crossbones tee shirt. He added in a voice heavy with sarcasm, 'Knowing Yogi Boy, he's probably standing on his head in front of a Buddha statue in the woods.'

They walked for a little over an hour and eventually arrived at a stone shrine, which was nestled in a narrow pass where two steep forested hills converged. It was a magical place. The small structure's wooden spire had been painted bright red. Strung onto it were Buddhist prayer flags that fluttered in the breeze. It was believed that the invocations, printed upon the coloured flags in black ink, were slowly being washed into the atmosphere by the elements, enabling the spirits to hear them.

Mist was filling the valley below. Four or five kilometres away, the Swayambhunath temple's golden tower rose out of white clouds like a cosmic beacon in a lost world.

The two psychonauts sat on the shrine's stone steps and for a while shared an unbroken silence. After about an hour, Angus remembered he had a voice and that he had something to say. For the first time since he'd found out about it, he broached the subject of Murphy having murdered the gangster, Jack Kilroy, back on the streets of Glasgow.

'I was wondering how long it was going to take before you brought that up,' said Murphy, smiling sardonically as he rolled a funnel-shaped joint. 'I have to admit, though, I didn't think you'd bring it up when we were out of our fucking heads on acid.' He shrugged. 'There's no time like the present, I suppose.'

'What compelled you to do such a thing?' Angus asked, glancing up at a corner of the shrine's roof, where a garishly painted wooden devil sneered back at him, its disproportionately large phallus erect. 'Don't you feel bad about it?'

Murphy raised his jaw and answered without hesitation. 'No man, I don't feel *bad* about it. We're all travelling on different trains to reach the same terminal station. I just helped that rotten bastard, Kilroy, reach his final destination a bit quicker, that's all. So why the fuck should I feel guilty about it?'

Angus replied, 'Because to kill another human being creates really heavy karma.'

'Fucking karma,' cursed Murphy. 'You sound like you're reading your lines from the same book as Raj. What is it with you guys and all of this religious bullshit?' He paused, as if waiting for an answer, but Angus understood that he didn't really want one. Murphy continued. 'The pair of you should away and shave your heads, join the God Squad up at the temple and then you can sit around with them, listening to the sound of one hand wanking.' Murphy made a masturbatory movement with his right hand. 'What with their rosaries, incense, dirge-like chants and uniform robes, those Buddhist monks remind me too much of those long-faced papist priests and Protestant ministers we left behind back in Scotland. You know,' he said, warming to his subject, 'control freaks who want to brainwash people into thinking life is a serious business for no other reason than making them ripe for exploitation. Let fun loose in the world and they'll all be out of a job, because nobody will bother listening to boring sermons about hell and damnation.' Murphy hacked up some phlegm and spat into the dust at his feet. 'Bunch of fucking hypocrites, telling everyone to pray for forgiveness for all the sins they've committed, while they're down in the rectory basement exercising their God-given right to have the choirboys suck their dicks.'

Murphy laughed loudly at his own words and used a match to light the joint he was holding. He smoked it through his fist, drawing the smoke deep into his lungs, coughed twice and then handed the spliff to Angus. He then ploughed on. 'I don't believe in all that karma shite. It's a big fat lie produced by the mind and if LSD has shown me one thing it is that the mind can declare anything to be true and pretend that it has proven it. In my opinion the idea of karma is nothing more than a guilt trip, and in my book guilt is the most useless human emotion. Nearly everyone has learned to distrust their body's intelligence and their feelings, to place their trust in authorities instead of their own inner power. Religions condition people into feeling guilty about natural tendencies and then programme those people to be scared of life. *Scared of life,*' he repeated loudly, shaking his head. 'Sounds absurd, doesn't it?' He paused for dramatic effect and slapped Angus on the back. 'Wake up, man. We don't *have* a life. We *are* life. We can't lose something that we never possessed in the first place. You just have to get out of the way and allow the universe to live through you, man. Anyway,' he concluded, 'it's birth that is the real cause of death and it might well be the case that when you're dead, you're dead, end of story. So, live today, do what has to be done and don't think too much about it.'

Angus exhaled hashish smoke through his nostrils. 'Is that a verse from the Murpanishads?'

Pundit Murphy glanced at Angus from the opposite side of an attitude, grinned and said nothing.

'Anyway, how can you be so sure of yourself?'

'Don't know,' answered Murphy. 'I just am.'

Angus looked at Murphy and wondered if his soul was possessed by a fierce, uncompromising demon. For a moment he could have sworn that his friend had sprouted horns. 'You know…I think you've got an evil streak in you.'

'I won't deny it,' said Murphy. 'Christ said, 'Resist not evil'. I believe he said that because he understood that resisting evil merely strengthens it.'

'I'm not so sure about that,' said Angus. 'Anyway, what do you think about Heaven and Hell?'

Murphy gave a derisive snort. *'Heaven and fuckin' Hell?'* He spat the words out, as if they were linguistic bullets. 'Listen to you,' he scoffed. 'You're starting to sound like a Jehovah's fuckin' Witness.' Murphy shook his head slowly. 'You'll be subscribing to *The Watchtower* next. Heaven and Hell are places that are created by your mind. It's all in your head.'

'You hope' said Angus, 'you hope.'

'What is hope?' Murphy asked, remembering a quote from Lord Byron. 'Nothing but the paint on the face of existence, the least touch of truth rubs it off, and then we see what a hollow-cheeked harlot we have got hold of.'

'Every harlot was a virgin once,' countered Angus, delivering a line penned by William Blake.

In response, Murphy slapped him on the back again and said, 'Not bad, not bad at all. You're good company. I'll say that for you. I'm glad to hear that you've been reading up on your quotations.' He turned and looked directly into Angus's eyes. 'You know the big difference between you and me, don't you?'

'No. Tell me,' requested Angus.

Murphy put an arm round him, leaned his mouth towards his left ear and said in a quiet voice, 'Okay I will. You're hooked on knowledge and I'm not.'

Angus scratched at a mosquito bite. 'What's that supposed to mean?'

'Unlike you,' said Murphy, 'I don't have that anxiety…that insecurity…that makes you want to seek knowledge so you can better understand why life is the way it is. I don't give a shit about, karma, reincarnation and the afterlife. All of those so-called spiritual questions are born out of fear.'

'Hey, Murph.'

Murphy looked at him. 'What?'

'Lighten up, man.'

'Okay then,' said Murphy, 'I will, and I'll do it by telling you a really good joke. Told to me the other day by – believe it or not – *The Prof.'*

Angus raised an eyebrow. 'I'm listening.'

Murphy tilted his head towards Angus, his lips bending into an archly playful smile. 'Three black guys,' he began, 'rob a bank in Manhattan. They're making a high-speed getaway in a stolen Cadillac when, all of a sudden, a fully loaded petrol tanker drives across an intersection in front of them. The getaway car hits it square on and *boom!'* Murphy threw his hands in the air. 'There's a huge fuckin' explosion. The three black guys are vaporized instantly and find themselves standing in front of a pair of solid gold gates, studded with diamonds and pearls – no prizes for guessing where they are. One of the guys pulls on a bell rope and they hear a distant ringing.

'A minute in eternity later, the gates creak open and an old fart with a long white beard steps out and says, 'What the fuck do you three want?'

'The black guys look at him in surprise and then one of them says, 'Hey, how ya doing?' He steps forward. 'Let us in, we want to check out the scene, man.'

'Saint Peter holds up his hands and says, 'You can't come in.'

'One of the other guys says, 'Be cool, man, be cool. We just want to come in, sit around, smoke a little weed and get a little high like everyone else. I promise we won't hassle the angels.'

'Saint Peter thinks for a minute, and then says, 'Wait here.' The gates close and the saint hurries up the stairway to heaven because he needs to speak to God and ask his advice.

'God's sitting in a wing-backed executive chair. He looks up from the big thick Bible he's reading with his third eye. He's thinking to himself that the good book needs some serious editing because, viewed from a modern scientific perspective, a lot of what he's written sounds unbelievable, especially that nonsense in Genesis about bringing all the world's creature's into existence, fully formed, in just six days.

'What is it Peter?' God asks, glowering at the saint. 'Can't you see I'm busy?'

'Saint Peter bows and then says, 'I'm sorry to disturb you, Lord, but there's three fucking niggers at the front gates and they want to come in.'

'God is outraged at the saint's ungodly language and demeanour. 'Good heavens, Peter!' God shouts, dropping his de-luxe first edition of the Bible on the floor as he jumps to his feet. 'How dare you speak about our dark-complexioned brethren in such a way. Have you forgotten that my son, Jesus, was a black man? Go back downstairs and welcome those three souls into heaven immediately.'

'Saint Peter rushes away and a minute later runs back up to God and cries, 'They're gone! They're gone! They're gone!'

God steps out from behind his desk and says, 'For Christ's sake, calm down.' He then asks, 'Who's gone, the three black guys?'

'Saint Peter shakes his head and says, 'No, *the fucking gates!*''

Murphy burst into laughter.

Angus stared at him, quietly marvelling at his friend's sense of humour.

Murphy quickly noticed that Angus was looking at him with an amused expression on his face. He stopped laughing and asked, 'What's up? Don't you get it?'

Angus gave him a wan smile. 'Yeah, man, I got it – the first time I heard it.'

'The first time you heard it?' Murphy repeated questioningly. 'You mean…you mean you've heard that joke before?'

'The Prof told it to me the other night down at the Rising Moon.'

'For fuck's sake, man, I'm tripping out of my head and straining my fucking brain trying to get a joke right, and then you tell me you've already heard it. What the fuck are you playing at?'

'I'm not playing at anything,' replied Angus, chewing on a blade of grass. 'I really enjoyed listening to you telling that joke because you told it very well. Your embellishments were brilliant.'

Murphy smiled. 'They were?'

'Sure, Murph, you're a very funny guy.'

'I am?'

'I just told you that you are.'

Murphy grinned from ear to ear. 'Fancy dropping another hit of acid?'

Angus looked into Murphy's fully dilated pupils. 'Does Pinocchio have wooden balls?'

Murphy chuckled and, after fishing in his black leather wallet, produced two windowpanes, one for Angus and one for himself.

The tiny gelatine squares did a four point landing on the tips of their sticky tongues and, just like Maltteasers, the LSD melted in their mouths and not in their hands.

'Wow!' Murphy exclaimed. 'I feel like *God.*'

God...God...God... The word echoed in Angus's rapidly expanding mind until he heard hooves scraping on loose gravel. He looked up, nodded to his left and said, 'Oh, oh.'

With that, their conversation slipped away and disappeared down a rabbit hole because trotting along a dirt track, and heading towards them, was a small herd of young black bulls. The animals' nostrils flared and snorted as they tossed their heads. Not wishing to attract the horned ones' aggressive attentions, the two trippers sat as still as stone Buddhas. Angus and Murphy closed their eyes and a silent moment lengthened into an hour as they slipped into a timeless psychedelic trance.

Next thing they knew it was late afternoon. A flock of startled yellow-crested parakeets took to the air when a line of copper-skinned village women emerged from a nearby hillside forest. They carried wicker baskets on their backs that were supported by a cloth strap running over their foreheads. Inside the large baskets were lengths of cut branches covered in leaves. The women were singing a work song to take their minds off the heavy loads that strained against their taut neck muscles.

'Look, walking bushes,' said Murphy, lighting a short-stemmed clay pipe loaded with hashish, 'and they know how to sing. Praise the Lord, it's a miracle.'

The sun dropped into the clouds. Angus and Murphy made their way home. As they walked they chatted about everything under the moon, full that evening and rising majestically, a disk of shining mercury in a mackerel sky. They stopped off at the house to collect Jenny and then continued on their way into the village. Their empty stomachs were rumbling at the prospect of finding something decent to eat.

'Hey, you guys, what happened to your Indian friend?' asked The Prof as soon as they arrived outside the *chai* (tea) shop.

Angus experienced a stab of guilt. He'd completely forgotten about Raj for what felt like a hundred years. 'Where is he?' he asked.

'I saw him about an hour ago. He was up in the trees behind the temple,' replied The Prof, whose dishevelled hair, drooping moustache and unshaven face lent him the look of a demented rabbi. 'He was as naked as the day he was born and howling at the moon.'

'For fuck's sake,' cursed Murphy. 'We better go and look for him. He must have flipped out big time.'

They heard Raj before they saw him. Emanating from within the shadows of a cluster of tall pine trees, a primeval scream cut through the moonlit night's still air.

Murphy hissed through his teeth. '*Ssshit!* The monks up at the temple will be freaking out about that fucking racket.'

They continued along a narrow track and then Jenny caught sight of Raj, perched high above them on a thick branch. 'There he is.' She pointed with one hand while the other shot to her mouth in shock.

Squatting on his haunches, Raj was silhouetted in front of a full moon, which had just popped out from behind rolling billows of cloud that looked to Angus like a family of giant silver-grey cabbages.

Still tripping, Angus exclaimed, 'Look at the sky! It's absolutely amazing!'

'Wow! I see what you mean,' agreed Murphy, giggling like a schoolboy watching a cartoon. 'Hey, man, far out, I'm seeing lime-green flouro trails everywhere.'

'Holy shit! Me too!' gasped Angus.

'Hey! For crying out loud,' said Jenny with a brittle voice, 'those flouro trails are fireflies. Will you two astronauts please try and get your space boots back on the ground. In case you haven't noticed, your pal's up a pine tree in Nepal impersonating Tarzan.'

As if to confirm Jenny's observation, Raj roared and proceeded to thump his fists on his chest cavity to produce a hollow drumming sound. Monkeys in the branches around him started to jabber excitedly. The Scots' eyes had become accustomed to the diffused light and they could now see that the mangy simians were sitting in close proximity to Raj. They looked down at the grounded Scots, their sharp teeth reflecting the occasional pale blue moonbeam. *'Yaka-yaka-yeek-yeek,'* they screeched.

'Hey Raj,' shouted Angus, 'come down out of there. That's enough of your monkey business. You'll be scaring the shit out of the monks up at the temple with the noise you're making.'

Murphy suddenly exclaimed, 'Oh wow!' He pointed at an oddly shaped boulder and said, 'Check out the size of that rock toad.'

Angus looked over at the rock and hallucinated a giant, vile-looking toad. 'Jesus,' he cried, 'is that thing dangerous?'

'Only during the mating season,' answered Murphy, taking a step back from the rock.

Angus asked urgently, 'When's the fucking mating season?'

Murphy tweaked his nose. 'During the full moon.'

Angus looked up at the moon and could have sworn it was scowling at him. 'For Christ's sake, let's get out of here.'

Murphy snickered.

'What's so funny about that?' Angus asked angrily.

Murphy spluttered. 'If...if...if you believe in rock toads, you'll believe anything.'

Angus punched him on the shoulder and shouted, 'You stupid asshole! You had me shit-scared for a minute there.'

The absurdity of the situation became all too apparent, infecting Angus and Murphy with a laughing fit. Oblivious to their presence, Raj howled.

A stream of warm liquid splattered over Murphy's head and shoulders. He jumped out of the way and bellowed in anger. 'For fuck's sake, the bastards are pissing on me.' He bent to pick up a rock.

'Cool it, Murph.' Angus raised a palm. 'We don't want to upset the monkeys or they might attack Raj.'

'You've got to be joking' said Murphy. 'He's sitting around up there like the king of the fucking apes.'

'I'm getting cold,' complained Jenny, heaving a ragged sigh of impatience. She draped a woollen shawl over her shoulders. 'Let's go back down to the chai shop. You two idiots can come back later.'

Two hours later, Angus and Murphy did just that. Raj had disappeared, but not for long.

Over the course of the next two days the ape-man of Swayambhunath became a local celebrity. The Nepalese villagers started to speak excitedly about Raj. They took him to be an incarnation of Hanuman, the big-jawed Hindu monkey god who is, among other things, the redeemer of causes bereft of hope.

Murphy tried climbing up into the trees to grab hold of Raj, but gave up when his friend scrambled higher up on to branches barely able to support his weight. The chattering monkeys had become aggressively protective of their human companion and set about attacking Murphy who had trespassed too far into their leafy domain. Fortunately for him, Murphy had his cudgel tucked into his belt. He knocked a large slavering male out of the trees with a lucky swing of his club. When he descended to the ground the agitated monkeys began to once again shower him with jets of urine.

Beneath the trees small crowds of locals gathered in the afternoon to light bundles of incense. Some sat to the side, closed their eyes and entered meditation. Most craned their necks hoping to catch a glimpse of the monkey god, who is credited with giving his blessings to anyone who approaches him with an open and pure heart. If the villagers saw Raj they threw small bananas up at him and cheered with delight if he caught one. After three days, such a large pile of fruit offerings had accumulated at the foot of Hanuman's lofty throne that even the voraciously hungry monkeys could not devour it, let alone their deity whose appetite was legendary.

Murphy had begun hanging out with a petite Nepalese woman called Dugma. She was a small-time LSD dealer who lived in an apartment in a downtown area of Kathmandu. Slim with high cheekbones, the Nepali was quite a catch for him. Like many a womanizer, Murphy had become bold, sassy and so relaxed in the company of beautiful women that he immediately put them at their ease; from there it was only a few steps to the bedroom. Dugma had introduced Murphy to the world of tantric sex practices. She'd taught him how to retain his semen by controlling his breath. This enabled him to make love to her, while she was tied spread-eagled to an iron bed, for hours on end without ejaculating. Important things first, Murphy, who was always hornier than a deep-sea sailor on a weekend's shore leave in Bangkok, disappeared for a couple of days during the period of Raj's monkey god incarnation.

Before heading into Kathmandu, Murphy passed on some of his newly discovered tantric secrets to Angus. After what seemed like a year in the life of a randy celibate, Angus was making love with Jenny again. It was a peculiarly one-sided affair because Jenny was not too keen on excessive physical movement. Nonetheless, it was a mutually satisfying exchange of energies.

One evening, four days after Raj had taken up residence in the treetops, Angus fell into a deep sleep after a strenuous workout on top of Jenny's receptive body. In the middle of the night he sat up wide-awake. He'd been wrenched from his dreams by an invisible signal that told him his attentions were required elsewhere. He sensed someone near. The front door was locked. It was therefore he reasoned that whoever it was must be outside.

Dressing quickly, Angus hurried downstairs with a premonition that something momentous was about to happen. The kitchen was dark. He could hear the building making the creaking noises of a wooden ship at anchor as it contracted in the cool night air. He lit a paraffin lamp and left it on the kitchen table, from where it cast a pale yellow arc over the room. He unbolted the front door. It creaked open. He went out into the garden and looked up. The cloudy sky was broken by rents in its vaporous fabric where silver-grey moonbeams cut through, sending down gentle fingers of light to caress the dormant landscape. His senses were alerted by a movement behind a thorny acacia shrub. It was Raj. He was cowering in the shadows like an overgrown brownie from the underworld. It took some coaxing on Angus's part to motivate his friend to enter the kitchen. Raj squinted in the murky yellow glow cast by the lamp. He was covered in scratches and stank of monkey excreta and stale sweat. His long black hair was in knots and as ragged as an untended hedge.

Raj drank a cup of hot cocoa, washed with warm water and then explained what had happened to him. He'd been in a confrontation with one of the monkeys' leaders, who had objected to his close physical proximity to some pregnant females. Survival of the fittest is the law of the jungle, where the killer instinct is paramount for self-preservation. Raj had strangled the big male with his bare hands. The emotional impact of what he'd done brought him back into the self-conscious world of his senses.

'Jesus, man!' Angus exclaimed. 'You didn't get bitten, did you?'

Raj examined his body under the dim light provided by the smoking paraffin lamp sitting on the centre of the wooden table. 'No, I don't think so.' He raised his right arm and groaned. 'I think I might've pulled something.'

Angus shook his head, not quite believing what his friend had been through. 'Well you know what they say, 'If it doesn't kill you, it can only make you stronger.''

Raj screwed up his face. 'Hey, do me a favour and spare me your homilies. If there was any truth in what you just said I'd be as strong as Hercules by now.'

Angus smiled awkwardly. 'Sorry. I was only trying to put a different slant on things. You flipped right out, didn't you?'

'Yeah,' replied Raj, 'you can say that again. I can remember looking up at the moon and feeling its magnetism effect the liquid in my brain. Man, you know, I actually had the hots for one of the females.'

'You're fucking well joking!'

'I am.' Raj chuckled. 'But I had you going there for a minute, didn't I?'

Their laughter woke Jenny. She came downstairs and put her arms around Raj. Her tear-filled eyes expressed her relief and joy at having their Indian brother back in their midst.

It was late afternoon when Murphy the Lothario returned the following day. His face broke into a grin as soon as he set eyes on Raj. 'Fucking hell, man, you really had us worried there for a while. I was starting to wonder if you were ever going to come down from your Tarzan trip.'

Raj laughed quietly, stepped forward and gave Murphy a hug. Rarely expressed physically, the affection between the two young men was often amusingly obvious.

'Man,' Raj said, 'I really lost it up in the trees. I fell in love with the monkey queen.'

'Wow, far out. Did you shag her?'

'Naw, Murph, I didn't, but I put in a good grunt for you.'

'What a pal you are, Raj. I always wondered how I was going to lose my virginity.' Murphy emptied the contents of a plastic bag he'd been carrying on to the table.

'What's this for?' Angus enquired, picking up a bubble strip of penicillin capsules, one of many now splayed out before him.

'Well,' Murphy explained, 'I've just returned from a visit to Kathmandu's VD clinic with some rather disturbing news. That fucking witch, Dugma, has managed to infect me with a particularly virulent strain of gonorrhoea.'

The Aids epidemic was still a long way off and therefore the second coming of condoms was not yet stretching over the penile horizon.

'For fuck's sake, man,' said Raj, 'you should be more careful.'

'Should I now? Well, fuck you big boy and the same goes for your advice,' said Murphy, without a trace of anger in his voice. 'Anyway, listen to who's talking, King fucking Kong himself. You wouldn't know a real sexual adventure if it grabbed you by the balls and bit the end of your dick off. *Showtime!*' Murphy took off his rattan coolie hat, threw it on the flagstone floor, leapt up onto the kitchen table and went down on all fours.

'*Howoooo!*' He howled like the lone wolf he was so very much an incarnation of, fell silent, stood and, looking down into his three friends wide-open eyes, bowed with a flourish of his right hand. The uproarious outburst of laughter that followed could be heard down at the Rising Moon Tea Shop.

Even before the monkey business, Raj's gentle character had endeared him to Swayambhu's inhabitants. A few days later, when he'd fully recovered from his escapade in the trees, he wandered down into the village. He was somewhat surprised to find that the Nepalis were still viewing him as an ethnic deity. Everywhere Raj turned he was offered bananas by the villagers, while the worshipful were bowing down to touch his feet. It took a fortnight for the novelty to wear off on both sides.

Today, in the twenty-first century, the legend of Raj's Hanuman incarnation is still recounted by Nepalese folklorists, the tale being an established favourite of adults and children alike.

16

WITHIN YOU AND WITHOUT YOU

The longer the Scots stayed in Swayambhu, the more they grew to love the village and the house.

'Maybe we should buy this place,' suggested Murphy over breakfast one morning. 'The landlord only wants ten grand for it.'

'We're only paying two hundred bucks rent a month,' said Angus, looking up from a half-finished plate of lumpy porridge. 'Buying it would mean a pile of paperwork? You want to deal with that?'

'Ehhh...yeah, maybe you're right, man,' mumbled Murphy through a mouthful of burnt chapatti and marmalade. 'It's just that I'm really starting to dig living here.'

'Me too,' chimed Raj, glancing up from a paperback copy of the *Bhagavad Gitā*. 'I haven't felt so at home since we left Scotland'

The rest of the day was spent in and around the house. Taped music drifted out of the kitchen's open door into the garden, where Angus was pulling weeds, trimming bushes dotted with purple morning glory flowers and lighting a fire to burn rubbish. *One pill makes you larger*... He leaned on a rake and began humming along to the haunting melody of Jefferson Airplane's 'White Rabbit'.

Foomp! Foomp! Foomp! Angus looked up when a squadron of low-flying pigeons passed overhead. He sighed through his nose, gazed around and gloried in his environment's unique beauty. In the distance, he could make out terraced paddy fields cutting steps in the sides of steep green hills. Through a space in the trees he could see the Swayambhunath temple standing with its Buddha eyes looking out over the verdant countryside's natural splendour. From the temple's direction drifted the sound of monks chanting, their dirge-like syncopation punctuated by someone blowing on a conch shell. A brass bell tolled, signalling that Swayambhunath's twelve-foot high prayer wheel had just completed another rotation. *You are the crown of creation*... Grace Slick's voice called from the kitchen. The Jefferson Airplane was in full flight, the San Francisco band's music soaring like a high-flying bird.

That evening, the Scots dined on one of Jenny's rare culinary experiments. She'd bought a live chicken from a Nepalese neighbour and then, much to everyone's surprise, slaughtered and plucked it herself. The curry that she made with it was succulent and filling. Over cups of cinnamon-flavoured chai, the four friends sat by the fire, smoking joints and gazing into the flames. Conversation was at a minimum. When the fire died down, the house was as still and quiet as a Zen monastery. They stayed up all night and drank in the peace. It was the last time they would experience such a satisfying feeling of family togetherness. Down in the valley the winds of change were starting to gather and strengthen.

Events were set in motion by a question.

'You guys wouldn't be interested in buying a load of top quality hash by any chance, would you?'

Professor Vogel pitched this interesting proposition one rainy September evening down at the Rising Moon tea shop. The MacDopes were all ears, except Jenny, who wasn't present, in all senses of the word. She was home riding the dragon and surrendering herself to the blissful world of secret dreams it flew her to in the land of Morpheus.

'Maybe,' said Murphy flatly, in answer to a question asked by a man he'd written off as a professional bullshit artist. He took a long sip on a bowl of warm *chang* and then said, 'It all depends on price and quality.'

The American ran his hands over thick, bushy sideburns, stood, took off his brown leather jerkin, draped it across the back of his chair, sat down again and out of nowhere produced a 250-gram plaque of glistening black hashish. The Prof made a show of placing it exactly on the centre of the circular wooden table they were gathered around. His eyes shone and his pointed face leered. He nodded towards the hashish and said, 'Check it out, amigos. Check it out.'

Angus had a nose for the business and he knew just what to do. He picked up the bendy oblong plaque and used his Swiss army knife to cut off a corner. He held the hashish under his nose and slowly inhaled its bouquet. It was fresh and smelled like a well-fertilized tropical garden on a hot summer's day. Suitably impressed, Angus tweaked his nose, leaned back, smiled and nodded to Murphy, who The Prof had been studying with the clinical air of a dental surgeon regarding a rotten molar in need of extraction.

'How much do you want for it?' asked Murphy directly, seeing no need for eloquence when it came to bargaining.

'Depends on how much you want to *buy*,' answered The Prof, emphasizing his last word. The American glanced around, secretive and cunning. He had a determined look about him, as if he were trying to reel in a prize-winning salmon he'd just hooked during an angling competition.

As part of his sales pitch The Prof went into a long, detailed explanation about how he'd come to be in possession of the hashish and why he now had to sell it. The bus that was supposed to arrive, in order to drive a ton of it back to Amsterdam, had been involved in a collision in Turkey that left it and its driver beyond repair.

After an intense bargaining session, it was agreed that the Scots would purchase half a metric ton at one-hundred and fifty dollars a kilo. It was expensive but, as the three Scots walked back to the house, they were excited about how much money they could make when they smuggled it into Europe.

Raj encapsulated it in a greenback nutshell. 'Man, we could cash in big time. That gear is pure connoisseur's dynamite.'

By the time they got home it had been decided that, if The Prof was as good as his word and came up with the goods, Angus and Jenny would stay in Nepal, while Raj and Murphy took care of business.

'We can keep the house on here,' suggested Angus, 'and meet up in Goa for Christmas.'

'At *Joe Bananas* chai shop on Anjuna Beach, under the December full moon, to be more precise,' added Murphy.

As is often the case in the drug-smuggling world, the plan they came up with wasn't the best scam ever conceived and it wasn't an original one either, but it was simple enough to work. Then again, like most smuggling ventures, it would help to have Lady Luck on their side when it came to crossing international borders. Murphy and Raj would visit a barber's shop for a haircut and a close shave. After that, they'd find and recruit a few respectable-looking, fare-paying passengers who wished to travel overland to Europe, preferably attractive women, so that the two philanderers would have something to amuse themselves with during the long journey and create a diversion when encountering customs officers, who were usually men.

'What's the spray paint for?' asked Angus, a week later, when Murphy returned from a shopping trip in the city.

'It breaks my heart to do it,' said Murphy, whose too short hair made him look like he'd just been discharged from the Marines, 'but we've got to get rid of that skull and crossbones on the front of the bus. It looks dead suspect.'

'Yeah, you're probably right, Murph. The old girl won't look quite the same though, will she?'

'No man, she won't,' answered Murphy, giving an experimental squirt with a can of dark blue gloss paint. 'Funny how we speak about Rolling Thunder like she's a lady isn't it?'

'Yeah, man, it is,' agreed Angus, who would have liked to accompany his two friends back to the West. Jenny had become an enormous weight around his neck, dragging him down as she descended into the murky realm of morphine and heroin addiction she now inhabited. Both her physical and mental conditions were in a serious state of deterioration. The day before, he'd taken her into Kathmandu's general hospital to have a festering wound on her left arm treated. She'd scratched the skin off her arm while dreaming about aliens. She'd screamed when a puzzled Nepali doctor injected an anti-tetanus shot into her right arm. On the taxi journey home she'd raved on about how the doctor was an undercover agent working for the Greys. When Angus discussed this with Murphy and Raj, both of them shook their heads and agreed that Jenny had crossed the bridge that leads into the world of drug-addled madness.

It was easy for Murphy to pick up on Angus's thoughts. 'I told you to dump her in Pakistan,' he said. 'Sometimes you have to act tough with people for their own good.'

Raj, who'd been replacing a broken indicator light and listening to the exchange, pointed a small screwdriver at Angus and said, 'I warned you, man. You should have put your foot down in Herat. If you'd have listened to me, maybe Jenny wouldn't have turned into a junkie.'

Angus said nothing, although he was thinking plenty. What a pair of fucking know-it-alls. How the hell was I supposed to know that Jenny would get hooked on that shit? There's no way I can take her overland on the bus. Any customs official who looks twice at her will twig immediately that she's on something illegal. Putting Jenny on a plane back to Britain is out of the question. She's so fucked up that going cold turkey might kill her. Shit! Shit! Shit!

Murphy, who could see how trapped in his mind Angus was, slapped him hard on the back and said, 'Can you remember that afternoon when Raj flipped out and we were tripping up in the hills beside that little temple?'

Angus nodded and replied, 'Yeah...yeah, sure I can.'

'Good,' said Murphy, 'then maybe you'll also be able to recall me saying to you, live today, do what has to be done and don't think too much about it.'

Angus smiled at Murphy and asked, 'What's your point, man?'

Murphy smiled back at Angus and replied, 'I really meant it.'

Raj laughed and then said, 'I do believe it's time for a cup of tea and a joint.' He turned and walked away with Murphy in the direction of the house.

Angus stood watching them until they disappeared into the kitchen. Shit, he thought, I'm going to miss them.

It was a grey morning when Murphy and Raj finally drove away. They were heading into Kathmandu to pick up four female passengers and from there begin their journey west. Angus had met one of the women who was going to travel with them, a tall, slender German chick in her early twenties, with fantastic long legs and tight buttocks that must have been shoehorned into her fashionably patched Levis, lending a whole new curvaceous dimension to the expression *Dharma bum*. The overall impression had been stylish, sophisticated and very sexy. The memory of her smiling confidently at him made Angus feel like he'd been dealt the second-best hand in a game of high stakes poker and, not for the first time that year, he felt like a loser.

The sky was a sheet of unbroken cloud and the threat of a heavy downpour hung in the muggy air. Swallows darted around, chirping excitedly as they feasted on tiny insects pushed down by a wave of low atmospheric pressure.

More comfortable with greetings than farewells, Angus gave his two closest friends a brief hug and wished them a safe journey. 'See you in December,' was all he said to Raj and Murphy before they boarded the bus. He had to support Jenny as she waved goodbye with a limp wrist. Due to her deteriorating condition she could no longer stand on her own two feet, unless buoyed up by something or someone.

Raj called to them from the driver's seat, 'You two be nice to each other.' He put on his Glasgow bus driver's hat. 'And don't worry about us, because everything is under—'

Angus cut him off. 'Don't say it, man!'

Raj laughed and turned the ignition key. The bus's engine came to life immediately. He gunned the motor for a few seconds. Rolling Thunder roared like a gigantic mechanical lion. Raj put the bus into gear and she began to rumble down the road, her tyres purring as their thick treads sucked at the damp asphalt. He honked the compressed air horn repeatedly and then loud music reverberated through the bus's aluminium frame and shook the side panels. Murphy had recently become obsessed with the Motown sound. *Money, who needs it...?* Junior Walker and the All Stars' dance floor classic, 'Road Runner', blared out. *Let me live my life free and easy...* Murphy's arm waved from an open back window. There was a red toothbrush in his hand.

As far as Angus was concerned 'The Tracks Of My Tears' by Smokey Robinson and the Miracles would have been a more appropriate Motown chartbuster for the occasion. *I'm a road runner, babe...* The music faded away. A distant peal of thunder rolled in the hills. Then, as if a big hole had been blown in the sky, it began to pour. A thick maudlin silence engulfed Angus. Dripping wet, he went into the house with Jenny; he with a heavy heart and she itching to inhale some morphine vapour in the privacy of her boudoir.

Half an hour later and in a foul mood, Angus went upstairs to have it out with her. When he opened the bedroom door the sickly sweet chemical smell of morphine smoke tingled in his nostrils. Pale and fragile, Jenny lay flaked out on the bed. She did not stir when he approached her. He sat on a wooden stool and studied her bleached face, smooth and white as if carved from chalk. The tendons in her throat stood out beneath her skin in such stark definition the visual impact was shocking. He glanced at a pillow. Maybe I should put her out of her fucking misery, he thought. His body shuddered. Man, what's happening to me? Rain slashed and pattered on the window, prompting a feeling of great sadness to rise in his heart. He still loved Jenny, even though she had drifted so very far away from him into a world where she walked through the shadow lands of her dreams alone. How different, he recalled, from when we first met, long ago in a Glasgow pub. She was so beautiful. Shit, it feels like another lifetime now. He stood up, turned away from her, slipped out of the room and gently closed the door behind him.

Down in the kitchen, he brewed a pot of tea, smoked a joint and lay around on a creaky settee. He read Tom Wolfe's *The Electric Kool Aid Acid Test* until he fell asleep and dreamt about when he was a little boy on Iona and the first time he saw his stepfather, Daniel, put pencil to paper to draw a boat on the sea, and how he'd believed he was witnessing magic.

It was dawn when Angus woke. He felt fresh and rejuvenated.

One peep into her bedroom's still shadows was all it took to ascertain that Jenny was off for another sojourn in the Land of Nod.

Angus decided to take a walk into Kathmandu. He went by way of a back road, which entered the city from the north. A thin layer of ground mist was being burned off by the sun, its warm slanting rays playing upon prismatic dewdrops, sparkling like tear-shaped diamonds as they dripped from wild flowers' petals. Outside of a small roadside temple, housing a stone deity so eroded by time that it had become a smooth cone-shaped boulder with a pug nose, Angus sat down for a spot of spontaneous meditation. He closed his eyes and centred on his breathing, a technique he'd learned from reading one of Raj's yoga books. Like the early morning mist, his worldly problems slowly began to evaporate, leaving him at peace with himself.

An hour passed. Angus's eyes blinked open. He felt clearer about his relationship with Jenny and made up his mind that, when he returned home, he would deliver her an ultimatum along the lines of, *if you don't clean up your act you can clear off out of my life.* Still turning this idea over in his mind, he approached the outskirts of Kathmandu.

When he'd first arrived in Nepal's capital over a year before, Angus had been fascinated by the city's Byzantine labyrinth of passages, flagstone alleyways, squares and choked streets that formed the downtown area. The novelty had worn off. As a result Kathmandu, rather than provoking fascination, was inducing revulsion. He stood for a moment and observed some mud-splattered black pigs rooting in pile of organic garbage, which had been dumped in an overflowing gutter that stank of decay. Bells rang out as bow-legged Nepalis prostrated themselves on the steps of ancient stone temples, housing brass deities covered in bright orange sindur powder. The idols were garlanded with flowers and surrounded by smoking incense sticks. The strongly perfumed smoke did little in the way of obscuring the damp stench that exuded from the very foundations of the city. Bright splotches of colour on a sepia background, hippies wandered around in their gaudy glad rags, looking bewildered and out of place on the wet and muddy streets. Many of them seemed to be suffering from some kind of narcosis. In other words, they looked like your everyday, garden-variety, stoned zombies. Everything began to appear to Angus like a hollow facade. A wave of negativity washed over him.

I need to eat something to recharge my batteries, he thought, as he sat down at a table in the Ying-Yang Restaurant on Durbar Square and ordered a late breakfast. While he was waiting for his coffee, he picked up a glass of water. He was about to take a sip when a beam of sunlight shone through an open window and illuminated the water. Tiny organisms, the kind of things one sees when looking at a drop of sewage under a microscope, were swimming around propelled by hairlike flaggela. It was while staring at the glass of water that it dawned on Angus that he'd had about enough of Kathmandu and its contaminated environment. Hunger prevented him from walking out the door in disgust. He picked up a rumpled copy of *Newsweek* and studied the cover picture of America's new president, Gerald Ford. Angus was not interested in politics but, like nearly everyone else on the planet, he was glad Richard Nixon had resigned.

The breakfast turned out to be a surprisingly good one. Revitalised by a plate of fried eggs on brown bread toast and a pot of fresh coffee, he reckoned a tasty joint of hashish might lift him out of his visions of doom and gloom.

Ten minutes later, Angus strolled along Freak Street and stopped for a moment to say hello to Gorda, a fat, deeply tanned woman from Barcelona who had bottle-blonde hair that stuck out from the sides of her head like wings, protruding lips and a face covered in symmetrical Maori tattoos. She was sitting on a wooden bench outside of what had once been the Royal Nepal Hash Shop, until it was closed when the sale of cannabis was made illegal during the previous autumn. Gorda was reading Carlos Castaneda's *The Teachings of Don Juan*.

Angus enquired, 'Good book?'

'Don Juan says to keep death present on one shoulder,' Gorda replied, smiling as she glanced up at him, 'and I think that is good advice, because it keeps you on your toes. Check this guy out, *hombre,*' she said, raising bleached eyebrows and looking towards a pavement dentist.

Naked from the waist up, a skeletal man was sitting cross-legged on a folded black blanket by an open sewer that was full of green iridescent sludge that smelled of rotten eggs. His only surgical instruments were a bent scalpel and a pair of rusty pliers. They were lying at his muddy feet beside a line of ivory-coloured teeth that were so big they might well have been extracted from the mouth of a yeti. The dentist smiled a toothless smile at Angus and called out, 'Toothache?'

Angus shook his head, said adios to Gorda and continued on his way. He paused for a moment to check out his reflection in the Hungry Eye restaurant's main window. He then walked round the corner, climbed up a set of rickety stairs and entered Laughing Sam's, a wood-floored café that Angus had visited at least once a week during the past six months. The café was a long, low-ceilinged room with thick pine beams, stained dark brown from years of hash and tobacco smoke. Cracked mildewed walls were decorated with framed photographs of Nepal's royal family, torn Bruce Lee posters and printed pictures of the blue-skinned Hindu deity, Lord Shiva, sitting cross-legged on a Himalayan mountain top. Overhead, a ceiling fan churned lazily but made little impression on the stuffy atmosphere. Diffused shafts of sunlight entered the room through two glass windows that had once been transparent but over time were rendered translucent by accumulated dust and grime. The casements faced away from the street and when open lent a view of a flagstoned courtyard where, during daylight hours, Nepalese housewives were often to be seen chattering amidst lines of washing that flapped in the breeze.

What Angus liked about Sam's was the music the Nepali owner played over a powerful sound system, serious enough to drown out the noise of traffic rising up from the congested street outside. Sambhava was the cheery proprietor's name. He was a demobbed Ghurkha and a big fan of rock music. The ex-soldier exuded a strong impression of physical discipline, suggested by his muscular shoulders, trim moustache, alert slanted eyes and his boots.

Sam's black leather boots were military issue and shone like polished granite. Even though Cannabis was now illegal, Sambhava still sold it under the counter and his café was never visited by the police.

Angus sat down at a low wooden table, surrounded by stained cotton cushions that felt like they were stuffed with pebbles. The squelchy guitar intro to Hendrix's 'Voodoo Chile' wah-wahed out of a pair of coffin-sized PA speakers and sent a shiver up Angus's spine. *Well I stand up next to a mountain...* It was still early and, apart from Sambhava, Angus and the spirit of James Marshall Hendrix, the only other people in the café were a longhaired couple who were seated at a corner table playing backgammon. Not wishing to smoke alone, Angus rose to his feet, approached them and then cupped his hands over his mouth. He shouted over the high volume bombardment of Hendrix's howling guitar as it ripped through a complex progression of chords. 'Mind if I join you?'

In response to his question the young man, wearing a long red shirt and black baggy pants, passed him a fat joint, which was combusting enough tobacco and hashish to smoke a box of herring. Angus sat down, took a long hit and exhaled a lengthy plume of aromatic smoke.

'Ah, that's better,' he sighed.

The couple proceeded to introduce themselves by informing Angus that they were both born on Christmas Day in 1949. It was obvious to Angus that Martin and Lulu were deeply in love. They looked to him like two hip peas in a space pod orbiting the mountains of Venus. Like Angus, they'd travelled overland from Britain in a bus, an orange-painted VW camper, affectionately referred to as 'Bertha'. Speaking a heavily accented form of English whereby things became 'thinks', Martin told Angus how he and his wife made their living on the road by playing rock n' roll music in pubs and small nightclubs. The duo called their band Black Maitreya.

Martin looked like Keith Richards with a lot more hair. His right arm showed a faded blue tattoo depicting skulls with worms in their eye sockets. Lulu was quick to laugh and, whenever an opportunity presented itself, enjoyed dancing around in a frenzied manner. A string of mini human skulls, carved from buffalo bone, hung around her slender neck. The macabre necklace helped cast the impression that Lulu was a good-looking incarnation of Kali, the long-tongued Hindu Goddess of Destruction, who chops demons' heads off with a scimitar. What Lulu didn't share in common with the bloodthirsty deity was her fair-skinned complexion, thick makeup, long black wavy hair with peroxide white streaks in it, two arms instead of four and the fact that she was not into butchery. Although, it must be said, she did have a maniacal gleam in her eyes. She was an astrology buff who could throw a mean tarot and liked to use her fortune-telling cards to play poker games in the evenings. Pentacles were always wild.

Within an hour of meeting Angus, she'd consulted her almanac and mapped out his birth chart. Lulu sounded concerned when she informed him that he was fast approaching a difficult period of transition in his life. Angus, who understood nothing about astrological divination methods, thanked Lulu for her efforts and paid little heed to what she said. A few days later, when he reflected upon their first meeting, he had to admit that Lulu had been right on the money with her forecast.

During the course of the afternoon, Angus hung out with the English couple and smoked one joint after another, while listening to Hendrix deliver surrealistic songs from *Electric Ladyland*. They talked about whatever passed through their turned-on minds. Amongst other things, Martin mentioned that he and his wife were preparing to leave Nepal. They planned to drive to Kanyakumari, Cape Comorin, the Indian subcontinent's southernmost tip.

The music intensified. *I saw a light just up ahead...* Sambhava faded Hendrix's *Rainbow Bridge* LP out and mixed in Robin Trower's seminal *Bridge of Sighs* album. 'Day Of The Eagle' roared from the straining speakers.

It was getting dark outside. Angus descended the creaking wooden stairs that led down from Laughing Sam's Cafe to the busy street. His steps were hesitant, because he felt sorry to leave the place. Late afternoon rainfall had left the asphalt wet enough to reflect the electrified scribble of neon shop signs and the glare of vehicle headlamps. Crowds of people were weaving between slow-moving traffic. Steel wheels grated as sweating coolies pulled overloaded trolleys alongside bullock carts, buses, taxis and diesel trucks, jammed together in a mish-mash that the builders who had constructed the city streets hundreds of years before could never have envisaged.

Heading in the general direction of Swayambhu, Angus cut through a foul-smelling back alley. It was lined by garbage piled high against festering damp walls. Rats twittered in the shadows. Scampering around in packs, the rodents were the size of well-fed piglets. Their eyes glowed neon pink.

Angus was halfway along the dimly lit lane when a scraping sound prompted him to look up from his feet. Up ahead, a big black bull with long pointed horns was pawing at the cobblestones. The beast lowered its head and charged at him Pamplona style. Angus escaped injury by quickly climbing up a convenient cast iron drainpipe, the rusty brackets of which were starting to come away from the rotting brick wall they were screwed into. A few feet below him, the enraged bull raised its head and bellowed. The beast's hooves clattered on stone as it continued along the alley. Angus waited until his arms ached before he lowered himself to the ground.

He'd only taken a few steps when something bounced off the crown of his head like a deflected meteorite. He looked down and saw a dead mouse with its guts oozing out of its swollen belly. He glanced up in time to see a third floor window slam shut. It cut off children's excited laughter. Although annoyed, Angus had to laugh because it reminded him of the kind of pranks he'd enjoyed as a youngster.

A fifteen minute walk later, city sounds faded and gave way to the heavy buzz of nocturnal insects. A night-bird called out from a roadside bush, startling Angus. There was no moon and little in the way of lighting on the winding country road that he had chosen as his route home. A couple of aggressive pye-dogs sneaked up from behind and yapped furiously at his heels. Wishing he'd remembered his stick, Angus bent down and picked up a rock and hurled it at their shadows. The dogs howled and disappeared.

Time, affected by smoking dope all afternoon, seemed to be crawling by on short arthritic legs. Angus trudged, one slow step at a time, up the steep hill leading to the village. It felt to him like he was walking on a treadmill set to a tortoise's pace. The darkness was so dense he began to imagine what it must be like to be blind.

He reached the Rising Moon's welcoming door. Its stout wooden frame was adorned with flashing fairy lights. Parched, he popped in for a cold drink. The café was host to a couple of local drunks and a small group of foreigners, among whom Angus recognized only The Prof.

The American looked up from where he was seated at a small wooden table and called out, 'Hey, Angus, you want to light this?' He held up a clay chillum that was as big as pint milk bottle.

It was impossible to enter that particular establishment in the evening without smoking hashish. A couple of smoke-filled hours were sucked into a black hole before Angus set off again into the night. He was so tired he could have slept standing up and had to struggle to keep his eyes open, as his feet stumbled over the last kilometre of tar road.

The house was quiet and, devoid of Raj and Murphy's boisterous presence, almost lifeless. Angus shucked off his denim jacket and draped it over the back of a kitchen chair. He then lit a few candles and set about starting a fire in the grate to boil some water for a pot of tea. The fire crackled into life and he hung a copper kettle above the flames on a hook set into the fireplace. He popped upstairs to see if Jenny was awake. Peeping in through the partly opened bedroom door, he saw that a candle stub with a small spear of flame by her bedside was sputtering as it neared extinction. Jenny lay with her eyes closed, hands interlocked upon her chest. She stirred for a moment, mumbled something from a dream and then fell silent.

Angus returned to the kitchen, brewed some tea, rolled a stiff joint and settled down on a mattress by the warmth of the fire. He picked up and then started to read the *Bardo Thödol* that Raj had given him as a goodbye present. Angus found the book both fascinating and informative, especially the sections describing what Tibetan lamas call the *Bardos*, the supposedly harrowing interim periods between death and rebirth that can also be viewed as representing different states of consciousness while still alive. It was while reading about the *Bardos* and the six *Lokas,* or six Realms that there is so much discussion about in the Buddhist tradition, that Angus came across a folded sheet of writing paper lodged between the book's middle pages. Written in Raj's distinctive looping handwriting, which looked like a botched attempt at calligraphy, there were a few lines from Shakespeare's Hamlet.

'To die, to sleep,
To sleep! Perchance to dream; Aye, there's the rub,
For in that sleep of death what dreams may come, when we have shuffled off this mortal coil, must give us pause.'

Angus nodded off as he read and the paper fell from his hand.

Early morning sunlight was streaming through the kitchen window when Angus awoke from a disturbing dream about his alcoholic uncle, Alfred Docherty, making coffins in his workshop on Iona. Angus awoke from the dream just as he was about to be buried alive in a wooden casket.

Slightly unsettled, he sat up and rubbed sleep from his eyes. The house was strangely silent. He shrugged off a sensation of foreboding by busying himself with practical matters. He restarted the fire to heat water for coffee. When it was ready he carried a mug full of the steaming brew upstairs to the bedroom. The room was in dark shadow, but retained enough light to see that Jenny was more or less lying on the double bed in the same position she had been the evening before when he'd peeked in.

'Good morning. I've made you some coffee,' said Angus brightly, setting down the mug by her bedside and walking over to the heavy wooden shutters that were blocking out the daylight. Their hinges creaked as he pulled them inward. Expansive September light flooded into the room, accompanied by a warm breeze scented with honeysuckle. Turning, the smile on his lips withered and then vanished as he sensed something was terribly wrong. He looked at Jenny's body, her hands neatly resting in the centre of her unmoving covered breasts. Ashen, her skin was lifeless. Angus's heart felt like a heavy iron spike had been driven through it to pin him in an awful moment of time.

'Oh, Jenny, no, please, God no.' Heartfelt, his words were little more than anguished exhalations of breath.

He moaned, sat down beside Jenny's prone form and touched her hands. They were as cold as frozen meat. A tidal wave of sadness collapsed in his chest. His body shook with the force of it. A dizzying nausea spread through his guts like a stain. The room began to spin around him. Muted sounds of disbelief croaked in his throat. The bitter taste of bile came to his dry mouth.

Twirls of cloud flitted across the face of the sun, affecting the available light in such a way as to make it appear like some unseen hand was rapidly twisting the control knob on an invisible dimmer switch.

He reached over and tried to close Jenny's staring eyes. As though in denial of their mistress's death, her eyelids would not stay shut. Her thin lips were tinged a light purplish blue and parted in the faintest of smiles, the kind of smile that carries upon it both a touch of sad acceptance and a hint of bliss. The sight of that smile affected Angus in a way that stilled his beating heart, but not his thoughts. Like a bleating, tethered billy goat, his mind was running in a loop, repeating the same predominant question: where has she gone?

He stood and made to go out the door, but turned back. At a total loss what to do, he circled the room, shook his head from side to side and asked out loud again and again, 'Jenny, Jenny, where have you gone? Where have you gone?' He tasted salty liquid on his lips and realized he was crying.

He returned to his dead lover's side and listened. Somewhere in the neighbourhood someone was practicing scales on a sitar. The distinctly Eastern sound brought the lyrics of a Beatle's song to Angus's mind. It was a George Harrison composition that was timeless. Within you and without you, within you and without you, the song's title repeated itself in Angus's mind like a paradoxical Zen koan. Without you! The golden penny of understanding dropped into Angus's consciousness. He thought, that song's about life and death. He hurried downstairs, found the recording, put the *Sgt. Pepper's Lonely Hearts Club Band* tape into the machine, searched for the song, pushed the repeat button and turned the volume up.

Angus picked up his mug from the kitchen table, walked over to the front door, unbolted it, stepped outside and sat down on the stone doorstep in the early morning sunshine. He sipped on lukewarm coffee and listened to the song as if hearing it for the first time. The Beatle's haunting voice delivered lyrics that, to Angus's ears, suited the moment so perfectly it seemed like they'd been written for it.

The cassette tape rewound itself for the eighth time. *We were talking about the space between us...* Angus felt that George Harrison was speaking directly to him and voicing one of life's intrinsic truths when he sang about seeing that we're only very small and that life really does go on within you and without you.

He bent forward and studied a single-file army of red ants marching by as they carried their eggs to a safe place in anticipation of more rain. Overhead, small birds flitted and chirped in the branches of an overgrown rhododendron, its pink bell-shaped flowers host to a swarm of black buzzing bees. In the distance he heard the shrill call of a peacock. It was a sad sound, which sent a chill through his body and made his mind scramble to fill the black hole of nothingness, opening up inside of him, with the illusion of something, in this instance physical activity. And, when he rose to his feet, it suddenly came to him how he was going to deal with Jenny's sudden departure from the world of the living.

Angus went back into the kitchen to collect two boxes of candles and a packet of sandalwood incense sticks. Before he went upstairs he switched off the music. *Try to realize it's all within yourself*— Click. He then retrieved the *Bardo Thödol* from where he'd left it on the flagstone floor.

Once he'd returned to Jenny's bedroom, he lit a packet of white candles and positioned them around the room. He then sat down cross-legged by Jenny's inert body. He closed his eyes and focused his attention on the rising and falling of his breath. Slowly the procession of thoughts passing through his mind faded until all that was left was a positive emptiness. He then opened his eyes, picked up *The Tibetan Book Of The Dead* and began to read out loud in a clear voice. 'Oh nobly born Jenny, the time has come for you to seek the path...'

The longer he read, the more the damp gloom that had filled the room receded.

'You are now experiencing what people call 'death'. You are now drifting away from this world, but you are not unique, for this happens to everybody. Though you feel longing and attachment to this life, you cannot stay here...'

The afternoon passed.

'Let the radiant glory of auspiciousness come to illuminate the world. Let this book be auspicious. Let virtue and goodness be perfected in every way.'

Angus fell silent. The last light of day was framed in the open window.

For a while he sat studying Jenny's features. Her expressionless eyes continued to stare up at the ceiling. Her face had become a fascinating mask formed by death's invisible hands. He caught a hint of patchouli, a scent he would always equate with Jenny.

He looked up in surprise when, heralded by the gentle beat of its wings, a snow-white dove landed on the windowsill.

Angus asked the bird, 'Is that you Jen?'

The dove responded by making a repetitive tonal sound, like a bamboo flute being played at the lower register.

He watched as the white bird preened her feathers. Angus was so captivated by the dove's natural beauty that his heart skipped a beat when it suddenly took to the air and flew away. A small, fluffy white feather drifted into the room. It slalomed slowly through the air and came to rest on the centre of Jenny's forehead.

'Oh, God!' Angus groaned.

In that moment three things imprinted themselves indelibly on his mind. His beloved had come back to bid him a final farewell. Her spirit had now left the earthly plane. He had not known how deep the love in his heart for Jenny was until she was gone forever.

'Right, Jen,' he said gently, lighting a thick candle and placing it on the wooden chair that served as a bedside table, 'I'm going to give you a wonderful send-off.'

The remainder of the evening was spent carrying armfuls of dry firewood up the stairs and stacking them around Jenny's corpse. He left her face uncovered and, before retiring for the night, used an embroidered handkerchief that he found amongst her things to wipe away green fluid that was seeping out of her nostrils.

'There you go, Jen,' he said softly. 'We want you looking your best now, don't we?'

Downstairs, Angus lay by the fire and stared into its flames. He felt like he was the only person in the world, an anchorless boat cast adrift in a fickle grey sea. The past year, he thought, being around Jenny was like living with a ghost under a cloud-filled sky, but when she flashed me a smile nothing else in the world made me happier. A wave of sentimentality rose in his chest. He emptied his lungs and let out a seamless cry of loss, a pitiful sound, like a lonely dog baying at the moon.

'Come to grips, Angus,' he said, speaking out loud to himself.

A guide should be fearless and confident in order to inspire the dying person. He remembered words from the *Bardo Thödol* that prompted him to control his emotions by breathing deeply. Sleep, when it came, was most welcome.

The following morning, Angus rose at dawn, showered, washed his waist-length hair and used a strip of black cloth to bind it into a ponytail. Wearing a fresh white muslin shirt, matching trousers and a battered straw hat he visited a general store in the village. He purchased twenty litres of paraffin and then carried it back to the house in two red plastic canisters. He went upstairs and placed the fuel containers at the foot of Jenny's bed. He then sat on the floor and began to read a few random passages from the *Bardo Thödol*.

'Listen, Jenny, the pure radiance of reality has dawned...'

Thirty minutes later, he locked the house up and, adopting a brisk pace, strode into Kathmandu.

Angus found Martin and Lulu where he expected them to be – getting stoked up in the shadows of Sambhava's café. *When I'm sad she comes to me...* The music was turned down low and, as bold as love, Jimi Hendrix was singing 'Little Wing'. Rock's greatest guitarist was dead, but his musical legacy was still very much alive. The song which, according to rumour, Hendrix had written in honour of his mother, sounded extremely poignant to Angus's emotionally sensitive ears that particular morning – it was one of Jenny's favourites. He stifled a sob rising in his throat.

'Hi, guys.' Angus greeted the English couple as if it were just another stoned day. 'When are you leaving for India?'

'This is our last day in Kathmandu, man,' replied Martin. 'Here, try some of this.' He passed a big, funnel-shaped joint to Angus that was so loaded with hashish it looked like a mini volcano with red-hot rocks tumbling out of its glowing cone. 'We're setting off first think tomorrow mornink.'

'I can't wait to get back on the road again,' added Lulu wistfully. 'We're thinkink of stoppink off in Goa. People are sayink the full moon parties down there are the wildest in the world. The dealers are dishink out free acid on Anjuna Beach. Can you imagine?'

Angus coughed and imagined Jenny's lifeless body back at the house. He pushed the image from his mind and elected not to mention what had happened. He smiled at Lulu's enthusiasm, passed the oversized joint to her and then made the couple an offer they could not refuse. 'Tell you what. I'll give you guys five hundred dollars if you'll give me a ride down to Benares.'

'Wow, Angus!' Martin exclaimed. He couldn't believe what he was hearing. 'That's a lot of bread, man. We'll be happy to take you, won't we?' His spouse nodded her head vigorously. 'But listen, man,' continued Martin, 'two hundred is more than enough.'

Touched by their kindness, Angus let out a short laugh. 'Don't even think about it. I can afford it.' He looked into the Englishman's slightly bloodshot eyes and asked, 'So then, where will I meet you tomorrow morning?'

'How about outside the Yink-Yank Restaurant at dawn?' suggested Martin.

Angus nodded, stood up and said, 'That's cool with me, man.'

'Hey, Angus,' said Lulu, blowing out smoke through her lipsticked mouth, 'what's the hurry? Sit down and share the rest of this spliff wiv us. Sam's playink great sounds this mornink.' She passed the joint to her husband and then called to the proprietor who was sitting by the bar, reading a newspaper. 'Hey, Sambhava, turn it up, man!'

Thrown like a star in my vast sleep...

Donovan's 'Hurdy Gurdy Man' droned out of the speakers. The guitar kicked in and whanged around the room like an electrified poltergeist. Angus listened and felt like Pavlov's dog. Whenever he heard that particular song he felt like getting high. 'Sorry guys,' he said, suppressing the feeling, 'I've got a few things to take care of. I'd like to keep moving.'

'No probs, man.' Martin coughed up a lungful of hash smoke. 'See you at dawn tomorrow.'

Angus raised a hand in farewell. 'Ying-Yang at sunrise, I'll be there for sure.'

Hurdy gurdy, hurdy gurdy, man... Donovan's voice followed him as he walked out the door.

Back on the street, Angus couldn't help smiling at the thought of the stoned English couple. He realized he was pretty stoned himself when he entered a hardware shop and it took him five minutes to remember what it was he wanted to purchase.

Twenty minutes later, he was walking along the pavement, carrying a brown paper bag with two clockwork alarm clocks in it and a big cardboard box which had once, according to the legend printed on it, contained a dozen hairdryers that had been manufactured in Hong Kong. The box was now filled with Chinese fireworks.

'Taxi!' He shouted at a battered, Morris Oxford-style, Hindustan Ambassador taxi. It stopped. He opened the passenger side front door and slid in beside the driver.

The turbaned driver asked, 'Where you go?'

'Swayambhu,' answered Angus, noticing that the man's white shirt collar was stained black from sweat.

'Hundred rupees, okay?'

'Ten, or I get out right now.' Angus reached for the door handle.

'Okay, okay, fifty okay?'

Angus began to open the moving car's door.

'No problem,' said the driver, an apologetic, almost sad expression on his bearded face. He gestured for Angus to remain seated. 'Ten is good.'

They sat for some time listening to the squeak of tired shock absorbers and the rattle of wheels on the bumpy, rough-paven streets.

Angus broke the monotony by asking, 'Are you a Sikh?'

'Yes,' answered the driver, slowing up to let a group of orange-clad monks cross the road. 'Guru Nanak very big man.' He reached up to surreptitiously pat his insurance policy, a small framed picture of the white-bearded guru that was dangling from the rear-view mirror.

'I was in Amritsar last year.'

'My home town,' said the driver upon hearing this, his chubby face bending into a grin.

'I've been in the Golden Temple.'

'Then you are very lucky fellow.' The Sikh glanced at the firework rockets, sticking out of the cardboard box on his passengers lap. 'You make boom-boom party?'

'Yeah, man, I suppose you could say that.'

'You want buy hashish?'

'No thanks. I'm leaving tomorrow.'

'Okay, no problem.'

The taxi driver's face frowned in concentration as he steered his clattering vehicle up the steep slope that led to the village. He turned to Angus, smiled and said, 'Twenty rupees last price…' He nodded encouragingly. '…okay?'

Angus did not want to deal with the bureaucratic hassles that would doubtless accompany the death of a foreign national in Nepal. Apart from that, there was something else that compelled him not to inform the authorities and that was the idea of giving Jenny a unique fiery farewell from this world. He believed she would have wanted it that way.

They spent their last evening together surrounded by dozens of lit candles. For some time Angus chanted *'Om mani padme hum'*, an ancient Tibetan mantra credited with having the power contained within its sacred syllables to help free an individual from the psychic shackles that bind him or her to the wheel of life and death, thereby liberating the deceased into spiritual oneness. Angus was so caught up in the immediate present that he did not pause for a single moment to consider the possible ramifications of what he was about to do.

It was late when he crept over to the landlord's house with a rusty tea tin containing ten thousand dollars in one-hundred dollar bills. He pressed tight against the walls as he edged around the building and held his breath as he passed under an open window. The tin with the money in it was left on top of a woodpile outside the back door. Fair enough, he reasoned, that's what the man wanted to sell his house for. Now he has the cash and still owns the land.

Dogs barked but did not approach as he returned home.

Using the two wind-up alarm clocks, strips of emery paper peeled from matchboxes, a few spots of adhesive, half a dozen matches and some rags soaked in paraffin, Angus constructed a primitive but effective timing device to ignite his dead beloved's funeral pyre. A lit cigarette tucked into a book of matches would have sufficed but only left him with ten minutes of getaway time at the maximum.

He picked up the box containing the fireworks and then tipped them out onto the floor. He sorted through them and placed some around the room. Rockets and Roman candles were set pointing outwards on the small balcony and open window.

Angus wished to travel light and carry only things that were either essential or very important to him. Two thick wads of hundred dollar bills, his passport, a leather-bound notebook containing addresses and phone numbers, fifty LSD trips, the remnants of his DMT stash, a chunk of Nepalese hashish, his Swiss army knife, a C90 cassette tape with The Beatle's *Sgt Peppers* recorded on one side and The Rolling Stones' *Exile On Main Street* on the other, a change of clothes, his straw hat, *The Tibetan Book of the Dead,* and a few toiletries were packed into a small rucksack.

He went upstairs and dowsed the woodpile covering Jenny's corpse with fuel oil. He wound up and then set the alarm clocks to ring in thirty minutes. Using a pocket flashlight, he looked at Jenny one last time. Her wavy blonde hair framed her serene face like a tangle of golden seaweed. In his imagination he saw her as a lean, flaxen-haired Viking queen lying in state on the deck of a dragon-prowed longboat waiting to depart for Valhalla. He kissed her on the forehead and tasted paraffin on his lips. A sense of deep loss gave wing to butterflies in his stomach. Reluctant to bid his friend and lover a final farewell, he stood silent and still, drinking in their last moments together.

'Goodbye, Jenny.' His voice cracked with emotion. 'May…may you rest in peace forever.' A tear tumbled down his cheek. And with that he was gone into the night.

Carrying his rucksack on his shoulders and a stout length of bamboo in his right hand, he took the back road into Kathmandu. He walked at a leisurely pace through the darkness. A song flared in his mind. He began to hum the Door's 'Light My Fire'; the line about love becoming a funeral pyre having taken on a new and special significance for him.

He fell silent when he noticed clouds of fireflies creating ghostly patches of green fluorescence over the rain ditches that flanked the narrow road. Wrapped up in his thoughts, Angus let his feet guide him. A spinning memory reel unspooled its contents and images of Jenny filled his mind: Jenny how she'd looked when he'd first met her, Jenny's lemon-shaped breasts, the rose tattooed on her thigh, Jenny sighing with pleasure as they made love, Jenny's laughing eyes, Jenny's comments on Adam and Eve when the bus was stuck in a blizzard in Turkey, Jenny's stoned smile as she drew on her opium pipe. When he heard the muted rumble of unseen flames and alarmed shouts, he turned and looked back. The mist hanging over Swayambhu glowed red. Thick clouds of smoke billowed up like thunderheads. Dull thuds signalled that the fireworks were beginning to go off. *Whoosh! Whoosh! Whoosh!* Three rockets scudded across the sky, sprayed the darkness with sparkling colour and then exploded with loud bangs that echoed over the valley. Dogs barked. Monkeys shrieked and gibbered in terror. The gilded surfaces of the Swayambhunath temple's spire reflected the blaze in glimmering golden tones. Angus sat for ten minutes on a roadside shrine's steps in order to admire his handiwork. The sound of cracking rafters came to his ears. Sparks spiralled up into the night sky, a sight which reminded him of how he'd once thought the fire in Jenny's eyes could have burnt a building down. Now the flames devouring her body were doing just that.

Angus felt like he'd left a part of his soul behind in the inferno. He would miss Jenny; even though in his heart he knew that she'd been absent from the world for so long that it had only been a matter of time before her body disappeared as well. He began to think about how he had become strongly identified with a number of things and people to give his life substance, not least of which was Rolling Thunder and his relationship with his two soul brothers, who were now steering the bus west on a winding transcontinental journey. Now, with his outward attachments in life stripped down to what he carried in a small bag upon his back, he felt unburdened.

The lyrics of a Robert Hunter song, put to music by Jerry Garcia and made famous by the Grateful Dead, rippled across his memory. He began to sing. 'There is a road, no simple highway…'

Angus rose to his feet and continued singing as he walked on into the night. 'That path is for your steps alone...'

17

MYSTICAL MEETINGS WITH REMARKABLE MEN

Cambodia.

'**F**ucking hell!' I roared.

The rain was so heavy it felt like I was sitting under a waterfall. *Ba-doom! Boom! Ba-doom!* Thunder rolled like tribal war drums, a sound so loud it gave palpable blows to my ears. Simultaneous forked lightning flashes transformed the sky into a huge three-dimensional topographical map, scarred by electric-blue rivers and edged by light-grey deltas. It was too much for my already shattered nerves. In urgent need of a nicotine fix, I unrolled my denim shirt and draped the sodden garment over my head. I quickly extracted one of the few remaining cigarettes from the damp packet and tried to light it. *Click! Click! Click!* 'Shit!' The lighter was wet. I adjusted the gas control. *Click! Click! 'Awooogh!'* A blue flame engulfed my right hand and shot up my nostrils. My nose stung and I could smell singed hair.

Karaaack! A bolt of lightning seared through the clouds. It narrowly missed the coconut tree, but succeeded in dislodging four coconuts. *Thump! Thump! Thump!* The first three thudded into the sand. *Whooomp!* The fourth glanced off my shoulder.

'Aaaargh!' I screamed out in shock and pain.

My right shoulder was throbbing when I finally managed to light the cigarette. I drew on it. It wasn't smoking properly. A lightning flash supplied enough illumination to see that the bent cigarette was cracked in the middle. I attempted to repair it, but my wet fingers caused the bloody thing to disintegrate.

'Fuck it!' I ripped the shirt off my head and threw it away in frustration.

The rain let up and gave way to a strong wind that raised goose pimples on my exposed arms and legs. My canvas training shoes were full of water. I wiggled my toes and they produced a squishing sound. My lips tasted of salt and my eyes stung. A cold void expanded in my soul. It was the most miserable moment in my life. I wept.

With an aching heart I stared at the churning waves. The sea was no longer an impersonal expanse, but a living being that was swelling with a pitiless force. I felt very small, tiny and then microscopic. A roll of surf crashed before me. I threw myself on to the raft of memory, drifted into the slipstream of the past and left the storm behind.

Angus arrived early, and waited for over an hour before the English couple showed up. Kathmandu was starting to rouse itself in preparation for another busy day. Temple bells pealed, filling the moisture-laden air with frequencies ranging from low dong to high zing. A herd of frisky bulls sported with each other on the deserted square's wet cobblestones. A barefoot Nepali girl wandered by. She was carrying a bleating lamb under an arm and stopped for a moment to stare at Angus as if he were some kind of extraterrestrial visitor. 'Namaste', said Angus in greeting. The girl's slanted eyes blinked in surprise. She smiled sheepishly and walked away without saying a word. His eyes followed her and noticed that, over to the east, the sky was beginning to lighten above the outline of the city's antiquated buildings.

Bertha, the bright orange VW camper, pulled up outside of the Ying-Yang restaurant. Its wipers were slapping to and fro as they tried to rid the windscreen of early morning condensation. Angus stepped forward and Martin rolled down the driver's side window.

The Englishman greeted him. 'Good mornink, man, it's goink to be a beautiful day.' There was an unlit joint stuck to the bottom lip of his lopsided mouth.

The first thing Angus noticed when he stepped into the camper's cramped interior was a little brass statue of Ganesha, the four-armed, elephant-headed Hindu deity. It was glued on to the centre of the dashboard. 'The Remover of Obstacles' was well positioned. The road out of town was littered with rocks and potholed to the extent that it looked like it had been carpet-bombed. The bumping brought Angus's attention to the total lack of upholstery on his seat. A broken spring was digging into his backside. He looked down to his feet. They were resting on a metal spar between rusted-out floor panels, through which he could see the blur of asphalt beneath his boot soles.

'I'll say this much, Bertha has plenty of character,' remarked Angus, leaning into Lulu as the camper swerved to avoid a holy cow sleeping in the middle of the road.

'You're not kiddink, mate,' she chuckled, 'and all of it bad.'

Martin overtook a line of toiling overloaded trucks on the outskirts of town. Driving too fast, he skidded into a curve, the camper's tyres slipping on a patch of smooth asphalt. Angus turned to glance out of the back window and had his last glimpse of Kathmandu.

In comparison to Rolling Thunder, Bertha was like a Dinky toy. This came as a novelty to Angus because it gave a sensation of being more in touch with the land they were driving through. Rolling Thunder's luxury had insulated and thus isolated her passengers from the outside world.

Lulu pushed a cassette tape into the player. *When the mist rolls in on Highway One...* Joan Baez's voice trilled out of a small dashboard speaker.

'We like to listen to folk songs when we're on the road,' Lulu explained. 'Stops us gettink uptight with other drivers and allows us to put in a bit of singink practice. We're into Baez and Leonard Cohen, but we love Bobby Dylan most of all.'

Angus joined the melodically voiced couple as they sang along to Dylan and soon songs like 'Blowing In The Wind', 'Watching The River Flow' and 'Don't Think Twice, It's All Right' began to take on a new meaning for him.

It was the second of October, 1974 when Bertha, the orange VW camper van with the world's most uncomfortable seats, crossed the borderline into India. Angus felt a thrill buzz through him.

By early afternoon of the following day Bertha was parked under a shady tree, across the street from the gold-domed Vishwanath Temple in the Old City area of Benares. Angus bid a fond farewell to the English couple before setting off on his own.

The familiarity of the city felt reassuring to Angus, who was excited as he hurried down a narrow, shop-lined alley, eager to once again set eyes on the Ganges. He was hoping for one thing, and that was to run into Swami Ram. His inquisitive mind was overflowing with questions and he knew in his heart that the enigmatic swami had the answers.

Angus's first few days in the sacred city were spent in the company of a group of sadhus who met each day on a stone platform and smoked marijuana from sunrise to sunset. The low-grade grass that the mendicants used to fuel their chillums was purchased for a few rupees an ounce from a government ganja shop. The marijuana smoke would not have succeeded in getting a mosquito high, but it worked wonders as a repellent during the evenings, when clouds of the blood-sucking malarial pests buzzed around in the damp air.

One morning, Angus gave his sadhu friends their first LSD trip. Strict vegetarians, they would have had a collective fit if they'd known that the little squares of windowpane acid they swallowed were made from gelatine extracted from boiled cow hooves. The spontaneous psychedelic get-together almost turned into a disaster when, two hours into the trip, Angus and his companions dived into the river, intent on swimming to the other side. The mid-stream current was strong and Gopal, a spindly ascetic, almost drowned. For a few minutes it was touch and go but, thanks to Angus and another strong swimmer, Gopal was dragged out of the river on to the far shore. Gasping for air, the sadhu heaved up a bellyful of dirty water and then, much to everyone's relief, proceeded to laugh about it.

After an eight-chillum salute in honour of Lord Shiva, the day-trippers hailed a passing ferryman, who then rowed them back across the river and dropped them off at the ghats. The afternoon passed in a swirling cloud of colour, sound and cannabis smoke.

Angus revelled in the sadhus' company. He saw them as the ultimate hippies, who seemed about as far from the normal world as one could care to wander. There was a childlike quality of innocence to their nature, normally only found in the very young or the very old. They were unconcerned about the future and owned nothing in the way of material possessions. They rarely stayed in the same place for more than a few days and never knew where their next meal was coming from. Yet, the sadhus were unabashedly happy, viewing the world as a caravanserai, a stopover for the night on the long journey home to God.

The comedian of the group was called Agni Baba. He was a tall man with a modest potbelly and a tearing cough that rattled in his concave chest like dice in a tin cup. His speciality was to lift heavy rocks with his penis. A brass ring had been inserted through a hole pierced in the head of his member. Looping a cotton prayer scarf through the thick ring, he'd bend down to wrap the cloth around a twenty-kilo rock, straighten his back and use his knees as springs to yank the rock off the ground. Angus had to look away when Agni Baba performed this painful act because the ascetic's flaccid sex organ stretched like a piece of thick elastic, casting the impression it might snap off at any moment.

'Very, very holy man with many *siddhis* (supernatural abilities),' said Gopal, who could speak a little English.

It was Gopal who informed Angus that Agni Baba was a Naga, a sect of warrior-like mendicants that had existed since time immemorial. In physical appearance there was nothing warlike about the Baba. Always smiling, his eyes shone with remarkable vitality, their whites as pure as Mount Kailash's snow-capped peak. His strong sense of personal hygiene prompted him to wash his long greying beard and dreadlocks daily. Round his neck he wore half a dozen strands of nut-like beads with little metal charms tied on to them. He wasn't shy and most days he walked around naked. When he wandered up into the city's gallies he used a long orange cloth, the flag of his renunciation, to swaddle his privates like a big nappy.

After spending almost a week in their company, it began to dawn on Angus that Baba was the only member of the small band who was a genuine spiritual aspirant. The others were little more than spaced-out vagabonds masquerading as holy men. All they really wanted to do was to get stoned all day and, after their first experience, they began to continuously pester Angus to supply them with more of the magic squares of LSD.

It was late afternoon and Angus was alone with Agni Baba in a relatively quiet corner of a ghat. Over countless years, the green granite flagstones they sat upon had been worn smooth by the feet of millions of worshipers making their way to the river. The sadhu was covered from head to foot in *vibhuti*, sacred grey ashes. A young Indian couple, with three noisy young children in tow, approached and then prostrated themselves at Agni Baba's thickly calloused feet. He stretched out his right arm and delivered a perfunctory pat on the crown of each of their heads. Grateful for the blessing, the woman pulled her blue sari tightly around herself, averted her eyes and placed a crumpled green five-rupee note in front of the holy man's crossed legs. Agni Baba glanced down at the generous offering and chuckled. With a gentle touch and a barely audible word the mother drew her children close and then, keeping their heads bowed and their hands raised prayer-like in the namaskar, the five-member family walked away backwards. The sadhu studied them for a moment, nodded thoughtfully and then picked up the five-rupee note and tucked it away in his *jholi*, a small woven eight-sided bag that he always carried with him. He then began to cough in small explosive bursts for about a minute. He spat to one side and Angus noticed Agni Baba's phlegm was speckled by blood. The baba observed the concerned expression on Angus's face, shrugged fatalistically and smiled.

Naked from the waist up, a couple of overweight Brahmin priests waddled by, carrying their big round bellies before them like proud eight-month pregnant mothers. In their wake followed an all-male group, composed of about two dozen Shaiva sect novitiates with freshly shaven scalps. They sang hymns in praise of their deity as they descended a wide set of stone steps that fronted the river. Standing waist deep in dark green water, they performed their early evening ablutions. The scene seemed steeped in mystery to Angus and he wished he could ask his ash-covered companion about the significance of what was taking place. The sadhu picked up on his thoughts. He turned to Angus, placed a gentle hand behind his neck and pulled him closer. Their foreheads touched and something hummed up from the base of Angus's spine. They stayed linked like this long enough to make Angus's lower back begin to ache. He did not want to pull away because his body was filling up with a soft neon-blue light that pulsed through his mind in waves, bringing with it a feeling of deep serenity. Laughing like a child with a new puppy, the Baba sat up straight and stared at Angus. The grey ash paste on his face was cracking and his striking grey eyes looked with an intensity that was deeply penetrating, as if he were peering into Angus's soul. This keen gaze had the edge taken off it by the tangible vibration of human kindness that constantly emanated from the ascetic's spiritual heart. Positively charged, Angus was suffused with a strong sense of brotherly love for Agni Baba, a man whose presence he never tired of. The communication that passed between them on a non-verbal level was far more profound than mere words could convey. The sadhu handed Angus his chillum, signalling that it was time for a smoke.

Angus made up a potent smoking mix, using sticky Nepalese hash mixed with natural tobacco and the last granules of his DMT stash for good measure. Sitting facing each other with their legs locked in the full lotus position, Angus passed Agni Baba the tubular clay pipe to give him the honour of lighting it and then struck a match. By way of salutation, the sadhu raised the pipe to his furrowed brow and then proceeded to puff up a thick cloud of smoke. When Angus took a long draw on the chillum the effects from the powerful concoction hit him right between the eyes with the force of a runaway train. Blood hissed in his ears as a tremendous rush of psychic energy blasted rainbow light through his rapidly expanding mind. As if obeying a subliminal command, the two men leaned forward and once more, for a few timeless minutes, touched foreheads with their eyes closed. Feeling disconnected from his body, Angus leaned back on his hands to steady himself. A wailing long distance saxophone called him back to corporeal awareness. He opened his eyes and saw that the Baba was blowing on a conch. The mendicant put the white spiral shell back in his bag, looked at Angus and bestowed a radiant smile upon him. For the second time that evening he gazed into Angus's eyes. There was such direct candour in his gaze that it felt like the man had reached into Angus's body and gently taken hold of his heart. A twinkling light radiated from the centres of Agni Baba's dilated pupils. The sight of him, like some ghostly apparition from the antediluvian past, made Angus stare back in fascination. The Baba appeared splendid. His hair, tied up in a top knot, was garlanded with small, yellow marigold flowers. On the middle of his forehead a triangle of vermilion-coloured sandalwood paste formed a tilak, a mark identifying the sadhu sect to which he belonged and also a symbol of his philosophical faith. Angus realized that the man was indeed a warrior, albeit a saintly one. A few years later, he would hear a discourse on the teachings of Lord Buddha, containing two eloquent sentences that captured Baba's spiritual essence: *'One may conquer a million men in a single battle; however, the greatest and best warrior conquers himself. Conquest of one's self is the greatest victory of all.'*

As dusk fell, they stood up. Agni Baba turned to his young companion and, taking hold of his right hand, spoke in a fusion of Hindi and strongly Indian-accented English. 'Ahcha, Angusji, ek dum good smoke.'

The ash-covered sadhu slapped his potbelly with delight and, chuckling to himself, walked away along the ghat without a backward glance, his gracefully balanced form melting into the shadows like a holy ghost.

The following morning, Angus rose from bed before dawn. He rubbed crusty sleep from his eyes as he looked out of his hotel room's window and watched the holy city awaken to the sound of cocks crowing. Red and orange flags hung limp on temple spires. A thin crescent moon floated like a mottled silver ornament in the roseate sky.

After breakfasting on buttered chapattis and a mug of Nescafé made with buffalo milk, Angus put on his battered straw hat and strolled down to the ghats, where he sat down on a stone step and watched the river flow.

His mountainous bright-red turban askew, a charming ferryman, with a neatly trimmed moustache, coaxed Angus into a boat trip over to the far side of the Ganges. Rowing at a leisurely pace, the boatman's oars creaked in their rowlocks. Angus looked back to see Benares appear out of quickly evaporating river mist. Ornately carved, tiered temple towers glowed orange-pink in the early morning light. Below them, hordes of devout worshippers swarmed over giant stone steps like a multi-coloured plague of locusts. They were on their way to perform their bathing rituals in a dreamlike panoramic vista that could have been an illustration from the *Mahābhārata,* the great epic saga which incorporates the *Bhagavad Gītā* and the *Ramayana.*

Shifted aslant by a breeze coming up from the river, columns of thick grey smoke were already beginning to rise into the pale-blue sky above the Manikarnika burning ghat. Living, it occurred to Angus, was a dying business.

The sun rose out of the mist and lit the sky with the promise of a hot day. A purple dragonfly zigzagged up to the ferryman's sweating face, circled his head twice and then flashed away. Angus scanned the river for body parts, something that foreign travellers he'd met in Nepal had taken a macabre delight in describing to him in great detail. The Ganges was as flat and reflective as a mirror with not a half-burnt, bloated corpse or dismembered limb in sight.

The ferryman beached his boat. He held out the calloused palm of his right hand and accepted with a smile the tired-looking ten-rupee note placed there by his passenger, who then began to make his way along the riverbank.

A flock of green-tailed parakeets screeched by a few feet above Angus's head, bringing his attention firmly into the present. Paddy fields, ploughed into regimented neat furrows, stretched away into the distance. Some of the paddies were flooded with irrigation water and reflected the rising sun in a sparkling tapestry of warm colours. Knee-deep in muddy water, a bull buffalo lowed. A pair of gangling cattle egrets stood perched on the bull's mud-caked back, using their long yellow beaks to probe for a parasitical breakfast in the deep folds of his neck. The birds' plumage was a spotless white, accentuated by the dark brown colour of the tilled earth behind them.

A man, dressed in a knee length ochre robe, was criss-crossing the paddy fields' narrow dykes. As he made his indirect way towards Angus a *kamandalu*, a brass multi-purpose utilitarian vessel with a hinged handle, swung in his left hand glinting gold. Angus's heart leapt when the man drew closer and he recognised him to be Swami Ram.

The swami drew closer. This was the first time Angus had seen him in daylight. He had the well-developed muscular calves of a marathon runner and the sprightly gait of a young man and therefore Angus was surprised to see that, close up, Swami Ram appeared to be in late middle age. Clean-shaven, his bright, slightly rheumy eyes were framed by a profusion of squint lines that were accentuated by sunburn. His hooked nose's nostrils were, like his ears, hosts to tufts of black hair. Smile lines and hollow cheeks flanked his dark-skinned lips. Crowned by shoulder-length, greying hair parted down the middle, the overall physical impression he gave off was that of a person who took good care of his health, but lacked the nutritional diet to ward off the premature onset of old age.

'Good morning, Angus,' said the swami as he approached, raising his right palm in greeting.

'Namaste, Swami Ram.' Angus raised his hands prayerfully in front of his face. He was overjoyed that he'd been recognized to the extent that his name had been remembered.

They walked together in the direction of a solitary banyan tree and then sat down between the towering giant's grey buttressed roots. In a matter of minutes, Angus was firing off a stream of questions about spiritual matters that had been accumulating in his mind over the past year. When the swami informed Angus that his guru had brought him to Benares, he was surprised because it was difficult to imagine this dignified man having a spiritual master. If anyone looked wise, it was Swami Ram, whose noble bearing was counterbalanced by an air of genuine humility.

'You have a guru?'

'Yes,' answered the swami, 'his name is *Sadguru*, the supreme master, and he resides here in my spiritual heart.' Swami Ram patted the centre of his chest. Perceiving rightly that the young man sitting cross-legged before him was puzzled by his declaration, he elaborated. 'The light, which shines peacefully and eternally in the innermost shrine of our heart, is the real guru. Anyone who tells you otherwise is a deceiver.'

'But why is your guru sad?'

'*Sad* is a word and prefix in India's ancient Sanskrit language. It's used in conjunction with a number of words, none of which has anything much to do with sorrow. The literal translation of *sad-guru* is good or virtuous teacher.'

'Oh,' said Angus. 'What about all those guys with long beards and blissful smiles who are called gurus?'

'Nothing wrong with them, they are best viewed as signposts on the path. Remember though, even if they give good directions on the twisting road that leads to the land of truth, it is you alone who must travel it. If they are authentic, they will tell you to look inside yourself to find your true nature, and that truth belongs to those who are their own masters.'

'How can I find the real guru? What should I do?'

'*Do?*' echoed the swami. 'The best thing you can do is ask who it is that believes they are doing.'

Angus gave a nervous laugh. 'Swami Ram, I haven't the faintest idea what that means. Do you think I need spiritual help? How will I find a guru to...to...to show me the way?'

The swami shook his head, laughed quietly and then replied, 'No need to feel concerned about finding a guru. When the seeker is ready, the guru appears. A real guru never invites anybody. He or she lets the seeker come. In other words, this means that when you are ready to discern it, you will find the teacher beside you and you'll recognize him or her by the silence which surrounds them, because realized people are nearly always quiet. Remember also that a stupid person can teach you, a beggar on a street corner, a thief, a fool, a wicked man, a child.' Ram smiled as if something pleasant had just occurred to him. 'In fact, everyone we meet, no matter how much life experience we think they might have or have not, can teach us something. That is, if we know how to watch and listen. Recognize all beings as mentors, including the animals. Learn love from the cooing doves, faithfulness from a gentle dog, how to move and stretch from a cat, patience from a web-spinning spider as she weaves her concentric net over the void and, last but not least, study Mother Nature in her totality for she is the source of endless creativity. In ancient times our early ancestors recognized that this world's natural environment was an integral part of life and death's great mystery and therefore treated nature with respect. We in turn do well if we follow their example, for every aspect of God's creation has something to teach us. If your heart is open, life will always provide you with the experiences that are necessary for the evolution of consciousness. As long as there is a need for an outer manifestation of that which is within, the guru will always appear.' He added wistfully, 'Once upon a time, self-realization was a way of life. Now it has become something secondary to be achieved after the primary goals of a material lifestyle have been fulfilled. During this current epoch that we find ourselves living in, good disciples have become a rarity.'

Angus wondered if he had the makings of a good disciple. 'Is there some place I could go…you know…an ashram or something, where I could learn to be a good disciple?'

'Mmmh,' Ram hummed. 'The only proper place to go is within. No ashram will take you to that place which is your heart's true goal. Stop looking out, start looking in and concentrate on the *now.'*

'What do you think about drugs?' Angus enquired, feeling the urge to move on to a more familiar topic.

'Medicine?'

Angus let out another nervous laugh. 'No. I mean drugs like *ganga (marijuana)*, hashish and LSD.'

'Oh, you mean intoxicants. Well…here in India man has had a relationship with such substances for thousands of years. Personally, I've never been interested in them. Many so-called mystics and misguided people use them to attain a state they call ecstasy. However, it is my opinion that these substances, at best, give a glimpse of the beyond and, at worst, destroy a man's vitality and cause all manner of sickness both physical and psychological. In some instances these *drugs*, as you refer to them, gain a man a certain fleeting sense of enlightenment or deep relaxation wherein he imagines that he has found the truth. The problem is that to gain these transient states a person can become dependent on something which is outside of himself and, in so doing, become a slave. Intoxicants give experiences. True spirituality has little or nothing to do with experiences, because it is the ego that is entertaining those experiences. Enlightenment is a state devoid of experiences. Man is not who he thinks he is, but is who he thinks he is not, and that is God. God is an alive presence that is everywhere. That aliveness exists in the present, and therefore it can never be experienced by the ego, because the ego is never found in the 'now'. It is as simple as that.'

After having had this explained to him, Angus, for obvious reasons, felt ill at ease. 'Swami Ram, how old are you?' he asked, quickly changing the subject to one that his mind would not have to run away from.

'Old enough to know that it's only a thought that I've been wearing this body for eighty-two years.'

'Eighty-two!' Angus was astonished.

Ram shook his head and chuckled. 'It's an old car, but I'm a good driver.' He nodded at Angus. 'And you?'

'I'll be twenty-four in December.'

Ram raised his bushy eyebrows and smiled.

Angus enquired, 'Have you always been a swami?'

'No, I haven't. I used to be a plumber.'

'A plumber!'

'Yes, and believe me, clearing blocked toilets in Mother India is not a job for the faint-hearted. I can smell the stink of human waste in my nostrils as I speak of it, even though its more than twenty years since I laid down my tool bag.'

'How did you become a swami?'

'Bharati, my beloved wife, died of leukaemia in nineteen fifty-six. My grief was such that I wished I'd died with her.' By way of further explanation Ram added, 'For months I mourned her passing. I sank into a deep valley of depression and lived there until inspiration broke through the darkness and lifted me into the light of understanding. It dawned on me that my grief was not due to Bharati's death, but rather because of my ego's insistence that death shouldn't have happened to someone I knew. It is difficult to say in so many words, but something inside of me knew that death did not really exist, that nothing is permanent in life except life itself and I just had to move beyond the limitations imposed by my ego to live that reality. It was this insight that urged me to give up everything so that I could dedicate my life to the pursuit, discovery and investigation of the enlightened condition. I signed over all of my worldly possessions to my two sons, shaved my head, put on an orange robe, kissed my five grandchildren goodbye and became a sannyasin. In Rishikesh—'

Angus cut him off by asking, 'What's a sannyasin?'

'A person, who renounces all worldly attachments,' answered Ram. 'The Hindu world-view recommends *sannyāsa* as a way of life for men who have fulfilled all their duties during the householder phase of life. A task, I must confess, that I haven't been entirely successful in. I still travel to Rishikesh at least once a year to visit my family.'

'My girlfriend died recently.'

The swami looked intently at Angus. 'And?'

'And…and…and I feel that I'd like to find something beautiful in life, something that can't be taken away from me.'

'Mmmh.' Swami Ram hummed again and looked away from Angus.

A bullock cart, stacked high with grey sacks of cement, rumbled on a nearby dirt track. *'Hup! Hup! Hup!'* cried the seated carter, who was using a length of knotted rope to whip at a white Brahmani bull's flanks. The long-horned beast's big black eyes rolled in its struggling head. Harnessed to a wooden yoke, the large hump muscle in its neck pulsed with concentrated strength.

Clearing his throat to catch Angus's attention, the swami said, 'It sounds to me like you're getting the call.'

'The call? What call?'

'Why, the call to awaken to your true self. The summons that tells you that it is now time to seek wholeheartedly that which is inside of you – your true nature, a state of timeless perfection which nothing can be added to or subtracted from.'

Angus scratched at his bearded chin. 'Swami Ram, I just want to know what the best thing is to do. I'm sorry, but all that stuff about getting a spiritual call sounds a bit old-fashioned and sentimental to me.'

The swami cocked his head, glanced sideways at him and, after a short, loaded silence, said. 'I see. *A bit old-fashioned and sentimental* is it? Mark my words…*young man,'* he added, with more than a hint of condescension, 'nostalgia for what is no longer current has nothing to do with what I am talking to you about. What I am trying to describe is eternal. Perhaps, in the years ahead, a day will dawn when you will look back to see that you've crossed the bridge of no return and it will be you who has to struggle with a sentimental longing for the good old days of your youth.'

Angus chuckled awkwardly. 'I don't think—'

'Please…let me finish,' said Ram, 'because it is due to too much thinking that a person lives a dead life, instead of living a life that is alive.' Angus nodded and the swami went on. 'Walking the spiritual path requires firm determination and guts. To be awake in a sleeping world inhabited by somnambulists can feel very lonely at times. To combat that sense of loneliness the seeker must learn to embrace his aloneness and grow to love it, for in that solitude you will find God. Apart from that there is, as I've already told you, nothing to do, other than enquiring who it is that believes themself to be doing. Just *be*. Do nothing. Moreover, you would do well to remember that to participate in God's greatness you also have to share His agony. It is better not to set off on the journey than to one day turn around and try to retrace your steps, because you will find it impossible to do. The inner guru will show you the way, but heed me well when I say that he can at times appear like a hard master indeed.'

Not sure what the swami was driving at, Angus said, 'Should I be afraid of the Sadguru? It all sounds a bit heavy.'

Swami Ram peered into Angus's eyes and said, gently, with an expression of the greatest kindness, 'You're mistaken.' He gave a slight nod, as if acknowledging the presence of a useful thought. 'Or perhaps I am not expressing myself clearly enough. That's one of the problems I have with English; it's not nearly as resourceful as Sanskrit when applied to metaphysics. The truth is lighter than a sunbeam and if your heart is in the right place there is no need to be fearful. The inner master will never overburden you, but he must be taken seriously. If he is denied for too long, his patience is not infinite and he will turn to more compelling methods to awaken you from your eternal sleep.'

'What kind of methods?'

'Why, he will employ his well-worn tools of human suffering, old age and approaching death. Powerful, but not always effective, they work well on the person who has a seeker's heart.'

This struck a clear note in Angus's excited mind. Full of emotion, he asked, 'Swami Ram, will you be my guru?'

Ram nodded sagely to demonstrate that this was not the most unintelligent question he'd ever been asked, which in turn made Angus wonder if perhaps it was.

The swami's eyes shone with a startling clarity and once more locked on to Angus's. 'I'm touched by your sincerity and enthusiasm, but there is no need for such a relationship between us. The truth be told, we are the same. The only difference is that you don't know it. Because of that you imagine yourself to be what you are not. I am a humble *Sadhak*, a spiritual aspirant. Perhaps one day I will attain *moksha*, or enlightenment as you Westerner's call that most exalted of states which, I might add, we all have the potential to realize in the course of our human lifetime. So, for now, our role is that of two travellers on life's road, spending a few enjoyable moments together by the banks of the Ganga.'

Angus looked past Ram towards the river. His eyes squinted against the midday sun's glare and he wished he'd remembered to bring his sunglasses. He pulled his straw hat's frayed brim down to shade the top half of his face.

His stomach rumbled and then he asked one more question. 'Who will guide me on the spiritual path if I decide to walk upon it?'

Swami Ram closed his eyes for a moment, opened them and then answered. 'I don't believe a person has a choice in such matters. Therefore, it's not really a case of deciding to lead a spiritual life or not.' Ram's brow creased as he peered up into the banyan tree's broad boughs, as if seeking the spirit of inspiration. He looked back to Angus and said, 'I'll put it to you like this. The true self is like a magnet which draws you gradually towards itself. That divine magnetism will guide you on the path. As I've already told you, the real guru lives in your heart. All others are merely fingers pointing at the moon. There's no need to become attached to a finger. Look at the moon directly and one day you will come to realize that it is the supreme being who is the real guru.' Swami Ram rose to his feet and dusted himself off. 'Come now, hunger beckons. Let us cross the holy river and seek that which will satisfy our empty bellies. *Annam Brahm* – food is God.'

They returned to Benares by employing the services of the same ferryman who'd rowed Angus over the river earlier that day. When they reached the ghats, the boatman would not accept any payment for his toil. He stooped and touched Swami Ram's bare feet, indicating to Angus that he was indeed sharing the company of a revered personage, although the swami made little of his own state of grace.

After dining together in a small tea shop on spicy lentil soup and fresh rotis, Swami Ram took his leave of Angus. Sensing finality in their farewell, Angus took a few deep breaths and tried to control the emotions threatening to bring tears to his eyes. He had not followed the swami's wise counsel and therefore had become attached to the finger pointing at the moon.

The holy man bowed and brought his palms together in front of his face. He then bent down to pick up his brass *kamandalu* from the chai shop's stone floor, stood up straight, smiled at Angus, turned and walked out into the dazzling mid-afternoon sunlight, where the ghats rippled with a blue shimmer of heat produced by a fierce sun.

Angus was not prepared to let go of his spiritual friend quite so easily. He hesitated for a minute, hurried out of the teashop and ran after Swami Ram. A question burned in his inquisitive mind. As he approached the swami's orange-clad back, the holy man turned around to face him.

'Yes, Angus, what is it?'

'I...I...I'm sorry,' puffed Angus, trying to catch his breath. 'I have to ask you one more question.'

'I'm listening.'

Wiping sweat from his brow with the end of a printed prayer scarf, Angus sighed and said, 'I think I've got it. We are born into this world alone and must one day die and leave alone. It's true isn't it?'

A hint of mild irritation flitted across the swami's calm features. 'My young friend, if you truly believe that, you are labouring under a misguided notion.'

A hole opened up inside Angus's guts, as if something terrible had just been revealed to him. He stammered, 'Wh...Wh...What do you mean?'

Raising his right arm, the swami placed a firm hand on Angus's left shoulder, gazed unblinking into his eyes for a few moments and then said, 'The idea that you come and go anywhere is perhaps life's greatest illusion. Try and realize that it is not you who moves from dream to dream, but rather the dreams that pass before you, the immutable witness. That is who you really are and nothing can affect your real being – this is the absolute truth.'

There was a firm note in Ram's voice and Angus knew in his heart that he would never see him again.

The swami gave a quick namaskar and then, once more, turned and walked away. This time Angus let him go unhindered. Physically, it was the last time that he saw Swami Ram, but he only had to close his eyes and think of him to conjure up his saintly presence.

Whether or not Swami Ram was an enlightened man, Angus never really knew, but he chose to believe he was because it suited his mindset at the time. He'd been strongly influenced by reading books like *Autobiography of a Yogi* and Paul Brunton's *A Search in Secret India*.

Angus had been in Benares for a fortnight. His feet were beginning to itch. He was just about ready to hit the road in search of new horizons. Thirst drew him into a back lane teashop. It was there that he reconnected with Martin and Lulu. They were seated on a wooden bench, drinking cardamom-flavoured tea from brown clay cups. In the background, a large, paraffin-powered primus stove roared like a jet engine. Dripping with sweat, a chai wallah, his thick black hair combed into a brilliantined quiff, used a wooden paddle to stir a brass pot full of caramel-coloured liquid that was coming to the boil. Over in a corner, below a big black and white framed photograph of Mahatma Gandhi, another man squatted as he baked chapattis in a brick bread oven.

'Hey, man, good to see you,' said Martin, as Angus approached their table. 'We were just talkink about you.'

As if to lend credence to her husband's statement, Lulu nodded her head. 'Yeah, man,' she said, 'it's true. We're leavink for Agra tomorrow to see the

Taj and we were hopink to see you again so we could ask you if you'd like to come along wiv us.'

A week had passed since Swami Ram pulled Maya's illusionary carpet out from under Angus's sandaled feet. He was feeling cast adrift and was pleased to see the English couple again because they came to him like a safe anchorage in a stormy sea of change. Martin and Lulu's love for each other was so strong they were positively glowing. Martin looked stoned as usual, a joint never far from his lips. His long unkempt brown hair hung down the sides of a face that was intelligent and goofy at the same time. Lulu leaned into her lover. Under her zebra-striped hairstyle's fringe a fluorescent pink, stick-on bindi sparkled on the middle of her broad forehead. Her thin black eyebrows were perfectly straight, like dashes, and her neatly applied, purple gloss lipstick and chalk white face were drawing curious stares from the chai shop's male clientele.

'Sit down, Angus,' said Lulu, moving over on the bench to make space for him. 'You're lookink a bit out of it. It's time for a cuppa, mate. Look at this.' She handed him a postcard with a garish photograph of the Taj Mahal printed on it. 'Doesn't that look absolutely far-out, man? It's goink to be fantastic to visit the Taj. Some famous guy said it looks like a teardrop on the face of eternity. It's full moon in six days and that's supposed to be the best time to view the most beautiful buildink in the world.'

It had never before occurred to Angus that the Taj Mahal might be worth visiting. He'd imagined it to be an overcrowded tourist trap and consequently off the map for a non-conformist rebel like himself.

'The Taj,' he said, turning the word over in his mouth. 'Yeah, man, it sounds good to me. Besides, I'd like to learn some more Dylan songs.'

'Like a rolling stone?' Martin asked. 'Just as long as you don't get the subterranean homesick blues.' He nuzzled Lulu's face with his nose and ran a long tongue over her slender neck, causing an instantaneous outbreak of excited chatter in the chai shop. 'Deee...licious,' sighed Martin. 'She tastes just like a woman.'

'I'll be your be your baby tonight,' chuckled Lulu.

18

IMAGINE

Cambodia.

I kept my eyes closed because I didn't want to see what was happening. Hearing it was bad enough. The wind was howling across the roiling sea. Waves were crashing on to the beach in front of me. Overhead, palm fronds clattered like a laundry basket full of angry rattlesnakes. My heart was pounding so hard that, despite the noise that surrounded me, I was aware of blood hissing through my ears.

I muttered, 'Come on, Jean, where the hell are you? How can you sleep with this bloody racket going on around you?'

'Easy,' answered a voice in my head. 'Jean could sleep through a hurricane – lying on a bed of nails.'

It was true.

A cloud of sea spray slapped my face. I ranted. 'I'll shave my head and become a Buddhist monk. I'll go to Africa and help feed the starving millions. I'll give all of my hard-earned money to cancer research. I'll start driving a more environmentally friendly car. Fuck it, I'll even give up smoking and go to church every Sunday. Please, God, I'll do anything you ask of me. Just get me off of this bloody thing.'

The wind shrieked and the door to the past blew open.

October, 1974, India.

National Highway 2 entered the sprawling industrial estates and dilapidated slum areas on Agra's northern outskirts. The three travellers were sitting in the VW camper's front seats. They were half way through singing Bob Dylan's 'When I Paint My Masterpiece'

'Someday, everythink is gonna be smooth like a—' Lulu broke off in mid-song when she caught sight of the Taj Mahal in the distance. 'Wow!' she exclaimed. 'Check that out. It looks like an upside down ice-cream sundae.' She jabbed an index finger in the direction she was gawking. Martin followed her gaze. His jaw dropped.

Angus shouted, 'Look out!'

Not a second too soon, Martin slammed on the brakes to prevent Bertha crashing into the back of a Tata articulated lorry, loaded with orange-painted steel girders.

It was late afternoon. The Taj Mahal rose up behind the familiar stage of India's urban sprawl of filthy streets, unrendered brick buildings and faded white houses with lines of dung patties pressed on to their walls. Angus suspected that the Indian Tourist Board actually encouraged Agra's population to keep the city's environs as untidy as possible to accentuate the Taj's extraordinary pristine beauty. Bathed in pastel colours, the white marble mausoleum looked unearthly, as if made of some alien material and transported to Planet Earth by an advanced civilization that created world wonders for galactic export.

An hour before closing time, Angus, Martin and Lulu paid the entrance fee and hurried through a red sandstone gateway that was framed with Koranic inscriptions. Moments later, they had their first uninterrupted view of the Taj Mahal. Against the perfect backdrop of a shifting sky, hundreds of sightseers thronged the neat ornamental gardens and walkways that front the Taj. Rather than tarnishing the environment, the crowds of tourists added an extra dimension to the place, appearing like a multicoloured army of ants in comparison to the massive architectural marvel and its four soaring minarets.

Suitably impressed, Angus and his two friends decided to save going inside the mausoleum for the following day. It would have been less strenuous on their neck muscles if they'd simply walked backwards when they left, because they continuously twisted their heads round to gaze back in amazement at the main dome, its colours fading to silver in the last light of day.

They returned the following morning and by ten o'clock they'd entered the Taj. After ascending a flight of curving marble stairs, they walked out onto a circular, railed gallery. A crowd of Indian tourists was calling out in order to hear the dome's echo. The resulting din formed a polyphonic cacophony that reverberated off the huge cupola, while it did its best to integrate the clamour into a resounding hum.

The rest of the day was spent wandering around in the grounds of what many consider to be the supreme epitome of love made manifest on the material plane. Towards sunset, Angus stuck a deal with a uniformed guard whereby, if he paid the man five hundred rupees, he and his two companions would be allowed into the mausoleum under the cover of darkness.

A perfect full moon rose above a line of trees.

'Please to be staying no longer than fifteen minutes,' said the guard, as he unlocked a small wooden door set into the Taj Mahal's main portal.

Once their eyes had adjusted to the almost pitch darkness inside, Angus, Martin and Lulu were amazed to find that the Taj's white marble interior glowed with a muted translucence – which may have had a lot to do with the fact that they were sky high on LSD. The slightest sound was many times multiplied by the mausoleum's hollow emptiness. Their bare feet slapped on the smooth floor as they made their way to a spot directly below the centre of the Taj's bulbous dome. They sat down cross-legged, joined hands to form a magic circle and began to chant 'Allah,' which seemed appropriate considering they were sitting at the centre of a monument inspired by a Muslim ideal and created by a cultured Moghul tyrant with the modern-day equivalent of a billion dollars to spend.

Auuuuuummm! The dome rang with a tremendous sound that made every cell in Angus's body vibrate in sympathetic resonance with the cosmos. The world dissolved into an infinite electric-blue void.

Having the mantric time of their lives, the trio began pumping out more ohms per second than a Van de Graff generator. 'Om, om, om, o—'

'Please...*please*...*please* to be leaving now...*now*...*now*. Sergeant... *sergeant*...*sergeant* is coming...*coming*...*coming* and I do not want to be punished...*punished*...*punished*.' The worried guard's echoing voice cut through the trippers' chanting like a supersonic wet blanket breaking the sound barrier. Rising unsteadily to their feet, the psychonauts quickly became reacquainted with their bodies and, guided by the guard's battery-powered torchlight, stumbled towards the exit.

Outside, moonbeams dazzled their eyes as they headed off to a convenient alcove to get blasted on hashish and drink in the lunar magic. Beneath the light of a silvery moon, the gem-encrusted Taj Mahal's beauty was unsurpassable.

Angus's last day in Agra was spent on the eastern bank of the languidly flowing Yamuna River. From there, the Taj could be viewed in all her magnificence, far away from the crowds of sightseers and the accompanying whirr of their motor-driven cameras. He looked upstream to where he could see the sixty-foot high red sandstone battlements of the Agra Fort where, over three centuries before, Emperor Shah Jahan, the man behind the Taj Mahal's construction, had been imprisoned for eight years in his own palace when Prince Aurangzeb, one of his sons, seized control of the empire. From a locked room with a view, the lecherous old monarch spent the last years of his life gazing out at the memorial he'd had constructed in honour of his dead beloved, Mumtaz Mahal, who had died while giving birth to their fourteenth child.

In days gone by, the Yamuna River was a mighty waterway with double-masted sailing vessels plying their trade between fertile riverbanks producing a wealth of agricultural products. In modern times, the once proud river has been reduced to little more than a shallow stream of effluent, thanks to man's catastrophic quest for economic growth and the side effects of overpopulation. Nonetheless, to Angus's non-too-discerning eyes, the scene appeared fantastic.

Due to their permanently stoned condition, Martin and Lulu found it extremely difficult to make their minds up about anything that went much further than who was rolling the next joint. They were constantly making plans that they would never implement. For a few days they'd been in half a mind whether to head for Goa or continue down south to Kanyakumari. After a conversation with some hardcore hippies, who they'd met the day before in a chai shop, the English couple finally made a decision. One of the hippy travellers, a crazy Welshman who let out a spluttering laugh after every sentence he spoke, had told them about a man called Hampi Baba who lived in the town he'd been named after. He was a chillum maker and his creations were the stuff of a hash smoker's pipe dreams. This news intrigued Angus and he decided to accompany his two friends south to Central Karnataka.

The road journey was a weeklong marathon of Indian style 'chicken', played with reckless, amphetamine-wired truckers, driving ten-ton dodgems, whose speciality was overtaking on hairpin bends. Near misses, soaring temperatures, thick clouds of dust, sleepless nights in mosquito-infested roadside hotels, bouts of gut-wrenching diarrhoea and bum-stabbing seat springs worked together to create a very unpleasant trip.

Angus shared the driving, leaving Martins' hands free to strum out lively songs on his battered acoustic guitar. Not far from Hampi, the Englishman began laying down a twelve bar chord sequence he'd learned by listening to his guru, Chuck Berry. It was the father of all rock and roll *bhajans*, 'Johnny B. Goode'. Martin employed an emotion-filled singing voice, similar in style to that of Jamaican reggae star, Peter Tosh. As Martin sang he added his own improvised lyrics:

> *'Deep down in Pondicherry, close to Auroville,*
> *Set back into the jungle on top of a hill,*
> *There is a little hut made out of mud and wood,*
> *Inside it lives a sage they call Swami-so-good.*

'He'd never been tricked by materialism's spell
But he could make his sitar ring just like a temple bell.
People said 'Om, Om Swami, Swami-so-good,
All right', they said, 'Om Swami, Swami-so-good'.'

'He was married to a yogini that he met way back,
Who'd sit with him under a tree by a dusty track.
Masters and disciples, their love never fades,
Chantink to the mantras that their gurus gave.

People would approach him, bow down and pray,
Cryink, 'Oh Lord, oh Lord, my soul you can play'.
They cried, 'Om, Om Swami, Swami-so-good.
All right, yes,' they cried, 'Om, om Swami-so-good'.'

Martin used a short stainless steel tube on his left hand's index finger to lay down a slide guitar solo which, had he been there to witness it, would have brought tears of appreciation to dear old John Lee Hooker's eyes. Solo over, Martin returned to his song:

'Swami said, 'I don't want no fans,
Go place your souls in the Creator's hands.
Seekers' minds will always be bound
Until their egos drop and the truth is found.

So come and join me here in the light,
Singink Swami, Swami-so-good. All right.'
They sang, 'Om, Om Swami, Swami-so-good,
All right, yes', they sang. 'Om, Om Swami.
Our guru is good all right. Om Swami-so-good'.'

Martin strummed out a crescendo that rattled Bertha's dirty windows, just as the orange VW camper trundled into Hampi's dusty town square at sunset.

Five hundred years before, Hampi was the capital of the Vijayanagar kingdom. A thriving population of 600,000 Hindus had lived inside the seven lines of fortified walls that ringed the city, until invading Mogul armies laid siege and eventually broke through the fortifications with war elephants to loot and destroy what was once one of ancient India's greatest empires.

When Angus arrived in the small village lying to the south of the Tungabhadra River, he stepped out of Bertha and sensed immediately he was in an enchanted place.

Within a day, he and his two companions had set up camp down by the river in the ruins of what had once been a huge temple. The river's waters were unpolluted, deep enough to swim in and relatively undiscovered as far as foreign travellers were concerned.

Lulu made enquiries and found out that Hampi's famous chillum maker had died and been cremated. The Baba's ashes, purported to bring visions when mixed with tobacco and smoked, were being sold under the counter for ten rupees a gram at the Shivadol chai shop.

For a week, the three friends walked around the ruins of Hampi's bygone empire, which once covered an area of fifty square kilometres. They explored ancient temples and tombs, some so worn and crumbling they looked more like strange geological accidents than buildings. The landscape was strewn with a profusion of massive rounded boulders that looked like the eggs of some extinct species of dinosaurian colossi.

Days passed by like the puffy white clouds that drifted across the bright blue sky. Martin and his wife decided to move on after Lulu experienced a very painful encounter with a poisonous arachnid.

They'd spent the day swimming in the river, smoking hashish and sunbathing on flat rocks, worn smooth by the natural elements. It was while laying on such a rock that Lulu put her hand on a scorpion. Its pointed stinger delivered a load of neurotoxic venom, which packed the wallop of a fist-sized wasp sting, into the palm of her right hand. Lulu screamed in pain and tears sprang from her eyes. She held her hand aloft and watched it swell up like a dark red balloon.

Angus caught sight of the creature as it scuttled off to hide in a crack out of harm's way. He was surprised by its relative largeness and was reminded of a scene in the James Bond film *Diamonds Are Forever*, which he'd seen two weeks before in Agra, where a couple of homosexual assassins, called Mr Wind and Mr Kid, use a scorpion to dispatch one of their victims.

Angus and Martin quickly bundled Lulu into Bertha and then drove in to Hampi. It took them ten minutes to find a local doctor, who, going by his filthy hands, tawdry appearance and bewildered facial expression, had never read a medical manual in his life. Nonetheless, he immediately informed Lulu that, although extremely painful, one black scorpion sting did not contain enough poison to make it lethal. Upon hearing this she calmed down and realized with some relief that she was not going to die. Well...at least not on that particular day.

'It is those pink, semi-transparent scorpions that you must be looking out for,' warned the unshaven doctor, lighting up a king-sized beedie. 'Those little devils can be killing a fellow.'

Later that evening, by the light of a blazing campfire and the sound of running water, Lulu referred to her astrological textbooks. Dissatisfied with the forecasts they provided, she moved on to consult her well-thumbed copy of the *I-Ching,* or *Book of Changes* as it is sometimes known. Dating back to 3,000 B.C., this ancient treasure may be the oldest book on the planet. What the *I-Ching* does best is communicate over the millennia with astounding clarity. The book has been used for thousands of years to isolate the present moment and predict possible futures. The *I-Ching* consists of 64 hexagrams, each of which has an explanation that can be taken as an answer to the enquirer's question. The hexagrams can be consulted by throwing three coins to determine which ones are appropriate.

Lulu invoked the spirit of the *I-Ching* with a solemn ritual replete with fluttering eyelids and mumbled incantations. Angus's unenlightened mind interpreted the rite as an advanced form of witchcraft. He and Martin looked on as she shook the coins in her bandaged right hand before throwing them on to a patch of sand by the campfire. After working it out with pen and paper, Lulu groaned when she saw the hexagram she'd thrown was number 23, 'Deterioration'. She burst into tears when she realized one of the changing lines in the hexagram was the fourth, indicating she was being exposed to danger.

'M...Ma...Martin,' she sobbed, 'we're goink to have to leave here immediately.'

'What? Right now?' he asked, poking at the fire with a long stick.

'Yes,' she replied, her spine ramrod straight, as if she'd just answered the million-dollar question on a televised quiz show.

Martin looked heavenwards, not knowing what to think. 'What about you, Angus?'

Angus had been watching Lulu's antics. Due to growing up on a small Scottish island, where he was surrounded by superstitious fishermen who were always on the lookout for omens and portents, he tended to pay close heed to auspicious signs that would have meant little to most people. However, he still thought that Lulu had completely lost the plot. He shrugged and said in answer to Martin's question, 'Depends on where you guys are headed, I suppose.'

'Lulu?' Martin looked over to his ashen-faced wife, who appeared to be labouring under a hex cast by an ancient Chinese sorcerer.

Lulu hurriedly leafed through the pages of an almanac until she found what she was looking for. 'South,' she proclaimed, wiping tears from her eyes. 'We have to drive south to Trivandrum.'

'Ehm…Lulu…' Martin hesitated. '…could we leave tomorrow mornink?'

The planets spinning in Lulu's mind shifted into a more favourable conjunction and she began to relax. She blinked like an owl. 'Of course, darlink, there's no need to rush off in the middle of the night.' She paused and looked at Angus. 'You're welcome to come wiv us, you know.'

Judging by the uneasy tilt of her head, Angus doubted her sincerity. Conditions on board the camper were cramped. On the road, there had been times when he'd felt like a wallflower getting in the way of the couple's on-going love affair. Apart from that, there were two other magnetic influences exerting their pull on his inner compass: Raj and Murphy. It was mid-November. If he was going to make a move, it would be towards Goa.

Angus smiled at Lulu. 'Thanks. I appreciate your offer but it looks like we've reached a fork in the road. I'm really looking forward to meeting up with my mates in Goa.'

Lulu laughed knowingly. 'Typical Sagittarius,' she announced, adjusting her position on top of a rolled up sleeping bag. 'Sagittarians like nothink better than to go their own way and do their own think. They hope to find those of like consciousness along the path they tread, but often as not they tend to be lonely souls because their journey takes them along the road less travelled. Your task is to set aside your prejudices, be open to new experiences and allow the light of others to enter your restless heart.' Lulu bestowed a warm smile upon Angus. 'That way your feelinks of loneliness will one day be alleviated.'

Angus set aside his prejudices and let her words into his restless heart. He had to admit that what she'd just told him pretty much summed up how he envisaged himself. 'Yeah, Lulu,' he said with a hint of resignation, 'I have to confess that sounds just like me.'

The prospect of parting company brought the three of them closer together. They sat in silence for some time, their eyes feasting on the spectacle of the campfire's flames performing their transient dance.

'I'm really goink to miss you, mate,' said Martin, passing a joint to Angus.

'Me, too,' chimed Lulu, her pale face glowing orange in the firelight.

'Cor-blimey!' Angus exclaimed. 'That's nothink compared to the way I'm goink to miss hangink out wiv you guys.'

They laughed together for the last time.

Angus woke up under a mosquito net and lay staring up at a slowly turning ceiling fan. Its dirty plastic blades were covered in splattered bugs. He'd been in Hampi for three days on his own and was just about ready to purchase a bus ticket and head for Goa. Tomorrow, he thought, rising out of bed.

After a cold shower that ran lukewarm, Angus slipped into a white cotton shirt and trousers. He locked his room door, descended a flight of concrete stairs, left his key on an unmanned reception desk and then walked out of the Arjuna Hotel into a deserted street. It could have been an abandoned film-set from a spaghetti western. The sun's crusty eye had only been open for an hour but it was already hot. A couple of mangy dogs were sunning themselves by an oxcart with a broken wooden wheel.

Angus's empty stomach led him round the corner and into the Shivadol chai shop, where the proprietor was busy moving a greasy rag back and forth over the dusty counter. When he looked over at him, Angus ordered a glass of lemon tea and a bowl of potato bhaji.

While he was sitting at a wobbly wooden table waiting on his breakfast, a bedraggled man with a sparse grey beard appeared out of nowhere like a scruffy genie out of a broken bottle.

'Mind if I join you?' he asked.

'Yeah sure. No prob—'

The freak, whose brown skin was dirt-streaked, sat down before the words were out of Angus's mouth. 'Say, can you pay for my breakfast, brother?'

'Ehm…well I—'

'Hey, Baba,' cried the man to the proprietor without waiting to hear Angus's answer, 'triple scrambled eggs on toast with two glasses of fresh chai, and make it fucking pronto.' He turned to Angus. 'You've got to let these assholes know who the boss is around here.' He offered his hand and introduced himself. 'Deek…Deek Burnnet.'

Angus ignored the offer of a handshake, hoping that would discourage conversation. Deek didn't seem to notice. Angus checked Deek out while the American, going by his accent, stuffed cheap powdered marijuana into a chillum. He looked like a dreadlocked Rasputin the Mad Monk with a Charles Manson stare, made more disconcerting by a cast in his left eye. His forehead was creased down the middle by a deep anger line. An old raised scar ran along his left cheekbone. Quasimodo's hump had been grafted on to his right shoulder, lending his appearance a bit of character. With Quasimodo in mind, Angus reckoned Deek could have found employment in Paris, as a replacement gargoyle under the eaves of Notre Dame Cathedral.

They shared a rough-tasting chillum and then Deek began talking faster than a speeding bigot. He narrated how he'd been decorated with a Purple

Heart after being wounded in action in Vietnam. 'I was in Special Forces,' he boasted. 'The survival rate was one in ten. I went up country solo…dozens of times…in Cambodia and Laos…for weeks on end. I learned to respect Charlie. Muthafucking yellowheads could smell American tobacco in the jungle from two-hundred yards away.' Deek smiled wistfully as he recalled a particular incident. 'My weapon of choice was a deer hunter's rifle with telescopic sight and a foot-long silencer. It was against the rules of war, but in 'Nam nobody gave a fuck. I'd been in north-eastern Cambodia for two weeks, without making a single kill, when I came across a gook with his pants down. He was taking a dump behind some bushes.'

Unsure whether to believe the man or not, Angus asked, 'What did you do?'

'I just stood there looking down into his slanted eyes. The Commie muthafucker smiled up at me, as his right hand slowly reached for his AK-forty-seven.' Deek formed an invisible rifle with his arms and clenched fists. 'I raised my weapon and then – *doof!*' Deek's right shoulder jerked back. 'I blew the cocksucker's face off.'

Angus allowed a muffled whistling sound to escape from between his teeth. 'Man, it must have been heavy in Vietnam.' He was pretending to be amiable, feigning interest while trying at the same time to think of a convenient way to end the spontaneous meeting.

Deek rambled on and told another far-fetched story about how he'd been born during a lunar eclipse, in a haunted cemetery on the banks of the Mississippi Delta. He said he'd grown up in New Orleans and claimed Howling Wolf had fathered him after a one-night stand with his mother, Lucille LaBelle. According to Deek, Lucille was a Haitian immigrant who, during the early forties, worked as a waitress in a juke joint on Congo Square, which the bluesman frequented from time to time when he was in town. Miss Labelle lured Mr Wolf into her arms by casting a spell on him with a juju stick because, in reality, she was a voodoo sorceress, who'd eventually passed her healing powers on to Deek, her seventh son.

Angus looked down to the pus-weeping tropical ulcers, circled by Mercurochrome, on the American's legs and it struck him that Deek's alleged capacity to be able to perform voodoo healing didn't appear to be doing him much good on a personal level. He could see the white of maggots hatching in the festering wounds.

Deek's dry red eyes darted around as he cleaned out his clay chillum with a strip of tar-stained cloth. 'You have to watch out for those sadhus down at the Virupaksha Temple,' he warned, scratching nervously at the thick scar on his left cheek.

Angus had noticed a group of ascetics hanging out in the shade of Hampi's oldest structure, but they'd never appeared threatening to him.

He asked, 'Why are you saying that?'

'Because, man,' replied Deek, patting a small, yellowed, cloth sachet tied around one of his scrawny biceps, 'if I didn't have this, those asswipes would have put a curse on me.'

An awkward moment passed. Angus felt ill at ease and suspected the man was flipping out from smoking too much marijuana in the brain-boiling heat. He decided to humour him. 'What is that?' he asked, raising his chin and pointing to Deek's dirt-streaked arm.

The American patted the little cloth bag on his arm a second time. 'This is an amulet given to me by Yogi Mayadwar Bakwaas in Dimapur. It contains holy gonad wax, peeled from a Shiva lingam, which protects me from the evil eye. That's why those sadhu muthafuckers can't harm me with their black magic shit.'

This was too much for Angus to take on-board. He laughed nervously and swallowed the last of his lemon tea. He was ready to move on.

'Nice talking to you, man,' said Angus, a laugh behind his words. He stood, opened a flap on his rucksack, took out his wallet and tossed enough money on to the wooden table to pay for both their breakfasts plus a healthy tip. He began to turn away, eager to escape from the empty chai shop where he'd been sitting with the madman for the last half hour.

'Sit down, man, sit down,' said Deek, grabbing hold of Angus's arm with a clawlike hand. Angus was pulled back on to the bench he'd vacated a moment before.

Deek gulped down a mouthful of scrambled egg and then said, 'You think I'm lying, don't you?' An edge entered the American's voice as his fierce eyes pinned Angus with an intensity that would have done credit to Vlad the Impaler. A flicker of annoyance flashed across his scarred countenance and his jaw muscles hardened. 'Shee-it! You dumb-ass, sonofabitch Scotsman, you think this is all some kinda fucking joke. Well it ain't, and I'll prove it to you. Look at this.' Deek held up his right hand in front of Angus's face. His hand was balled in a fist. He opened it palm up to reveal a few grams of fine grey powder.

'What the fuck is that supposed be?' asked Angus, who was by now feeling extremely uncomfortable.

'*Gris-gris*', hissed the American, blowing the dust from an evil priest's grave into Angus's eyes.

Angus felt like he'd been hit in the face by a red-hot frying pan. He reeled from the impact and tried to stand up, but instead tumbled backwards over the wooden bench he'd been sitting on.

'Fuck you, asshole,' sneered Deek over his shoulder, as he snatched the money from the table and made a hasty exit out into the street.

Angus's eyes were on fire. He called out for help. The moustachioed proprietor rose up off the three-legged wooden stool he'd been sitting upon. He'd been idly watching the foreigners in the hope that they'd order some more tea or coffee. He hurried over to see what had befallen the longhaired young man writhing about on his establishment's filthy floor.

'Pani lal, pani, pani!' Angus yelled, begging for clean water.

The proprietor did as requested and handed him a big jug of drinking water.

Twenty minutes and five pitchers of water later, Angus could see clearly enough to envisage himself throttling Deek Burnett, if the American was crazy enough to let him catch up with him. After thanking the proprietor for his aid and paying the bill for a second time, Angus decided to go for a long hike to help him come to terms with his run in with Hampi's gris-gris man.

It was just after ten when he set off in a westerly direction, walking at a brisk pace. The small town was soon left behind and, finding himself enjoying the exercise, he kept walking for a couple of hours. By midday his cotton clothes were soaked with sweat. He ambled through a banana plantation and came across a ruined crypt, webbed in grey creepers as if in testimony to nature's dominion over the works of man. The small stone structure's roof was partly intact and provided a rectangle of welcome shade.

Angus kicked off his rubber flip-flops, then removed his wet shirt and draped it over a broken limestone column to dry in the sun. He'd purchased a small stainless steel Thermos flask the day before. Unscrewing its black plastic top, he poured himself a cup of cold water to wash down a vegetable samosa. Time for a spliff, he thought, searching in his rucksack for rolling papers.

Two puffs into his joint, a shadow appeared on the ground in front of him. He looked up from his bare feet to see an old crone dressed in a filthy black lunghi, which was hiked up above her cracked, knobbly knees. She looked like a skinny potato woman, who'd been stuck together with tar. Naked from the waist up, her withered dugs hung down to her navel. Her ancient nipples resembled squashed dates. Her milky grey eyes were like those of a crow.

What does this old bird want? he wondered.

In answer to his unspoken question, the woman extended her right hand to display a mouldy apple. Puzzled, Angus looked from the bruised fruit to the hag's scowling face and didn't see much difference.

'Rupee,' she cawed, as if her measly offering were a bargain.

Angus shook his head, annoyed to find himself being harassed by this pinch-faced harridan, who could have been an Indian incarnation of Typhoid Mary for all he knew.

'Rupee, *rupee!*' Her voice intensified and the ligature of her neck stood out like taut cables.

Angus waggled his head more vigorously.

'*Bah!*' She spat through lips that looked like a septic wound, her rotten teeth grinding like rusty cogs on a machine. She raised a scrawny arm and threw the apple at Angus's feet, where it spread out on the ground like a diarrhoea pancake. She hurried off. The small metal tools and talismans tied around her waist rattling as she disappeared out of sight.

'Man, that was really weird,' said Angus, marvelling at the scene's absurdity.

He returned to his abandoned joint, now extinct. He was relighting it with a burning match when a large rock bounced off the broken column his shirt was drying on. Fuelled by a spurt of adrenaline, his heart lurched and began to throb in his chest. He jumped to his feet.

'*Gurdy, gurdy, gurdy!*'

He could hear the old crone's voice calling out.

Crack! A large chunk of stone whizzed by his head and shattered on a fallen block of masonry behind him. Accompanied by the agitated rustling of leaves, the shadowy form of a large monkey or ape flitted through the trees. Angus focused his eyes and saw more of them moving closer by the second. Two more rocks landed in the dust at his feet. He realized they'd been launched from above. *Rock-throwing monkeys?* Angus thought in alarm, remembering a scene from Stanley Kubrick's *2001* sci-fi epic, where a troop of prehistoric carnivorous apes receive a high frequency message from a giant black monolith that shows up one sunny morning down at the waterhole. The time had come for Kubrick's apes to get tooled up, kill the members of a rival troop of territorial monkeys and prepare for the next evolutionary leap – space travel just around the corner. The image of a circular space station orbiting Planet Earth fled from Angus's mind when he ducked to avoid a buffalo's thighbone that had been aimed at his head. He crouched and looked up into the trees. There were now at least a dozen black apes in sight, hurling stones, pieces of wood and handfuls of their own excrement. Angus glanced around, half-expecting to see a sabre-toothed wild cat with glowing eyes.

'*Gurdy, gurdy, gurdy!*' The old hag's call echoed out.

Angus twigged she was none other than the apes' mistress, ordering them into action. He grabbed his rucksack and shirt. In his haste to escape the situation, he abandoned his flip-flops. He took off like a startled deer and started running as if it were the first day of the hunting season.

Angus ran barefoot through the banana grove and glanced over his shoulder to see that about twenty ferocious, long-tailed monkeys were bounding over the ground in hot pursuit, their rabid eyes reflecting bright sunlight like obsidian chips.

'Gurdy, gurdy—!'

Yeeeeka! Yeeeeka! The monkey matriarch's call was drowned out by her slavering simian cohorts' sub-human howls.

Angus sprinted along a barely discernable cow path flanked by thick bushes. Briars and glossy thorns scratched and tore at his pumping arms.

'Fuuuck!'

A large brown cobra was shedding its skin on the middle of the narrow path. A spurt of adrenaline kicked Angus's reflexes into top gear. He leapt over the venomous snake. It hissed, spat and lashed at his heels. Fortunately for Angus he was moving too quickly.

Fire scorched his lungs with each burning breath as he merged in the frantic activity of panic-driven escape. He broke through the vegetation, ran along a dirt track and headed east in the general direction of Hampi. He kept going until his lungs were ready to explode. He stopped running, turned around and saw the road behind him was deserted. He'd lost his pursuers. Gasping for breath, faint with shock, he sat on a boulder by the wayside and tried to calm down. Dripping sweat, it soon became apparent he'd have to seek shade or suffer a heatstroke.

Up ahead, about half a kilometre away, he saw that the track he was on intersected with another. Rippled by a heat haze rising from the roasting earth, there stood a lone tree, offering abundant shade. Its thick foliage was peppered with brilliant red flowers.

He staggered towards the tree, noticing as he did so that a figure, dressed in an ochre robe, was approaching from the other direction. It registered in Angus's mind that the person was a wandering mendicant. As he drew closer he realized that the orange-clad figure was a *sadhvi*, a female sadhu.

They converged under the tree and stood gazing at each other across creation's most primordial divide. She appeared to be in her mid-thirties. Her eyes, dark and sensual, shone with a lust she could not conceal as they looked out at him from a narrow face. Her forehead was marked with three horizontal lines of white sandalwood paste. At her side hung a shoulder bag made from coarse jute fibre. Laying this at her bare feet, the woman reached up to undo her black hair, tied in a knot on top of her head. Thick and shiny, it cascaded down her back. Her eyes never left his for a moment.

Deek the freak had already been locked up in a dark dungeon in Angus's consciousness but he'd barely come to terms with the fact that he'd just been chased by a troop of rock-throwing monkeys. Sex was the last thing on his mind but his body thought otherwise. The heat of sensuality rising from the woman bore her savage scent to him, a bittersweet musk that reminded him of overripe jackfruit. His heart was beating so hard he thought she must hear it. He felt like a horny buck sniffing out a hind in oestrus. His groin was throbbing. He glanced down to see if his feelings were showing under the folds of his dust-covered, white cotton trousers. They were.

The sadhvi gave the slightest of nods. Her full lips formed a lascivious smile and with one graceful movement she removed her thin robe and let it fall on top of her gunnysack bag. Her smooth copper-coloured skin, slightly separated legs, tapering waist and conical breasts, with pointed, dark brown nutty nipples as eager as the expression on her face, added up to a vision of femininity that affected him in the most fundamental of ways. His balls ached and sent a lust-filled pulse through his body. Angus did not need to look to know that he was rock hard.

Swaying erotically, her breasts wobbled engagingly as she moved closer to him. She lay down in the dust before him and, propping herself up on her elbows, motioned for him to join her with a beckoning hand movement.

Angus could not believe his good fortune. He'd forgotten how long it had been since he'd last made love. A powerful force enveloped him as the hot primal spirit flowing from the sadhvi evaporated all civilized thought from his mind, leaving his body free to respond like a beast. He jumped out of his trousers as if they were on fire. Sexual energy shot between them like an electrical current. The air crackled and turned blue from the static. He knelt beside her. She grabbed a handful of his hair and guided his head to her crotch. Her pubic hair's dark, wiry ringlets reminded him of an exotic seaweed dish he'd eaten in an Amsterdam sushi restaurant. She rubbed his face against her slit. It was dripping hot syrup with a pungent scent, which ribboned his brain and sent a signal to his heart to begin pumping faster. He parted her labia with his tongue. The woman mumbled something incomprehensible. Long nails clawed into his naked back. Her hips rose off the ground. She arched her body and balanced on the back of her head and heels. He was nothing but hard cock as he knelt before her. He hesitated for a moment, and then thrust into the fire between her dark muscular thighs as if he were an animal in rut.

'*Ugh!*' He grunted, breathing in her spicy scent.

'*Oogh! Oogh! Oogh!*' She moaned loudly as the rhythm of life took possession of their bodies, pumping like the pistons of a tugboat's engine pulling an ocean liner into deeper waters.

He pushed harder, wanting to plumb her depths.

She began to orgasm almost immediately. Hot juice splashed his balls. He controlled himself, wishing to make the spontaneous convergence last. The sadhvi rolled Angus over and started riding him like she was out to win the Grand National by a few furlongs. She cried out with joy and laughed like a madwoman when he tweaked her nipples until they shrank, hardened and stuck out like mini, chocolate-coloured, ice cream cones. Angus was so mesmerized by her bouncing breasts that he hardly noticed the sharp stones digging in to his back.

Angus and the sadhvi became the only man and woman on earth, meeting for the first time, a feeling so primeval that he started to accompany her passionate cries. A swelling wave of hot energy began to envelope him and, for a brief moment, he was unsure if he was plunging into the deepest hell or rising to the highest heaven. He could hear strange bestial sounds erupting from his throat. He let go. Screaming in ecstasy, they joined in a mind blowing sexual climax that eclipsed anything he'd experienced. The defining line between pleasure and pain dissolved. He gave every drop of himself. The sadhvi kept moving until she let out a gut-wrenching screech that threatened to shatter his eardrums. The whites of her eyes were showing like she was watching a pleasure bomb detonating in her brain. 'Ugh!' She gasped and then collapsed on top of him.

After fucking like a pair of wild things on the ground for over half an hour, their sweat-soaked bodies were covered in mud-coloured dust, adding to the primordial nature of the scene. The sadhvi let out a quiet groan and rose slowly to her feet. Her breasts were slick with dirt and perspiration. The sweat carved furrows over her belly. Semen traced rivulets down the inside of her thighs. She stared bewitchingly at Angus. He rose to his feet and faced her. She was the wildest looking woman he'd ever set his eyes on.

He stood naked, while she squatted on her haunches and slipped on her ochre robe. She picked up her bag and in the same moment pulled a monochrome photograph out of it that was framed behind glass. It was then Angus had one of the strangest experiences in his life. The sadhvi held the photograph in front of her face and Angus found himself looking into a pair of hypnotic eyes. The bald man they belonged to had a long black beard. There was a circle of light in the centre of his unlined forehead. Angus watched as his reflection merged with the black and white image of the bearded man's face.

Accompanied by the physical sensation of a snake uncoiling at the base of his spine, a wave of vital energy shot up through Angus's body and stuck in his throat. His attention was magnetically held to the picture. He was choking. A river of tears flowed from his eyes in an emotional outpouring stronger than anything he'd ever known. The sadhvi lowered the framed picture and Angus felt like he was about to die.

He stood rooted to the spot, held by a penetrating stare that could have pierced the armoured hull of a battleship. The woman's physical form melted away to reveal an astral angel bathed in turquoise light. A violet nimbus circled her head. The female he'd just made wild unconstrained love with had been replaced with a creature whose presence was apocalyptic. Irradiant lime-green eyes cut to the very core of his being, seeing in an instant everything there was to know about him. Behind the androgynous angel, golden wings rose and fell in slow motion, projecting a cool draught in Angus's direction. He shivered. The emotional knot in Angus's throat exploded. He screamed, blacked out and fell to the ground.

Insects chirped, whirred and chorused. Somewhere in the distance a distressed mother goat bleated for a lost kid. Angus came to and gazed up into a dimming sky. The sun had descended behind a jungle-clad hill. He looked around. The sadhvi was nowhere in sight. She'd left a small brown rock with an orange flower placed on top of it. Etched in the dust in front of the stone was written one word: PUNE. Pune? Angus wondered. What's a pune? Was that her name?

He scratched his hairy chin, pulled on his trousers and shirt, and then retrieved his Thermos from his rucksack. Unscrewing the flask top, he drained it of the remaining mouthful of water.

It was dark when Angus returned to the Arjuna Hotel. The entrance hall was lit by a high wattage overhead bulb whose electricity source was fluctuating. Standing behind a pink, Formica-topped counter and dressed in loose-fitting, grey satin pyjamas, the hotel owner's demure teenage daughter handed Angus his key when he approached. Her young face was vacant, as if her soul had left her body.

'Do you know what a pune is?' he asked.

She stared up at the brown water stains on the low ceiling as if Angus had used Mongolian to enquire about the mating habits of termites. After a shy glance, she hooked a slender finger over her tight lips like a question mark, shook her head and then directed her attention towards an untuned mini TV set. It was hissing in a corner and showing a flickering static blizzard, which provided her with the visual entertainment equivalent of watching paint dry.

'Pune, pune!' Angus persisted, writing the word on a scrap of paper with a ballpoint pen. 'Look, it's spelled like this,' he said, pushing the slip of paper across the counter top towards her.

For a few moments she studied the word with the intensity of an archaeologist deciphering cuneiform writing. Then, as if searching for inspiration, she eyed a tall can of mosquito repellent standing on the warped counter. She picked up the spray can and squirted a vaporous, lemon-scented jet over Angus's head and, without so much as a word, raised her pointed chin in the direction of a large map of India, stuck to a peeling wall with aged strips of transparent sticky tape.

Accompanied by the cloying artificial smell of chemical lemon, Angus ambled over to the map. It was old and faded, in places worn through where countless travellers before him had traced their prospective routes with their dirty fingers. He found Pune (Poona) in Maharashtra State, not far from Bombay, and stood staring at the red spot on the map for a few moments before going upstairs to his room.

Early the next morning, Angus caught a bus to Hospet, the first leg of a journey that would bring him eventually to Goa. He had to spend six hours in the regional hub waiting for a train connection to Hubli. Three delicious masala dosas covered in coconut chutney later, he stood for some time on the railway station's concrete platform, watching big brown rats forage for food scraps on the rubbish-strewn railway tracks.

His foreign presence caught a beggar's attention. Wearing soiled rags, the man's hair was shaved close to his dirty scalp. His fleshless shoulders were so bent he looked like a hunchback. He extended a grubby paw with fingers like gnarled yellow bamboo roots and waved it under Angus's nose. It smelled putrid, a stink of life lived at its most spirit-crushing level.

An announcement in Hindi came over the station's crackling PA system. A klaxon hooted. Angus looked to his left and saw an ancient British steam engine, chugging towards the platform like a venerable, pipe-smoking chieftain with his rolling clan of maroon-coloured carriages in tow.

The beggar persisted and Angus decided to make his day. He deposited a crisp one-hundred dollar bill in the skeletal outstretched hand. The emaciated unfortunate glanced at it, crushed it into a ball, muttered something undecipherable and cast the money away. The little paper ball bounced off the platform and landed in the path of the oncoming locomotive. The beggar stuck out his hand again, cried, '*Rupeeee!*', and then gestured to his toothless mouth.

'Aw, for fuck's sake,' cursed Angus, edging past the man.

'Rupee! Rupee!' The beggar pursued him, his left arm swinging from its socket like a rogue pendulum.

There was a loud hiss of pressurized air followed by the screech of metal rubbing against metal. The Hampi Express jolted to a halt and the platform was enveloped in a thick, grey pall of coal smoke, adding a pea soup fog of surrealism to the scene. Angus coughed and spluttered as he turned a brass handle and pulled open a metal door. Rare for an Indian passenger train, it was easy to find a seat. He sat down by a window. 'Rupee! Rupee!' called the desperate beggar from the other side of the dirty glass. The locomotive moved forward and jerked the carriages when the slack was pulled from their couplings.

Hospet railway station was left behind in a cloud of smoke. Two stops later, Angus had the whole carriage to himself. He began to review the events that had transpired the day before. It felt to him like he'd been on a crazy acid trip and that he'd hallucinated Deek the freak, the rock-throwing apes, the crone who commanded them and making wild animal love with the sexy sadhvi. He only needed a mirror to see the red-flecked swollen eyes caused by Deek's gris-gris powder or look at the scratches on his arms from when he was pursued by the monkeys and feel the aching bruises on his back from his intense sexual encounter to know these incidents had really happened. Yet it all seemed unreal. For the first time in Angus's hippy incarnation he thought perhaps he should cool it on his acid taking. Although he hadn't been high on LSD in three weeks, his reality was starting to become a little too warped for his liking. As if to counter his idea of psychedelic abstinence, Lulu's voice chattered in his head. *The dealers are dishink out free acid on Anjuna Beach. Can you imagine?* 'Yes,' Angus mumbled to himself, 'I can imagine.' The carriage lurched and he grabbed the edge of his seat to steady himself.

The ticket-collector came and went. Angus mulled over his thoughts as the moving picture that was rural India rolled by outside. He gazed out of the barred window and saw crows wheeling in the air above the heads of gaunt, white-clad farmers, coaxing skinny oxen into pulling wooden ploughshares over parched fields. Wrapped in brightly coloured cotton sarees, womenfolk walked behind, casting seeds from woven baskets. Angus wondered how on earth people managed to eek out a living from such bone-dry land, a land so arid you could feel it ache.

Click-clack, clickety-clack, sounded the train's pounding steel wheels on the railroad tracks, one line running into the future, the other going back. Angus was looking forward to meeting up with Murphy and Raj on Anjuna Beach. Many travellers had told him that Goa was a beautiful place. Now he was on the way to find out for himself.

Hoo! Hoo! Hoo! The train whistle hooted, as the locomotive steamed towards the setting sun.

19

WAVES OF CHANGE

Cambodia.

'Oh, God, no, please God, *no!*'
A wave roared on to the beach, broke in front of me, rushed over my legs and almost succeeded in dragging me off the landmine. The water bubbled, hissed and drew back, leaving me high but not dry. If the sea continued to rise I was doomed.

My mind screamed, 'Where the hell are you, Jean?' Then I thought about how our rented beach hut was built on a slight rise and that the sea must be breaking only a few feet from the front door. Surely she can't be sleeping through this, I reasoned.

'Oh yes she could,' said a suspicious thought, employing a pantomimic voice.

I shouted, my voice high-pitched and raw with terror. '*Jeeeean!* Wake up! Wake up! Wake—'

Another wave crashed in. Although not quite as big as the last, it was large enough to fill my lap with water and leave me shivering like a leaf in the wind.

'Please God, help me!' I yelled, unable to come to terms with the sea's onslaught.

Clouds began to separate, allowing moonlight to filter through. I stared at the waves as they tumbled towards me. It was only during the last week that I'd finally made peace with the sea, after the terrible events that had unfolded when its massive force unleashed itself along Sri Lanka's coastline two months earlier.

Sri Lanka.

It was eight in the morning on December 26, 2004, when my brother and I sat down for our routine breakfast together in 'Serendipity', Angus and Lara's beachfront restaurant.

We were in the midst of a conversation when Angus suddenly announced from his side of the table, 'By the way, I've been listening to the BBC World Service on my short wave radio.'

I already knew that Angus did this every morning while he shaved and showered. 'So,' I said, looking up from a bowl of fruit salad, 'what's new in the world?'

'There's been a powerful seaquake off the West Coast of Sumatra,' replied Angus, pouring coffee into our waiting mugs.

I had paid little attention at the time to this seemingly unimportant snippet of news. I wasn't exactly sure where Sumatra was, although I knew enough geography to figure out that it was a great distance away to the east in Indonesia.

It was a pleasant, sunny morning with a few small bone-white clouds being blown along the horizon by an offshore breeze. There had been a full moon beach party the night before. From my slightly elevated position in the restaurant I could see a few late-night revellers, lying crashed out on the beach. Lara and Jean had gone for a walk along Unawantuna Bay's curving shoreline, something they did together most mornings. I turned to my left and could just make out their suntanned forms, receding into the distance as they strode southwards along the golden sands. The conversation that Angus and I were involved in had begun halfway through our breakfast of egg *hoppers,* a native dish cooked in a hemispherical wok-like pan. Angus had broached the subject of himself and Lara leaving Sri Lanka and performing a disappearing act.

More than a little surprised to hear this, my mind filled with questions that I then verbalized. 'What exactly do you mean by *a disappearing act?* Why on earth would you and Lara want to leave *The Retreat?* Aren't your meditation centre and this fabulous restaurant the fulfilment of all your dreams? My God,' I continued before Angus had a chance to respond, 'the pair of you have created such a wonderful lifestyle here in Unawantuna. You have everything that life can offer. Don't you love it here in Sri Lanka?'

'Yes, of course we do,' answered Angus, a hint of regret in his voice. 'It's just that it's becoming a wee bit too hot for us around here.'

I gave him a bewildered look and said, 'But I thought you both enjoyed the tropical temperatures.'

'Hamish, I'm not referring to the climate. I'm talking about the cops.'

'The police?' I nearly gagged on a mouthful of half-chewed food. 'I thought your life of crime was a thing of the past.'

'I did too,' said Angus. 'Unfortunately, I'm sorry to say, the past has caught up with us.'

'Good God, man, how?' I asked.

'It began when Murphy and Raj were busted in the process of carrying out a big, ill-fated coke deal in Spain.'

'But I remember you saying you never dealt in cocaine. You said it was against your moral principles.'

Angus's shrugged. 'I had absolutely nothing to do with it.'

'So, why are the police looking for you?'

'Well...what it all boils down to is this. Lara and I had been staying in the lads' finca in Ibiza and, after the shit hit the fan and splattered the walls, the Guardia Civil dusted the farmhouse and found our fingerprints all over the place.'

'I thought you said you were a professional.'

'Very funny,' said Angus. 'I was a professional, but I had no idea what the guys were up to at the time.'

'Judging by what you've told me about your friend Murphy, you should have known better.'

'Yes, that is a valid point.' Angus nodded in agreement. 'But you have to understand Murphy and Raj were, for one reason or another, holding their cards close to their chests at the time. Probably because they knew I wouldn't approve of their business activities.'

'And now the police have found out about your whereabouts?' I concluded.

'Yes, that is exactly what has happened.'

'That's terrible news,' I said. 'What are you going to do?'

'I've already told you. We're going to perform a disappearing act. Its success will of course hinge on everyone concerned being distracted by something completely unexpected, while Lara and I discreetly slip out the back door and make our escape.'

'Where to?' I enquired.

'We have a number of options.' A little hungover from the previous evening, Angus rubbed his temples with stiffened fingers. 'We haven't quite made up our minds yet which one to go for.'

'What about the meditation centre and this place?'

Angus leaned on his elbows, still massaging his head. 'That's all taken care of. Legally nothing is in either of our names. The whole business is owned by a group of offshore companies whose managing director is Donald McGuffin, a close friend of mine and a legitimate businessman. It would take a genius in international banking law to figure out who's who and who owns what.'

I still couldn't quite believe what I was hearing. 'You mean to say that after all the time, work and money you've poured into this place, you and Lara are just going to turn your backs and walk away from it?'

'Yes, that's precisely what we're going to do,' confirmed Angus. 'Apart from anything else,' he added, 'I believe that life is in many ways a preparation for letting go of it. So I might as well put in a spot of practice.'

'That,' I remarked, 'sounds completely crazy.'

Angus smiled at my bewilderment. 'Maybe so, but, crazy or not, that's what we're going to do. If we stay here much longer it's more than likely we'll be arrested and deported to Spain to face serious criminal charges.'

'When do you plan to leave?'

'Soon, Hamish, soon. Perhaps we'll be gone by the time you and Jean return from your trip to Cambodia.' Angus pushed his empty breakfast plate to one side and poured himself another mug of black coffee. 'You know,' he continued, 'back in the seventies I read a book called *The Way of The White Cloud*. That book changed the direction of my life forever. It's only now that I can really appreciate what it means to move through life like a white cloud.'

'Like a white cloud?' I echoed in perplexity, wiping beads of perspiration from my brow with a napkin.

Angus pointed to the clouds drifting across the azure sky. 'All you have to do in order to understand is observe those clouds. They move, leaving no trace of their passage. It's an ancient Tibetan meditation technique to sit on the side of a mountain and focus on a single cloud until it disappears.'

'That sounds like ancient nonsense to me,' I said.

'How come I'm not in the least bit surprised to hear you say that?' Angus asked, squinting as he looked out over the calm sea's reflective waters. 'Perhaps because it is *non-sense*,' he said, answering his own question. 'However, I can assure you that both Lara and I have spent a lot of time discussing the matter and there is nothing foolish or unacceptable about the decision we've come to.'

A group of young children ran along the shore in front of us. Shouts of joy accompanied their antics as they turned cartwheels on the sand, drawing our attention away from our conversation for a moment as our eyes followed the youngsters' gymnastics along the beach.

'You see how carefree they are?' said Angus. 'Those kids know how to live in the here and now, in a way that we adults have forgotten.'

'Yes,' I agreed, 'I know what you mean, but we aren't children anymore'

'That all depends on how you look at it,' commented Angus. 'For years I've lived a life surrounded by all the luxuries that money can buy. I've come to understand that money has nothing whatsoever to do with real happiness as a direct consequence of having it. I find myself looking forward to the day when Lara and I can condense our needs into a couple of small travel bags.'

'Well, you are in the fortunate position of being able to have a choice in the matter,' I remarked. 'It sounds to me like you have a desire to return to your hippy roots.'

'Yes, I suppose it does,' concurred Angus. 'It has been my lot in life to possess large quantities of money and expensive things that I don't really need. As a consequence what I really find myself wanting to do is return to a simple life, unencumbered by the weight of material possessions. The more one has in this world the more one has to take care of, meanwhile life's more important experiences are passing you by.'

'Don't tell me you're thinking of returning to India to become a pair of wandering sadhus.'

'I've no desire to swing in to such an extreme change of lifestyle. Lara and I are thinking more along the lines of a two-bedroom cottage on a palm-covered hill, overlooking the Pacific in a remote part of Costa Rica. Who knows? We might eventually settle in New Zealand or the West Coast of Scotland. As I—'

I cut him off by saying, *'Scotland?'*

'Why not?' Angus asked. 'It's one of the most beautiful countries in the world.'

'I know that,' I said. 'Why do you think I've been living there since I was born? That's not the point, though. The problem with bonnie Scotland is the bloody weather.'

'There's no such thing as bad weather,' said Angus, 'if you have on the right clothes.'

'You're starting to sound like Billy Connolly.' I raised my chin in the beach's direction. 'Here come the girls.'

Angus turned in his seat and watched our wives as they walked towards the restaurant. Jean, a little taller than Lara, was laughing. She had her long black hair piled on top of her head in a tight plaited coil. Lara looked tomboyish next to her, due to her short, almost masculine, hairstyle. Wearing pastel coloured bikinis, they both appeared remarkably youthful, fit and trim considering they shared over a century of living between them.

'My God, they're beautiful, aren't they?' said Angus half to himself, his face a study in contentment.

'They sure are,' I agreed. 'We're very lucky men indeed.'

It was just then that something extraordinary started to unfold before our eyes. The sea began to recede. For a few moments the pair of us stared in disbelief, until Angus leapt to his feet and knocked over his wicker chair. 'C'mon,' he said in a voice that was close to a shout, 'there's going to be a tidal surge. We haven't a second to waste.'

'Wh...Wh...What?' I stammered.

Angus hauled me out of my chair and pushed me in the direction of the beach. By the time we reached our wives, the sea had gone back twenty metres. Hands on hips, Lara and Jean stood open-mouthed, gawking at multicoloured tropical fish flapping around on the waterless seabed amidst grey piles of broken-off coral from the nearby reef. A large hawk-billed turtle was floundering on wet sand where only a minute before it had been swimming around in crystal clear water.

Angus quickly took command of the situation. 'Lara,' he said, 'there's been a massive earthquake under the sea off the coast of Sumatra. I think there is a strong possibility of the sea rising up in a tidal wave.'

'Are you sure?' Lara asked anxiously, her brow creasing.

'As sure as I need to be.' Angus answered impatiently. 'Quick, gather everyone together from the restaurant and drive them up to *The Retreat*.'

Lara planted her feet firmly in the sand and folded her arms across her chest in a show of defiance. 'And what, might I ask, are you going to be doing?'

Everything was becoming unusually still, as if life were grounding to a halt. The cawing crows that inhabited the coconut trees skirting the bay had fallen silent and were beginning to fly inland. Existing in unconscious harmony with nature, all the fauna living on or near the coastline had sensed something was amiss and, unlike their human counterparts, intuitively sought out higher ground. Dozens of people were standing on the beach watching the sea draw back. Children were picking up seashells. Local villagers were collecting turquoise-coloured parrot fish for the cooking pot, thinking it was their lucky day. How wrong they were would become horribly apparent a few minutes later.

Angus pointed north along the beach. Fifty metres out, jagged spikes were emerging from the sea. A small group of teenagers, with snorkelling gear on, were standing on top of the reef. They were looking around in astonishment.

'That's Mike's daughter, Karuna,' said Angus, turning to Lara. 'Those kids are from *The Retreat*. I have to get them away from there.'

Lara unfolded her arms. 'Right then, I'm coming with you.'

I glanced at her. The determined set of her mouth and eyes made it perfectly clear that it was either going to be her way or no way at all.

'There's no time to waste arguing,' said Angus urgently.

The sea had continued to recede and was by this time a long way from the shoreline.

Angus turned to face me 'Hamish,' he said, 'get going, man. The keys are in the pickup. Gather everyone in the restaurant together and get them away from the beach.'

I stammered again, 'B…B…But I—'

Angus shouted at me. 'Hamish, just fucking well do what you're told.' He looked at my wife and gave her an order. 'Jean, you go with him…*now!*'

It was then that I realized why some of my brother's close friends called him 'The Commander'. There was a power in his voice that compelled you to obey him without question.

Angus and Lara sprinted away and headed north along the beach. Angst hung in the air like a negative electrical charge. Jean and I rushed into the restaurant. Everyone in the place was standing with their mouths open, gazing at the receding sea as if hypnotized.

'Wakey! Wakey!' called Jean. 'We're going to get out of here right now.' She put on a Scottish tour guide's gentle accent. 'If you would please be so kind as to follow me in this direction.' She pointed towards the side exit.

Nobody moved.

Jean screamed at the top of her voice, *'Now! You fuckin' idiots!'*

Chairs toppled as everybody moved at once and began piling into the back of the Mitsubishi pickup. Before I followed them, I stopped to take one last look at the ocean. The water was over a hundred metres from the shore. I knew then that Angus was right. Something awful was about to happen. I looked along the beach. Angus and Lara were running across the dry seabed, leaving footprints in the sand behind them and shouting to the kids on the exposed reef in front of them. Sensing my eyes on him, Angus stopped and turned in his tracks. From his position, half a kilometre away, he waved to me in such a way that it indicated it was time for me to get a move on.

I did not see the tsunami crashing into Unawantuna Bay but, as I drove away from the beach, I did hear its arrival. The ten-metre-high wave's approach was heralded by a sound that I will remember for as long as I live. Hundreds of people screamed in terror when the tidal wave surged up out of the sea and roared towards the land to engulf them. With a thunderous crash, the massive wall of water exploded over the beach and rammed into the many restaurants built along the shore. It sounded like the bay was being bombed. The noise was extremely loud because I could hear it over the Mitsubishi's whining engine, which I was driving in second gear, and the anguished cries of the passengers, who were hanging on for their lives as we sped along a narrow village lane toward the Galle road.

When the pickup screeched on to the coastal highway, I spun the wheel to the right and manoeuvred between traffic that had ground to a standstill. Drivers, passengers, cyclists and pedestrians were running in panic.

Unawantuna Bay fronts a small peninsula. Four-metre high waves were rolling along the Galle road from both north and south, swallowing up motorists and pedestrians in their path. The pickup's tyres squealed for purchase as I took a hard left on to the steep asphalt track leading up to *The Retreat*. I heard the boom when, seconds later, the two walls of water collided behind me.

When the four-by-four reached the meditation centre's main building, I slammed on the brakes and skidded to a halt. I jumped out of the vehicle's cabin and, followed closely by Jean, ran over to a rocky outcrop which provided a commanding view of the southwest coastline.

What I saw from that vantage point was to remain forever burnt into my memory. Unawantuna village was submerged under dark grey water. All along the coast, the sea was sandy brown and already littered with flotsam. The first wave was beginning to draw back. Bile rose from my guts when the full realization struck me that my brother and Lara were down there somewhere. Jean stood silently by my side. My wife is a strong woman and she does not cry easily, but in that moment tears were streaming down her face.

I watched as a second tidal wave rolled in five minutes later. It was half as high as the first, but no less devastating to the village, still submerged in filthy water.

I did not know it then, but I'd just become one of the many millions who came to be known as tsunami survivors, each with an incredible tale to tell, more often than not filled with loss, heartbreak and wonder at still being alive.

The next twenty-four hours flew by in a sleepless blur. Because of *The Retreat's* elevated position the meditation centre became a rallying point for foreigners and Sinhalese alike. Many people were in a state of shock or badly injured. Due to misinformation broadcast on Sri Lankan radio stations, rumours were rife about the possibility of more tidal waves rising out of the sea.

The first representatives of foreign agencies to arrive on the scene were news reporters. It was mid-afternoon and I was sitting in the kitchen, consoling a young man who worked in *The Retreat* as a gardener. He was a Tamil from Jaffna who'd just been informed by mobile phone that his entire family had been wiped out. A film crew sauntered in to the room. Small enamel badges were pinned to their clothes and recording equipment, leaving it in no doubt that they worked for an independent British TV channel. A cameraman with one eye jammed into his shoulder camera's viewer approached the stricken Tamil. A red light glowed beneath a turning automatic zoom lens.

'What the bloody hell do you think you're doing?' I asked, my voice seething with anger.

'We…we…we're making a documentary about the disaster,' blurted out a young woman with a makeup-caked face. She was holding up a microphone that looked like a ball of black wool impaled on a stick. 'Would you like—?'

'Bugger off right now,' I said, cutting her off. I glared at her colleagues and shouted, 'Where the bloody hell do you think you are? A pop festival?'

The stunned film crew froze on the spot. I stood, took a couple of steps towards them and then I went ballistic. Spittle flew out of my mouth as I ranted, 'Don't you see what's going on here? People have lost their loved ones. Get out of here right now or so help me God…' I grabbed a kitchen chair and hurled it at the news crew. They ducked and the wooden chair shattered against a wall. I then picked up a frying pan and screamed, *'You fucking news scavenging vultures!'*

The reporters did not hang around to hear anything more. They quickly scurried off to their air-conditioned Land Cruiser. A greasy frying pan bounced off its back bumper as it sped away.

Nobody in *The Retreat* was aware of the colossal human tragedy they were part of because everyone was preoccupied with taking care of the injured, the bereaved and, in many cases, themselves. The Germans were getting things organized. The Dutch were being sociable. The Brits were stoically cheerful. The Scandinavians were getting drunk. The Italians were becoming more emotional by the minute and the French were complaining, while they took care of providing everyone with a hot meal. A retired American couple were wandering about, assuring everyone that there was nothing to worry about because their wonderful president, George W. Bush, was bound to send in the Marines. A handful of hatchet-faced Chinese hookers, who'd been working the local hotels, sat around by the pool manicuring their nails and jabbering into mobile phones. Meanwhile, the Sinhalese were displaying what wonderful people they were on every level one could care to imagine.

Two hours after the British news crew left in a hurry, another team of reporters showed up. Three bearded men approached me cautiously and then informed me that they were from Al-Jazeera, the Arab world's international TV network. The eldest of the trio, bald, gaunt and in his early forties, told me he'd just flown in from Baghdad. It soon became obvious to me that the bespectacled man was accustomed to the face of tragedy. I could tell this by the level of sensitivity he displayed when talking with me. I took to him almost immediately, sensing that this particular correspondent was a dedicated professional and a humanitarian to boot. During the course of our conversation it was agreed that I'd give an interview, imploring the international community to fly in urgently needed medical supplies. The interview was broadcast the following day.

Immersing myself in caring for others prevented me from dwelling overmuch on the shattering thought that my brother and Lara were in all probability amongst the many fatalities. It was late at night when exhaustion overcame me. I lay down on a foam rubber mattress in a quiet corner of the wooden-floored meditation hall and drifted into unconsciousness.

After a few hours of fitful sleep, I woke up and immediately went in search of my wife.

Jean had not slept a wink and, although haggard and fatigued, she refused to rest. Human catastrophes can serve to bring out the very best in people. Jean was a perfect example. She'd been transformed from a middle-aged material girl into a modern-day Florence Nightingale wearing a hip-hugging short dress, her long black hair crowned by a red bandanna. She hurried from one casualty to the next, possessed by the desire to help others less fortunate than herself.

Although deeply moved by my wife's selfless behaviour, I had reached the point of being emotionally overwhelmed by the situation. Hundreds of people were wandering around *The Retreat* in a state of distress and my own personal loss was gnawing at my bowels like an avaricious parasite. Absorbed in my own suffering, I needed some time on my own to digest what was happening to me.

All around the world everyone who had a television set had by this time seen the horrific images that the tsunami had left behind in its wake. Unless one was actually there, it is impossible to comprehend the emotional impact of what was to later be described as one of the greatest natural disasters in human history.

It was nine in the morning on December 27 when I walked down to the Galle road. The highway was covered in a thick layer of grey mud that had quickly developed a sun-baked crust. Wrecked vehicles lay abandoned like children's broken toys. The local populace had already begun to rise to the challenge presented by the daunting task of cleaning up the mess.

Foreign aid convoys were beginning to arrive on the scene, delivering drinking water and badly needed food supplies. Through no fault of their own, the well-intentioned aid-workers were distributing food to people who were the least in need of it and, unknown to them, these commodities were being resold within hours from retail outlets.

I approached a Buddhist temple, where saffron-clad monks invited me in for a bowl of rice. Hunger was a sensation that was still some time away from returning to my empty stomach and therefore I declined the monks' kind offer, thanked them and moved on. When I turned into the narrow road that led down to Unawantuna Bay, there was a feeling of dread in my guts.

I'd been living in the area for over two months and was well acquainted with quite a few of the local villagers. Many of them were now dead or missing. The death toll in the bay would come to a final tally of over two hundred Sri Lankans and fifty foreign nationals. Three kilometres north in Galle, six thousand people had been wiped out in less than a minute.

Nothing could have prepared me for the scene of devastation that awaited me on the coast. The place looked like it had been nuked. Bulldozers had not yet arrived to clear the road, which was completely blocked by piles of debris, smashed cars, dead livestock and the occasional bloated corpse. All around, arising from within shattered homes, came the anguished cries of villagers mourning the loss of family members. Closer to the sea, an Indian film crew was busy taking dramatic shots of a battered taxi – suspended five metres above the ground by a bent coconut palm.

I turned on to the beach, hardly noticing that it was a beautiful, clear morning. A breath of wind brought coolness to my sweating body. Every time a small wave broke on the shore a jolt of adrenaline shot through me, exacerbating my already nervous condition. 'Serendipity', Angus and Lara's once beautiful seafront restaurant, had been reduced to a brown tiled rectangle, edged by dozens of palm trees that had been snapped off like the masts of wrecked sailing ships. The many species of birds that normally filled the air with their calls had flown elsewhere, leaving an unnatural silence. Large chunks of concrete with rusty rebar sticking out of them, smashed furniture, broken glass and pieces of clothing littered the beach. The many cafés that had once lined the shore looked as if they'd been blown up, or flattened by a giant steamroller.

I hunted desperately for signs of my brother and Lara. I picked up a sodden white shirt; similar in style to the one Angus had been wearing when I last saw him. I looked at the label. It said M for medium. Angus's size was

XXL. I dropped the dripping wet cotton shirt on the sand and then walked up to a solitary figure, sitting naked on the beach gazing out to sea. Her name was Helga. She was a plump woman from Düsseldorf, who I'd noticed in the Serendipity restaurant two days earlier, devouring a huge plate of pancakes. In German-accented English she told her survival story. Unawantuna Bay is one of the few places on Sri Lanka's southern coastline where there are no strong currents or undertows. This makes it possible to swim safely for a long distance. Helga had been swimming half a kilometre from the shore when the tsunami had lifted her, carried her three-hundred metres inland and dumped her in the garden of the guesthouse in which she was lodging. I couldn't help noticing that Helga's pale body carried little in the way of cuts and bruises. It was the first of many remarkable survival stories I was to have recounted to me during the next few days. I hoped and prayed that Angus and Lara could have been so lucky.

I looked away from Helga's face and she sensed that I was ready to move on. She promptly stood up and gave me a hug. Her flabby breasts pressed against my chest. There was nothing sexual about the encounter but I still felt uncomfortable. It came as a relief when she dropped her hands to her sides and took a step back from me. I said goodbye to her and then walked over to a spot on the beach, close to where I'd last seen my brother. I looked towards the sea and blew out a long sigh of despair. The reef was submerged. Further out, a small deserted island appeared as little more than a bubble of rock protruding from the water. *No man is an island, entire of itself.* The truth contained within John Donne's timeless statement came to me with a force that made my body shudder.

I wandered back into the wrecked village and came across a gang of looters breaking into a jeweller's shop, one of the few buildings still remaining relatively intact. I turned away from the scene in revulsion and headed towards the bay's northern end, where a white-painted Buddhist temple sat amid pink granite boulders streaked black by time. Outside the temple's splintered wooden gate, I encountered three villagers who I knew on first name terms. Each had their personal tale to tell and two of them had lost relatives. None of them had any news of Angus and Lara.

I walked away from the beach and followed a dirt track that flanked a stream of filthy oil-slicked water. A large, charcoal-grey monitor lizard lumbered across my path. Its jet black eyes blinked at me and then, flicking its tail like a bullwhip, the cumbersome reptile picked up speed and crashed into the undergrowth.

I sat down on the steps of a ruined café called 'The Blowhole' and listened patiently to the distraught proprietor as he explained how the sea had washed away his new deep freeze, which he'd purchased a week earlier on credit. 'I am a ruined man and not only that...' With not a scratch on his body, the café owner was in the midst of recounting an apparently endless list of material woes when a blonde-haired Swedish couple approached us. Their arms were covered in bloodstained bandages. They told me how they'd come to Sri Lanka on their honeymoon. They'd been in bed when the tsunami's waters had crashed through their hotel room's door. The small room had filled with swirling grey water in seconds. Floating against the ceiling, they'd clutched each other's hands, taking what they believed to be their last breath, when the building collapsed and they were washed outside. Bruised and bleeding they'd used a cotton sarong to tie themselves to a tree trunk and thus prevent being dragged out to sea.

After bidding the young honeymooners farewell, I made my way further inland and then walked up an incline to visit the Browns, a retired English couple who Angus had introduced me to some weeks earlier. They owned a small guesthouse that, due to its elevation, lay beyond the tsunami's destructive reach. The grey-haired pensioners made me most welcome and sat me down on an overstuffed sofa. Within five minutes, Mrs Brown had put on a fresh apron and was serving me tea in a delicate porcelain cup and chocolate biscuits from a bone-china platter. An air of calm unreality permeated the stone building. A grandfather clock ticked in a corner. Had it not been for the humidity and heat, I could easily have imagined that I was in a semi-detached bungalow somewhere in England.

Sitting below a framed colour photograph of The Queen on horseback, Mr Brown lit a briar pipe that was filled with fragrant-smelling tobacco. He blew a cloud of smoke across the sitting room towards me and proceeded to tell me a most remarkable survival story. A well-known personality around the village was a small longhaired man called Chandrika who, due to being crippled, got around on a wonky wheelchair. In spite of his disability, the middle-aged Sri Lankan always had a joyous smile on his face. His optimism was infectious, making him a very popular fellow with everyone he rolled into. He'd been on the beach when the tidal wave rose out of the sea and took him. The water tumbled, spun and dragged him inland until he was slammed against a stout tree at the foot of the hill where the pensioners lived. Reaching up, Chandrika grabbed on to a thick branch. When the sea drew back he found himself hanging several metres above a pile of jagged boulders. Not having much in the way of legs, he daren't have let go of the branch because serious injury awaited him if he did. He hung there for an hour, a physical feat made possible by his highly developed arm muscles, formed by thirty years of powering a wheelchair. When the elderly couple came across him, the cripple was hoarse from shouting. With the help of a few villagers, they'd set about the task of bringing him back to earth. They did this by forming a circle and stretching a handheld tarpaulin below Chandrika. It had taken a few minutes of coaxing to persuade the invalid to let go of the branch that had doubtless saved his life. He screamed when he released his grip and fell to safety.

'Mister Brown! Mister Brown! Come quick, please!'

We were interrupted when an overanxious employee rushed into the pensioners' living room to inform them that a dead female foreigner had been discovered at the bottom of their well.

I helped to recover the body by hauling on a rope and experienced a confusing mix of emotions when I saw it wasn't Lara. I felt relieved, while on the other hand I paled at the tragedy of a young woman whose existence had been cut short before she'd had a chance to experience life's fullness.

'Only the good die young,' said Mrs Brown, kneeling in the mud by the battered corpse as her husband covered it with a sheet of black plastic.

Standing beside a formless pile of blue-painted fibreglass debris, which had been a fishing boat until the tsunami crushed it, I told the pensioners about when I'd last seen Angus and Lara.

Mr Brown, who was an exceptionally tall man, stood next to me and turned the disturbing news over in his mind. 'You mustn't give up hope,' he said, draping a conciliatory arm over my shoulders. 'If anyone has a chance of surviving such a calamity it will be that rogue Angus and his charming wife.'

That rogue Angus...Angus...Angus and his charming wife...wife...wife. I had a lump in my throat as Mr Brown's encouraging statement echoed in my mind, while I made my way along a rubbish-strewn single-track road. It was there that I stumbled upon the cadavers of dozens of drowning victims. They'd been recovered from the thick undergrowth which lay at the foot of the hills that rose up to form a green wall of jungle at the back of the bay. Covered in stained bed sheets, the discoloured corpses lay lined up by the wayside awaiting burial. Swarms of buzzing flies rose off them as I approached. Rigor mortis had locked the swollen bodies in unnatural poses, adding to the surreal horror of the scene. I looked against hope at the swollen limbs extending from beneath their shrouds. Their purplish blue colour signified all of them were natives.

One body in particular caught my attention. It was that of a young girl, whose finger and toe nails were painted with glitter varnish. Death's wanton hands had deformed her, but it was still apparent that she'd been pretty and her nail varnish fresh. Lines of black ants marched in and out of her open mouth. The ghastly sight prompted me to contemplate that, only one day before, this innocent lass had been a vibrant member of the community, her mind filled with dreams of the future.

As I stood staring down at the corpse, a gut-wrenching feeling took hold of me. I experienced my first bout of survivor's guilt. I vomited tea and the sludge of chocolate biscuits. My head spun like a top. Gasping, I staggered away along the debris-strewn track.

Before long, I came upon a scene that was to haunt me for weeks. Mr Lal was a villager who ran a small dairy farm. I was acquainted with him because every day the farmer delivered jars of goat's milk yoghurt up to *The Retreat*. A pious Buddhist, Mr Lal took great pride in his three young children, one of whom, a little boy with the eyes of an angel, often accompanied him on his daily delivery run.

When I came across Mr Lal he was filling in the last of four graves, dug in the ruined garden in front of his wrecked home. Three of the graves had white bed sheets stretched over them, white being the colour of mourning in Sri Lanka. Transfixed, I looked on in a state of shocked consternation as the dairyman shovelled lumps of reddish brown earth into a hole in the ground. Filling the still air with its fragrance, frankincense smoke rose from a perforated tin can near to the graves. When he sensed someone's presence, the bereaved villager dropped his spade and looked over towards me. Mr Lal's grief-stricken, bulging eyes glistened with tears.

Grey smoke drifted between the coconut trees and made blue rays out of sunbeams. One of the rays shone down upon Mr Lal, accentuating the vivid salmon-pink pigmentation of his facial discolorations, caused by vitiligo. A terrible groan escaped from the man's throat, a self-pitying sound that cut deep into my soul, unlocking the door to my own personal grief. Mr Lal beat his chest with clenched hands and then lifted his outstretched arms towards the impartial sky, his face twisted like a Sri Lankan devil mask worn at an exorcism. He stood unmoving in this position, forming a living sculpture of utter desolation.

I reeled away, feeling like I'd been dealt a mortal blow. My body was wracked by sobs. Tears clouded my eyes as I stumbled over piles of wreckage. On the village's outskirts my pace quickened, spurred on by an urgent need to be reunited with my wife's precious and sacred living form.

My heart pounded in my ears as I hurried up the steep track that led to *The Retreat*. I felt overwhelmed by a mixture of disconcerting thoughts and the feeling that my whole life had been a build up in preparation for witnessing the events surrounding the tsunami's aftermath. *You mustn't give up hope*. All the while the English pensioner's hopeful message that Angus and Lara could somehow have survived burned in the back of my mind.

'Hello, Mister Macleod.'

I stopped dead in my tracks and looked up.

'How are you doing?'

The voice belonged to Jeeps, Angus's Scottish friend, who looked like an obese garden gnome. He was sitting cross-legged on a flat boulder by the roadside.

'I...I...I'm not quite sure how I'm doing,' I replied. 'How about yourself?'

'Sit down Hamish, sit down,' said Jeeps, motioning with a hand. He plucked a long blade of grass and began to chew on it.

I did as requested and sat at his feet. We remained silent for some time and I listened to the breeze blowing in the eucalyptus trees. I recalled when my brother had first introduced me to Jeeps. Angus had told me that Jeeps was a crazy Buddha. I'd only found it possible to believe the crazy part at the time. Now, looking up into his deep blue eyes, I started to wonder if perhaps what my brother had said was true. There was a feeling of serenity emanating from the chubby little man that I experienced as extraordinary. The events of the morning began to slip away from my mind.

Jeeps chuckled as if sensing my mental state. He ran a hand over his long grey beard and said, 'No need to worry about Angus and Lara.'

'What do you mean?' I asked.

His blue eyes twinkled. 'What I mean is this. Even if those two are dead, which I very much doubt, there is nothing to be worried about, because worrying is like praying for what you do not want.'

'How on earth can you say that?' I asked, my stomach suddenly churning with anger. 'My brother and his wife were in the water when the tsunami came in. Now you're telling me not to worry about it. That...that's outrageous.'

Jeeps began to laugh uproariously.

'What's so bloody well funny about that?'

There were tears of laughter in Jeeps eyes when he answered. 'Angus told me you had a tendency towards taking life too seriously. Death too, it would seem. He also—'

'Oh, he did, did he?'

'Yes he did, *Mister* Macleod. He also told me how much he loved you and your wife, Jean.'

'Oh!' My emotional pendulum was swinging from one extreme to another – in the space of seconds. My anger was replaced by a deep sense of loss. I saw in a flash how delicate the fabric of human existence actually is.

'What you have to understand,' continued Jeeps, 'is that death does not really exist. Death simply means that the visible form has disappeared. Energy cannot die and life is energy at its most vital. The people you find yourself related to in this life, you have in some mysterious way known in another form. When they die in this life, you will meet up with them again somewhere in another life. It's all a matter of patience. Therefore—'

Suddenly, for some unaccountable reason, I felt exceedingly angry again. 'Aw come off it,' I said, cutting Jeeps off for a second time by raising my voice. 'I don't believe in all that bloody reincarnation mumbo-jumbo. In my book anyone who does is...is...*stupid!*'

'Is that so?' said Jeeps. 'It might be wise to abstain from judging or criticizing anyone you meet, for you never really know who anyone is until you've gone beyond the world of appear—'

'*Aaaagh!*' A wave broke over my knees, ripping away the memory of that fateful day. 'Jesus,' I gasped.

The saviour was not around. Instead, Angus's voice spoke to me. 'Listen, Hamish, you have to learn how to visualize things. People who think the end of the world is nigh are simply people who lack the imagination to envision what the future holds. You have the power to dream what you want into existence.'

I heard Angus's words in my ears, as lucid as the sound of the water rushing around me. Even if it were true that death is an illusion I still was not ready to let go of life. I spat salty water out of my mouth and shouted at the roaring sea. 'I want to see my wife and family again and you're not going to fucking well stop— *Ooofh!* '

As if in response to a challenge, a breaking wave crashed into me and knocked the air out of my lungs. I gagged on seawater.

A stark animal terror gnawed at my bone marrow. My mind filled with the blackest of thoughts.

The one that shouted loudest said, 'I've fucking well had it.'

Paranoia screamed, 'I'm going to die!'

Angus's voice broke through the darkness. 'Visualize it, Hamish, visualize the light. Imagine a beautiful day with not a cloud in the sky. A day when simply being alive makes life's trials and tribulations seem worthwhile.'

'Don't listen to him,' advised a doubtful thought

'It's fucking bullshit!' yelled an aggressive one.

'You must pray to God for forgiveness,' whispered a guilt-ridden Christian sentiment.

'I'm going fucking nuts,' confessed the voice of insanity.

'Use your mind as a tool, Hamish. Don't let your mind use you.' Angus's words shone through like a beacon of hope.

Casting around in my memory for a picture of where I would like to be transported to, I recalled Angus's description of Goa's sun-kissed beaches the first time he'd set eyes on them. It wasn't much to go on, but so immersed was I in my brother's experiences it was the straw I chose to grasp. There were no others, except The Lord's Prayer, and I wasn't quite ready for that.

20

THE GOA TRIANGLE

November 1974.

When Angus arrived in Panjim, Goa State's capital, he liked the feel of the place and checked into a small hotel on January Road. He was immediately impressed by the Goans' affable nature and the fact that many of them spoke English. This was a pleasant change from Hindi, of which he only understood a few words, although the Goans employed the same paradoxical body language as their Indian neighbours, whereby a nod of the head was a negative and an animated shake a yes.

It was late afternoon. Angus set off to explore the old Portuguese quarter's narrow streets. Solid whitewashed buildings roofed with curved terracotta tiles, ornate balconies, louvered window shutters and imposing brass-studded oak doors, opening on to shady fountained courtyards, created an overall impression of being in a southern European town. This distinct architectural style had been imported by the colonists who'd occupied Goa for almost five centuries before finally relinquishing control of the now independent state in 1961.

A swelling cluster of Goanese pedestrians was gathering on a paved square in front of an immense Catholic Church, its central tower home to a huge brass bell. Curious, Angus strolled over to investigate.

Surrounded by people and twirling a four-foot-long fluorescent light tube above his head, a shirtless man, wearing a shapeless turban formed from a dirty blue towel, was turning tight circles on a rusty bicycle and calling out, *'Magic show! Magic show!'* He dismounted from his bike and pushed it up on its stand. A space opened up in front of Angus. Hoping for a better view, he moved forward to join the spectators' front ranks.

After placing the fluorescent tube on the ground, the street performer lay down on it and used his naked back to shatter it. When he stood up, shards of white glass were embedded in his skin. Women put their hands to their mouths in shock upon seeing what the bleeding man had done to himself.

319

Apparently immune to pain, he took a generous slug of strong-smelling alcohol from a half-pint bottle and, using a small plastic brush and dustpan, proceeded to sweep up the broken glass. Next, he sat cross-legged on the ground and began eating splinters of glass. Angus's healthy scepticism was sucked into a whirlwind of irrationality. He had to believe the unbelievable, taking place right before his astonished eyes. Halfway through his crunchy lunch the glass eater stood up and singled out Angus for a spot of audience participation. The crowd took a few steps back from the longhaired foreigner when the magician approached him. Clucking like an aggressive rooster, the crazy performer's rabid, bloodshot eyes bulged as he waved a six-inch sliver of white glass in front of Angus's bewildered face.

'Eat, eat, very tasty!' he cawed, so close that Angus could smell the cheap booze on his fetid breath.

'No thanks, man,' declined Angus, raising his hands in front of him. 'I'm not that hungry right now.' He let out a burst of nervous laughter.

A few of the transfixed onlookers laughed, purging the tension that had accumulated in the air.

'*Ha!*' spat the drunken man, a thick blue vein pulsing in his throat. 'I will eat.'

Angus could hear the sickening crunch as the man bit down hard on the brittle splinter. This was no optical illusion. The madman was gnawing at the broken glass with his bloodied yellow teeth.

For a finale, a packet of rusty razor blades was swallowed one by one, followed by a large light bulb that was smashed before being munched up, brass fitting included.

A small boy broke through the circle of enthralled spectators and began collecting coins in a tin can. Angus peeped into the rusty can and then deposited a brown ten-rupee note. Including his donation, he reckoned that the magic show had pulled in fifteen rupees at an absolute maximum, enough to feed the glass-eater and his helper for a couple of days. Angus watched the bleeding street performer gather a few discarded items together, mount his rattletrap bicycle and turn to his little assistant. He took the money that the lad offered him and patted him affectionately on the head, demonstrating that their relationship was probably that of father and son.

Turning to a bystander, an elderly gentleman dressed in a double-breasted, white cotton suit, Angus asked what he made of the spectacle.

The old gent's reply was spoken with a refined Indian accent. 'This man is a drunken fakir. He is a good-for-nothing fellow and only doing this for the money.' He looked Angus in the eye and added in what was evidently an attempt to make sure he got his point across, 'The rascal should be taken off the street immediately and locked up in jail.'

Angus thanked the old man when he realized that was all he had to say on the matter, which had of course shed absolutely no light whatsoever on how it was possible for a human being to swallow a quarter pound of broken glass, three brass light fittings and a packet of razor blades, then ride away on a bicycle as if it were nothing at all.

It was early morning of the following day. Angus caught an overcrowded bus that was bound for Mapusa, the main commercial centre in Goa's northern districts. He had to stand and therefore saw very little apart from the back of peoples' heads and the Mandoui River as the bus trundled over the Nehru Bridge.

An hour later, he caught another bus in Mapusa. It was no less crowded than the first. Shoehorned into a back seat, he looked out between the bars of an open window at a landscape that grew more enchanting by the minute. White-painted churches and houses stood by verdant paddy fields, bordered by swaying coconut trees, creating a scene of lush tranquillity that was a far cry from the parched plains of India.

Angus alighted from the bus at the north end of Anjuna and watched as it sped off around a corner, headed for its terminal stop in Chapora village. Once the dust settled and the stench of diesel fumes dissolved, he took a deep breath. The sea air was tinged with the sweet scent of cashew trees and, much to his surprise, roses. He turned, glanced up and saw a blue sign with painted red flowers surrounding the words 'Rose Garden Café'.

He entered the establishment, sat at a table by a rose bush and ordered a lemon soda from an unshaven waiter who reeked of rum. Ten minutes later, he asked a couple of vacant-faced hippies for directions to Joe Bananas, a well-known chai shop.

It was almost midday when Angus realized that he was completely lost. He stood on a narrow cattle path that wound its way through a coconut tree plantation and gazed around him, wondering if perhaps he should try to retrace his steps. The sound of voices made him look up. Barefoot toddy wallahs were calling to each other as they collected sap from the treetops for making fenny, the local alcoholic beverage.

A young man, wearing a pair of bright-red Bermuda shorts, came wandering along the sandy path towards Angus. His skin was the colour of coffee beans. Black kinky hair hung over his shoulders and glistened with oil. There was a shark's teeth necklace strung around his neck and he was whittling a piece of wood with a penknife.

'Excuse me, man,' said Angus. 'Do you know the way to Joe Bananas?'

'Boom, boom,' said the carver. 'Yeah, man, keep going this way,' he pointed with his knife, 'until you see a big white stone with a black metal cross sticking out of it. Then you take a left and boom, boom, you're there.' He raised his handiwork in front of Angus's eyes. 'You interested in buying a hairpin, man? I made it myself.'

'How much?'

'Twelve rupees, man,' replied the carver, his brown face breaking into a charming smile that displayed a big gap between his front teeth.

'Okay, it's a deal,' said Angus, rummaging in his pocket for some loose change.

'C'mon, man,' said the carver, handing over the hairpin in return for a sweat-dampened ten rupee note and two one-rupee coins, 'I'll get you down to Joe Bananas. I haven't had any breakfast yet but now, thanks to you, I can go buy myself some porridge down on the beach.'

They walked along the path together.

'I'm Jamaican,' said the young man, who let it be known that he was a Londoner who'd been born in Kingston – Kingston-upon-Thames. 'My friends call me Atom.'

'That's an unusual name,' remarked Angus.

'My real name's Albert, but I like Atom better. It sounds more cosmic,' the Englishman remarked. 'I used to work as a cleaner in a nuclear power plant.'

'Weren't you worried about the radiation?'

'No way, man, I like atomic energy. It makes you glow in the dark.' He chuckled and grabbed the crotch of his red shorts. 'The chicks love it.' A big green coconut fell from a tree and thudded to the ground. 'Got to watch out for those,' warned Atom, nodding towards the fallen nut. 'I was just reading that ten thousand people a year get killed by falling coconuts.'

'That sounds a bit exaggerated,' commented Angus.

Atom said, 'One too many if it happens to be you...right?'

Angus nodded. 'Right.'

They were chatting like old friends by the time they arrived outside a small, whitewashed house. There were a few tables and chairs set out on a porch shaded by woven palm leaves.

'There you go, man, Joe Bananas,' said Atom, walking off in the direction of the beach. 'See you around, man. Boom, boom.'

'Eh...ehm, thanks, Atom, boom, boom,' said Angus, wondering what all this *'boom, boom'* business was about. He would soon discover that 'boom, boom' was the traditional way that chillum smokers greeted each other in

Goa. The greeting came from the cry that went up when a hash pipe was being lit, as in *'Alack! Boom Shanker!'*

Just as he was about to enter Joe Bananas, a female voice shrieked, *'Angus!'* He turned around and a suntanned woman in a yellow bikini with a shaved head slammed into his chest. She embraced him with a tight bear hug that almost succeeded in snapping his spine. When he finally managed to free himself, he held her at arm's length and realized she had a familiar face, which looked a little wiser around the eyes since the last time he'd seen it.

'Alice?'

Someone else hugged him from behind. She said in an excited voice, 'Oh wow, this is really amazingly far-fucking-out, man!'

Angus instantly recognised Nina's distinct Glaswegian brogue. He turned in her circling arms and saw that she too had shaved her head. Her dark bronze skin made her look like a curvaceous Nubian slave girl. He laughed, surprised and overjoyed to have run into Alice and Nina so soon after arriving in Anjuna. All three rocked together in a spontaneous waltz. A gentle sea breeze rustled palm fronds to provide the music.

'How come you shaved your heads?' he asked.

'Och,' replied Alice, 'when you're on the beach all day its easier not to have any hair to take care of. That's why we went for the Kojak look.' She ran a tanned hand over the glistening crown of her head. 'What do you think?'

Angus stood back and gazed steadily at Alice and Nina for a moment. Alice's torn earlobe had healed and the faint scar that remained on her cheek added to her wild-woman-of-the-jungle look. Nina had put on a little weight since he'd last seen her in Peshawar.

He let out a soft whistle. 'The pair of you look drop-dead gorgeous.'

'Wow thanks, man,' said Nina, giving him a wink, her broad smile seraphic. 'We've been here just over a month now and I never want to leave. This place is paradise. The parties are pure mental. Come on, man.'

'Where to?' asked Angus, stepping in a fresh cowpat.

Alice looked down at his dung-covered, sandaled right foot and smiled. 'Hey, Angus, it's your lucky day, man.'

'It's beginning to feel like that,' he agreed.

'We're going to the beach,' said Nina. 'Wait till you see it, man. It's absolutely out of this world.' She took hold of his hand and pulled him forward behind her.

Nina was right. Anjuna Beach was a little slice of tropical heaven. Deserted, except for a few nude sunbathers, gently curving waves broke on to the shoreline's white sands. Out on the sea, a two-masted dhow's reddish-brown triangular sails bellied out in the wind.

'Last one in is a rotten kipper,' yelled Alice, pulling off her bikini top.

Angus's eyebrows shot up. It wasn't only the beach that looked wonderful. He watched the two naked nymphs run into the sea, feeling like a castaway in paradise who'd just discovered a pair of treasure chests. He stripped and dived into a breaking wave. The water was lukewarm and crystal clear. Alice and Nina swam over and hugged him, their eyes sparkling in the sunlight.

'It's great to see you again,' said Nina holding on to his neck.

Angus looked down at her round breasts and pulled her closer. 'It's good to see you too, Nina.'

'Och, you men are all the same, so you are.' She giggled and ran the fingers of her right hand through the short, wiry hair on his chest.

Back on the beach, they lazed around on the warm sand, smoking joints, laughing and nibbling on succulent papaya and watermelon purchased from 'fruit ladies'. Dressed in saris, these sturdy women patrolled the sun-kissed beaches, their heavy baskets cocked on their hips while they stopped to haggle over the price of a fresh coconut or ripe pineapple.

When the girls asked about Jenny, Angus told them, as gently as possible, about her deterioration and eventual death.

'I knew Jen was going to OD sooner or later,' said Alice.

'Me, too,' commented Nina, 'but it's still a drag, man. Do you miss her a lot?'

'Yes and no,' he replied, Jenny's loss having become for him a dull ache buried beneath the surface of his wandering life. 'I loved Jenny but, towards the end, there wasn't anybody left to love anymore. I know it sounds callous, but in a way it was a relief when she died because I'd reached a point where I didn't know how to handle it any more. She was in a right mess.' He paused and for a moment his eyes became thoughtful. 'When I found her dead it broke my heart. I still flash on it nearly every day. Sometimes I look up, half-expecting her to appear. Like what happened was some kind of weird dream.' He nodded. 'So yes, I miss Jenny. I...I didn't know how capable I was of missing another person until she disappeared out of my life.' He then added. 'The strange thing is, I met this really amazing swami in Benares, who told me that death does not really exist.'

'Huh,' said Alice, obviously unconvinced by this statement, 'what is that supposed to mean?'

'I'm not quite sure,' confessed Angus. 'He also told me that nothing is permanent in life except life itself and that I just had to move beyond my ego to live that reality.'

'Mmmh,' Alice hummed and looked out to sea.

'Anyway,' Angus concluded, 'meeting that swami really helped me come to terms with Jenny's death because he'd also lost someone he loved and kept going. He was a beautiful guy.'

'Wow, man, that's really far out,' said Nina, a tear ready to escape from the corner of an eye.

Alice changed the subject. 'What about those male chauvinist pigs, Raj and Murphy?'

'They drove back to Europe before Jenny died,' answered Angus. 'I'm supposed to meet them at Joe Bananas on December full—'

Nina cut him off. 'I don't care if I never see those fucking assholes again.'

'Me too,' added Alice. 'We both felt used by those selfish bastards.'

'Hey, come on, those selfish bastards happen to be my—'

'Don't take it personally,' said Nina, punching Angus lightly on the shoulder. 'We're really happy to see you, man.' She turned to Alice. 'Aren't we?'

Alice said nothing. She was tracing a figure of eight in the sand with a finger. She raised her head, looked into Angus's eyes and shot him a smile.

Carried on friendship's wings, the afternoon flew by. Large yellow-beaked gulls pranced on the beach like avian shamans, casting elongated shadows as an orange-gold sun sank towards the sea's horizon. When daylight softened into dusk, the sky turned deep purple.

'Let's go back to our place,' Nina suggested, standing up and collecting their things. 'Wait till you see our house. It's only five minutes away and for three-hundred rupees a month, it's got to be the deal of the century.'

When Angus was shown around the Portuguese-style villa that the girls rented, he was impressed. Set in the centre of a walled-off garden, the house was airy and spacious. On the wide porch, a couple of nylon cord hammocks were strung on hooks between smooth coconut-wood pillars. Inside the house, thick high walls rose up to the underside of a sloping terracotta-tiled roof, set on a lattice of thin timber joists. The smooth cement floors were painted dark red and in places covered by patterned straw mats. The whole house smelled of lavender-scented furniture polish.

Alice popped a music cassette into a portable player. An evening raga by Ravi Shankar started twanging and pattering in the background.

Nina applied a burning match to a brass oil lamp and a handful of Nag Champa incense. She knelt by a small alcove and inserted the smouldering joss sticks into a wooden holder that sat at the foot of a bronze Shiva Nataraj statue adorned with wilted frangipani flowers strung on thread.

'This is our puja, man,' she explained. 'Do you like it?'

Angus spread his arms in front of the makeshift altar. 'Nina, I like everything about the place. You guys have done a brilliant job of doing it up.'

Naked except for a thin cotton scarf wrapped around her waist and a silver om suspended from her neck, which swung to and fro below her breasts like a circus acrobat, Nina continued to kneel on the floor. She gazed up at him, deep dimples framing a broad smile. An infectious enthusiasm streamed from her large blue eyes.

'Thanks darling,' she purred, stretching her limbs like a cat. 'It feels even better now that you're here,' she said in a honey-laced tone. 'We've been missing a man around the house.'

'Angus!' Alice called from a candlelit room. 'Come 'ere and see this, man.'

He entered the bedroom. Set on the middle of the oblong room's shiny red floor was a queen-sized, four-poster bed, the folds of a pink mosquito net draped around it. Alice lay naked on top of a white satin bed sheet. Her smooth head and narrow shoulders were propped up by a pile of black cotton pillows. She looked like a darkly tanned and wickedly mischievous princess, turned high-class hooker.

'So, what do you think?' she asked. 'Beats the hell out of the Hotel Rumi, doesn't it?'

'You can say that again,' he gulped, taking in the scene, centred on the shaved mound at the top of Alice's streamlined thighs.

Nina's bare feet slapped over the floor behind him, beating in time with the tabla player, who was picking up the rhythm on the taped music playing in the background. She put her arms around him. Her warm breasts pressed into the middle of his back. He swallowed hard. The air was by now filled with sweet-smelling incense smoke and buzzing with energy.

'Hey, Angus,' called Alice, bringing his attention back to her shapely reclining form.

'Yeah,' he said, hardly able to breathe, his muscles tightening with a surge of lust.

'Me and Nina haven't made love in a very long time. We're absolutely gagging for it.' She bent her knees up. 'We were kind of hoping you were going to supply us with what we so desperately need.' She made a feminine, wet, snickering sound, intensifying the charge building up in the room.

Ravi Shankar's frenetic sitar playing shifted into top gear.

Nina giggled as she slipped a probing hand under the elastic waistband of his cotton trousers, so baggy the crotch hung between his knees. 'Oh,' she groaned, gripping his semi-erect penis. 'Alice, if I rub this, maybe a big genie will appear to fulfil all our wishes.'

A short blur of time later, Angus was entwined in the warm embrace of his two sex-hungry girlfriends. He sucked on one of Alice's dark brown nipples.

She licked his ear and whispered, 'I've been waiting for this for a long time.'

'Me first,' moaned Nina, straddling his hips.

The trio's sweating bodies gradually welded together in the total intimacy that is sexual magic, laying the foundation for a tantric triangle that was to last for the duration of their stay in Goa.

The next morning, over a late breakfast, Nina was combing Angus's hair, while he sat drinking coffee and smoking a strong-smelling joint of Kerala grass.

'Mmmh,' she sighed, 'that was so good last night, like really cosmic, man.'

'I know what you mean.' Alice smiled a lusty smile from across the breakfast table. 'Do you think Angus might be able to conjure up that wish-fulfilling genie of his again?'

Five minutes later they were back in bed, involved in a lively ménage à trois that, boosted by the powerful doses of LSD that Alice had spiked the coffee with, went on until after midnight.

Much of what is credited to the sixties didn't actually come to fruition until well into the seventies. Nowhere was this more apparent than at the sky-isn't-the-limit, full moon parties held under star-spangled skies on Anjuna Beach. Although the wooden ships of the hippy dream would soon capsize and sink in a sea of unsupportable excess, Angus was later to recall the November full moon party of 1974 as one of the best ever.

In an age of knob-twiddling, beat-matching DJs, who insist that their turntable trickery, which sounds like the soundtrack for a documentary about automated car assembly plants, is the music of the future, it may be difficult for some to imagine that, once upon a lysergic time, when people still believed that music was a force powerful enough to change the world, party people used to dance to the guitar-driven rock of Hendrix, Santana and The Stones.

As Angus walked hand in hand with Alice and Nina towards the party zone's periphery, he could hear a squelchy wah-wah guitar and a squeaky harmonica playing the intro to 'The Cisco Kid' by War. The pre-recorded music was blasting out of a powerful PA system – donated by The Who – and was a pre-cursor to the main musical event of the evening – to be delivered by none other than the splendiferous Big Dipper Band.

When the boys in the band appeared on the wooden stage, facing a wild crowd backed by a moonlit Arabian Sea, a euphoric roar of approval rose into the dust-filled air above the dance floor. The tribal stomping ground was packed with hundreds of colourfully dressed revellers who'd travelled from all over the world to be there that night. Newcomers to the scene rubbed shoulders with well known super-freak personalities from the acidocracy. The stuff of legend, some of their names have, in modern times, achieved cult status – even if only in their own mind.

Over to the right of the stage and dressed in a multicoloured dream cloak, a psychedelic alchemist was using a dropper to dispense liquid LSD on to partygoers' extended tongues, as they fuelled up in preparation for an intergalactic ride on the Milky Way Express. Angus joined the queue.

Badoooooom! Up on the stage, the bass player hit a long booming note and let it float out into the charged atmosphere. *Da-da-doom, da-da-doom!* Like a musical locomotive running down the tracks, the band picked up on the drummers' pounding rhythms. A repetitive, fuzz box power chord buzzed through a guitarist's amp, cranked out of the speakers and took possession of the dancers, working them up into an ecstatic frenzy. In true musical shamanistic fashion, the vocalist hollered out provocative lyrics, inciting the writhing groovers to take it higher and higher. Weaving to and fro, the dancers moved around each other in a cosmic parody of an army of speeded up Tai Chi masters dressed in tribal outfits. Elated screams cut through the sound of the polyrhythmic music. The loudspeakers shook as an amplified full range spectrum of frequencies bombarded the dancers and turned the celebration into one orgasmic whole of high-decibel funk 'n' roll.

Angus was only a few steps away from a megadose of acid. He was so keyed up his intestines were performing a loop-the-loop, like he was moving on a high speed escalator. He looked around nervously and caught sight of Nina and Alice just before they hit the packed dance floor. His mind was doing interdimensional pole vaults and he began to think about how, over the centuries, the priests of organized religion had suppressed and outlawed the age-old tradition of dancing into ecstasy. His excited musings were interrupted by a gentle male voice.

'How much do you want, brother?'

'Oh…ehm…three please,' replied Angus, sticking out his tongue.

'You sure?'

Angus kept his tongue out and nodded three times.

'Boom, boom, boom,' said the man with the dropper.

One hyper-intense hour later, Angus stopped dancing and looked up at the stage, where a lone trumpet player was blowing a series of echoing high notes – Miles Davis Bitches Brew-style. It sounded like an alarmed electric owl hooting at the moon. Angus gazed up at the sky and saw that the moon was in the midst of an eclipse. The milky shadows on the moon's surface were slowly changing from sickly yellow to blood red as the earth moved between its satellite and the sun. Angus began to wonder if there was any truth in the saying that man is food for the moon, something he'd read in a Gurdjieff book. A hallucinatory crimson skull formed from the moon's shadows. He shuddered at the sight of it and suddenly had a vision of the moon behaving like a giant electromagnetic parasite, pulling upon all organic life on earth and sucking up the soul essence of dying creatures through an etheric umbilical cord. He felt something being drawn out of the crown of his head. *'Wow!'* He gasped in astonishment and tore his eyes away from the eclipse.

Meanwhile, back on Planet Earth, the Big Dipper Band kicked in again and Angus returned to surfing the sonic waves crashing over the dance floor, out of his mind on the three drops of pure LSD that had been dropped on the end of his tongue by the psychedelic witchdoctor.

'I want to take you higher,' cried the vocalist, invoking the spirit of Sly Stone.

'Higher!' chorused the crowd.

Angus raised his arms in the air and threw himself totally into the rhythm of the music. He moved as if possessed. Time disappeared. The sensory borderline between the dance and the dancer began to dissolve. The awareness of his existence vanished as he experienced total ego meltdown and became a pulsating cell in the organism of the musical beast unleashed.

Hours later, Angus opened his eyes and realised he was in bed. He couldn't remember how he'd come to be there. His lovers were lying peacefully by his side. Alice was snoring. He could hear music in the distance. The beach party was still going on. A rooster crowed. Angus rolled over to go back to sleep, but Nina had something more energetic in mind.

21

OLD SCHOOL REUNION AT THE CROSSROADS

O ne day flowed into the next, each more wonderful than the last. The Christmas and New Year parties passed, but there was still no sign of Raj and Murphy. Angus began to wonder if something untoward had happened to them, but relaxed knowing from experience that they were probably labouring under the modern-day curse of waiting for phone calls. Disorganized crime always takes longer than planned when it comes to committing it.

Life with Alice and Nina was a surrealistic dream come true. During the day they hung out together on the beach and swam in the sea. In the evenings the girls cooked delicious spicy meals for Angus, while their insatiable sexual appetites provided him with more lovemaking than he, at times, was able to keep up with.

Anjuna Beach was a magnet for international travellers, many of them fascinating people. But their presence didn't quite fill the vacuum that Angus experienced every once in a while, an empty space in his heart that only his Scottish mates could fill.

It was mid-January when Acid Mike showed up one evening in Joe Bananas. He was cast in the double role of bearer of sad tidings and blighter of dreams. Angus was happy to see his old business acquaintance again and, judging by the way Mike's face creased into a delighted bullfrog grin, the feeling was mutual. Mike was surprised when he discovered that Angus was unaware of what had befallen his two partners on their journey west on Rolling Thunder.

'You mean to say you don't know?' Mike asked, his tone reflecting the puzzled expression on his face.

The hair on the back of Angus's neck prickled in anticipation. 'Know what?'

The Englishman averted his eyes, and Angus knew that bad news was about to be delivered.

'It was in the papers some weeks back,' said Mike. 'There was a small photograph and that's how I knew it was them. Murphy and Raj were busted driving into Iran with half a ton of hash hidden on the bus. The incident caused a stir in the British press because one of their passengers was a society family's daughter. Anyway,' he concluded, 'Raj and Murphy were sentenced to twenty years in prison.'

The colour drained from Angus's face. 'For fuck's sake,' he rasped, bile rising in his throat, 'don't tell me.'

'I'm sorry to be the one who had to drop that one on you, man,' said Mike, placing a consolatory hand on Angus's shoulder. 'Thing is, there's more.'

Angus shifted uneasily on his creaking bamboo chair, not quite knowing what to expect. He gulped back a mouthful of ice-cold banana lassi laced with fenny.

'Your name's been in the newspapers as well,' declared Mike.

'*My name!* How the fuck did my name get in the papers?' Angus asked, steel bands tightening around his chest. He was just about ready to head for the smelly squat-down toilet round the back of Joe Bananas.

'There was an article about your girlfriend, Jennifer Fraser, reporting that she'd been killed in a deliberately lit fire in Nepal.' Mike paused for a moment as he searched for concise phrases to deliver a message that he knew was bound to cause further upset. 'Scotland Yard is working in conjunction with the Nepalese authorities, investigating what they described as a drug-related murder and you're their main suspect.'

'You...you're fucking well joking.'

Mike frowned. 'Do I look like I'm joking?'

'Sorry, man, but that's really not what happened. Well...well in a way it was, but...but not like *that*.' Angus went on to explain the story surrounding Jenny's death and how he'd burnt a house down in the process of cremating her corpse. His narration was accompanied by a sinking feeling that told him his desire to give his girlfriend a spectacular farewell had completely eclipsed his common sense.

Mike stared blankly at him. Then, shaking his head, he muttered, 'Man, oh man, that was a bloody stupid thing to do.'

Angus felt irritated, the way one does when criticism is too close. 'Yeah, maybe so,' he said, hiding his annoyance, 'but it seemed like the right thing to do at the time. I...I just wanted to give her a good send-off.'

'*A good send-off,*' mimicked Acid Mike, looking at Angus with the kind of wry expression that he reserved for moments when confronted by incredible foolishness. 'Are you off your bloody rocker? If the sodding Old

Bill get hold of you, you're the one who's going to get the good bloody send off – to a cell in Wormwood Scrubs maximum security prison.'

Mike's comment acted like a shocking revelation on Angus's mind and prompted him to say, 'Fucking shit, man, what do you think I should do?'

'Well…you can stay in India for a start. You're lucky Commonwealth passport holders don't need a visa.' Mike thought for a minute, and then added, 'You'll have to get a new book.'

The gravity of the situation was really beginning to sink in for Angus. His head felt like it was filled with a ton of lead. 'Where will I get a false passport from? I don't know anybody in that line of business.'

Mike leaned toward Angus and placed a warm hand over his. 'Piece of cake, old son,' he said, sounding like a cockney Etonian. 'I'll get one together for you. I'm flying back to London at the end of the month. All you need to do is provide some mug shots. I'll do the rest.'

'How?' asked Angus, moving a little closer to Mike.

'Man, don't you know that the British Passport Office's system is full of holes? All that's needed is a dead man's birth certificate, someone who was born round about the same time as you, something the Registrar's Office is only too happy to issue, and a new passport is yours for the sum of twenty-five quid.'

'I can't believe it's that easy,' said Angus, hoping that it was.

'Believe me, it's true. If you don't want to do it that way, you buy a new identity by simply dropping some nobody a monkey (£500), if his travel plans don't go any further than the white cliffs of Dover, and get him to apply for a passport using your photograph.'

Angus heaved a sigh, turned to Mike and said, 'Man, if you can sort that out for me, we're friends for life.'

Mike took his right hand off of Angus's and used it to slap him on the back. He laughed and enquired, with a gracious generosity never before witnessed by Angus, 'How are you doing for dosh?'

Angus took a double take on Acid Mike when he asked this because he was most definitely not renowned for his handouts. He was tighter than a penguin's arsehole in a blizzard.

'I'm all right for the moment,' said Angus in response to Mike's unexpected enquiry. 'I did have a lot of money invested in that fucking bus, though.'

'Can't win 'em all, Angus. You should know that by now. At least you're not banged up in an Iranian prison with your mates.'

'I can't argue with that but, even though I'm still a free man, I'm also now in a situation where I will have to wait things out. I'm terrible at that sort of thing. I'm impatient at the best of times and waiting a long time on anything makes me edgy.' Angus laughed nervously and then said, 'Man, I can get uptight waiting for a kettle to boil.'

Mike nodded. 'I can relate to that,' he said. 'Patience isn't one of my virtues either. Waiting has always had a negative quality to it for me also.' He added, 'I can't stand being in drawn-out iffy situations, especially when the cops are involved. I've been through that number a few times and I had to stop my bloody imagination from locking me up in a claustrophobic hell. If you ask me, it's best to try and not think too much about it.'

'Easier said than done, Mike, easier said than done.'

'I know, man, I know.'

There was a moment of silence between them, underscored by the background crash of waves breaking on the nearby beach and the conversational hum created by the half-a-dozen languages being spoken by the café's international clientele.

Angus's mind was busy trying to assimilate the new and unexpected developments in his life, which did little to relieve the uneasiness he felt about Murphy and Raj's predicament. He looked at Mike and said, 'Iranian prisons aren't exactly famous for treating their inmates well, are they? What on earth can I do to help Raj and Murphy?'

'Pray,' Mike suggested, raising his joined hands in front of his bearded face.

Angus cocked an eye. 'Getting religious in your old age?'

Mike shook his head and gave a wry smile. 'Uh-uh, not me, not like some of the folks round here.' He raised his bearded chin in the direction of a neighbouring table, where a group of orange-clad foreigners, each with a string of black wooden beads around their neck, were laughing loudly.

Now that Mike had brought them to his attention Angus realized that, during the past month, he'd seen quite a few Westerners wandering along the beach dressed in saffron-coloured clothes. 'What's with the Jaffa convention?' he asked.

'They call themselves sannyasins,' answered Mike. 'They belong to a new religious cult led by an Indian guru called Bhagwan Shree Rajneesh. He's set up shop and opened an ashram in Poona.'

Angus's ears pricked up when he heard the word Poona. 'They seem happy enough. What do you know about this Rajneesh guy?'

'Maybe I'm not the one to ask about guru trips,' said Mike. 'I'm dead against the idea of surrendering to some Indian geezer who claims to have all the answers and says that the keys to the door of spiritual salvation are in his hands. I see—'

'Does he?' Angus asked, cutting him off.

'Does he what?' Mike asked back.

'Claim to have all the answers.'

'Of course he does,' replied Mike. 'That's what all the supposed masters say, and that's why I think the whole guru trip is a bloody con that leaves the so-called 'seeker' childishly dependent on second-hand experience. The big flaw in adopting Eastern spiritual perspectives is the wide-ranging condemnation of thought that comes with those views which, paradoxically, is a perfect example of rigid thinking. The practice of negating thought to transcend it brings with it the danger of destroying one's critical faculties. This leaves a person wide-open to many forms of manipulation and mind control. I suspect that is why the gurus say it is better not to judge which, if you think about it, is highly ironic because a judgement has to have been made in order to come to such a conclusion.'

Mike turned his intense gaze on Angus for a few seconds. When there was an outburst of laughter from the sannyasins' direction, he glanced over at them and then continued. 'If you ask me, any guiding principle that delivers fixed ideas about the nature of perfection and enlightenment creates its own illusions, and that's another reason why I'm not interested in gurus and the whole surrender trip that goes with them. If there is such a thing as the road to salvation, I'll walk it on my own.' He chuckled to himself and concluded, 'It takes guts and discipline to go it alone on the path of the free spirit. Looking for liberation in another person's enlightenment seems to me like a lazy way to go about seeking the truth.' Mike produced a small, transparent plastic, 35mm film canister, containing little red pills. He shook it like a Polaroid picture and it made a sound like an aggravated rattlesnake. 'If I have a spiritual teacher, it's LSD twenty-five. Take a good dose of acid and experience God directly. That's my philosophy.'

In that case, Angus thought, I'd better keep my mouth shut about Swami Ram. He looked at Mike. There was no doubt in his mind that, as far as mind-blowing experiences went, Acid Mike was a true veteran of altered states. Below his tie-dye headband Mike's smouldering blue eyes stared back at Angus, who inwardly acknowledged the respect he had for the man, for in his opinion Mike was a courageous psychedelic adventurer.

Angus rose from his chair and then ambled over to the bamboo counter that served as a bar in Joe Bananas. He paid the bill with a hundred-rupee note and stood around waiting for his change. It was late and he was ready to go home. His eyes drifted over to the sannyasins' table. Glancing up from her companions, one of them made eye contact with him. Not particularly attractive, the young woman's most outstanding facial features were her thick pouting lips. They parted in a salacious smile. Angus was not sure why, but he just stood there gawking at her. She rose, walked over to him, put her arms around his waist and embraced him. Her tactile response seemed so natural he simply surrendered to the situation by returning her hug. Her right hand squeezed his left buttock and he felt a familiar tightening between his legs. A strong sexual current coursed through his body. In the background, Steve Miller's voice was crackling out of a pair of tinny speakers. *Go on, take the money and run...* As far as Angus was concerned it wasn't exactly a new idea, but when he saw his change on the bar counter from the corner of his eye, the song's sentiment suddenly appealed to him. He was beginning to feel extremely self-conscious about standing in the middle of the café, hugging a total stranger like she was a long lost relative. Sensing his unease, the woman broke the embrace. Her open face looked up into his. 'Enjoy,' she said with a hint of merriment in her voice. Turning away, she rejoined her friends, none of whom had paid the slightest bit of attention to the impromptu hugging session taking place beside them.

Mike walked over to Angus and spoke softly in his ear, 'Thinking of joining the Poonatics?'

'The what?'

'The sannyasins.'

Angus shook his head. 'No, man, I'm not. I've never seen her before in my life. I have to admit, though, that for a moment there it felt kind of good to be hugged like that. It made me feel like a kid again.'

'How do you think the Rajneeshies enlist new recruits, man?'

'C'mon, Mike, you're being cynical now.'

'Am I?' Acid Mike paused and glanced into Angus's eyes. 'Maybe I am, but I don't think Bhagwan Shree Rajneesh earned himself the reputation of being India's 'Sex Guru' for nothing.'

Over the next few days, Angus came to terms with the three new, unsettling facts that had entered into his life: his two closest friends were locked up in an Iranian prison, Rolling Thunder was now history and, most difficult to accept of all, he was a murder suspect.

He discussed his problems with Alice and Nina. They were good listeners, but when it came to advice they did not offer anything that went any further than telling him to live in the moment, which was exactly what he needed to hear. Although still prone to the occasional fit of the giggles, the girls had matured a lot since they'd parted company with Raj and Murphy back in Pakistan over eighteen months earlier. Apart from being exceptionally attractive, excellent housekeepers, great cooks and fun company, they were without doubt a phenomenal pair of lovers. This was something that Angus took a great deal of gratification from, the arrangement being one of mutual sexual fulfilment.

Angus spent a lot of time smoking hashish with Acid Mike. They both loved to get stoned on the beach and engage each other in drawn-out conversations about the nature of reality and discuss the role that Mike saw psychedelic drugs playing in human evolution. In between esoteric discussions, Mike delivered glowing descriptions of the finca he'd bought in Ibiza and spoke enthusiastically about his plans to move there permanently, once renovations on his rustic farmhouse had been completed.

'Sounds amazing,' said Angus one evening in response to his friend's description of life on the Balearic Island.

'It is,' added Mike, who was rocking back and forth in a hammock on Alice and Nina's porch. 'Mark my words, one day soon Ibiza is really going to be on the map. It's a truly magical place and one of the most unspoiled spots in Europe to live in, cheap too.' His face became thoughtful. 'Once we get your new book sorted, you can come and check it out for yourself. As they say in Spain, *mi casa* is *tu casa.*'

'*Aww*, now I get it,' said Angus from his perch on a windowsill, 'a *casa* is a house. I always wondered what that meant. Thanks for the offer, Mike, I appreciate it.'

'Dinner's ready,' called Nina from the kitchen.

The day before the January full moon, Alice and Nina came down with a nasty stomach bug that left them too weak to attend the following night's party on Anjuna Beach. Mike had met up with a beautiful blonde Londoner called Candy. She'd flown out to India on a BOAC flight from Heathrow – two days after being released from Holloway Prison. Candy had been busted for drug dealing and sentenced to five years imprisonment. She'd been given time off for good conduct. Judging by the way she was doing lines of coke, Candy was endeavouring to catch up on some bad behaviour as quickly as possible. Mike was only too happy to accommodate her in the small house he'd rented, along the coast in the Vagator Beach vicinity, and as a result they'd both disappeared from the scene.

Angus sat down and meditated for an hour, something he'd begun practising on an almost daily basis since he'd decided to follow Swami Ram's advice. When he'd finished, he went out in to the garden and hauled buckets of water from the well. By the light of a flickering candle, he took a shower under a papaya tree, trimmed his beard in front of a cracked mirror and then tied his wet hair into a ponytail. Before leaving the house, he drank a pot of local coffee and swallowed two small tablets of LSD that Mike had given him a few days earlier. They were dark pink and indented with a little strawberry.

Angus ambled along a sandy path that led to the beach, singing quietly to himself as he walked. 'Let me take you down, 'cause I'm going to—'

He fell silent when a small snake slithered across the path in front of him. He watched as it disappeared under a bush. The warm air was crystal clear. The moon shone like an opalescent eye that varnished everything it could see with a cool alien light. Through thick stands of palm trees, Angus could make out the sea, where reflected moonbeams played and danced on its surface like radioactive particles. In the midnight-blue sky only the brightest of stars sparkled, their more diminutive stellar companions' twinkle obscured by lunar glare.

Music thrummed, buzzed and phased over the airwaves. *Oooh a hooo, oooh a hooo, zoo zoo mamoo...* When Angus heard the voodoo chant of Doctor John the Night Tripper's 'Zu Zu Mamou', carried to his ears on a filtering breeze, he continued on his way, walking a little faster than previously.

He drew closer to the party and passed by the only manifestation of commercialism at the event. Local entrepreneurs had set up temporary tea stalls to provide warm beverages, cold drinks and sweet snacks on the perimeters of the party zone. A very good idea indeed, because judging by the clouds of hash smoke rising above the circles of longhaired freaks, seated around candles stuck into the sand, a communal Pavlovian sugar-seeking response was imminent.

Papa was a rolling stone... The Temptations blared from the sound system.

Out on the dance area, the previous month's full moon party was repeating itself with twice as many people moving their feet to the funky beat. There was so much dust being kicked up into the air everything stationary had a fine layer of grey powder on it, which lent the scene an unearthly quality and succeeded in making Angus imagine that he'd arrived in the world of the *Gandharvas* (fairy-like celestial musicians of Buddhist mythology), wherein music is the predominant quality of existence.

When Acid Mike's latest product kicked in good and proper, Angus shimmied on to the dance floor and was soon spinning in the centre of a psychic cyclone. Pre-recorded music gave way to a live band, whose spiralling rhythms lifted the gyrating dancers' spirits far above the confines of the three dimensional world.

Time passed. Angus had no idea how long he'd been dancing, but he was aware that if he didn't get some liquid in his body soon he might faint due to a severe case of dehydration. Soaked in sweat, he made his way over to the line of improvised chai stalls and sat down on a woven mat, near to a group of orange-clad Rajneesh sannyasins.

It was that stage of the night when the concept of verbal communication is remote and difficult to grasp. Angus looked over at the sannyasins. He reckoned they were tripping too because their eyes were shining like black diamonds and they were laughing hysterically.

It took Angus a few minutes of concentrated effort to summon up the appropriate words to order tea and a small packet of Padma biscuits from the expectant stall owner, a corpulent lady with a big smile who was dressed in a blue saree and breastfeeding an infant from her exposed and swollen left nipple.

Angus was on to his second glass of steaming-hot, cardamom-flavoured chai when he realized he hadn't smoked any dope since sunset. Two days earlier, he'd purchased a small, embroidered sadhu bag at the Anjuna flea market to carry his money and smoking implements in. He opened it, retrieved a nifty little mixing bowl made from a polished baby coconut shell that he'd bought from Atom, a chillum, a pack of Cavenders cigarettes and a piece of resinous Manali hashish. While he sat preparing a smoking mixture, one of the sannyasins disengaged himself from his companions.

'Hey, mate, mind if I join you?' he asked, sounding as English as Yorkshire pudding. 'I'm dying for a smoke.'

'Eh…sure, man,' replied Angus, patting a space on the mat beside him.

The longhaired Englishman sat down and said, '*Shanti.*'

Angus knew this to be the Hindi word for peace and took it as a form of greeting.

'Shanti Deva,' said the sannyasin, offering his hand.

Realising that Shanti was the young man's name, Angus pressed flesh and introduced himself.

'Angus!' exclaimed Shanti as if he'd just found a gold nugget in the sand. 'You've got to be a Scotsman, laddie.'

Angus gave him a high wattage smile and handed Shanti the chillum. There was a piece of damp cotton cloth wrapped around its narrow end to act as a filter.

'You want to light this?'

'Boom, boom, yeah, man, I'd love to,' replied the sannyasin as he took the pipe from Angus and raised it to his mouth.

'*Alack, Boom Shankar!*' cried Angus, entering into the spirit of the occasion as he applied a burning match to the end of the chillum.

Shanti Deva proceeded to puff up a thundercloud of sweet-smelling charas smoke. He passed the smoking cannon back to Angus, who took a massive hit on it. The rush of fresh Manali hashish entering his bloodstream was fantastic. His surroundings lit up as if illuminated by a fireworks display. He looked into Shanti's wide-open bioluminescent eyes and for a fleeting moment he and the young Englishman shared a wild ecstatic grin. The two smokers passed the chillum until it had been smoked down to ashes and then adopted the spaced-out monkey mudra.

An amplified voice echoed over from the party zone. '*Ladies and gentlemen, The Big Bang Dada Band.*'

There was an excited roar of approval and then a wave of high-octane acid funk crashed over the dance area when the musicians on stage slammed into sonic overdrive.

'That sounds magic,' said Angus, uncrossing his legs. 'I've got to move.'

'Yeah...yeah, me too.' Shanti rose unsteadily to his feet. 'Great to meet you, man.'

'Likewise, Shanti. Maybe see you around.'

'Insh'allah.' The Englishman raised his hands in a namaskar.

Back on the dance floor, the party was going ballistic. Over in one corner a group of sannyasins were doing the pogo, half of them completely naked. The rest of the crowd was kicking up dust in an acid-fuelled freak-out. Joining the action, Angus merged with the sound belting out from the stacks of black speaker boxes at each side of the stage.

Hours later, his frazzled brain registered that the sky was lightening in the east. His tired legs felt like worn shock absorbers. He stumbled over to the base of a coconut tree, sat down heavily and leaned back against it. The tree trunk was reassuringly solid in an otherwise fluid reality.

Breaking free from the psychological no-man's land inside of his head, he observed the scene around him. The partygoers had thinned out, leaving about two-hundred hardcore ravers. Those still on the dance floor were all mirroring in their own way a personal physical interpretation of the extended solos that the improvising musicians on the stage had drifted into. Every few minutes a musical junction, formed by a riff, beat or a chord, would be reached and once again the sound would meld into one electric groove that kept the enthralled dancers moving. The dusty party zone looked like it had been lifted from Fellini's *Satyricon*. Had a bull-headed Minotaur trotted out of the sea to sit down beside him, Angus would've passed him the joint he was puffing on.

He glanced up at the palm fronds. They looked like frozen explosions from fused shells above a Napoleonic battlefield.

A blistering, melt-your-face-off guitar duel screamed from the stage. It sounded to Angus like electrified cats yowling in agony.

He could feel a weary numbness beginning to creep into his arms and legs. He looked over to the front of the stage and noticed that there was a naked flip-out crawling around in the sand. The forlorn figure made him feel uneasy in his skin, knowing full well that going over the edge into the abyss was something every true psychonaut had to face at some point in their inner journey. The less fortunate became lost in the void, where they inhabited the schizoid world of the acid casualty.

Angus cringed and swallowed a bubble of dread when the madman picked up on his curious attention and began crawling across the powdered sand towards him. Had he not felt so zapped himself, Angus's sense of self-preservation would have perhaps motivated him to move elsewhere. As it happened, he just sat where he was, propped up against the trunk of the tree. He witnessed himself undergo a quick mood change which, amplified by LSD, projected itself on to his surroundings and bleached the colour from the scene to leave it looking like a sepia photograph. The spirit of celebration left him and was replaced by apprehension.

The flip-out reached Angus's feet and touched them as if they were sacred relics. Angus pulled his knees up and studied him. The poor devil was in a terrible state. He was as skinny as a pipe cleaner and his unfocused eyes were staring in opposite directions. He constantly scratched his right temple as if he'd lost something but couldn't remember what it was. It was all too obvious to Angus that what the man had lost was his mind. He reached out to him, placed both hands on his dusty shoulders and gave him a shake. It was then that Angus noticed that the man had a barely visible line of scar tissue running horizontally across his dirt-caked forehead.

'Hey, are...are you okay?' Angus's words were hollow and sounded absurd, like a schoolboy naïvely enquiring about his pet hamster − after it had been run over by a steamroller. He knew without thinking about it that the human wreck, kneeling in the sand before him, was a very long way from anything that could remotely be described as being okay.

He watched in dumbstruck fascination as the flip-out filled his mouth with sand and proceeded to swallow it. 'Oh, no,' Angus moaned, flashing on the glass-eater he'd encountered on the square in Panjim a few weeks earlier. Before he could say anything else to him, the nutcase scuttled away sideways like a giant spider crab.

A chill shot down Angus's spine and pierced his testicles. Not knowing what to think, he stayed where he was until an invisible finger flipped the switch of a football stadium's worth of floodlights in the centre of his brain. The dazzling glare illuminated a crossroads on the faded map of his past. His long-term memory banks had been jolted into life by the scar on the madman's forehead. He knew him. It was Jimmy Bradley. Angus shouted, 'Holy fucking shit!' A couple of sadhu types glanced over at him like he was behaving uncool. He ignored them, sprang to his feet and went in search of his long-lost friend from his early teenage years in Glasgow.

Jimmy had disappeared. Angus skirted the party's perimeters, but his flipped-out Glaswegian pal was nowhere to be found. Urgency ran through his body. He had to control his bowels. They felt like they were filling up with ice-cold oil. The sun was beginning to rise by the time he gave up the search.

Feeling somewhat dejected, Angus started to make his way home. He was walking along a winding cow path when he a heard a whimpering from within a thick thorn bush. It was Jimmy. Angus had to struggle to haul him out of the prickly foliage. When he finally succeeded, he was horrified to see that Jimmy was covered in dozens of bleeding puncture wounds inflicted by needle-sharp thorns.

'Aargha garga grooo.' Sounds gurgled in Jimmy's throat. He panicked and tried to flee. Angus grabbed hold of him and held him tight.

'Jimmy, Jimmy, for fuck's sake, man,' he pleaded, 'it's me, Angus, Angus Macleod.'

Jimmy's body appeared to relax a little. Taking hold of a trembling hand, Angus led him along the sandy path in the direction of Alice and Nina's home.

'Naaaaagh!' Jimmy began to scream when Angus tried to lead him up the red-painted stairs into the house.

Alerted by the commotion, a pale-faced Alice came to investigate. 'What's going on, Angus?' she asked, rubbing sleep from eyes that sprang open when she saw Jimmy's dust-covered, bleeding mess of a shivering body. 'Jesus!' she exclaimed. 'Where did you find this guy? He looks like he's been crucified.'

Angus explained as best he could.

Alice came to his assistance by taking hold of one of Jimmy's torn arms and coaxing him into the kitchen. She spoke gently to him. 'Don't worry, Jimmy. You're with friends now. We'll take care of you.'

Thus began Angus's reunion with his accident-prone friend. It was to take Jimmy over a week to gain enough control of his mind to remember where the guest house in Calangute Beach was that he'd left his personal belongings in. Slowly, he began to piece together sentences coherent enough to form an explanation of what had befallen him.

22

VIGILANTES

During the mid-seventies in Goa, long-distance call boxes, let alone mobile phones, were a convenience that was still a long way off. When Jimmy was fit enough to travel, he and Angus caught a bus into Panjim to make an international phone call.

The antiquated telephone system was just a couple of steps above rusty tin cans connected by waxed twine. Angus and Jimmy had to sit for two hours on a wooden bench outside the central telegraph office, waiting for a call to go through. During that time, they brought each other up to date about what course their lives had taken since they'd last seen each other on the streets of Glasgow.

Jimmy explained how, before catching the overnight ferry down to Goa from Bombay (Mumbai), he'd spent a week in the city taking care of some business that he made a point of being vague about.

'Listen, pal,' he said, 'I'll never forget what you and the girls have done for me. I want you to come and work in a great scam that I've got going.'

'Where?' Angus asked, swatting at a mosquito that had landed on the back of his hand.

'Bombay.'

'What kind of scam?'

'It's something that's running on a need-to-know basis,' answered Jimmy, wiping sweat from his scarred brow with a crumpled handkerchief. 'I don't want to say much more about it unless you agree to come in on the deal. The last guy who worked with me was too old for the game and had to pack it in because his nerves couldn't handle it. I think you're the man to take his place, because you've got the balls to do it and I know you'll enjoy making a shitload of money.'

It only took a second for the thought of lots of money to ring a positive note on Angus's mental cash register. 'I'm most definitely interested,' he said, 'but what exactly will I have to do to earn it?'

'Well, pal, you can begin by learning how to scuba dive.'

'What, you mean like Jacques Cousteau?'

'Yes, exactly, but you won't need to study French or eat snails. All you have to do is put on a pair of flippers and learn how to swim around in the depths of the big blue, courtesy of the deep dive corporation.'

'Where am I going to learn that?'

'From an acquaintance of mine,' said Jimmy. 'His name's Manni and he lives in a village called Palolem in the South of Goa. He'll show you the ropes.'

'You'll have to give me his address.'

'So, you're in then?'

'Big bucks, you say?'

'Aye, pal, the kind of cash you only get a crack at once in a tartan moon.'

'I haven't seen one of those lately.'

'You soon will, if you shake hands with me,' said Jimmy. 'This deal is incomparable.'

'That's easy for you to say when I don't have any others to compare it to.'

'You can always check out poverty as an alternative.'

Angus pursed his lips and nodded thoughtfully. 'Okay, I'm in. I just wish you'd tell me a bit more about this scam of yours.'

'Let's just say it's an undercover, underwater operation and patience will be rewarded most generously. You've got my word on it.'

The two prospective business partners exchanged a firm handshake.

'Mister Bradley,' called a female voice with an Indian accent, 'your call to England is going through now. Please to be proceeding to number six.'

Jimmy rose to his feet and hurried into a plywood booth, home to a solitary black bakelite phone with a rotary dial. He was eager to speak to his wife and two children, who hadn't heard from him in almost a month.

Angus remained seated on the wooden bench, wondering what he'd just gotten himself into. Money, he thought. Since Raj and Murphy disappeared out of the picture, my financial prospects have not exactly been looking too rosy. If I keep living the way I am just now, without some cash coming in, I'll be skint in a year or so. Just as well Jimmy appeared…or is it? There's bound to be a price. There always is in that kind of game…whatever kind of game it is. Undercover, underwater operation my ass…it will be serious business for sure. Nobody, not even old pals, give you a lot of money for nothing. They always want something. Probably a lot if I'm going to be well paid for getting involved in it. On top of that I can't leave India because of this Jenny story. Mike was right. I must've been off my rocker.

'Shit,' he said out loud, his mind still chattering. Here am I in sunny Goa, caught up in my stupid little movie and worrying about my problems, while my two closest friends are locked up in some Iranian hellhole. Man, that's something else that will require my urgent attention as soon as I can move again. He looked up from his sandaled feet. Why can't I just be here now?

Bzzzzzzzt...!

Angus slapped himself on the face when a kamikaze mosquito whined and took a nosedive into his cheek.

On the return journey to Anjuna, the two friends sat in the back seat of a black and yellow Ambassador taxi, discussing what had knocked Jimmy into the realm of insanity and what they were going to do about it.

When Jimmy first arrived in Goa, he'd spent a week in Anjuna before deciding to take a lengthy walk north along the palm-fringed coastline. It took him all afternoon to reach a remote beach called Arambol. It was early evening when he joined a group of naked hippies who were sitting on the beach, smoking dope and watching the red sun disappear behind the horizon. By midnight, he'd fallen asleep on the sand next to a small freshwater lake that was fed by a rivulet running out of the jungle.

He woke at dawn and, feeling the need to stretch his legs, followed the stream up into the thick tangle of bushes that formed the base of the vine-choked jungle. After a fifteen-minute uphill walk, he entered a small clearing and met three Frenchmen, who were camped out under a towering banyan tree. Jimmy's first impression was that he'd stumbled upon holy men. All three were covered from head to foot in grey ash and were sitting beside a *dhüni* (small fire before which a sadhu meditates). One of them was brewing up a pot of tea, while another fried vegetables in a pan.

'*Bonjour*, boom, boom,' said the third man, who was beating eggs in a plastic bowl. 'Come and join us for breakfast, *mon ami*.'

Jimmy sat down beside him and, to the accompanying chirps and coughs of insects arising from within the undergrowth, began chatting about what a fine place they'd chosen as a campsite.

'Would you like something to eat?' asked the bearded man, who was frying the vegetables, his grey dreadlocks hanging down in much the same way as the banyan's twisted branch roots.

It sounded like a great offer to Jimmy. The smell of fried onions had coaxed his digestive system into performing a percussive symphony on the walls of his empty stomach.

Quarter of an hour of belly rumbles and intestinal groans later, he was handed an aluminium plate with a steaming, inch-thick omelette on it. Jimmy was by then ravenous and therefore devoured his breakfast quickly. Unfortunately for him, he'd just become the victim of a wicked prank. One of the Frenchmen had sprinkled a handful of powdered *Datura metel* seeds into the omelette mix.

Ubiquitous in the region and considered weeds by the uninitiated, the broad-leafed datura plant is made distinct in appearance by its trumpet-shaped white flowers and the green spiky balls it produces as seedpods. Inside the hard fruit are hundreds of smooth, black, kidney-shaped seeds that, if ingested, produce long-lasting and unpredictable psychoactive effects that can transport the user to frightening worlds. New World shamans maintain a reverential affinity for datura even though its effects can be lethal.

After a cup of coffee and sharing a chillum of hand-rubbed hashish, Jimmy thanked the Frenchmen for their hospitality and left them sitting around their *dhūni* at the foot of the ancient tree. As he bid them farewell, one of the men laughed and called out, '*Bon voyage, mon ami Ecossais.*'

There was a note of sarcasm in the man's voice that Jimmy had thought nothing of at the time, being more concerned about the difficulty he was experiencing focusing his eyes and the extreme tingling sensation in his lips and fingertips.

An hour later, Jimmy collapsed on Arambol beach. Soon he was frothing at the mouth and convinced that he was about to die. He watched as his spirit helicoptered out of his body and soared over Goa's coastline. That was the last thing he could remember until Angus and the girls nursed him back to health.

'Those bastards need to be taught a lesson,' said Angus, after listening to his friend's story for the second time.

'Aye, pal, you're right, but what kind of a fuckin' lesson?'

'I don't know, Jimmy. It'll come to me.'

Angus was struck by inspiration while staring at a plate of black bean bhaji in Chandrika's chai shop over in Chapora village. Why not? Angus thought, spooning up a mouthful of spicy gravy.

Two days later, Angus, Jimmy, Acid Mike and the English sannyasin, Shanti Deva, set off in the direction of Arambol. Shanti carried a small wooden drum and played a beat for their marching feet as they headed north along the coast. Except for flocks of squawking gulls and the occasional Goan fisherman, repairing nylon nets beside high-prowed fishing boats, the beach was deserted.

Shanti had come along because a young woman he knew had also fallen foul of the French omelette makers. Two months earlier, the woman had ended up in the locked ward of Panjim's mental hospital after slashing her breasts with a broken bottle. He'd visited her a week before her parents flew over from London to collect her.

'You know,' said Shanti to Angus, 'I think she believed that she was in charge of maintaining Goa's climate system or something like that. I sat in that crazy house watching her adjust invisible controls with an invisible bloody spanner. At one point she was crying her eyes out and babbling on about a noseless witch who'd taken her prisoner and locked her in a rat-infested dungeon.' He spat on the sand, as if disgusted by what he was describing. 'Man, she didn't even know I was there. I've never seen anybody that freaked out before. It scared the shit out of me.'

Angus liked Shanti Deva. The sannyasin was well named, being an unhurried affable man whose peaceful presence made people relax. His long dark brown hair was cut in a fringe, framing eyes that shone light blue, like those of a merchant seaman accustomed to viewing the endless horizons of the world's oceans.

As they marched along the beach in time to Shanti's beating drum, the Englishman filled Angus's head with amazing stories about his guru in Poona, Bhagwan Shree Rajneesh. 'He's the master of masters,' proclaimed Shanti. 'You'd love him. His energy is amazing and practicing the meditation techniques he's devised is an absolute blast, man.'

Round his neck Shanti wore a *mala*, a string of 108 wooden beads with a transparent plastic locket hanging from it. Encased in the oval locket was a tiny picture of the bearded master. Shanti fingered it and said, 'You just have to hold this and you're in direct communication with Bhagwan.'

Upon hearing this preposterous claim, Angus stopped in his tracks. Reaching out, he asked, 'Can I try it?'

Shanti shook his head. 'Sorry, man, you've got to be a sannyasin to do that.'

'Aye, right,' Angus said, laughing.

Mike, who'd been listening in on their conversation, asked Shanti, 'Has Rajneesh told you that if you surrender to him he'll take care of everything else?'

'Yes, he did. How come you know that?' Shanti asked back.

Mike gave the wryest of smiles and said nothing.

Arambol Beach was a splendidly beautiful place, a remote, unspoiled strip of natural paradise. There were no signs of civilization or commercialism, not even a chai shop. Naked sun-worshipers sat on the sand, playing on guitars and drums, blowing chillums and laughing with their children who, going by their squeals of delight and shouts of joy, were enjoying themselves immensely.

Angus and his friends dived into the sea to cool off and then set up camp under a fruitless mango tree that was situated by the small freshwater lake.

Early the next morning, after sleeping out under the stars, Acid Mike and Angus set off in search of the French pseudo-sadhus. Like barking dogs, they heard the pranksters before they saw them. The ash-covered freaks were sitting around their campfire, talking and laughing loudly. True to form, as soon as the two strangers appeared on the scene, one of the Frenchmen invited Angus and Mike to join them for breakfast.

'No thanks,' said Angus, straining to reign in his anger. 'We're both fasting just now, but it's nice of you to offer.'

With that, he and Mike continued on their way until they were out of sight. Doubling back, they hid in the undergrowth and observed the three dreadlocked men until they'd seen enough.

That night, under the cover of darkness that a moonless sky provided, the four vigilantes ambushed the Frenchmen. Within minutes, the three terrified men were bound and propped up against the trunk of the banyan tree.

'Remember me, *mon fuckin' amis*?' Jimmy shouted, glaring into his captives' frightened eyes. 'If you don't, you fucking well will by the time I've finished with you tonight. You shit-arsed bastards that you are.'

'Look at this.' Shanti held up a glass jar and shone torchlight on it. The transparent container was full to the top with powdered datura seeds. 'Catch.' He tossed it to Jimmy, who handed it to Angus.

Angus emptied the jar's contents into a cooking pot, added water and stirred with a wooden spoon. He glanced over at the Frenchmen, held the aluminium pot up and announced, 'Voila, mes froggies, revenge might be a dish that's best served cold but in this case lukewarm will have to do.'

The three Frenchmen were by now, quite understandably, shitting themselves. Shanti held their noses closed, while Jimmy poured the black sludge from the soot-covered pot down each of their throats. Close on their heels came Acid Mike, plastic torch in hand, popping half a dozen tabs of LSD into each of the gagging men's gullets. He cursed, 'Fucking waste of good acid, man.'

Jimmy spoke over his shoulder. 'Don't worry about it, pal. It will do these fuckers the world of good.' He held an electric torch under his chin and illuminated his face for the Frenchmen's benefit. 'My name's Jimmy Bradley,' he announced, opening his short farewell speech, 'and if I ever see one of you fucking wankers again you better run like fuck, unless you want to spend the rest of your rotten life in traction.' His voice shrieked, *'Shake your fucking heads if you understand!'*

The three Frenchmen nodded their heads vigorously, although, judging by their spinning eyeballs, understanding was something that was swiftly slipping away from them.

Ssssshhhh! Jimmy stood to the side of the ritual fire and pissed into it. He squatted down in front of the three petrified men and spat into each of their faces in turn.

Rough justice done, the vigilantes made their way back down to the beach.

It was January 28, 1975, when Jimmy Bradley and Acid Mike left Anjuna to catch the ferry up to Bombay. Angus accompanied them to Panjim to see them off.

During the taxi drive, Mike promised he'd return to Goa in December with a new name and passport for Angus.

Down on the waterfront, Jimmy handed Angus a piece of paper and said, 'Phone this number on the fourth of July. That's the day your journey to becoming independently wealthy begins.' Jimmy stepped forward and gave his old friend a manly hug at the foot of a sun-bleached, wooden gangway. He then picked up his canvas bag. 'Okay pal, thanks for everything. Those girls of yours are the tops. Take good care of them and yourself. See you in Bombay.'

Dressed in a creme-coloured lightweight suit, which made his scuffed sports shoes look more worn than they actually were, Jimmy walked up the gangway and joined Mike under a canvas awning on the steamer's stern. The gangplank was rolled back and passengers threw streaming toilet rolls down to friends for good luck. The ship's propeller churned up mud as it pulled away from the pier. With a loud hoot from its claxon, the *Konkan Shakti* picked up speed as it steamed down the Mandoui River. Jimmy and Mike waved until the ship was a kilometre downstream. Angus turned and hailed a motorbike taxi to take him back to Anjuna.

Over the course of the next two weeks, Angus settled into a comfortable domestic existence with his two insatiable lovers. Shanti Deva was a regular visitor round at the house. His *'spaghetti à la Shanti'* became an almost nightly culinary experience, because it never had the same flavour twice.

It was due to the congenial Englishman's influence that Angus and the girls became acquainted with a number of Rajneesh's disciples, the most notable of whom was Arihantha, a bearded wild man who ran *Prem Kutira*, a small meditation centre situated on the Chapora Beach Road. He was a man whose multifaceted spiritual vision was so all-encompassing it denied any attempt at pigeonholeing. English by birth, Arihantha had lived in Goa for years and liked nothing better than to smoke chillums of potent Manali hashish and holler out Beatles' songs, while he strummed the chords on a battered twelve-string Rickenbacker acoustic guitar. A dynamic personality, who shunned most social conventions – with the exception of hospitality – Arihantha made Angus most welcome when he first visited him in his smoke-filled kitchen, where he was busy boiling goat's milk to make yoghurt.

Taking Angus firmly by the elbow, Arihantha pulled a maroon velvet curtain aside and led him into a shadow-filled meditation room's cool interior. He then let go of Angus's arm, knelt by a small alter, lit a candle in front of a picture of Rajneesh and said, 'Sit here with your eyes open and stare into Bhagwan's eyes.' Angus did as instructed. Arihantha patted him gently on the back and added, 'Remember, there are only two possibilities: you can refuse the master or refuse the mind. It's up to you. Try not to blink.'

Arihantha left the room and pulled the curtain closed behind him. The sound of baby goats, bleating outside in the garden, came to Angus's ears as he studied the Indian guru's photograph. It quickly dawned on him that he'd seen it before. The sadhvi had shown him the same picture in Hampi. His first thoughts were, Man, this is weird. What the hell is going on? Then, because of the respect he felt for Arihantha, he began to settle into the situation, knowing there must be a good reason for the centre leader to have positioned him just so.

Angus sat as still as a granite boulder embedded in a Scottish mountainside and stared into the black-bearded, bald-headed Indian guru's hypnotic eyes. Much to his surprise, Rajneesh's expressionless face began to morph. The facial changes quickly accelerated to the point that Angus saw a different face with every beat of his heart. The faces' common denominator was intelligence. Within the space of an hour, Angus felt like he'd gazed into the eyes of every wise man who had ever graced the face of the planet with his presence. Angus's eyes watered as he strained to keep them from blinking and then, suddenly, something extraordinary happened. The guru's face disappeared completely. No stranger to mysterious phenomena, Angus began to laugh. With that, Rajneesh's face reappeared in front of him. The photograph now appeared as if it were alive, amused and smiling at Angus. 'What the—?'

The velvet curtain swished on its rail and Arihantha strode into the room. 'Right then,' he announced, bubbling over with infectious enthusiasm, 'it's time for the Kundalini Meditation.'

Sannyasins began to silently filter into the room.

Five minutes later, Angus had removed all of his clothing and, surrounded by a dozen naked people, started shaking in time to what sounded like a snake charmer's flute, which was being played over a stereo system at high volume. When the meditation entered a fifteen-minute, let-go dancing session, Angus began to enjoy himself immensely. The meditation ended after everyone involved had been sitting in silence for a quarter-hour. People began to put on their clothes and leave the room. Angus continued to sit cross-legged on the floor. Although the meditation technique was unconventional by anyone's standards, it had worked for him. Free of thought, he wanted to remain in that empty and peaceful space for as long as it lasted.

Within earshot, Arihantha whispered to one of the other meditators, 'He got it.'

Later that evening, Angus sat around on the meditation centre's porch with Arihantha, his feisty wife, Puja, and a small group of friends, singing along to the centre leader's endless repertoire of Beatles songs. It was after midnight by the time Angus decided to head for home. As he walked along a moonlit jungle path, he could still hear Arihantha's voice, calling out into the darkness as he sang, 'I'll never dance with another, *ooooh!*' The combined chorus of '*ooooh*' brought images of the Fab Four from Liverpool shaking their moptops in front of screaming fans and contained so much unconstrained joy that Angus was tempted to turn in his tracks and hurry back to join in before the song ended.

Chuckling to himself, Angus had to admit that most of the Rajneesh disciples he'd met were fun-loving people, who didn't fit into his patchy preconceived notions of how he'd imagined members of a religious cult might behave. Not only that, all of the female sannyasins had an air of uninhibited sexual relaxedness about them. One in particular had caught his eye. German, he imagined – or maybe Danish – with short ash-blonde hair and a willowy body that moved like liquid when she danced.

By the time he reached home, Angus had other things on his mind. He'd decided to head south and find out who Manni was.

23

OM, MANNI, PADI AND PREM

T he express bus let out a roar of low-gear compression and then squealed when its driver pushed down hard on the brake pedal, bringing the vehicle to a lurching halt.

'*Palolem, Palolem, Palolem!*' cried the bus boy, sounding like a market vendor offering some exotic fruit for sale.

Angus had been lulled into sleep by the bus's monotonous motion and the accompanying drone of its engine. Disorientated, he picked up his rucksack and headed for the door. Stepping out of the cool temperatures provided by the bus's air-conditioning system, Southern Goa's late afternoon heat came to his face with the humidity of a hothouse in a botanical garden. Bullets of sweat shot from his brow.

A short walk later, he was on the beach, peeling off his damp clothes as if they were a cumbersome layer of dead skin. He walked naked into a sea that was as clear as glass. Colourful tropical fish scooted around his legs. He swam out in the light blue shallows, turned around and wolf-whistled, much in the way a labourer on a building site might do upon seeing a pretty girl in a short skirt passing by. Palolem's broad lagoon stretched in a gentle crescent of spotless white sands, upon which lay a few beached fishing boats. A half dozen or so thatched huts, peeping out from between tall coconut trees, were the only other signs that the area was inhabited. In the background were palm-forested hills, covered with dense vegetation and dotted with vine-strung boulders. To the north lay the small hump of a palm-studded island, separated from the coast by a narrow strip of water. Palolem was an idyllic spot and the few manmade creations only added to a scene that was resplendently perfect.

Angus swam back to the shore. There was a profusion of coloured shells embedded in the sand. He could not resist the idea of collecting some to take home as presents for Alice and Nina. After half an hour, he'd made a pile of seashells that would have filled a sack. He recognized the impractical nature of what he was doing, sat down and began selecting a half dozen or so of what he deemed to be the prettiest. It struck him that he hadn't felt so happy and carefree in ages.

'*Yeeeeah!*' He let out a joyous yell, startling a pair of grey gulls, who squawked a complaint before taking to the air and gliding gracefully away on a warm breeze.

He dressed and watched as the sun sank towards a horizon unmarred by a dhow's sail or smoke from a merchant hulk.

Angus walked back to the main road and asked directions from a decrepit man who was bent over double from ninety years of exposure to the earth's gravity. He had on short trousers. His spindly legs were scored with varicose veins. He looked like a sickly plucked stork and smelled like a urinal. The old man sighed, as if Angus's request entailed performing the most exhausting task imaginable. An elbow joint creaked as he raised his walking stick, a knobbly length of yellow bamboo with part of the root as a handle, and pointed to a strip of red-tiled roof set back in the jungle.

'*Ja, ja*, I've been expecting you,' were Manni's first words when Angus stepped on to the porch of his small house. He spoke with more than a hint of the Teutonic in his voice.

Seated on a creaking wicker armchair, he was dandling a dark-skinned infant, with kohl around its eyes, upon his bouncing knees. When Manni stood up and shook hands with him, Angus was struck by the German's physique. He had well-developed shoulders and arms, a trim waist and the thick muscular neck of a heavyweight boxer. There were deep wrinkles around his sky-blue eyes. Angus used these creases as a chronological yardstick and gauged Manni to be about sixty. He would never know for certain, because the German soon made it clear that he did not like personal questions, and only supplied facts about his life when he felt like it.

'I grew up in a small village by the banks of the River Elbe,' Manni said by way of an introduction, 'within sight of Hamburg's green copper church spires. I worked as a docker before joining the navy, where I served on a recovery ship and eventually become a master diver. I took early retirement after an accident.' He raised a crooked right hand without a thumb and shook it, as if to give credence to his words.

Angus found it easy to imagine the grizzled German commanding a wolf pack in Hitler's Northern Fleet during the Second World War. He saw Captain Manni standing in his U-boat's conning tower as waves crashed over the bow and deck gun, a big pair of rubber-coated binoculars glued to his eyes, while he scanned the North Atlantic's endless horizons in search of an Allied convoy to torpedo.

Running a hand over his short iron-grey hair, Manni motioned for Angus to enter the candlelit interior of his home saying, '*Ja, ja*, it's that time of the evening when a bottle of ice-cold beer is most appreciated.' He called out, 'Maria, *zwei Bier, Liebling.*'

A few moments later, a short Goanese woman, with skin the colour of chocolate milk and a face like a teddy bear, shuffled out of the kitchen carrying a tray with a pair of dimpled beer mugs and two dark brown bottles beaded by condensation.

Maria was Manni's wife and bearer of their seven children. Wide-hipped, her breasts were the size of bowling balls. She was built to be a mother – just as well, because she was heavily pregnant with number eight.

From the way they smiled into each other's eyes, it was clear to Angus that the couple adored each other; an odd match, but in terms of a loving relationship, it worked well for them as far as he was able to ascertain.

Maria had filigreed silver anklets with little bells attached that produced a tinkling accompaniment to all of her movements.

'Keeps the snakes away,' said Manni, when he noticed Angus looking towards Maria's feet.

'Is it okay if I smoke?' Angus asked, producing his cigarette papers.

Manni gave a knowing chuckle. 'If you have to,' he nodded, 'go ahead.'

It was just after dawn on the following morning when Manni and his new student walked down to the beach. Angus was shocked at how out of shape he'd become. He was gasping for breath and sweating like a lump of cheese left out in the sun. He dropped the heavy oxygen bottle that he was carrying on to the sand

Manni's gaze fixed on Angus. '*Ja, ja, mein Junge,*' he said, 'it would be a good idea for you to drop your hashish smoking instead of that aluminium bottle. Inhaling the smoke from one of your filthy joints is like smoking ten cigarettes. Life only gave us one set of lungs, thinking that would be sufficient. You can't buy another pair if you damage them.' Manni slapped his student on the back and almost succeeded in knocking him over. 'Besides,' he continued, 'you obviously haven't realized yet that taking drugs is for foolish people. And it's not just the physical effects that I'm talking about.' Manni turned away from Angus, gently lowered the oxygen bottle that he'd been carrying from his shoulder, looked out to sea and spoke half to himself. '*Damned hashish,* clouds a man's mind, weakens his willpower and drags his spirit down into the darkness like a lead weight belt.'

Angus stared at the German's broad back. Fists wedged into narrow hips, Manni was the epitome of vigour and health. Look at this guy, Angus thought, he's got to be nearly three times older than me and the big bastard's twice as fit.

Over the course of the morning Manni explained in detail how the diving gear worked. It was the only time in their brief relationship that Manni actually encouraged Angus to ask questions.

Angus's initiation into the fascinating world of scuba diving had begun. How Jimmy Bradley came to know Manni in the first place was to forever remain a mystery to Angus. Jimmy's motive for sending him to a dive master would, of course, be revealed in time. All he knew then was that the big German was a great tutor who soon had his full respect and, as far as the deep blue sea was concerned, his total trust.

Angus's most memorable moments with Manni took place twenty metres below the calm surface of the cerulean sea. They were sitting together on the ribbed sand of the seabed exchanging regulators, practicing for the emergency of a buddy diver running out of air. A pair of curious, two-metre long, black-tip reef sharks circled above them at close quarters, compounding the intensity of the exercise. Aware of the likelihood that the territorial sharks might put in appearance, Manni had informed him earlier that morning that these streamlined predators posed no threat, as they were nocturnal feeders and human beings did not register on their menu radar. 'Too much bone and muscle, and not enough protein for a shark's appetite,' was how he'd put it. Nonetheless, Angus controlled his breathing to prevent panic. As they glided by overhead, he could see clearly that the pelagic sharks' curving mouths were full of sharp teeth. They were never still for a moment because their gills needed motion to keep them supplied with oxygen. Looking into Manni's masked face it struck him how wholly dependent one is on oxygen for survival. After holding his breath for a very long minute, the metal-flavoured compressed air tasted great when his teacher handed him back his supply. He exhaled and watched the bubbles streaming from his regulator expand and rise to the surface.

Four days and ten dives later, Manni told Angus he was as ready as he'd ever be to go it alone.

South of Palolem Beach, a short distance out from a small rock-strewn cove called Colomb Bay, Angus descended to twenty-five metres and adjusted his buoyancy vest. Visibility was excellent and, when a solitary black-tip shark cruised by at a distance, he patted the large stainless-steel diver's knife in a rubber sheath, which was strapped to his right thigh, for reassurance, took a couple of deep breaths and kept his cool.

Propelled by a paddle-shaped tail, a black and white-banded sea snake swam by at close range, its graceful movement fascinating to behold. Manni had told him that sea snakes can be dangerous but, left alone, they seldom attack. Angus followed the aquatic serpent's zigzag course until he found himself approaching a school of striped barracudas. With not so much as a blink, their big black eyes stared back lifelessly, their sharp serrated teeth clicking out a warning that prompted him to turn around and head back towards the shore. In shallower waters, a squadron of inquisitive squid flanked him, their myriad, subtle colour changes almost imperceptible. Coasting along the sea bottom, brown rays' feline eyes blinked shyly as he passed overhead.

Angus's flippers began to stir up sand on the bottom as he drew close to the shore. He walked backwards onto the beach and sat down clumsily. 'Man, that was absolutely brilliant,' he said to himself, exhaling with a chuckle.

On his last night with Manni and his family, Angus bowed his head as his teacher said grace and thanked The Lord for what he'd provided – a king prawn curry, prepared by Maria. An exotic aroma wafted off the succulent meal, whose delicate flavours were brought out by the superb use of Indian spices and the delicious seafood taste of the prawns themselves. The food was washed down with half a dozen bottles of ice-cold Kingfisher beer.

Satiated, Angus, Manni and his wife slumped around the candlelit table, while a noisy tribe of children played by their feet. Every once in a while, the German would grab one of his kids by a limb, toss them up into the air, shout in surprise as if they'd just fallen through the roof and then catch them with a skill born of practice and love. Angus laughed along with his teacher, wondering if perhaps one day he would play the role of father.

'So, *mein junger Schotte*, where will you go from here?' Manni asked, opening a bottle of beer with his teeth.

Angus shrugged. 'Back up to Anjuna, I suppose. I don't really have anything planned.'

'Ah, *ja*, such is life when you're young. I've enjoyed your company, Angus. You've been a diligent pupil. Undisciplined at times, but I put that down to enthusiasm. I must say, you have the makings of a first class diver.'

Angus felt honoured to receive such a compliment from a person who had earned his total respect. In his eyes the dive master was a real man, a rugged individual whose life made sense. Manni's ongoing love affair with the sea had infected Angus and, in the years to come, he'd continue to dive on a regular basis.

'Thanks,' said Angus, shaking Manni's calloused hand. 'It's been great learning from you. You're a great teacher, man. Maybe you should think about calling this place the Om Manni Padi Hum Diving Centre.'

'*Ja, ja,*' said the dive master, who like many a seaman was frugal with his words and weighed them carefully before employing them. He smiled and a gold incisor, set in a line of even teeth, glinted in the candlelight. 'Next time you see Jimmy, say hello to him for me and tell him I was asking for him.'

A year later, struggling for balance on the heaving deck of a small tugboat in Bombay harbour, Jimmy Bradley explained how it happened that Angus came to be wearing Manni's flippers. The German had worked with Jimmy for three months, after which time the dive master had decided to quit. It was not so much the task that he had been performing that had gotten to his nerves, but rather the idea of being caught and thrown into an Indian prison for an indeterminate period of time that made him throw in his fins. Being a family man at heart, Manni simply saw that he had too much to forfeit to be participating in such a dangerous scenario, wherein lay the possibility of being separated from his family for years, a psychological burden too heavy for his well-developed swimmer's shoulders to bear.

A bright sickle moon hung in the sky above the coconut trees. Feathered fronds rasped in the breeze. Below, in the palms' trembling and shifting shadows, Angus wound his way along the path that led to Alice and Nina's house in Anjuna. His nose vibrated as he hummed the melody from a Simon and Garfunkel song and, just like the lyrics echoing in his head suggested, he could hear music playing – sombre classical music. It was Beethoven's 'Eroica'.

As Angus approached the Portuguese villa, he could see warm yellow light filtering through cracks in the closed wooden shutters. Home, he mused, where my lovers wait silently for me. Full breasts and firm buttocks jiggled and rippled in his mind. He was as amorous as a male dolphin in mating season from all the exercise he'd had learning to dive and was now ready to plunge into a different kind of waters.

Angus started to whistle 'Homeward Bound'. He crossed the porch and pushed against the stout wooden door, which was weathered to the point that its grain stood out in curving ridges like a huge fingerprint. The door was locked. He stopped whistling and, with more force than was required to draw attention, banged the brass knocker. Somebody switched off Beethoven. A moment later, bolts rattled and a tumbler clattered when an iron key turned in a well-oiled lock. The wooden door swung inwards.

Standing in the doorway, framed by candlelight, was a tall skinny fellow with a mop of frizzy fair hair. Angus judged him to be no more than thirty years old. There was a thin down on the man's lean face, which lent his appearance a soft and tender look. His lips were so thin they made his mouth look like a pink slash. Angus left his manners on the doorstep as he pushed by him, eager to set eyes on Alice and Nina. They were nowhere in sight.

'Who the fuck are you?' Angus asked.

Cocking his head to one side, the stranger answered in a slightly effeminate voice. 'Welcome home. My name is Prem.'

Angus glanced at the man and in the same moment realized how boorish he must appear.

'Hi, I'm Angus.'

'Yes, I know.'

'Where are Alice and Nina?'

'I'm sorry old chap. They left with Shanti Deva for Poona two days ago.' Prem drew out his vowels on a palate shaped and formed in an upper-crust, fee-paying public school.

The indelibly imprinted phonetic calling card of the rich and privileged grated on Angus's working class ears. Old chap, he thought, who the fuck does this toffee-nosed prat think he's talking to? It was then that the message conveyed by the Englishman's words landed in the information received basket in Angus's mind. His voice ratcheted up a notch. *'Poona! Shanti Deva!'* He shot Prem an angry look. 'Man, you've got to be fuckin' well joking.'

Prem's deadpan expression confirmed that he wasn't.

Angus noticed that Prem had on a faded pair of orange shorts and a red tee shirt. 'What about you, are you one of Rajneesh's sannyasins?'

'Yes, I am. Can I make you a cup of tea, old chap?'

'Stop calling me *old fucking chap!* My name's Angus,' he declared, loathing Prem for his Oxbridge accent.

The Englishman passed a hand across his forehead. 'All right, *Angus*. As you wish. Now, do you want a cup of tea or don't you?'

'Yeah, go ahead and make me a cup of tea, and don't forget the fuckin' hot buttered crumpets, man.'

'Angus, I'd feel more comfortable if you addressed me as Prem, not man.'

'Okay, *Prem*, I get the picture. I'm acting like a shit and I know it.'

'You're just a teensy-weensy bit upset, that's all. Think nothing of it.'

Teensy-weensy, thought Angus, wondering, who the hell is this guy?

Prem went into the kitchen at the back of the house.

Angus entered the main bedroom, which was illuminated by a solitary thick-stemmed candle. He'd envisioned his homecoming in a very different light. Alice and Nina would rush into his waiting arms and soon they'd tumble laughing onto the nearest bed and make wild, sweaty love.

'What a drag!' The scene struck him as depressingly empty. He tossed his rucksack on the bed and heard the seashells that he'd collected on Palolem Beach clatter. He sat down on the floor and put his face between his hands.

Prem's effete voice echoed out. 'Tea's ready.'

Angus rose wearily to his feet and returned to the adjoining room, where he stood for a moment, vacantly staring up at the underside of the tiled roof.

'Sit down,' said Prem. 'You're making me feel uncomfortable.'

Angus sat down on a mirrored Rajasthani cushion beside a low, oblong-shaped, teakwood table and began to sip on a cup of jasmine tea, absorbed in his own thoughts.

A few silent minutes passed

'I'm *gay*,' Prem suddenly announced, enunciating the word gay.

Angus looked up from his teacup and glanced across the table at Prem's androgynous features. 'Oh yeah? Well, so was I until I walked in here ten minutes ago.'

He could see a thought forming in Prem's mind as the Englishman's brow knitted in bafflement. 'I'm sorry. Perhaps I'm not making myself understood. What I mean to say is that I'm a homosexual.' Prem paused, and then added, 'There, I've said it.'

Angus thought about this for a moment, having never before heard the expression 'gay'.

'You don't need to feel sorry, Prem. We all have our problems.' Angus gave a nervous chuckle. 'I'm only joking, man. Listen, I don't care what your sexual preferences are. Just don't try climbing into my bed when I'm in it. I'm not into stubbly chins.'

Prem ran a delicate hand over his smooth chin and laughed self-consciously. 'Relax, Angus. It always amazes me how straight guys think that gay men immediately want to pull them into bed. I mean to say, do you jump into bed with every woman you meet?'

'Ehm...well...no, not really.'

'So, don't worry. I won't touch you.'

'Ehm...sorry. I suppose I was being a bit presumptuous. But why did you tell me you were gay?'

'I just had to tell you. You see, I only came out six month ago.'

'Came out of where?'

'The closet.'

'What? Somebody locked you up in a fucking wardrobe? Have you been in prison?'

Indecision rippled across Prem's face before he said, 'Oh bother, never mind, it's not important.' He glanced shyly at Angus. 'I've been looking forward to meeting you. Nina and Alice told me so much about you. They absolutely love you to bits. Both of them told me to tell you that.'

'Is that so? Well how come the sneaky bitches aren't here to tell me themselves?'

Prem cocked a plucked eyebrow. 'I say, steady on old boy – I mean Angus – that's absolute balderdash. There's a time and a place for everything. You should have at least learnt that by now.'

'I'm sorry. You're right,' admitted Angus. 'Alice and Nina are beautiful people. It's just...it's just... *Aww* shit, let's drop the subject.' Warming to Prem, he produced a packet of rolling papers and asked, 'You want to smoke a joint with me?'

Prem shook his head. 'Good Lord, no thanks. Hashish doesn't do a thing for me, except make me cough.' He stood up and disappeared into the kitchen. He returned a moment later with an unopened bottle of Glenfiddich single malt whisky and two glasses. 'I am partial to a wee tipple now and then. Would you care to join me?'

Angus raised his head, his shiny blue eyes reflecting the candlelight. 'Is Liberace gay?'

That broke the ice. They both chuckled as Prem poured out two large shots of twelve-year-old malt. Slowly, but surely, during the course of the evening, they got very drunk and in the process became friends of a kind.

Angus fell asleep with a contented smile on his lips.

Late the following morning, he woke up with an erection and a head that felt like a blender with pieces of his brain ricocheting around inside of it. He staggered into the kitchen, where he found Prem solemnly drinking coffee.

The Englishman was also suffering from the same alcohol-induced affliction. 'My brain feels too big for my skull,' he complained, directing a curious stare towards the protuberance straining against the crotch of Angus's red baggy pants.

Angus fried eggs while Prem filled in the details leading up to Alice and Nina's departure from Goa.

'They felt called by the master,' he said, summing up his short account.

Angus frowned. 'Kidnapped by that randy bastard Shanti more like,' he commented sourly, still unable to accept the idea that his lovers had done a bunk on him. 'What about you?' he enquired. 'When are you going back to Poona?'

'Have you tired of me already, darling?' pouted Prem.

'You won't have to ask if I am, because I'll let you know about it.' Angus sprinkled salt over the sizzling eggs. 'I didn't mean it like that. I dig you, man...even if you are gay.'

Their laughter was cut short by the pain it caused in their heads.

Angus slid a greasy fried egg from the frying pan on to a slice of burnt toast and Prem explained to him how, in his opinion, some sannyasin men had adopted a very narrow-minded standpoint in regards to his homosexuality. 'I mean to say,' he concluded, 'Bhagwan told me to accept who I am, but some of those macho pricks in Poona have a problem accepting what I am.'

It was obvious to Angus that this was a very touchy subject for the young Englishman and therefore he changed the subject by asking, 'Where are you going to go during the hot season? Back west?'

Prem shook his head and screwed up his pale face. 'Lord no, I couldn't face going back to England right now, not to mention the weather. I've been thinking for some time to visit Pushkar in Rajasthan.

'I've never heard of the place,' mumbled Angus through a mouthful of runny egg and black toast. 'What's special about it?'

Prem stood up and stretched his arms above his head. 'Well, I can only go on what other people have told me and I must say it sounds terrific. Pushkar is an ancient town in the middle of the desert with lots of temples and a freshwater lake'

Angus envisaged a still lake, surrounded by sand dunes, with a couple of camels bowing their heads to drink fresh water. 'Sounds interesting, man,' he said, before biting into his second slice of toast and egg.

'Why don't you accompany me?' Prem suggested.

Angus chewed on his breakfast, thought about the proposal for a few moments and then said, 'Okay, I will.'

'Oh great!' Prem exclaimed, resuming his seat. He reached over and took one of Angus hands between his. 'I've a feeling we're going to get along like old friends.'

Angus withdrew his hand from Prem's gentle grasp and wondered if he'd just made a big mistake.

That evening, Angus locked up the house and left the keys with Angela de Souza, the cigar-smoking landlady. Then he and Prem caught the last bus into Panjim. One long bumpy ride later, they checked into a cheap hotel that was situated within sight of the harbour.

The following morning at eight-thirty, Angus and Prem stood around on the pier waiting to board the Bombay ferry. They had just been informed that tickets for cabin accommodation were sold out. It had only been light for two hours and it was already hot.

'For fuck's sake, Priscilla, where did you find that get-up?' Angus asked.

Prem's ankle length, bubblegum-pink robe matched his floppy fedora hat, which was decorated with yellow plastic flowers, two more of which adorned his red rubber flip-flops.

'Crikey, look who's talking,' retorted Prem from behind an enormous pair of white-rimmed, rose-tinted glasses. 'You look like a cross between the thief of Baghdad and Robinson Crusoe.'

Angus was wearing purple satin baggy pants and a gold embroidered waistcoat. A broad leather belt, patterned by brass studs, girdled his slim waist. On his head was a tattered straw hat, from under which his thick wavy brown hair cascaded over his muscular shoulders and reached down to the midpoint of his back. Perched on the end of his nose was a pair of tiny, blue-tinted sunglasses. A bushy beard covered most of his face.

'It's a free world,' countered Angus, 'but I still think you look like a reject from central casting.'

They ascended the gangway arm and arm.

The *Konkan Shakti* pulled out into the river and began steaming towards the sea.

Cries of *Boom Shanker* rose from within clouds of hashish smoke. Sitting cross-legged amidst a small gathering of international hippies, Angus passed a smoking chillum to a dark-skinned tie-dye princess who was wearing a slightly addled expression on her Latin-featured face.

Meanwhile, Prem was flitting around the second-class passengers' deck like a lost guest at a flouro-dress cocktail party.

Out on the open sea, the ship's prow cleaved through dark blue water with a hiss. Grey dolphins shot out of the bow waves in pursuit of silver flying fish. Goa was left behind and the coast became a green line separating sea from sky. Every few kilometres an intermittent stretch of deserted beach broke up the monotony. It was late March and the sea breeze came as a welcome relief which diluted the soaring temperatures. The motley crew of Goa-freaks on board were making their exodus from the heat. Many of them were either heading north to the Himalaya's cooler climes, or on their way to catch a flight back West with an illicit stash of hash to make the dollars, Deutschmarks or pounds sterling necessary to finance another trip east.

After dining on a lunch composed of a soggy rice plate served with chapattis that tasted like they'd been made from cardboard, it was time for the social highlight of the afternoon. The ship's stewards organized a game of housey-housey. Throwaway lines don't always ring true, and so it was in Angus's case when the caller shouted out, 'Unlucky for some – thirteen', because this number completed the lucky Scotsman's card.

'*Bingo!*' cried Angus, surprisingly carried away for having just won the rupee equivalent of three dollars.

The sun slipped below the horizon and tropical darkness descended with its customary speed. Glaring fluorescent light illuminated the second-class deck, which shuddered and throbbed as the ferry ploughed through the sea. Angus and Prem fell asleep in the shadow provided by a suspended lifeboat. They were awoken at dawn when the spray thrown up from a big wave soaked them to the skin. Shivering, they huddled together. Angus began to question Prem about his homosexuality.

'So how come you're gay?'

'Why do you ask?'

'I've never really met a gay guy before. So, curious, I suppose.'

'You're not the first straight man to ask such a question of me. Difficult to understand, *I suppose*,' said Prem, tilting his head and raising his eyebrows in a deliberately exaggerated manner.

'I'd never thought about it until I ran into you.'

'Well, you would have if you'd had the tendency towards it. I've been gay for as long as I can remember.'

Angus turned to face the Englishman under the harsh light thrown off by a lime-coloured neon strip. '*What!*' he blurted. 'Even when you were a kid?'

'Yes.'

'You mean you liked boys better than girls?'

'Yes, I did. Didn't you?'

'Yeah…I…I mean *no*, well not like that anyway.'

'Like *what* anyway?'

'Come off it, man, you know what I mean.'

Prem smiled mischievously and leaned back against the base of a davit. 'I adored my father,' he said, adopting a wistful air. 'He was a professional soldier until he was forced into early retirement due to health problems. He died of a heart attack four years ago. I still think of him almost every day. Colonel Trevor Prendergast was his name. I loved to watch Daddy shaving when he was home on leave from Cyprus, where he was stationed for some years. That small morning ritual somehow succeeded in making me feel secure in the world. I can still remember the smell of his sweat mixed with the scent of soap and the hair on his—'

'Aw, for fucks sake,' complained Angus. 'You mean to tell me you had the hots for your dad?'

'Well... I wouldn't quite put it like that,' said Prem in a God-save-me-from-this-cretin voice. 'Let's just say I felt sexually attracted to him.'

'Right then, you felt *sexually attracted* to your dad.' Angus made inverted commas above his head with his index fingers. 'What about your mum?'

'I didn't have a *mum*. I had a domineering bitch of a mother, an heiress who inherited a fortune when she turned twenty-one. She was so self-centred that every time she was given a choice between pleasing herself and pleasing someone else – something that happened often – she always pleased herself, believing she'd just made the whole world happy with her decision. Just thinking about her makes me feel sick.' The ship juddered when its bow crashed into a particularly high wave. Spray flew over the deck. Prem dabbed moisture from his face with a red handkerchief and then continued. 'My mother was the kind of person who wasn't happy unless she had a fawning crowd of sycophants around her, especially during the garden parties and hunt balls she organized at her family's Sixteenth Century country seat, Elsfield Hall in Oxfordshire.' Angus pictured a line of black Bentleys and a fan of gold credit cards. 'It was there that the rich and famous were invited to rub shoulders, get drunk and converse about what they always talk about, London, Paris, New York, fashion, their favourite charity, horses, real estate and of course business, but never money as such...oh no, never money, for that would have been considered very bad form indeed. My mother manipulated people with her wealth, including my father, who I now believe was more in love with her title and megabucks than he was with her. That's the distinct advantage the poor have over the rich – they know their friends aren't after their money.'

'Yeah, right,' commented Angus, 'I wouldn't mind being rich so that I could find that out for myself.'

'Believe me, being rich isn't all it's cracked up to be. The wealthy are no different than the poor in that they are constantly thinking of having more money. My mother was fascinated by money in much the same way as I was fascinated by men. Over the years that fascination grew until it possessed me.'

'Did anybody know about this?'

'My parents suspected of course, but somehow managed to convince themselves that being a member of a stinking rich family guaranteed vigorous heterosexuality.' He laughed to himself, remembering something. 'I preferred to play with the girls in my neighbourhood, instead of playing football and war games with their brothers. The boys' world seemed so...so crude and tense.'

'You must have felt lonely.'

'That's a major understatement. I was a complete misfit as a child. It was being *different…*' Prem took his turn at adding emphasis to something he'd said by making inverted commas with his index fingers. '…that helped break my identification with social conditioning patterns and behaviour. This also applies to gay society. I've done the gay bars and sauna thing, where I soon became bored with the skin-deep attitudes. Therefore, in a way, being gay helped bring me on to the spiritual path. You see, life was difficult for me from an early age and this turned out to be a blessing in disguise.' Angus looked sceptical. Prem noticed this and clarified what he meant by saying, 'It was beneficial because I was forced to enquire deeply about who I really am, and I know in my heart…' He paused and patted the centre of his narrow chest. '…that if I can find the answer to that question I'll also find the answer to all the other important questions, such as: Where did I come from? What is the purpose of my life? What happens when you die?' He concluded. 'You might say that I've changed from being an outsider to being an insider.'

Angus nodded. 'I get the picture,' he said, glancing at Prem, whose eyes were obscured by shadow. 'Have you ever had sex with a woman?'

'Yes, I've had sexual intercourse with women. In comparison to men most women have a more submissive nature, something which appeals to me. I have lots of wonderful female friends. But women's bodies never really turned me on.'

Angus asked, 'What was it like the first time you did it with a guy?'

Prem asked back, 'What was it like the first time you made love with a woman?'

Angus remembered a night long ago, the night he'd jumped into bed with Jenny and quickly lost his virginity. 'A bit of a premature ejaculation disaster at first,' he confessed, 'that turned into something beautiful in the end.' He smiled, as if acknowledging the presence of a fond memory. 'I suppose it was a lot of things.'

'In that case,' said Prem, 'it was by definition a unique experience for both of us.'

Angus moved closer to the Englishman. 'You know,' he said, 'there's something I've been dying to ask you.'

Prem's eyes narrowed. 'What's that, Angus?'

'Would you like to make love with me?'

'Sure. You can suck my dick immediately…don't hesitate.' Prem laughed nervously and then said, 'Only joking. That beard of yours is an absolute turn-off.'

'Aw, now you've gone and hurt my feelings.'

'My bloody oath!' Prem exclaimed. 'Are you pulling my leg?'

'Dead fucking right I am, and it's not your middle one.'

Whack! Angus received a hard slap on the face.

The penetrating thrum rising from the diesel engines in the ferry's belly lessened and, silhouetted against a hazy sunrise, Bombay's seafront skyline came into sight.

Angus and Prem stepped out of a taxi in the Colaba, Bombay's main tourist area, and found themselves standing in front of the Gateway of India, the city's architectural icon. Angus listened as Prem explained to him how the yellow basalt archway had been built by the British as a symbol of triumph in the early twentieth century. 'It was here,' said Prem, facing the harbour and pointing under the towering arch, 'that the last regiment of departing British soldiers marched when India broke free of the colonial yoke and gained its independence in 1947.'

Angus was not impressed by Prem's history lecture or the filthy beggars, who were swarming around them and pestering them for bakshish.

A short walk later, the two travellers checked into the Rex Hotel and caught up on their sleep.

It was late afternoon when Angus took a shower with a family of cockroaches under tepid water that smelled of bleach. He put on fresh clothes, exited the hotel, crossed the road and entered Dipti's Milkshake Bar, where he spent over an hour reading old copies of *Time* and drinking ice cold drinks. The sky was darkening when Prem wandered into Dipti's and joined him. The streets were alive with the sound of heavily amplified Bollywood music, throngs of irate drivers honking their horns and muezzins' haunting voices calling the faithful to prayer.

Dinner was eaten in the Kailash Prabat restaurant. Angus and Prem gorged themselves on vegetarian dishes served by stressed-out, sweating waiters who rushed around under whirring electric ceiling fans.

An endless stream of hustlers and vagrants, with grubby hands outstretched begging for small change, enlivened a digestive stroll along Marine Drive. By midnight, Angus and Prem were back in the Rex, fast asleep in preparation for an early start.

It was still dark when they boarded a packed train in the Victoria Terminus railway station. The carriage's atmosphere was hot, claustrophobic and filled with the grimy reek of freshly burned coal. They squeezed past milling passengers and porters in faded red jackets who were carrying huge suitcases and rolled up mattresses on their turbaned heads.

'Here we are,' said Prem when he located their first class seats, obtained with the assistance of Lord Bakshish.

'Garam chai! Garam chai! Garam chai!' called a platform tea seller.

From his window seat, Angus passed a few coins to the rake-thin vendor and in return received two clay cups filled to the brim with scalding hot tea.

After an interminable wait, the steam train panted out of the station. The passengers let out a collective sigh of relief when a cool draught rushed in through the open windows. Dilapidated slum dwellings lined the sides of the tracks. The locomotive belched boiler smoke and strained as it pulled a line of about twenty rusty-wheeled carriages along equally oxidized rails. Angus peered out between the metal window bars and pitied the thousands upon thousands of poor people who lived in very close proximity to the tracks, where they were constantly bombarded with noise, lumps of burning coal and litter thrown from passing carriages.

The city's urban sprawl and twelve million inhabitants were left behind as the train chugged into lush open countryside.

It was twenty-one hours later when it rumbled into the pink city of Jaipur, Rajasthan's State Capital. From there, a three-hour taxi ride was required to ferry Angus and Prem to their final destination. Eyelids heavy, the travellers sat in the taxi's back seat and stared absently out of the windows at a barren landscape, illuminated by the dim grey of faint daylight that was tinging the eastern skyline. They passed by crumbling Rajput forts, crowning hills that had in antiquity been surrounded by high, fortified, stone walls, now reduced to formless piles of rubble. They arrived at Pushkar's outskirts just in time to see a pale sun float up from the early morning mist that hung over the small town like a gossamer veil.

Exhausted, they checked into the Lake View Guest House. Prem was snoring as soon as he lay horizontal on a lumpy mattress. Angus stared up and watched lime green geckos scurrying across the ceiling until he fell asleep.

Angus awoke in the late afternoon. For a few alien moments he hadn't a clue where he was. He turned on his side and saw that Prem's cot was empty. Warm sunlight flooded into the room through a flimsy torn curtain. He stretched, groaned, stood and walked unsteadily towards the window. As the hotel's name implied, Angus found himself looking out at a stunning view of Pushkar Lake's leaden waters.

Pushkar is renowned for a number of reasons. During the month of November, the small town hosts an annual camel fair, when ships of the desert are steered into town in staggering numbers by brightly turbaned herders. Although principally a fair in which the humped beasts can be traded and sold, horses, goats, cows and sheep are also driven across central Rajasthan's arid wastelands to converge in and around the town's environs.

For Hindus, Pushkar is the Lourdes of the sub-continent. The semicircular lake's sacred waters are credited with having curative properties, especially in respect to skin infections and diseases. After a holy healing dip, devotees line up in long queues outside of the famous Brahma Temple to take their turn in worshipping Lord Brahma, who is the vehicle of expression for the divine intelligence's creative impulse. In the Hindu Pantheon, the Lord of Creation receives relatively little attention from worshipers as he lives in the shadow of his two divine colleagues Shiva, Lord of Destruction, and his workmate Vishnu, The Preserver, who acts as the cosmos's maintenance man. Paying little heed to Brahma's power is viewed by his worshippers as a spiritual blunder. They believe he has four faces on top of his Mister Universe shoulders, meaning that he quite literally has eyes on the back of his head and, every breath you take, God, like a cosmic peeping Tom, will be watching you. Pushkar's Brahma temple is purported to be one of only a few in the whole of India and is often crammed with pilgrims paying respects to their all-seeing maker.

What Angus found most enjoyable about the holy town was the purity of its air. On a clear day you could see for miles and during the night, stars shone in the heavens with an exceptional brilliance, the likes of which he had never before witnessed.

During the day, the fifty-two ghats that lead down to the sacred lake were the stage for busloads of devout Hindus, who created a spectacle of clashing colours, vocal noise and chaotic movement, which somehow succeeded in turning into a harmonious social event.

On his second afternoon in Pushkar, Angus sat in a lakeside temple's shade and looked on as the worshipful submerged themselves in the consecrated waters. As he observed the relieved expressions on people's faces he began to suspect that many of the eager bathers were more concerned with escaping the ferocious mid-day heat than washing away their sins in the communal karma-cleansing bathtub.

After a two-day absence, Prem returned to the Lake View Guest House, hand in hand with Harold, a distinguished-looking gentleman from Berlin. The fair-haired Berliner was a week into a see-everything-in-India-in-a-month whirlwind tour. He had fallen in love with Prem and asked if the Englishman would like to accompany him – all five star expenses paid for. Prem was blushing like an eight-month pregnant bride and chomping at the bit like a frisky colt when he stood in front of Angus, who was lying in bed reading a book, and told him he was going to Western Rajasthan's Golden City, Jaisalmer.

'You mean to say that you came all the way here with me just to say adios, amigo?' Angus asked, looking up from a worn paperback copy of Chögyam Trungpa's *Cutting Through Spiritual Materialism*.

'Bhagwan says you have to follow your feelings,' blurted Prem.

'Oh, he does, does he?' Angus said. 'In that case I hope you never feel suicidal.'

'Bhagwan says it's sannyas or suicide.'

'*Bhagwan says, Bhagwan says,* you sound like a fucking parrot,' said Angus, the tension rising in his voice. 'What the fuck do you say?'

Prem merely shrugged and looked over to Harold who, dressed in a light tan-coloured Armani suit, stood in the doorway glancing at his slimline watch, as if there was a plane to catch.

Angus smiled and stood up. 'Come 'ere,' he said, spreading his arms.

Prem stumbled forward and stammered, 'I…I…I'm sorry Angus. I…I didn't mean to let you down.'

Angus chuckled, embraced him, patted him on the back and said, 'Relax, Prem. It's been fun hanging out with you. Maybe we'll run into each other some other time.'

'Maybe in Poona,' suggested Prem, standing back from him.

Angus shook his head and said, 'I doubt it.'

He went down to the street to see Prem and Harold off. He waved goodbye to the happy couple as they stepped into a white, chauffeur-driven Ambassador car and sped away, enveloped by an aura of rainbow-coloured hearts.

Alone once more and suddenly feeling it, Angus missed Prem – for about two seconds.

Angus settled into what was to become his daily routine for the next few weeks. Each morning at dawn, he strolled down to the lake and swam for half an hour. He then hurried back to his room for a hot shower, where he used pink carbolic soap, Dettol and a stiff bristle brush to scrub his skin, just in case he'd been exposed to contagious leprosy bacteria. Red raw and smelling like a hospital toilet, he then dressed and nipped around the corner to a terraced restaurant with a questionable hygiene standard. It was there that he would breakfast on masala tea and crispy wafer-thin dosa. Once he had eaten his fill, he'd then set off to explore the town and its sun-drenched environs. By late afternoon, he'd use a winding series of stone steps to trek up a steep hill and reach the Savitri Temple, from where he'd enjoy the fantastic sunset view over the mirror-like lake and listen to the thud of drums echoing up from the ghats.

There were plenty of foreign travellers passing through the town. Angus kept to himself for the most part, entering only into light conversation with people when visiting a chai shop to satisfy his need for a sociable chat.

It was during his third week in Pushkar that Angus took a break from his predictable routine. He awoke before dawn one morning and decided to storm heaven and hell's gates by ingesting two saucer-shaped, White Lightning LSD tabs, given to him as a parting gift by Acid Mike.

Before heading out of town, he went into an early morning café to purchase two plastic bottles of drinking water and a half-dozen vegetable samosas.

By the time he'd passed through a cultivated area, dotted by a few neem and ashoka trees, and reached Pushkar's arid outskirts, the sky was flashing in unusual colour combinations. The desert landscape began to look like Vincent Van Gogh might have painted it – if the Dutch artist had seen a desert. High above, a lone hawk wheeled, its shrill cry cutting through the air like a high-pitched dog whistle.

An hour later, the white clouds in the distance had been transformed into galleons, their huge sails billowing out as they crossed a turquoise-blue ocean. The temperature was soaring. The ancient lizard that lay nestled in the reptilian folds behind the frontal lobes of Angus's brain hissed a warning and urged him to seek shade immediately. Looking over to a sun-blasted hill, void of any form of vegetation, he spotted a dark shadow halfway up its sloping sides.

The shade was further than he imagined. He was wiping sweat from his eyes when he stepped into a shallow cave that smelled of bat excrement. His throat felt parched and narrow as he gasped for breath. There was a strong metallic taste in his mouth. He threw back his head, gulped down half a litre of water from a plastic bottle and studied the tapering tips of a family of ivory-coloured crystalline stalactites. He looked down at the fine powder on the ground and noticed that concentric rings were rippling out from under his sandaled feet. Then, as if a thick cloud had passed in front of the sun, the cave darkened. Suddenly the floor shook. 'Huh!' Angus gasped and wondered if it was an earthquake. He heard a motorized buzz, looked around and, much to his astonishment, found himself in a tropical rain forest. There was a shout and then a tremendous crash. A huge tree had fallen in an explosion of branches and leaves. The mechanical whirring intensified. It was the sound of an industrial chain saw. Its linked teeth were zipping through thousand-year-old timber like a red-hot scalpel slicing through butter. Another huge tree toppled over and crashed to the forest floor.

A green veil lifted from Angus's eyes. Wearing nothing but flower necklaces on their red-painted bodies, a tribe of frightened Amazonian Indians were crouched in front of him. They were shrouded in dust and seemed unaware of his presence. It occurred to Angus that he might be invisible. Impulsively he looked at his watch. It was gone. So was his arm.

Where's my body? Angus silently asked himself. Mike warned me that this acid was strong, but this is fuckin' well ridiculous!

'Jeeesussss!' he hissed.

A soft voice in his head tried to educate him. 'Cowering before you, these terrified natives are deemed primitive by technological society because they own little in the way of material possessions and live in close contact with—'

'What the hell's going on?'

Vroooop! The rainforest and the Indios disappeared.

Car horns blared. He looked around and found himself standing in the middle of a busy street that was host to a massive traffic jam. Well-dressed people streamed around him. They were hurrying to work in office blocks and the factories that Angus could see on the horizon, made hazy by the smoke belching from chimneystacks. Flanked by towering skyscrapers that were circled by elevated monorails, he began to float along the street. Oblivious to his presence, pedestrians moved around him, their eyes focused on hand-held telecommunication devices. The people appeared unable to look at each other, as though they were afraid of seeing what they had become reflected in each other's eyes, biological robots, content to do their masters' bidding as they rushed from here to there with no other purpose than attending to the superficial. Angus could hear their noisy thoughts. Almost everyone was looking forward to getting their feet up in the evening. He could see them sitting on sofas, with a bottle of fresh oxygen in one hand and a TV remote in the other. They sat as if hypnotized, heads nodding to and fro like metronomes, their dull eyes watching state-sponsored entertainment channels and news broadcasts, delivered by cables right into their living rooms, and hosted by anchormen and women whose names were more familiar to them than those of their next-door neighbours. Mass frustration ruled the nation and the news was always bad, because the programmes that fed negative emotions captured unconscious viewers' attention better than anything else. Angus looked on and observed how, as the news worsened and the films became more insanely violent, the audience's love of these horrible images increased. The shocking realization came to him that people found it entertaining to watch other human beings inflict pain and suffering upon each other, because it delivers the quick fix that feeds their addiction to unhappiness.

Outside of the air-conditioned nightmare bubble, Angus watched Inuit Indians in Greenland, chewing on mouldy blubber in their melting igloos. Their irradiated skin was peeling off. They jabbered excitedly to each other about the hungry polar bears floating by on ice flows, as the huge animals drifted towards extinction, the planet's life-support systems exhausted.

A silence, long enough for the polar caps to melt, enveloped Angus. He staggered over to the mouth of the cave, looked up at the sky and saw that it was filled with black clouds, red and yellow flames licking around their edges. The understanding came to him that Earth's natural resources would not be able to sustain man's gluttony forever. It wasn't the planet that needed saving it was the human beings, who were just another failed mutation entering an evolutionary cul-de-sac as far as their spinning host was concerned. The air grew thick with smoke and the iceberg Angus believed himself to be standing on started to sink under an ocean of contaminated water.

So caught up was he in his vision, Angus imagined himself to be drowning. As he went under for the third time, he began to panic. His heartbeat quickened and his breath came in short, sharp, shallow gasps. The choking sensation brought him back in touch with his body. He was relieved to find himself back in his earth suit, but the awareness of how attached he was to it came as a shock. He sank to the floor and shuddered as a powerful lysergic wave crashed over him. He was scared stiff and wasn't in the least bit consoled by the knowledge that the only way to transcend his fear was to reach the end of the terrifying road that ran through it.

He sat taking deep breaths in through his mouth in the hope that this would straighten him out. His upper lip and fingertips began to tingle from the effects of hyperventilation. Trying to control the LSD didn't work. It was way too powerful and getting stronger by the second. It was time to let go, face ego meltdown and wander the *bardos* in a psychological no man's land.

Using his rucksack as a pillow, he lay down spread-eagled in the fine grey powder that covered the hollow's floor. He closed his eyes and let his expanded consciousness swim along the orange and scarlet Celtic knotwork of his blood vessels, pulsating in time to his heartbeat.

He entered an exalted state wherein he became hyper-receptive to any form of stimuli, external or internal. Drawn to a white circle in the centre of his forehead, his heart's rhythmic echo faded into a dull primordial thud. He merged with the disc and an unsettling feeling crept over him. This was not the cosmic rainbow light of the acid tripper's dreams, but rather a disconcerting, amorphous blankness containing no colour at all. Angus sat up and opened his eyes, or at least he thought he did, for he was still in the centre of a blank, empty space and for the second time that afternoon he lost contact with his physical body. There was a loud tearing sound, as if a hurricane had ripped a sailing ship's mainsail, followed by humming, rolling and crackling noises. A dark moaning shadow flitted across the colourless, incorporeal nothingness. Angus was in a void where his mind and all its suppressed imaginings could run free.

In a state of delirium, he heard a confusion of human sounds as grey misshapen entities whirled around him. The message their cries, whimpers and urgent talking conveyed to him was none too clear but he reckoned it wasn't a happy one. His disembodied consciousness registered that he knew what he was about to encounter – the ghosts of his past. In the blink of an inner eye his whole life danced before him clad in forgotten incidents, embroidered with various colours of emotional thread. He sailed off on the tide of memory and drifted across an ocean composed of sparkling particles where kaleidoscopic images spun out of nowhere, one superimposed upon the other. Figures loomed and faded on the screen of his memory, the mirror of karma. Everyone he'd ever met in the world passed through him, their psychic imprint living on in the heart of his soul.

Jenny was here, there and everywhere. Angus looked at her face and saw whatever he projected on it. Angel, demon from hell, child of God, daughter of Satan, she embodied them all. Her eyes were wide open and shone like white opals. Her pointed tongue flicked across her gently curving lips, making them glisten in the ethereal light. An air of tragedy shrouded her in swirling mist.

Alice and Nina skipped by. Naked and provocative, their full breasts wobbled as they called out in stereo, 'Oh, Angus, we're absolutely gagging for it.'

'*He-haw, he-haw, he-haw!*' Dirty Ali's trousers were bundled at his ankles as he impaled a female donkey on the end of his massive, swollen, brown cock. Grey goo seeped from Ali's smashed left eye. '*Heee-hawwww!*' The Persian howled and ejaculated a steaming jet of sperm into the braying ass. Ali's good eye rolled up into his head and the donkey's tongue hung languidly from the side of a mouth full of rotten yellow teeth.

Wearing a red pleated kilt, made from the Macleod clan's tartan, a solitary piper played a lament on his bagpipes. He stood amidst purple heather on the shores of a deep Scottish loch. A woman in black shrouds drifted over the water towards him and Angus knew intuitively that this was his mother, Margaret, whose love he'd never known. Her sad eyes radiated waves of emotion that he welcomed with a river of crystal raindrop tears. Rocking to and fro, a tall man in oilskins appeared beside her. His strong hands curled around the wooden wheel of his doomed trawler. Angus watched as his father, Captain Norman Macleod, descended into the darkest depths of his cruel mistress, the sea.

Highland clansmen swung claymores in the air and shouted encouragement as Daniel, Angus's beloved stepfather, played a jig on his fiddle. An icy wave washed over him and in his place stood the wicked schoolteacher from Angus's childhood on Iona, Hitler. 'Up with them, boy, I said, up with them,' ordered the tyrant. Nessie, the leather belt, smashed down on Angus's fingertips and destroyed their nerve endings in a burning instant.

'No son of mine would have ended up in prison...*prison...prison*,' echoed his stepmother's voice from long ago, as she spoke the last words Angus ever heard from her mouth on the afternoon she disowned him.

Light faded and it became as dark as a tomb.

Angus was beginning to wonder if this was some kind of prelude to meeting people in the realm of the dead. It crossed his mind that he was dead himself. Then, suddenly, he heard Murphy's voice call out in desperation, 'Angus, you've got to help us. Bust us out of here, man, or we'll die.'

Echoing footsteps grew louder and louder, then stopped when a bloodshot eye peeped through a Judas spy-hole to observe Raj and Murphy, sitting on the dirty floor of a stifling cell. Above their lice-infested heads, sunlight shone through a barred window and illuminated a trapezium of dun-coloured sandstone wall covered in flowing, Arabic script graffiti. Names, dates and prayers had been written in blood and excrement by the generations of prisoners who'd left a psychological imprint behind while doing hard time in Iran. Angus heard a heavy steel door slam shut and an iron key rasp against metal as it turned a lock's clattering tumblers.

Air bubbles burst on the surface of filthy oil-slicked water. Jimmy Bradley's head appeared. He pulled a fogged-up diver's mask off his face, laughed and then said, 'Hey pal, it'll take more than a smack on the head to kill me. Let's get cracking. This only happens once in a tartan moon.'

Angus saw a tartan moon rising out of a sea of mercury and found himself sitting on a beach. He felt wretched. There was something hard and round pressing into his right buttock. He reached down into the sand and touched whatever it was. It occurred to him that he was sitting on a bomb and if he moved it would explode. What the fuck is going on? Angus asked himself anxiously. I'm freaking, man, I'm freaking. Words like 'bummer' and 'flipping out' came to mind and, for the first time in his life, he wondered if he was having a bad trip.

Something rattled and he heard Mike's voice saying, 'Take a good dose of acid and experience God directly.'

There was a flash of blue light and then Angus saw a beautiful young woman, standing beside a pile of smouldering ashes. She raised her head and asked with the trace of an Irish accent, 'Where are you? I've been waiting my whole life for you. Don't you remember who I am?'

Angus tried to draw closer to the mysterious woman, but she merged with the shadows and disappeared. He had no idea who she was but intuited that he was destined to find out one day in some kind of déjà voodoo.

His paranoia level ratcheted up a notch when he smelt the malodorous reek of sulphur. The suffocating smell launched his brain into a dark galaxy. The inside of his cranium was suffused with blood red light and a malevolent form began to manifest. A goat-headed beast sat in the centre of his consciousness. Yellow saurian eyes shone with cunning light. A grinning mouth opened to reveal serrated teeth, its long pointed incisors dripping with blood-flecked saliva. A vile voice whispered, 'Come to me, Angus, my son. I'll give you everything.' It was an invitation both tempting and sinister. From between black hairy legs and cloven hooves rose a crimson, eel-like phallus, its head that of a vicious fanged viper. Blazing with fire, its eyes nailed Angus. Hissing, the phallic snake lashed out.

'*Aaagh!*' Angus yelled out in terror, jumped up and banged his head on a stalactite. Shocked back into his senses, his body felt like it was made from hot jelly.

'Fucking hell,' he whispered sharply, rubbing the bump that was rapidly developing on the crown of his head. His heart hammered, about ready to burst.

'You belong to me,' the beast's voice called from behind him. Angus spun around but there was nothing there except crumbling green boulders embedded in their own detritus.

'Pull yourself together, man,' said Angus, speaking out loud. 'You're freaking out.'

Trembling and sweaty, as if he were emerging from a nightmare, he sat down on a flat rock and gazed beyond the cave's mouth. Heat waves were rising from an outlandish wilderness that looked like it was radioactive. Dust devils spiralled up from the hot desert floor like whirling dervishes incarnated as baby tornadoes. The bright morning had drifted into late afternoon. The descending sun's unobstructed rays burnished the desert sand with a golden patina. The air was so close and heavy it bore down upon

Angus with palpable weight. He didn't think it wise to venture out of the shade yet, although the idea of vacating the spooky chamber appealed greatly. He stared out over the wilderness's vast expanse and studied the swirling, petrol-blue sky. For the first time since he'd left Britain, Angus missed Scotland, especially his homeland's cool, fresh air.

While he sat cross-legged on the rock the unsettling feeling of standing outside of himself stayed with him. In a detached way he could see what a strange figure he made, sitting in a dusty cave in the middle of roasting hot nowhere.

'Come to me.' The voice was no more than a faint whisper. Angus ignored it, having reached the point where a devilish figment of his imagination was a lot less frightening than the face of chaos, the great unknown, a huge burning question mark, which in that moment his fragile world seemed to be revolving around.

He reached for his bag in search of something to smoke and it struck him that he couldn't feel any higher than he already was. His body craved nicotine. Fucking fags, he thought, that shit's as bad as smack. He made a resolution to stop smoking tobacco.

He ate a greasy vegetable samosa and washed it down with water. He drank deeply and heard his breath return when he drained the plastic bottle of a litre of lukewarm water in eleven seconds. His stomach felt like it had mysteriously liquefied.

Suddenly, a recollection exploded in his head. The last words Dawn said to him in Kabul echoed through a memory vault. 'Remember...*remember*, India...*India*...*India* is not a country. It's an exalted state of mind...*mind*...*mind* that has to be dreamed...*dreamed*...*dreamed* into existence...*existence*...*existence*.'

He placed a smidgen of hashish in his little glass pipe, lit it with a match, inhaled a lungful of smoke, held his breath for as long as possible, exhaled with a cough, closed his eyes and slipped into a dream. He could see Swami Ram, strolling along the banks of the Ganges. The holy man stretched out a hand. A white dove landed in his palm, cooed for a moment and then flew off. Ram's soft melodious voice called out a greeting. *'Om Namo Narayan.'* He raised his right hand and said, 'You are a prisoner of the mind, living in a dream world that you alone have created. The light of awareness will lead you out of this trap. Bear in mind, the difficulty lies not with finding the guru. Be he inner or outer, he is always available. Remember also that a real spiritual master is not the one with the most followers. That kind of teacher, although claiming to voice the truth, is in reality bogged down in the mire of commerce. The real preceptor is the one who creates masters who are no longer in need of his or her guidance, masters whose sole purpose in life is to create love where love did not exist before, and in so doing help mankind ascend the ladder of spiritual evolution. It's not worshiping a guru that is important, but the depth of your devotion to the pursuit of truth. Your task now is that of becoming a sincere and valiant seeker. This is the reason you've lived up until now, the genesis of your being born into this world. Be aware that what the future holds for you will be determined by your state of consciousness in this very moment. Use your time well, so as not to mourn its passing, knowing that a human lifetime is but a flutter of Lord Brahma's eyelids.'

Swami Ram put his palms together, bowed reverently and then continued on his way along the riverbank. Spine ramrod straight, he was a quintessential embodiment of the spiritual warrior.

'*Ja, ja.*' Out of the blue, another voice spoke inside Angus's head and he remembered a morning not so long ago when he'd been with his diving instructor, Manni, and how the big German had said something to him which he hadn't paid much attention to at the time. '*Damned hashish,* clouds a man's mind, weakens his willpower and drags his spirit down into the darkness like a lead weight belt.'

Swami Ram's voice was but a whisper when it repeated one last time. 'Be he inner or outer, he is always available.'

Angus snapped open his eyes and realized he was crying. He was crying because he knew with certainty that up until that moment he'd been wandering through life like a sleepwalker. It was time to wake up.

'Right, then,' he said, tipping his canvas rucksack's contents out on to the dust.

He balanced a packet of cigarettes, rolling papers, chillum, a chunk of hashish, glass pipe and a box of matches to form a small cairn on top of a boulder that for some reason reminded him of Ben Nevis, Scotland's highest mountain. He stood back, took one last look at his old companions and said a fond farewell to them. 'It was great hanging out with you. We had some high times together. Goodbye.'

He slung his rucksack over his shoulder and stepped out of the cave's shadow into the early evening light. He felt like he'd been liberated from a cramped prison cell. He began to make his way down the hillside and then retraced his footsteps from earlier that day.

By the time Angus reached Pushkar's outskirts night had descended. He was covered in dust and extremely thirsty. The idea of a cold shower splashed in his mind. He was almost tempted to head directly for the Lake View Hotel but there was one more thing he wanted to do. He took a right turn down a narrow alley and walked in the direction of the red-spired Brahma Temple. Rats scurried for cover as he hurried by.

That particular evening there were no queues outside the Jagat Pita Brahma Mandir. Angus glanced up at the goose, a symbol of knowledge, carved on the temple's gateway as he passed under it. He removed his sandals and left them outside on the white marble stairs that lead up to the main building. He crossed a black and white-tiled courtyard, walked up a short flight of steps, passed between blue-painted pillars and entered the small main shrine, which was illuminated by brass oil lamps, suspended on iron chains. There was a large silver turtle on the floor that faced towards the sanctum sanctorum, where the metre-high, four-headed statue of the Lord of Creation sat cross-legged in a silver-lined arched recess. Angus inhaled incense smoke and it filled his mind with the fragrance of infinite possibilities. He approached the marigold-garlanded stone deity and gazed into one of its rounded faces. He had the uncanny feeling that the statue's eyes were watching him from multiple angles. His perceptions still strongly affected by LSD, he could have sworn that Lord Brahma winked conspiratorially at him, as if to say that life was a hugely complex joke and getting it was the purpose of being born into the world that he had created.

Behind him, a male voice whispered. 'The world is illusionary. Brahma alone is real. Brahma is the world.'

Angus turned to see who had uttered the gently spoken words. There was nobody there. The temple was deserted and, for the first time in his life, he felt a real sense of his own destiny that told him the path he'd stumbled on to was the right one.

24

TERMINAL JUNCTION

Cambodia

'*Oof!*' A wave crashed into me. It hit me squarely on the chest and shocked me back to physical reality. Visualizing a better scenario had not helped to alleviate my predicament, but rather only made me forget where I was for a short while. Air bubbles rushed around me in the swirling water, hissing a complaint as they popped and expired.

'No, no, no!' I cried, trying to steady myself with clawing hands as the surf sucked sand out from under me. My backside remained on top of the landmine, but only just. I reached to it and could feel that the round detonator button had shifted position. I knew with certainty that time was running out and it would only require a few more waves as big as the last to wash me off the mine and blow me to pieces in the process.

My imagination ran wild and presented me with a horrific mental picture of some of my body parts being dragged out to sea, where they were then devoured by sharks. A few charred remains, left smouldering beneath the coconut tree, were being pecked upon by a flock of hoarsely cawing carrion crows.

So this is the end, I thought, Terminal Junction. I could never have imagined that this was how my life was going to finish.

My voice quavered as I began to recite the Lord's Prayer. 'Ou...Our father who art in heaven hallowed be—'

The dark sea tumbled and roared. Another wave broke against me. *'Ugh!'* I gagged on seawater. I could feel the sand shifting beneath me like liquid mud. I spat out the brine, squeezed my eyes shut and continued with the only prayer I knew by heart. 'Thy kingdom come, thy will be done, on earth as it is in Heaven...'

The inside of my eyelids lit up when a white slash of lightning splintered the charged atmosphere, followed almost immediately by a tremendous bang. At first I thought the mine had exploded but, when I realized it hadn't, my memory began to sieve fractured thoughts and disjointed images into my brain's frontal lobes, where they coalesced into a bizarre vision. Part dream, part Bollywood farce, it was a fantastic amalgam composed of exaggerated interpretations of Angus's stories.

Brahma, the Lord of Creation, was reclining on a giant pink lotus flower when his prayer phone rang. Tutting in annoyance, he pressed the pause button on his digital movie player's remote control, picked up a cordless diamond-studded receiver and listened for a moment to my desperate plea.

'But deliver us from evil. For thine is the kingdom, and the…'

'Good heavens!' Brahma exclaimed, before hanging up.

His eight eyelids blinked as three pairs of eyes stared at the huge IMAX screen in front of him. Projected on the curving silver screen was a frozen image of Marlon Brando's shaved head. Brahma had been in the midst of viewing Francis Ford Coppola's 1979 Vietnam War epic, *Apocalypse Now*. The Lord had watched this particular movie on countless occasions. It was one of his favourite creations, especially the title, something which he'd dreamt up one night back in '69 when he was in a bad mood – after a flaming row with his four-armed wife, Savitri – and projected into a Hollywood scriptwriter's subconscious. Now, just when Captain Willard was creeping out of a slimy Cambodian river and getting ready to chop Colonel Walter E. Kurtz up with a whopping great knife to the sound of Doors vocalist, Jim Morrison, singing 'The End', he'd been interrupted by a mere mortal's distressed prayer.

Brahma stood up and paced around on his lotus trying to make up his universal mind what to do. He leaned over the pink flower's petals and looked down at the casual waters of the Ocean of Infinite Possibilities swirling below him. Lord Brahma knew that somewhere upon those churning waters lay his cosmic counterpart, Lord Vishnu, ensconced in his throne room, formed from an infinitely long, multi-headed serpent. It was there, just beyond the mundane universe, that Vishnu dreamt into existence the reality of waking experiences. Well and good, thought Brahma, Vishnu can have his metaphysical malarkey for all eternity. I have more urgent matters that require my attention. Lord Brahma surrendered to the creative impulse, the very essence of his limitless being, grabbed a ruby-encrusted emergency phone and dialled 0800 Aum Mani Padme Hum.

'Om, Shanti, Shanti,' echoed a saintly voice, with a distinctly Indian accent, on the other end of the cosmic hotline. 'Life is God's breath within us.'

'Listen, you can drop the holy bullshit for a start,' barked Lord Brahma. 'Do you know anything about a third-dimensional carbon entity named Hamish Macleod? The poor creature is on Earth, a small planet in a backwater of the Milky Way Galaxy, in some god-forsaken place called Cambodia, suffering through the illusion that he's sitting on top of an explosive device.'

'Yes, Lord Brahma, I do know something about Hamish Macleod,' replied the soothing voice. 'In fact, I'm working on him right now.'

'So, Sadguru, it's just as I thought. I had a feeling this hanky-panky had your hallmark on it. Are you aware that this Hamish Macleod's soul has been sending out an anguished prayer to me and in so doing disturbed me in my free time?'

'No, Lord Brahma, I'm sorry to say that I wasn't aware of this.'

'Typical,' huffed God, all of his suspicions confirmed. 'And what exactly is the purpose of putting this tiny entity through such a hellish experience that he bothers me about it?'

'Well, Lord Brahma, I thought Hamish might be a good candidate for enlightenment.'

'Enlightenment?' repeated Brahma in dismay. 'Sadguru, of all my creations, you, more than anyone else, should have realized by now that self-realization simply happens.'

Sadguru started to protest. 'I know…I know…but…but—'

'No, I will hear none of it,' shouted Brahma who, in spite of his annoyance, was taking pleasure in making the supreme master squirm. 'Now you listen to me, Sadguru. This is the last time I'm going to tell you this. Everything started from pure consciousness and will ultimately end in pure consciousness. Awakening to this reality brings the ultimate freedom. As I've told you time and again, it's just like when an earthen pot is shattered and it is realized that the space within is one with the space without. It will happen for everyone when the appointed moment rolls around, because all of my creation is cyclical and all beings will one day close their individual circle and return to me, having gone beyond the ridiculous notion that the ego can seek spiritual enlightenment.'

Sadguru felt compelled to object, persistence being a core element of his divine nature. 'Yes…but—'

'Yes but, nothing!' Brahma's voice thundered out across the multiverse. 'You will do as I command. You will stop this nonsense of yours right now and give Hamish Macleod a break. If you don't, I might be tempted to summon Lord Shiva and command him to perform his dance of destruction as a precursor to a new cycle of creation.'

Upon hearing this, Sadguru knew that God was in no mood for fooling around. He'd gone as far as he dared. He bit the metaphysical bullet. It tasted of mango chutney.

'Do you hear me?' Lord Brahma's tone was growing impatient.

'Yes…yes my Lord, I do.'

'Very well, get on with it and do as I command.' God was about to hang up when he heard Sadguru's voice say his name in a questioning manner.

'Lord Brahma?' Not wishing for the exchange to end on a sour note, the supreme spiritual master was endeavouring to steer things in a more positive direction.

'Yes, what is it now?'

'I'd just like to know where the story goes from here.'

'What are you referring to exactly?'

'Well…I'm a bit concerned about the rumours that are circulating in regard to life on Planet Earth. Things are in a terrible mess down there, what with global warming, oil spills, floods, massive storms, famines, disease, wars, rampant materialism and nuclear weapons in the hands of idiots. Why…the situation's out of control. My God!' Sadguru sighed in exasperation. 'People are living in such a godless state down there that they've started worshiping television screens, computers, automobiles, money and…and…and…' Sadguru couldn't summon up the courage to say the worst part.

'And what? Out with it!' Brahma demanded.

Sadguru took a deep breath and let it out slowly. 'I'm sorry to have to inform you that human beings have started to worship The God of Corruption.'

Brahma's eight eyes blinked in astonishment. 'Lord Bakshish?'

'Yes, my lord.'

'It's come to that has it?'

'Yes, Lord Brahma, I'm afraid it has. Object proliferation and corruption on Planet Earth have reached saturation levels that are unheard of in any other region of the multiverse.' He paused briefly. 'The word is that you're planning something big during this current *Kali Yug* (age of disintegration). Is it true?'

'Heavens above,' cried an incredulous Lord Brahma, who was beginning to long for the good old days that had existed just after the dawn of creation, when there was not a single being beside himself to witness the endless silence. 'You'll just have to be patient like everyone else and wait for everything to click into place as my divine plan unfolds.'

Unable to restrain his curiosity, of which he possessed an abundant supply, Sadguru ventured, 'Not even a hint?'

Lord Brahma chuckled. 'Well, I'll say this much, it's going to be a surprise. You see, of late, many of my creations are saying that I've gone mad because of the crazy dimensions I've manifested for them to inhabit. Why, they rarely even bother to worship me anymore, or build temples in my honour.' Brahma's voice became stern. 'That is all going to change. I want to instil knowledge in my subjects' minds and return faith to their hearts. That way they will understand that ultimately God is good and all is as it should be.' He added. 'I've just remembered something. I incarnated on Earth for a short time quite recently. It...it turned out to be a disaster. Those imbeciles down there stuck a crown of thorns on my head and nailed me to a cross. I forgave—'

'I know, I know. They wrote a bestselling book about your—'

'Don't interrupt me, Sadguru.'

'Sorry, my Lord.'

'As I was saying, I forgave the poor fools because they hadn't a clue who it was that they were crucifying. I also told them that the meek will one day inherit their planet. The time is drawing near for that to happen. *Homo Novus*, a new, less egocentric, more conscious species of man is about to appear on Planet Earth. Of course in the initial stages there will be ramifications – growing pains you might say – but, in the end, what is destined to happen shall prevail.'

The supreme master was touched upon hearing this. 'Thank you, Lord Brahma. Your wisdom is infinite.'

'Come off it, Sadguru. I'm not above making a mistake, you know. I'm still not sure what to do with those black holes that resulted from one of my failed experiments.' Brahma chuckled into the phone, making the receiver's membrane on the other end of the line buzz in the supreme master's ear. 'Just remember to inform my third-dimensional creations that everything in their lives is predetermined. Remind them also that they are always free not to identify with the body and not be affected by the pains and pleasures that come as a consequence of the body's activities. Now, if you don't mind, I'd like to return to watching *Apocalypse Now*.'

'Thank you for all and everything,' said the supreme master.

'Think nothing of it, my son. Now, run along and take care of this Hamish Macleod business.'

With that, the Lord of Creation hung up the cosmic emergency telephone. Sadguru listened to the dialling tone as it sounded out across the omniverse in one long drawn out Om.

I shook my head and for a moment I thought I'd gone insane. I could hear a deep hum, the vibration of which seemed to permeate everything. I wondered why I'd never noticed it before, or if it had just begun. My eyes blinked open.

The moon broke out from behind the clouds and cast my shadow in front of me. I shouted, 'I don't believe it!' The wind had abated and the waves were drawing back. The fear of a tidal surge rose in my mind, but no, the sea was calm. I looked to my right and saw a slither of lightning pierce the sky. Seconds later I heard a distant grumble of thunder. The storm was far away and receding east in the direction of Sihanoukville.

So amazed was I at this miraculous turn of events, it took some time for me to notice that my watch had been washed up by the sea and now lay in my lap. Flabbergasted, I picked it up and looked at its face. Time was up to its mischievous tricks again. The digital numbers shone forth in soft blue light – 19:51. 'What the...' I gasped in disbelief. 1951 was the year that Angus and I were born on Iona.

In slow motion the watch tumbled from my hand on to the sand.

The moon turned yellow as it descended towards the horizon. I was shivering. It felt to me like I'd been sitting there forever, as though this night was all there was, all there ever had been and all there ever would be.

A blank eternity passed. When I next looked at my watch, I found that it was 05:25. I did not even bother to think about why the watch had resumed telling the time with what I presumed was accuracy, because time was bearing down on my soul with the weight of an anvil. I could feel that my spirit was beginning to buckle. The after-effects of the adrenaline rushes that had flooded my system during the storm had now completely worn off. Sleep called to me like a siren song. My mind went numb, as if it had been injected with novocaine. I'd reached a point of psychological exhaustion where it was no longer possible to recall any of Angus's stories for inspiration. My eyelids felt like lead. It required all of my remaining will power to keep them open. I stared out to sea.

A faint rustling and sense of movement behind me brought my body and mind to full alert. I slowly turned and saw a lizard that was as long as my arm. It was about two metres away and stood dead still on a large flat rock. The reptile stared back at me with unblinking black eyes. Then, with a flick of its pointed tail, the scaly creature scuttled off and disappeared.

I used my hands to pad sand around my backside to prevent shifting position on top of the mine. This kept me occupied for a while. I looked to my left and saw a crimson hue had appeared on the distant horizon above the dark blue sea. 'Thank God,' I sighed.

Somewhere in the distance a cockerel crowed as my mind bobbed in and out of reality, in and out of dream and thought as I fought an overwhelming sensation of fatigue.

I began to nod off.

'Ugh!' I let out a startled cry when my body jerked awake.

Thin fingers of light were probing the eastern sky. The two islands in the sea in front of me had shed their shadowy outlines and taken on a green-tinged depth of field within their clearly defined contours. About four kilometres away and crossing the wide channel that separated the uninhabited islands, I could see a small sailboat. The sight of it made me feel like I'd been cast adrift on an ocean of time, extremely lonely, utterly helpless and completely lost. All of the fear within me had been expended. I slowly drew my knees up, clasped my hands on top of them, bent forward and rested my heavy head. My wife loomed in my mind like a lifeboat on a sinking ship. The last thought I can remember before falling asleep was, *Jean, where are you?*

25

JEAN

B rilliant early-morning sunlight slanted through cracks in the beach hut's bamboo walls. Jean woke up and lay staring up at the roof's crosshatched palm leaves. The bed sheets felt damp. She stretched her arms until her elbow joints cracked and then turned on her left side to face Hamish. He wasn't there. 'Och, bloody hell,' she said out loud, assuming correctly that her husband had slipped out for a secret smoke. What she didn't know was that the earth had turned half a revolution since Hamish had left the hut to smoke a cigarette and he was now over a kilometre away, sitting on top of a landmine.

A hangover made its presence felt by jabbing Jean's right temple with a sharp pain. She sat up and groaned. There was a bottle of drinking water next to the bed. She picked the plastic bottle up, brought it to her dry lips, tilted her head back and drained it. 'Never again,' she said, making a resolution to abstain from swallowing another drop of alcohol for the rest of her life.

Jean stood up and began rummaging through her rucksack, in search of a packet of Aspirin. She came across her pink battery-powered shaver and decided to shave her armpits. This isn't exactly Marbella, she thought, but one has to keep up appearances.

She stepped out of the bamboo hut's doorway and saw a long line of flotsam, composed of driftwood dotted by green coconuts, tangled lumps of black seaweed and plastic waste, washed up on the shoreline. She realized there had been a storm during the night. Hamish was nowhere in sight.

Naked except for an orange-coloured bathing cap to keep her thick black hair dry, she ran into the murky sea and swam out from the shore in a straight line. She floated on her back for a while and stared up at the sky. It was clear, virtually cloudless except for a wispy grey streak of high altitude cirrus drifting north. Turning round in the water, she began to swim back towards the beach. Her eyes scanned the coast. To the right she noticed a tall coconut tree in the distance, but it was too far away to see her husband sitting under it. Where on earth is he? Jean wondered. How can he just wander off and leave me alone in a deserted place like this? Selfish bugger! Something bad could happen to me.

Her feet touched the bottom. She pulled off her bathing cap, shook her long hair loose, then walked up on to the beach and sat down on the warm white sand. Gazing at the calm sea, Jean was suddenly overcome by homesickness. She saw the streets of Oban on a rainy afternoon and her grandchildren playing by an open fire in her living room. 'Scotland,' she sighed, 'I wish I was back where I belong, going for a walk in the hills with the kids.' The thought inspired her to do some hatha yoga.

Jean stood up straight and began performing the sun salutation, a series of gentle movements synchronized with the breath. She'd been practising this exercise for over twenty years and was positively addicted to it because it never failed to lift her spirits. She was fifty-three, a material girl and she knew how to make herself feel good. She moaned with pleasure as she stretched muscles and tendons. An increase of blood circulation caused a stimulating rush in her brain.

Feeling invigorated and revitalized, she went into the hut and tried to make up her mind what to wear. Her choices were limited and she decided on a tartan bikini, something she hadn't worn since she tried it on Edinburgh, four months earlier in a sport shop's changing room. They're beginning to sag, she thought as she tucked her breasts into the bikini top. Not for the first time, she contemplated whether it was time to take the jump and go for silicone implants.

'Right then,' she said, leaping through the doorway and landing in a crouch on the sand, 'no rest for the wicked.' She sprang up and began jogging barefoot along the beach – in the opposite direction from where her husband was sitting under the coconut tree.

Ten minutes later, she was beginning to break out in a sweat. She turned in her tracks and retraced her footprints in the sand. When Jean reached the hut she popped in for a drink of water. She drained another plastic bottle of its lukewarm contents, burped and then noticed her glass spray dispenser of Chanel №5 lying beside her makeup bag. The perfume was a birthday present from Hamish. She picked it up, gave her cleavage a light squirt and dabbed a little of the scent behind her ears. A quick glance in a compact mirror was all it took to help her decide that the natural look would suffice today. She broke into song. 'Like a virgin...' Jean was Madonna's oldest teenage fan.

Back on the beach, she started jogging again – in Hamish's direction. 'There he is,' she muttered under her breath, when she spotted him sitting under the coconut tree. She veered to her left and slowly stepped in to the waist-high undergrowth. She went down on her haunches and then crept closer to him. From a distance of about twenty metres, she peeped out from behind a small clump of Ephedra pine saplings and observed her husband. *What on earth is he doing?* Jean asked herself. *He'll get sunstroke.* Hamish had his legs pulled up and was resting his head on his knees. He was shirtless and appeared to be fast asleep. *The silly bugger's smoked too many of those bloody fags and feels dizzy from the nicotine,* she reasoned. *I'll teach him a lesson,* she thought, an idea forming in the back of her mind.

Jean got down on all fours and, moving as silently as a cat stalking a mouse, slinked round behind her husband. There was a flat rock between her and Hamish's back. She stole stealthily towards it. Jean stepped on a dry twig.

Hamish woke up when he heard a faint crack. He sat up straight.

Smell is our most immediate sense. It directly affects the limbic system, a complex of nerves in the brain that control basic emotions, which is why memory and smell are so closely related. Hamish could smell Chanel №5, his wife's perfume of choice.

Jean? He twisted around and saw her standing on the rock, knees bent, ready to pounce. Hamish looked up into his wife's bright, mischievous eyes. 'No!' he screamed.

His warning came too late. She jumped.

26

HENG PICH

Cambodia, April Fool's Day, 2005.

My name is Heng Pich. It was me who discovered the two pale-skinned farangs just over six weeks ago. They'd been seriously injured by a landmine. I felt very bad about it because it was partly my fault that the accident occurred.

You see, some months earlier, Samphy Souanarith caught me stealing coconuts from his tree. Samphy was very angry about this at the time because he is a poor man who often doesn't have enough to feed himself and his family. I am not by nature a thief. I knew it was wrong to take something that didn't belong to me, but I am very partial to drinking fresh coconut juice and I couldn't resist the temptation. Samphy knew how many nuts were on his tree. When they continued to go missing he knew I was the culprit. Things came to a head when, one afternoon, we ran into each other outside of our village's general store. Samphy Souanarith swore at me and then hit me hard in the face. I am a practicing Buddhist and I've learnt to abhor violence, but my body struck back automatically. I landed a lucky punch and broke Samphy's nose. He started to cry and lots of passers-by stopped to stare at us. Samphy Souanarith swore that he'd take revenge and that's how I knew it was him who'd planted the mine at the foot of the coconut tree, hoping that I would stand on it. Don't ask me where he got hold of a mine, because I have no idea.

I own a small strip of land that is situated about a quarter of a kilometre from the beach. Every morning I walk for twenty minutes with two buckets of well water in hand to nourish my vegetable patch. That particular morning, I remember feeling anxious because during the night there had been a violent storm and I was worried about my tomato plants. Sure enough, when I arrived at my vegetable garden there was quite a mess to be tidied up. I'd just finished watering my cucumbers and was searching in my satchel for a piece of newspaper to roll a cigarette with when I heard a dull thud. I recognized the sound straight away because it wasn't the first time I'd heard a mine explode. Why, it was only last month when that fat pig, Kun Thea, had her head blown off by a landmine. Narith Rithisak, my nearest neighbour and closest friend, was heartbroken at the loss of his prize sow. Everyone else in the village was overjoyed because they got to eat pork chops.

I looked over towards the sea and saw a small cloud of grey smoke rising up in to the sky. A second later, there was a loud crack and then I saw something that I'll never forget for the remainder of my life. Samphy Souanarith's coconut tree toppled over and crashed on to the beach. He'd lost what he'd wanted to protect by trying to take revenge on me. I dropped my bag and began running towards the sea. This was not as easy as it sounds due to the arthritis in my ankles.

When I arrived on the scene, I saw a lot of things in the space of a minute. There was a small smoking crater in the sand. Quite near to it were two people lying by the shoreline. I hurried over to them. I could tell by the colour of their skin that the man and woman were foreigners, probably Europeans or Americans. The man was, like many farangs, overweight. He was bleeding badly and had a big twisted shard of shrapnel embedded in his right shoulder. His back and legs were peppered with smaller wounds. He was unconscious and lying on top of the woman. I glanced over at the smouldering tree stump. It had been severed at about the height of a man's groin. From this I gauged that it was an anti-personnel mine that had been detonated, perhaps a Russian-made POMZ-2, but more likely some kind of Chinese-manufactured 'Bouncing Betty'. The Chinks have a proverb that's tailor-made for those horrible things: 'One false step can bring everlasting grief.'

'Oh,' I can hear you saying, 'how is it that an ignorant Cambodian peasant knows so much about mines?' Well, let me tell you. I haven't always been a peasant. Thirty years ago I was an officer in Pol Pot's communist army. 'Aha,' you're thinking, 'Mr Pich was in the Khymer Rouge.' Yes, it's true. I'm not ashamed of it. I'm no stranger to war's barbaric countenance. I know how, when confronted with that savage face, it can serve to bring out the very worst and the finest in people. War brought out the best in me. I risked my life on countless occasions to save hundreds, perhaps thousands, of innocent men, women and children's lives. The infantry soldiers under my command only killed enemy combatants, never civilians. I earned my men's respect and when the time came they fought with me like Trojans against overwhelming odds. Many sacrificed their lives. For what? Honour? Vengeance? Freedom? You may well ask. I'll tell you − absolutely nothing, because there is nothing in this world that's worth killing for.

I almost lost my life. I was stabbed in the guts by a bayonet when our pestilent neighbours, the Vietnamese, invaded Cambodia.

The truth be told, nobody survives a war. Anybody who enters that horrible theatre is a completely different person by the time the curtain falls on the final scene and the light of normal life is restored. When the war ended, I saw only darkness. In those times of blackest despair I had some of my most honest and lucid moments, as if a thick veil was lifted that allowed me to see life as it really is. Slowly, thanks to the Lord Buddha's teachings, the light began to return to my life. Now I feel compassion for my fellow man. Well...most of the time, although it's not always easy.

I knelt beside the foreigners and looked at the woman. Even though she was covered in blood, I could see that she was a beautiful buxom specimen. Her right breast was exposed. It was so ripe I almost reached over and touched it. I could easily appreciate why the man had shielded her body with his own in order to protect her from the blast.

Suddenly, the woman's eyes sprang open. She pinned me with a stare that was as sharp as a needle. She pushed the man off her and began shouting at me, using a harsh language that I could not understand. She tried to stand up. Both she and I noticed, in the same instant, that a piece of shrapnel had penetrated her left calf and was now sticking out of her shin. The woman shrieked, fell back onto the sand and passed out. Well now, as I said, I saw a lot in a minute. During the next five minutes, I did a lot.

I tended to the farang woman first. The wound on the back of her leg was pumping blood. I knew this in all likelihood meant that the shrapnel had pierced an artery. I removed her brassiere. 'Dirty devil,' you might be thinking, but you're wrong if you are. I needed her brassiere to make a tourniquet. I tied it around her thigh and used a piece of driftwood to tighten it. I'm no doctor but I learned battlefield first aid in the army. The tourniquet worked a treat. The flow of blood was reduced to a trickle. I turned the injured woman on her side, examined the rest of her wounds and found them to be of a relatively superficial nature. As for the man, well, he was in a sorry state. There were pieces of metal embedded in his back and legs. But it was the big shard of shrapnel in his shoulder which worried me the most. I put an ear to the left side of his upper back and listened for a heartbeat. I couldn't hear one. The man let out a faint groan and it was therefore that I knew he was still alive. He'd lost a lot of blood but, as far as I could determine, there was no damage to the arteries.

'So, Heng,' I can hear you asking, 'what did you do next?' That's hardly a surprising question and the answer is I did nothing at first. I just stood there like an imbecile staring at the sea and then I looked up at something bigger –

the sky. There wasn't a cloud to be seen. It was hot and I was sweating like a pig although, I must say, I've never, in all my fifty-one years, seen a pig sweating. Have you?

They say that the Lord Buddha reached the door to Nirvana two thousand five hundred years ago. I believe that, but I don't believe he entered Nirvana. I think he is standing in the doorway waiting for the rest of us to catch up with him. The Buddha taught compassion. It is that virtue which inspires him to wait patiently on us, the suffering billions who live in the world of illusion. I glanced down at the poor bleeding foreigners and felt great pity in my heart for them. I saw it as my karmic duty to do everything I could to help them. I hurried off along the beach and eventually headed inland towards my village.

To take my mind off my aching ankles I began to think about something that was puzzling me. How did the foreigners manage to get a few metres away from the mine before it exploded? In the end I decided that the mine, due perhaps to its being old, hadn't gone off immediately and the foreigners, realizing that they'd tripped the detonator, dived and rolled away from it.

When I reached the village I found Hun Kui sitting on his porch, eating a watermelon. Hun thinks he's a big shot because he's the only man in the village who owns a motorized vehicle. I told him what had happened and we jumped into his ancient jeep. It was a miracle that the rusty heap started as soon as Hun Kui connected two wires under the steering column.

The foreigners were still unconscious when we pulled up beside them. Hun Kui, who is very fat, huffed and puffed as we lifted the injured farangs into the back of the jeep. We set off on the road to Khum Angkol, the nearest town of any importance. Halfway there the jeep started spluttering and then the engine stopped.

'We're out of petrol,' says Hun.

I said, 'What do you mean, *we're out of petrol?* It's your jeep.'

We started arguing. Just when our dispute was at the point where it might come to blows, the injured woman cried out, bringing us back to the urgency of our mission of mercy.

'Listen,' I said to Hun, 'you go and search for fuel and I'll take care of the foreigners.'

'Don't you start bossing me around,' says he, 'I'm in charge.'

'Whatever you say Hun Kui,' I said, trying to keep the situation under control, 'but please – just this once – do what I say or these farangs might die.'

Hun might be stubborn but he's not altogether stupid. He knew that there would be hell to pay if he was caught with two dead foreigners in the back of a vehicle that belonged to him. 'Okay,' he says, getting his fat arse in gear. He set off and trudged down the road with a plastic canister in his right hand.

I turned to the foreigners. The woman's eyelashes fluttered, prompting me to clamber into the back of the jeep and loosen the tourniquet on her leg. I looked at her husband…well, at least that's what I took him to be, you never know with these foreigners and their immoral ways…had blood running out of his ears. His skin was the colour of curdled milk. I thought to myself, this poor man might die in the back of Hun Kui's jeep. I covered their bodies with a filthy tarpaulin that I found behind the driver's seat. You see, by this time I was starting to worry about what I'd gotten myself into.

After what seemed like an eternity in hell, Hun returned with a full canister of fuel. 'I had to leave my precious Seiko watch as a deposit, because I didn't have any money with me. This is your damned fault,' says he, complaining as usual.

Less than thirty minutes later, we drove in to Khum Angkol and pulled up outside of a small police station. I rushed into the office and saw two uniformed men, sitting with their feet up on a metal desk. They were drinking liquor from plastic cups. The placed reeked of cheap booze, stale tobacco smoke and sweaty socks. I shouted, 'We've got two seriously injured foreigners outside in the back of Hun Kui's jeep.' The two cops were ugly drunk and wanted to lock me up in a cell for running over two foreign tourists. I explained what had happened. That sobered them up.

To cut a long story short, the two farangs were eventually taken to the general hospital in Sihanoukville and that's the last I saw of them – that is, until a week ago.

The sun was sinking behind a clump of tall bamboos when a brand new Toyota Landcruiser drew up in front of my garden gate. At the time, I was playing with Srey Leak, my youngest daughter. I told her to go in to the house and tell Veata, my wife, that something strange was going on. I didn't realize it immediately, but it was to be the luckiest day of my life.

The foreigners had driven all the way from Sihanoukville to thank me, Heng Pich, for saving their lives. I didn't recognize the man at first. The last time I'd seen him, he was covered in blood. He'd lost a lot of weight and now looked very frail. His wife looked wonderful, so much so I would have given everything I owned to spend a night with her, which wasn't very much now that I think about it, a dozen scrawny chickens, an aggressive red rooster who has lost every fight he's ever been in and a little wooden house with a leaky roof. Anyway, it doesn't matter, because I could tell by the haughty look in her eye that she wouldn't have paid the slightest bit of attention to a poor peasant like me had I not saved their lives.

Samlain was the name of the effeminate motorbike taxi driver the foreign couple had hired as an interpreter. The young man smelled of perfume and spoke very well of his newfound employers, who, he informed me, paid him generously for his services. It was through Samlain that I learned the farangs names, Jean something-or-other and Ham Ish.

I invited the three of them into my humble home and ordered Veata to make a pot of tea. We sat on the floor and, with Samlain's assistance, began a conversation. It was then that I learnt how Mister Ham Ish had spent a night sitting on top of a landmine. It sounded incredible, but I believed it because Mister Ish had an honest face. He also told me how his wife had crept up on him from behind and knocked him off of the mine. Whereupon, a few seconds later, it had exploded. Hearing this confirmed that my earlier deductions were more or less accurate.

When the tea was ready, Veata joined us. She whispered a question into my ear. 'Dear Heng,' she says, 'do you think the farang woman would be offended if I ask to touch her hair. It is so long, black and shiny, surely it can't be real.' I shook my head vigorously and that was the end of that.

Missus Jean handed me a small paper parcel bound with ribbon.

'What's this,' I asked the interpreter.

He answered, 'My employers wish to give you this as a token of their gratitude for saving their lives.'

I laid the parcel to one side.

'Open it, fool,' hissed the interpreter, who I'd taken a disliking to from the moment I set eyes on him.

I did as the impertinent ladyboy ordered and found myself staring at the largest amount of money I'd ever seen in my entire life. Lost for words, I glanced at my wife. Her eyes were as wide as full moons and she looked like she'd just seen the ghosts of our ancestors.

My first reaction was to tell a lie. 'There's no way I can accept this,' said I, looking into Mister Ham Ish's striking blue eyes.

'Don't be a fucking idiot,' says that ignorant two-legged snake of a taxi driver from Sihanoukville.

It only took a little persuasion for me to accept the money. Veata started crying a river of tears. There was a lump in my throat and, try as I might, I couldn't prevent myself from crying like a baby also. Then, a very strange thing occurred. Tears began to roll down Mister Ham Ish's cheeks. I glanced at his wife and low and behold tears were gushing from her eyes and making her makeup run, which only succeeded in making Missus Jean appear more attractive. She looked so feminine and vulnerable I can feel a stirring in my pants just thinking about her. Unfortunately, I'm sorry to say, that's not something which happens very often these days.

It was beginning to get dark when the foreigners said they had to return to Sihanoukville. They informed me that they were catching a plane from Phnom Penh to Bangkok in a couple of days and from there they would fly home to a place called Scotland, which I believe I'm correct in assuming is somewhere in America, the country where all the fat people live.

Had it not been for my taking offence at the way their interpreter spoke to me I would have offered Mister Ham Ish and his lovely wife my bed to sleep in. In a way, it was maybe just as well that things worked out the way they did. The wealthy foreigners were no doubt accustomed to a standard of living beyond my wildest imaginings, not only that, they smelled of medicine and sour milk.

Before a final farewell, Mister Ham Ish and Missus Jean stepped forward and embraced both me and my wife. I'll always cherish that moment because those people made me feel important, like I was somebody worth knowing.

The couple got in to the back of the Toyota, rolled down a grey-tinted window and waved goodbye. Samlain tooted the horn and smiled. It was then that I realized he wasn't such a creep after all.

Thanks to the money that the foreigners gave me, I'm planning to open a grocery shop in Khum Angkol and send my four children to a good school. Now that I'm rich there's no need to tend to my vegetable garden anymore, I suppose that's the nature of progress.

I have a feeling that I'll never see Mister Ham Ish and his beautiful wife, Missus Jean something-or-other, again. During the early evening, when I sit on the porch of my new three-bedroomed house, looking to the west as the sun sets, I often say a prayer for those kind people, because I know in my heart that they would not have survived such a terrible accident had not life wanted it so for a special reason. Then again, now that I think about it, one never really knows for sure what is a blessing or a curse in this world.

Acknowledgements

T o my beloved Prita, who must have the patience of a saint to put up with me. To the three Helens, Gosch, Watts and Mitchell, for their invaluable help. To Simon Abbot for making me run the gauntlet of his acerbic sarcasm and helping me to let go of what I did not need. Salvador Harguindey and Anita Avey for their energetic and positive input. Mr P, Tosh, Premal, Murphy, Salim, Gita, Ardha, Kelly Cooper Barr, 'Big Boy' Miguel, Jeeps, Miss Gupta, Walter, Scottish Yogi, Silvia and Tomas San Miguel, Ines Hartz, Barry Page, The Prof and all the friends who lent me their ear and gave me their creative and critical feedback. My teachers past, present and future. And last but not least, Dirty Ali for inspiring me to create such a wicked character, may his pipe never be empty.

Lightning Source UK Ltd.
Milton Keynes UK
17 January 2011

165834UK00001B/365/P